C0050 41048

Dan Brown is the bestselling author of *Digital Fortress*, *Angels and Demons*, *Deception Point* and *The Da Vinci Code*. He lives in New England.

Praise for the novels of Dan Brown:

'Wow . . . Blockbuster perfection . . . An exhilaratingly brainy thriller. Not since the advent of Harry Potter has an author so flagrantly delighted in leading readers on a breathless chase.'
New York Times

'Brown's novel adroitly blends the chase-scene-stuffed thrillers of Robert Ludlum and the learned romps of Umberto Eco . . . For anyone who wants more brain-food than thrillers normally provide.'
Sunday Times

'Exceedingly clever . . . Both fascinating and fun . . . a considerable achievement.'
Washington Post

'A gripping bestseller . . . Brown has cracked the bestseller code.'
Guardian

'A heart-racing thriller. This story has so many twists that it would be a sin to reveal too much of the plot in advance. Let's just say that if this novel doesn't get your pulse racing, you need to check your meds.'
San Francisco Chronicle

'Some genuinely fascinating insights into Grail history make this the best thriller *FHM* has read in yonks.'
FHM

'A thundering, tantalizing, extremely smart fun ride. Brown doesn't slow down this tremendously powerful narrative engine despite transmitting several doctorates' worth of fascinating history and learned speculation.'
Chicago Tribune

www.booksattransworld.co.uk

ANGELS AND DEMONS

THE DA VINCI CODE

A ROBERT LANGDON OMNIBUS

DAN BROWN

BANTAM PRESS

LONDON · TORONTO · SYDNEY · AUCKLAND · JOHANNESBURG

TRANSWORLD PUBLISHERS
61–63 Uxbridge Road, London W5 5SA
a division of The Random House Group Ltd

RANDOM HOUSE AUSTRALIA (PTY) LTD
20 Alfred Street, Milsons Point, Sydney,
New South Wales 2061, Australia

RANDOM HOUSE NEW ZEALAND LTD
18 Poland Road, Glenfield, Auckland 10, New Zealand

RANDOM HOUSE SOUTH AFRICA (PTY) LTD
Isle of Houghton, Corner Boundary Road & Carse O'Gowrie,
Houghton 2198, South Africa

A catalogue record for this book is available from the British Library.
ISBN 0593 054601

Typeset in 11/12.5pt Ehrhardt

Printed in Great Britain by
Mackays of Chatham plc, Chatham, Kent

1 3 5 7 9 10 8 6 4 2

Papers used by Transworld Publishers are natural, recyclable products
made from wood grown in sustainable forests. The manufacturing
processes conform to the environmental regulations of the country of origin.

Contents

ANGELS AND DEMONS

For Blythe . . .

Acknowledgements

A debt of gratitude to Emily Bestler, Jason Kaufman, Ben Kaplan, and everyone at Pocket Books for their belief in this project.

To my friend and agent, Jake Elwell, for his enthusiasm and unflagging effort.

To the legendary George Wieser, for convincing me to write novels.

To my dear friend Irv Sittler, for facilitating my audience with the Pope, secreting me into parts of Vatican City few ever see, and making my time in Rome unforgettable.

To one of the most ingenious and gifted artists alive, John Langdon, who rose brilliantly to my impossible challenge and created the ambigrams for this novel.

To Stan Planton, head librarian, Ohio University – Chillicothe, for being my number one source of information on countless topics.

To Sylvia Cavazzini, for her gracious tour through the secret *Passetto*.

And to the best parents a kid could hope for, Dick and Connie Brown . . . for everything.

Thanks also to CERN, Henry Beckett, Brett Trotter, the Pontifical Academy of Science, Brookhaven Institute, FermiLab Library, Olga Wieser, Don Ulsch of the National Security Institute, Caroline H. Thompson at University of Wales, Kathryn Gerhard and Omar Al Kindi, John Pike and the Federation of American Scientists, Heimlich Viserholder, Corinna and Davis Hammond, Aizaz Ali, the Galileo Project of Rice University, Julie Lynn and Charlie Ryan at Mockingbird Pictures, Gary Goldstein, Dave (Vilas) Arnold and Andra Crawford, the Global Fraternal Network, the Phillips Exeter Academy Library, Jim Barrington, John Maier, the exceptionally keen eye of Margie Wachtel, alt.masonic. members, Alan Wooley, the Library of Congress Vatican Codices Exhibit, Lisa Callamaro and the Callamaro Agency, Jon A. Stowell, Musei Vaticani, Aldo Baggia, Noah Alireza, Harriet Walker, Charles Terry, Micron Electrics, Mindy Renselaer, Nancy and Dick Curtin, Thomas D. Nadeau, NuvoMedia and Rocket E-books, Frank and Sylvia Kennedy, Simon Edwards, Rome Board of Tourism, Maestro Gregory Brown, Val Brown,

Werner Brandes, Paul Krupin at Direct Contact, Paul Stark, Tom King at Computalk Network, Sandy and Jerry Nolan, Web guru Linda George, the National Academy of Art in Rome, physicist and fellow scribe Steve Howe, Robert Weston, the Water Street Bookstore in Exeter, New Hampshire, and the Vatican Observatory.

Fact

The world's largest scientific research facility – Switzerland's *Conseil Européen pour la Recherche Nucléaire* (CERN) – recently succeeded in producing the first particles of antimatter. Antimatter is identical to physical matter except that it is composed of particles whose electric charges are *opposite* to those found in normal matter.

Antimatter is the most powerful energy source known to man. It releases energy with 100 per cent efficiency (nuclear fission is 1.5 per cent efficient). Antimatter creates no pollution or radiation, and a droplet could power New York City for a full day.

There is, however, one catch . . .

Antimatter is highly unstable. It ignites when it comes in contact with absolutely anything . . . even air. A single gram of antimatter contains the energy of a 20-kiloton nuclear bomb – the size of the bomb dropped on Hiroshima.

Until recently antimatter has been created only in very small amounts (a few atoms at a time). But CERN has now broken ground on its new Antiproton Decelerator – an advanced antimatter production facility that promises to create antimatter in much larger quantities.

One question looms: Will this highly volatile substance save the world, or will it be used to create the most deadly weapon ever made?

Author's Note

References to all works of art, tombs, tunnels, and architecture in Rome are entirely factual (as are their exact locations). They can still be seen today. The brotherhood of the Illuminati is also factual.

MODERN ROME

Santa Maria del Popolo

Spanish Steps

Via Sistina

Via Due Macelli

Via del Corso

Via della Scofra

Via Zanardelli

Via dei Coronari

Bridge of Angels

Tiber River

Via del Tritone

Hotel Bernini

Piazza Barberini

Quirinale

Via del Quirinale

Via Nationale

Santa Maria della Vittoria

Trevi Fountain

Pantheon

Piazza della Rotunda

Piazza Navona

St Agnes in Agony

Corso Vittorio Emanuelle

Piazza Venezia

Coliseum

Aremula

Hospital Tiberina

Tiberina Island

Castel Sant' Angelo

Piazza Cavour

Via Crescenzio

Via della Conciliazione

Vatican City

St Peter's Basilica

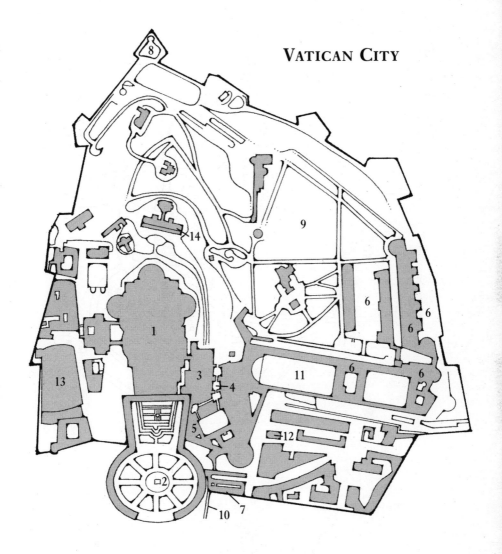

VATICAN CITY

1 St Peter's Basilica	7 Office of the Swiss Guard	11 Courtyard of the Belvedere
2 St Peter's Square	8 heliport	12 Central Post Office
3 Sistine Chapel	9 gardens	13 Papal Audience Hall
4 Borgia Courtyard	10 the *Passetto*	14 Government Palace
5 Office of the Pope		
6 Vatican Museums		

Prologue

Physicist Leonardo Vetra smelled burning flesh, and he knew it was his own. He stared up in terror at the dark figure looming over him. 'What do you want!'

'*La chiave*,' the raspy voice replied. 'The password.'

'But . . . I don't—'

The intruder pressed down again, grinding the white hot object deeper into Vetra's chest. There was the hiss of broiling flesh.

Vetra cried out in agony. 'There *is* no password!' He felt himself drifting toward unconsciousness.

The figure glared. '*Ne avevo paura*. I was afraid of that.'

Vetra fought to keep his senses, but the darkness was closing in. His only solace was in knowing his attacker would never obtain what he had come for. A moment later, however, the figure produced a blade and brought it to Vetra's face. The blade hovered. Carefully. Surgically.

'For the love of God!' Vetra screamed. But it was too late.

1

High atop the steps of the Great Pyramid of Giza, a young woman laughed and called down to him. 'Robert, hurry up! I knew I should have married a younger man!' Her smile was magic.

He struggled to keep up, but his legs felt like stone. 'Wait,' he begged. 'Please . . .'

As he climbed, his vision began to blur. There was a thundering in his ears. *I must reach her!* But when he looked up again, the woman had disappeared. In her place stood an old man with rotting teeth. The man stared down, curling his lips into a lonely grimace. Then he let out a scream of anguish that resounded across the desert.

Robert Langdon awoke with a start from his nightmare. The phone beside his bed was ringing. Dazed, he picked up the receiver.

'Hello?'

'I'm looking for Robert Langdon,' a man's voice said.

Langdon sat up in his empty bed and tried to clear his mind. 'This . . . is Robert Langdon.' He squinted at his digital clock. It was 5.18 a.m.

'I must see you immediately.'

'Who is this?'

'My name is Maximilian Kohler. I'm a discrete particle physicist.'

'A *what*?' Langdon could barely focus. 'Are you sure you've got the right Langdon?'

'You're a professor of religious iconology at Harvard University. You've written three books on symbology and—'

'Do you know what time it is?'

'I apologize. I have something you need to see. I can't discuss it on the phone.'

A knowing groan escaped Langdon's lips. This had happened before. One of the perils of writing books about religious symbology was the calls from religious zealots who wanted him to confirm their latest sign from God. Last month, a stripper from Oklahoma had promised Langdon the best sex of his life if he would fly down and verify the authenticity of a cruciform that had magically appeared on her bed sheets. *The Shroud of Tulsa*, Langdon had called it.

'How did you get my number?' Langdon tried to be polite, despite the hour.

'On the Worldwide Web. The site for your book.'

Langdon frowned. He was damn sure his book's site did not include his home phone number. The man was obviously lying.

'I need to see you,' the caller insisted. 'I'll pay you well.'

Now Langdon was getting mad. 'I'm sorry, but I really—'

'If you leave immediately, you can be here by—'

'I'm not going anywhere! It's five o'clock in the morning!' Langdon hung up and collapsed back in bed. He closed his eyes and tried to fall back asleep. It was no use. The dream was emblazoned in his mind. Reluctantly, he put on his robe and went downstairs.

Robert Langdon wandered barefoot through his deserted Massachusetts Victorian home and nursed his ritual insomnia remedy – a mug of steaming Nestlé's Quik. The April moon filtered through the bay windows and played on the oriental carpets. Langdon's colleagues often joked that his place looked more like an anthropology museum than a home. His shelves were packed with religious artifacts from around the world – an *ekuaba* from Ghana, a gold cross from Spain, a cycladic idol from the Aegean, and even a rare woven *boccus* from Borneo, a young warrior's symbol of perpetual youth.

As Langdon sat on his brass Maharishi's chest and savored the warmth of the chocolate, the bay window caught his reflection. The image was distorted and pale ... like a ghost. *An aging ghost*, he thought, cruelly reminded that his youthful spirit was living in a mortal shell.

Although not overly handsome in a classical sense, the forty-five-year-old Langdon had what his female colleagues referred to as an 'erudite' appeal – wisps of gray in his thick brown hair, probing blue eyes, an arrestingly deep voice, and the strong, carefree smile of a collegiate athlete. A varsity diver in prep school and college, Langdon still had the body of a swimmer, a toned, six-foot physique that he vigilantly maintained with fifty laps a day in the university pool.

Langdon's friends had always viewed him as a bit of an enigma – a man caught between centuries. On weekends he could be seen lounging on the quad in blue jeans, discussing computer graphics or religious history with students; other times he could be spotted in his Harris tweed and paisley vest, photographed in the pages of upscale art magazines at museum openings where he had been asked to lecture.

Although a tough teacher and strict disciplinarian, Langdon was the first to embrace what he hailed as the 'lost art of good clean fun.' He relished recreation with an infectious fanaticism that had earned him a fraternal acceptance among his students. His campus nickname – 'The Dolphin' – was a reference both to his affable nature and his legendary ability to dive into a pool and outmaneuver the entire opposing squad in a water polo match.

As Langdon sat alone, absently gazing into the darkness, the silence of his home was shattered again, this time by the ring of his fax machine. Too exhausted to be annoyed, Langdon forced a tired chuckle.

God's people, he thought. *Two thousand years of waiting for their Messiah, and they're still persistent as hell.*

Wearily, he returned his empty mug to the kitchen and walked slowly to his oak-paneled study. The incoming fax lay in the tray. Sighing, he scooped up the paper and looked at it.

Instantly, a wave of nausea hit him.

The image on the page was that of a human corpse. The body had been stripped naked, and its head had been twisted, facing completely backward. On the victim's chest was a terrible burn. The man had been branded . . . imprinted with a single word. It was a word Langdon knew well. Very well. He stared at the ornate lettering in disbelief.

Illuminati

'Illuminati,' he stammered, his heart pounding. *It can't be . . .*

In slow motion, afraid of what he was about to witness, Langdon rotated the fax 180 degrees. He looked at the word upside down.

Instantly, the breath went out of him. It was like he had been hit by a truck. Barely able to believe his eyes, he rotated the fax again, reading the brand right-side up and then upside down.

'Illuminati,' he whispered.

Stunned, Langdon collapsed in a chair. He sat a moment in utter bewilderment. Gradually, his eyes were drawn to the blinking red light on his fax machine. Whoever had sent this fax was still on the line . . . waiting to talk. Langdon gazed at the blinking light a long time.

Then, trembling, he picked up the receiver.

2

'Do I have your attention now?' the man's voice said when Langdon finally answered the line.

'Yes, sir, you damn well do. You want to explain yourself?'

'I tried to tell you before.' The voice was rigid, mechanical. 'I'm a physicist. I run a research facility. We've had a murder. You saw the body.'

'How did you find me?' Langdon could barely focus. His mind was racing from the image on the fax.

'I already told you. The Worldwide Web. The site for your book, *The Art of the Illuminati*.'

Langdon tried to gather his thoughts. His book was virtually unknown in mainstream literary circles, but it had developed quite a following on-line. Nonetheless, the caller's claim still made no sense. 'That page has no contact information,' Langdon challenged. 'I'm certain of it.'

'I have people here at the lab very adept at extracting user information from the Web.'

Langdon was skeptical. 'Sounds like your lab knows *a lot* about the Web.'

'We should,' the man fired back. 'We *invented* it.'

Something in the man's voice told Langdon he was not joking.

'I must see you,' the caller insisted. 'This is not a matter we can discuss on the phone. My lab is only an hour's flight from Boston.'

Langdon stood in the dim light of his study and analyzed the fax in his hand. The image was overpowering, possibly representing the epigraphical find of the century, a decade of his research confirmed in a single symbol.

'It's urgent,' the voice pressured.

Langdon's eyes were locked on the brand. *Illuminati*, he read over and over. His work had always been based on the symbolic equivalent of fossils – ancient documents and historical hearsay – but this image before him was today. Present tense. He felt like a paleontologist coming face to face with a living dinosaur.

'I've taken the liberty of sending a plane for you,' the voice said. 'It will be in Boston in twenty minutes.'

Langdon felt his mouth go dry. *An hour's flight . . .*

'Please forgive my presumption,' the voice said. 'I need you here.'

Langdon looked again at the fax – an ancient myth confirmed in black and white. The implications were frightening. He gazed absently through the bay window. The first hint of dawn was sifting through the birch trees in his backyard, but the view looked somehow different this morning. As an odd combination of fear and exhilaration settled over him, Langdon knew he had no choice.

'You win,' he said. 'Tell me where to meet the plane.'

3

Thousands of miles away, two men were meeting. The chamber was dark. Medieval. Stone.

'*Benvenuto*,' the man in charge said. He was seated in the shadows, out of sight. 'Were you successful?'

'*Si*,' the dark figure replied. '*Perfettamente*.' His words were as hard as the rock walls.

'And there will be no doubt who is responsible?'

'None.'

'Superb. Do you have what I asked for?'

The killer's eyes glistened, black like oil. He produced a heavy electronic device and set it on the table.

The man in the shadows seemed pleased. 'You have done well.'

'Serving the brotherhood is an honor,' the killer replied.

'Phase two begins shortly. Get some rest. Tonight we change the world.'

4

Robert Langdon's Saab 900S tore out of the Callahan Tunnel and emerged on the east side of Boston Harbor near the entrance to Logan Airport. Checking his directions Langdon found Aviation Road and turned left past the old Eastern Airlines Building. Three hundred yards down the access road a hangar loomed in the darkness. A large number '4' was painted on it. He pulled into the parking lot and got out of his car.

A round-faced man in a blue flight suit emerged from behind the building. 'Robert Langdon?' he called. The man's voice was friendly. He had an accent Langdon couldn't place.

'That's me,' Langdon said, locking his car.

'Perfect timing,' the man said. 'I've just landed. Follow me, please.'

As they circled the building, Langdon felt tense. He was not accustomed to cryptic phone calls and secret rendezvous with strangers. Not knowing what to expect he had donned his usual classroom attire – a pair of chinos, a turtleneck, and a Harris tweed suit jacket. As they walked, he thought about the fax in his jacket pocket, still unable to believe the image it depicted.

The pilot seemed to sense Langdon's anxiety. 'Flying's not a problem for you, is it, sir?'

'Not at all,' Langdon replied. *Branded corpses are a problem for me. Flying I can handle.*

The man led Langdon the length of the hangar. They rounded the corner onto the runway.

Langdon stopped dead in his tracks and gaped at the aircraft parked on the tarmac. 'We're riding in *that*?'

The man grinned. 'Like it?'

Langdon stared a long moment. 'Like it? What the hell *is* it?'

The craft before them was enormous. It was vaguely reminiscent of the space shuttle except that the top had been shaved off, leaving it perfectly flat. Parked there on the runway, it resembled a colossal wedge. Langdon's first impression was that he must be dreaming. The vehicle looked as airworthy as a Buick. The wings were practically nonexistent – just two

7

stubby fins on the rear of the fuselage. A pair of dorsal guiders rose out of the aft section. The rest of the plane was hull – about 200 feet from front to back – no windows, nothing but hull.

'Two hundred fifty thousand kilos fully fueled,' the pilot offered, like a father bragging about his newborn. 'Runs on slush hydrogen. The shell's a titanium matrix with silicon carbide fibers. She packs a 20:1 thrust/weight ratio; most jets run at 7:1. The director must be in one helluva hurry to see you. He doesn't usually send the big boy.'

'This thing *flies?*' Langdon said.

The pilot smiled. 'Oh yeah.' He led Langdon across the tarmac toward the plane. 'Looks kind of startling, I know, but you better get used to it. In five years, all you'll see are these babies – HSCT's – High Speed Civil Transports. Our lab's one of the first to own one.'

Must be one hell of a lab, Langdon thought.

'This one's a prototype of the Boeing X-33,' the pilot continued, 'but there are dozens of others – the National Aero Space Plane, the Russians have Scramjet, the Brits have HOTOL. The future's here, it's just taking some time to get to the public sector. You can kiss conventional jets good-bye.'

Langdon looked up warily at the craft. 'I think I'd prefer a conventional jet.'

The pilot motioned up the gangplank. 'This way, please, Mr Langdon. Watch your step.'

Minutes later, Langdon was seated inside the empty cabin. The pilot buckled him into the front row and disappeared toward the front of the aircraft.

The cabin itself looked surprisingly like a wide-body commercial airliner. The only exception was that it had no windows, which made Langdon uneasy. He had been haunted his whole life by a mild case of claustrophobia – the vestige of a childhood incident he had never quite overcome.

Langdon's aversion to closed spaces was by no means debilitating, but it had always frustrated him. It manifested itself in subtle ways. He avoided enclosed sports like racquetball or squash, and he had gladly paid a small fortune for his airy, high-ceilinged Victorian home even though economical faculty housing was readily available. Langdon had often suspected his attraction to the art world as a young boy sprang from his love of museums' wide open spaces.

The engines roared to life beneath him, sending a deep shudder through the hull. Langdon swallowed hard and waited. He felt the plane start taxiing. Piped-in country music began playing quietly overhead.

A phone on the wall beside him beeped twice. Langdon lifted the receiver.

'Hello?'

'Comfortable, Mr Langdon?'

'Not at all.'

'Just relax. We'll be there in an hour.'

'And where exactly is *there*?' Langdon asked, realizing he had no idea where he was headed.

'Geneva,' the pilot replied, revving the engines. 'The lab's in Geneva.'

'Geneva,' Langdon repeated, feeling a little better. 'Upstate New York. I've actually got family near Seneca Lake. I wasn't aware Geneva had a physics lab.'

The pilot laughed. 'Not Geneva, *New York*, Mr Langdon. Geneva, *Switzerland*.'

The word took a long moment to register. 'Switzerland?' Langdon felt his pulse surge. 'I thought you said the lab was only an hour away!'

'It is, Mr Langdon.' The pilot chuckled. 'This plane goes Mach fifteen.'

5

On a busy European street, the killer serpentined through a crowd. He was a powerful man. Dark and potent. Deceptively agile. His muscles still felt hard from the thrill of his meeting.

It went well, he told himself. Although his employer had never revealed his face, the killer felt honored to be in his presence. *Had it really been only fifteen days since his employer had first made contact?* The killer still remembered every word of that call . . .

'My name is Janus,' the caller had said. 'We are kinsmen of a sort. We share an enemy. I hear your skills are for hire.'

'It depends whom you represent,' the killer replied.

The caller told him.

'Is this your idea of a joke?'

'You have heard our name, I see,' the caller replied.

'Of course. The brotherhood is legendary.'

'And yet you find yourself doubting I am genuine.'

'Everyone knows the brothers have faded to dust.'

'A devious ploy. The most dangerous enemy is that which no one fears.'

The killer was skeptical. 'The brotherhood endures?'

'Deeper underground than ever before. Our roots infiltrate everything you see . . . even the sacred fortress of our most sworn enemy.'

'Impossible. They are invulnerable.'

'Our reach is far.'

'No one's reach is that far.'

'Very soon, you will believe. An irrefutable demonstration of the brotherhood's power has already transpired. A single act of treachery and proof.'

'What have you done?'

The caller told him.

The killer's eyes went wide. 'An impossible task.'

The next day, newspapers around the globe carried the same headline. The killer became a believer.

Now, fifteen days later, the killer's faith had solidified beyond the shadow of a doubt. *The brotherhood endures*, he thought. *Tonight they will surface to reveal their power.*

As he made his way through the streets, his black eyes gleamed with foreboding. One of the most covert and feared fraternities ever to walk the earth had called on him for service. *They have chosen wisely*, he thought. His reputation for secrecy was exceeded only by that of his deadliness.

So far, he had served them nobly. He had made his kill and delivered the item to Janus as requested. Now, it was up to Janus to use his power to ensure the item's placement.

The placement . . .

The killer wondered how Janus could possibly handle such a staggering task. The man obviously had connections on the inside. The brotherhood's dominion seemed limitless.

Janus, the killer thought. *A code name, obviously*. Was it a reference, he wondered, to the Roman two-faced god . . . or to the moon of Saturn? Not that it made any difference. Janus wielded unfathomable power. He had proven that beyond a doubt.

As the killer walked, he imagined his ancestors smiling down on him. Today he was fighting *their* battle, he was fighting the same enemy they had fought for ages, as far back as the eleventh century . . . when the enemy's crusading armies had first pillaged his land, raping and killing his people, declaring them unclean, defiling their temples and gods.

His ancestors had formed a small but deadly army to defend themselves. The army became famous across the land as protectors – skilled executioners who wandered the countryside slaughtering any of the enemy they could find. They were renowned not only for their brutal killings, but also for celebrating their slayings by plunging themselves into drug-induced stupors. Their drug of choice was a potent intoxicant they called *hashish*.

As their notoriety spread, these lethal men became known by a single word – *Hassassin* – literally 'the followers of hashish.' The name *Hassassin* became synonymous with death in almost every language on earth. The word was still used today, even in modern English . . . but like the craft of killing, the word had evolved.

It was now pronounced *assassin*.

6

Sixty-four minutes had passed when an incredulous and slightly airsick Robert Langdon stepped down the gangplank onto the sun-drenched runway. A crisp breeze rustled the lapels of his tweed jacket. The open space felt wonderful. He squinted out at the lush green valley rising to snow-capped peaks all around them.

I'm dreaming, he told himself. *Any minute now I'll be waking up.*

'Welcome to Switzerland,' the pilot said, yelling over the roar of the X-33's misted-fuel HEDM engines winding down behind them.

Langdon checked his watch. It read 7.07 a.m.

'You just crossed six time zones,' the pilot offered. 'It's a little past 1 p.m. here.'

Langdon reset his watch.

'How do you feel?'

He rubbed his stomach. 'Like I've been eating Styrofoam.'

The pilot nodded. 'Altitude sickness. We were at sixty thousand feet. You're thirty per cent lighter up there. Lucky we only did a puddle jump. If we'd gone to Tokyo I'd have taken her all the way up – a hundred miles. Now *that'll* get your insides rolling.'

Langdon gave a wan nod and counted himself lucky. All things considered, the flight had been remarkably ordinary. Aside from a bone-crunching acceleration during take off, the plane's motion had been fairly typical – occasional minor turbulence, a few pressure changes as they'd climbed, but nothing at all to suggest they had been hurtling through space at the mind-numbing speed of 11,000 miles per hour.

A handful of technicians scurried onto the runway to tend to the X-33. The pilot escorted Langdon to a black Peugeot sedan in a parking area beside the control tower. Moments later they were speeding down a paved road that stretched out across the valley floor. A faint cluster of buildings rose in the distance. Outside, the grassy plains tore by in a blur.

Langdon watched in disbelief as the pilot pushed the speedometer up around 170 kilometers an hour – over 100 miles per hour. *What is it with this guy and speed?* he wondered.

'Five kilometers to the lab,' the pilot said. 'I'll have you there in two minutes.'

Langdon searched in vain for a seat belt. *Why not make it three and get us there alive?*

The car raced on.

'Do you like Reba?' the pilot asked, jamming a cassette into the tape deck. A woman started singing. 'It's just the fear of being alone . . .'

No fear here, Langdon thought absently. His female colleagues often ribbed him that his collection of museum-quality artifacts was nothing more than a transparent attempt to fill an empty home, a home they insisted would benefit greatly from the presence of a woman. Langdon always laughed it off, reminding them he already had three loves in his life – symbology, water polo, and bachelorhood – the latter being a freedom that enabled him to travel the world, sleep as late as he wanted, and enjoy quiet nights at home with a brandy and a good book.

'We're like a small city,' the pilot said, pulling Langdon from his day-dream. 'Not just labs. We've got supermarkets, a hospital, even a cinema.'

Langdon nodded blankly and looked out at the sprawling expanse of buildings rising before them.

'In fact,' the pilot added, 'we possess the largest machine on earth.'

'Really?' Langdon scanned the countryside.

'You won't see it out there, sir.' The pilot smiled. 'It's buried six stories below the earth.'

Langdon didn't have time to ask. Without warning the pilot jammed on the brakes. The car skidded to a stop outside a reinforced sentry booth.

Langdon read the sign before them. SECURITE. ARRETEZ. He suddenly felt a wave of panic, realizing where he was. 'My God! I didn't bring my passport!'

'Passports are unnecessary,' the driver assured. 'We have a standing arrangement with the Swiss government.'

Langdon watched dumbfounded as his driver gave the guard an ID. The sentry ran it through an electronic authentication device. The machine flashed green.

'Passenger name?'

'Robert Langdon,' the driver replied.

'Guest of?'

'The director.'

The sentry arched his eyebrows. He turned and checked a computer printout, verifying it against the data on his computer screen. Then he returned to the window. 'Enjoy your stay, Mr Langdon.'

The car shot off again, accelerating another 200 yards around a sweeping rotary that led to the facility's main entrance. Looming before them was a rectangular, ultramodern structure of glass and steel. Langdon was amazed by the building's striking transparent design. He had always had a fond love of architecture.

'The Glass Cathedral,' the escort offered.

'A church?'

'Hell, no. A church is the one thing we *don't* have. Physics is the religion around here. Use the Lord's name in vain all you like,' he laughed, 'just don't slander any quarks or mesons.'

Langdon sat bewildered as the driver swung the car around and brought it to a stop in front of the glass building. *Quarks and mesons? No border control? Mach 15 jets? Who the hell ARE these guys?* The engraved granite slab in front of the building bore the answer:

(CERN)
*Conseil Européen pour la
Recherche Nucléaire*

'Nuclear Research?' Langdon asked, fairly certain his translation was correct.

The driver did not answer. He was leaning forward, busily adjusting the car's cassette player. 'This is your stop. The director will meet you at this entrance.'

Langdon noted a man in a wheelchair exiting the building. He looked to be in his early sixties. Gaunt and totally bald with a sternly set jaw, he wore a white lab coat and dress shoes propped firmly on the wheelchair's footrest. Even at a distance his eyes looked lifeless – like two gray stones.

'Is that him?' Langdon asked.

The driver looked up. 'Well, I'll be . . .' He turned and gave Langdon an ominous smile. 'Speak of the devil.'

Uncertain what to expect, Langdon stepped from the vehicle.

The man in the wheelchair accelerated toward Langdon and offered a clammy hand. 'Mr Langdon? We spoke on the phone. My name is Maximilian Kohler.'

7

Maximilian Kohler, director general of CERN, was known behind his back as *König* – King. It was a title more of fear than reverence for the figure who ruled over his dominion from a wheelchair throne. Although few knew him personally, the horrific story of how he had been crippled was lore at CERN, and there were few there who blamed him for his bitterness . . . nor for his sworn dedication to pure science.

Langdon had only been in Kohler's presence a few moments and already sensed the director was a man who kept his distance. Langdon found himself practically jogging to keep up with Kohler's electric wheelchair as it sped silently toward the main entrance. The wheelchair was like none Langdon had ever seen – equipped with a bank of electronics including a multiline phone, a paging system, computer screen, even a small, detachable video camera. King Kohler's mobile command center.

Langdon followed through a mechanical door into CERN's voluminous main lobby.

The Glass Cathedral, Langdon mused, gazing upward toward heaven.

Overhead, the bluish glass roof shimmered in the afternoon sun, casting rays of geometric patterns in the air and giving the room a sense of grandeur. Angular shadows fell like veins across the white tiled walls and down to the marble floors. The air smelled clean, sterile. A handful of scientists moved briskly about, their footsteps echoing in the resonant space.

'This way, please, Mr Langdon.' His voice sounded almost computerized. His accent was rigid and precise, like his stern features. Kohler coughed and wiped his mouth on a white handkerchief as he fixed his dead gray eyes on Langdon. 'Please hurry.' His wheelchair seemed to leap across the tiled floor.

Langdon followed past what seemed to be countless hallways branching off the main atrium. Every hallway was alive with activity. The scientists who saw Kohler seemed to stare in surprise, eyeing Langdon as if wondering who he must be to command such company.

'I'm embarrassed to admit,' Langdon ventured, trying to make conversation, 'that I've never heard of CERN.'

'Not surprising,' Kohler replied, his clipped response sounding harshly efficient. 'Most Americans do not see Europe as the world leader in scientific research. They see us as nothing but a quaint shopping district – an odd perception if you consider the nationalities of men like Einstein, Galileo, and Newton.'

Langdon was unsure how to respond. He pulled the fax from his pocket. 'This man in the photograph, can you—'

Kohler cut him off with a wave of his hand. 'Please. Not here. I am taking you to him now.' He held out his hand. 'Perhaps I should take that.'

Langdon handed over the fax and fell silently into step.

Kohler took a sharp left and entered a wide hallway adorned with awards and commendations. A particularly large plaque dominated the entry. Langdon slowed to read the engraved bronze as they passed.

ARS ELECTRONICA AWARD
For Cultural Innovation in the Digital Age
Awarded to Tim Berners Lee and CERN
for the invention of the
WORLDWIDE WEB

Well I'll be damned, Langdon thought, reading the text. *This guy wasn't kidding.* Langdon had always thought of the Web as an American invention. Then again, his knowledge was limited to the site for his own book and the occasional on-line exploration of the Louvre or El Prado on his old Macintosh.

'The Web,' Kohler said, coughing again and wiping his mouth, 'began here as a network of in-house computer sites. It enabled scientists from different departments to share daily findings with one another. Of course, the entire world is under the impression the Web is U.S. technology.'

Langdon followed down the hall. 'Why not set the record straight?'

Kohler shrugged, apparently disinterested. 'A petty misconception over a petty technology. CERN is far greater than a global connection of computers. Our scientists produce miracles almost daily.'

Langdon gave Kohler a questioning look. '*Miracles?*' The word 'miracle' was certainly not part of the vocabulary around Harvard's Fairchild Science Building. *Miracles* were left for the School of Divinity.

'You sound skeptical,' Kohler said. 'I thought you were a religious symbologist. Do you not believe in miracles?'

'I'm undecided on miracles,' Langdon said. *Particularly those that take place in science labs.*

'Perhaps miracle is the wrong word. I was simply trying to speak your language.'

'My language?' Langdon was suddenly uncomfortable. 'Not to disappoint you, sir, but I study religious *symbology* – I'm an academic, not a priest.'

Kohler slowed suddenly and turned, his gaze softening a bit. 'Of course.

16

How simple of me. One does not need to have cancer to analyze its symptoms.'

Langdon had never heard it put quite that way.

As they moved down the hallway, Kohler gave an accepting nod. 'I suspect you and I will understand each other perfectly, Mr Langdon.'

Somehow Langdon doubted it.

As the pair hurried on, Langdon began to sense a deep rumbling up ahead. The noise got more and more pronounced with every step, reverberating through the walls. It seemed to be coming from the end of the hallway in front of them.

'What's that?' Langdon finally asked, having to yell. He felt like they were approaching an active volcano.

'Free fall tube,' Kohler replied, his hollow voice cutting the air effortlessly. He offered no other explanation.

Langdon didn't ask. He was exhausted, and Maximilian Kohler seemed disinterested in winning any hospitality awards. Langdon reminded himself why he was here. *Illuminati.* He assumed somewhere in this colossal facility was a body . . . a body branded with a symbol he had just flown thousands of miles to see.

As they approached the end of the hall, the rumble became almost deafening, vibrating up through Langdon's soles. They rounded the bend, and a viewing gallery appeared on the right. Four thick-paned portals were embedded in a curved wall, like windows in a submarine. Langdon stopped and looked through one of the holes.

Professor Robert Langdon had seen some strange things in his life, but this was the strangest. He blinked a few times, wondering if he was hallucinating. He was staring into an enormous circular chamber. Inside the chamber, floating as though weightless, were *people.* Three of them. One waved and did a somersault in midair.

My God, he thought. *I'm in the land of Oz.*

The floor of the room was a mesh grid, like a giant sheet of chicken wire. Visible beneath the grid was the metallic blur of a huge propeller.

'Free fall tube,' Kohler said, stopping to wait for him. 'Indoor skydiving. For stress relief. It's a vertical wind tunnel.'

Langdon looked on in amazement. One of the free fallers, an obese woman, maneuvered toward the window. She was being buffeted by the air currents but grinned and flashed Langdon the thumbs-up sign. Langdon smiled weakly and returned the gesture, wondering if she knew it was the ancient phallic symbol for masculine virility.

The heavyset woman, Langdon noticed, was the only one wearing what appeared to be a miniature parachute. The swathe of fabric billowed over her like a toy. 'What's her little chute for?' Langdon asked Kohler. 'It can't be more than a yard in diameter.'

'Friction,' Kohler said. 'Decreases her aerodynamics so the fan can lift

17

her.' He started down the corridor again. 'One square yard of drag will slow a falling body almost twenty per cent.'

Langdon nodded blankly.

He never suspected that later that night, in a country hundreds of miles away, the information would save his life.

8

When Kohler and Langdon emerged from the rear of CERN's main complex into the stark Swiss sunlight, Langdon felt as if he'd been transported home. The scene before him looked like an Ivy League campus.

A grassy slope cascaded downward onto an expansive lowlands where clusters of sugar maples dotted quadrangles bordered by brick dormitories and footpaths. Scholarly looking individuals with stacks of books hustled in and out of buildings. As if to accentuate the collegiate atmosphere, two longhaired hippies hurled a Frisbee back and forth while enjoying Mahler's Fourth Symphony blaring from a dorm window.

'These are our residential dorms,' Kohler explained as he accelerated his wheelchair down the path toward the buildings. 'We have over three thousand physicists here. CERN single-handedly employs more than half of the world's particle physicists – the brightest minds on earth – Germans, Japanese, Italians, Dutch, you name it. Our physicists represent over five hundred universities and sixty nationalities.'

Langdon was amazed. 'How do they all communicate?'

'English, of course. The universal language of science.'

Langdon had always heard *math* was the universal language of science, but he was too tired to argue. He dutifully followed Kohler down the path.

Halfway to the bottom, a young man jogged by. His T-shirt proclaimed the message: NO GUT, NO GLORY!

Langdon looked after him, mystified. 'Gut?'

'General Unified Theory,' Kohler quipped. 'The theory of everything.'

'I see,' Langdon said, not seeing at all.

'Are you familiar with particle physics, Mr Langdon?'

Langdon shrugged. 'I'm familiar with general physics – falling bodies, that sort of thing.' His years of high-diving experience had given him a profound respect for the awesome power of gravitational acceleration. 'Particle physics is the study of atoms, isn't it?'

Kohler shook his head. 'Atoms look like planets compared to what we deal with. Our interests lie with an atom's *nucleus* – a mere ten-thousandth the size of the whole.' He coughed again, sounding sick. 'The men and women of CERN are here to find answers to the same questions man has been asking since the beginning of time. Where did we come from? What are we made of?'

'And these answers are in a physics lab?'

'You sound surprised.'

'I am. The questions seem spiritual.'

'Mr Langdon, all questions were once spiritual. Since the beginning of time, spirituality and religion have been called on to fill in the gaps that science did not understand. The rising and setting of the sun was once attributed to *Helios* and a flaming chariot. Earthquakes and tidal waves were the wrath of Poseidon. Science has now proven those gods to be false idols. Soon *all* Gods will be proven to be false idols. Science has now provided answers to almost every question man can ask. There are only a few questions left, and they are the esoteric ones. Where do we come from? What are we doing here? What is the meaning of life and the universe?'

Langdon was amazed. 'And these are questions CERN is trying to answer?'

'Correction. These are questions we *are* answering.'

Langdon fell silent as the two men wound through the residential quadrangles. As they walked, a Frisbee sailed overhead and skidded to a stop directly in front of them. Kohler ignored it and kept going.

A voice called out from across the quad. '*S'il vous plaît!*'

Langdon looked over. An elderly white-haired man in a COLLEGE PARIS sweatshirt waved to him. Langdon picked up the Frisbee and expertly threw it back. The old man caught it on one finger and bounded it a few times before whipping it over his shoulder to his partner. 'Merci!' he called to Langdon.

'Congratulations,' Kohler said when Langdon finally caught up. 'You just played toss with a Nobel prize-winner, Georges Charpak, inventor of the multiwire proportional chamber.'

Langdon nodded. *My lucky day.*

It took Langdon and Kohler three more minutes to reach their destination – a large, well-kept dormitory sitting in a grove of aspens. Compared to the other dorms, this structure seemed luxurious. The carved stone sign in front read BUILDING C.

Imaginative title, Langdon thought.

But despite its sterile name, Building C appealed to Langdon's sense of architectural style – conservative and solid. It had a red brick façade, an ornate balustrade, and sat framed by sculpted symmetrical hedges. As the two men ascended the stone path toward the entry, they passed under a gateway formed by a pair of marble columns. Someone had put a sticky-note on one of them.

THIS COLUMN IS IONIC

Physicist graffiti? Langdon mused, eyeing the column and chuckling to himself. 'I'm relieved to see that even brilliant physicists make mistakes.'

Kohler looked over. 'What do you mean?'

'Whoever wrote that note made a mistake. That column isn't Ionic. Ionic columns are uniform in width. That one's tapered. It's Doric – the Greek counterpart. A common mistake.'

Kohler did not smile. 'The author meant it as a joke, Mr Langdon. *Ionic* means containing ions – electrically charged particles. Most objects contain them.'

Langdon looked back at the column and groaned.

Langdon was still feeling stupid when he stepped from the elevator on the top floor of Building C. He followed Kohler down a well-appointed corridor. The decor was unexpected – traditional colonial French – a cherry divan, porcelain floor vase, and scrolled woodwork.

'We like to keep our tenured scientists comfortable,' Kohler explained.

Evidently, Langdon thought. 'So the man in the fax lived up here? One of your upper-level employees?'

'Quite,' Kohler said. 'He missed a meeting with me this morning and did not answer his page. I came up here to locate him and found him dead in his living room.'

Langdon felt a sudden chill realizing that he was about to see a dead body. His stomach had never been particularly stalwart. It was a weakness he'd discovered as an art student when the teacher informed the class that Leonardo da Vinci had gained his expertise in the human form by exhuming corpses and dissecting their musculature.

Kohler led the way to the far end of the hallway. There was a single door. 'The Penthouse, as you would say,' Kohler announced, dabbing a bead of perspiration from his forehead.

Langdon eyed the lone oak door before them. The name plate read:

LEONARDO VETRA

'Leonardo Vetra,' Kohler said, 'would have been fifty-eight next week. He was one of the most brilliant scientists of our time. His death is a profound loss for science.'

For an instant Langdon thought he sensed emotion in Kohler's hardened face. But as quickly as it had come, it was gone. Kohler reached in his pocket and began sifting through a large key ring.

An odd thought suddenly occurred to Langdon. The building seemed deserted. 'Where is everyone?' he asked. The lack of activity was hardly what he expected considering they were about to enter a murder scene.

'The residents are in their labs,' Kohler replied, finding the key.

'I mean the *police*,' Langdon clarified. 'Have they left already?'

Kohler paused, his key halfway into the lock. 'Police?'

Langdon's eyes met the director's. 'Police. You sent me a fax of a homicide. You *must* have called the police.'

'I most certainly have not.'

'What?'

Kohler's gray eyes sharpened. 'The situation is complex, Mr Langdon.'

Langdon felt a wave of apprehension. 'But . . . certainly someone else knows about this!'

'Yes. Leonardo's adopted daughter. She is also a physicist here at CERN. She and her father share a lab. They are partners. Ms Vetra has been away this week doing field research. I have notified her of her father's death, and she is returning as we speak.'

'But a man has been murd—'

'A formal investigation,' Kohler said, his voice firm, 'will take place. However, it will most certainly involve a search of Vetra's lab, a space he and his daughter hold most private. Therefore, it will wait until Ms Vetra has arrived. I feel I owe her at least that modicum of discretion.'

Kohler turned the key.

As the door swung open, a blast of icy air hissed into the hall and hit Langdon in the face. He fell back in bewilderment. He was gazing across the threshold of an alien world. The flat before him was immersed in a thick, white fog. The mist swirled in smoky vortexes around the furniture and shrouded the room in opaque haze.

'What the . . . ?' Langdon stammered.

'Freon cooling system,' Kohler replied. 'I chilled the flat to preserve the body.'

Langdon buttoned his tweed jacket against the cold. *I'm in Oz*, he thought. *And I forgot my magic slippers.*

9

The corpse on the floor before Langdon was hideous. The late Leonardo Vetra lay on his back, stripped naked, his skin bluish-gray. His neck bones were jutting out where they had been broken, and his head was twisted completely backward, pointing the wrong way. His face was out of view, pressed against the floor. The man lay in a frozen puddle of his own urine, the hair around his shriveled genitals spidered with frost.

Fighting a wave of nausea, Langdon let his eyes fall to the victim's chest. Although Langdon had stared at the symmetrical wound a dozen times on the fax, the burn was infinitely more commanding in real life. The raised, broiled flesh was perfectly delineated . . . the symbol flawlessly formed.

Langdon wondered if the intense chill now raking through his body was the air-conditioning or his utter amazement with the significance of what he was now staring at.

His heart pounded as he circled the body, reading the word upside down, reaffirming the genius of the symmetry. The symbol seemed even less conceivable now that he was staring at it.

'Mr Langdon?'

Langdon did not hear. He was in another world . . . his world, his element, a world where history, myth, and fact collided, flooding his senses. The gears turned.

'Mr Langdon?' Kohler's eyes probed expectantly.

Langdon did not look up. His disposition now intensified, his focus total. 'How much do you already know?'

'Only what I had time to read on your website. The word *Illuminati* means "the enlightened ones." It is the name of some sort of ancient brotherhood.'

Langdon nodded. 'Had you heard the name before?'

'Not until I saw it branded on Mr Vetra.'

'So you ran a web search for it?'

'Yes.'

'And the word returned hundreds of references, no doubt.'

'Thousands,' Kohler said. 'Yours, however, contained references to Harvard, Oxford, a reputable publisher, as well as a list of related publications. As a scientist I have come to learn that information is only as valuable as its source. Your credentials seemed authentic.'

Langdon's eyes were still riveted on the body.

Kohler said nothing more. He simply stared, apparently waiting for Langdon to shed some light on the scene before them.

Langdon looked up, glancing around the frozen flat. 'Perhaps we should discuss this in a warmer place?'

'This room is fine.' Kohler seemed oblivious to the cold. 'We'll talk here.'

Langdon frowned. The Illuminati history was by no means a simple one. *I'll freeze to death trying to explain it.* He gazed again at the brand, feeling a renewed sense of awe.

Although accounts of the Illuminati emblem were legendary in modern symbology, no academic had ever actually *seen* it. Ancient documents described the symbol as an *ambigram* – *ambi* meaning 'both' – signifying it was legible *both* ways. And although ambigrams were common in symbology – swastikas, yin yang, Jewish stars, simple crosses – the idea that a *word* could be crafted into an ambigram seemed utterly impossible. Modern symbologists had tried for years to forge the word 'Illuminati' into a perfectly symmetrical style, but they had failed miserably. Most academics had now decided the symbol's existence was a myth.

'So who are the Illuminati?' Kohler demanded.

Yes, Langdon thought, *who indeed?* He began his tale.

'Since the beginning of history,' Langdon explained, 'a deep rift has existed between science and religion. Outspoken scientists like Giordano Bruno—'

'Were murdered,' Kohler interjected. 'Murdered by the church for revealing scientific truths. Religion has always persecuted science.'

'Yes. But in the 1500s, a group of men in Rome fought back against the church. Some of Italy's most enlightened men – physicists, mathematicians, astronomers – began meeting secretly to share their concerns about the church's inaccurate teachings. They feared that the church's monopoly on "truth" threatened academic enlightenment around the world. They founded the world's first scientific think tank, calling themselves "the enlightened ones."'

'The Illuminati.'

'Yes,' Langdon said. 'Europe's most learned minds . . . dedicated to the quest for scientific truth.'

Kohler fell silent.

'Of course, the Illuminati were hunted ruthlessly by the Catholic Church. Only through rites of extreme secrecy did the scientists remain safe. Word spread through the academic underground, and the Illuminati brotherhood grew to include academics from all over Europe. The scientists met regularly in Rome at an ultrasecret lair they called the *Church of Illumination.*'

Kohler coughed and shifted in his chair.

'Many of the Illuminati,' Langdon continued, 'wanted to combat the church's tyranny with acts of violence, but their most revered member persuaded them against it. He was a pacifist, as well as one of history's most famous scientists.'

Langdon was certain Kohler would recognize the name. Even nonscientists were familiar with the ill-fated astronomer who had been arrested and almost executed by the church for proclaiming that the *sun*, not the earth, was the center of the solar system. Although his data were incontrovertible, the astronomer was severely punished for implying that God had placed mankind somewhere other than at the *center* of His universe.

'His name was Galileo Galilei,' Langdon said.

Kohler looked up. 'Galileo?'

'Yes. Galileo was an Illuminatus. And he was also a devout Catholic. He tried to soften the church's position on science by proclaiming that science did not undermine the existence of God, but rather *reinforced* it. He wrote once that when he looked through his telescope at the spinning planets, he could hear God's voice in the music of the spheres. He held that science and religion were not enemies, but rather *allies* – two different languages telling the same story, a story of symmetry and balance . . . heaven and hell, night and day, hot and cold, God and Satan. Both science and religion rejoiced in God's symmetry . . . the endless contest of light and dark.' Langdon paused, stamping his feet to stay warm.

Kohler simply sat in his wheelchair and stared.

'Unfortunately,' Langdon added, 'the unification of science and religion was not what the church wanted.'

'Of course not,' Kohler interrupted. 'The union would have nullified the church's claim as the *sole* vessel through which man could understand God. So the church tried Galileo as a heretic, found him guilty, and put him under permanent house arrest. I am quite aware of scientific history, Mr Langdon. But this was all centuries ago. What does it have to do with Leonardo Vetra?'

The million dollar question. Langdon cut to the chase. 'Galileo's arrest threw the Illuminati into upheaval. Mistakes were made, and the church discovered the identities of four members, whom they captured and interrogated. But the four scientists revealed nothing . . . even under torture.'

'Torture?'

Langdon nodded. 'They were branded alive. On the chest. With the symbol of a cross.'

Kohler's eyes widened, and he shot an uneasy glance at Vetra's body.

'Then the scientists were brutally murdered, their dead bodies dropped in the streets of Rome as a warning to others thinking of joining the Illuminati. With the church closing in, the remaining Illuminati fled Italy.'

Langdon paused to make his point. He looked directly into Kohler's eyes. 'The Illuminati went deep underground, where they began mixing with other refugee groups fleeing the Catholic purges – mystics, alchemists, occultists, Muslims, Jews. Over the years, the Illuminati began absorbing new members. A new Illuminati emerged. A darker Illuminati. A deeply anti-Christian Illuminati. They grew very powerful, employing mysterious rites, deadly secrecy, vowing someday to rise again and take revenge on the Catholic Church. Their power grew to the point where the church considered them the single most dangerous anti-Christian force on earth. The Vatican denounced the brotherhood as *Shaitan*.'

'*Shaitan?*'

'It's Islamic. It means "adversary" . . . *God's* adversary. The church chose Islam for the name because it was a language they considered dirty.' Langdon hesitated. '*Shaitan* is the root of an English word . . . *Satan*.'

An uneasiness crossed Kohler's face.

Langdon's voice was grim. 'Mr Kohler, I do not know how this marking appeared on this man's chest . . . or why . . . but you are looking at the long-lost symbol of the world's oldest and most powerful satanic cult.'

10

The alley was narrow and deserted. The Hassassin strode quickly now, his black eyes filling with anticipation. As he approached his destination, Janus's parting words echoed in his mind. *Phase two begins shortly. Get some rest.*

The Hassassin smirked. He had been awake all night, but sleep was the last thing on his mind. Sleep was for the weak. He was a warrior like his ancestors before him, and his people never slept once a battle had begun. This battle had most definitely begun, and he had been given the honor of spilling first blood. Now he had two hours to celebrate his glory before going back to work.

Sleep? There are far better ways to relax . . .

An appetite for hedonistic pleasure was something bred into him by his ancestors. His ascendants had indulged in hashish, but he preferred a different kind of gratification. He took pride in his body – a well-tuned, lethal machine, which, despite his heritage, he refused to pollute with narcotics. He had developed a more nourishing addiction than drugs . . . a far more healthy and satisfying reward.

Feeling a familiar anticipation swelling within him, the Hassassin moved faster down the alley. He arrived at the nondescript door and rang the bell. A view slit in the door opened, and two soft brown eyes studied him appraisingly. Then the door swung open.

'Welcome,' the well-dressed woman said. She ushered him into an impeccably furnished sitting room where the lights were low. The air was laced with expensive perfume and musk. 'Whenever you are ready.' She handed him a book of photographs. 'Ring me when you have made your choice.' Then she disappeared.

The Hassassin smiled.

As he sat on the plush divan and positioned the photo album on his lap, he felt a carnal hunger stir. Although his people did not celebrate Christmas, he imagined that this is what it must feel like to be a Christian child, sitting before a stack of Christmas presents, about to discover the miracles inside. He opened the album and examined the photos. A lifetime of sexual fantasies stared back at him.

Marisa. An Italian goddess. Fiery. A young Sophia Loren.

Sachiko. A Japanese geisha. Lithe. No doubt skilled.

Kanara. A stunning black vision. Muscular. Exotic.

He examined the entire album twice and made his choice. He pressed a button on the table beside him. A minute later the woman who had greeted him reappeared. He indicated his selection. She smiled. 'Follow me.'

After handling the financial arrangements, the woman made a hushed phone call. She waited a few minutes and then led him up a winding marble staircase to a luxurious hallway. 'It's the gold door on the end,' she said. 'You have expensive taste.'

I should, he thought. *I am a connoisseur.*

The Hassassin padded the length of the hallway like a panther anticipating a long overdue meal. When he reached the doorway he smiled to himself. It was already ajar . . . welcoming him in. He pushed, and the door swung noiselessly open.

When he saw his selection, he knew he had chosen well. She was exactly as he had requested . . . nude, lying on her back, her arms tied to the bedposts with thick velvet cords.

He crossed the room and ran a dark finger across her ivory abdomen. *I killed last night*, he thought. *You are my reward.*

11

'Satanic?' Kohler wiped his mouth and shifted uncomfortably. 'This is the symbol of a *satanic* cult?'

Langdon paced the frozen room to keep warm. 'The Illuminati were satanic. But not in the modern sense.'

Langdon quickly explained how most people pictured satanic cults as devil-worshiping fiends, and yet Satanists historically were educated men who stood as adversaries to the church. *Shaitan.* The rumors of satanic black-magic animal sacrifices and the pentagram ritual were nothing but lies spread by the church as a smear campaign against their adversaries. Over time, opponents of the church, wanting to emulate the Illuminati, began believing the lies and acting them out. Thus, modern Satanism was born.

Kohler grunted abruptly. 'This is all ancient history. I want to know how this symbol got *here*.'

Langdon took a deep breath. 'The symbol itself was created by an anonymous sixteenth-century Illuminati artist as a tribute to Galileo's love of symmetry – a kind of sacred Illuminati logo. The brotherhood kept the design secret, allegedly planning to reveal it only when they had amassed enough power to resurface and carry out their final goal.'

Kohler looked unsettled. 'So this symbol means the Illuminati brother-hood is resurfacing?'

Langdon frowned. 'That would be impossible. There is one chapter of Illuminati history that I have not yet explained.'

Kohler's voice intensified. 'Enlighten me.'

Langdon rubbed his palms together, mentally sorting through the hundreds of documents he'd read or written on the Illuminati. 'The Illuminati were survivors,' he explained. 'When they fled Rome, they traveled across Europe looking for a safe place to regroup. They were taken in by another secret society . . . a brotherhood of wealthy Bavarian stone craftsmen called the Freemasons.'

Kohler looked startled. 'The Masons?'

Langdon nodded, not at all surprised that Kohler had heard of the group. The brotherhood of the Masons currently had over five million members worldwide, half of them residing in the United States, and over one million of them in Europe.

'Certainly the Masons are not satanic,' Kohler declared, sounding suddenly skeptical.

'Absolutely not. The Masons fell victim of their own benevolence. After harboring the fleeing scientists in the 1700s, the Masons unknowingly became a front for the Illuminati. The Illuminati grew within their ranks, gradually taking over positions of power within the lodges. They quietly reestablished their scientific brotherhood deep within the Masons – a kind of secret society within a secret society. Then the Illuminati used the worldwide connection of Masonic lodges to spread their influence.'

Langdon drew a cold breath before racing on. 'Obliteration of Catholicism was the Illuminati's central covenant. The brotherhood held that the superstitious dogma spewed forth by the church was mankind's greatest enemy. They feared that if religion continued to promote pious myth as absolute fact, scientific progress would halt, and mankind would be doomed to an ignorant future of senseless holy wars.'

'Much like we see today.'

Langdon frowned. Kohler was right. Holy wars were still making headlines. *My God is better than your God.* It seemed there was always close correlation between true believers and high body counts.

'Go on,' Kohler said.

Langdon gathered his thoughts and continued. 'The Illuminati grew more powerful in Europe and set their sights on America, a fledgling government many of whose leaders were Masons – George Washington, Ben Franklin – honest, God-fearing men who were unaware of the Illuminati stronghold on the Masons. The Illuminati took advantage of the infiltration and helped found banks, universities, and industry to finance their ultimate quest.' Langdon paused. 'The creation of a single unified world state – a kind of secular New World Order.'

Kohler did not move.

'A New World Order,' Langdon repeated, 'based on scientific enlightenment. They called it their Luciferian Doctrine. The church claimed Lucifer was a reference to the devil, but the brotherhood insisted Lucifer was intended in its literal Latin meaning – *bringer of light.* Or *Illuminator.*'

Kohler sighed, and his voice grew suddenly solemn. 'Mr Langdon, please sit down.'

Langdon sat tentatively on a frost-covered chair.

Kohler moved his wheelchair closer. 'I am not sure I understand everything you have just told me, but I do understand this. Leonardo Vetra was one of CERN's greatest assets. He was also a friend. I need you to help me locate the Illuminati.'

Langdon didn't know how to respond. 'Locate the Illuminati?' *He's kidding, right?* 'I'm afraid, sir, that will be utterly impossible.'

Kohler's brow creased. 'What do you mean? You won't—'

'Mr Kohler,' Langdon leaned toward his host, uncertain how to make him understand what he was about to say, 'I did not finish my story. Despite appearances, it is extremely unlikely that this brand was put here by the Illuminati. There has been no evidence of their existence for over half a century, and most scholars agree the Illuminati have been defunct for many years.'

The words hit silence. Kohler stared through the fog with a look somewhere between stupefaction and anger. 'How the hell can you tell me this group is extinct when their name is seared into this man!'

Langdon had been asking himself that question all morning. The appearance of the Illuminati ambigram was astonishing. Symbologists worldwide would be dazzled. And yet, the academic in Langdon understood that the brand's reemergence proved absolutely nothing about the Illuminati.

'Symbols,' Langdon said, 'in no way confirm the presence of their original creators.'

'What is *that* supposed to mean?'

'It means that when organized philosophies like the Illuminati go out of existence, their symbols remain . . . available for adoption by other groups. It's called *transference*. It's very common in symbology. The Nazis took the swastika from the Hindus, the Christians adopted the cruciform from the Egyptians, the—'

'This morning,' Kohler challenged, 'when I typed the word "Illuminati" into the computer, it returned thousands of current references. Apparently a lot of people think this group is still active.'

'Conspiracy buffs,' Langdon replied. He had always been annoyed by the plethora of conspiracy theories that circulated in modern pop culture. The media craved apocalyptic headlines, and self-proclaimed 'cult specialists' were still cashing in on millennium hype with fabricated stories that the Illuminati were alive and well and organizing their New World Order. Recently the *New York Times* had reported the eerie Masonic ties of countless famous men – Sir Arthur Conan Doyle, the Duke of Kent, Peter Sellers, Irving Berlin, Prince Philip, Louis Armstrong, as well as a pantheon of well-known modern-day industrialists and banking magnates.

Kohler pointed angrily at Vetra's body. 'Considering the evidence, I would say perhaps the conspiracy buffs are correct.'

'I realize how it appears,' Langdon said as diplomatically as he could. 'And yet a far more plausible explanation is that some *other* organization has taken control of the Illuminati brand and is using it for their own purposes.'

'What purposes? What does this murder prove?'

Good question, Langdon thought. He was also having trouble imagining where anyone could have turned up the Illuminati brand after 400 years. 'All I can tell you is that even if the Illuminati were still active today, which I am virtually positive they are not, they would never be involved in Leonardo Vetra's death.'

'No?'

'No. The Illuminati may have believed in the abolition of Christianity, but they wielded their power through political and financial means, not through terrorist acts. Furthermore, the Illuminati had a strict code of morality regarding who they saw as enemies. They held men of science in the highest regard. There is no way they would have murdered a fellow scientist like Leonardo Vetra.'

Kohler's eyes turned to ice. 'Perhaps I failed to mention that Leonardo Vetra was anything but an ordinary scientist.'

Langdon exhaled patiently. 'Mr Kohler, I'm sure Leonardo Vetra was brilliant in many ways, but the fact remains—'

Without warning, Kohler spun in his wheelchair and accelerated out of the living room, leaving a wake of swirling mist as he disappeared down a hallway.

For the love of God, Langdon groaned. He followed. Kohler was waiting for him in a small alcove at the end of the hallway.

'This is Leonardo's study,' Kohler said, motioning to the sliding door. 'Perhaps when you see it you'll understand things differently.' With an awkward grunt, Kohler heaved, and the door slid open.

Langdon peered into the study and immediately felt his skin crawl. *Holy mother of Jesus*, he said to himself.

12

In another country, a young guard sat patiently before an expansive bank of video monitors. He watched as images flashed before him – live feeds from hundreds of wireless video cameras that surveyed the sprawling complex. The images went by in an endless procession.

An ornate hallway.

A private office.

An industrial-size kitchen.

As the pictures went by, the guard fought off a daydream. He was nearing the end of his shift, and yet he was still vigilant. Service was an honor. Someday he would be granted his ultimate reward.

As his thoughts drifted, an image before him registered alarm. Suddenly, with a reflexive jerk that startled even himself, his hand shot out and hit a button on the control panel. The picture before him froze.

His nerves tingling, he leaned toward the screen for a closer look. The reading on the monitor told him the image was being transmitted from camera #86 – a camera that was supposed to be overlooking a hallway.

But the image before him was most definitely *not* a hallway.

13

Langdon stared in bewilderment at the study before him. 'What *is* this place?' Despite the welcome blast of warm air on his face, he stepped through the door with trepidation.

Kohler said nothing as he followed Langdon inside.

Langdon scanned the room, not having the slightest idea what to make of it. It contained the most peculiar mix of artifacts he had ever seen. On the far wall, dominating the decor, was an enormous wooden crucifix, which Langdon placed as fourteenth-century Spanish. Above the cruciform, suspended from the ceiling, was a metallic mobile of the orbiting planets. To the left was an oil painting of the Virgin Mary, and beside that was a laminated periodic table of elements. On the side wall, two additional brass cruciforms flanked a poster of Albert Einstein, his famous quote reading, GOD DOES NOT PLAY DICE WITH THE UNIVERSE.

Langdon moved into the room, looking around in astonishment. A leather-bound Bible sat on Vetra's desk beside a plastic Bohr model of an atom and a miniature replica of Michelangelo's Moses.

Talk about eclectic, Langdon thought. The warmth felt good, but something about the decor sent a new set of chills through his body. He felt like he was witnessing the clash of two philosophical titans . . . an unsettling blur of opposing forces. He scanned the titles on the bookshelf:

The God Particle
The Tao of Physics
God: The Evidence

One of the bookends was etched with a quote:

TRUE SCIENCE DISCOVERS GOD
WAITING BEHIND EVERY DOOR.
—POPE PIUS XII

'Leonardo was a Catholic priest,' Kohler said.
Langdon turned. 'A priest? I thought you said he was a physicist.'

'He was both. Men of science and religion are not unprecedented in history. Leonardo was one of them. He considered physics "God's natural law". He claimed God's handwriting was visible in the natural order all around us. Through science he hoped to prove God's existence to the doubting masses. He considered himself a theo-physicist.'

Theo-physicist? Langdon thought it sounded impossibly oxymoronic.

'The field of particle physics,' Kohler said, 'has made some shocking discoveries lately – discoveries quite spiritual in implication. Leonardo was responsible for many of them.'

Langdon studied CERN's director, still trying to process the bizarre surroundings. 'Spirituality and physics?' Langdon had spent his career studying religious history, and if there was one recurring theme, it was that science and religion had been oil and water since day one . . . archenemies . . . unmixable.

'Vetra was on the cutting edge of particle physics,' Kohler said. 'He was starting to fuse science and religion . . . showing that they complement each other in most unanticipated ways. He called the field *New Physics*.' Kohler pulled a book from the shelf and handed it to Langdon.

Langdon studied the cover. *God, Miracles, and the New Physics* – by Leonardo Vetra.

'The field is small,' Kohler said, 'but it's bringing fresh answers to some old questions – questions about the origin of the universe and the forces that bind us all. Leonardo believed his research had the potential to convert millions to a more spiritual life. Last year he categorically proved the existence of an energy force that unites us all. He actually demonstrated that we are all physically connected . . . that the molecules in your body are intertwined with the molecules in mine . . . that there is a single force moving within all of us.'

Langdon felt disconcerted. *And the power of God shall unite us all.* 'Mr Vetra actually found a way to *demonstrate* that particles are connected?'

'Conclusive evidence. A recent *Scientific American* article hailed *New Physics* as a surer path to God than religion itself.'

The comment hit home. Langdon suddenly found himself thinking of the antireligious Illuminati. Reluctantly, he forced himself to permit a momentary intellectual foray into the impossible. If the Illuminati were indeed still active, would they have killed Leonardo to stop him from bringing his religious message to the masses? Langdon shook off the thought. *Absurd! The Illuminati are ancient history! All academics know that!*

'Vetra had plenty of enemies in the scientific world,' Kohler went on. 'Many scientific purists despised him. Even here at CERN. They felt that using analytical physics to support religious principles was a treason against science.'

'But aren't scientists today a bit less defensive about the church?'

Kohler grunted in disgust. 'Why *should* we be? The church may not be burning scientists at the stake anymore, but if you think they've released their reign over science, ask yourself why half the schools in your country are not allowed to teach evolution. Ask yourself why the U.S. Christian Coalition is the most influential lobby against scientific progress in the world. The battle between science and religion is still raging, Mr Langdon. It has moved from the battlefields to the boardrooms, but it is still raging.'

Langdon realized Kohler was right. Just last week the Harvard School of Divinity had marched on the Biology Building, protesting the genetic engineering taking place in the graduate program. The chairman of the Bio Department, famed ornithologist Richard Aaronian, defended his curriculum by hanging a huge banner from his office window. The banner depicted the Christian 'fish' modified with four little feet – a tribute, Aaronian claimed, to the African lung-fishes' evolution onto dry land. Beneath the fish, instead of the word 'Jesus', was the proclamation 'DARWIN!'

A sharp beeping sound cut the air, and Langdon looked up. Kohler reached down into the array of electronics on his wheelchair. He slipped a beeper out of its holder and read the incoming message.

'Good. That is Leonardo's daughter. Ms Vetra is arriving at the helipad right now. We will meet her there. I think it best she not come up here and see her father this way.'

Langdon agreed. It would be a shock no child deserved.

'I will ask Ms Vetra to explain the project she and her father have been working on . . . perhaps shedding light on why he was murdered.'

'You think Vetra's *work* is why he was killed?'

'Quite possibly. Leonardo told me he was working on something groundbreaking. That is all he said. He had become very secretive about the project. He had a private lab and demanded seclusion, which I gladly afforded him on account of his brilliance. His work had been consuming huge amounts of electric power lately, but I refrained from questioning him.' Kohler rotated toward the study door. 'There is, however, one more thing you need to know before we leave this flat.'

Langdon was not sure he wanted to hear it.

'An item was stolen from Vetra by his murderer.'

'An item?'

'Follow me.'

The director propelled his wheelchair back into the fog-filled living room. Langdon followed, not knowing what to expect. Kohler maneuvered to within inches of Vetra's body and stopped. He ushered Langdon to join him. Reluctantly, Langdon came close, bile rising in his throat at the smell of the victim's frozen urine.

'Look at his face,' Kohler said.

Look at his face? Langdon frowned. *I thought you said something was stolen.*

Hesitantly, Langdon knelt down. He tried to see Vetra's face, but the head was twisted 180 degrees backward, his face pressed into the carpet.

Struggling against his handicap Kohler reached down and carefully twisted Vetra's frozen head. Cracking loudly, the corpse's face rotated into view, contorted in agony. Kohler held it there for a moment.

'Sweet Jesus!' Langdon cried, stumbling back in horror. Vetra's face was covered in blood. A single hazel eye stared lifelessly back at him. The other socket was tattered and empty. 'They stole his *eye*?'

14

Langdon stepped out of Building C into the open air, grateful to be outside Vetra's flat. The sun helped dissolve the image of the empty eye socket emblazoned into his mind.

'This way, please,' Kohler said, veering up a steep path. The electric wheelchair seemed to accelerate effortlessly. 'Ms Vetra will be arriving any moment.'

Langdon hurried to keep up.

'So,' Kohler asked. 'Do you still doubt the Illuminati's involvement?'

Langdon had no idea what to think anymore. Vetra's religious affiliations were definitely troubling, and yet Langdon could not bring himself to abandon every shred of academic evidence he had ever researched. Besides, there was the eye . . .

'I still maintain,' Langdon said, more forcefully than he intended, 'that the Illuminati are *not* responsible for this murder. The missing eye is proof.'

'What?'

'Random mutilation,' Langdon explained, 'is very . . . *un*-Illuminati. Cult specialists see desultory defacement from inexperienced fringe sects – zealots who commit random acts of terrorism – but the Illuminati have always been more deliberate.'

'Deliberate? Surgically removing someone's eyeball is not deliberate?'

'It sends no clear message. It serves no higher purpose.'

Kohler's wheelchair stopped short at the top of the hill. He turned. 'Mr Langdon, believe me, that missing eye does *indeed* serve a higher purpose . . . a much higher purpose.'

As the two men crossed the grassy rise, the beating of helicopter blades became audible to the west. A chopper appeared, arching across the open valley toward them. It banked sharply, then slowed to a hover over a helipad painted on the grass.

Langdon watched, detached, his mind churning circles like the blades, wondering if a full night's sleep would make his current disorientation any clearer. Somehow, he doubted it.

As the skids touched down, a pilot jumped out and started unloading gear. There was a lot of it – duffels, vinyl wet bags, scuba tanks, and crates of what appeared to be high-tech diving equipment.

Langdon was confused. 'Is that Ms Vetra's gear?' he yelled to Kohler over the roar of the engines.

Kohler nodded and yelled back, 'She was doing biological research in the Balearic Sea.'

'I thought you said she was a *physicist*!'

'She is. She's a Bio Entanglement Physicist. She studies the interconnectivity of life systems. Her work ties closely with her father's work in particle physics. Recently she disproved one of Einstein's fundamental theories by using atomically synchronized cameras to observe a school of tuna fish.'

Langdon searched his host's face for any glint of humor. *Einstein and tuna fish?* He was starting to wonder if the X-33 space plane had mistakenly dropped him off on the wrong planet.

A moment later, Vittoria Vetra emerged from the fuselage. Robert Langdon realized today was going to be a day of endless surprises. Descending from the chopper in her khaki shorts and white sleeveless top, Vittoria Vetra looked nothing like the bookish physicist he had expected. Lithe and graceful, she was tall with chestnut skin and long black hair that swirled in the backwind of the rotors. Her face was unmistakably Italian – not overly beautiful, but possessing full, earthy features that even at twenty yards seemed to exude a raw sensuality. As the air currents buffeted her body, her clothes clung, accentuating her slender torso and small breasts.

'Ms Vetra is a woman of tremendous personal strength,' Kohler said, seeming to sense Langdon's captivation. 'She spends months at a time working in dangerous ecological systems. She is a strict vegetarian and CERN's resident guru of Hatha yoga.'

Hatha yoga? Langdon mused. The ancient Buddhist art of meditative stretching seemed an odd proficiency for the physicist daughter of a Catholic priest.

Langdon watched Vittoria approach. She had obviously been crying, her deep sable eyes filled with emotions Langdon could not place. Still, she moved toward them with fire and command. Her limbs were strong and toned, radiating the healthy luminescence of Mediterranean flesh that had enjoyed long hours in the sun.

'Vittoria,' Kohler said as she approached. 'My deepest condolences. It's a terrible loss for science . . . for all of us here at CERN.'

Vittoria nodded gratefully. When she spoke, her voice was smooth – a throaty, accented English. 'Do you know who is responsible yet?'

'We're still working on it.'

She turned to Langdon, holding out a slender hand. 'My name is Vittoria Vetra. You're from Interpol, I assume?'

Langdon took her hand, momentarily spellbound by the depth of her watery gaze. 'Robert Langdon.' He was unsure what else to say.

'Mr Langdon is not with the authorities,' Kohler explained. 'He is a specialist from the U.S. He's here to help us locate who is responsible for this situation.'

Vittoria looked uncertain. 'And the police?'

Kohler exhaled but said nothing.

'Where is his body?' she demanded.

'Being attended to.'

The white lie surprised Langdon.

'I want to see him,' Vittoria said.

'Vittoria,' Kohler urged, 'your father was brutally murdered. You would be better to remember him as he was.'

Vittoria began to speak but was interrupted.

'Hey, Vittoria!' voices called from the distance. 'Welcome home!'

She turned. A group of scientists passing near the helipad waved happily. 'Disprove any more of Einstein's theories?' one shouted.

Another added, 'Your dad must be proud!'

Vittoria gave the men an awkward wave as they passed. Then she turned to Kohler, her face now clouded with confusion. 'Nobody *knows* yet?'

'I decided discretion was paramount.'

'You haven't told the staff my father was *murdered*?' Her mystified tone was now laced with anger.

Kohler's tone hardened instantly. 'Perhaps you forget, Ms Vetra, as soon as I report your father's murder, there will be an investigation of CERN. Including a thorough examination of his lab. I have always tried to respect your father's privacy. Your father told me only two things about your current project. One, that it has the potential to bring CERN millions of francs in licensing contracts in the next decade. And two, that it is not ready for public disclosure because it is still hazardous technology. Considering these two facts, I would prefer that strangers not poke around inside his lab and either steal his work or kill themselves in the process and hold CERN liable. Do I make myself clear?'

Vittoria stared, saying nothing. Langdon sensed in her a reluctant respect and acceptance of Kohler's logic.

'Before we report anything to the authorities,' Kohler said, 'I need to know what you two were working on. I need you to take us to your lab.'

'The lab is irrelevant,' Vittoria said. 'Nobody knew what my father and I were doing. The experiment could not possibly have anything to do with my father's murder.'

Kohler exhaled a raspy, ailing breath. 'Evidence suggests otherwise.'

'Evidence? What evidence?'

Langdon was wondering the same thing.

Kohler was dabbing his mouth again. 'You'll just have to trust me.'

It was clear, from Vittoria's smoldering gaze, that she did not.

15

Langdon strode silently behind Vittoria and Kohler as they moved back into the main atrium where Langdon's bizarre visit had begun. Vittoria's legs drove in fluid efficiency – like an Olympic diver – a potency, Langdon figured, no doubt born from the flexibility and control of yoga. He could hear her breathing slowly and deliberately, as if somehow trying to filter her grief.

Langdon wanted to say something to her, offer his sympathy. He too had once felt the abrupt hollowness of unexpectedly losing a parent. He remembered the funeral mostly, rainy and gray. Two days after his twelfth birthday. The house was filled with gray-suited men from the office, men who squeezed his hand too hard when they shook it. They were all mumbling words like *cardiac* and *stress*. His mother joked through teary eyes that she'd always been able to follow the stock market simply by holding her husband's hand . . . his pulse her own private ticker tape.

Once, when his father was alive, Langdon had heard his mom begging his father to 'stop and smell the roses.' That year, Langdon bought his father a tiny blown-glass rose for Christmas. It was the most beautiful thing Langdon had ever seen . . . the way the sun caught it, throwing a rainbow of colours on the wall. 'It's lovely,' his father had said when he opened it, kissing Robert on the forehead. 'Let's find a safe spot for it.' Then his father had carefully placed the rose on a high dusty shelf in the darkest corner of the living room. A few days later, Langdon got a stool, retrieved the rose, and took it back to the store. His father never noticed it was gone.

The ping of an elevator pulled Langdon back to the present. Vittoria and Kohler were in front of him, boarding the lift. Langdon hesitated outside the open doors.

'Is something wrong?' Kohler asked, sounding more impatient than concerned.

'Not at all,' Langdon said, forcing himself toward the cramped carriage. He only used elevators when absolutely necessary. He preferred the more open spaces of stairwells.

'Dr Vetra's lab is subterranean,' Kohler said.

Wonderful, Langdon thought as he stepped across the cleft, feeling an icy

41

wind churn up from the depths of the shaft. The doors closed, and the car began to descend.

'Six stories,' Kohler said blankly, like an analytical engine.

Langdon pictured the darkness of the empty shaft below them. He tried to block it out by staring at the numbered display of changing floors. Oddly, the elevator showed only two stops. GROUND LEVEL and LHC.

'What's LHC stand for?' Langdon asked, trying not to sound nervous.

'Large Hadron Collider,' Kohler said. 'A particle accelerator.'

Particle accelerator? Langdon was vaguely familiar with the term. He had first heard it over dinner with some colleagues at Dunster House in Cambridge. A physicist friend of theirs, Bob Brownell, had arrived for dinner one night in a rage.

'The bastards canceled it!' Brownell cursed.

'Canceled what?' they all asked.

'The SSC!'

'The what?'

'The Superconducting Super Collider!'

Someone shrugged. 'I didn't know Harvard was building one.'

'Not Harvard!' he exclaimed. 'The U.S.! It was going to be the world's most powerful particle accelerator! One of the most important scientific projects of the century! Two *billion* dollars into it and the Senate sacks the project! Damn Bible-Belt lobbyists!'

When Brownell finally calmed down, he explained that a particle accelerator was a large, circular tube through which subatomic particles were accelerated. Magnets in the tube turned on and off in rapid succession to 'push' particles around and around until they reached tremendous velocities. Fully accelerated particles circled the tube at over 180,000 miles per *second*.

'But that's almost the speed of light,' one of the professors exclaimed.

'Damn right,' Brownell said. He went on to say that by accelerating two particles in opposite directions around the tube and then colliding them, scientists could shatter the particles into their constituent parts and get a glimpse of nature's most fundamental components. 'Particle accelerators,' Brownell declared, 'are critical to the future of science. Colliding particles is the key to understanding the building blocks of the universe.'

Harvard's *Poet in Residence*, a quiet man named Charles Pratt, did not look impressed. 'It sounds to me,' he said, 'like a rather Neanderthal approach to science . . . akin to smashing clocks together to discern their internal workings.'

Brownell dropped his fork and stormed out of the room.

So CERN has a particle accelerator? Langdon thought, as the elevator dropped. *A circular tube for smashing particles.* He wondered why they had buried it underground.

When the elevator thumped to a stop, Langdon was relieved to feel terra firma beneath his feet. But when the doors slid open, his relief evaporated. Robert Langdon found himself standing once again in a totally alien world.

The passageway stretched out indefinitely in both directions, left and right. It was a smooth cement tunnel, wide enough to allow passage of an eighteen wheeler. Brightly lit where they stood, the corridor turned pitch black further down. A damp wind rustled out of the darkness – an unsettling reminder that they were now deep in the earth. Langdon could almost sense the weight of the dirt and stone now hanging above his head. For an instant he was nine years old . . . the darkness forcing him back . . . back to the five hours of crushing blackness that haunted him still. Clenching his fists, he fought it off.

Vittoria remained hushed as she exited the elevator and strode off without hesitation into the darkness without them. Overhead the fluorescents flickered on to light her path. The effect was unsettling, Langdon thought, as if the tunnel were alive . . . anticipating her every move. Langdon and Kohler followed, trailing a distance behind. The lights extinguished automatically behind them.

'This particle accelerator,' Langdon said quietly. 'It's down this tunnel someplace?'

'That's it there.' Kohler motioned to his left where a polished, chrome tube ran along the tunnel's inner wall.

Langdon eyed the tube, confused. '*That's* the accelerator?' The device looked nothing like he had imagined. It was perfectly straight, about three feet in diameter, and extended horizontally the visible length of the tunnel before disappearing into the darkness. *Looks more like a high-tech sewer*, Langdon thought. 'I thought particle accelerators were *circular*.'

'This accelerator *is* a circle,' Kohler said. 'It appears straight, but that is an optical illusion. The circumference of this tunnel is so large that the curve is imperceptible – like that of the earth.'

Langdon was flabbergasted. *This is a circle?* 'But . . . it must be enormous!'

'The LHC is the largest machine in the world.'

Langdon did a double take. He remembered the CERN driver saying something about a huge machine buried in the earth. *But—*

'It is over eight kilometers in diameter . . . and twenty-seven kilometres long.'

Langdon's head whipped around. 'Twenty-seven kilometers?' He stared at the director and then turned and looked into the darkened tunnel before him. 'This tunnel is twenty-seven kilometers long? That's . . . that's over sixteen miles!'

Kohler nodded. 'Bored in a perfect circle. It extends all the way into France before curving back here to this spot. Fully accelerated particles will circle the tube more than ten thousand times in a single second before they collide.'

Langdon's legs felt rubbery as he stared down the gaping tunnel. 'You're telling me that CERN dug out millions of tons of earth just to smash tiny particles?'

Kohler shrugged. 'Sometimes to find truth, one must move mountains.'

16

Hundreds of miles from CERN, a voice crackled through a walkie-talkie. 'Okay, I'm in the hallway.'

The technician monitoring the video screens pressed the button on his transmitter. 'You're looking for camera #86. It's supposed to be at the far end.'

There was a long silence on the radio. The waiting technician broke a light sweat. Finally his radio clicked.

'The camera isn't here,' the voice said. 'I can see where it was mounted, though. Somebody must have removed it.'

The technician exhaled heavily. 'Thanks. Hold on a second, will you?'

Sighing, he redirected his attention to the bank of video screens in front of him. Huge portions of the complex were open to the public, and wireless cameras had gone missing before, usually stolen by visiting pranksters looking for souvenirs. But as soon as a camera left the facility and was out of range, the signal was lost, and the screen went blank. Perplexed, the technician gazed up at the monitor. A crystal clear image was still coming from camera #86.

If the camera was stolen, he wondered, *why are we still getting a signal?* He knew, of course, there was only one explanation. The camera was still inside the complex, and someone had simply moved it. *But who? And why?*

He studied the monitor a long moment. Finally he picked up his walkie-talkie. 'Are there any closets in that stairwell? Any cupboards or dark alcoves?'

The voice replying sounded confused. 'No. Why?'

The technician frowned. 'Never mind. Thanks for your help.' He turned off his walkie-talkie and pursed his lips.

Considering the small size of the video camera and the fact that it was wireless, the technician knew that camera #86 could be transmitting from just about *anywhere* within the heavily guarded compound – a densely packed collection of thirty-two separate buildings covering a half-mile radius. The only clue was that the camera seemed to have been placed somewhere dark. Of course, that wasn't much help. The complex contained endless dark locations – maintenance closets, heating ducts, gardening sheds, bedroom wardrobes, even a labyrinth of underground tunnels. Camera #86 could take weeks to locate.

But that's the least of my problems, he thought.

Despite the dilemma posed by the camera's relocation, there was another far more unsettling matter at hand. The technician gazed up at the image the lost camera was transmitting. It was a stationary object. A modern-looking device like nothing the technician had ever seen. He studied the blinking electronic display at its base.

Although the guard had undergone rigorous training preparing him for tense situations, he still sensed his pulse rising. He told himself not to panic. There had to be an explanation. The object appeared too small to be of significant danger. Then again, its presence inside the complex was troubling. *Very* troubling, indeed.

Today of all days, he thought.

Security was always a top priority for his employer, but *today*, more than any other day in the past twelve years, security was of the utmost importance. The technician stared at the object for a long time and sensed the rumblings of a distant gathering storm.

Then, sweating, he dialed his superior.

17

Not many children could say they remembered the day they met their father, but Vittoria Vetra could. She was eight years old, living where she always had, *Orfanotrofio di Siena*, a Catholic orphanage near Florence, deserted by parents she never knew. It was raining that day. The nuns had called for her twice to come to dinner, but as always she pretended not to hear. She lay outside in the courtyard, staring up at the raindrops . . . feeling them hit her body . . . trying to guess where one would land next. The nuns called again, threatening that pneumonia might make an insufferably headstrong child a lot less curious about nature.

I can't hear you, Vittoria thought.

She was soaked to the bone when the young priest came out to get her. She didn't know him. He was new there. Vittoria waited for him to grab her and drag her back inside. But he didn't. Instead, to her wonder, he lay down beside her, soaking his robes in a puddle.

'They say you ask a lot of questions,' the young man said.

Vittoria scowled. 'Are questions bad?'

He laughed. 'Guess they were right.'

'What are you doing out here?'

'Same thing you're doing . . . wondering why raindrops fall.'

'I'm not wondering why they fall! I already know!'

The priest gave her an astonished look. 'You *do*?'

'Sister Francisca says raindrops are angels' tears coming down to wash away our sins.'

'Wow!' he said, sounding amazed. 'So *that* explains it.'

'No it doesn't!' the girl fired back. 'Raindrops fall because *everything* falls! *Everything* falls! Not just rain!'

The priest scratched his head, looking perplexed. 'You know, young lady, you're right. Everything *does* fall. It must be gravity.'

'It must be *what*?'

He gave her an astonished look. 'You haven't heard of *gravity*?'

'No.'

The priest shrugged sadly. 'Too bad. Gravity answers a *lot* of questions.'

Vittoria sat up. 'What's gravity?' she demanded. 'Tell me!'

The priest gave her a wink. 'What do you say I tell you over dinner.'

The young priest was Leonardo Vetra. Although he had been an award-winning physics student while in university, he'd heard another call and gone into the seminary. Leonardo and Vittoria became unlikely best friends in the lonely world of nuns and regulations. Vittoria made Leonardo laugh, and he took her under his wing, teaching her that beautiful things like rainbows and the rivers had many explanations. He told her about light, planets, stars, and all of nature through the eyes of both God and science. Vittoria's innate intellect and curiosity made her a captivating student. Leonardo protected her like a daughter.

Vittoria was happy too. She had never known the joy of having a father. When every other adult answered her questions with a slap on the wrist, Leonardo spent hours showing her books. He even asked what *her* ideas were. Vittoria prayed Leonardo would stay with her forever. Then one day, her worst nightmare came true. Father Leonardo told her he was leaving the orphanage.

'I'm moving to Switzerland,' Leonardo said. 'I have a grant to study physics at the University of Geneva.'

'Physics?' Vittoria cried. 'I thought you loved *God*!'

'I do, very much. Which is why I want to study his divine rules. The laws of physics are the canvas God laid down on which to paint his masterpiece.'

Vittoria was devastated. But Father Leonardo had some other news. He told Vittoria he had spoken to his superiors, and they said it was okay if Father Leonardo adopted her.

'Would you *like* me to adopt you?' Leonardo asked.

'What's *adopt* mean?' Vittoria said.

Father Leonardo told her.

Vittoria hugged him for five minutes, crying tears of joy. 'Oh yes! Yes!'

Leonardo told her he had to leave for a while and get their new home settled in Switzerland, but he promised to send for her in six months. It was the longest wait of Vittoria's life, but Leonardo kept his word. Five days before her ninth birthday, Vittoria moved to Geneva. She attended Geneva International School during the day and learned from her father at night.

Three years later Leonardo Vetra was hired by CERN. Vittoria and Leonardo relocated to a wonderland the likes of which the young Vittoria had never imagined.

Vittoria Vetra's body felt numb as she strode down the LHC tunnel. She saw her muted reflection in the LHC and sensed her father's absence. Normally she existed in a state of deep calm, in harmony with the world around her. But now, very suddenly, nothing made sense. The last three hours had been a blur.

It had been 10 a.m. in the Balearic Islands when Kohler's call came through. *Your father has been murdered. Come home immediately.* Despite the sweltering heat on the deck of the dive boat, the words had chilled her to the bone. Kohler's emotionless tone hurting as much as the news.

Now she had returned home. *But home to what?* CERN, her world since she was twelve, seemed suddenly foreign. Her father, the man who had made it magical, was gone.

Deep breaths, she told herself, but she couldn't calm her mind. The questions circled faster and faster. Who killed her father? And why? Who was this American 'specialist'? Why was Kohler insisting on seeing the lab?

Kohler had said there was evidence that her father's murder was related to the current project. *What evidence? Nobody knew what we were working on! And even if someone found out, why would they kill him?*

As she moved down the LHC tunnel toward her father's lab, Vittoria realized she was about to unveil her father's greatest achievement without him there. She had pictured this moment much differently. She had imagined her father calling CERN's top scientists to his lab, showing them his discovery, watching their awestruck faces. Then he would beam with fatherly pride as he explained to them how it had been one of *Vittoria's* ideas that had helped him make the project a reality . . . that his *daughter* had been integral in his breakthrough. Vittoria felt a lump in her throat. *My father and I were supposed to share this moment together.* But here she was alone. No colleagues. No happy faces. Just an American stranger and Maximilian Kohler.

Maximilian Kohler. Der König.

Even as a child, Vittoria had disliked the man. Although she eventually came to respect his potent intellect, his icy demeanor always seemed inhuman, the exact antithesis of her father's warmth. Kohler pursued science for its immaculate logic . . . her father for its spiritual wonder. And yet oddly there had always seemed to be an unspoken respect between the two men. *Genius*, someone had once explained to her, *accepts genius unconditionally*.

Genius, she thought. *My father . . . Dad. Dead.*

The entry to Leonardo Vetra's lab was a long sterile hallway paved entirely in white tile. Langdon felt like he was entering some kind of underground insane asylum. Lining the corridor were dozens of framed, black–and–white images. Although Langdon had made a career of studying images, these were entirely alien to him. They looked like chaotic negatives of random streaks and spirals. *Modern art?* he mused. *Jackson Pollock on amphetamines?*

'Scatter plots,' Vittoria said, apparently noting Langdon's interest. 'Computer representations of particle collisions. That's the Z-particle,' she said, pointing to a faint track that was almost invisible in the confusion. 'My father discovered it five years ago. Pure energy – no mass at all. It may well be the smallest building block in nature. Matter is nothing but trapped energy.'

Matter is energy? Langdon cocked his head. *Sounds pretty Zen.* He gazed at the tiny streak in the photograph and wondered what his buddies in the Harvard physics department would say when he told them he'd spent the weekend hanging out in a Large Hadron Collider admiring Z-particles.

'Vittoria,' Kohler said, as they approached the lab's imposing steel door, 'I should mention that I came down here this morning looking for your father.'

Vittoria flushed slightly. 'You did?'

'Yes. And imagine my surprise when I discovered he had replaced CERN's standard keypad security with something else.' Kohler motioned to an intricate electronic device mounted beside the door.

'I apologize,' she said. 'You know how he was about privacy. He didn't want anyone but the two of us to have access.'

Kohler said, 'Fine. Open the door.'

Vittoria stood for a long moment. Then, pulling a deep breath, she walked to the mechanism on the wall.

Langdon was in no way prepared for what happened next.

Vittoria stepped up to the device and carefully aligned her right eye with a protruding lens that looked like a telescope. Then she pressed a button. Inside the machine, something clicked. A shaft of light oscillated back and forth, scanning her eyeball like a copy machine.

'It's a retina scan,' she said. 'Infallible security. Authorized for two retina patterns only. Mine and my father's.'

Robert Langdon stood in horrified revelation. The image of Leonardo Vetra came back in grisly detail – the bloody face, the solitary hazel eye staring back, and the empty eye socket. He tried to reject the obvious truth, but then he saw it . . . beneath the scanner on the white tile floor . . . faint droplets of crimson. Dried blood.

Vittoria, thankfully, did not notice.

The steel door slid open and she walked through.

Kohler fixed Langdon with an adamant stare. His message was clear: *As I told you . . . the missing eye serves a higher purpose.*

18

The woman's hands were tied, her wrists now purple and swollen from chafing. The mahogany-skinned Hassassin lay beside her, spent, admiring his naked prize. He wondered if her current slumber was just a deception, a pathetic attempt to avoid further service to him.

He did not care. He had reaped sufficient reward. Sated, he sat up in bed.

In *his* country women were possessions. Weak. Tools of pleasure. Chattel to be traded like livestock. And they understood their place. But *here*, in Europe, women feigned a strength and independence that both amused and excited him. Forcing them into physical submission was a gratification he always enjoyed.

Now, despite the contentment in his loins, the Hassassin sensed another appetite growing within him. He had killed last night, killed and mutilated, and for him killing was like heroin . . . each encounter satisfying only temporarily before increasing his longing for more. The exhilaration had worn off. The craving had returned.

He studied the sleeping woman beside him. Running his palm across her neck, he felt aroused with the knowledge that he could end her life in an instant. What would it matter? She was subhuman, a vehicle only of pleasure and service. His strong fingers encircled her throat, savoring her delicate pulse. Then, fighting desire, he removed his hand. There was work to do. Service to a higher cause than his own desire.

As he got out of bed, he reveled in the honor of the job before him. He still could not fathom the influence of this man named Janus and the ancient brotherhood he commanded. Wondrously, the brotherhood had chosen *him*. Somehow they had learned of his loathing . . . and of his skills. How, he would never know. *Their roots reach wide.*

Now they had bestowed on him the ultimate honor. He would be their hands and their voice. Their assassin and their messenger. The one his people knew as *Malk al-haq* – the Angel of Truth.

19

Vetra's lab was wildly futuristic.

Stark white and bounded on all sides by computers and specialized electronic equipment, it looked like some sort of operating room. Langdon wondered what secrets this place could possibly hold to justify cutting out someone's eye to gain entrance.

Kohler looked uneasy as they entered, his eyes seeming to dart about for signs of an intruder. But the lab was deserted. Vittoria moved slowly too . . . as if the lab felt unknown without her father there.

Langdon's gaze landed immediately in the center of the room, where a series of short pillars rose from the floor. Like a miniature Stonehenge, a dozen or so columns of polished steel stood in a circle in the middle of the room. The pillars were about three feet tall, reminding Langdon of museum displays for valuable gems. These pillars, however, were clearly not for precious stones. Each supported a thick, transparent canister about the size of a tennis ball can. They appeared empty.

Kohler eyed the canisters, looking puzzled. He apparently decided to ignore them for the time being. He turned to Vittoria. 'Has anything been stolen?'

'Stolen? *How?*' she argued. 'The retina scan only allows entry to us.'

'Just look around.'

Vittoria sighed and surveyed the room for a few moments. She shrugged. 'Everything looks as my father always leaves it. Ordered chaos.'

Langdon sensed Kohler weighing his options, as if wondering how far to push Vittoria . . . how much to tell her. Apparently he decided to leave it for the moment. Moving his wheelchair toward the center of the room, he surveyed the mysterious cluster of seemingly empty canisters.

'Secrets,' Kohler finally said, 'are a luxury we can no longer afford.'

Vittoria nodded in acquiescence, looking suddenly emotional, as if being here brought with it a torrent of memories.

Give her a minute, Langdon thought.

As though preparing for what she was about to reveal, Vittoria closed her eyes and breathed. Then she breathed again. And again. And again . . .

Langdon watched her, suddenly concerned. *Is she okay?* He glanced at

Kohler, who appeared unfazed, apparently having seen this ritual before. Ten seconds passed before Vittoria opened her eyes.

Langdon could not believe the metamorphosis. Vittoria Vetra had been transformed. Her full lips were lax, her shoulders down, and her eyes soft and assenting. It was as though she had realigned every muscle in her body to accept the situation. The resentful fire and personal anguish had been quelled somehow beneath a deeper, watery cool.

'Where to begin . . .' she said, her accent unruffled.

'At the beginning,' Kohler said. 'Tell us about your father's experiment.'

'Rectifying science with religion has been my father's life dream,' Vittoria said. 'He hoped to prove that science and religion are two totally compatible fields – two different approaches to finding the same truth.' She paused as if unable to believe what she was about to say. 'And recently . . . he conceived of a way to do that.'

Kohler said nothing.

'He devised an experiment, one he hoped would settle one of the most bitter conflicts in the history of science and religion.'

Langdon wondered which conflict she could mean. There were so many.

'Creationism,' Vittoria declared. 'The battle over how the universe came to be.'

Oh, Langdon thought. *THE debate.*

'The Bible, of course, states that God created the universe,' she explained. 'God said, "Let there be light," and everything we see appeared out of a vast emptiness. Unfortunately, one of the fundamental laws of physics states that matter cannot be created out of nothing.'

Langdon had read about this stalemate. The idea that God allegedly created 'something from nothing' was totally contrary to accepted laws of modern physics and therefore, scientists claimed, Genesis was scientifically absurd.

'Mr Langdon,' Vittoria said, turning, 'I assume you are familiar with the Big Bang Theory?'

Langdon shrugged. 'More or less.' The Big Bang, he knew, was *the* scientifically accepted model for the creation of the universe. He didn't really understand it, but according to the theory, a single point of intensely focused energy erupted in a cataclysmic explosion, expanding outward to form the universe. Or something like that.

Vittoria continued. 'When the Catholic Church first proposed the Big Bang Theory in 1927, the—'

'I'm sorry?' Langdon interrupted, before he could stop himself. 'You say the Big Bang was a *Catholic* idea?'

Vittoria looked surprised by his question. 'Of course. Proposed by a Catholic monk, Georges Lemaître in 1927.'

'But, I thought . . .' he hesitated. 'Wasn't the Big Bang proposed by Harvard astronomer Edwin Hubble?'

Kohler glowered. 'Again, American scientific arrogance. Hubble published in 1929, two years *after* Lemaître.'

Langdon scowled. *It's called the Hubble Telescope, sir – I've never heard of any Lemaître Telescope!*

'Mr Kohler is right,' Vittoria said, 'the idea belonged to Lemaître. Hubble only *confirmed* it by gathering the hard evidence that proved the Big Bang was scientifically probable.'

'Oh,' Langdon said, wondering if the Hubble-fanatics in the Harvard Astronomy Department ever mentioned Lemaître in their lectures.

'When Lemaître first proposed the Big Bang Theory,' Vittoria continued, 'scientists claimed it was utterly ridiculous. Matter, science said, could not be created out of nothing. So, when Hubble shocked the world by scientifically proving the Big Bang was accurate, the church claimed victory, heralding this as *proof* that the Bible was scientifically accurate. The divine truth.'

Langdon nodded, focusing intently now.

'Of course scientists did not appreciate having their discoveries used by the church to promote religion, so they immediately mathematicized the Big Bang Theory, removed all religious overtones, and claimed it as their own. Unfortunately for science, however, their equations, even today, have one serious deficiency that the church likes to point out.'

Kohler grunted. 'The *singularity*.' He spoke the word as if it were the bane of his existence.

'Yes, the singularity,' Vittoria said. 'The exact moment of creation. Time zero.' She looked at Langdon. 'Even today, science cannot grasp the initial moment of creation. Our equations explain the *early* universe quite effectively, but as we move back in time, approaching time zero, suddenly our mathematics disintegrates, and everything becomes meaningless.'

'Correct,' Kohler said, his voice edgy, 'and the church holds up this deficiency as proof of God's miraculous involvement. Come to your point.'

Vittoria's expression became distant. 'My point is that my father had always believed in God's involvement in the Big Bang. Even though science was unable to comprehend the divine moment of creation, he believed someday it *would*.' She motioned sadly to a laser-printed memo tacked over her father's work area. 'My dad used to wave that in my face every time I had doubts.'

Langdon read the message:

SCIENCE AND RELIGION ARE NOT AT ODDS.
SCIENCE IS SIMPLY TOO YOUNG TO UNDERSTAND.

'My dad wanted to bring science to a higher level,' Vittoria said, 'where science supported the concept of God.' She ran a hand through her long hair, looking melancholy. 'He set out to do something no scientist had ever thought to do. Something that no one has ever had the *technology* to do.'

She paused, as though uncertain how to speak the next words. 'He designed an experiment to prove Genesis was possible.'

Prove Genesis? Langdon wondered. *Let there be light? Matter from nothing?*

Kohler's dead gaze bore across the room. 'I beg your pardon?'

'My father created a universe . . . from nothing at all.'

Kohler snapped his head around. 'What!'

'Better said, he recreated the Big Bang.'

Kohler looked ready to jump to his feet.

Langdon was officially lost. *Creating a universe? Recreating the Big Bang?*

'It was done on a much smaller scale, of course,' Vittoria said, talking faster now. 'The process was remarkably simple. He accelerated two ultra-thin particle beams in opposite directions around the accelerator tube. The two beams collided head-on at enormous speeds, driving into one another and compressing all their energy into a single pinpoint. He achieved extreme energy densities.' She started rattling off a stream of units, and the director's eyes grew wider.

Langdon tried to keep up. *So Leonardo Vetra was simulating the compressed point of energy from which the universe supposedly sprang.*

'The result,' Vittoria said, 'was nothing short of wondrous. When it is published, it will shake the very foundation of modern physics.' She spoke slowly now, as though savoring the immensity of her news. 'Without warning, inside the accelerator tube, at this point of highly focused energy, particles of matter began appearing out of nowhere.'

Kohler made no reaction. He simply stared.

'*Matter*,' Vittoria repeated. 'Blossoming out of nothing. An incredible display of subatomic fireworks. A miniature universe springing to life. He proved not only that matter *can* be created from nothing, but that the Big Bang *and* Genesis can be explained simply by accepting the presence of an enormous source of energy.'

'You mean *God?*' Kohler demanded.

'God, Buddha, The Force, Yahweh, the singularity, the unicity point – call it whatever you like – the result is the same. Science and religion support the same truth – pure *energy* is the father of creation.'

When Kohler finally spoke, his voice was somber. 'Vittoria, you have me at a loss. It sounds like you're telling me your father *created* matter . . . out of nothing?'

'Yes.' Vittoria motioned to the canisters. 'And there is the proof. In those canisters are specimens of the matter he created.'

Kohler coughed and moved towards the canisters like a wary animal circling something he instinctively sensed was wrong. 'I've obviously missed something,' he said. 'How do you expect anyone to believe these canisters contain particles of matter your father actually *created?* They could be particles from anywhere at all.'

'Actually,' Vittoria said, sounding confident, 'they couldn't. These particles are unique. They are a type of matter that does not exist anywhere on earth . . . hence they *had* to be created.'

Kohler's expression darkened. 'Vittoria, what do you mean a certain *type* of matter? There is only *one* type of matter, and it—' Kohler stopped short.

Vittoria's expression was triumphant. 'You've lectured on it yourself, director. The universe contains *two* kinds of matter. Scientific fact.' Vittoria turned to Langdon. 'Mr Langdon, what does the Bible say about the Creation? What did God create?'

Langdon felt awkward, not sure what this had to do with anything. 'Um, God created . . . light and dark, heaven and hell—'

'Exactly,' Vittoria said. 'He created everything in opposites. Symmetry. Perfect balance.' She turned back to Kohler. 'Director, science claims the same thing as religion, that the Big Bang created everything in the universe with an opposite.'

'Including *matter* itself,' Kohler whispered, as if to himself.

Vittoria nodded. 'And when my father ran his experiment, sure enough, *two* kinds of matter appeared.'

Langdon wondered what this meant. *Leonardo Vetra created matter's opposite?*

Kohler looked angry. 'The substance you're referring to only exists *elsewhere* in the universe. Certainly not on earth. And possibly not even in our galaxy!'

'Exactly,' Vittoria replied, 'which is proof that the particles in these canisters had to be *created*.'

Kohler's face hardened. 'Vittoria, surely you can't be saying those canisters contain actual specimens?'

'I am.' She gazed proudly at the canisters. 'Director, you are looking at the world's first specimens of *antimatter*.'

20

Phase two, the Hassassin thought, striding into the darkened tunnel.

The torch in his hand was overkill. He knew that. But it was for effect. Effect was everything. Fear, he had learned, was his ally. *Fear cripples faster than any implement of war.*

There was no mirror in the passage to admire his disguise, but he could sense from the shadow of his billowing robe that he was perfect. Blending in was part of the plan . . . part of the depravity of the plot. In his wildest dreams he had never imagined playing this part.

Two weeks ago, he would have considered the task awaiting him at the far end of this tunnel impossible. A suicide mission. Walking naked into a lion's lair. But Janus had changed the definition of impossible.

The secrets Janus had shared with the Hassassin in the last two weeks had been numerous . . . this very tunnel being one of them. Ancient, and yet still perfectly passable.

As he drew closer to his enemy, the Hassassin wondered if what awaited him inside would be as easy as Janus had promised. Janus had assured him someone on the inside would make the necessary arrangements. *Someone on the inside. Incredible.* The more he considered it, the more he realized it was child's play.

Wahad . . . tintain . . . thalatha . . . arbaa, he said to himself in Arabic as he neared the end. *One . . . two . . . three . . . four . . .*

21

'I sense you've heard of antimatter, Mr Langdon?' Vittoria was studying him, her dark skin in stark contrast to the white lab.

Langdon looked up. He felt suddenly numb. 'Yes. Well . . . sort of.'

A faint smile crossed her lips. 'You watch *Star Trek*.'

Langdon flushed. 'Well, my students enjoy . . .' He frowned. 'Isn't antimatter what fuels the *U.S.S. Enterprise*?'

She nodded. 'Good science fiction has its roots in good science.'

'So antimatter is *real*?'

'A fact of nature. Everything has an opposite. Protons have electrons. Up-quarks have down-quarks. There is a cosmic symmetry at the sub-atomic level. Antimatter is *yin* to matter's *yang*. It balances the physical equation.'

Langdon thought of Galileo's belief of duality.

'Scientists have known since 1918,' Vittoria said, 'that *two* kinds of matter were created in the Big Bang. One matter is the kind we see here on earth, making up rocks, trees, people. The other is its inverse – identical to matter in all respects except that the charges of its particles are reversed.'

Kohler spoke as though emerging from a fog. His voice sounded suddenly precarious. 'But there are enormous technological barriers to actually *storing* antimatter. What about neutralization?'

'My father built a reverse polarity vacuum to pull the antimatter positrons out of the accelerator before they could decay.'

Kohler scowled. 'But a vacuum would pull out the *matter* also. There would be no way to separate the particles.'

'He applied a magnetic field. Matter arced right, and antimatter arced left. They are polar opposites.'

At that instant, Kohler's wall of doubt seemed to crack. He looked up at Vittoria in clear astonishment and then without warning was overcome by a fit of coughing. 'Incred . . . ible . . .' he said, wiping his mouth, 'and yet . . .' It seemed his logic was still resisting. 'Yet even if the vacuum *worked*, these canisters are made of matter. Antimatter cannot be stored inside canisters made out of *matter*. The antimatter would instantly react with—'

'The specimen is not touching the canister,' Vittoria said, apparently expecting the question. 'The antimatter is suspended. The canisters are called "antimatter traps" because they literally trap the antimatter in the center of the canister, suspending it at a safe distance from the sides and bottom.'

'Suspended? But . . . *how?*'

'Between two intersecting magnetic fields. Here, have a look.'

Vittoria walked across the room and retrieved a large electronic apparatus. The contraption reminded Langdon of some sort of cartoon ray gun – a wide cannonlike barrel with a sighting scope on top and a tangle of electronics dangling below. Vittoria aligned the scope with one of the canisters, peered into the eyepiece, and calibrated some knobs. Then she stepped away, offering Kohler a look.

Kohler looked nonplussed. 'You collected *visible* amounts?'

'Five thousand nanograms,' Vittoria said. 'A liquid plasma containing millions of positrons.'

'Millions? But a few *particles* is all anyone has ever detected . . . *anywhere.*'

'Xenon,' Vittoria said flatly. 'He accelerated the particle beam through a jet of xenon, stripping away the electrons. He insisted on keeping the exact procedure a secret, but it involved simultaneously injecting raw electrons into the accelerator.'

Langdon felt lost, wondering if their conversation was still in English.

Kohler paused, the lines in his brow deepening. Suddenly he drew a short breath. He slumped like he'd been hit with a bullet. 'Technically that would leave . . .'

Vittoria nodded. 'Yes. *Lots* of it.'

Kohler returned his gaze to the canister before him. With a look of uncertainty, he hoisted himself in his chair and placed his eye to the viewer, peering inside. He stared a long time without saying anything. When he finally sat down, his forehead was covered with sweat. The lines on his face had disappeared. His voice was a whisper. 'My God . . . you really did it.'

Vittoria nodded. 'My *father* did it.'

'I . . . I don't know what to say.'

Vittoria turned to Langdon. 'Would you like a look?' She motioned to the viewing device.

Uncertain what to expect, Langdon moved forward. From two feet away, the canister appeared empty. Whatever was inside was infinitesimal. Langdon placed his eye to the viewer. It took a moment for the image before him to come into focus.

Then he saw it.

The object was not on the bottom of the container as he expected, but rather it was floating in the center – suspended in midair – a shimmering globule of mercurylike liquid. Hovering as if by magic, the liquid tumbled in space. Metallic wavelets rippled across the droplet's surface. The suspended fluid reminded Langdon of a video he had once seen of a water droplet in zero G. Although he knew the globule was microscopic, he could see every changing gorge and undulation as the ball of plasma rolled slowly in suspension.

'It's . . . floating,' he said.

'It had better be,' Vittoria replied. 'Antimatter is highly unstable. Energetically speaking, antimatter is the mirror of matter, so the two instantly cancel each other out if they come in contact. Keeping antimatter isolated from matter is a challenge, of course, because *everything* on earth is made of matter. The samples have to be stored without ever touching anything at all – even air.'

Langdon was amazed. *Talk about working in a vacuum.*

'These antimatter traps?' Kohler interrupted, looking amazed as he ran a pallid finger around one's base. 'They are your father's design?'

'Actually,' she said, 'they are mine.'

Kohler looked up.

Vittoria's voice was unassuming. 'My father produced the first particles of antimatter but was stymied by how to store them. I suggested these. Airtight nanocomposite shells with opposing electromagnets at each end.'

'It seems your father's genius has rubbed off.'

'Not really. I borrowed the idea from nature. Portuguese man-o'-wars trap fish between their tentacles using nematocystic charges. Same principle here. Each canister has two electromagnets, one at each end. Their opposing magnetic fields intersect in the center of the canister and hold the antimatter there, suspended in midvacuum.'

Langdon looked again at the canister. Antimatter floating in a vacuum, not touching anything at all. Kohler was right. It was genius.

'Where's the power source for the magnets?' Kohler asked.

Vittoria pointed. 'In the pillar beneath the trap. The canisters are screwed into a docking port that continuously recharges them so the magnets never fail.'

'And if the field fails?'

'The obvious. The antimatter falls out of suspension, hits the bottom of the trap, and we see an annihilation.'

Langdon's ears pricked up. 'Annihilation?' He didn't like the sound of it.

Vittoria looked unconcerned. 'Yes. If antimatter and matter make contact, both are destroyed instantly. Physicists call the process "annihilation."'

Langdon nodded. 'Oh.'

'It is nature's simplest reaction. A particle of matter and a particle of antimatter combine to release two *new* particles – called photons. A photon is effectively a tiny puff of light.'

Langdon had read about photons – light particles – the purest form of energy. He decided to refrain from asking about Captain Kirk's use of photon torpedoes against the Klingons. 'So if the antimatter falls, we see a tiny puff of light?'

Vittoria shrugged. 'Depends what you call tiny. Here, let me demonstrate.' She reached for the canister and started to unscrew it from its charging podium.

Without warning, Kohler let out a cry of terror and lunged forward, knocking her hands away. 'Vittoria! Are you insane!'

22

Kohler, incredibly, was standing for a moment, teetering on two withered legs. His face was white with fear. 'Vittoria! You can't remove that trap!'

Langdon watched, bewildered by the director's sudden panic.

'Five hundred nanograms!' Kohler said. 'If you break the magnetic field—'

'Director,' Vittoria assured, 'it's perfectly safe. Every trap has a failsafe – a back-up battery in case it is removed from its recharger. The specimen remains suspended even if I remove the canister.'

Kohler looked uncertain. Then, hesitantly, he settled back into his chair.

'The batteries activate automatically,' Vittoria said, 'when the trap is removed from the recharger. They work for twenty-four hours. Like a reserve tank of gas.' She turned to Langdon, as if sensing his discomfort. 'Antimatter has some astonishing characteristics, Mr Langdon, which make it quite dangerous. A ten milligram sample – the volume of a grain of sand – is hypothesized to hold as much energy as about two hundred metric tons of conventional rocket fuel.'

Langdon's head was spinning again.

'It is the energy source of tomorrow. A thousand times more powerful than nuclear energy. One hundred per cent efficient. No byproducts. No radiation. No pollution. A few grams could power a major city for a week.'

Grams? Langdon stepped uneasily back from the podium.

'Don't worry,' Vittoria said. '*These* samples are minuscule fractions of a gram – *millionths*. Relatively harmless.' She reached for the canister again and twisted it from its docking platform.

Kohler twitched but did not interfere. As the trap came free, there was a sharp bleep, and a small LED display activated near the base of the trap. The red digits blinked, counting down from twenty-four hours.

24:00:00 . . .
23:59:59 . . .
23:59:58 . . .

Langdon studied the descending counter and decided it looked unsettlingly like a bomb.

'The battery,' Vittoria explained, 'will run for the full twenty-four hours before dying. It can be recharged by placing the trap back on the podium. It's designed as a safety measure, but it's also convenient for transport.'

'Transport?' Kohler looked thunderstruck. 'You take this stuff out of the lab?'

'Of course not,' Vittoria said. 'But the mobility allows us to study it.'

Vittoria led Langdon and Kohler to the far end of the room. She pulled a curtain aside to reveal a window, beyond which was a large room. The walls, floors, and ceiling were entirely plated in steel. The room reminded Langdon of the holding tank of an oil freighter he had once taken to Papua New Guinea to study *Hanta* body graffiti.

'It's an annihilation tank,' Vittoria declared.

Kohler looked up. 'You actually *observe* annihilations?'

'My father was fascinated with the physics of the Big Bang – large amounts of energy from minuscule kernels of matter.' Vittoria pulled open a steel drawer beneath the window. She placed the trap inside the drawer and closed it. Then she pulled a lever beside the drawer. A moment later, the trap appeared on the other side of the glass, rolling smoothly in a wide arc across the metal floor until it came to a stop near the center of the room.

Vittoria gave a tight smile. 'You're about to witness your first antimatter-matter annihilation. A few millionths of a gram. A relatively minuscule specimen.'

Langdon looked out at the antimatter trap sitting alone on the floor of the enormous tank. Kohler also turned toward the window, looking uncertain.

'Normally,' Vittoria explained, 'we'd have to wait the full twenty-four hours until the batteries died, but this chamber contains magnets beneath the floor that can override the trap, pulling the antimatter out of suspension. And when the matter and antimatter touch . . .'

'Annihilation,' Kohler whispered.

'One more thing,' Vittoria said. 'Antimatter releases pure energy. A one hundred per cent conversion of mass to photons. So don't look directly at the sample. Shield your eyes.'

Langdon was wary, but he now sensed Vittoria was being overly dramatic. *Don't look directly at the canister?* The device was more than thirty yards away, behind an ultrathick wall of tinted Plexiglas. Moreover, the speck in the canister was invisible, microscopic. *Shield my eyes?* Langdon thought. *How much energy could that speck possibly—*

Vittoria pressed the button.

Instantly, Langdon was blinded. A brilliant point of light shone in the canister and then exploded outward in a shock wave of light that radiated in all directions, erupting against the window before him with thunderous force. He stumbled back as the detonation rocked the vault. The light burned bright for a moment, searing, and then, after an instant, it rushed back inward, absorbing in on itself, and collapsing into a tiny speck that disappeared to nothing. Langdon blinked in pain, slowly recovering his eyesight. He squinted into the smoldering chamber. The canister on the floor had entirely disappeared. Vaporized. Not a trace.

He stared in wonder. 'G . . . God.'

Vittoria nodded sadly. 'That's precisely what my father said.'

23

Kohler was staring into the annihilation chamber with a look of utter amazement at the spectacle he had just seen. Robert Langdon was beside him, looking even more dazed.

'I want to see my father,' Vittoria demanded. 'I showed you the lab. Now I want to see my father.'

Kohler turned slowly, apparently not hearing her. 'Why did you wait so long, Vittoria? You and your father should have told me about this discovery immediately.'

Vittoria stared at him. *How many reasons do you want?* 'Director, we can argue about this later. Right now, I want to see my father.'

'Do you know what this technology implies?'

'Sure,' Vittoria shot back. 'Revenue for CERN. A lot of it. Now I want—'

'Is that why you kept it secret?' Kohler demanded, clearly baiting her. 'Because you feared the board and I would vote to license it out?'

'It *should* be licensed,' Vittoria fired back, feeling herself dragged into the argument. 'Antimatter is important technology. But it's also dangerous. My father and I wanted time to refine the procedures and make it safe.'

'In other words, you didn't trust the board of directors to place prudent science before financial greed.'

Vittoria was surprised by the indifference in Kohler's tone. 'There were other issues as well,' she said. 'My father wanted time to present antimatter in the appropriate light.'

'Meaning?'

What do you think I mean? 'Matter from energy? Something from nothing? It's practically proof that Genesis is a scientific possibility.'

'So he didn't want the religious implications of his discovery lost in an onslaught of commercialism?'

'In a manner of speaking.'

'And you?'

Vittoria's concerns, ironically, were somewhat the opposite. Commercialism was critical for the success of any new energy source. Although antimatter technology had staggering potential as an efficient and nonpolluting energy source – if unveiled prematurely, antimatter ran the risk of being vilified by the politics and PR fiascos that had killed nuclear and solar power. Nuclear had proliferated before it was safe, and there were accidents. Solar had proliferated before it was efficient, and people lost money. Both technologies got bad reputations and withered on the vine.

'My interests,' Vittoria said, 'were a bit less lofty than uniting science and religion.'

'The environment,' Kohler ventured assuredly.

'Limitless energy. No strip mining. No pollution. No radiation. Antimatter technology could save the planet.'

'Or destroy it,' Kohler quipped. 'Depending on who uses it for what.' Vittoria felt a chill emanating from Kohler's crippled form. 'Who else knew about this?' he asked.

'No one,' Vittoria said. 'I told you that.'

'Then why do you think your father was killed?'

Vittoria's muscles tightened. 'I have no idea. He had enemies here at CERN, you know that, but it couldn't have had anything to do with anti-matter. We swore to each other to keep it between us for another few months, until we were ready.'

'And you're certain your father kept his vow of silence?'

Now Vittoria was getting mad. 'My father has kept tougher vows than that!'

'And *you* told no one?'

'Of course not!'

Kohler exhaled. He paused, as though choosing his next words carefully. 'Suppose someone *did* find out. And suppose someone gained access to this lab. What do you imagine they would be after? Did your father have notes down here? Documentation of his processes?'

'Director, I've been patient. I need some answers now. You keep talking about a break-in, but you saw the retina scan. My father has been vigilant about secrecy and security.'

'Humor me,' Kohler snapped, startling her. 'What would be missing?'

'I have no idea.' Vittoria angrily scanned the lab. All the antimatter spec-imens were accounted for. Her father's work area looked in order. 'Nobody came in here,' she declared. 'Everything up here looks fine.'

Kohler looked surprised. '*Up* here?'

Vittoria had said it instinctively. 'Yes, here in the upper lab.'

'You're using the lower lab too?'

'For storage.'

Kohler rolled towards her, coughing again. 'You're using the Haz-Mat chamber for storage? Storage of *what*?'

Hazardous material, what else! Vittoria was losing her patience. 'Antimatter.'

Kohler lifted himself on the arms of his chair. 'There are *other* speci-mens? Why the hell didn't you tell me!'

'I just did,' Vittoria fired back. 'And you've barely given me a chance!'

'We need to check those specimens,' Kohler said. 'Now.'

'Specimen,' Vittoria corrected. 'Singular. And it's fine. Nobody could ever—'

'Only one?' Kohler hesitated. 'Why isn't it up here?'

'My father wanted it below the bedrock as a precaution. It's larger than the others.'

The look of alarm that shot between Kohler and Langdon was not lost on Vittoria. Kohler rolled toward her again. 'You created a specimen *larger* than five hundred nanograms?'

'A necessity,' Vittoria defended. 'We had to prove the input/yield threshold could be safely crossed.' The question with new fuel sources, she knew, was always one of input vs. yield – how much money one had to expend to harvest the fuel. Building an oil rig to yield a single barrel of oil was a losing endeavor. However, if that same rig, with minimal added expense, could deliver millions of barrels, then you were in business. Antimatter was the same way. Firing up sixteen miles of electromagnets to create a tiny specimen of antimatter expended more energy than the resulting antimatter contained. In order to prove antimatter efficient and viable, one had to create specimens of a larger magnitude.

Although Vittoria's father had been hesitant to create a large specimen, Vittoria had pushed him hard. She argued that in order for antimatter to be taken seriously, she and her father had to prove two things. First, that cost-effective amounts could be produced. And second, that the specimens could be safely stored. In the end she had won, and her father had acquiesced against his better judgment. Not, however, without some firm guidelines regarding secrecy and access. The antimatter, her father had insisted, would be stored in Haz-Mat – a small granite hollow, an additional seventy-five feet below ground. The specimen would be their secret. And only the two of them would have access.

'Vittoria?' Kohler insisted, his voice tense. 'How large a specimen did you and your father create?'

Vittoria felt a wry pleasure inside. She knew the amount would stun even the great Maximilian Kohler. She pictured the antimatter below. An incredible sight. Suspended inside the trap, perfectly visible to the naked eye, danced a tiny sphere of antimatter. This was no microscopic speck. This was a droplet the size of a BB.

Vittoria took a deep breath. 'A full quarter of a gram.'

The blood drained from Kohler's face. 'What!' He broke into a fit of coughing. 'A quarter of a gram? That converts to . . . almost five kilotons!'

Kilotons. Vittoria hated the word. It was one she and her father never used. A kiloton was equal to 1,000 metric tons of TNT. Kilotons were for weaponry. Payload. Destructive power. She and her father spoke in electron volts and joules – constructive energy output.

'That much antimatter could literally liquidate everything in a half-mile radius!' Kohler exclaimed.

'Yes, if annihilated all at once,' Vittoria shot back, 'which nobody would ever do!'

'Except someone who didn't know better. Or if your power source failed!' Kohler was already heading for the elevator.

'Which is why my father kept it in Haz-Mat under a fail-safe power and a redundant security system.'

Kohler turned, looking hopeful. 'You have additional security on Haz-Mat?'

'Yes. A second retina-scan.'

Kohler spoke only two words. 'Downstairs. Now.'

The freight elevator dropped like a rock.

Another seventy-five feet into the earth.

Vittoria was certain she sensed fear in both men as the elevator fell deeper. Kohler's usually emotionless face was taut. *I know*, Vittoria thought, *the sample is enormous, but the precautions we've taken are—*

They reached the bottom.

The elevator opened, and Vittoria led the way down the dimly lit corridor. Up ahead the corridor dead-ended at a huge steel door. HAZ-MAT. The retina device beside the door was identical to the one upstairs. She approached. Carefully, she aligned her eye with the lens.

She pulled back. Something was wrong. The usually spotless lens was splattered . . . smeared with something that looked like . . . *blood?* Confused she turned to the two men, but her gaze met waxen faces. Both Kohler and Langdon were white, their eyes fixed on the floor at her feet.

Vittoria followed their line of sight . . . down.

'No!' Langdon yelled, reaching for her. But it was too late.

Vittoria's vision locked on the object on the floor. It was both utterly foreign and intimately familiar to her.

It took only an instant.

Then, with a reeling horror, she knew. Staring up at her from the floor, discarded like a piece of trash, was an eyeball. She would have recognized that shade of hazel anywhere.

24

The security technician held his breath as his commander leaned over his shoulder, studying the bank of security monitors before them. A minute passed.

The commander's silence was to be expected, the technician told himself. The commander was a man of rigid protocol. He had not risen to command one of the world's most elite security forces by talking first and thinking second.

But what is he thinking?

The object they were pondering on the monitor was a canister of some sort – a canister with transparent sides. That much was easy. It was the rest that was difficult.

Inside the container, as if by some special effect, a small droplet of metallic liquid seemed to be *floating* in midair. The droplet appeared and disappeared in the robotic red blinking of a digital LED descending resolutely, making the technician's skin crawl.

'Can you lighten the contrast?' the commander asked, startling the technician.

The technician heeded the instruction, and the image lightened somewhat. The commander leaned forward, squinting closer at something that had just come visible on the base of the container.

The technician followed his commander's gaze. Ever so faintly, printed next to the LED was an acronym. Four capital letters gleaming in the intermittent spurts of light.

'Stay here,' the commander said. 'Say nothing. I'll handle this.'

25

Haz-Mat. Fifty meters below ground.

Vittoria Vetra stumbled forward, almost falling into the retina scan. She sensed the American rushing to help her, holding her, supporting her weight. On the floor at her feet, her father's eyeball stared up. She felt the air crushed from her lungs. *They cut out his eye!* Her world twisted. Kohler pressed close behind, speaking. Langdon guided her. As if in a dream, she found herself gazing into the retina scan. The mechanism beeped.

The door slid open.

Even with the terror of her father's eye boring into her soul, Vittoria sensed an additional horror awaited inside. When she leveled her blurry gaze into the room, she confirmed the next chapter of the nightmare. Before her, the solitary recharging podium was empty.

The canister was gone. They had cut out her father's eye to steal it. The implications came too fast for her to fully comprehend. Everything had backfired. The specimen that was supposed to prove antimatter was a safe and viable energy source had been stolen. *But nobody knew this specimen even existed!* The truth, however, was undeniable. Someone had found out. Vittoria could not imagine who. Even Kohler, whom they said knew everything at CERN, clearly had no idea about the project.

Her father was dead. Murdered for his genius.

As the grief strafed her heart, a new emotion surged into Vittoria's consciousness. This one was far worse. Crushing. Stabbing at her. The emotion was guilt. Uncontrollable, relentless guilt. Vittoria knew it had been *she* who convinced her father to create the specimen. Against his better judgment. And he had been killed for it.

A quarter of a gram . . .

Like any technology – fire, gunpowder, the combustion engine – in the wrong hands, antimatter could be deadly. Very deadly. Antimatter was a lethal weapon. Potent, and unstoppable. Once removed from its recharging platform at CERN, the canister would count down inexorably. A runaway train.

And when time ran out . . .

A blinding light. The roar of thunder. Spontaneous incineration. Just the flash . . . and an empty crater. A *big* empty crater.

The image of her father's quiet genius being used as a tool of destruction was like poison in her blood. Antimatter was the ultimate terrorist weapon. It had no metallic parts to trip metal detectors, no chemical signature for dogs to trace, no fuse to deactivate if the authorities located the canister. The countdown had begun . . .

Langdon didn't know what else to do. He took his handkerchief and laid it on the floor over Leonardo Vetra's eyeball. Vittoria was standing now in the doorway of the empty Haz-Mat chamber, her expression wrought with grief and panic. Langdon moved toward her again, instinctively, but Kohler intervened.

'Mr Langdon?' Kohler's face was expressionless. He motioned Langdon out of earshot. Langdon reluctantly followed, leaving Vittoria to fend for herself. 'You're the specialist,' Kohler said, his whisper intense. 'I want to know what these Illuminati bastards intend to do with this antimatter.'

Langdon tried to focus. Despite the madness around him, his first reaction was logical. Academic rejection. Kohler was still making assumptions. Impossible assumptions. 'The Illuminati are defunct, Mr Kohler. I stand by that. This crime could be anything – maybe even another CERN employee who found out about Mr Vetra's breakthrough and thought the project was too dangerous to continue.'

Kohler looked stunned. 'You think this is a crime of *conscience*, Mr Langdon? Absurd. Whoever killed Leonardo wanted one thing – the antimatter specimen. And no doubt they have plans for it.'

'You mean terrorism.'

'Plainly.'

'But the Illuminati were not terrorists.'

'Tell that to Leonardo Vetra.'

Langdon felt a pang of truth in the statement. Leonardo Vetra had indeed been branded with the Illuminati symbol. Where had it come from? The sacred brand seemed too difficult a hoax for someone trying to cover his tracks by casting suspicion elsewhere. There had to be another explanation.

Again, Langdon forced himself to consider the implausible. *If the Illuminati were still active, and if they stole the antimatter, what would be their intention? What would be their target?* The answer furnished by his brain was instantaneous. Langdon dismissed it just as fast. True, the Illuminati had an obvious enemy, but a wide-scale terrorist attack against that enemy was inconceivable. It was entirely out of character. Yes, the Illuminati had killed people, but *individuals*, carefully conscripted targets. Mass destruction was somehow heavy-handed. Langdon paused. Then again, he thought, there would be a rather majestic eloquence to it – antimatter, the ultimate scientific achievement, being used to vaporize—

He refused to accept the preposterous thought. 'There is,' he said suddenly, 'a logical explanation other than terrorism.'

Kohler stared, obviously waiting.

Langdon tried to sort out the thought. The Illuminati had always wielded tremendous power through *financial* means. They controlled banks. They owned gold bullion. They were even rumored to possess the single most valuable gem on earth – the Illuminati Diamond, a flawless diamond of enormous proportions. 'Money,' Langdon said. 'The antimatter could have been stolen for financial gain.'

Kohler looked incredulous. 'Financial gain? Where does one sell a droplet of antimatter?'

'Not the specimen,' Langdon countered. 'The technology. Antimatter technology must be worth a mint. Maybe someone stole the specimen to do analysis and R and D.'

'Industrial espionage? But that canister has twenty-four hours before the batteries die. The researchers would blow themselves up before they learned anything at all.'

'They could recharge it before it explodes. They could build a compatible recharging podium like the ones here at CERN.'

'In twenty-four hours?' Kohler challenged. 'Even if they stole the schematics, a recharger like that would take *months* to engineer, not hours!'

'He's right.' Vittoria's voice was frail.

Both men turned. Vittoria was moving toward them, her gait as tremulous as her words.

'He's right. Nobody could reverse engineer a recharger in time. The interface alone would take weeks. Flux filters, servo–coils, power conditioning alloys, all calibrated to the specific energy grade of the locale.'

Langdon frowned. The point was taken. An antimatter trap was not something one could simply plug into a wall socket. Once removed from CERN, the canister was on a one-way, twenty-four-hour trip to oblivion.

Which left only one, very disturbing, conclusion.

'We need to call Interpol,' Vittoria said. Even to herself, her voice sounded distant. 'We need to call the proper authorities. Immediately.'

Kohler shook his head. 'Absolutely not.'

The words stunned her. 'No? What do you mean?'

'You and your father have put me in a very difficult position here.'

'Director, we need help. We need to find that trap and get it back here before someone gets hurt. We have a responsibility!'

'We have a responsibility to *think*,' Kohler said, his tone hardening. 'This situation could have very, very serious repercussions for CERN.'

'You're worried about CERN's *reputation*? Do you know what that canister could do to an urban area? It has a blast radius of a half mile! Nine city blocks!'

'Perhaps you and your father should have considered that before you created the specimen.'

Vittoria felt like she'd been stabbed. 'But . . . we took every precaution.'

'Apparently, it was not enough.'

'But nobody *knew* about the antimatter.' She realized, of course, it was an absurd argument. Of course somebody knew. Someone had found out.

Vittoria had told no one. That left only two explanations. Either her father had taken someone into his confidence without telling her, which made no sense because it was her *father* who had sworn them both to secrecy, or she and her father had been monitored. The cell phone maybe? She knew they had spoken a few times while Vittoria was traveling. Had they said too much? It was possible. There was also their E-mail. But they had been discreet, hadn't they? CERN's security system? Had they been monitored somehow without their knowledge? She knew none of that mattered anymore. What was done, was done. *My father is dead.*

The thought spurred her to action. She pulled her cell phone from her shorts pocket.

Kohler accelerated toward her, coughing violently, eyes flashing anger. 'Who . . . are you calling?'

'CERN's switchboard. They can connect us to Interpol.'

'Think!' Kohler choked, screeching to a halt in front of her. 'Are you really so naïve? That canister could be anywhere in the world by now. No intelligence agency on earth could possibly mobilize to find it in time.'

'So we do *nothing*?' Vittoria felt compunction challenging a man in such frail health, but the director was so far out of line she didn't even know him anymore.

'We do what is *smart*,' Kohler said. 'We don't risk CERN's reputation by involving the authorities who cannot help anyway. Not yet. Not without thinking.'

Vittoria knew there was logic somewhere in Kohler's argument, but she also knew that logic, by definition, was bereft of moral responsibility. Her father had *lived* for moral responsibility – careful science, accountability, faith in man's inherent goodness. Vittoria believed in those things too, but she saw them in terms of *karma*. Turning away from Kohler, she snapped open her phone.

'You can't do that,' he said.

'Just try and stop me.'

Kohler did not move.

An instant later, Vittoria realized why. This far underground, her cell phone had no dial tone.

Fuming, she headed for the elevator.

26

The Hassassin stood at the end of the stone tunnel. His torch still burned bright, the smoke mixing with the smell of moss and stale air. Silence surrounded him. The iron door blocking his way looked as old as the tunnel itself, rusted but still holding strong. He waited in the darkness, trusting.

It was almost time.

Janus had promised someone on the inside would open the door. The Hassassin marveled at the betrayal. He would have waited all night at that door to carry out his task, but he sensed it would not be necessary. He was working for determined men.

Minutes later, exactly at the appointed hour, there was a loud clank of heavy keys on the other side of the door. Metal scraped on metal as multiple locks disengaged. One by one, three huge deadbolts ground open. The locks creaked as if they had not been used in centuries. Finally all three were open.

Then there was silence.

The Hassassin waited patiently, five minutes, exactly as he had been told. Then, with electricity in his blood, he pushed. The great door swung open.

27

'Vittoria, I will not allow it!' Kohler's breath was labored and getting worse as the Haz-Mat elevator ascended.

Vittoria blocked him out. She craved sanctuary, something familiar in this place that no longer felt like home. She knew it was not to be. Right now, she had to swallow the pain and act. *Get to a phone.*

Robert Langdon was beside her, silent as usual. Vittoria had given up wondering who the man was. *A specialist?* Could Kohler be any less specific? *Mr Langdon can help us find your father's killer.* Langdon was being no help at all. His warmth and kindness seemed genuine, but he was clearly hiding something. They both were.

Kohler was at her again. 'As director of CERN, I have a responsibility to the future of science. If you amplify this into an international incident and CERN suffers—'

'Future of science?' Vittoria turned on him. 'Do you really plan to escape accountability by never admitting this antimatter came from CERN? Do you plan to ignore the people's lives we've put in danger?'

'Not *we*,' Kohler countered. '*You*. You and your father.'

Vittoria looked away.

'And as far as endangering lives,' Kohler said, '*life* is exactly what this is about. You know antimatter technology has enormous implications for life on this planet. If CERN goes bankrupt, destroyed by scandal, *everybody* loses. Man's future is in the hands of places like CERN, scientists like you and your father, working to solve tomorrow's problems.'

Vittoria had heard Kohler's Science-as-God lecture before, and she never bought it. Science *itself* caused half the problems it was trying to solve. 'Progress' was Mother Earth's ultimate malignancy.

'Scientific advancement carries risk,' Kohler argued. 'It always has. Space programs, genetic research, medicine – they all make mistakes. Science needs to survive its own blunders, at any cost. For *everyone's* sake.'

Vittoria was amazed at Kohler's ability to weigh moral issues with scientific detachment. His intellect seemed to be the product of an icy divorce from his inner spirit. 'You think CERN is so critical to the earth's future that we should be immune from moral responsibility?'

'Do not argue *morals* with me. You crossed a line when you made that specimen, and you have put this entire facility at risk. I'm trying to protect not only the jobs of the three thousand scientists who work here, but also your father's reputation. Think about *him*. A man like your father does not deserve to be remembered as the creator of a weapon of mass destruction.'

Vittoria felt his spear hit home. *I am the one who convinced my father to create that specimen. This is my fault!*

When the door opened, Kohler was still talking. Vittoria stepped out of the elevator, pulled out her phone, and tried again.

Still no dial tone. *Damn!* She headed for the door.

'Vittoria, stop.' The director sounded asthmatic now, as he accelerated after her. 'Slow down. We need to talk.'

'*Basta parlare!*'

'Think of your father,' Kohler urged. 'What would he do?'

She kept going.

'Vittoria, I haven't been totally honest with you.'

Vittoria felt her legs slow.

'I don't know what I was thinking,' Kohler said. 'I was just trying to protect you. Just tell me what you want. We need to work together here.'

Vittoria came to a full stop halfway across the lab, but she did not turn. 'I want to find the antimatter. And I want to know who killed my father.' She waited.

Kohler sighed. 'Vittoria, we already know who killed your father. I'm sorry.'

Now Vittoria turned. 'You what?'

'I didn't know how to tell you. It's a difficult—'

'You *know* who killed my father?'

'We have a very good idea, yes. The killer left somewhat of a calling card. That's the reason I called Mr Langdon. The group claiming responsibility is his specialty.'

'The group? A terrorist group?'

'Vittoria, they stole a quarter *gram* of antimatter.'

Vittoria looked at Robert Langdon standing there across the room. Everything began falling into place. *That explains some of the secrecy.* She was amazed it hadn't occurred to her earlier. Kohler had called the authorities after all. *The* authorities. Now it seemed obvious. Robert Langdon was American, clean-cut, conservative, obviously very sharp. Who else could it be? Vittoria should have guessed from the start. She felt a newfound hope as she turned to him.

'Mr Langdon, I want to know who killed my father. And I want to know if your agency can find the antimatter.'

Langdon looked flustered. 'My agency?'

'You're with U.S. Intelligence, I assume.'

'Actually . . . no.'

76

Kohler intervened. 'Mr Langdon is a professor of art history at Harvard University.'

Vittoria felt like she had been doused with ice water. 'An art teacher?'

'He is a specialist in cult symbology.' Kohler sighed. 'Vittoria, we believe your father was killed by a satanic cult.'

Vittoria heard the words in her mind, but she was unable to process them. *A satanic cult.*

'The group claiming responsibility calls themselves the Illuminati.'

Vittoria looked at Kohler and then at Langdon, wondering if this was some kind of perverse joke. 'The Illuminati?' she demanded. 'As in the *Bavarian* Illuminati?'

Kohler looked stunned. 'You've *heard* of them?'

Vittoria felt the tears of frustration welling right below the surface. '*Bavarian Illuminati: New World Order.* Steve Jackson computer games. Half the techies here play it on the Internet.' Her voice cracked. 'But I don't understand . . .'

Kohler shot Langdon a confused look.

Langdon nodded. 'Popular game. Ancient brotherhood takes over the world. Semihistorical. I didn't know it was in Europe too.'

Vittoria was bewildered. 'What are you talking about? The Illuminati? It's a computer game!'

'Vittoria,' Kohler said, 'the Illuminati is the group claiming responsibility for your father's death.'

Vittoria mustered every bit of courage she could find to fight the tears. She forced herself to hold on and assess the situation logically. But the harder she focused, the less she understood. Her father had been murdered. CERN had suffered a major breach of security. There was a bomb counting down somewhere that *she* was responsible for. And the director had nominated an art teacher to help them find a mythical fraternity of Satanists.

Vittoria felt suddenly all alone. She turned to go, but Kohler cut her off. He reached for something in his pocket. He produced a crumpled piece of fax paper and handed it to her.

Vittoria swayed in horror as her eyes hit the image.

'They branded him,' Kohler said. 'They branded his goddamn chest.'

28

Secretary Sylvie Baudeloque was now in a panic. She paced outside the director's empty office. *Where the hell is he? What do I do?*

It had been a bizarre day. Of course, any day working for Maximilian Kohler had the potential to be strange, but Kohler had been in rare form today.

'Find me Leonardo Vetra!' he had demanded when Sylvie arrived this morning.

Dutifully, Sylvie paged, phoned, and E-mailed Leonardo Vetra.

Nothing.

So Kohler had left in a huff, apparently to go find Vetra himself. When he rolled back in a few hours later, Kohler looked decidedly not well . . . not that he ever actually looked *well*, but he looked worse than usual. He locked himself in his office, and she could hear him on his modem, his phone, faxing, talking. Then Kohler rolled out again. He hadn't been back since.

Sylvie had decided to ignore the antics as yet another Kohlerian melodrama, but she began to get concerned when Kohler failed to return at the proper time for his daily injections; the director's physical condition required regular treatment, and when he decided to push his luck, the results were never pretty – respiratory shock, coughing fits, and a mad dash by the infirmary personnel. Sometimes Sylvie thought Maximilian Kohler had a death wish.

She considered paging him to remind him, but she'd learned charity was something Kohler's pride despised. Last week, he had become so enraged with a visiting scientist who had shown him undue pity that Kohler clambered to his feet and threw a clipboard at the man's head. King Kohler could be surprisingly agile when he was *pissé*.

At the moment, however, Sylvie's concern for the director's health was taking a back burner . . . replaced by a much more pressing dilemma. The CERN switchboard had phoned five minutes ago in a frenzy to say they had an urgent call for the director.

'He's not available,' Sylvie had said.

Then the CERN operator told her who was calling.

Sylvie half laughed aloud. 'You're kidding, right?' She listened, and her face clouded with disbelief. 'And your caller ID confirms—' Sylvie was frowning. 'I see. Okay. Can you ask what the—' She sighed. 'No. That's fine. Tell him to hold. I'll locate the director right away. Yes, I understand. I'll hurry.'

But Sylvie had not been able to find the director. She had called his cell line three times and each time gotten the same message: 'The mobile customer you are trying to reach is out of range.' *Out of range? How far could he go?* So Sylvie had dialed Kohler's beeper. Twice. No response. Most unlike him. She'd even E-mailed his mobile computer. Nothing. It was like the man had disappeared off the face of the earth.

So what do I do? she now wondered.

Short of searching CERN's entire complex herself, Sylvie knew there was only one other way to get the director's attention. He would not be pleased, but the man on the phone was not someone the director should keep waiting. Nor did it sound like the caller was in any mood to be told the director was unavailable.

Startled with her own boldness, Sylvie made her decision. She walked into Kohler's office and went to the metal box on his wall behind his desk. She opened the cover, stared at the controls, and found the correct button.

Then she took a deep breath and grabbed the microphone.

29

Vittoria did not remember how they had gotten to the main elevator, but they were there. Ascending. Kohler was behind her, his breathing labored now. Langdon's concerned gaze passed through her like a ghost. He had taken the fax from her hand and slipped it in his jacket pocket away from her sight, but the image was still burned into her memory.

As the elevator climbed, Vittoria's world swirled into darkness. *Papa!* In her mind she reached for him. For just a moment, in the oasis of her memory, Vittoria was with him. She was nine years old, rolling down hills of edelweiss flowers, the Swiss sky spinning overhead.

Papa! Papa!

Leonardo Vetra was laughing beside her, beaming. 'What is it, angel?'

'Papa!' she giggled, nuzzling close to him. 'Ask me what's the matter!'

'But you look happy, sweetie. Why would I ask you what's the matter?'

'Just ask me.'

He shrugged. 'What's the matter?'

She immediately started laughing. 'What's the matter? *Everything* is the matter! Rocks! Trees! Atoms! Even anteaters! Everything is the matter!'

He laughed. 'Did you make that up?'

'Pretty smart, huh?'

'My little Einstein.'

She frowned. 'He has stupid hair. I saw his picture.'

'He's got a smart head, though. I told you what he proved, right?'

Her eyes widened with dread. 'Dad! No! You *promised!*'

'$E=MC^2$!' He tickled her playfully. '$E=MC^2$!'

'No *math*! I told you! I hate it!'

'I'm glad you hate it. Because girls aren't even *allowed* to do math.'

Vittoria stopped short. 'They *aren't*?'

'Of course not. Everyone knows that. Girls play with dollies. Boys do math. No math for girls. I'm not even *permitted* to talk to little girls about math.'

'What! But that's not fair!'

'Rules are rules. Absolutely no math for little girls.'

Vittoria looked horrified. 'But dolls are boring!'

'I'm sorry,' her father said. 'I could tell you about math, but if I got caught . . .' He looked nervously around the deserted hills.

Vittoria followed his gaze. 'Okay,' she whispered, 'just tell me quietly.'

The motion of the elevator startled her. Vittoria opened her eyes. He was gone.

Reality rushed in, wrapping a frosty grip around her. She looked to Langdon. The earnest concern in his gaze felt like the warmth of a guardian angel, especially in the aura of Kohler's chill.

A single sentient thought began pounding at Vittoria with unrelenting force.

Where is the antimatter?

The horrifying answer was only a moment away.

30

'Maximilian Kohler. Kindly call your office immediately.'

Blazing sunbeams flooded Langdon's eyes as the elevator doors opened into the main atrium. Before the echo of the announcement on the intercom overhead faded, every electronic device on Kohler's wheelchair started beeping and buzzing simultaneously. His pager. His phone. His E-mail. Kohler glanced down at the blinking lights in apparent bewilderment. The director had resurfaced, and he was back in range.

'Director Kohler. Please call your office.'

The sound of his name on the PA seemed to startle Kohler.

He glanced up, looking angered and then almost immediately concerned. Langdon's eyes met his, and Vittoria's too. The three of them were motionless a moment, as if all the tension between them had been erased and replaced by a single, unifying foreboding.

Kohler took his cell phone from the armrest. He dialed an extension and fought off another coughing fit. Vittoria and Langdon waited.

'This is . . . Director Kohler,' he said, wheezing. 'Yes? I was subterranean, out of range.' He listened, his gray eyes widening. *'Who?* Yes, patch it through.' There was a pause. 'Hello? This is Maximilian Kohler. I am the director of CERN. With whom am I speaking?'

Vittoria and Langdon watched in silence as Kohler listened.

'It would be unwise,' Kohler finally said, 'to speak of this by phone. I will be there immediately.' He was coughing again. 'Meet me . . . at Leonardo da Vinci Airport. Forty minutes.' Kohler's breath seemed to be failing him now. He descended into a fit of coughing and barely managed to choke out the words. 'Locate the canister immediately . . . I am coming.' Then he clicked off his phone.

Vittoria ran to Kohler's side, but Kohler could no longer speak. Langdon watched as Vittoria pulled out her cell phone and paged CERN's infirmary. Langdon felt like a ship on the periphery of a storm . . . tossed but detached.

Meet me at Leonardo da Vinci Airport. Kohler's words echoed.

The uncertain shadows that had fogged Langdon's mind all morning, in a single instant, solidified into a vivid image. As he stood there in the swirl of confusion, he felt a door inside him open . . . as if some mystic threshold had just been breached. *The ambigram. The murdered priest/scientist. The antimatter. And now . . . the target.* Leonardo da Vinci Airport could only mean one thing. In a moment of stark realization, Langdon knew he had just crossed over. He had become a believer.

Five kilotons. Let there be light.

Two paramedics materialized, racing across the atrium in white smocks. They knelt by Kohler, putting an oxygen mask on his face. Scientists in the hall stopped and stood back.

Kohler took two long pulls, pushed the mask aside, and still gasping for air, looked up at Vittoria and Langdon. 'Rome.'

'Rome?' Vittoria demanded. 'The antimatter is in Rome? Who called?'

Kohler's face was twisted, his gray eyes watering. 'The Swiss . . .' He choked on the words, and the paramedics put the mask back over his face. As they prepared to take him away, Kohler reached up and grabbed Langdon's arm.

Langdon nodded. He knew.

'Go . . .' Kohler wheezed beneath his mask. 'Go . . . call me . . .' Then the paramedics were rolling him away.

Vittoria stood riveted to the floor, watching him go. Then she turned to Langdon. 'Rome? But . . . what was that about *the Swiss?*'

Langdon put a hand on her shoulder, barely whispering the words. 'The Swiss Guard,' he said. 'The sworn sentinels of Vatican City.'

31

The X-33 space plane roared into the sky and arched south toward Rome. On board, Langdon sat in silence. The last fifteen minutes had been a blur. Now that he had finished briefing Vittoria on the Illuminati and their covenant against the Vatican, the scope of this situation was starting to sink in.

What the hell am I doing? Langdon wondered. *I should have gone home when I had the chance!* Deep down, though, he knew he'd never had the chance.

Langdon's better judgment had screamed at him to return to Boston. Nonetheless, academic astonishment had somehow vetoed prudence. Everything he had ever believed about the demise of the Illuminati was suddenly looking like a brilliant sham. Part of him craved proof. Confirmation. There was also a question of conscience. With Kohler ailing and Vittoria on her own, Langdon knew that if his knowledge of the Illuminati could assist in any way, he had a moral obligation to be here.

There was more, though. Although Langdon was ashamed to admit it, his initial horror on hearing about the antimatter's location was not only the danger to human life in Vatican City, but for something else as well.

Art.

The world's largest art collection was now sitting on a time bomb. The Vatican Museum housed over 60,000 priceless pieces in 1,407 rooms – Michelangelo, da Vinci, Bernini, Botticelli. Langdon wondered if all of the art could possibly be evacuated if necessary. He knew it was impossible. Many of the pieces were sculptures weighing tons. Not to mention, the greatest treasures were architectural – the Sistine Chapel, St Peter's Basilica, Bramante's famed spiral staircase leading to the *Museo Vaticano* – priceless testaments to man's creative genius. Langdon wondered how much time was left on the canister.

'Thanks for coming,' Vittoria said, her voice quiet.

Langdon emerged from his daydream and looked up. Vittoria was sitting across the aisle. Even in the stark fluorescent light of the cabin, there was an aura of composure about her – an almost magnetic radiance of wholeness. Her breathing seemed deeper now, as if a spark of self-preservation had ignited within her . . . a craving for justice and retribution, fueled by a daughter's love.

Vittoria had not had time to change from her shorts and sleeveless top, and her tawny legs were now goose-bumped in the cold of the plane. Instinctively Langdon removed his jacket and offered it to her.

'American chivalry?' She accepted, her eyes thanking him silently.

The plane jostled across some turbulence, and Langdon felt a surge of danger. The windowless cabin felt cramped again, and he tried to imagine himself in an open field. The notion, he realized, was ironic. He had been in an open field when it had happened. *Crushing darkness.* He pushed the memory from his mind. *Ancient history.*

Vittoria was watching him. 'Do you believe in God, Mr Langdon?'

The question startled him. The earnestness in Vittoria's voice was even more disarming than the inquiry. *Do I believe in God?* He had hoped for a lighter topic of conversation to pass the trip.

A spiritual conundrum, Langdon thought. *That's what my friends call me.* Although he'd studied religion for years, Langdon was not a religious man. He respected the power of faith, the benevolence of churches, the strength religion gave so many people . . . and yet, for him, the intellectual suspension of disbelief that was imperative if one were truly going to 'believe' had always proved too big an obstacle for his academic mind. 'I *want* to believe,' he heard himself say.

Vittoria's reply carried no judgment or challenge. 'So why *don't* you?'

He chuckled. 'Well, it's not that easy. *Having* faith requires *leaps* of faith, cerebral acceptance of miracles – immaculate conceptions and divine interventions. And then there are the codes of conduct. The Bible, the Koran, Buddhist scripture . . . they all carry similar requirements – and similar penalties. They claim that if I don't live by a specific code I will go to hell. I can't imagine a God who would rule that way.'

'I hope you don't let your students dodge questions that shamelessly.'

The comment caught him off guard. 'What?'

'Mr Langdon, I did not ask if you believe what *man* says about God. I asked if you believe in God. There is a difference. Holy scripture is stories . . . legends and history of man's quest to understand his own need for meaning. I am not asking you to pass judgment on literature. I am asking if you believe in *God*. When you lie out under the stars, do you sense the divine? Do you feel in your gut that you are staring up at the work of God's hand?'

Langdon took a long moment to consider it.

'I'm prying,' Vittoria apologized.

'No, I just . . .'

'Certainly you must debate issues of faith with your classes.'

'Endlessly.'

'And you play devil's advocate, I imagine. Always fueling the debate.'

Langdon smiled. 'You must be a teacher too.'

'No, but I learned from a master. My father could argue two sides of a Möbius Strip.'

Langdon laughed, picturing the artful crafting of a Möbius Strip – a twisted ring of paper, which technically possessed only *one* side. Langdon had first seen the single-sided shape in the artwork of M. C. Escher. 'May I ask you a question, Ms Vetra?'

'Call me Vittoria. Ms Vetra makes me feel old.'

He sighed inwardly, suddenly sensing his own age. 'Vittoria, I'm Robert.'

'You had a question.'

'Yes. As a scientist and the daughter of a Catholic priest, what do *you* think of religion?'

Vittoria paused, brushing a lock of hair from her eyes. 'Religion is like language or dress. We gravitate toward the practices with which we were raised. In the end, though, we are all proclaiming the same thing. That life has meaning. That we are grateful for the power that created us.'

Langdon was intrigued. 'So you're saying that whether you are a Christian or a Muslim simply depends on where you were born?'

'Isn't it obvious? Look at the diffusion of religion around the globe.'

'So faith is random?'

'Hardly. Faith is universal. Our specific methods for understanding it are arbitrary. Some of us pray to Jesus, some of us go to Mecca, some of us study subatomic particles. In the end we are all just searching for truth, that which is greater than ourselves.'

Langdon wished his students could express themselves so clearly. Hell, he wished *he* could express himself so clearly. 'And God?' he asked. 'Do you believe in God?'

Vittoria was silent for a long time. 'Science tells me God must exist. My mind tells me I will never understand God. And my heart tells me I am not meant to.'

How's that for concise, he thought. 'So you believe God is fact, but we will never understand Him.'

'*Her*,' she said with a smile. 'Your Native Americans had it right.'

Langdon chuckled. 'Mother Earth.'

'*Gaea*. The planet is an organism. All of us are cells with different purposes. And yet we are intertwined. Serving each other. Serving the whole.'

Looking at her, Langdon felt something stir within him that he had not felt in a long time. There was a bewitching clarity in her eyes . . . a purity in her voice. He felt drawn.

'Mr Langdon, let me ask you another question.'

'Robert,' he said. *Mr Langdon makes me feel old. I am old!*

'If you don't mind my asking, Robert, how did you get involved with the Illuminati?'

Langdon thought back. 'Actually, it was money.'

Vittoria looked disappointed. 'Money? Consulting, you mean?'

Langdon laughed, realizing how it must have sounded. 'No. Money as in *currency*.' He reached in his pants pocket and pulled out some money. He found a one-dollar bill. 'I became fascinated with the cult when I first learned that U.S. currency is covered with Illuminati symbology.'

Vittoria's eyes narrowed, apparently not knowing whether or not to take him seriously.

Langdon handed her the bill. 'Look at the back. See the Great Seal on the left?'

Vittoria turned the one-dollar bill over. 'You mean the pyramid?'

'The pyramid. Do you know what pyramids have to do with U.S. history?'

Vittoria shrugged.

'Exactly,' Langdon said. 'Absolutely *nothing*.'

Vittoria frowned. 'So why is it the *central* symbol of your Great Seal?'

'An eerie bit of history,' Langdon said. 'The pyramid is an occult symbol representing a convergence upward, toward the ultimate source of Illumination. See what's above it?'

Vittoria studied the bill. 'An eye inside a triangle.'

'It's called the *trinacria*. Have you ever seen that eye in a triangle anywhere else?'

Vittoria was silent a moment. 'Actually, yes, but I'm not sure . . .'

'It's emblazoned on Masonic lodges around the world.'

'The symbol is Masonic?'

'Actually, no. It's Illuminati. They called it their "shining delta." A call for enlightened change. The eye signifies the Illuminati's ability to infiltrate and watch all things. The shining triangle represents enlightenment. And the triangle is also the Greek letter delta, which is the mathematical symbol for—'

'Change. Transition.'

Langdon smiled. 'I forgot I was talking to a scientist.'

'So you're saying the U.S. Great Seal is a call for enlightened, all-seeing change?'

'Some would call it a New World Order.'

Vittoria seemed startled. She glanced down at the bill again. 'The writing under the pyramid says *Novus . . . Ordo . . .*'

'*Novus Ordo Seclorum*,' Langdon said. 'It means New Secular Order.'

'Secular as in *non*religious?'

'Nonreligious. The phrase not only clearly states the Illuminati objective, but it also blatantly contradicts the phrase beside it. In God We Trust.'

Vittoria seemed troubled. 'But how could all this symbology end up on the most powerful currency in the world?'

'Most academics believe it was through Vice President Henry Wallace. He was an upper echelon Mason and certainly had ties to the Illuminati. Whether it was as a member or innocently under their influence, nobody knows. But it was Wallace who sold the design of the Great Seal to the president.'

'How? Why would the president have agreed to—'

'The president was Franklin D. Roosevelt. Wallace simply told him *Novus Ordo Seclorum* meant *New Deal*.'

Vittoria seemed skeptical. 'And Roosevelt didn't have anyone *else* look at the symbol before telling the Treasury to print it?'

'No need. He and Wallace were like brothers.'

'Brothers?'

'Check your history books,' Langdon said with a smile. 'Franklin D. Roosevelt was a well-known Mason.'

32

Langdon held his breath as the X-33 spiraled into Rome's Leonardo da Vinci International Airport. Vittoria sat across from him, eyes closed as if trying to will the situation into control. The craft touched down and taxied to a private hangar.

'Sorry for the slow flight,' the pilot apologized, emerging from the cockpit. 'Had to trim her back. Noise regulations over populated areas.'

Langdon checked his watch. They had been airborne thirty-seven minutes.

The pilot popped the outer door. 'Anybody want to tell me what's going on?'

Neither Vittoria nor Langdon responded.

'Fine,' he said, stretching. 'I'll be in the cockpit with the air-conditioning and my music. Just me and Garth.'

The late-afternoon sun blazed outside the hangar. Langdon carried his tweed jacket over his shoulder. Vittoria turned her face skyward and inhaled deeply, as if the sun's rays somehow transferred to her some mystical replenishing energy.

Mediterraneans, Langdon mused, already sweating.

'Little old for cartoons, aren't you?' Vittoria asked, without opening her eyes.

'I'm sorry?'

'Your wristwatch. I saw it on the plane.'

Langdon flushed slightly. He was accustomed to having to defend his timepiece. The collector's edition Mickey Mouse watch had been a childhood gift from his parents. Despite the contorted foolishness of Mickey's outstretched arms designating the hour, it was the only watch Langdon had ever worn. Waterproof and glow-in-the-dark, it was perfect for swimming laps or walking unlit college paths at night. When Langdon's students questioned his fashion sense, he told them he wore Mickey as a daily reminder to stay young at heart.

'It's six o'clock,' he said.

Vittoria nodded, eyes still closed. 'I think our ride's here.'

Langdon heard the distant whine, looked up, and felt a sinking feeling. Approaching from the north was a helicopter, slicing low across the runway. Langdon had been on a helicopter once in the Andean Palpa Valley looking at the *Nazca* sand drawings and had not enjoyed it one bit. *A flying shoebox.* After a morning of space plane rides, Langdon had hoped the Vatican would send a car.

Apparently not.

The chopper slowed overhead, hovered a moment, and dropped toward the runway in front of them. The craft was white and carried a coat of arms emblazoned on the side – two skeleton keys crossing a shield and papal crown. He knew the symbol well. It was the traditional seal of the Vatican – the sacred symbol of the *Holy See* or 'holy seat' of government, the *seat* being literally the ancient throne of St Peter.

The Holy Chopper, Langdon groaned, watching the craft land. He'd forgotten the Vatican owned one of these things, used for transporting the Pope to the airport, to meetings, or to his summer palace in Gandolfo. Langdon definitely would have preferred a car.

The pilot jumped from the cockpit and strode toward them across the tarmac.

Now it was Vittoria who looked uneasy. '*That's* our pilot?'

Langdon shared her concern. 'To fly, or not to fly. That is the question.'

The pilot looked like he was festooned for a Shakespearean melodrama. His puffy tunic was vertically striped in brilliant blue and gold. He wore matching pantaloons and spats. On his feet were black flats that looked like slippers. On top of it all, he wore a black felt beret.

'Traditional Swiss Guard uniforms,' Langdon explained. 'Designed by Michelangelo himself.' As the man drew closer, Langdon winced. 'I admit, *not* one of Michelangelo's better efforts.'

Despite the man's garish attire, Langdon could tell the pilot meant business. He moved toward them with all the rigidity and dignity of a U.S. Marine. Langdon had read many times about the rigorous requirements for becoming one of the elite Swiss Guard. Recruited from one of Switzerland's four Catholic cantons, applicants had to be Swiss males between nineteen and thirty years old, at least 5 feet 6 inches, trained by the Swiss Army, and unmarried. This imperial corps was envied by world governments as the most allegiant and deadly security force in the world.

'You are from CERN?' the guard asked, arriving before them. His voice was steely.

'Yes, sir,' Langdon replied.

'You made remarkable time,' he said, giving the X–33 a mystified stare. He turned to Vittoria. 'Ma'am, do you have any other clothing?'

'I beg your pardon?'

He motioned to her legs. 'Short pants are not permitted inside Vatican City.'

Langdon glanced down at Vittoria's legs and frowned. He had forgotten.

Vatican City had a strict ban on visible legs above the knee – both male and female. The regulation was a way of showing respect for the sanctity of God's city.

'This is all I have,' she said. 'We came in a hurry.'

The guard nodded, clearly displeased. He turned next to Langdon. 'Are you carrying any weapons?'

Weapons? Langdon thought. *I'm not even carrying a change of underwear!* He shook his head.

The officer crouched at Langdon's feet and began patting him down, starting at his socks. *Trusting guy*, Langdon thought. The guard's strong hands moved up Langdon's legs, coming uncomfortably close to his groin. Finally they moved up to his chest and shoulders. Apparently content Langdon was clean, the guard turned to Vittoria. He ran his eyes up her legs and torso.

Vittoria glared. 'Don't even think about it.'

The guard fixed Vittoria with a gaze clearly intended to intimidate. Vittoria did not flinch.

'What's that?' the guard said, pointing to a faint square bulge in the front pocket of her shorts.

Vittoria removed an ultrathin cell phone. The guard took it, clicked it on, waited for a dial tone, and then, apparently satisfied that it was indeed nothing more than a phone, returned it to her. Vittoria slid it back into her pocket.

'Turn around, please,' the guard said.

Vittoria obliged, holding her arms out and rotating a full 360 degrees.

The guard carefully studied her. Langdon had already decided that Vittoria's form-fitting shorts and blouse were not bulging anywhere they shouldn't have been. Apparently the guard came to the same conclusion.

'Thank you. This way please.'

The Swiss Guard chopper churned in neutral as Langdon and Vittoria approached. Vittoria boarded first, like a seasoned pro, barely even stooping as she passed beneath the whirling rotors. Langdon held back a moment.

'No chance of a car?' he yelled, half-joking to the Swiss Guard, who was climbing in the pilot's seat.

The man did not answer.

Langdon knew that with Rome's maniacal drivers, flying was probably safer anyway. He took a deep breath and boarded, stooping cautiously as he passed beneath the spinning rotors.

As the guard fired up the engines, Vittoria called out, 'Have you located the canister?'

The guard glanced over his shoulder, looking confused. 'The what?'

'The canister. You called CERN about a canister?'

The man shrugged. 'No idea what you're talking about. We've been busy today. My commander told me to pick you up. That's all I know.'

Vittoria gave Langdon an unsettled look.

'Buckle up, please,' the pilot said as the engine revved.

Langdon reached for his seat belt and strapped himself in. The tiny fuselage seemed to shrink around him. Then with a roar, the craft shot up and banked sharply north toward Rome.

Rome . . . the *caput mundi*, where Caesar once ruled, where St Peter was crucified. The cradle of modern civilization. And at its core . . . a ticking bomb.

33

Rome from the air is a labyrinth – an indecipherable maze of ancient roadways winding around buildings, fountains, and crumbling ruins.

The Vatican chopper stayed low in the sky as it sliced northwest through the permanent smog layer coughed up by the congestion below. Langdon gazed down at the mopeds, sight-seeing buses, and armies of miniature Fiat sedans buzzing around rotaries in all directions. *Koyaanisqatsi*, he thought, recalling the Hopi term for 'life out of balance.'

Vittoria sat in silent determination in the seat beside him.

The chopper banked hard.

His stomach dropping, Langdon gazed farther into the distance. His eyes found the crumbling ruins of the Roman Coliseum. The Coliseum, Langdon had always thought, was one of history's greatest ironies. Now a dignified symbol for the rise of human culture and civilization, the stadium had been built to host centuries of barbaric events – hungry lions shredding prisoners, armies of slaves battling to the death, gang rapes of exotic women captured from far-off lands, as well as public beheadings and castrations. It was ironic, Langdon thought, or perhaps fitting, that the Coliseum had served as the architectural blueprint for Harvard's Soldier Field – the football stadium where the ancient traditions of savagery were reenacted every fall . . . crazed fans screaming for bloodshed as Harvard battled Yale.

As the chopper headed north, Langdon spied the Roman Forum – the heart of pre-Christian Rome. The decaying columns looked like toppled gravestones in a cemetery that had somehow avoided being swallowed by the metropolis surrounding it.

To the west the wide basin of the Tiber River wound enormous arcs across the city. Even from the air Langdon could tell the water was deep. The churning currents were brown, filled with silt and foam from heavy rains.

'Straight ahead,' the pilot said, climbing higher.

Langdon and Vittoria looked out and saw it. Like a mountain parting the morning fog, the colossal dome rose out of the haze before them: St Peter's Basilica.

'Now *that*,' Langdon said to Vittoria, 'is something Michelangelo got right.'

Langdon had never seen St Peter's from the air. The marble façade blazed like fire in the afternoon sun. Adorned with 140 statues of saints, martyrs, and angels, the Herculean edifice stretched two football fields wide and a staggering *six* long. The cavernous interior of the basilica had room for over 60,000 worshipers ... over one hundred times the population of Vatican City, the smallest country in the world.

Incredibly, though, not even a citadel of this magnitude could dwarf the piazza before it. A sprawling expanse of granite, St Peter's Square was a staggering open space in the congestion of Rome, like a classical Central Park. In front of the basilica, bordering the vast oval common, 284 columns swept outward in four concentric arcs of diminishing size ... an architectural *trompe l'oeil* used to heighten the piazza's sense of grandeur.

As he stared at the magnificent shrine before him, Langdon wondered what St Peter would think if he were here now. The saint had died a gruesome death, crucified upside down on this very spot. Now he rested in the most sacred of tombs, buried five stories down, directly beneath the central cupola of the basilica.

'Vatican City,' the pilot said, sounding anything but welcoming.

Langdon looked out at the towering stone bastions that loomed ahead – impenetrable fortifications surrounding the complex ... a strangely earthly defense for a spiritual world of secrets, power and mystery.

'Look!' Vittoria said suddenly, grabbing Langdon's arm. She motioned frantically downward toward St Peter's Square directly beneath them. Langdon put his face to the window and looked.

'Over there,' she said, pointing.

Langdon looked. The rear of the piazza looked like a parking lot crowded with a dozen or so trailer trucks. Huge satellite dishes pointed skyward from the roof of every truck. The dishes were emblazoned with familiar names:

TELEVISOR EUROPEA
VIDEO ITALIA
BBC
UNITED PRESS INTERNATIONAL

Langdon felt suddenly confused, wondering if the news of the anti-matter had already leaked out.

Vittoria seemed suddenly tense. 'Why is the press here? What's going on?'

The pilot turned and gave her an odd look over his shoulder. 'What's going on? You don't know?'

'No,' she fired back, her accent husky and strong.

'*Il Conclave*,' he said. 'It is to be sealed in about an hour. The whole world is watching.'

Il Conclave.

The word rang a long moment in Langdon's ears before dropping like a brick to the pit of his stomach. *Il Conclave. The Vatican Conclave.* How could he have forgotten? It had been in the news recently.

Fifteen days ago, the Pope, after a tremendously popular twelve-year reign, had passed away. Every paper in the world had carried the story about the Pope's fatal stroke while sleeping – a sudden and unexpected death many whispered was suspicious. But now, in keeping with the sacred tradition, fifteen days after the death of a Pope, the Vatican was holding *Il Conclave* – the sacred ceremony in which the 165 cardinals of the world – the most powerful men in Christendom – gathered in Vatican City to elect the new Pope.

Every cardinal on the planet is here today, Langdon thought as the chopper passed over St Peter's Basilica. The expansive inner world of Vatican City spread out beneath him. *The entire power structure of the Roman Catholic Church is sitting on a time bomb.*

34

Cardinal Mortati gazed up at the lavish ceiling of the Sistine Chapel and tried to find a moment of quiet reflection. The frescoed walls echoed with the voices of cardinals from nations around the globe. The men jostled in the candlelit tabernacle, whispering excitedly and consulting with one another in numerous languages, the universal tongues being English, Italian and Spanish.

The light in the chapel was usually sublime – long rays of tinted sun slicing through the darkness like rays from heaven – but not today. As was the custom, all of the chapel's windows had been covered in black velvet in the name of secrecy. This ensured that no one on the inside could send signals or communicate in any way with the outside world. The result was a profound darkness lit only by candles ... a shimmering radiance that seemed to purify everyone it touched, making them all ghostly ... like saints.

What privilege, Mortati thought, *that I am to oversee this sanctified event.* Cardinals over eighty years of age were too old to be eligible for election and did not attend conclave, but at seventy-nine years old, Mortati was the most senior cardinal here and had been appointed to oversee the proceedings.

Following tradition, the cardinals gathered here two hours before conclave to catch up with friends and engage in last-minute discussion. At 7 p.m., the late Pope's chamberlain would arrive, give opening prayer, and then leave. Then the Swiss Guard would seal the doors and lock all the cardinals inside. It was then that the oldest and most secretive political ritual in the world would begin. The cardinals would not be released until they decided who among them would be the next Pope.

Conclave. Even the name was secretive. '*Con clave*' literally meant 'locked with a key.' The cardinals were permitted no contact whatsoever with the outside world. No phone calls. No messages. No whispers through doorways. Conclave was a vacuum, not to be influenced by anything in the outside world. This would ensure that the cardinals kept *Solum Deum prae oculis* ... only God before their eyes.

Outside the walls of the chapel, of course, the media watched and

96

waited, speculating as to which of the cardinals would become the ruler of one billion Catholics worldwide. Conclaves created an intense, politically charged atmosphere, and over the centuries they had turned deadly; poisonings, fist fights, and even murder had erupted within the sacred walls. *Ancient history*, Mortati thought. *Tonight's conclave will be unified, blissful, and above all . . . brief.*

Or at least that had been his speculation.

Now, however, an unexpected development had emerged. Mystifyingly, four cardinals were absent from the chapel. Mortati knew that all the exits to Vatican City were guarded, and the missing cardinals could not have gone far, but still, with less than an hour before opening prayer, he was feeling disconcerted. After all, the four missing men were no *ordinary* cardinals. They were *the* cardinals.

The chosen four.

As overseer of the conclave, Mortati had already sent word through the proper channels to the Swiss Guard alerting them to the cardinals' absence. He had yet to hear back. Other cardinals had now noticed the puzzling absence. The anxious whispers had begun. Of *all* cardinals, these *four* should be on time! Cardinal Mortati was starting to fear it might be a long evening after all.

He had no idea.

35

The Vatican's helipad, for reasons of safety and noise control, is located in the northwest tip of Vatican City, as far from St Peter's Basilica as possible.

'Terra firma,' the pilot announced as they touched down. He exited and opened the sliding door for Langdon and Vittoria.

Langdon descended from the craft and turned to help Vittoria, but she had already dropped effortlessly to the ground. Every muscle in her body seemed tuned to one objective – finding the antimatter before it left a horrific legacy.

After stretching a reflective sun tarp across the cockpit window, the pilot ushered them to an oversized electric golf cart waiting near the helipad. The cart whisked them silently alongside the country's western border – a fifty-foot-tall cement bulwark thick enough to ward off attacks even by tanks. Lining the interior of the wall, posted at fifty-meter intervals, Swiss Guards stood at attention, surveying the interior of the grounds. The cart turned sharply right onto Via dell'Osservatorio. Signs pointed in all directions:

PALAZZO GOVERNATORIO
COLLEGIO ETIOPE
BASILICA SAN PIETRO
CAPELLA SISTINA

They accelerated up the manicured road past a squat building marked RADIO VATICANA. This, Langdon realized to his amazement, was the hub of the world's most listened-to radio programming – *Radio Vaticana* – spreading the word of God to millions of listeners around the globe.

'*Attenzione*,' the pilot said, turning sharply into a rotary.

As the cart wound round, Langdon could barely believe the sight now coming into view. *Giardini Vaticani*, he thought. The heart of Vatican City. Directly ahead rose the rear of St Peter's Basilica, a view, Langdon realized, most people never saw. To the right loomed the Palace of the Tribunal, the lush papal residence rivaled only by Versailles in its baroque embellishment. The severe-looking Governatorato building was now behind them, housing Vatican City's administration. And up ahead on the left, the massive rectangular edifice of the Vatican Museum. Langdon knew there would be no time for a museum visit this trip.

'Where is everyone?' Vittoria asked, surveying the deserted lawns and walkways.

The guard checked his black, military-style chronograph – an odd anachronism beneath his puffy sleeve. 'The cardinals are convened in the Sistine Chapel. Conclave begins in a little under an hour.'

Langdon nodded, vaguely recalling that before conclave the cardinals spent two hours inside the Sistine Chapel in quiet reflection and visitations with their fellow cardinals from around the globe. The time was meant to renew old friendships among the cardinals and facilitate a less heated election process. 'And the rest of the residents and staff?'

'Banned from the city for secrecy and security until the conclave concludes.'

'And when does it conclude?'

The guard shrugged. 'God only knows.' The words sounded oddly literal.

After parking the cart on the wide lawn directly behind St Peter's Basilica, the guard escorted Langdon and Vittoria up a stone escarpment to a marble plaza off the back of the basilica. Crossing the plaza, they approached the rear wall of the basilica and followed it through a triangular courtyard, across Via Belvedere, and into a series of buildings closely huddled together. Langdon's art history had taught him enough Italian to pick out signs for the Vatican Printing Office, the Tapestry Restoration Lab, Post Office Management, and the Church of St Ann. They crossed another small square and arrived at their destination.

The Office of the Swiss Guard is housed adjacent to Il Corpo di Vigilanza, directly northeast of St Peter's Basilica. The office is a squat, stone building. On either side of the entrance, like two stone statues, stood a pair of guards.

Langdon had to admit, these guards did not look quite so comical. Although they also wore the blue and gold uniform, each wielded the traditional 'Vatican long sword' – an eight-foot spear with a razor-sharp scythe – rumored to have decapitated countless Muslims while defending the Christian crusaders in the fifteenth century.

As Langdon and Vittoria approached, the two guards stepped forward, crossing their long swords, blocking the entrance. One looked up at the pilot in confusion. '*I pantaloni corti*,' he said, motioning to Vittoria's shorts.

The pilot waved them off. '*Il comandante vuole vederli subito.*'

The guards frowned. Reluctantly they stepped aside.

Inside, the air was cool. It looked nothing like the administrative security offices Langdon would have imagined. Ornate and impeccably furnished, the hallways contained paintings Langdon was certain any museum world-wide would gladly have featured in its main gallery.

The pilot pointed down a steep set of stairs. 'Down, please.'

Langdon and Vittoria followed the white marble treads as they descended between a gauntlet of nude male sculptures. Each statue wore a fig leaf that was lighter in color than the rest of the body.

The Great Castration, Langdon thought.

It was one of the most horrific tragedies in Renaissance art. In 1857, Pope Pius IX decided that the accurate representation of the male form might incite lust inside the Vatican. So he got a chisel and mallet and hacked off the genitalia of every single male statue inside Vatican City. He defaced works by Michelangelo, Bramante, and Bernini. Plaster fig leaves were used to patch the damage. Hundreds of sculptures had been emasculated. Langdon had often wondered if there was a huge crate of stone penises someplace.

'Here,' the guard announced.

They reached the bottom of the stairs and dead-ended at a heavy, steel door. The guard typed an entry code, and the door slid open. Langdon and Vittoria entered.

Beyond the threshold was absolute mayhem.

36

The Office of the Swiss Guard.

Langdon stood in the doorway, surveying the collision of centuries before them. *Mixed media.* The room was a lushly adorned Renaissance library complete with inlaid bookshelves, oriental carpets, and colorful tapestries . . . and yet the room bristled with high-tech gear – banks of computers, faxes, electronic maps of the Vatican complex, and televisions tuned to CNN. Men in colorful pantaloons typed feverishly on computers and listened intently in futuristic headphones.

'Wait here,' the guard said.

Langdon and Vittoria waited as the guard crossed the room to an exceptionally tall, wiry man in a dark blue military uniform. He was talking on a cellular phone and stood so straight he was almost bent backward. The guard said something to him, and the man shot a glance over at Langdon and Vittoria. He nodded, then turned his back on them and continued his phone call.

The guard returned. 'Commander Olivetti will be with you in a moment.'

'Thank you.'

The guard left and headed back up the stairs.

Langdon studied Commander Olivetti across the room, realizing he was actually the Commander in Chief of the armed forces of an entire country. Vittoria and Langdon waited, observing the action before them. Brightly dressed guards bustled about yelling orders in Italian.

'*Continua a cercare!*' one yelled into a telephone.

'*Hai provato il museo?*' another asked.

Langdon did not need fluent Italian to discern that the security center was currently in intense search mode. This was the good news. The bad news was that they obviously had not yet found the antimatter.

'You okay?' Langdon asked Vittoria.

She shrugged, offering a tired smile.

When the commander finally clicked off his phone and approached across the room, he seemed to grow with each step. Langdon was tall himself and not accustomed to looking up at many people, but Commander

Olivetti demanded it. Langdon sensed immediately that the commander was a man who had weathered tempests, his face hale and steeled. His dark hair was cropped in a military buzz cut, and his eyes burned with the kind of hardened determination only attainable through years of intense training. He moved with ramrod exactness, the earpiece hidden discreetly behind one ear making him look more like U.S. Secret Service than Swiss Guard.

The commander addressed them in accented English. His voice was startlingly quiet for such a large man, barely a whisper. It bit with a tight, military efficiency. 'Good afternoon,' he said. 'I am Commander Olivetti – *Comandante Principale* of the Swiss Guard. I'm the one who called your director.'

Vittoria gazed upward. 'Thank you for seeing us, sir.'

The commander did not respond. He motioned for them to follow and led them through the tangle of electronics to a door in the side wall of the chamber. 'Enter,' he said, holding the door for them.

Langdon and Vittoria walked through and found themselves in a darkened control room where a wall of video monitors was cycling lazily through a series of black-and-white images of the complex. A young guard sat watching the images intently.

'*Fuori,*' Olivetti said.

The guard packed up and left.

Olivetti walked over to one of the screens and pointed to it. Then he turned toward his guests. 'This image is from a remote camera hidden somewhere inside Vatican City. I'd like an explanation.'

Langdon and Vittoria looked at the screen and inhaled in unison. The image was absolute. No doubt. It was CERN's antimatter canister. Inside, a shimmering droplet of metallic liquid hung ominously in the air, lit by the rhythmic blinking of the LED digital clock. Eerily, the area around the canister was almost entirely dark, as if the antimatter were in a closet or darkened room. At the top of the monitor flashed superimposed text: LIVE FEED – CAMERA #86.

Vittoria looked at the time remaining on the flashing indicator on the canister. 'Under six hours,' she whispered to Langdon, her face tense.

Langdon checked his watch. 'So we have until . . .' He stopped, a knot tightening in his stomach.

'Midnight,' Vittoria said, with a withering look.

Midnight, Langdon thought. *A flair for the dramatic.* Apparently whoever stole the canister last night had timed it perfectly. A stark foreboding set in as he realized he was currently sitting at ground zero.

Olivetti's whisper now sounded more like a hiss. 'Does this object belong to your facility?'

Vittoria nodded. 'Yes, sir. It was stolen from us. It contains an extremely combustible substance called antimatter.'

Olivetti looked unmoved. 'I am quite familiar with incendiaries, Ms Vetra. I have not heard of antimatter.'

'It's new technology. We need to locate it immediately or evacuate Vatican City.'

Olivetti closed his eyes slowly and reopened them, as if refocusing on Vittoria might change what he just heard. 'Evacuate? Are you aware what is going on here this evening?'

'Yes, sir. And the lives of your cardinals are in danger. We have about six hours. Have you made any headway locating the canister?'

Olivetti shook his head. 'We haven't started looking.'

Vittoria choked. 'What? But we expressly heard your guards talking about searching the—'

'Searching, *yes*,' Olivetti said, 'but not for your canister. My men are looking for something else that does not concern you.'

Vittoria's voice cracked. 'You haven't even *begun* looking for this canister?'

Olivetti's pupils seemed to recede into his head. He had the passionless look of an insect. 'Ms Vetra, is it? Let me explain something to you. The director of your faculty refused to share any details about this object with me over the phone except to say that I needed to find it immediately. We are exceptionally busy, and I do not have the luxury of dedicating manpower to a situation until I get some facts.'

'There is only one relevant fact at this moment, sir,' Vittoria said, 'that being that in six hours that device is going to vaporize this entire complex.'

Olivetti stood motionless. 'Ms Vetra, there is something you need to know.' His tone hinted at patronizing. 'Despite the archaic appearance of Vatican City, every single entrance, both public and private, is equipped with the most advanced sensing equipment known to man. If someone tried to enter with any sort of incendiary device it would be detected instantly. We have radioactive isotope scanners, olfactory filters designed by the American DEA to detect the faintest chemical signatures of combustibles and toxins. We also use the most advanced metal detectors and X-ray scanners available.'

'Very impressive,' Vittoria said, matching Olivetti's cool. 'Unfortunately, antimatter is nonradioactive, its chemical signature is that of pure hydrogen, and the canister is plastic. None of those devices would have detected it.'

'But the device has an energy source,' Olivetti said, motioning to the blinking LED. 'Even the smallest trace of nickel–cadmium would register as—'

'The batteries are also plastic.'

Olivetti's patience was clearly starting to wane. 'Plastic batteries?'

'Polymer gel electrolyte with Teflon.'

Olivetti leaned towards her, as if to accentuate his height advantage. '*Signorina*, the Vatican is the target of dozens of bomb threats a month. I personally train every Swiss Guard in modern explosive technology. I am well aware that there is no substance on earth powerful enough to do what you are describing unless you are talking about a nuclear warhead with a fuel core the size of a baseball.'

Vittoria framed him with a fervent stare. 'Nature has many mysteries yet to unveil.'

Olivetti leaned closer. 'Might I ask exactly *who* you are? What is your position at CERN?'

'I am a senior member of the research staff and appointed liaison to the Vatican for this crisis.'

'Excuse me for being rude, but if there is indeed a *crisis*, why am I dealing with *you* and not your director? And what disrespect do you intend by coming into Vatican City in short pants?'

Langdon groaned. He couldn't believe that under the circumstances the man was being a stickler for dress code. Then again, he realized, if stone penises could induce lustful thoughts in Vatican residents, Vittoria Vetra in shorts could *certainly* be a threat to national security.

'Commander Olivetti,' Langdon intervened, trying to defuse what looked like a second bomb about to explode. 'My name is Robert Langdon. I'm a professor of religious studies in the U.S. and unaffiliated with CERN. I have seen an antimatter demonstration and will vouch for Ms Vetra's claim that it is exceptionally dangerous. We have reason to believe it was placed inside your complex by an antireligious cult hoping to disrupt your conclave.'

Olivetti turned, peering down at Langdon. 'I have a woman in shorts telling me that a droplet of liquid is going to blow up Vatican City, and I have an American professor telling me we are being targeted by some antireligious cult. What exactly is it you expect me to do?'

'Find the canister,' Vittoria said. 'Right away.'

'Impossible. That device could be anywhere. Vatican City is enormous.'

'Your cameras don't have GPS locators on them?'

'They are not generally *stolen*. This missing camera will take days to locate.'

'We don't have *days*,' Vittoria said adamantly. 'We have six hours.'

'Six hours until what, Ms Vetra?' Olivetti's voice grew louder suddenly. He pointed to the image on the screen. 'Until these numbers count down? Until Vatican City disappears? Believe me, I do not take kindly to people tampering with my security system. Nor do I like mechanical contraptions appearing mysteriously inside my walls. I *am* concerned. It is my *job* to be concerned. But what you have told me here is unacceptable.'

Langdon spoke before he could stop himself. 'Have you heard of the Illuminati?'

The commander's icy exterior cracked. His eyes went white, like a shark about to attack. 'I am warning you. I do not have time for this.'

'So you *have* heard of the Illuminati?'

Olivetti's eyes stabbed like bayonets. 'I am a sworn defendant of the Catholic Church. *Of course* I have heard of the Illuminati. They have been dead for decades.'

Langdon reached in his pocket and pulled out the fax image of Leonardo Vetra's branded body. He handed it to Olivetti.

'I am an Illuminati scholar,' Langdon said as Olivetti studied the picture. 'I am having a difficult time accepting that the Illuminati are still active, and yet the appearance of this brand combined with the fact that the Illuminati have a well-known covenant against Vatican City has changed my mind.'

'A computer-generated hoax.' Olivetti handed the fax back to Langdon.

Langdon stared, incredulous. 'Hoax? Look at the symmetry! You of all people should realize the authenticity of—'

'Authenticity is precisely what you lack. Perhaps Ms Vetra has not informed you, but CERN scientists have been criticizing Vatican policies for decades. They regularly petition us for retraction of Creationist theory, formal apologies for Galileo and Copernicus, repeal of our criticism against dangerous or immoral research. What scenario seems more likely to you – that a four-hundred-year-old satanic cult has resurfaced with an advanced weapon of mass destruction, or that some prankster at CERN is trying to disrupt a sacred Vatican event with a well-executed fraud?'

'That photo,' Vittoria said, her voice like boiling lava, 'is of my father. *Murdered.* You think this is my idea of a *joke?*'

'I don't know, Ms Vetra. But I do know until I get some answers that make *sense*, there is no way I will raise any sort of alarm. Vigilance and discretion are my duty . . . such that spiritual matters can take place here with clarity of mind. Today of all days.'

Langdon said, 'At least postpone the event.'

'Postpone?' Olivetti's jaw dropped. 'Such arrogance! A conclave is not some American baseball game you call off on account of rain. This is a sacred event with a strict code and process. Never mind that one billion Catholics in the world are waiting for a leader. Never mind that the world media is outside. The protocols for this event are holy – *not* subject to modification. Since 1179, conclaves have survived earthquakes, famines, and even the plague. Believe me, it is not about to be canceled on account of a murdered scientist and a droplet of God knows what.'

'Take me to the person in charge,' Vittoria demanded.

Olivetti glared. 'You've got him.'

'No,' she said. 'Someone in the *clergy*.'

The veins on Olivetti's brow began to show. 'The clergy has gone. With the exception of the Swiss Guard, the only ones present in Vatican City at this time are the College of Cardinals. And they are inside the Sistine Chapel.'

'How about the *chamberlain?*' Langdon stated flatly.

'Who?'

'The late Pope's *chamberlain*.' Langdon repeated the word self-assuredly, praying his memory served him. He recalled reading once about the curious arrangement of Vatican authority following the death of a Pope. If Langdon was correct, during the interim between Popes, complete autonomous power shifted temporarily to the late Pope's personal assistant – his chamberlain – a secretarial underling who oversaw conclave until the cardinals chose the new Holy Father. 'I believe the *chamberlain* is the man in charge at the moment.'

'*Il camerlengo?*' Olivetti scowled. 'The camerlengo is only a priest here. He is the late Pope's hand servant.'

'But he is here. And you answer to him.'

Olivetti crossed his arms. 'Mr Langdon, it is true that Vatican rule dictates the camerlengo assume chief executive office during conclave, but it is only because his lack of eligibility for the papacy ensures an unbiased election. It is as if your president died, and one of his aides temporarily sat in the oval office. The camerlengo is young, and his understanding of security, or anything else for that matter, is extremely limited. For all intents and purposes, I am in charge here.'

'Take us to him,' Vittoria said.

'Impossible. Conclave begins in forty minutes. The camerlengo is in the Office of the Pope preparing. I have no intention of disturbing him with matters of security.'

Vittoria opened her mouth to respond but was interrupted by a knocking at the door. Olivetti opened it.

A guard in full regalia stood outside, pointing to his watch. '*É l'ora, comandante.*'

Olivetti checked his own watch and nodded. He turned back to Langdon and Vittoria like a judge pondering their fate. 'Follow me.' He led them out of the monitoring room across the security center to a small clear cubicle against the rear wall. 'My office.' Olivetti ushered them inside. The room was unspecial – a cluttered desk, file cabinets, folding chairs, a water cooler. 'I will be back in ten minutes. I suggest you use the time to decide how you would like to proceed.'

Vittoria wheeled. 'You can't just leave! That canister is—'

'I do not have time for this,' Olivetti seethed. 'Perhaps I should detain you until after the conclave when I *do* have time.'

'Signore,' the guard urged, pointing to his watch again. '*È l'ora di spazzare la cappella.*'

Olivetti nodded and started to leave.

'*Spazzare la cappella?*' Vittoria demanded. 'You're leaving to *sweep* the chapel?'

Olivetti turned, his eyes boring through her. 'We sweep for electronic bugs, Miss Vetra – a matter of *discretion*.' He motioned to her legs. 'Not something I would expect you to understand.'

With that he slammed the door, rattling the heavy glass. In one fluid motion he produced a key, inserted it, and twisted. A heavy deadbolt slid into place.

'*Idiòta!*' Vittoria yelled. 'You can't keep us in here!'

Through the glass, Langdon could see Olivetti say something to the guard. The sentinel nodded. As Olivetti strode out of the room, the guard spun and faced them on the other side of the glass, arms crossed, a large sidearm visible on his hip.

Perfect, Langdon thought. *Just bloody perfect.*

37

Vittoria glared at the Swiss Guard standing outside Olivetti's locked door. The sentinel glared back, his colorful costume belying his decidedly ominous air.

Che fiasco, Vittoria thought. *Held hostage by an armed man in pajamas.*

Langdon had fallen silent, and Vittoria hoped he was using that Harvard brain of his to think them out of this. She sensed, however, from the look on his face, that he was more in shock than in thought. She regretted getting him so involved.

Vittoria's first instinct was to pull out her cell phone and call Kohler, but she knew it was foolish. First, the guard would probably walk in and take her phone. Second, if Kohler's episode ran its usual course, he was probably still incapacitated. Not that it mattered . . . Olivetti seemed unlikely to take anybody's word on anything at the moment.

Remember! she told herself. *Remember the solution to this test!*

Remembrance was a Buddhist philosopher's trick. Rather than asking her mind to search for a solution to a potentially impossible challenge, Vittoria asked her mind simply to remember it. The presupposition that one once *knew* the answer created the mindset that the answer must *exist* . . . thus eliminating the crippling conception of hopelessness. Vittoria often used the process to solve scientific quandaries . . . those that most people thought had no solution.

At the moment, however, her remembrance trick was drawing a major blank. So she measured her options . . . her needs. She needed to warn someone. Someone at the Vatican needed to take her seriously. But who? The camerlengo? How? She was in a glass box with one exit.

Tools, she told herself. *There are always tools. Reevaluate your environment.*

Instinctively she lowered her shoulders, relaxed her eyes, and took three deep breaths into her lungs. She sensed her heart rate slow and her muscles soften. The chaotic panic in her mind dissolved. *Okay*, she thought, *let your mind be free. What makes this situation positive? What are my assets?*

The analytical mind of Vittoria Vetra, once calmed, was a powerful force. Within seconds she realized their incarceration was actually their key to escape.

'I'm making a phone call,' she said suddenly.

Langdon looked up. 'I was about to suggest you call Kohler, but—'

'Not Kohler. Someone else.'

'Who?'

'The camerlengo.'

Langdon looked totally lost. 'You're calling the chamberlain? How?'

'Olivetti said the camerlengo was in the Pope's office.'

'Okay. You know the Pope's private number?'

'No. But I'm not calling on *my* phone.' She nodded to a high-tech phone system on Olivetti's desk. It was riddled with speed dial buttons. 'The head of security *must* have a direct line to the Pope's office.'

'He also has a weight lifter with a gun planted six feet away.'

'And we're locked in.'

'I was actually aware of that.'

'I mean the *guard* is locked out. This is Olivetti's private office. I doubt anyone else has a key.'

Langdon looked out at the guard. 'This is pretty thin glass, and that's a pretty big gun.'

'What's he going to do, shoot me for using the phone?'

'Who the hell knows! This is a pretty strange place, and the way things are going—'

'Either that,' Vittoria said, 'or we can spend the next five hours and forty-eight minutes in Vatican Prison. At least we'll have a front-row seat when the antimatter goes off.'

Langdon paled. 'But the guard will get Olivetti the second you pick up that phone. Besides, there are twenty buttons on there. And I don't see any identification. You going to try them all and hope to get lucky?'

'Nope,' she said, striding to the phone. 'Just one.' Vittoria picked up the phone and pressed the top button. 'Number *one*. I bet you one of those Illuminati U.S. dollars you have in your pocket that this is the Pope's office. What else would take primary importance for a Swiss Guard commander?'

Langdon did not have time to respond. The guard outside the door started rapping on the glass with the butt of his gun. He motioned for her to set down the phone.

Vittoria winked at him. The guard seemed to inflate with rage.

Langdon moved away from the door and turned back to Vittoria. 'You damn well better be right, 'cause this guy does not look amused!'

'Damn!' she said, listening to the receiver. 'A recording.'

'Recording?' Langdon demanded. 'The Pope has an answering machine?'

'It wasn't the Pope's office,' Vittoria said, hanging up. 'It was the damn weekly menu for the Vatican commissary.'

Langdon offered a weak smile to the guard outside who was now glaring angrily through the glass while he hailed Olivetti on his walkie-talkie.

38

The Vatican switchboard is located in the Ufficio di Communicazione behind the Vatican post office. It is a relatively small room containing an eight-line Corelco 141 switchboard. The office handles over 2,000 calls a day, most routed automatically to the recording information system.

Tonight, the sole communications operator on duty sat quietly sipping a cup of caffeinated tea. He felt proud to be one of only a handful of employees still allowed inside Vatican City tonight. Of course the honor was tainted somewhat by the presence of the Swiss Guards hovering outside his door. *An escort to the bathroom*, the operator thought. *Ah, the indignities we endure in the name of Holy Conclave.*

Fortunately, the calls this evening had been light. Or maybe it was not so *fortunate*, he thought. World interest in Vatican events seemed to have dwindled in the last few years. The number of press calls had thinned, and even the crazies weren't calling as often. The press office had hoped tonight's event would have more of a festive buzz about it. Sadly, though, despite St Peter's Square being filled with press trucks, the vans looked to be mostly standard Italian and Euro press. Only a handful of global cover-all networks were there . . . no doubt having sent their *giornalisti secondarii.*

The operator gripped his mug and wondered how long tonight would last. *Midnight or so*, he guessed. Nowadays, most insiders already knew who was favored to become Pope well before conclave convened, so the process was more of a three- or four-hour ritual than an actual election. Of course, last-minute dissension in the ranks could prolong the ceremony through dawn . . . or beyond. The conclave of 1831 had lasted fifty-four days. *Not tonight*, he told himself; rumor was *this* conclave would be a 'smoke-watch.'

The operator's thoughts evaporated with the buzz of an inside line on his switchboard. He looked at the blinking red light and scratched his head. *That's odd*, he thought. *The zero-line. Who on the inside would be calling operator information tonight? Who is even inside?*

'*Città del Vaticano, per favore?*' he said, picking up the phone.

The voice on the line spoke in rapid Italian. The operator vaguely recognized the accent as that common to Swiss Guards – fluent Italian tainted by the Franco-Swiss influence. This caller, however, was most definitely not Swiss Guard.

On hearing the woman's voice, the operator stood suddenly, almost spilling his tea. He shot a look back down at the line. He had not been mistaken. *An internal extension.* The call was from the inside. *There must be some mistake!* he thought. *A woman inside Vatican City? Tonight?*

The woman was speaking fast and furiously. The operator had spent enough years on the phones to know when he was dealing with a *pazzo*. This woman did not sound crazy. She was urgent but rational. Calm and efficient. He listened to her request, bewildered.

'*Il camerlengo?*' the operator said, still trying to figure out where the hell the call was coming from. 'I cannot possibly connect . . . yes, I am aware he is in the Pope's office but . . . who are you again? . . . and you want to warn him of . . .' He listened, more and more unnerved. *Everyone is in danger? How? And where are you calling from?* 'Perhaps I should contact the Swiss . . .' The operator stopped short. 'You say you're *where? Where?*'

He listened in shock, then made a decision. 'Hold, please,' he said, putting the woman on hold before she could respond. Then he called Commander Olivetti's direct line. *There is no way that woman is really—*

The line picked up instantly.

'*Per l'amore di Dio!*' a familiar woman's voice shouted at him. 'Place the damn call!'

The door of the Swiss Guards' security center hissed open. The guards parted as Commander Olivetti entered the room like a rocket. Turning the corner to his office, Olivetti confirmed what his guard on the walkie-talkie had just told him; Vittoria Vetra was standing at his desk talking on the commander's private telephone.

Che coglioni che ha questa! he thought. *The balls on this one!*

Livid, he strode to the door and rammed the key into the lock. He pulled open the door and demanded, 'What are you doing!'

Vittoria ignored him. 'Yes,' she was saying into the phone. 'And I must warn—'

Olivetti ripped the receiver from her hand, and raised it to his ear. 'Who the hell is this!'

For the tiniest of an instant, Olivetti's inelastic posture slumped. 'Yes, camerlengo . . .' he said. 'Correct, signore . . . but questions of security demand . . . of course not . . . I am holding her here for . . . certainly, but . . .' He listened. 'Yes, sir,' he said finally. 'I will bring them up immediately.'

39

The Apostolic Palace is a conglomeration of buildings located near the Sistine Chapel in the northeast corner of Vatican City. With a commanding view of St Peter's Square, the palace houses both the Papal Apartments and the Office of the Pope.

Vittoria and Langdon followed in silence as Commander Olivetti led them down a long rococo corridor, the muscles in his neck pulsing with rage. After climbing three sets of stairs, they entered a wide, dimly lit hallway.

Langdon could not believe the artwork on the walls – mint-condition busts, tapestries, friezes – works worth hundreds of thousands of dollars. Two-thirds of the way down the hall they passed an alabaster fountain. Olivetti turned left into an alcove and strode to one of the largest doors Langdon had ever seen.

'*Ufficio del Papa*,' the commander declared, giving Vittoria an acrimonious scowl. Vittoria didn't flinch. She reached over Olivetti and knocked loudly on the door.

Office of the Pope, Langdon thought, having difficulty fathoming that he was standing outside one of the most sacred rooms in all of world religion.

'*Avanti!*' someone called from within.

When the door opened, Langdon had to shield his eyes. The sunlight was blinding. Slowly, the image before him came into focus.

The Office of the Pope seemed more of a ballroom than an office. Red marble floors sprawled out in all directions to walls adorned with vivid frescoes. A colossal chandelier hung overhead, beyond which a bank of arched windows offered a stunning panorama of the sun-drenched St Peter's Square.

My God, Langdon thought. *This is a room with a view.*

At the far end of the hall, at a carved desk, a man sat writing furiously. '*Avanti*,' he called out again, setting down his pen and waving them over.

Olivetti led the way, his gait military. '*Signore*,' he said apologetically. '*No ho potuto—*'

The man cut him off. He stood and studied his two visitors.

The camerlengo was nothing like the images of frail, beatific old men Langdon usually imagined roaming the Vatican. He wore no rosary beads or pendants. No heavy robes. He was dressed instead in a simple black cassock that seemed to amplify the solidity of his substantial frame. He looked to be in his late-thirties, indeed a child by Vatican standards. He had a surprisingly handsome face, a swirl of coarse brown hair, and almost radiant green eyes that shone as if they were somehow fueled by the mysteries of the universe. As the man drew nearer, though, Langdon saw in his eyes a profound exhaustion – like a soul who had been through the toughest fifteen days of his life.

'I am Carlo Ventresca,' he said, his English perfect. 'The late Pope's camerlengo.' His voice was unpretentious and kind, with only the slightest hint of Italian inflection.

'Vittoria Vetra,' she said, stepping forward and offering her hand. 'Thank you for seeing us.'

Olivetti twitched as the camerlengo shook Vittoria's hand.

'This is Robert Langdon,' Vittoria said. 'A religious historian from Harvard University.'

'*Padre*,' Langdon said, in his best Italian accent. He bowed his head as he extended his hand.

'No, no,' the camerlengo insisted, lifting Langdon back up. 'His Holiness's office does not make me holy. I am merely a priest – a chamberlain serving in a time of need.'

Langdon stood upright.

'Please,' the camerlengo said, 'everyone sit.' He arranged some chairs around his desk. Langdon and Vittoria sat. Olivetti apparently preferred to stand.

The camerlengo seated himself at the desk, folded his hands, sighed, and eyed his visitors.

'Signore,' Olivetti said. 'The woman's attire is my fault. I—'

'Her attire is *not* what concerns me,' the camerlengo replied, sounding too exhausted to be bothered. 'When the Vatican operator calls me a half hour before I begin conclave to tell me a woman is calling from *your* private office to warn me of some sort of major security threat of which I have not been informed, *that* concerns me.'

Olivetti stood rigid, his back arched like a soldier under intense inspection.

Langdon felt hypnotized by the camerlengo's presence. Young and wearied as he was, the priest had the air of some mythical hero – radiating charisma and authority.

'Signore,' Olivetti said, his tone apologetic but still unyielding. 'You should not concern yourself with matters of security. You have other responsibilities.'

'I am well aware of my other responsibilities. I am also aware that as *direttore intermediario*, I have a responsibility for the safety and wellbeing of everyone at this conclave. What is going on here?'

'I have the situation under control.'

'Apparently not.'

'Father,' Langdon interrupted, taking out the crumpled fax and handing it to the camerlengo, 'please.'

Commander Olivetti stepped forward, trying to intervene. 'Father, please do not trouble your thoughts with—'

The camerlengo took the fax, ignoring Olivetti for a long moment. He looked at the image of the murdered Leonardo Vetra and drew a startled breath. 'What is this?'

'That is my father,' Vittoria said, her voice wavering. 'He was a priest and a man of science. He was murdered last night.'

The camerlengo's face softened instantly. He looked up at her. 'My dear child. I'm so sorry.' He crossed himself and looked again at the fax, his eyes seeming to pool with waves of abhorrence. 'Who would . . . and this burn on his . . .' The camerlengo paused, squinting closer at the image.

'It says *Illuminati*,' Langdon said. 'No doubt you are familiar with the name.'

An odd look came across the camerlengo's face. 'I have heard the name, yes, but . . .'

'The Illuminati murdered Leonardo Vetra so they could steal a new technology he was—'

'Signore,' Olivetti interjected. 'This is absurd. The Illuminati? This is clearly some sort of elaborate hoax.'

The camerlengo seemed to ponder Olivetti's words. Then he turned and contemplated Langdon so fully that Langdon felt the air leave his lungs. 'Mr Langdon, I have spent my life in the Catholic Church. I am familiar with the Illuminati lore . . . and the legend of the brandings. And yet I must warn you, I am a man of the present tense. Christianity has enough real enemies without resurrecting ghosts.'

'The symbol is authentic,' Langdon said, a little too defensively he thought. He reached over and rotated the fax for the camerlengo.

The camerlengo fell silent when he saw the symmetry.

'Even modern computers,' Langdon added, 'have been unable to forge a symmetrical ambigram of this word.'

The camerlengo folded his hands and said nothing for a long time. 'The Illuminati are dead,' he finally said. 'Long ago. That is historical fact.'

Langdon nodded. 'Yesterday, I would have agreed with you.'

'Yesterday?'

'Before today's chain of events. I believe the Illuminati have resurfaced to make good on an ancient pact.'

'Forgive me. My history is rusty. What ancient pact is this?'

Langdon took a deep breath. 'The destruction of Vatican City.'

'*Destroy* Vatican City?' The camerlengo looked less frightened than confused. 'But that would be impossible.'

Vittoria shook her head. 'I'm afraid we have some more bad news.'

40

'Is this *true*?' the camerlengo demanded, looking amazed as he turned from Vittoria to Olivetti.

'Signore,' Olivetti assured, 'I'll admit there is some sort of device here. It is visible on one of our security monitors, but as for Ms Vetra's claims as to the power of this substance, I cannot possibly—'

'Wait a minute,' the camerlengo said. 'You can *see* this thing?'

'Yes, signore. On wireless camera #86.'

'Then why haven't you recovered it?' The camerlengo's voice echoed anger now.

'Very difficult, signore.' Olivetti stood straight as he explained the situation.

The camerlengo listened, and Vittoria sensed his growing concern. 'Are you certain it is inside Vatican City?' the camerlengo asked. 'Maybe someone took the camera out and is transmitting from somewhere else.'

'Impossible,' Olivetti said. 'Our external walls are shielded electronically to protect our internal communications. This signal can *only* be coming from the inside or we would not be receiving it.'

'And I assume,' he said, 'that you are now looking for the missing camera with all available resources?'

Olivetti shook his head. 'No, signore. Locating that camera could take hundreds of man hours. We have a number of other security concerns at the moment, and with all due respect to Ms Vetra, this droplet she talks about is very small. It could not possibly be as explosive as she claims.'

Vittoria's patience evaporated. 'That droplet is enough to level Vatican City! Did you even listen to a word I told you?'

'Ma'am,' Olivetti said, his voice like steel, 'my experience with explosives is extensive.'

'Your experience is obsolete,' she fired back, equally tough. 'Despite my attire, which I realize you find troublesome, I am a senior level physicist at the world's most advanced subatomic research facility. I personally designed the antimatter trap that is keeping that sample from annihilating right now. And I am warning you that unless you find that canister in the next six hours, your guards will have nothing to protect for the next century but a big hole in the ground.'

Olivetti wheeled to the camerlengo, his insect eyes flashing rage. 'Signore, I cannot in good conscience allow this to go any further. Your time is being wasted by pranksters. The Illuminati? A droplet that will destroy us all?'

'*Basta*,' the camerlengo declared. He spoke the word quietly and yet it seemed to echo across the chamber. Then there was silence. He continued in a whisper. 'Dangerous or not, Illuminati or no Illuminati, whatever this thing is, it most certainly should not be inside Vatican City . . . no less on the eve of the conclave. I want it found and removed. Organize a search immediately.'

Olivetti persisted. 'Signore, even if we used all the guards to search the complex, it could take days to find this camera. Also, after speaking to Ms Vetra, I had one of my guards consult our most advanced ballistics guide for any mention of this substance called antimatter. I found no mention of it anywhere. Nothing.'

Pompous ass, Vittoria thought. *A ballistics guide? Did you try an encyclopedia? Under A!*

Olivetti was still talking. 'Signore, if you are suggesting we make a naked-eye search of the entirety of Vatican City then I must object.'

'Commander.' The camerlengo's voice simmered with rage. 'May I remind you that when you address me, you are addressing this office. I realize you do not take my position seriously – nonetheless, by law, I am in charge. If I am not mistaken, the cardinals are now safely within the Sistine Chapel, and your security concerns are at a minimum until the conclave breaks. I do not understand why you are hesitant to look for this device. If I did not know better it would appear that you are causing this conclave intentional danger.'

Olivetti looked scornful. 'How dare you! I have served your Pope for twelve years! And the Pope before that for fourteen years! Since 1438 the Swiss Guard have—'

The walkie-talkie on Olivetti's belt squawked loudly, cutting him off. '*Comandante?*'

Olivetti snatched it up and pressed the transmitter. '*Sono occupato! Cosa vuoi!!*'

'*Scusi*,' the Swiss Guard on the radio said. 'Communications here. I thought you would want to be informed that we have received a bomb threat.'

Olivetti could not have looked less interested. 'So handle it! Run the usual trace, and write it up.'

'We did, sir, but the caller . . .' The guard paused. 'I would not trouble you, commander, except that he mentioned the substance you just asked me to research. *Antimatter*.'

Everyone in the room exchanged stunned looks.

'He mentioned *what?*' Olivetti stammered.

'Antimatter, sir. While we were trying to run a trace, I did some additional research on his claim. The information on antimatter is . . . well, frankly, it's quite troubling.'

'I thought you said the ballistics guide showed no mention of it.'

'I found it on-line.'

Alleluia, Vittoria thought.

'The substance appears to be quite explosive,' the guard said. 'It's hard to imagine this information is accurate but it says here that pound for pound antimatter carries about a hundred times more payload than a nuclear warhead.'

Olivetti slumped. It was like watching a mountain crumble. Vittoria's feeling of triumph was erased by the look of horror on the camerlengo's face.

'Did you trace the call?' Olivetti stammered.

'No luck. Cellular with heavy encryption. The SAT lines are interfused, so triangulation is out. The IF signature suggests he's somewhere in Rome, but there's really no way to trace him.'

'Did he make demands?' Olivetti said, his voice quiet.

'No, sir. Just warned us that there is antimatter hidden inside the complex. He seemed surprised I didn't know. Asked me if I'd *seen* it yet. You'd asked me about antimatter, so I decided to advise you.'

'You did the right thing,' Olivetti said. 'I'll be down in a minute. Alert me immediately if he calls back.'

There was a moment of silence on the walkie-talkie. 'The caller is still on the line, sir.'

Olivetti looked like he'd just been electrocuted. 'The line is open?'

'Yes, sir. We've been trying to trace him for ten minutes, getting nothing but splayed ferreting. He must know we can't touch him because he refuses to hang up until he speaks to the camerlengo.'

'Patch him through,' the camerlengo commanded. 'Now!'

Olivetti wheeled. 'Father, no. A trained Swiss Guard negotiator is much better suited to handle this.'

'*Now!*'

Olivetti gave the order.

A moment later, the phone on Camerlengo Ventresca's desk began to ring. The camerlengo rammed his fingers down on the speaker-phone button. 'Who in the name of God do you think you are?'

41

The voice emanating from the camerlengo's speaker phone was metallic and cold, laced with arrogance. Everyone in the room listened.

Langdon tried to place the accent. *Middle Eastern, perhaps?*

'I am a messenger of an ancient brotherhood,' the voice announced in an alien cadence. 'A brotherhood you have wronged for centuries. I am a messenger of the Illuminati.'

Langdon felt his muscles tighten, the last shreds of doubt withering away. For an instant he felt the familiar collision of thrill, privilege, and dead fear that he had experienced when he first saw the ambigram this morning.

'What do you want?' the camerlengo demanded.

'I represent men of science. Men who like yourselves are searching for the answers. Answers to man's destiny, his purpose, his creator.'

'Whoever you are,' the camerlengo said, 'I—'

'*Silenzio.* You will do better to listen. For two millennia your church has dominated the quest for truth. You have crushed your opposition with lies and prophecies of doom. You have manipulated the truth to serve your needs, murdering those whose discoveries did not serve your politics. Are you surprised you are the target of enlightened men from around the globe?'

'Enlightened men do not resort to blackmail to further their causes.'

'Blackmail?' The caller laughed. 'This is not blackmail. We have no demands. The abolition of the Vatican is nonnegotiable. We have waited four hundred years for this day. At midnight, your city will be destroyed. There is nothing you can do.'

Olivetti stormed toward the speaker phone. 'Access to this city is impossible! You could not possibly have planted explosives in here!'

'You speak with the ignorant devotion of a Swiss Guard. Perhaps even an officer? Surely you are aware that for centuries the Illuminati have infiltrated elitist organizations across the globe. Do you really believe the Vatican is immune?'

Jesus, Langdon thought, *they've got someone on the inside.* It was no secret that infiltration was the Illuminati trademark of power. They had infiltrated the Masons, major banking networks, government bodies. In fact, Churchill had once told reporters that if English spies had infiltrated the Nazis to the degree the Illuminati had infiltrated English Parliament, the war would have been over in one month.

'A transparent bluff,' Olivetti snapped. 'Your influence cannot possibly extend so far.'

'Why? Because your Swiss Guards are vigilant? Because they watch every corner of your private world? How about the Swiss Guards themselves? Are they not men? Do you truly believe they stake their lives on a fable about a man who walks on water? Ask yourself how else the canister could have entered your city. Or how four of your most precious assets could have disappeared this afternoon.'

'Our assets?' Olivetti scowled. 'What do you mean?'

'One, two, three, four. You haven't missed them by now?'

'What the hell are you talk—' Olivetti stopped short, his eyes rocketing wide as though he'd just been punched in the gut.

'Light dawns,' the caller said. 'Shall I read their names?'

'What's going on?' the camerlengo said, looking bewildered.

The caller laughed. 'Your officer has not yet informed you? How sinful. No surprise. Such pride. I imagine the disgrace of telling you the truth . . . that four cardinals he had sworn to protect seem to have disappeared . . .'

Olivetti erupted. 'Where did you get this information!'

'Camerlengo,' the caller gloated, 'ask your commander if *all* your cardinals are present in the Sistine Chapel.'

The camerlengo turned to Olivetti, his green eyes demanding an explanation.

'Signore,' Olivetti whispered in the camerlengo's ear, 'it is true that four of our cardinals have not yet reported to the Sistine Chapel, but there is no need for alarm. Every one of them checked into the residence hall this morning, so we know they are safely inside Vatican City. You yourself had tea with them only hours ago. They are simply late for the fellowship preceding conclave. We are searching, but I'm sure they just lost track of time and are still out enjoying the grounds.'

'Enjoying the grounds?' The calm departed from the camerlengo's voice. 'They were due in the chapel over an hour ago!'

Langdon shot Vittoria a look of amazement. *Missing cardinals? So that's what they were looking for downstairs?*

'Our inventory,' the caller said, 'you will find quite convincing. There is Cardinal Lamassé from Paris, Cardinal Guidera from Barcelona, Cardinal Ebner from Frankfurt . . .'

Olivetti seemed to shrink smaller and smaller after each name was read.

The caller paused, as though taking special pleasure in the final name. 'And from Italy . . . Cardinal Baggia.'

The camerlengo loosened like a tall ship that had just run sheets first into a dead calm. His frock billowed, and he collapsed in his chair. '*I preferiti*,' he whispered. 'The four favorites . . . including Baggia . . . the most likely successor as Supreme Pontiff . . . how is it possible?'

Langdon had read enough about modern papal elections to understand the look of desperation on the camerlengo's face. Although technically *any* cardinal under eighty years old could become Pope, only a very few had the respect necessary to command a two-thirds majority in the ferociously partisan balloting procedure. They were known as the *preferiti*. And they were all gone.

Sweat dripped from the camerlengo's brow. 'What do you intend with these men?'

'What do you think I intend? I am a descendant of the Hassassin.'

Langdon felt a shiver. He knew the name well. The church had made some deadly enemies through the years – the Hassassin, the Knights Templar, armies that had been either hunted by the Vatican or betrayed by them.

'Let the cardinals go,' the camerlengo said. 'Isn't threatening to destroy the City of God enough?'

'Forget your four cardinals. They are lost to you. Be assured their deaths will be remembered though . . . by millions. Every martyr's dream. I will make them media luminaries. One by one. By midnight the Illuminati will have everyone's attention. Why change the world if the world is not watching? Public killings have an intoxicating horror about them, don't they? You proved that long ago . . . the inquisition, the torture of the Knights Templar, the Crusades.' He paused. 'And of course, *la purga*.'

The camerlengo was silent.

'Do you not recall *la purga*?' the caller asked. 'Of course not, you are a child. Priests are poor historians, anyway. Perhaps because their history shames them?'

'*La purga*,' Langdon heard himself say. 'Sixteen sixty-eight. The church branded four Illuminati scientists with the symbol of the cross. To purge their sins.'

'Who is speaking?' the voice demanded, sounding more intrigued than concerned. 'Who else is there?'

Langdon felt shaky. 'My name is not important,' he said, trying to keep his voice from wavering. Speaking to a living Illuminatus was disorienting for him . . . like speaking to George Washington. 'I am an academic who has studied the history of your brotherhood.'

'Superb,' the voice replied. 'I am pleased there are still those alive who remember the crimes against us.'

'Most of us think you are dead.'

'A misconception the brotherhood has worked hard to promote. What else do you know of *la purga*?'

Langdon hesitated. *What else do I know? That this whole situation is insanity, that's what I know!* 'After the brandings, the scientists were murdered, and their bodies were dropped in public locations around Rome as a warning to other scientists not to join the Illuminati.'

'Yes. So we shall do the same. *Quid pro quo.* Consider it symbolic retribution for our slain bothers. Your four cardinals will die, one every hour starting at eight. By midnight the whole world will be enthralled.'

Langdon moved toward the phone. 'You actually intend to *brand* and kill these four men?'

'History repeats itself, does it not? Of course, we will be more elegant and bold than the church was. They killed privately, dropping bodies when no one was looking. It seems so cowardly.'

'What are you saying?' Langdon asked. 'That you are going to brand and kill these men in *public?*'

'Very good. Although it depends what you consider public. I realize not many people go to church anymore.'

Langdon did a double take. 'You're going to kill them in *churches?*'

'A gesture of kindness. Enabling God to commend their souls to heaven more expeditiously. It seems only right. Of course the press will enjoy it too, I imagine.'

'You're bluffing,' Olivetti said, the cool back in his voice. 'You cannot kill a man in a church and expect to get away with it.'

'Bluffing? We move among your Swiss Guard like ghosts, remove four of your cardinals from within your walls, plant a deadly explosive at the heart of your most sacred shrine, and you think this is a bluff? As the killings occur and the victims are found, the media will swarm. By midnight the world will know the Illuminati cause.'

'And if we stake guards in every church?' Olivetti said.

The caller laughed. 'I fear the prolific nature of your religion will make that a trying task. Have you not counted lately? There are over four hundred Catholic churches in Rome. Cathedrals, chapels, tabernacles, abbeys, monasteries, convents, parochial schools . . .'

Olivetti's face remained hard.

'In ninety minutes it begins,' the caller said with a note of finality. 'One an hour. A mathematical progression of death. Now I must go.'

'Wait!' Langdon demanded. 'Tell me about the brands you intend to use on these men.'

The killer sounded amused. 'I suspect you know what the brands will be already. Or perhaps you are a skeptic? You will see them soon enough. Proof the ancient legends are true.'

Langdon felt light-headed. He knew exactly what the man was claiming. Langdon pictured the brand on Leonardo Vetra's chest. Illuminati folklore spoke of five brands in all. *Four brands are left*, Langdon thought, *and four missing cardinals.*

'I am sworn,' the camerlengo said, 'to bring a new Pope tonight. Sworn by God.'

'Camerlengo,' the caller said, 'the world does not need a new Pope. After midnight he will have nothing to rule over but a pile of rubble. The Catholic Church is finished. Your run on earth is done.'

Silence hung.

The camerlengo looked sincerely sad. 'You are misguided. A church is more than mortar and stone. You cannot simply erase two thousand years of faith . . . *any* faith. You cannot crush faith simply by removing its earthly manifestations. The Catholic Church will continue with or without Vatican City.'

'A noble lie. But a lie all the same. We both know the truth. Tell me, why is Vatican City a walled citadel?'

'Men of God live in a dangerous world,' the camerlengo said.

'How young *are* you? The Vatican is a fortress because the Catholic Church holds half of its equity *inside* its walls – rare paintings, sculpture, devalued jewels, priceless books . . . then there is the gold bullion and the real estate deeds inside the Vatican Bank vaults. Inside estimates put the raw value of Vatican City at 48.5 billion dollars. Quite a nest egg you're sitting on. Tomorrow it will be ash. Liquidated assets as it were. You will be bankrupt. Not even men of cloth can work for nothing.'

The accuracy of the statement seemed to be reflected in Olivetti's and the camerlengo's shell-shocked looks. Langdon wasn't sure what was more amazing, that the Catholic Church had that kind of money, or that the Illuminati somehow knew about it.

The camerlengo sighed heavily. 'Faith, not money, is the backbone of this church.'

'More lies,' the caller said. 'Last year you spent 183 million dollars trying to support your struggling dioceses worldwide. Church attendance is at an all-time low – down forty-six per cent in the last decade. Donations are half what they were only seven years ago. Fewer and fewer men are entering the seminary. Although you will not admit it, your church is dying. Consider this a chance to go out with a bang.'

Olivetti stepped forward. He seemed less combative, as if he now sensed the reality facing him. He looked like a man searching for an out. Any out. 'And what if some of that bullion went to fund *your* cause?'

'Do not insult us both.'

'We have money.'

'As do we. More than you can fathom.'

Langdon flashed on the alleged Illuminati fortunes, the ancient wealth of the Bavarian stone masons, the Rothschilds, the Bilderbergers, the legendary Illuminati Diamond.

'*I preferiti*,' the camerlengo said, changing the subject. His voice was pleading. 'Spare them. They are old. They—'

'They are virgin sacrifices.' The caller laughed. 'Tell me, do you think they are *really* virgins? Will the little lambs squeal when they die? *Sacrifici vergini all'altare della scienza.*'

The camerlengo was silent for a long time. 'They are men of faith,' he finally said. 'They do not fear death.'

The caller sneered. 'Leonardo Vetra was a man of faith, and yet I saw fear in his eyes last night. A fear I removed.'

Vittoria, who had been silent, was suddenly airborne, her body taut with hatred. '*Asino!* He was my father!'

A cackle echoed from the speaker. 'Your father? What is this? Vetra has a daughter? You should know your father whimpered like a child at the end. Pitiful really. A pathetic man.'

Vittoria reeled as if knocked backward by the words. Langdon reached for her, but she regained her balance and fixed her dark eyes on the phone. 'I swear on my life, before this night is over, I will find you.' Her voice sharpened like a laser. 'And when I do . . .'

The caller laughed coarsely. 'A woman of spirit. I am aroused. Perhaps before this night is over, I will find *you*. And when I do . . .'

The words hung like a blade. Then he was gone.

42

Cardinal Mortati was sweating now in his black robe. Not only was the Sistine Chapel starting to feel like a sauna, but conclave was scheduled to begin in twenty minutes, and there was still no word on the four missing cardinals. In their absence, the initial whispers of confusion among the other cardinals had turned to outspoken anxiety.

Mortati could not imagine where the truant men could be. *With the camerlengo perhaps?* He knew the camerlengo had held the traditional private tea for the four *preferiti* earlier that afternoon, but that had been hours ago. *Were they ill? Something they ate?* Mortati doubted it. Even on the verge of death the *preferiti* would be here. It was once in a lifetime, usually *never*, that a cardinal had the chance to be elected Supreme Pontiff, and by Vatican Law the cardinal had to be *inside* the Sistine Chapel when the vote took place. Otherwise, he was ineligible.

Although there were four *preferiti*, few cardinals had any doubt who the next Pope would be. The past fifteen days had seen a blizzard of faxes and phone calls discussing potential candidates. As was the custom, four names had been chosen as *preferiti*, each of them fulfilling the unspoken requisites for becoming Pope.

Multilingual in Italian, Spanish, and English.
No skeletons in his closet.
Between sixty-five and eighty years old.

As usual, one of the *preferiti* had risen above the others as the man the college proposed to elect. Tonight that man was Cardinal Aldo Baggia from Milan. Baggia's untainted record of service, combined with unparalleled language skills and the ability to communicate the essence of spirituality, had made him the clear favorite.

So where the devil is he? Mortati wondered.

Mortati was particularly unnerved by the missing cardinals because the task of supervising this conclave had fallen to him. A week ago, the College of Cardinals had unanimously chosen Mortati for the office known as *The Great Elector* – the conclave's internal master of ceremonies. Even though the camerlengo was the church's ranking official, the camerlengo was only a priest and had little familiarity with the complex election process, so one cardinal was selected to oversee the ceremony from within the Sistine Chapel.

Cardinals often joked that being appointed The Great Elector was the cruelest honor in Christendom. The appointment made one *ineligible* as a candidate during the election, and it also required one spend many days prior to conclave poring over the pages of the *Universi Dominici Gregis* reviewing the subtleties of conclave's arcane rituals to ensure the election was properly administered.

Mortati held no grudge, though. He knew he was the logical choice. Not only was he the senior cardinal, but he had also been a confidant of the late Pope, a fact that elevated his esteem. Although Mortati was technically still within the legal age window for election, he was getting a bit old to be a serious candidate. At seventy-nine years old he had crossed the unspoken threshold beyond which the college no longer trusted one's health to withstand the rigorous schedule of the papacy. A Pope usually worked fourteen-hour days, seven days a week, and died of exhaustion in an average of 6.3 years. The inside joke was that accepting the papacy was a cardinal's 'fastest route to heaven.'

Mortati, many believed, could have been Pope in his younger days had he not been so broad-minded. When it came to pursuing the papacy, there was a Holy Trinity – Conservative. Conservative. Conservative.

Mortati had always found it pleasantly ironic that the late Pope, God rest his soul, had revealed himself as surprisingly liberal once he had taken office. Perhaps sensing the modern world progressing away from the church, the Pope had made overtures, softening the church's position on the sciences, even donating money to selective scientific causes. Sadly, it had been political suicide. Conservative Catholics declared the Pope 'senile,' while scientific purists accused him of trying to spread the church's influence where it did not belong.

'So where are they?'

Mortati turned.

One of the cardinals was tapping him nervously on the shoulder. 'You know where they are, don't you?'

Mortati tried not to show too much concern. 'Perhaps still with the camerlengo.'

'At this hour? That would be highly unorthodox!' The cardinal frowned mistrustingly. 'Perhaps the camerlengo lost track of time?'

Mortati sincerely doubted it, but he said nothing. He was well aware that most cardinals did not much care for the camerlengo, feeling he was too young to serve the Pope so closely. Mortati suspected much of the cardinals' dislike was jealousy, and Mortati actually admired the young man, secretly applauding the late Pope's selection for chamberlain. Mortati saw only conviction when he looked in the camerlengo's eyes, and unlike many of the cardinals, the camerlengo put church and faith before petty politics. He was truly a man of God.

Throughout his tenure, the camerlengo's steadfast devotion had become legendary. Many attributed it to the miraculous event in his childhood . . . an event that would have left a permanent impression on any man's heart. *The miracle and wonder of it*, Mortati thought, often wishing his own childhood had presented an event that fostered that kind of doubtless faith.

Unfortunately for the church, Mortati knew, the camerlengo would never become Pope in his elder years. Attaining the papacy required a certain amount of political ambition, something the young camerlengo apparently lacked; he had refused his Pope's offers for higher clerical stations many times, saying he preferred to serve the church as a simple man.

'What next?' The cardinal tapped Mortati, waiting.

Mortati looked up. 'I'm sorry?'

'They're late! What shall we do!'

'What *can* we do?' Mortati replied. 'We wait. And have faith.'

Looking entirely unsatisfied with Mortati's response, the cardinal shrunk back into the shadows.

Mortati stood a moment, dabbing his temples and trying to clear his mind. *Indeed, what shall we do?* He gazed past the altar up to Michelangelo's renowned fresco, 'The Last Judgment.' The painting did nothing to soothe his anxiety. It was a horrifying, fifty-foot-tall depiction of Jesus Christ separating mankind into the righteous and sinners, casting the sinners into hell. There was flayed flesh, burning bodies, and even one of Michelangelo's rivals sitting in hell wearing ass's ears. Guy de Maupassant had once written that the painting looked like something painted for a carnival wrestling booth by an ignorant coal heaver.

Cardinal Mortati had to agree.

43

Langdon stood motionless at the Pope's bulletproof window and gazed down at the bustle of media trailers in St Peter's Square. The eerie phone conversation had left him feeling turgid . . . distended somehow. Not himself.

The Illuminati, like a serpent from the forgotten depths of history, had risen and wrapped themselves around an ancient foe. No demands. No negotiation. Just retribution. Demonically simple. Squeezing. A revenge 400 years in the making. It seemed that after centuries of persecution, science had bitten back.

The camerlengo stood at his desk, staring blankly at the phone. Olivetti was the first to break the silence. 'Carlo,' he said, using the camerlengo's first name and sounding more like a weary friend than an officer. 'For twenty-six years, I have sworn my life to the protection of this office. It seems tonight I am dishonored.'

The camerlengo shook his head. 'You and I serve God in different capacities, but service always brings honor.'

'These events . . . I can't imagine how . . . this situation . . .' Olivetti looked overwhelmed.

'You realize we have only one possible course of action. I have a responsibility for the safety of the College of Cardinals.'

'I fear that responsibility was mine, signore.'

'Then your men will oversee the immediate evacuation.'

'Signore?'

'Other options can be exercised later – a search for this device, a manhunt for the missing cardinals and their captors. But first the cardinals must be taken to safety. The sanctity of human life weighs above all. Those men are the foundation of this church.'

'You suggest we cancel conclave right now?'

'Do I have a choice?'

'What about your charge to bring a new Pope?'

The young chamberlain sighed and turned to the window, his eyes drifting out onto the sprawl of Rome below. 'His Holiness once told me that a Pope is a man torn between two worlds . . . the real world and the divine.

He warned that any church that ignored reality would not survive to enjoy the divine.' His voice sounded suddenly wise for its years. 'The real world is upon us tonight. We would be vain to ignore it. Pride and precedent cannot overshadow reason.'

Olivetti nodded, looking impressed. 'I have underestimated you, signore.'

The camerlengo did not seem to hear. His gaze was distant on the window.

'I will speak openly, signore. The real world is *my* world. I immerse myself in its ugliness every day such that others are unencumbered to seek something more pure. Let me advise you on the present situation. It is what I am trained for. Your instincts, though worthy . . . could be disastrous.'

The camerlengo turned.

Olivetti sighed. 'The evacuation of the College of Cardinals from the Sistine Chapel is the worst possible thing you could do right now.'

The camerlengo did not look indignant, only at a loss. 'What do you suggest?'

'Say nothing to the cardinals. Seal conclave. It will buy us time to try other options.'

The camerlengo looked troubled. 'Are you suggesting I lock the entire College of Cardinals on top of a time bomb?'

'Yes, signore. For now. Later, if need be, we can arrange evacuation.'

The camerlengo shook his head. 'Postponing the ceremony *before* it starts is grounds alone for an inquiry, but after the doors are sealed nothing intervenes. Conclave procedure obligates—'

'*Real* world, signore. You're in it tonight. Listen closely.' Olivetti spoke now with the efficient rattle of a field officer. 'Marching one hundred sixty-five cardinals unprepared and unprotected into Rome would be reckless. It would cause confusion and panic in some very old men, and frankly, one fatal stroke this month is enough.'

One fatal stroke. The commander's words recalled the headlines Langdon had read over dinner with some students in the Harvard Commons: POPE SUFFERS STROKE. DIES IN SLEEP.

'In addition,' Olivetti said, 'the Sistine Chapel is a fortress. Although we don't advertise the fact, the structure is heavily reinforced and can repel any attack short of missiles. As preparation we searched every inch of the chapel this afternoon, scanning for bugs and other surveillance equipment. The chapel is clean, a safe haven, and I am confident the antimatter is not inside. There is no safer place those men can be right now. We can always discuss emergency evacuation later if it comes to that.'

Langdon was impressed. Olivetti's cold, smart logic reminded him of Kohler.

'Commander,' Vittoria said, her voice tense, 'there are other concerns. Nobody has ever created this much antimatter. The blast radius, I can only estimate. Some of surrounding Rome may be in danger. If the canister is in one of your central buildings or underground, the effect outside these walls may be minimal, but if the canister is near the perimeter . . . in *this* building for example . . .' She glanced warily out the window at the crowd in St Peter's Square.

'I am well aware of my responsibilities to the outside world,' Olivetti replied, 'and it makes this situation no more grave. The protection of this sanctuary has been my sole charge for over two decades. I have no intention of allowing this weapon to detonate.'

Camerlengo Ventresca looked up. 'You think you can *find* it?'

'Let me discuss our options with some of my surveillance specialists. There is a possibility, if we kill power to Vatican City, that we can eliminate the background RF and create a clean enough environment to get a reading on that canister's magnetic field.'

Vittoria looked surprised, and then impressed. 'You want to *black out* Vatican City?'

'Possibly. I don't yet know if it's possible, but it is one option I want to explore.'

'The cardinals would certainly wonder what happened,' Vittoria remarked.

Olivetti shook his head. 'Conclaves are held by candlelight. The cardinals would never know. After conclave is sealed, I could pull all except a few of my perimeter guards and begin a search. A hundred men could cover a lot of ground in five hours.'

'*Four* hours,' Vittoria corrected. 'I need to fly the canister back to CERN. Detonation is unavoidable without recharging the batteries.'

'There's no way to recharge here?'

Vittoria shook her head. 'The interface is complex. I'd have brought it if I could.'

'*Four* hours then,' Olivetti said, frowning. 'Still time enough. Panic serves no one. Signore, you have ten minutes. Go to the chapel, seal conclave. Give my men some time to do their job. As we get closer to the critical hour, we will make the critical decisions.'

Langdon wondered how close to 'the critical hour' Olivetti would let things get.

The camerlengo looked troubled. 'But the college will ask about the *preferiti* . . . especially about Baggia . . . where they are.'

'Then you will have to think of something, signore. Tell them you served the four cardinals something at tea that disagreed with them.'

The camerlengo looked riled. 'Stand on the altar of the Sistine Chapel and lie to the College of Cardinals?'

'For their own safety. *Una bugia veniale.* A white lie. Your job will be to keep the peace.' Olivetti headed for the door. 'Now if you will excuse me, I need to get started.'

'Commandante,' the camerlengo urged, 'we cannot simply turn our backs on missing cardinals.'

Olivetti stopped in the doorway. 'Baggia and the others are currently outside our sphere of influence. We must let them go . . . for the good of the whole. The military calls it *triage*.'

'Don't you mean *abandonment*?'

His voice hardened. 'If there were *any* way, signore . . . any way in heaven to locate those four cardinals, I would lay down my life to do it. And yet . . .' He pointed across the room at the window where the early evening sun glinted off an endless sea of Roman rooftops. 'Searching a city of five million is not within my power. I will not waste precious time to appease my conscience in a futile exercise. I'm sorry.'

Vittoria spoke suddenly. 'But if we *caught* the killer, couldn't you make him talk?'

Olivetti frowned at her. 'Soldiers cannot afford to be saints, Ms Vetra. Believe me, I empathize with your personal incentive to catch this man.'

'It's not only personal,' she said. 'The *killer* knows where the antimatter is . . . *and* the missing cardinals. If we could somehow find him . . .'

'Play into their hands?' Olivetti said. 'Believe me, removing all protection from Vatican City in order to stake out hundreds of churches is what the Illuminati *hope* we will do . . . wasting precious time and manpower when we should be searching . . . or worse yet, leaving the Vatican Bank totally unprotected. Not to mention the remaining cardinals.'

The point hit home.

'How about the Roman Police?' the camerlengo asked. 'We could alert citywide enforcement of the crisis. Enlist their help in finding the cardinals' captor.'

'Another mistake,' Olivetti said. 'You know how the Roman *Carabinieri* feel about us. We'd get a half-hearted effort of a few men in exchange for their selling our crisis to the global media. Exactly what our enemies want. We'll have to deal with the media soon enough as it is.'

I will make your cardinals media luminaries, Langdon thought, recalling the killer's words. *The first cardinal's body appears at eight o'clock. Then one every hour. The press will love it.*

The camerlengo was talking again, a trace of anger in his voice. 'Commander, we cannot in good conscience do *nothing* about the missing cardinals!'

Olivetti looked the camerlengo dead in the eye. 'The prayer of St Francis, signore. Do you recall it?'

The young priest spoke the single line with pain in his voice. 'God, grant me strength to accept those things I cannot change.'

'Trust me,' Olivetti said. '*This* is one of those things.' Then he was gone.

44

The central office of the British Broadcasting Corporation (BBC) is in London just west of Piccadilly Circus. The switchboard phone rang, and a junior content editor picked up.

'BBC,' she said, stubbing out her Dunhill cigarette.

The voice on the line was raspy, with a Mid-East accent. 'I have a breaking story your network might be interested in.'

The editor took out a pen and a standard Lead Sheet. 'Regarding?'

'The papal election.'

She frowned wearily. The BBC had run a preliminary story yesterday to mediocre response. The public, it seemed, had little interest in Vatican City. 'What's the angle?'

'Do you have a TV reporter in Rome covering the election?'

'I believe so.'

'I need to speak to him directly.'

'I'm sorry, but I cannot give you that number without some idea—'

'There is a threat to the conclave. That is all I can tell you.'

The editor took notes. 'Your name?'

'My name is immaterial.'

The editor was not surprised. 'And you have proof of this claim?'

'I do.'

'I would be happy to take the information, but it is not our policy to give out our reporters' numbers unless—'

'I understand. I will call another network. Thank you for your time. Good-b—'

'Just a moment,' she said. 'Can you hold?'

The editor put the caller on hold and stretched her neck. The art of screening out potential crank calls was by no means a perfect science, but this caller had just passed the BBC's two tacit tests for authenticity of a phone source. He had refused to give his name, and he was eager to get off the phone. Hacks and glory hounds usually whined and pleaded.

Fortunately for her, reporters lived in eternal fear of missing the big story, so they seldom chastised her for passing along the occasional delusional psychotic. Wasting five minutes of a reporter's time was forgivable. Missing a headline was not.

Yawning, she looked at her computer and typed in the keywords 'Vatican City.' When she saw the name of the field reporter covering the papal election, she chuckled to herself. He was a new guy the BBC had just brought up from some trashy London tabloid to handle some of the BBC's more mundane coverage. Editorial had obviously started him at the bottom rung.

He was probably bored out of his mind, waiting all night to record his ten-second video spot. He would most likely be grateful for a break in the monotony.

The BBC content editor copied down the reporter's satellite extension in Vatican City. Then, lighting another cigarette, she gave the anonymous caller the reporter's number.

45

'It won't work,' Vittoria said, pacing the Pope's office. She looked up at the camerlengo. 'Even if a Swiss Guard team can filter electronic interference, they will have to be practically *on top* of the canister before they detect any signal. And that's if the canister is even accessible . . . unenclosed by other barriers. What if it's buried in a metal box somewhere on your grounds? Or up in a metal ventilating duct. There's no way they'll trace it. And what if the Swiss Guards *have* been infiltrated? Who's to say the search will be clean?'

The camerlengo looked drained. 'What are you proposing, Ms Vetra?'

Vittoria felt flustered. *Isn't it obvious!* 'I am proposing, sir, that you take other precautions *immediately*. We can hope against all hope that the commander's search is successful. At the same time, look out the window. Do you see those people? Those buildings across the piazza? Those media vans? The tourists? They are quite possibly within range of the blast. You need to act *now*.'

The camerlengo nodded vacantly.

Vittoria felt frustrated. Olivetti had convinced everyone there was plenty of time. But Vittoria knew if news of the Vatican predicament leaked out, the entire area could fill with onlookers in a matter of minutes. She had seen it once outside the Swiss Parliament building. During a hostage situation involving a bomb, thousands had congregated outside the building to witness the outcome. Despite police warnings that they were in danger, the crowd packed in closer and closer. Nothing captured human interest like human tragedy.

'Signore,' Vittoria urged, 'the man who killed my father is out there somewhere. Every cell in this body wants to run from here and hunt him down. But I am standing in your office . . . because I have a responsibility to you. To you and others. Lives are in danger, signore. Do you hear me?'

The camerlengo did not answer.

Vittoria could hear her own heart racing. *Why couldn't the Swiss Guard trace that damn caller? The Illuminati assassin is the key! He knows where the antimatter is . . . hell, he knows where the cardinals are! Catch the killer, and everything is solved.*

Vittoria sensed she was starting to come unhinged, an alien distress she recalled only faintly from childhood, the orphanage years, frustration with no tools to handle it. *You have tools*, she told herself, *you always have tools*. But it was no use. Her thoughts intruded, strangling her. She was a researcher and problem solver. But this was a problem with no solution. *What data do you require? What do you want?* She told herself to breathe deeply, but for the first time in her life, she could not. She was suffocating.

Langdon's head ached, and he felt like he was skirting the edges of rationality. He watched Vittoria and the camerlengo, but his vision was blurred by hideous images: explosions, press swarming, cameras rolling, four branded humans.

Shaitan ... Lucifer ... Bringer of light ... Satan ...

He shook the fiendish images from his mind. *Calculated terrorism*, he reminded himself, grasping at reality. *Planned chaos.* He thought back to a Radcliffe seminar he had once audited while researching praetorian symbolism. He had never seen terrorists the same way since.

'Terrorism,' the professor had lectured, 'has a singular goal. What is it?'

'Killing innocent people?' a student ventured.

'Incorrect. Death is only a *byproduct* of terrorism.'

'A show of strength?'

'No. A weaker persuasion does not exist.'

'To cause terror?'

'Concisely put. Quite simply, the goal of terrorism is to create terror and fear. Fear undermines faith in the establishment. It weakens the enemy from within ... causing unrest in the masses. Write this down. Terrorism is *not* an expression of rage. Terrorism is a political weapon. Remove a government's façade of infallibility, and you remove its people's faith.'

Loss of faith ...

Is that what this was all about? Langdon wondered how Christians of the world would react to cardinals being laid out like mutilated dogs. If the faith of a priest did not protect him from the evils of Satan, what hope was there for the rest of us? Langdon's head was pounding louder now ... tiny voices playing tug of war.

Faith does not protect you. Medicine and airbags ... those are things that protect you. God does not protect you. Intelligence protects you. Enlightenment. Put your faith in something with tangible results. How long has it been since someone walked on water? Modern miracles belong to science ... computers, vaccines, space stations ... even the divine miracle of creation. Matter from nothing ... in a lab. Who needs God? No! Science is God.

The killer's voice resonated in Langdon's mind. *Midnight ... mathematical progression of death ... sacrifici vergini all'altare della scienza.*

Then suddenly, like a crowd dispersed by a single gunshot, the voices were gone.

Robert Langdon bolted to his feet. His chair fell backward and crashed on the marble floor.

Vittoria and the camerlengo jumped.

'I missed it,' Langdon whispered, spellbound. 'It was right in front of me . . .'

'Missed what?' Vittoria demanded.

Langdon turned to the priest. 'Father, for three years I have petitioned this office for access to the Vatican Archives. I have been denied seven times.'

'Mr Langdon, I am sorry, but this hardly seems the moment to raise such complaints.'

'I need access immediately. The four missing cardinals. I may be able to figure out where they're going to be killed.'

Vittoria stared, looking certain she had misunderstood.

The camerlengo looked troubled, as if he were the brunt of a cruel joke. 'You expect me to believe this information is in our *archives*?'

'I can't promise I can locate it in time, but if you let me in . . .'

'Mr Langdon, I am due in the Sistine Chapel in four minutes. The archives are across Vatican City.'

'You're serious aren't you?' Vittoria interrupted, staring deep into Langdon's eyes, seeming to sense his earnestness.

'Hardly a joking time,' Langdon said.

'Father,' Vittoria said, turning to the camerlengo, 'if there's a chance . . . any at all of finding where these killings are going to happen, we could stake out the locations and—'

'But the archives?' the camerlengo insisted. 'How could they possibly contain any clue?'

'Explaining it,' said Langdon, 'will take longer than you've got. But if I'm right, we can use the information to catch the Hassassin.'

The camerlengo looked as though he wanted to believe but somehow could not. 'Christianity's most sacred codices are in that archive. Treasures I myself am not privileged enough to see.'

'I am aware of that.'

'Access is permitted only by written decree of the curator and the Board of Vatican Librarians.'

'*Or*,' Langdon declared, 'by *papal* mandate. It says so in every rejection letter your curator ever sent me.'

The camerlengo nodded.

'Not to be rude,' Langdon urged, 'but if I'm not mistaken a papal mandate comes from *this* office. As far as I can tell, tonight you hold the trust of his station. Considering the circumstances . . .'

The camerlengo pulled a pocket watch from his cassock and looked at it. 'Mr Langdon, I am prepared to give my life tonight, quite literally, to save this church.'

Langdon sensed nothing but truth in the man's eyes.

'This document,' the camerlengo said, 'do you truly believe it is here? And that it can help us locate these four churches?'

'I would not have made countless solicitations for access if I were not convinced. Italy is a bit far to come on a lark when you make a teacher's salary. The document you have is an ancient—'

'Please,' the camerlengo interrupted. 'Forgive me. My mind cannot process any more details at the moment. Do you know where the secret archives are located?'

Langdon felt a rush of excitement. 'Just behind the Santa Ana Gate.'

'Impressive. Most scholars believe it is through the secret door behind St Peter's Throne.'

'No. That would be the Archivio della Reverenda di Fabbrica di S. Pietro. A common misconception.'

'A librarian docent accompanies every entrant at all times. Tonight, the docents are gone. What you are requesting is carte blanche access. Not even our cardinals enter alone.'

'I will treat your treasures with the utmost respect and care. Your librarians will find not a trace that I was there.'

Overhead the bells of St Peter's began to toll. The camerlengo checked his pocket watch. 'I must go.' He paused a taut moment and looked up at Langdon. 'I will have a Swiss Guard meet you at the archives. I am giving you my trust, Mr Langdon. Go now.'

Langdon was speechless.

The young priest now seemed to possess an eerie poise. Reaching over, he squeezed Langdon's shoulder with surprising strength. 'I want you to find what you are looking for. And find it quickly.'

46

The Secret Vatican Archives are located at the far end of the Belvedere Courtyard directly up a hill from the Gate of Santa Ana. They contain over 20,000 volumes and are rumored to hold such treasures as Leonardo da Vinci's missing diaries and even unpublished books of the Holy Bible.

Langdon strode powerfully up the deserted Via della Fondamenta toward the archives, his mind barely able to accept that he was about to be granted access. Vittoria was at his side, keeping pace effortlessly. Her almond-scented hair tossed lightly in the breeze, and Langdon breathed it in. He felt his thoughts straying and reeled himself back.

Vittoria said, 'You going to tell me what we're looking for?'

'A little book written by a guy named Galileo.'

She sounded surprised. 'You don't mess around. What's in it?'

'It is supposed to contain something called *il segno*.'

'The sign?'

'Sign, clue, signal . . . depends on your translation.'

'Sign to *what*?'

Langdon picked up the pace. 'A secret location. Galileo's Illuminati needed to protect themselves from the Vatican, so they founded an ultra-secret Illuminati meeting place here in Rome. They called it The Church of Illumination.'

'Pretty bold calling a satanic lair a *church*.'

Langdon shook his head. 'Galileo's Illuminati were not the least bit satanic. They were scientists who revered enlightenment. Their meeting place was simply where they could safely congregate and discuss topics forbidden by the Vatican. Although we know the secret lair existed, to this day nobody has ever located it.'

'Sounds like the Illuminati know how to keep a secret.'

'Absolutely. In fact, they never revealed the location of their hideaway to anyone outside the brotherhood. This secrecy protected them, but it also posed a problem when it came to recruiting new members.'

'They couldn't grow if they couldn't advertise,' Vittoria said, her legs and mind keeping perfect pace.

'Exactly. Word of Galileo's brotherhood started to spread in the 1630s, and scientists from around the world made secret pilgrimages to Rome hoping to join the Illuminati ... eager for a chance to look through Galileo's telescope and hear the master's ideas. Unfortunately, though, because of the Illuminati's secrecy, scientists arriving in Rome never knew where to go for the meetings or to whom they could safely speak. The Illuminati wanted new blood, but they could not afford to risk their secrecy by making their whereabouts known.'

Vittoria frowned. 'Sounds like a *situazione senza soluzione.*'

'Exactly. A catch-22, as we would say.'

'So what did they do?'

'They were scientists. They examined the problem and found a solution. A brilliant one, actually. The Illuminati created a kind of ingenious *map* directing scientists to their sanctuary.'

Vittoria looked suddenly skeptical and slowed. 'A map? Sounds careless. If a copy fell into the wrong hands . . .'

'It couldn't,' Langdon said. 'No copies existed anywhere. It was not the kind of map that fit on paper. It was enormous. A blazed trail of sorts across the city.'

Vittoria slowed even further. 'Arrows painted on sidewalks?'

'In a sense, yes, but much more subtle. The map consisted of a series of carefully concealed symbolic markers placed in public locations around the city. One marker led to the next . . . and the next . . . a trail . . . eventually leading to the Illuminati lair.'

Vittoria eyed him askance. 'Sounds like a treasure hunt.'

Langdon chuckled. 'In a manner of speaking, it is. The Illuminati called their string of markers "The Path of Illumination," and anyone who wanted to join the brotherhood had to follow it all the way to the end. A kind of test.'

'But if the Vatican wanted to find the Illuminati,' Vittoria argued, 'couldn't *they* simply follow the markers?'

'No. The path was hidden. A puzzle, constructed in such a way that only certain people would have the ability to track the markers and figure out where the Illuminati church was hidden. The Illuminati intended it as a kind of initiation, functioning not only as a security measure but also as a screening process to ensure that only the brightest scientists arrived at their door.'

'I don't buy it. In the 1600s the clergy were some of the most educated men in the world. If these markers were in public locations, certainly there existed members of the Vatican who could have figured it out.'

'Sure,' Langdon said, 'if they had *known* about the markers. But they didn't. And they never noticed them because the Illuminati designed them in such a way that clerics would never suspect what they were. They used a method known in symbology as *dissimulation.*'

'Camouflage.'

Langdon was impressed. 'You know the term.'

'*Dissimulazione*,' she said. 'Nature's best defense. Try spotting a trumpet fish floating vertically in seagrass.'

'Okay,' Langdon said. 'The Illuminati used the same concept. They created markers that faded into the backdrop of ancient Rome. They couldn't use ambigrams or scientific symbology because it would be far too conspicuous, so they called on an Illuminati artist – the same anonymous prodigy who had created their ambigrammatic symbol "Illuminati" – and they commissioned him to carve four sculptures.'

'Illuminati *sculptures?*'

'Yes, sculptures with two strict guidelines. First, the sculptures had to look like the rest of the artwork in Rome . . . artwork that the Vatican would *never* suspect belonged to the Illuminati.'

'*Religious* art.'

Langdon nodded, feeling a tinge of excitement, talking faster now. 'And the *second* guideline was that the four sculptures had to have very specific themes. Each piece needed to be a subtle tribute to one of the four elements of science.'

'*Four* elements?' Vittoria said. 'There are over a hundred.'

'Not in the 1600s,' Langdon reminded her. 'Early alchemists believed the entire universe was made up of only four substances: Earth, Air, Fire, and Water.'

The early cross, Langdon knew, was the most common symbol of the four elements – four arms representing Earth, Air, Fire, and Water. Beyond that, though, there existed literally *dozens* of symbolic occurrences of Earth, Air, Fire, and Water throughout history – the Pythagorean cycles of life, the Chinese *Hong-Fan*, the Jungian male and female rudiments, the quadrants of the Zodiac, even the Muslims revered the four ancient elements . . . although in Islam they were known as 'squares, clouds, lightning, and waves.' For Langdon, though, it was a more modern usage that always gave him chills – the Mason's four mystic grades of Absolute Initiation: Earth, Air, Fire, and Water.

Vittoria seemed mystified. 'So this Illuminati artist created four pieces of art that *looked* religious, but were actually tributes to Earth, Air, Fire, and Water?'

'Exactly,' Langdon said, quickly turning up Via Sentinel toward the archives. 'The pieces blended into the sea of religious artwork all over Rome. By donating the artwork anonymously to specific churches and then using their political influence, the brotherhood facilitated placement of these four pieces in carefully chosen churches in Rome. Each piece of course was a marker . . . subtly pointing to the next church . . . where the next marker awaited. It functioned as a trail of clues disguised as religious art. If an Illuminati candidate could find the first church and the marker for Earth, he could follow it to Air . . . and then to Fire . . . and then to Water . . . and finally to the Church of Illumination.'

Vittoria was looking less and less clear. 'And this has something to do with catching the Illuminati assassin?'

Langdon smiled as he played his ace. 'Oh, yes. The Illuminati called these four churches by a very special name. *The Altars of Science.*'

Vittoria frowned. 'I'm sorry, that means noth—' She stopped short. '*Gli altari della scienza?*' she exclaimed. 'The Illuminati assassin. He warned that the cardinals would be virgin sacrifices on the altars of science!'

Langdon gave her a smile. 'Four cardinals. Four churches. The four altars of science.'

She looked stunned. 'You're saying the four churches where the cardinals will be sacrificed are the *same* four churches that mark the ancient Path of Illumination?'

'I believe so, yes.'

'But why would the killer have given us that clue?'

'Why not?' Langdon replied. 'Very few historians know about those sculptures. Even fewer believe they exist. And their locations have remained secret for four hundred years. No doubt the Illuminati trusted the secret for another five hours. Besides, the Illuminati don't *need* their Path of Illumination anymore. Their secret lair is probably long gone anyway. They live in the modern world. They meet in bank boardrooms, eating clubs, private golf courses. Tonight they *want* to make their secrets public. This is their moment. Their grand unveiling.'

Langdon feared the Illuminati unveiling would have a special symmetry to it that he had not yet mentioned. *The four brands.* The killer had sworn each cardinal would be branded with a different symbol. *Proof the ancient legends are true*, the killer had said. The legend of the four ambigrammatic brands was as old as the Illuminati itself: earth, air, fire, water – four words crafted in perfect symmetry. Just like the word Illuminati. Each cardinal was to be branded with one of the ancient elements of science. The rumor that the four brands were in *English* rather than Italian remained a point of debate among historians. English seemed a random deviation from their natural tongue . . . and the Illuminati did nothing randomly.

Langdon turned up the brick pathway before the archive building. Ghastly images thrashed in his mind. The overall Illuminati plot was starting to reveal its patient grandeur. The brotherhood had vowed to stay silent as long as it took, amassing enough influence and power that they could resurface without fear, make their stand, fight their cause in broad daylight. The Illuminati were no longer about hiding. They were about flaunting their power, confirming the conspiratorial myths as fact. Tonight was a global publicity stunt.

Vittoria said, 'Here comes our escort.' Langdon looked up to see a Swiss Guard hurrying across an adjacent lawn toward the front door.

When the guard saw them, he stopped in his tracks. He stared at them, as though he thought he was hallucinating. Without a word he turned away and pulled out his walkie-talkie. Apparently incredulous at what he was

141

being asked to do, the guard spoke urgently to the person on the other end. The angry bark coming back was indecipherable to Langdon, but its message was clear. The guard slumped, put away the walkie-talkie, and turned to them with a look of discontent.

Not a word was spoken as the guard guided them into the building. They passed through four steel doors, two passkey entries, down a long stairwell, and into a foyer with two combination keypads. Passing through a high-tech series of electronic gates, they arrived at the end of a long hallway outside a set of wide oak double doors. The guard stopped, looked them over again and, mumbling under his breath, walked to a metal box on the wall. He unlocked it, reached inside, and pressed a code. The doors before them buzzed, and the deadbolt fell open.

The guard turned, speaking to them for the first time. 'The archives are beyond that door. I have been instructed to escort you this far and return for briefing on another matter.'

'You're leaving?' Vittoria demanded.

'Swiss Guards are not cleared for access to the Secret Archives. You are here only because my commander received a direct order from the camerlengo.'

'But how do we get *out*?'

'Monodirectional security. You will have no difficulties.' That being the entirety of the conversation, the guard spun on his heel and marched off down the hall.

Vittoria made some comment, but Langdon did not hear. His mind was fixed on the double doors before him, wondering what mysteries lay beyond.

47

Although he knew time was short, Camerlengo Carlo Ventresca walked slowly. He needed the time alone to gather his thoughts before facing opening prayer. So much was happening. As he moved in dim solitude down the Northern Wing, the challenge of the past fifteen days weighed heavy in his bones.

He had followed his holy duties to the letter.

As was Vatican tradition, following the Pope's death the camerlengo had personally confirmed expiration by placing his fingers on the Pope's carotid artery, listening for breath, and then calling the Pope's name three times. By law there was no autopsy. Then he had sealed the Pope's bedroom, destroyed the papal fisherman's ring, shattered the die used to make lead seals, and arranged for the funeral. That done, he began preparations for the conclave.

Conclave, he thought. *The final hurdle.* It was one of the oldest traditions in Christendom. Nowadays, because the outcome of conclave was usually known before it began, the process was criticized as obsolete – more of a burlesque than an election. The camerlengo knew, however, this was only a lack of understanding. Conclave was not an election. It was an ancient, mystic transference of power. The tradition was timeless . . . the secrecy, the folded slips of paper, the burning of the ballots, the mixing of ancient chemicals, the smoke signals.

As the camerlengo approached through the Loggias of Gregory XIII, he wondered if Cardinal Mortati was in a panic yet. Certainly Mortati had noticed the *preferiti* were missing. Without them the voting would go on all night. Mortati's appointment as the Great Elector, the camerlengo assured himself, was a good one. The man was a free-thinker and could speak his mind. The conclave would need a leader tonight more than ever.

As the camerlengo arrived at the top of the Royal Staircase, he felt as though he were standing on the precipice of his life. Even from up here he could hear the rumble of activity in the Sistine Chapel below – the uneasy chatter of 165 cardinals.

One hundred sixty-one cardinals, he corrected.

For an instant the camerlengo was falling, plummeting toward hell, people screaming, flames engulfing him, stones and blood raining from the sky.

And then silence.

When the child awoke, he was in heaven. Everything around him was white. The light was blinding and pure. Although some would say a ten year old could not possibly understand heaven, the young Carlo Ventresca understood heaven very well. He was in heaven right now. Where else would he be? Even in his short decade on earth Carlo had felt the majesty of God – the thundering pipe organs, the towering domes, the voices raised in song, the stained glass, shimmering bronze and gold. Carlo's mother, Maria, brought him to Mass every day. The church was Carlo's home.

'Why do we come to Mass every single day?' Carlo asked, not that he minded at all.

'Because I promised God I would,' she replied. 'And a promise to God is the most important promise of all. Never break a promise to God.'

Carlo promised her he would never break a promise to God. He loved his mother more than anything in the world. She was his holy angel. Sometimes he called her *Maria benedetta* – the Blessed Mary – although she did not like that at all. He knelt with her as she prayed, smelling the sweet scent of her flesh and listening to the murmur of her voice as she counted the rosary. *Hail Mary, Mother of God . . . pray for us sinners . . . now and at the hour of our death.*

'Where is my father?' Carlo asked, already knowing his father had died before he was born.

'God is your father, now,' she would always reply. 'You are a child of the church.'

Carlo loved that.

'Whenever you feel frightened,' she said, 'remember that God is your father now. He will watch over you and protect you forever. God has *big plans* for you, Carlo.' The boy knew she was right. He could already feel God in his blood.

Blood . . .

Blood raining from the sky!

Silence. Then heaven.

His heaven, Carlo learned as the blinding lights were turned off, was actually the Intensive Care Unit in *Santa Clara Hospital* outside of Palermo. Carlo had been the sole survivor of a terrorist bombing that had collapsed a chapel where he and his mother had been attending Mass while on vacation. Thirty-seven people had died, including Carlo's mother. The papers called Carlo's survival *The Miracle of St Francis*. Carlo had, for some unknown reason, only moments before the blast, left his mother's side and ventured into a protected alcove to ponder a tapestry depicting the story of St Francis.

God called me there, he decided. *He wanted to save me.*

Carlo was delirious with pain. He could still see his mother, kneeling at the pew, blowing him a kiss, and then with a concussive roar, her sweet-smelling flesh was torn apart. He could still taste man's *evil*. Blood showered down. His mother's blood! The blessed Maria!

God will watch over you and protect you forever, his mother had told him. *But where was God now!*

Then, like a worldly manifestation of his mother's truth, a clergyman had come to the hospital. He was not any clergyman. He was a bishop. He prayed over Carlo. The Miracle of St Francis. When Carlo recovered, the bishop arranged for him to live in a small monastery attached to the cathedral over which the bishop presided. Carlo lived and tutored with the monks. He even became an altar boy for his new protector. The bishop suggested Carlo entered public school, but Carlo refused. He could not have been more happy with his new home. He now truly lived in the house of God.

Every night Carlo prayed for his mother.

God saved me for a reason, he thought. *What is the reason?*

When Carlo turned sixteen, he was obliged by Italian law to serve two years of reserve military training. The bishop told Carlo that if he entered seminary he would be exempt from this duty. Carlo told the priest that he planned to enter seminary but that first he needed to understand *evil*.

The bishop did not understand.

Carlo told him that if he was going to spend his life in the church fighting evil, first he had to understand it. He could not think of any better place to understand evil than in the army. The army used guns and bombs. *A bomb killed my Blessed mother!*

The bishop tried to dissuade him, but Carlo's mind was made up.

'Be careful, my son,' the bishop had said. 'And remember the church awaits you when you return.'

Carlo's two years of military service had been dreadful. Carlo's youth had been one of silence and reflection. But in the army there was no quiet for reflection. Endless noise. Huge machines everywhere. Not a moment of peace. Although the soldiers went to Mass once a week at the barracks, Carlo did not sense God's presence in any of his fellow soldiers. Their minds were too filled with chaos to see God.

Carlo hated his new life and wanted to go home. But he was determined to stick it out. He had yet to understand evil. He refused to fire a gun, so the military taught him how to fly a medical helicopter. Carlo hated the noise and the smell, but at least it let him fly up in the sky and be closer to his mother in heaven. When he was informed his pilot's training included learning how to parachute, Carlo was terrified. Still, he had no choice.

God will protect me, he told himself.

Carlo's first parachute jump was the most exhilarating physical experience of his life. It was like flying with God. Carlo could not get enough . . .

the silence . . . the floating . . . seeing his mother's face in the billowing white clouds as he soared to earth. *God has plans for you, Carlo.* When he returned from the military, Carlo entered the seminary.

That had been twenty-three years ago.

Now, as Camerlengo Carlo Ventresca descended the Royal Staircase, he tried to comprehend the chain of events that had delivered him to this extraordinary crossroads.

Abandon all fear, he told himself, *and give this night over to God.*

He could see the great bronze door of the Sistine Chapel now, dutifully protected by four Swiss Guards. The guards unbolted the door and pulled it open. Inside, every head turned. The camerlengo gazed out at the black robes and red sashes before him. He understood what God's plans for him were. The fate of the church had been placed in his hands.

The camerlengo crossed himself and stepped over the threshold.

48

BBC journalist Gunther Glick sat sweating in the BBC network van parked on the eastern edge of St Peter's Square and cursed his assignment editor. Although Glick's first monthly review had come back filled with superlatives – resourceful, sharp, dependable – here he was in Vatican City on 'Pope-Watch.' He reminded himself that reporting for the BBC carried a hell of a lot more credibility than fabricating fodder for the *British Tatler*, but still, this was *not* his idea of reporting.

Glick's assignment was simple. Insultingly simple. He was to sit here waiting for a bunch of old farts to elect their next chief old fart, then he was to step outside and record a fifteen-second 'live' spot with the Vatican as a backdrop.

Brilliant.

Glick couldn't believe the BBC still sent reporters into the field to cover this schlock. *You don't see the American networks here tonight. Hell no!* That was because the big boys did it right. They watched CNN, synopsized it, and then filmed their 'live' report in front of a blue screen, superimposing stock video for a realistic backdrop. MSNBC even used in-studio wind and rain machines to give that on-the-scene authenticity. Viewers didn't want truth anymore; they wanted entertainment.

Glick gazed out through the windshield and felt more and more depressed by the minute. The imperial mountain of Vatican City rose before him as a dismal reminder of what men could accomplish when they put their minds to it.

'What have I accomplished in my life?' he wondered aloud. 'Nothing.'

'So give up,' a woman's voice said from behind him.

Glick jumped. He had almost forgotten he was not alone. He turned to the back seat, where his camerawoman, Chinita Macri, sat silently polishing her glasses. She was always polishing her glasses. Chinita was black, although she preferred African American, a little heavy and smart as hell. She wouldn't let you forget it either. She was an odd bird, but Glick liked her. And Glick could sure as hell use the company.

'What's the problem, Gunth?' Chinita asked.

'What are we doing here?'

She kept polishing. 'Witnessing an exciting event.'

'Old men locked in the dark is exciting?'

'You *do* know you're going to hell, don't you?'

'Already there.'

'Talk to me.' She sounded like his mother.

'I just feel like I want to leave my mark.'

'You wrote for the *British Tatler*.'

'Yeah, but nothing with any resonance.'

'Oh, come on, I heard you did a groundbreaking article on the queen's secret sex life with aliens.'

'Thanks.'

'Hey, things are looking up. Tonight you make your first fifteen seconds of TV history.'

Glick groaned. He could hear the news anchor already. 'Thanks Gunther, great report.' Then the anchor would roll his eyes and move on to the weather. 'I should have tried for an anchor spot.'

Macri laughed. 'With no experience? And *that* beard? Forget it.'

Glick ran his hands through the reddish gob of hair on his chin. 'I think it makes me look clever.'

The van's cell phone rang, mercifully interrupting yet another one of Glick's failures. 'Maybe that's editorial,' he said, suddenly hopeful. 'You think they want a live update?'

'On *this* story?' Macri laughed. 'You keep dreaming.'

Glick answered the phone in his best anchorman voice. 'Gunther Glick, BBC, Live in Vatican City.'

The man on the line had a thick Arabic accent. 'Listen carefully,' he said. 'I am about to change your life.'

49

Langdon and Vittoria stood alone now outside the double doors that led to the inner sanctum of the Secret Archives. The decor in the colonnade was an incongruous mix of wall-to-wall carpets over marble floors and wireless security cameras gazing down from beside carved cherubs in the ceiling. Langdon dubbed it *Sterile Renaissance*. Beside the arched ingress hung a small bronze plaque.

ARCHIVIO DEL VATICANO
Curatore, Padre Jaqui Tomaso

Father Jaqui Tomaso. Langdon recognized the curator's name from the rejection letters at home in his desk. *Dear Mr Langdon, It is with regret that I am writing to deny . . .*

Regret. *Bullshit.* Since Jaqui Tomaso's reign had begun, Langdon had never met a single non-Catholic American scholar who had been given access to the Secret Vatican Archives. *Il guardiano*, historians called him. Jaqui Tomaso was the toughest librarian on earth.

As Langdon pushed the doors open and stepped through the vaulted portal into the inner sanctum, he half expected to see Father Jaqui in full military fatigues and helmet standing guard with a bazooka. The space, however, was deserted.

Silence. Soft lighting.

Archivio del Vaticano. One of his life dreams.

As Langdon's eyes took in the sacred chamber, his first reaction was one of embarrassment. He realized what a callow romantic he was. The images he had held for so many years of this room could not have been more inaccurate. He had imagined dusty bookshelves piled high with tattered volumes, priests cataloging by the light of candles and stained-glass windows, monks poring over scrolls . . .

Not even close.

At first glance the room appeared to be a darkened airline hangar in which someone had built a dozen free-standing racquetball courts. Langdon knew of course what the glass-walled enclosures were. He was not surprised to see them; humidity and heat eroded ancient vellums and parchments, and proper preservation required hermetic vaults like these – airtight cubicles that kept out humidity and natural acids in the air. Langdon had been inside hermetic vaults many times, but it was always an unsettling experience ... something about entering an airtight container where the oxygen was regulated by a reference librarian.

The vaults were dark, ghostly even, faintly outlined by tiny dome lights at the end of each stack. In the blackness of each cell, Langdon sensed the phantom giants, row upon row of towering stacks, laden with history. This was one hell of a collection.

Vittoria also seemed dazzled. She stood beside him staring mutely at the giant transparent cubes.

Time was short, and Langdon wasted none of it scanning the dimly lit room for a book catalog – a bound encyclopedia that cataloged the library's collection. All he saw was the glow of a handful of computer terminals dotting the room. 'Looks like they've got a Biblion. Their index is computerized.'

Vittoria looked hopeful. 'That should speed things up.'

Langdon wished he shared her enthusiasm, but he sensed this was bad news. He walked to a terminal and began typing. His fears were instantly confirmed. 'The old-fashioned method would have been better.'

'Why?'

He stepped back from the monitor. 'Because *real* books don't have password protection. I don't suppose physicists are natural born hackers?'

Vittoria shook her head. 'I can open oysters, that's about it.'

Langdon took a deep breath and turned to face the eerie collection of diaphanous vaults. He walked to the nearest one and squinted into the dim interior. Inside the glass were amorphous shapes Langdon recognized as the usual bookshelves, parchment bins, and examination tables. He looked up at the indicator tabs glowing at the end of each stack. As in all libraries, the tabs indicated the contents of that row. He read the headings as he moved down the transparent barrier.

PIETRO L'EREMITA ... LE CROCIATE ... URBANO II ... LEVANT ...

'They're labeled,' he said, still walking. 'But it's not alpha-author.' He wasn't surprised. Ancient archives were almost never cataloged alphabetically because so many of the authors were unknown. Titles didn't work either because many historical documents were untitled letters or parchment fragments. Most cataloging was done chronologically. Disconcertingly, however, *this* arrangement did not appear to be chronological.

Langdon felt precious time already slipping away. 'Looks like the Vatican has its own system.'

'What a surprise.'

He examined the labels again. The documents spanned centuries, but all the keywords, he realized, were interrelated. 'I think it's a thematic classification.'

'Thematic?' Vittoria said, sounding like a disapproving scientist. 'Sounds inefficient.'

Actually . . . Langdon thought, considering it more closely. *This may be the shrewdest cataloging I've ever seen.* He had always urged his students to understand the overall tones and motifs of an artistic period rather than getting lost in the minutia of dates and specific works. The Vatican Archives, it seemed, were cataloged on a similar philosophy. *Broad strokes* . . .

'Everything in this vault,' Langdon said, feeling more confident now, 'centuries of material, has to do with the Crusades. That's this vault's theme.' It was all here, he realized. *Historical accounts, letters, artwork, socio-political data, modern analyses. All in one place . . . encouraging a deeper understanding of a topic. Brilliant.*

Vittoria frowned. 'But data can relate to *multiple* themes simultaneously.'

'Which is why they cross-reference with proxy markers.' Langdon pointed through the glass to the colorful plastic tabs inserted among the documents. 'Those indicate secondary documents located elsewhere with their primary themes.'

'Sure,' she said, apparently letting it go. She put her hands on her hips and surveyed the enormous space. Then she looked at Langdon. 'So, Professor, what's the name of this Galileo thing we're looking for?'

Langdon couldn't help but smile. He still couldn't fathom that he was standing in this room. *It's in here*, he thought. *Somewhere in the dark, it's waiting.*

'Follow me,' Langdon said. He started briskly down the first aisle, examining the indicator tabs of each vault. 'Remember how I told you about the Path of Illumination? How the Illuminati recruited new members using an elaborate test?'

'The treasure hunt,' Vittoria said, following closely.

'The challenge the Illuminati had was that after they placed the markers, they needed some way to tell the scientific community the path existed.'

'Logical,' Vittoria said. 'Otherwise nobody would know to look for it.'

'Yes, and even if they *knew* the path existed, scientists would have no way of knowing where the path began. Rome is huge.'

'Okay.'

Langdon proceeded down the next aisle, scanning the tabs as he talked. 'About fifteen years ago, some historians at the Sorbonne and I uncovered a series of Illuminati letters filled with references to the *segno*.'

'The sign. The announcement about the path and where it began.'

'Yes. And since then, plenty of Illuminati academics, myself included, have uncovered other references to the *segno*. It is accepted theory now that the clue exists and that Galileo distributed it to the scientific community without the Vatican ever knowing.'

'How?'

'We're not sure, but most likely printed publications. He published many books and newsletters over the years.'

'That the Vatican no doubt saw. Sounds dangerous.'

'True. Nonetheless the *segno* was distributed.'

'But nobody has ever actually found it?'

'No. Oddly though, wherever allusions to the *segno* appear – Masonic diaries, ancient scientific journals, Illuminati letters – it is often referred to by a number.'

'666?'

Langdon smiled. 'Actually it's 503.'

'Meaning?'

'None of us could ever figure it out. I became fascinated with 503, trying everything to find meaning in the number – numerology, map references, latitudes.' Langdon reached the end of the aisle, turned the corner, and hurried to scan the next row of tabs as he spoke. 'For many years the only clue seemed to be that 503 began with the number five . . . one of the sacred Illuminati digits.' He paused.

'Something tells me you recently figured it out, and that's why we're here.'

'Correct,' Langdon said, allowing himself a rare moment of pride in his work. 'Are you familiar with a book by Galileo called *Diàlogo*?'

'Of course. Famous among scientists as the ultimate scientific sellout.'

Sellout wasn't quite the word Langdon would have used, but he knew what Vittoria meant. In the early 1630s, Galileo had wanted to publish a book endorsing the Copernican heliocentric model of the solar system, but the Vatican would not permit the book's release unless Galileo included equally persuasive evidence for the church's *geo*centric model – a model Galileo knew to be dead wrong. Galileo had no choice but to acquiesce to the church's demands and publish a book giving equal time to both the accurate and inaccurate models.

'As you probably know,' Langdon said, 'despite Galileo's compromise, *Diàlogo* was still seen as heretical, and the Vatican placed him under house arrest.'

'No good deed goes unpunished.'

Langdon smiled. 'So true. And yet Galileo was persistent. While under house arrest, he secretly wrote a lesser-known manuscript that scholars often confuse with *Diàlogo*. That book is called *Discorsi*.'

Vittoria nodded. 'I've heard of it. *Discourses on the Tides*.'

Langdon stopped short, amazed she had heard of the obscure publication about planetary motion and its effect on the tides.

'Hey,' she said, 'you're talking to an Italian marine physicist whose father worshiped Galileo.'

Langdon laughed. *Discorsi* however was not what they were looking for. Langdon explained that *Discorsi* had not been Galileo's only work while under house arrest. Historians believed he had also written an obscure booklet called *Diagramma*.

'*Diagramma della Verità*,' Langdon said. '*Diagram of Truth*.'

'Never heard of it.'

'I'm not surprised. *Diagramma* was Galileo's most secretive work – supposedly some sort of treatise on scientific facts he held to be true but was not allowed to share. Like some of Galileo's previous manuscripts, *Diagramma* was smuggled out of Rome by a friend and quietly published in Holland. The booklet became wildly popular in the European scientific underground. Then the Vatican caught wind of it and went on a book-burning campaign.'

Vittoria now looked intrigued. 'And you think *Diagramma* contained the clue? The *segno*. The information about the Path of Illumination.'

'*Diagramma* is how Galileo got the word out. That I'm sure of.' Langdon entered the third row of vaults and continued surveying the indicator tabs. 'Archivists have been looking for a copy of *Diagramma* for years. But between the Vatican burnings and the booklet's low permanence rating, the booklet has disappeared off the face of the earth.'

'Permanence rating?'

'Durability. Archivists rate documents one through ten for their structural integrity. *Diagramma* was printed on sedge papyrus. It's like tissue paper. Life span of no more than a century.'

'Why not something stronger?'

'Galileo's behest. To protect his followers. This way any scientists caught with a copy could simply drop it in water and the booklet would dissolve. It was great for destruction of evidence, but terrible for archivists. It is believed that only *one* copy of *Diagramma* survived beyond the eighteenth century.'

'One?' Vittoria looked momentarily starstruck as she glanced around the room. 'And it's *here*?'

'Confiscated from the Netherlands by the Vatican shortly after Galileo's death. I've been petitioning to see it for years now. Ever since I realized what was in it.'

As if reading Langdon's mind, Vittoria moved across the aisle and began scanning the adjacent bay of vaults, doubling their pace.

'Thanks,' he said. 'Look for reference tabs that have anything to do with Galileo, science, scientists. You'll know it when you see it.'

'Okay, but you still haven't told me how you figured out *Diagramma* contained the clue. It had something to do with the number you kept seeing in Illuminati letters? 503?'

Langdon smiled. 'Yes. It took some time, but I finally figured out that 503 is a simple code. It clearly points to *Diagramma*.'

For an instant Langdon relived his moment of unexpected revelation:

August 16. Two years ago. He was standing lakeside at the wedding of the son of a colleague. Bagpipes droned on the water as the wedding party made their unique entrance . . . across the lake on a barge. The craft was festooned with flowers and wreaths. It carried a Roman numeral painted proudly on the hull – DCII.

Puzzled by the marking Langdon asked the father of the bride, 'What's with 602?'

'602?'

Langdon pointed to the barge. 'DCII is the Roman numeral for 602.'

The man laughed. 'That's not a Roman numeral. That's the name of the barge.'

'The DCII?'

The man nodded. '*The Dick and Connie II.*'

Langdon felt sheepish. Dick and Connie were the wedding couple. The barge obviously had been named in their honor. 'What happened to the *DCI?*'

The man groaned. 'It sank yesterday during the rehearsal luncheon.'

Langdon laughed. 'Sorry to hear that.' He looked back out at the barge. *The DCII*, he thought. *Like a miniature QEII.* A second later, it had hit him.

Now Langdon turned to Vittoria. '503,' he said, 'as I mentioned, is a code. It's an Illuminati trick for concealing what was actually intended as a Roman numeral. The number 503 in Roman numerals is—'

'DIII.'

Langdon glanced up. 'That was fast. Please don't tell me you're an Illuminatus.'

She laughed. 'I use Roman numerals to codify pelagic strata.'

Of course, Langdon thought. *Don't we all.*

Vittoria looked over. 'So what is the meaning of DIII?'

'DI and DII and DIII are very odd abbreviations. They were used by ancient scientists to distinguish between the three Galilean documents most commonly confused.'

Vittoria drew a quick breath. '*Diàlogo* . . . *Discorsi* . . . *Diagramma.*'

'D-one. D-two. D-three. All scientific. All controversial. 503 is DIII. *Diagramma.* The third of his books.'

Vittoria looked troubled. 'But one thing still doesn't make sense. If this *segno*, this clue, this advertisement about the Path of Illumination was really in Galileo's *Diagramma*, why didn't the Vatican see it when they repossessed all the copies?'

'They may have seen it and not noticed. Remember the Illuminati markers? Hiding things in plain view? Dissimulation? The *segno* apparently was hidden the same way – in plain view. Invisible to those who were not looking for it. And also invisible to those who didn't *understand* it.'

'Meaning?'

'Meaning Galileo hid it well. According to historic record, the *segno* was revealed in a mode the Illuminati called *lingua pura*.'

'The pure language?'

'Yes.'

'Mathematics?'

'That's my guess. Seems pretty obvious. Galileo was a scientist after all, and he was writing *for* scientists. Math would be a logical language in which to lay out the clue. The booklet is called *Diagramma*, so mathematical diagrams may also be part of the code.'

Vittoria sounded only slightly more hopeful. 'I suppose Galileo could have created some sort of mathematical code that went unnoticed by the clergy.'

'You don't sound sold,' Langdon said, moving down the row.

'I'm not. Mainly because *you* aren't. If you were so sure about DIII, why didn't you publish? Then someone who *did* have access to the Vatican Archives could have come in here and checked out *Diagramma* a long time ago.'

'I didn't *want* to publish,' Langdon said. 'I had worked hard to find the information and—' He stopped himself, embarrassed.

'You wanted the *glory*.'

Langdon felt himself flush. 'In a manner of speaking. It's just that—'

'Don't look so embarrassed. You're talking to a scientist. Publish or perish. At CERN we call it "Substantiate or suffocate."'

'It wasn't only wanting to be the first. I was also concerned that if the wrong people found out about the information in *Diagramma*, it might disappear.'

'The wrong people being the Vatican?'

'Not that they are wrong, per se, but the church has always downplayed the Illuminati threat. In the early 1900s the Vatican went so far as to say the Illuminati were a figment of overactive imaginations. The clergy felt, and perhaps rightly so, that the last thing Christians needed to know was that there was a very powerful anti-Christian movement infiltrating their banks, politics, and universities.' *Present tense, Robert*, he reminded himself. *There IS a powerful anti-Christian force infiltrating their banks, politics, and universities.*

'So you think the Vatican would have buried any evidence corroborating the Illuminati threat?'

'Quite possibly. Any threat, real or imagined, weakens faith in the church's power.'

'One more question.' Vittoria stopped short and looked at him like he was an alien. 'Are you *serious*?'

Langdon stopped. 'What do you mean?'

'I mean is this *really* your plan to save the day?'

Langdon wasn't sure whether he saw amused pity or sheer terror in her eyes. 'You mean finding *Diagramma*?'

'No, I mean finding *Diagramma*, locating a four-hundred-year-old *segno*, deciphering some mathematical code, and following an ancient trail of art that only the most brilliant scientists in history have ever been able to follow . . . all in the next four hours.'

Langdon shrugged. 'I'm open to other suggestions.'

50

Robert Langdon stood outside Archive Vault 9 and read the labels on the stacks.

BRAHE . . . CLAVIUS . . . COPERNICUS . . . KEPLER . . . NEWTON . . .

As he read the names again, he felt a sudden uneasiness. *Here are the scientists . . but where is Galileo?*

He turned to Vittoria, who was checking the contents of a nearby vault. 'I found the right theme, but Galileo's missing.'

'No he isn't,' she said, frowning as she motioned to the next vault. 'He's over here. But I hope you brought your reading glasses, because this *entire* vault is his.'

Langdon ran over. Vittoria was right. Every indicator tab in Vault 10 carried the same keyword.

IL PROCESSO GALILEANO

Langdon let out a low whistle, now realizing why Galileo had his own vault. 'The Galileo Affair,' he marveled, peering through the glass at the dark outlines of the stacks. 'The longest and most expensive legal proceedings in Vatican history. Fourteen years and six hundred million lire. It's all here.'

'Have a few legal documents.'

'I guess lawyers haven't evolved much over the centuries.'

'Neither have sharks.'

Langdon strode to a large yellow button on the side of the vault. He pressed it, and a bank of overhead lights hummed on inside. The lights were deep red, turning the cube into a glowing crimson cell . . . a maze of towering shelves.

'My God,' Vittoria said, looking spooked. 'Are we tanning or working?'

'Parchment and vellum fades, so vault lighting is always done with dark lights.'

'You could go mad in here.'

Or worse, Langdon thought, moving toward the vault's sole entrance. 'A quick word of warning. Oxygen is an oxidant, so hermetic vaults contain very little of it. It's a partial vacuum inside. Your breathing will feel strained.'

'Hey, if old cardinals can survive it.'

True, Langdon thought. *May we be as lucky.*

The vault entrance was a single electronic revolving door. Langdon noted the common arrangement of four access buttons on the door's inner shaft, one accessible from each compartment. When a button was pressed, the motorized door would kick into gear and make the conventional half rotation before grinding to a halt – a standard procedure to preserve the integrity of the inner atmosphere.

'After I'm in,' Langdon said, 'just press the button and follow me through. There's only eight per cent humidity inside, so be prepared to feel some dry mouth.'

Langdon stepped into the rotating compartment and pressed the button. The door buzzed loudly and began to rotate. As he followed its motion, Langdon prepared his body for the physical shock that always accompanied the first few seconds in a hermetic vault. Entering a sealed archive was like going from sea level to 20,000 feet in an instant. Nausea and light-headedness were not uncommon. *Double vision, double over*, he reminded himself, quoting the archivist's mantra. Langdon felt his ears pop. There was a hiss of air, and the door spun to a stop.

He was in.

Langdon's first realization was that the air inside was thinner than he had anticipated. The Vatican, it seemed, took their archives a bit more seriously than most. Langdon fought the gag reflex and relaxed his chest while his pulmonary capillaries dilated. The tightness passed quickly. *Enter the Dolphin*, he mused, gratified his fifty laps a day were good for something. Breathing more normally now, he looked around the vault. Despite the transparent outer walls, he felt a familiar anxiety. *I'm in a box*, he thought. *A blood red box.*

The door buzzed behind him, and Langdon turned to watch Vittoria enter. When she arrived inside, her eyes immediately began watering, and she started breathing heavily.

'Give it a minute,' Langdon said. 'If you get light-headed, bend over.'

'I . . . feel . . .' Vittoria choked, 'like I'm . . . scuba diving . . . with the wrong . . . mixture.'

Langdon waited for her to acclimatize. He knew she would be fine. Vittoria Vetra was obviously in terrific shape, nothing like the doddering ancient Radcliffe alumnae Langdon had once squired through Widener Library's hermetic vault. The tour had ended with Langdon giving mouth-to-mouth to an old woman who'd almost aspirated her false teeth.

'Feeling better?' he asked.

Vittoria nodded.

'I rode your damn space plane, so I thought I owed you.'

This brought a smile. '*Touché.*'

Langdon reached into the box beside the door and extracted some white cotton gloves.

'Formal affair?' Vittoria asked.

'Finger acid. We can't handle the documents without them. You'll need a pair.'

Vittoria donned some gloves. 'How long do we have?'

Langdon checked his Mickey Mouse watch. 'It's just past seven.'

'We have to find this thing within the hour.'

'Actually,' Langdon said, 'we don't have that kind of time.' He pointed overhead to a filtered cut. 'Normally the curator would turn on a reoxygenation system when someone is inside the vault. Not today. Twenty minutes, we'll both be sucking wind.'

Vittoria blanched noticeably in the reddish glow.

Langdon smiled and smoothed his gloves. 'Substantiate or suffocate, Ms Vetra. Mickey's ticking.'

51

BBC reporter Gunther Glick stared at the cell phone in his hand for ten seconds before he finally hung up.

Chinita Macri studied him from the back of the van. 'What happened? Who was that?'

Glick turned, feeling like a child who had just received a Christmas gift he feared was not really for him. 'I just got a tip. Something's going on inside the Vatican.'

'It's called conclave,' Chinita said. 'Helluva tip.'

'No, something else.' *Something big.* He wondered if the story the caller had just told him could possibly be true. Glick felt ashamed when he realized he was praying it was. 'What if I told you four cardinals have been kidnapped and are going to be murdered at different churches tonight.'

'I'd say you're being hazed by someone at the office with a sick sense of humor.'

'What if I told you we were going to be given the exact location of the first murder?'

'I'd want to know who the hell you just talked to.'

'He didn't say.'

'Perhaps because he's full of shit?'

Glick had come to expect Macri's cynicism, but what she was forgetting was that liars and lunatics had been Glick's business for almost a decade at the *British Tatler*. This caller had been neither. This man had been coldly sane. Logical. *I will call you just before eight*, the man had said, *and tell you where the first killing will occur. The images you record will make you famous.* When Glick had demanded why the caller was giving him this information, the answer had been as icy as the man's Mideastern accent. *The media is the right arm of anarchy.*

'He told me something else too,' Glick said.

'What? That Elvis Presley was just elected Pope?'

'Dial into the BBC database, will you?' Glick's adrenaline was pumping now. 'I want to see what other stories we've run on these guys.'

'What guys?'

'Indulge me.'

Macri sighed and pulled up the connection to the BBC database. 'This'll take a minute.'

Glick's mind was swimming. 'The caller was very intent to know if I had a cameraman.'

'Videographer.'

'And if we could transmit live.'

'One point five three seven megahertz. What is this about?' The database beeped. 'Okay, we're in. Who is it you're looking for?'

Glick gave her the keyword.

Macri turned and stared. 'I sure as hell hope you're kidding.'

52

The internal organization of Archival Vault 10 was not as intuitive as Langdon had hoped, and the *Diagramma* manuscript did not appear to be located with other similar Galilean publications. Without access to the computerized Biblion and a reference locator, Langdon and Vittoria were stuck.

'You're sure *Diagramma* is in here?' Vittoria asked.

'Positive. It's a confirmed listing in both the *Ufficio della Propaganda delle Fede—*'

'Fine. As long as you're sure.' She headed left, while he went right.

Langdon began his manual search. He needed every bit of self-restraint not to stop and read every treasure he passed. The collection was staggering. *The Assayer . . . The Starry Messenger . . . The Sunspot Letters . . . Letter to the Grand Duchess Christina . . . Apologia pro Galileo . . .* On and on.

It was Vittoria who finally struck gold near the back of the vault. Her throaty voice called out, *'Diagramma della Verità!'*

Langdon dashed through the crimson haze to join her. 'Where?'

Vittoria pointed, and Langdon immediately realized why they had not found it earlier. The manuscript was in a folio bin, not on the shelves. Folio bins were a common means of storing unbound pages. The label on the front of the container left no doubt about the contents.

DIAGRAMMA DELLA VERITA
Galileo Galilei, 1639

Langdon dropped to his knees, his heart pounding, *'Diagramma.'* He gave her a grin. 'Nice work. Help me pull out this bin.'

Vittoria knelt beside him, and they heaved. The metal tray on which the bin was sitting rolled toward them on castors, revealing the top of the container.

'No lock?' Vittoria said, sounding surprised at the simple latch.

'Never. Documents sometimes need to be evacuated quickly. Floods and fires.'

'So open it.'

Langdon didn't need any encouragement. With his academic life's dream right in front of him and the thinning air in the chamber, he was in no mood to dawdle. He unsnapped the latch and lifted the lid. Inside, flat on the floor of the bin, lay a black, duck-cloth pouch. The cloth's breathability was critical to the preservation of its contents. Reaching in with both hands and keeping the pouch horizontal, Langdon lifted it out of the bin.

'I expected a treasure chest,' Vittoria said. 'Looks more like a pillow-case.'

'Follow me,' he said. Holding the bag before him like a sacred offering, Langdon walked to the center of the vault where he found the customary glass-topped archival exam table. Although the central location was intended to minimize in-vault travel of documents, researchers appreciated the privacy the surrounding stacks afforded. Career-making discoveries were uncovered in the top vaults of the world, and most academics did not like rivals peering through the glass as they worked.

Langdon laid the pouch on the table and unbuttoned the opening. Vittoria stood by. Rummaging through a tray of archivist tools, Langdon found the felt-pad pincers archivists called *finger cymbals* – oversized tweezers with flattened disks on each arm. As his excitement mounted, Langdon feared at any moment he might awake back in Cambridge with a pile of test papers to grade. Inhaling deeply, he opened the bag. Fingers trembling in their cotton gloves, he reached in with his tongs.

'Relax,' Vittoria said. 'It's paper, not plutonium.'

Langdon slid the tongs around the stack of documents inside and was careful to apply even pressure. Then, rather than pulling out the documents, he held them in place while he slid off the bag – an archivist's procedure for minimizing torque on the artifact. Not until the bag was removed and Langdon had turned on the exam darklight beneath the table did he begin breathing again.

Vittoria looked like a specter now, lit from below by the lamp beneath the glass. 'Small sheets,' she said, her voice reverent.

Langdon nodded. The stack of folios before them looked like loose pages from a small paperback novel. Langdon could see that the top sheet was an ornate pen and ink cover sheet with the title, the date, and Galileo's name in his own hand.

In that instant, Langdon forgot the cramped quarters, forgot his exhaustion, forgot the horrifying situation that had brought him here. He simply stared in wonder. Close encounters with history always left Langdon numbed with reverence . . . like seeing the brushstrokes on the Mona Lisa.

The muted, yellow papyrus left no doubt in Langdon's mind as to its age and authenticity, but excluding the inevitable fading, the document was in superb condition. *Slight bleaching of the pigment. Minor sundering and cohesion of the papyrus. But all in all . . . in damn fine condition.* He studied the ornate hand etching of the cover, his vision blurring in the lack of humidity. Vittoria was silent.

'Hand me a spatula, please.' Langdon motioned beside Vittoria to a tray filled with stainless-steel archival tools. She handed it to him. Langdon took the tool in his hand. It was a good one. He ran his fingers across the face to remove any static charge and then, ever so carefully, slid the blade beneath the cover. Then, lifting the spatula, he turned over the cover sheet.

The first page was written in longhand, the tiny, stylized calligraphy almost impossible to read. Langdon immediately noticed that there were no diagrams or numbers on the page. It was an essay.

'Heliocentricity,' Vittoria said, translating the heading on folio one. She scanned the text. 'Looks like Galileo renouncing the geocentric model once and for all. Ancient Italian, though, so no promises on the translation.'

'Forget it,' Langdon said. 'We're looking for math. The pure language.' He used the spatula tool to flip the next page. Another essay. No math or diagrams. Langdon's hands began to sweat inside his gloves.

'Movement of the Planets,' Vittoria said, translating the title.

Langdon frowned. On any other day, he would have been fascinated to read it; incredibly NASA's current model of planetary orbits, observed through high-powered telescopes, was supposedly almost identical to Galileo's original predictions.

'No math,' Vittoria said. 'He's talking about retrograde motions and elliptical orbits or something.'

Elliptical orbits. Langdon recalled that much of Galileo's legal trouble had begun when he described planetary motion as *elliptical*. The Vatican exalted the perfection of the *circle* and insisted heavenly motion must be only circular. Galileo's Illuminati, however, saw perfection in the ellipse as well, revering the mathematical duality of its twin foci. The Illuminati's ellipse was prominent even today in modern Masonic tracing boards and footing inlays.

'Next,' Vittoria said.

Langdon flipped.

'Lunar phases and tidal moon,' she said. 'No numbers. No diagrams.'

Langdon flipped again. Nothing. He kept flipping through a dozen or so pages. Nothing. Nothing. Nothing.

'I thought this guy was a mathematician,' Vittoria said. 'This is all text.'

Langdon felt the air in his lungs beginning to thin. His hopes were thinning too. The pile was waning.

'Nothing here,' Vittoria said. 'No math. A few dates, a few standard figures, but nothing that looks like it could be a clue.'

Langdon flipped over the last folio and sighed. It, too, was an essay.

'Short book,' Vittoria said, frowning.

Langdon nodded.

'*Merda*, as we say in Rome.'

Shit is right, Langdon thought. His reflection in the glass seemed mocking, like the image staring back at him this morning from his bay window. *An aging ghost.* 'There's *got* to be something,' he said, the hoarse desperation in his voice surprising him. 'The *segno* is here somewhere. I know it!'

'Maybe you were wrong about DIII?'

Langdon turned and stared at her.

'Okay,' she agreed, 'DIII makes perfect sense. But maybe the clue isn't mathematical?'

'*Lingua pura*. What else would it be?'

'Art?'

'Except there are no diagrams or pictures in the book.'

'All I know is that *lingua pura* refers to something other than Italian. Math just seems logical.'

'I agree.'

Langdon refused to accept defeat so quickly. 'The numbers must be written longhand. The math must be in words rather than equations.'

'It'll take some time to read all the pages.'

'Time's something we don't have. We'll have to split the work.' Langdon flipped the stack back over to the beginning. 'I know enough Italian to spot numbers.' Using his spatula, he cut the stack like a deck of cards and laid the first half-dozen pages in front of Vittoria. 'It's in here somewhere. I'm sure.'

Vittoria reached down and flipped her first page by hand.

'Spatula!' Langdon said, grabbing her an extra tool from the tray. 'Use the spatula.'

'I'm wearing gloves,' she grumbled. 'How much damage could I cause?'

'Just use it.'

Vittoria picked up the spatula. 'You feeling what I'm feeling?'

'Tense?'

'No. Short of breath.'

Langdon was definitely starting to feel it too. The air was thinning faster than he had imagined. He knew they had to hurry. Archival conundrums were nothing new for him, but usually he had more than a few minutes to work them out. Without another word, Langdon bowed his head and began translating the first page in his stack.

Show yourself, damn it! Show yourself!

53

Somewhere beneath Rome the dark figure prowled down a stone ramp into the underground tunnel. The ancient passageway was lit only by torches, making the air hot and thick. Up ahead the frightened voices of grown men called out in vain, echoing in the cramped spaces.

As he rounded the corner he saw them, exactly as he had left them – four old men, terrified, sealed behind rusted iron bars in a stone cubicle.

'*Qui êtes-vous?*' one of the men demanded in French. 'What do you want with us?'

'*Hilfe!*' another said in German. 'Let us go!'

'Are you aware who we are?' one asked in English, his accent Spanish.

'Silence,' the raspy voice commanded. There was a finality about the word.

The fourth prisoner, an Italian, quiet and thoughtful, looked into the inky void of his captor's eyes and swore he saw hell itself. *God help us*, he thought.

The killer checked his watch and then returned his gaze to the prisoners. 'Now then,' he said. 'Who will be first?'

54

Inside Archive Vault 10 Robert Langdon recited Italian numbers as he scanned the calligraphy before him. *Mille . . . cento . . . uno, duo, tre . . . cinquanta. I need a numerical reference! Anything, damnit!*

When he reached the end of his current folio, he lifted the spatula to flip the page. As he aligned the blade with the next page, he fumbled, having difficulty holding the tool steady. Minutes later, he looked down and realized he had abandoned his spatula and was turning pages by hand. *Oops*, he thought, feeling vaguely criminal. The lack of oxygen was affecting his inhibitions. *Looks like I'll burn in archivist's hell.*

'About damn time,' Vittoria choked when she saw Langdon turning pages by hand. She dropped her spatula and followed suit.

'Any luck?'

Vittoria shook her head. 'Nothing that looks purely mathematical. I'm skimming . . . but none of this reads like a clue.'

Langdon continued translating his folios with increasing difficulty. His Italian skills were rocky at best, and the tiny penmanship and archaic language were making it slow going. Vittoria reached the end of her stack before Langdon and looked disheartened as she flipped the pages over. She hunkered down for another more intense inspection.

When Langdon finished his final page, he cursed under his breath and looked over at Vittoria. She was scowling, squinting at something on one of her folios. 'What is it?' he asked.

Vittoria did not look up. 'Did you have any footnotes on your pages?'

'Not that I noticed. Why?'

'This page has a footnote. It's obscured in a crease.'

Langdon tried to see what she was looking at, but all he could make out was the page number in the upper right-hand corner of the sheet. Folio 5. It took a moment for the coincidence to register, and even when it did the connection seemed vague. *Folio Five. Five, Pythagoras, pentagrams, Illuminati.* Langdon wondered if the Illuminati would have chosen page five on which to hide their clue. Through the reddish fog surrounding them, Langdon sensed a tiny ray of hope. 'Is the footnote mathematical?'

Vittoria shook her head. 'Text. One line. Very small printing. Almost illegible.'

His hopes faded. 'It's supposed to be math. *Lingua pura.*'

'Yeah, I know.' She hesitated. 'I think you'll want to hear this, though.' Langdon sensed excitement in her voice.

'Go ahead.'

Squinting at the folio, Vittoria read the line. 'The path of light is laid, the sacred test.'

The words were nothing like what Langdon had imagined. 'I'm sorry?'

Vittoria repeated the line. 'The path of light is laid, the sacred test.'

'Path of light?' Langdon felt his posture straightening.

'That's what it says. Path of light.'

As the words sank in, Langdon felt his delirium pierced by an instant of clarity. *The path of light is laid, the sacred test.* He had no idea how it helped them, but the line was as direct a reference to the Path of Illumination as he could imagine. *Path of light. Sacred test.* His head felt like an engine revving on bad fuel. 'Are you sure of the translation?'

Vittoria hesitated. 'Actually . . .' She glanced over at him with a strange look. 'It's not technically a translation. The line is written in *English.*'

For an instant, Langdon thought the acoustics in the chamber had affected his hearing. '*English?*'

Vittoria pushed the document over to him, and Langdon read the minuscule printing at the bottom of the page. '*The path of light is laid, the sacred test.* English? What is *English* doing in an Italian book?'

Vittoria shrugged. She too was looking tipsy. 'Maybe English is what they meant by the *lingua pura*? It's considered the international language of science. It's all we speak at CERN.'

'But this was in the 1600s,' Langdon argued. 'Nobody spoke English in Italy, not even—' He stopped short, realizing what he was about to say. 'Not even . . . the *clergy.*' Langdon's academic mind hummed in high gear. 'In the 1600s,' he said, talking faster now, '*English* was one language the Vatican had not yet embraced. They dealt in Italian, Latin, German, even Spanish and French, but English was totally foreign inside the Vatican. They considered English a polluted, free-thinkers language for profane men like Chaucer and Shakespeare.' Langdon flashed suddenly on the Illuminati brands of Earth, Air, Fire, Water. The legend that the brands were in *English* now made a bizarre kind of sense.

'So you're saying maybe Galileo considered English *la lingua pura* because it was the one language the Vatican did not control?'

'Yes. Or maybe by putting the clue in English, Galileo was subtly restricting the readership away from the Vatican.'

'But it's not even a clue,' Vittoria argued. '*The path of light is laid, the sacred test?* What the hell does that mean?'

She's right, Langdon thought. The line didn't help in any way. But as he spoke the phrase again in his mind, a strange fact hit him. *Now that's odd*, he thought. *What are the chances of that?*

'We need to get out of here,' Vittoria said, sounding hoarse.

Langdon wasn't listening. *The path of light is laid, the sacred test.* 'It's a damn line of iambic pentameter,' he said suddenly, counting the syllables again. 'Five couplets of alternating stressed and unstressed syllables.'

Vittoria looked lost. 'Iambic who?'

For an instant Langdon was back at Phillips Exeter Academy sitting in a Saturday morning English class. *Hell on earth.* The school baseball star, Peter Greer, was having trouble remembering the number of couplets necessary for a line of Shakespearean iambic pentameter. Their professor, an animated schoolmaster named Bissell, leapt onto the table and bellowed, 'Penta-meter, Greer! Think of home plate! A pentagon! Five sides! Penta! Penta! Penta! Jeeeesh!'

Five couplets, Langdon thought. Each couplet, by definition, having *two* syllables. He could not believe in his entire career he had never made the connection. Iambic pentameter was a symmetrical meter based on the sacred Illuminati numbers of 5 and 2!

You're reaching! Langdon told himself, trying to push it from his mind. *A meaningless coincidence!* But the thought stuck. *Five . . . for Pythagoras and the pentagram. Two . . . for the duality of all things.*

A moment later, another realization sent a numbing sensation down his legs. Iambic pentameter, on account of its simplicity, was often called 'pure verse' or 'pure meter.' *La lingua pura?* Could this have been the pure language the Illuminati had been referring to? *The path of light is laid, the sacred test . . .*

'Uh oh,' Vittoria said.

Langdon wheeled to see her rotating the folio upside down. He felt a knot in his gut. *Not again.* 'There's no way that line is an ambigram!'

'No, it's not an ambigram . . . but it's . . .' She kept turning the document, 90 degrees at every turn.

'It's what?'

Vittoria looked up. 'It's not the *only* line.'

'There's another?'

'There's a different line on every margin. Top, bottom, left, and right. I think it's a poem.'

'Four lines?' Langdon bristled with excitement. *Galileo was a poet?* 'Let me see!'

Vittoria did not relinquish the page. She kept turning the page in quarter turns. 'I didn't see the lines before because they're on the edges.' She cocked her head over the last line. 'Huh. You know what? Galileo didn't even write this.'

'What!'

'The poem is signed John Milton.'

'John *Milton*?' The influential English poet who wrote *Paradise Lost* was a contemporary of Galileo's and a savant who conspiracy buffs put at the top of their list of Illuminati suspects. Milton's alleged affiliation with Galileo's Illuminati was one legend Langdon suspected was true. Not only had Milton made a well-documented 1638 pilgrimage to Rome to 'commune with enlightened men,' but he had held meetings with Galileo during the scientist's house arrest, meetings portrayed in many Renaissance paintings, including Annibale Gatti's famous *Galileo and Milton*, which hung even now in the IMSS Museum in Florence.

'Milton knew Galileo, didn't he?' Vittoria said, finally pushing the folio over to Langdon. 'Maybe he wrote the poem as a favor?'

Langdon clenched his teeth as he took the sheathed document. Leaving it flat on the table, he read the line at the top. Then he rotated the page 90 degrees, reading the line in the right margin. Another twist, and he read the bottom. Another twist, the left. A final twist completed the circle. There were four lines in all. The first line Vittoria had found was actually the third line of the poem. Utterly agape, he read the four lines again, clockwise in sequence: top, right, bottom, left. When he was done, he exhaled. There was no doubt in his mind. 'You found it, Ms Vetra.'

She smiled tightly. 'Good, now can we get the hell out of here?'

'I have to copy these lines down. I need to find a pencil and paper.'

Vittoria shook her head. 'Forget it, professor. No time to play scribe. Mickey's ticking.' She took the page from him and headed for the door.

Langdon stood up. 'You can't take that outside! It's a—'

But Vittoria was already gone.

55

Langdon and Vittoria exploded onto the courtyard outside the Secret Archives. The fresh air felt like a drug as it flowed into Langdon's lungs. The purple spots in his vision quickly faded. The guilt, however, did not. He had just been accomplice to stealing a priceless relic from the world's most private vault. The camerlengo had said, *I am giving you my trust.*

'Hurry,' Vittoria said, still holding the folio in her hand and striding at a half-jog across *Via Borgia* in the direction of Olivetti's office.

'If any water gets on that papyrus—'

'Calm down. When we decipher this thing, we can return their sacred Folio 5.'

Langdon accelerated to keep up. Beyond feeling like a criminal, he was still dazed over the document's spellbinding implications. *John Milton was an Illuminatus. He composed the poem for Galileo to publish in Folio 5 . . . far from the eyes of the Vatican.*

As they left the courtyard, Vittoria held out the folio for Langdon. 'You think you can decipher this thing? Or did we just kill all those brain cells for kicks?'

Langdon took the document carefully in his hands. Without hesitation he slipped it into one of the breast pockets of his tweed jacket, out of the sunlight and dangers of moisture. 'I deciphered it already.'

Vittoria stopped short. 'You *what?*'

Langdon kept moving.

Vittoria hustled to catch up. 'You read it *once*! I thought it was supposed to be hard!'

Langdon knew she was right, and yet he had deciphered the *segno* in a single reading. A perfect stanza of iambic pentameter, and the first altar of science had revealed itself in pristine clarity. Admittedly, the ease with which he had accomplished the task left him with a nagging disquietude. He was a child of the Puritan work ethic. He could still hear his father speaking the old New England aphorism: *If it wasn't painfully difficult, you did it wrong.* Langdon hoped the saying was false. 'I deciphered it,' he said, moving faster now. 'I know where the first killing is going to happen. We need to warn Olivetti.'

Vittoria closed in on him. 'How could you already know? Let me see that thing again.' With the sleight of a boxer, she slipped a lissome hand into his pocket and pulled out the folio again.

'Careful!' Langdon said. 'You can't—'

Vittoria ignored him. Folio in hand, she floated beside him, holding the document up to the evening light, examining the margins. As she began reading aloud, Langdon moved to retrieve the folio but instead found himself bewitched by Vittoria's accented alto speaking the syllables in perfect rhythm with her gait.

For a moment, hearing the verse aloud, Langdon felt transported in time . . . as though he were one of Galileo's contemporaries, listening to the poem for the first time . . . knowing it was a test, a map, a clue unveiling the four altars of science . . . the four markers that blazed a secret path across Rome. The verse flowed from Vittoria's lips like a song.

> *From Santi's earthly tomb with demon's hole,*
> *'Cross Rome the mystic elements unfold.*
> *The path of light is laid, the sacred test,*
> *Let angels guide you on your lofty quest.*

Vittoria read it twice and then fell silent, as if letting the ancient words resonate on their own.

From Santi's earthly tomb, Langdon repeated in his mind. The poem was crystal clear about that. The Path of Illumination began at Santi's tomb. From there, across Rome, the markers blazed the trail.

> *From Santi's earthly tomb with demon's hole,*
> *'Cross Rome the mystic elements unfold.*

Mystic elements. Also clear. *Earth, Air, Fire, Water.* Elements of science, the four Illuminati markers disguised as religious sculpture.

'The first marker,' Vittoria said, 'sounds like it's at Santi's tomb.'

Langdon smiled. 'I told you it wasn't that tough.'

'So who is Santi?' she asked, sounding suddenly excited. 'And where's his tomb?'

Langdon chuckled to himself. He was amazed how few people knew *Santi*, the last name of one of the most famous Renaissance artists ever to live. His first name was world renowned . . . the child prodigy who at the age of twenty-five was already doing commissions for Pope Julius II, and when he died at only thirty-eight, left behind the greatest collection of frescoes the world had ever seen. Santi was a behemoth in the art world, and being known solely by one's first name was a level of fame achieved only by an elite few . . . people like Napoleon, Galileo, and Jesus . . . and, of course, the demigods Langdon now heard blaring from Harvard dormitories – Sting, Madonna, Jewel, and

172

the artist formerly known as Prince, who had changed his name to the symbol ♀, causing Langdon to dub him 'The Tau Cross With Intersecting Hermaphroditic Ankh.'

'Santi,' Langdon said, 'is the last name of the great Renaissance master, Raphael.'

Vittoria looked surprised. 'Raphael? As in *the* Raphael?'

'The one and only.' Langdon pushed on toward the Office of the Swiss Guard.

'So the path starts at Raphael's tomb?'

'It actually makes perfect sense,' Langdon said as they rushed on. 'The Illuminati often considered great artists and sculptors honorary brothers in enlightenment. The Illuminati could have chosen Raphael's tomb as a kind of tribute.' Langdon also knew that Raphael, like many other religious artists, was a suspected closet atheist.

Vittoria slipped the folio carefully back in Langdon's pocket. 'So where is he buried?'

Langdon took a deep breath. 'Believe it or not, Raphael's buried in the Pantheon.'

Vittoria looked skeptical. '*The* Pantheon?'

'*The* Raphael at *the* Pantheon.' Langdon had to admit, the Pantheon was not what he had expected for the placement of the first marker. He would have guessed the first altar of science to be at some quiet, out of the way church, something subtle. Even in the 1600s, the Pantheon, with its tremendous, holed dome, was one of the best known sites in Rome.

'Is the Pantheon even a *church*?' Vittoria asked.

'Oldest Catholic church in Rome.'

Vittoria shook her head. 'But do you really think the first cardinal could be killed at the Pantheon? That's got to be one of the busiest tourist spots in Rome.'

Langdon shrugged. 'The Illuminati said they wanted the whole world watching. Killing a cardinal at the Pantheon would certainly open some eyes.'

'But how does this guy expect to kill someone at the Pantheon and get away unnoticed? It would be impossible.'

'As impossible as kidnapping four cardinals from Vatican City? The poem is precise.'

'And you're *certain* Raphael is buried inside the Pantheon?'

'I've seen his tomb many times.'

Vittoria nodded, still looking troubled. 'What time is it?'

Langdon checked. 'Seven-thirty.'

'Is the Pantheon far?'

'A mile maybe. We've got time.'

'The poem said Santi's *earthly* tomb. Does that mean anything to you?'

Langdon hastened diagonally across the Courtyard of the Sentinel. 'Earthly? Actually, there's probably no more earthly place in Rome than the

Pantheon. It got its name from the original religion practiced there – Pantheism – the worship of all gods, specifically the pagan gods of Mother Earth.'

As a student of architecture, Langdon had been amazed to learn that the dimensions of the Pantheon's main chamber were a tribute to Gaea – the goddess of the Earth. The proportions were so exact that a giant spherical globe could fit perfectly inside the building with less than a millimeter to spare.

'Okay,' Vittoria said, sounding more convinced. 'And demon's hole? *From Santi's earthly tomb with demon's hole?*'

Langdon was not quite as sure about this. '*Demon's hole* must mean the *oculus*,' he said, making a logical guess. 'The famous circular opening in the Pantheon's roof.'

'But it's a *church*,' Vittoria said, moving effortlessly beside him. 'Why would they call the opening a *demon's* hole?'

Langdon had actually been wondering that himself. He had never heard the term 'demon's hole,' but he did recall a famous sixth-century critique of the Pantheon whose words seemed oddly appropriate now. The Venerable Bede had once written that the hole in the Pantheon's roof had been bored by demons trying to escape the building when it was consecrated by Boniface IV.

'And why,' Vittoria added as they entered a smaller courtyard, 'would the Illuminati use the name Santi if he was really known as *Raphael?*'

'You ask a lot of questions.'

'My dad used to say that.'

'Two possible reasons. One, the word *Raphael* has too many syllables. It would have destroyed the poem's iambic pentameter.'

'Sounds like a stretch.'

Langdon agreed. 'Okay, then maybe using "Santi" was to make the clue more obscure, so only very enlightened men would recognize the reference to Raphael.'

Vittoria didn't appear to buy this either. 'I'm sure Raphael's last name was very well known when he was alive.'

'Surprisingly not. Single name recognition was a status symbol. Raphael shunned his last name much like pop stars do today. Take Madonna, for example. She never uses her surname, Ciccone.'

Victoria looked amused. 'You know Madonna's last name?'

Langdon regretted the example. It was amazing the kind of garbage a mind picked up living with 10,000 adolescents.

As he and Vittoria passed the final gate toward the Office of the Swiss Guard, their progress was halted without warning.

'*Alt!*' a voice bellowed behind them.

Langdon and Vittoria wheeled to find themselves looking into the barrel of a rifle.

'*Attento!*' Vittoria exclaimed, jumping back. 'Watch it with—'

'*Non spostarti!*' the guard snapped, cocking the weapon.

'*Soldato!*' a voice commanded from across the courtyard. Olivetti was emerging from the security center. 'Let them go!'

The guard looked bewildered. '*Ma, signore, è una donna—*'

'Inside!' he yelled at the guard.

'Signore, *non posso—*'

'Now! You have new orders. Captain Rocher will be briefing the corps in two minutes. We will be organizing a search.'

Looking bewildered, the guard hurried into the security center. Olivetti marched toward Langdon, rigid and steaming. 'Our most secret archives? I'll want an explanation.'

'We have good news,' Langdon said.

Olivetti's eyes narrowed. 'It better be *damn* good.'

56

The four unmarked Alfa Romeo 155 T-Sparks roared down Via dei Coronari like fighter jets off a runway. The vehicles carried twelve plain-clothed Swiss Guards armed with Cherchi-Pardini semiautomatics, local-radius nerve gas canisters, and long-range stun guns. The three sharpshooters carried laser-sighted rifles.

Sitting in the passenger seat of the lead car, Olivetti turned backward toward Langdon and Vittoria. His eyes were filled with rage. 'You assured me a sound explanation, and *this* is what I get?'

Langdon felt cramped in the small car. 'I understand your—'

'No, you don't understand!' Olivetti never raised his voice, but his intensity tripled. 'I have just removed a dozen of my best men from Vatican City on the eve of conclave. And I have done this to stake out the Pantheon based on the testimony of some American I have never met who has just interpreted a four-hundred-year-old poem. I have also just left the search for this antimatter weapon in the hands of secondary officers.'

Langdon resisted the urge to pull Folio 5 from his pocket and wave it in Olivetti's face. 'All I know is that the information we found refers to Raphael's tomb, and Raphael's tomb is inside the Pantheon.'

The officer behind the wheel nodded. 'He's right, commander. My wife and I—'

'Drive,' Olivetti snapped. He turned back to Langdon. 'How could a killer accomplish an assassination in such a crowded place and escape unseen?'

'I don't know,' Langdon said. 'But the Illuminati are obviously highly resourceful. They've broken into both CERN and Vatican City. It's only by luck we know where the first kill zone is. The Pantheon is your one chance to catch this guy.'

'More contradictions,' Olivetti said. '*One* chance? I thought you said there was some sort of pathway. A series of markers. If the Pantheon is the right spot, we can follow the pathway to the other markers. We will have *four* chances to catch this guy.'

'I had hoped so,' Langdon said. 'And we *would* have . . . a century ago.'

Langdon's realization that the Pantheon was the first altar of science had been a bittersweet moment. History had a way of playing cruel tricks on those who chased it. It was a long shot that the Path of Illumination would be intact after all of these years, with all of its statues in place, but part of Langdon had fantasized about following the path all the way to the end and coming face to face with the sacred Illuminati lair. Alas, he realized, it was not to be. 'The Vatican had all the statues in the Pantheon removed and destroyed in the late 1600s.'

Vittoria looked shocked. 'Why?'

'The statues were pagan Olympian Gods. Unfortunately, that means the first marker is gone . . . and with it—'

'Any hope,' Vittoria said, 'of finding the Path of Illumination and additional markers?'

Langdon shook his head. 'We have *one* shot. The Pantheon. After that, the path disappears.'

Olivetti stared at them both a long moment and then turned and faced front. 'Pull over,' he barked to the driver.

The driver swerved the car toward the curb and put on the brakes. Three other Alfa Romeos skidded in behind them. The Swiss Guard convoy screeched to a halt.

'What are you doing!' Vittoria demanded.

'My job,' Olivetti said, turning in his seat, his voice like stone. 'Mr Langdon, when you told me you would explain the situation en route, I assumed I would be approaching the Pantheon with a clear idea of why my men are here. That is not the case. Because I am abandoning critical duties by being here, and because I have found very little that makes sense in this theory of yours about virgin sacrifices and ancient poetry, I cannot in good conscience continue. I am recalling this mission immediately.' He pulled out his walkie-talkie and clicked it on.

Vittoria reached across the seat and grabbed his arm. 'You can't!'

Olivetti slammed down the walkie-talkie and fixed her with a red-hot stare. 'Have you been to the Pantheon, Ms Vetra?'

'No, but I—'

'Let me tell you something about it. The Pantheon is a single room. A circular cell made of stone and cement. It has *one* entrance. No windows. One *narrow* entrance. That entrance is flanked at all times by no less than four armed Roman policemen who protect this shrine from art defacers, anti-Christian terrorists, and gypsy tourist scams.'

'Your point?' she said coolly.

'My point?' Olivetti's knuckles gripped the seat. 'My point is that what you have just told me is going to happen is utterly impossible! Can you give me one plausible scenario of how someone could kill a cardinal *inside* the Pantheon? How does one even get a hostage past the guards *into* the Pantheon in the first place? Much less actually kill him and get away?' Olivetti leaned over the seat, his coffee breath now in Langdon's face. 'How, Mr Langdon? *One* plausible scenario.'

Langdon felt the tiny car shrink around him. *I have no idea! I'm not an assassin! I don't know how he will do it! I only know—*

'*One* scenario?' Vittoria quipped, her voice unruffled. 'How about this? The killer flies over in a helicopter and drops a screaming, branded cardinal down through the hole in the roof. The cardinal hits the marble floor and dies.'

Everyone in the car turned and stared at Vittoria. Langdon didn't know what to think. *You've got one sick imagination, lady, but you are quick.*

Olivetti frowned. 'Possible, I admit . . . but hardly—'

'Or the killer drugs the cardinal,' Vittoria said, 'brings him to the Pantheon in a wheelchair like some old tourist. He wheels him inside, quietly slits his throat, and then walks out.'

This seemed to wake up Olivetti a bit.

Not bad! Langdon thought.

'Or,' she said, 'the killer could—'

'I heard you,' Olivetti said. 'Enough.' He took a deep breath and blew it out. Someone rapped sharply on the window, and everyone jumped. It was a soldier from one of the other cars. Olivetti rolled down the window.

'Everything all right, commander?' The soldier was dressed in street clothes. He pulled back the sleeve of his denim shirt to reveal a black chronograph military watch. 'Seven-forty, commander. We'll need time to get in position.'

Olivetti nodded vaguely but said nothing for many moments. He ran a finger back and forth across the dash, making a line in the dust. He studied Langdon in the side-view mirror, and Langdon felt himself being measured and weighed. Finally Olivetti turned back to the guard. There was reluctance in his voice. 'I'll want separate approaches. Cars to Piazza della Rotunda, Via degli Orfani, Piazza Sant'Ignacio, and Sant'Eustachio. No closer than two blocks. Once you're parked, gear up and await my orders. Three minutes.'

'Very good, sir.' The soldier returned to his car.

Langdon gave Vittoria an impressed nod. She smiled back, and for an instant Langdon felt an unexpected connection . . . a thread of magnetism between them.

The commander turned in his seat and locked eyes with Langdon. 'Mr Langdon, this had better not blow up in our faces.'

Langdon smiled uneasily. *How could it?*

57

The director of CERN, Maximilian Kohler, opened his eyes to the cool rush of cromolyn and leukotriene in his body, dilating his bronchial tubes and pulmonary capillaries. He was breathing normally again. He found himself lying in a private room in the CERN infirmary, his wheelchair beside the bed.

He took stock, examining the paper robe they had put him in. His clothing was folded on the chair beside the bed. Outside he could hear a nurse making the rounds. He lay there a long minute listening. Then, as quietly as possible, he pulled himself to the edge of the bed and retrieved his clothing. Struggling with his dead legs, he dressed himself. Then he dragged his body onto his wheelchair.

Muffling a cough, he wheeled himself to the door. He moved manually, careful not to engage the motor. When he arrived at the door he peered out. The hall was empty.

Silently, Maximilian Kohler slipped out of the infirmary.

58

'Seven forty-six and thirty . . . *mark*.' Even speaking into his walkie-talkie, Olivetti's voice never seemed to rise above a whisper.

Langdon felt himself sweating now in his Harris tweed in the backseat of the Alfa Romeo, which was idling in Piazza de la Concorde, three blocks from the Pantheon. Vittoria sat beside him, looking engrossed by Olivetti, who was transmitting his final orders.

'Deployment will be an eight-point hem,' the commander said. 'Full perimeter with a bias on the entry. Target may know you visually, so you will be *pas visible*. Nonmortal force only. We'll need someone to spot the roof. Target is primary. Asset secondary.'

Jesus, Langdon thought, chilled by the efficiency with which Olivetti had just told his men the cardinal was expendable. *Asset secondary*.

'I repeat. Nonmortal procurement. We need the target alive. Go.' Olivetti snapped off his walkie-talkie.

Vittoria looked stunned, almost angry. 'Commander, isn't anyone going *inside*?'

Olivetti turned. 'Inside?'

'Inside the Pantheon! Where this is supposed to happen?'

'*Attento*,' Olivetti said, his eyes fossilizing. 'If my ranks have been infiltrated, my men may be known by sight. Your colleague has just finished warning me that *this* will be our sole chance to catch the target. I have no intention of scaring anyone off by marching my men inside.'

'But what if the killer is *already* inside?'

Olivetti checked his watch. 'The target was specific. Eight o'clock. We have fifteen minutes.'

'He said he would *kill* the cardinal at eight o'clock. But he may already have gotten the victim inside somehow. What if your men see the target come out but don't know who he is? Someone needs to make sure the inside is clean.'

'Too risky at this point.'

'Not if the person going in was unrecognizable.'

'Disguising operatives is time consuming and—'

'I meant *me*,' Vittoria said.

Langdon turned and stared at her.

Olivetti shook his head. 'Absolutely not.'

'He killed my father.'

'Exactly, so he may know who you are.'

'You heard him on the phone. He had no idea Leonardo Vetra even *had* a daughter. He sure as hell doesn't know what I look like. I could walk in like a tourist. If I see anything suspicious, I could walk into the square and signal your men to move in.'

'I'm sorry, I cannot allow that.'

'*Comandante?*' Olivetti's receiver crackled. 'We've got a situation from the north point. The fountain is blocking our line of sight. We can't see the entrance unless we move into plain view on the piazza. What's your call? Do you want us blind or vulnerable?'

Vittoria apparently had endured enough. 'That's it. I'm going.' She opened her door and got out.

Olivetti dropped his walkie-talkie and jumped out of the car, circling in front of Vittoria.

Langdon got out too. *What the hell is she doing!*

Olivetti blocked Vittoria's way. 'Ms Vetra, your instincts are good, but I cannot let a civilian interfere.'

'Interfere? You're flying blind. Let me help.'

'I would love to have a recon point inside, but . . .'

'But what?' Vittoria demanded. 'But I'm a *woman?*'

Olivetti said nothing.

'That had better not be what you were going to say, Commander, because you know damn well this is a good idea, and if you let some archaic *macho* bullshit—'

'Let us do our job.'

'Let me help.'

'Too dangerous. We would have no lines of communication with you. I can't let you carry a walkie-talkie, it would give you away.'

Vittoria reached in her shirt pocket and produced her cell phone. 'Plenty of tourists carry phones.'

Olivetti frowned.

Vittoria unsnapped the phone and mimicked a call. 'Hi, honey, I'm standing in the Pantheon. You should see this place!' She snapped the phone shut and glared at Olivetti. 'Who the hell is going to know? It is a no-risk situation. Let me be your eyes!' She motioned to the cell phone on Olivetti's belt. 'What's your number?'

Olivetti did not reply.

The driver had been looking on and seemed to have some thoughts of his own. He got out of the car and took the commander aside. They spoke in hushed tones for ten seconds. Finally Olivetti nodded and returned. 'Program this number.' He began dictating digits.

Vittoria programmed her phone.

'Now call the number.'

Vittoria pressed the auto dial. The phone on Olivetti's belt began ringing. He picked it up and spoke into the receiver. 'Go into the building, Ms Vetra, look around, exit the building, then call and tell me what you see.'

Vittoria snapped the phone shut. 'Thank you, sir.'

Langdon felt a sudden, unexpected surge of protective instinct. 'Wait a minute,' he said to Olivetti. 'You're sending her in there *alone*.'

Vittoria scowled at him. 'Robert, I'll be fine.'

The Swiss Guard driver was talking to Olivetti again.

'It's dangerous,' Langdon said to Vittoria.

'He's right,' Olivetti said. 'Even my best men don't work alone. My lieutenant has just pointed out that the masquerade will be more convincing with both of you anyway.'

Both of us? Langdon hesitated. *Actually, what I meant—*

'Both of you entering together,' Olivetti said, 'will look like a couple on holiday. You can also back each other up. I'm more comfortable with that.'

Vittoria shrugged. 'Fine, but we'll need to go fast.'

Langdon groaned. *Nice move, cowboy.*

Olivetti pointed down the street. 'First street you hit will be Via degli Orfani. Go left. It takes you directly to the Pantheon. Two-minute walk, tops. I'll be here, directing my men and waiting for your call. I'd like you to have protection.' He pulled out his pistol. 'Do either of you know how to use a gun?'

Langdon's heart skipped. *We don't need a gun!*

Vittoria held her hand out. 'I can tag a breaching porpoise from forty meters off the bow of a rocking ship.'

'Good.' Olivetti handed the gun to her. 'You'll have to conceal it.'

Vittoria glanced down at her shorts. Then she looked at Langdon.

Oh no you don't! Langdon thought, but Vittoria was too fast. She opened his jacket, and inserted the weapon into one of his breast pockets. It felt like a rock dropping into his coat, his only consolation being that *Diagramma* was in the other pocket.

'We look harmless,' Vittoria said. 'We're leaving.' She took Langdon's arm and headed down the street.

The driver called out, 'Arm in arm is good. Remember, you're tourists. *Newlyweds* even. Perhaps if you held hands?'

As they turned the corner Langdon could have sworn he saw on Vittoria's face the hint of a smile.

59

The Swiss Guard 'staging room' is located adjacent to the Corpo di Vigilanza barracks and is used primarily for planning the security surrounding papal appearances and public Vatican events. Today, however, it was being used for something else.

The man addressing the assembled task force was the second-in-command of the Swiss Guard, Captain Elias Rocher. Rocher was a barrel-chested man with soft, puttylike features. He wore the traditional blue captain's uniform with his own personal flair – a red beret cocked sideways on his head. His voice was surprisingly crystalline for such a large man, and when he spoke, his tone had the clarity of a musical instrument. Despite the precision of his inflection, Rocher's eyes were cloudy like those of some nocturnal mammal. His men called him 'orso' – grizzly bear. They sometimes joked that Rocher was 'the bear who walked in the viper's shadow.' Commander Olivetti was the viper. Rocher was just as deadly as the viper, but at least you could see him coming.

Rocher's men stood at sharp attention, nobody moving a muscle, although the information they had just received had increased their aggregate blood pressure by a few thousand points.

Rookie Lieutenant Chartrand stood in the back of the room wishing he had been among the 99 per cent of applicants who had *not* qualified to be here. At twenty years old, Chartrand was the youngest guard on the force. He had been in Vatican City only three months. Like every man there, Chartrand was Swiss Army trained and had endured two years of additional *Ausbildung* in Bern before qualifying for the grueling Vatican *pròva* held in a secret barracks outside of Rome. Nothing in his training, however, had prepared him for a crisis like this.

At first Chartrand thought the briefing was some sort of bizarre training exercise. *Futuristic weapons? Ancient cults? Kidnapped cardinals?* Then Rocher had shown them the live video feed of the weapon in question. Apparently this was no exercise.

'We will be killing power in selected areas,' Rocher was saying, 'to eradicate extraneous magnetic interference. We will move in teams of four. We will wear infrared goggles for vision. Reconnaissance will be done with traditional bug sweepers, recalibrated for sub-three-ohm flux fields. Any questions?'

None.

Chartrand's mind was on overload. 'What if we don't find it in time?' he asked, immediately wishing he had not.

The grizzly bear gazed out at him from beneath his red beret. Then he dismissed the group with a somber salute. 'Godspeed, men.'

60

Two blocks from the Pantheon, Langdon and Vittoria approached on foot past a line of taxis, their drivers sleeping in the front seats. Nap time was eternal in the Eternal City – the ubiquitous public dozing a perfected extension of the afternoon siestas born of ancient Spain.

Langdon fought to focus his thoughts, but the situation was too bizarre to grasp rationally. Six hours ago he had been sound asleep in Cambridge. Now he was in Europe, caught up in a surreal battle of ancient titans, packing a semiautomatic in his Harris tweed, and holding hands with a woman he had only just met.

He looked at Vittoria. She was focused straight ahead. There was a strength in her grasp – that of an independent and determined woman. Her fingers wrapped around his with the comfort of innate acceptance. No hesitation. Langdon felt a growing attraction. *Get real*, he told himself.

Vittoria seemed to sense his uneasiness. 'Relax,' she said, without turning her head. 'We're supposed to look like newlyweds.'

'I'm relaxed.'

'You're crushing my hand.'

Langdon flushed and loosened up.

'Breathe through your eyes,' she said.

'I'm sorry?'

'It relaxes the muscles. It's called *pranayama*.'

'Piranha?'

'Not the fish. *Pranayama*. Never mind.'

As they rounded the corner into Piazza della Rotunda, the Pantheon rose before them. Langdon admired it, as always, with awe. *The Pantheon. Temple to all gods. Pagan gods. Gods of Nature and Earth.* The structure seemed boxier from the outside than he remembered. The vertical pillars and triangular *pronaus* all but obscured the circular dome behind it. Still, the bold and immodest inscription over the entrance assured him they were in the right spot. M AGRIPPA L F COS TERTIUM FECIT. Langdon translated it, as always, with amusement. *Marcus Agrippa, Consul for the third time, built this.*

So much for humility, he thought, turning his eyes to the surrounding area. A scattering of tourists with video cameras wandered the area. Others sat enjoying Rome's best iced coffee at *La Tazza d'Oro*'s outdoor café. Outside the entrance to the Pantheon, four armed Roman policemen stood at attention just as Olivetti had predicted.

'Looks pretty quiet,' Vittoria said.

Langdon nodded, but he felt troubled. Now that he was standing here in person, the whole scenario seemed surreal. Despite Vittoria's apparent faith that he was right, Langdon realized he had put everyone on the line here. The Illuminati poem lingered. *From Santi's earthly tomb with demon's hole. YES*, he told himself. This was the spot. Santi's tomb. He had been here many times beneath the Pantheon's *oculus* and stood before the grave of the great Raphael.

'What time is it?' Vittoria asked.

Langdon checked his watch. 'Seven-fifty. Ten minutes till show time.'

'Hope these guys are good,' Vittoria said, eyeing the scattered tourists entering the Pantheon. 'If anything happens inside that dome, we'll all be in the crossfire.'

Langdon exhaled heavily as they moved toward the entrance. The gun felt heavy in his pocket. He wondered what would happen if the policemen frisked him and found the weapon, but the officers did not give them a second look. Apparently the disguise was convincing.

Langdon whispered to Vittoria. 'Ever fire anything other than a tranquilizer gun?'

'Don't you trust me?'

'Trust you? I barely know you.'

Vittoria frowned. 'And here I thought we were newlyweds.'

61

The air inside the Pantheon was cool and damp, heavy with history. The sprawling ceiling hovered overhead as though weightless – the 141-foot unsupported span larger even than the cupola at St Peter's. As always, Langdon felt a chill as he entered the cavernous room. It was a remarkable fusion of engineering and art. Above them the famous circular hole in the roof glowed with a narrow shaft of evening sun. *The oculus*, Langdon thought. *The demon's hole.*

They had arrived.

Langdon's eyes traced the arch of the ceiling sloping outward to the columned walls and finally down to the polished marble floor beneath their feet. The faint echo of footfalls and tourist murmurs reverberated around the dome. Langdon scanned the dozens or so tourists wandering aimlessly in the shadows. *Are you here?*

'Looks pretty quiet,' Vittoria said, still holding his hand.

Langdon nodded.

'Where's Raphael's tomb?'

Langdon thought for a moment, trying to get his bearings. He surveyed the circumference of the room. Tombs. Altars. Pillars. Niches. He motioned to a particularly ornate funerary across the dome and to the left. 'I think that's Raphael's over there.'

Vittoria scanned the rest of the room. 'I don't see anyone who looks like an assassin about to kill a cardinal. Shall we look around?'

Langdon nodded. 'There's only one spot in here where anyone could be hiding. We better check the *rientranze*.'

'The recesses?'

'Yes.' Langdon pointed. 'The recesses in the wall.'

Around the perimeter, interspersed with the tombs, a series of semi-circular niches were hewn in the wall. The niches, although not enormous, were big enough to hide someone in the shadows. Sadly, Langdon knew they once contained statues of the Olympian gods, but the pagan sculptures had been destroyed when the Vatican converted the Pantheon to a Christian church. He felt a pang of frustration to know he was standing at the first altar of science, and the marker was gone. He wondered which statue it had been, and where it had pointed. Langdon could imagine no greater thrill than finding an Illuminati marker – a statue that surreptitiously pointed the way down the Path of Illumination. Again he wondered *who* the anonymous Illuminati sculptor had been.

'I'll take the left arc,' Vittoria said, indicating the left half of the circumference. 'You go right. See you in a hundred and eighty degrees.'

Langdon smiled grimly.

As Vittoria moved off, Langdon felt the eerie horror of the situation seeping back into his mind. As he turned and made his way to the right, the killer's voice seemed to whisper in the dead space around him. *Eight o'clock. Virgin sacrifices on the altars of science. A mathematical progression of death. Eight, nine, ten, eleven ... and at midnight.* Langdon checked his watch: 7.52. Eight minutes.

As Langdon moved toward the first recess, he passed the tomb of one of Italy's Catholic kings. The sarcophagus, like many in Rome, was askew with the wall, positioned awkwardly. A group of visitors seemed confused by this. Langdon did not stop to explain. Formal Christian tombs were often misaligned with the architecture so they could lie facing *east*. It was an ancient superstition that Langdon's Symbology 212 class had discussed just last month.

'That's totally incongruous!' a female student in the front had blurted when Langdon explained the reason for east-facing tombs. 'Why would Christians want their tombs to face the rising *sun*? We're talking about Christianity ... not *sun* worship!'

Langdon smiled, pacing before the blackboard, chewing an apple. 'Mr Hitzrot!' he shouted.

A young man dozing in back sat up with a start. 'What! Me?'

Langdon pointed to a Renaissance art poster on the wall. 'Who is that man kneeling before God?'

'Um ... some saint?'

'Brilliant. And how do you *know* he's a saint?'

'He's got a halo?'

'Excellent, and does that golden halo remind you of anything?'

Hitzrot broke into a smile. 'Yeah! Those Egyptian things we studied last term. Those ... um ... *sun disks!*'

'Thank you, Hitzrot. Go back to sleep.' Langdon turned back to the class. 'Halos, like much of Christian symbology, were borrowed from the ancient Egyptian religion of *sun* worship. Christianity is filled with examples of sun worship.'

'Excuse me?' the girl in front said. 'I go to church all the time, and I don't see much sun worshiping going on!'

'Really? What do you celebrate on December twenty-fifth?'

'Christmas. The birth of Jesus Christ.'

'And yet according to the Bible, Christ was born in March, so what are we doing celebrating in late December?'

Silence.

Langdon smiled. 'December twenty-fifth, my friends, is the ancient pagan holiday of *sol invictus* – Unconquered Sun – coinciding with the winter solstice. It's that wonderful time of year when the sun returns, and the days start getting longer.'

Langdon took another bite of apple.

'Conquering religions,' he continued, 'often adopt existing holidays to make conversion less shocking. It's called *transmutation*. It helps people acclimatize to the new faith. Worshipers keep the same holy dates, pray in the same sacred locations, use a similar symbology . . . and they simply substitute a different god.'

Now the girl in front looked furious. 'You're implying Christianity is just some kind of . . . repackaged *sun worship!*'

'Not at all. Christianity did not borrow *only* from sun worship. The ritual of Christian canonization is taken from the ancient "god-making" rite of Euhemerus. The practice of "god-eating" – that is, Holy Communion – was borrowed from the Aztecs. Even the concept of Christ dying for our sins is arguably not exclusively Christian; the self-sacrifice of a young man to absolve the sins of his people appears in the earliest tradition of the Quetzalcoatl.'

The girl glared. 'So, is *anything* in Christianity original?'

'Very little in *any* organized faith is truly original. Religions are not born from scratch. They grow from one another. Modern religion is a collage . . . an assimilated historical record of man's quest to understand the divine.'

'Um . . . hold on,' Hitzrot ventured, sounding awake now. 'I know something Christian that's original. How about our *image* of God? Christian art never portrays God as the hawk sun god, or as an Aztec, or as anything weird. It always shows God as an old man with a white beard. So our *image* of God is original, right?'

Langdon smiled. 'When the early Christian converts abandoned their former deities – pagan gods, Roman gods, Greek, sun, Mithraic, whatever – they asked the church what their new Christian God looked like. Wisely, the church chose the most feared, powerful . . . and familiar face in all of recorded history.'

Hitzrot looked skeptical. 'An old man with a white, flowing beard?'

Langdon pointed to a hierarchy of ancient gods on the wall. At the top sat an old man with a white, flowing beard. 'Does Zeus look familiar?'

The class ended right on cue.

'Good evening,' a man's voice said.

Langdon jumped. He was back in the Pantheon. He turned to face an elderly man in a blue cape with a red cross on the chest. The man gave him a gray-toothed smile.

'You're English, right?' The man's accent was thick Tuscan.

Langdon blinked, confused. 'Actually, no. I'm American.'

The man looked embarrassed. 'Oh heavens, forgive me. You were so nicely dressed, I just figured . . . my apologies.'

'Can I help you?' Langdon asked, his heart beating wildly.

'Actually I thought perhaps I could help *you*. I am the *cicerone* here.' The man pointed proudly to his city-issued badge. 'It is my job to make your visit to Rome more interesting.'

More interesting? Langdon was certain this particular visit to Rome was *plenty* interesting.

'You look like a man of distinction,' the guide fawned, 'no doubt more interested in culture than most. Perhaps I can give you some history on this fascinating building.'

Langdon smiled politely. 'Kind of you, but I'm actually an art historian myself, and—'

'Superb!' The man's eyes lit up like he'd hit the jackpot. 'Then you will no doubt find this delightful!'

'I think I'd prefer to—'

'The Pantheon,' the man declared, launching into his memorized spiel, 'was built by Marcus Agrippa in 27 B.C.'

'Yes,' Langdon interjected, 'and rebuilt by Hadrian in 119 A.D.'

'It was the world's largest free-standing dome until 1960 when it was eclipsed by the Superdome in New Orleans!'

Langdon groaned. The man was unstoppable.

'And a fifth-century theologian once called the Pantheon the *House of the Devil*, warning that the hole in the roof was an entrance for demons!'

Langdon blocked him out. His eyes climbed skyward to the oculus, and the memory of Vittoria's suggested plot flashed a bone-numbing image in his mind . . . a branded cardinal falling through the hole and hitting the marble floor. *Now* that *would be a media event*. Langdon found himself scanning the Pantheon for reporters. None. He inhaled deeply. It was an absurd idea. The logistics of pulling off a stunt like that would be ridiculous.

As Langdon moved off to continue his inspection, the babbling docent followed like a love-starved puppy. *Remind me*, Langdon thought to himself, *there's nothing worse than a gung ho art historian*.

Across the room, Vittoria was immersed in her own search. Standing all alone for the first time since she had heard the news of her father, she felt the stark reality of the last eight hours closing in around her. Her father had been murdered – cruelly and abruptly. Almost equally painful was that her father's creation had been corrupted – now a tool of terrorists. Vittoria was plagued with guilt to think that it was *her* invention that had enabled the antimatter to be transported . . . *her* canister that was now counting down inside the Vatican. In an effort to serve her father's quest for the simplicity of truth . . . she had become a conspirator of chaos.

Oddly, the only thing that felt right in her life at the moment was the presence of a total stranger. Robert Langdon. She found an inexplicable refuge in his eyes . . . like the harmony of the oceans she had left behind early that morning. She was glad he was there. Not only had he been a source of strength and hope for her, Langdon had used his quick mind to render this one chance to catch her father's killer.

Vittoria breathed deeply as she continued her search, moving around the perimeter. She was overwhelmed by the unexpected images of personal revenge that had dominated her thoughts all day. Even as a sworn lover of all life . . . she wanted this executioner *dead*. No amount of good *karma* could make her turn the other cheek today. Alarmed and electrified, she sensed something coursing through her Italian blood that she had never felt before . . . the whispers of Sicilian ancestors defending family honor with brutal justice. *Vendetta*, Vittoria thought, and for the first time in her life understood.

Visions of reprisal spurred her on. She approached the tomb of Raphael Santi. Even from a distance she could tell this guy was special. His casket, unlike the others, was protected by a Plexiglas shield and recessed into the wall. Through the barrier she could see the front of the sarcophagus.

RAPHAEL SANTI, 1483–1520

Vittoria studied the grave and then read the one-sentence description plaque beside Raphael's tomb.

Then she read it again.

Then . . . she read it again.

A moment later, she was dashing in horror across the floor. 'Robert! *Robert!*'

62

Langdon's progress around his side of the Pantheon was being hampered somewhat by the guide on his heels, now continuing his tireless narration as Langdon prepared to check the final alcove.

'You certainly seem to be enjoying those niches!' the docent said, looking delighted. 'Were you aware that the tapering thickness of the walls is the reason the dome appears weightless?'

Langdon nodded, not hearing a word as he prepared to examine another niche. Suddenly someone grabbed him from behind. It was Vittoria. She was breathless and tugging at his arm. From the look of terror on her face, Langdon could only imagine one thing. *She found a body.* He felt an upswelling of dread.

'Ah, your wife!' the docent exclaimed, clearly thrilled to have another guest. He motioned to her short pants and hiking boots. 'Now *you* I can tell are American!'

Vittoria's eyes narrowed. 'I'm Italian.'

The guide's smile dimmed. 'Oh, dear.'

'Robert,' Vittoria whispered, trying to turn her back on the guide. 'Galileo's *Diagramma.* I need to see it.'

'*Diagramma?*' the docent said, wheedling back in. 'My! You two certainly know your history! Unfortunately that document is not viewable. It is under secret preservation in the Vatican Arc—'

'Could you excuse us?' Langdon said. He was confused by Vittoria's panic. He took her aside and reached in his pocket, carefully extracting the *Diagramma* folio. 'What's going on?'

'What's the date on this thing?' Vittoria demanded, scanning the sheet.

The docent was on them again, staring at the folio, mouth agape. 'That's not . . . really . . .'

'Tourist reproduction,' Langdon quipped. 'Thank you for your help. Please, my wife and I would like a moment alone.'

The docent backed off, eyes never leaving the paper.

'Date,' Vittoria repeated to Langdon. 'When did Galileo publish . . .'

Langdon pointed to the Roman numeral in the lower line. 'That's the pub date. What's going on?'

Vittoria deciphered the number. '1639?'

'Yes. What's wrong?'

Vittoria's eyes filled with foreboding. 'We're in trouble, Robert. Big trouble. The dates don't match.'

'What dates don't match?'

'Raphael's tomb. He wasn't buried here until 1759. A century *after Diagramma* was published.'

Langdon stared at her, trying to make sense of the words. 'No,' he replied. 'Raphael died in 1520, long *before Diagramma.*'

'Yes, but he wasn't buried *here* until much later.'

Langdon was lost. 'What are you talking about?'

'I just read it. Raphael's body was relocated to the Pantheon in 1758. It was part of some historic tribute to eminent Italians.'

As the words settled in, Langdon felt like a rug had just been yanked out from under him.

'When that poem was written,' Vittoria declared, 'Raphael's tomb was somewhere *else*. Back then, the Pantheon had nothing at all to do with Raphael!'

Langdon could not breathe. 'But that . . . means . . .'

'Yes! It means we're in the wrong place!'

Langdon felt himself sway. *Impossible . . . I was certain . . .*

Vittoria ran over and grabbed the docent, pulling him back. 'Signore, excuse us. Where was Raphael's body in the 1600s?'

'Urb . . . Urbino,' he stammered, now looking bewildered. 'His birth-place.'

'Impossible!' Langdon cursed to himself. 'The Illuminati altars of science were here in Rome. I'm certain of it!'

'Illuminati?' The docent gasped, looking again at the document in Langdon's hand. 'Who *are* you people?'

Vittoria took charge. 'We're looking for something called Santi's earthly tomb. In Rome. Can you tell us what that might be?'

The docent looked unsettled. 'This was Raphael's only tomb in Rome.'

Langdon tried to think, but his mind refused to engage. If Raphael's tomb wasn't in Rome in 1655, then what was the poem referring to? *Santi's earthly tomb with demon's hole? What the hell is it? Think!*

'Was there another artist called Santi?' Vittoria asked.

The docent shrugged. 'Not that I know of.'

'How about *anyone* famous at all? Maybe a scientist or a poet or an astronomer named Santi?'

The docent now looked like he wanted to leave. 'No, ma'am. The only Santi I've heard of is Raphael the architect.'

'Architect?' Vittoria said. 'I thought he was a painter!'

'He was both, of course. They all were. Michelangelo, da Vinci, Raphael.'

Langdon didn't know whether it was the docent's words or the ornate tombs around him that brought the revelation to mind, but it didn't matter. The thought occurred. *Santi was an architect.* From there the progression of thoughts fell like dominoes. Renaissance architects lived for only two reasons – to glorify God with big churches, and to glorify dignitaries with lavish tombs. *Santi's tomb. Could it be?* The images came faster now . . .

da Vinci's *Mona Lisa.*

Monet's *Water Lilies.*

Michelangelo's *David.*

Santi's *earthly tomb* . . .

'Santi *designed* the tomb,' Langdon said.

Vittoria turned. 'What?'

'It's not a reference to where Raphael is buried, it's referring to a tomb he *designed*.'

'What are you talking about?'

'I misunderstood the clue. It's not Raphael's burial site we're looking for, it's a tomb Raphael designed for someone *else*. I can't believe I missed it. Half of the sculpting done in Renaissance and Baroque Rome was for the funeraries.' Langdon smiled with the revelation. 'Raphael must have designed hundreds of tombs!'

Vittoria did not look happy. 'Hundreds?'

Langdon's smile faded. 'Oh.'

'Any of them *earthly*, professor?'

Langdon felt suddenly inadequate. He knew embarrassingly little about Raphael's work. Michelangelo he could have helped with, but Raphael's work had never captivated him. Langdon could only name a couple of Raphael's more famous tombs, but he wasn't sure what they looked like.

Apparently sensing Langdon's stymie, Vittoria turned to the docent, who was now inching away. She grabbed his arm and reeled him in. 'I need a tomb. Designed by Raphael. A tomb that could be considered *earthly*.'

The docent now looked distressed. 'A tomb of Raphael's? I don't know. He designed so many. And you probably would mean a *chapel* by Raphael, not a tomb. Architects always designed the chapels in conjunction with the tomb.'

Langdon realized the man was right.

'Are any of Raphael's tombs or chapels considered *earthly*?'

The man shrugged. 'I'm sorry. I don't know what you mean. *Earthly* really doesn't describe anything I know of. I should be going.'

Vittoria held his arm and read from the top line of the folio. 'From Santi's earthly tomb with demon's hole. Does that mean anything to you?'

'Not a thing.'

Langdon looked up suddenly. He had momentarily forgotten the second part of the line. *Demon's hole?* 'Yes!' he said to the docent. 'That's it! Do any of Raphael's chapels have an oculus in them?'

194

The docent shook his head. 'To my knowledge the Pantheon is unique.'
He paused. 'But . . .'

'But what!' Vittoria and Langdon said in unison.

Now the docent cocked his head, stepping toward them again. 'A
demon's hole?' He muttered to himself and picked at his teeth. 'Demon's
hole . . . that is . . . *buca del diàvolo?*'

Vittoria nodded. 'Literally, yes.'

The docent smiled faintly. 'Now there's a term I have not heard in a
while. If I'm not mistaken, a *buca del diàvolo* refers to an undercroft.'

'An undercroft?' Langdon asked. 'As in a *crypt?*'

'Yes, but a specific kind of crypt. I believe a demon's hole is an ancient
term for a massive burial cavity located in a chapel . . . underneath another
tomb.'

'An ossuary annex?' Langdon demanded, immediately recognizing what
the man was describing.

The docent looked impressed. 'Yes! That is the term I was looking for!'

Langdon considered it. Ossuary annexes were a cheap ecclesiastic fix to
an awkward dilemma. When churches honored their most distinguished
members with ornate tombs inside the sanctuary, surviving family members often demanded the family be buried together . . . thus ensuring they
too would have a coveted burial spot inside the church. However, if the
church did not have space or funds to create tombs for an entire family,
they sometimes dug an ossuary annex – a hole in the floor near the tomb
where they buried the less worthy family members. The hole was then
covered with the Renaissance equivalent of a manhole cover. Although
convenient, the ossuary annex went out of style quickly because of the
stench that often wafted up into the cathedral. *Demon's hole*, Langdon
thought. He had never heard the term. It seemed eerily fitting.

Langdon's heart was now pounding fiercely. *From Santi's earthly tomb
with demon's hole.* There seemed to be only one question left to ask. 'Did
Raphael design any tombs that had one of these demon's holes?'

The docent scratched his head. 'Actually, I'm sorry . . . I can only think
of one.'

Only one? Langdon could not have dreamed of a better response.

'Where!' Vittoria almost shouted.

The docent eyed them strangely. 'It's called the Chigi Chapel. Tomb of
Agostino Chigi and his brother, wealthy patrons of the arts and sciences.'

'*Sciences?*' Langdon said, exchanging looks with Vittoria.

'Where?' Vittoria asked again.

The docent ignored the question, seeming enthusiastic again to be
of service. 'As for whether or not the tomb is *earthly*, I don't know, but
certainly it is . . . shall we say *differènte.*'

'Different?' Langdon said. 'How?'

'Incoherent with the architecture. Raphael was only the architect. Some
other sculptor did the interior adornments. I can't remember who.'

Langdon was now all ears. *The anonymous Illuminati master, perhaps?*

'Whoever did the interior monuments lacked taste,' the docent said. *'Dio mio! Che atrocità!* Who would want to be buried beneath *piramidi?'*

Langdon could scarcely believe his ears. 'Pyramids? The chapel contains pyramids?'

'I know,' the docent scoffed. 'Terrible, isn't it?'

Vittoria grabbed the docent's arm. 'Signore, *where* is this Chigi Chapel?'

'About a mile north. In the church of Santa Maria del Popolo.'

Vittoria exhaled. 'Thank you. Let's—'

'Hey,' the docent said, 'I just thought of something. What a fool I am.'

Vittoria stopped short. 'Please don't tell me you made a mistake.'

He shook his head. 'No, but it should have dawned on me earlier. The Chigi Chapel was not always known as the Chigi. It used to be called Capella della Terra.'

'Chapel of the Land?' Langdon asked.

'No,' Vittoria said, heading for the door. 'Chapel of the *Earth*.'

Vittoria Vetra whipped out her cell phone as she dashed into Piazza della Rotunda. 'Commander Olivetti,' she said. 'This is the wrong place!'

Olivetti sounded bewildered. 'Wrong? What do you mean?'

'The first altar of science is at the Chigi Chapel!'

'Where?' Now Olivetti sounded angry. 'But Mr Langdon said—'

'Santa Maria del Popolo! One mile north. Get your men over there now! We've got four minutes!'

'But my men are in position *here*! I can't possibly—'

'Move!' Vittoria snapped the phone shut.

Behind her, Langdon emerged from the Pantheon, dazed.

She grabbed his hand and pulled him toward the queue of seemingly driverless taxis waiting by the curb. She pounded on the hood of the first car in line. The sleeping driver bolted upright with a startled yelp. Vittoria yanked open the rear door and pushed Langdon inside. Then she jumped in behind him.

'Santa Maria del Popolo,' she ordered. *'Presto!'*

Looking delirious and half terrified, the driver hit the accelerator, peeling out down the street.

63

Gunther Glick had assumed control of the computer from Chinita Macri, who now stood hunched in the back of the cramped BBC van staring in confusion over Glick's shoulder.

'I told you,' Glick said, typing some more keys. 'The *British Tatler* isn't the only paper that runs stories on these guys.'

Macri peered closer. Glick was right. The BBC database showed their distinguished network as having picked up and run six stories in the past ten years on the brotherhood called the Illuminati. *Well, paint me purple*, she thought. 'Who are the journalists who ran the stories,' Macri asked.'Schlock jocks?'

'BBC doesn't hire schlock jocks.'

'They hired *you*.'

Glick scowled. 'I don't know why you're such a skeptic. The Illuminati are well documented throughout history.'

'So are witches, UFOs, and the Loch Ness Monster.'

Glick read the list of stories. 'You ever heard of a guy called Winston Churchill?'

'Rings a bell.'

'BBC did a historical a while back on Churchill's life. Staunch Catholic by the way. Did you know that in 1920 Churchill published a statement condemning the Illuminati and warning Brits of a worldwide conspiracy against morality?'

Macri was dubious. 'Where did it run? In the *British Tatler*?'

Glick smiled. '*London Herald*. February 8, 1920.'

'No way.'

'Feast your eyes.'

Macri looked closer at the clip. *London Herald, Feb. 8, 1920. I had no idea*. 'Well, Churchill was a paranoid.'

'He wasn't alone,' Glick said, reading further. 'Looks like Woodrow Wilson gave three radio broadcasts in 1921 warning of growing Illuminati control over the U.S. banking system. You want a direct quote from the radio transcript?'

'Not really.'

Glick gave her one anyway. 'He said, "There is a power so organized, so subtle, so complete, so pervasive, that none had better speak above their breath when they speak in condemnation of it."'

'I've never heard anything about this.'

'Maybe because in 1921 you were just a kid.'

'Charming.' Macri took the jab in stride. She knew her years were showing. At forty-three, her bushy black curls were streaked with gray. She was too proud for dye. Her mom, a Southern Baptist, had taught Chinita contentedness and self-respect. *When you're a black woman,* her mother said, *ain't no hiding what you are. Day you try, is the day you die. Stand tall, smile bright, and let 'em wonder what secret's making you laugh.*

'Ever heard of Cecil Rhodes?' Glick asked.

Macri looked up. 'The British financier?'

'Yeah. Founded the Rhodes Scholarships.'

'Don't tell me—'

'Illuminatus.'

'BS.'

'BBC, actually. November 16, 1984.'

'*We* wrote that Cecil Rhodes was Illuminati?'

'Sure did. And according to our network, the Rhodes Scholarships were funds set up centuries ago to recruit the world's brightest young minds into the Illuminati.'

'That's ridiculous! My uncle was a Rhodes Scholar!'

Glick winked. 'So was Bill Clinton.'

Macri was getting mad now. She had never had tolerance for shoddy, alarmist reporting. Still, she knew enough about the BBC to know that every story they ran was carefully researched and confirmed.

'Here's one you'll remember,' Glick said. 'BBC, March 5, 1998. Parliament Committee Chair, Chris Mullin, required all members of British Parliament who were Masons to declare their affiliation.'

Macri remembered it. The decree had eventually extended to include policemen and judges as well. 'Why was it again?'

Glick read. '. . . concern that secret factions within the Masons exerted considerable control over political and financial systems.'

'That's right.'

'Caused quite a bustle. The Masons in parliament were furious. Had a right to be. The vast majority turned out to be innocent men who joined the Masons for networking and charity work. They had no clue about the brotherhood's past affiliations.'

'Alleged affiliations.'

'Whatever.' Glick scanned the articles. 'Look at this stuff. Accounts tracing the Illuminati back to Galileo, the *Guerenets* of France, the *Alumbrados* of Spain. Even Karl Marx and the Russian Revolution.'

'History has a way of rewriting itself.'

'Fine, you want something current? Have a look at this. Here's an Illuminati reference from a recent *Wall Street Journal*.'

This caught Macri's ear. 'The *Journal*?'

'Guess what the most popular Internet computer game in America is right now?'

'Pin the tail on Pamela Anderson.'

'Close. It's called, *Illuminati: New World Order*.'

Macri looked over his shoulder at the blurb. '*Steve Jackson Games has a runaway hit* ... *a quasi-historical adventure in which an ancient satanic brotherhood from Bavaria sets out to take over the world. You can find them on-line at* ...' Macri looked up, feeling ill. 'What do these Illuminati guys have against Christianity?'

'Not just Christianity,' Glick said. 'Religion in general.' Glick cocked his head and grinned. 'Although from the phone call we just got, it appears they *do* have a special spot in their hearts for the Vatican.'

'Oh, come on. You don't *really* think that guy who called is who he claims to be, do you?'

'A messenger of the Illuminati? Preparing to kill four cardinals?' Glick smiled. 'I sure hope so.'

64

Langdon and Vittoria's taxi completed the one-mile sprint up the wide Via della Scrofa in just over a minute. They skidded to a stop on the south side of the Piazza del Popolo just before eight. Not having any lire, Langdon overpaid the driver in U.S. dollars. He and Vittoria jumped out. The piazza was quiet except for the laughter of a handful of locals seated outside the popular Rosati Café – a hot spot of the Italian literati. The breeze smelled of espresso and pastry.

Langdon was still in shock over his mistake at the Pantheon. With a cursory glance at this square, however, his sixth sense was already tingling. The piazza seemed subtly filled with Illuminati significance. Not only was it laid out in a perfectly *elliptical* shape, but dead center stood a towering Egyptian obelisk – a square pillar of stone with a distinctively pyramidal tip. Spoils of Rome's imperial plundering, obelisks were scattered across Rome and referred to by symbologists as 'Lofty Pyramids' – skyward extensions of the sacred pyramidal form.

As Langdon's eyes moved up the monolith, though, his sight was suddenly drawn to something else in the background. Something even more remarkable.

'We're in the right place,' he said quietly, feeling a sudden exposed wariness. 'Have a look at that.' Langdon pointed to the imposing Porta del Popolo – the high stone archway at the far end of the piazza. The vaulted structure had been overlooking the piazza for centuries. Dead center of the archway's highest point was a symbolic engraving. 'Look familiar?'

Vittoria looked up at the huge carving. 'A shining star over a triangular pile of stones?'

Langdon shook his head. 'A source of Illumination over a pyramid.'

Vittoria turned, her eyes suddenly wide. 'Like . . . the Great Seal of the United States.'

'Exactly. The Masonic symbol on the one-dollar bill.'

Vittoria took a deep breath and scanned the piazza. 'So where's this damn church?'

*

The Church of Santa Maria del Popolo stood out like a misplaced battleship, askew at the base of a hill on the southeast corner of the piazza. The eleventh-century stone aerie was made even more clumsy by the tower of scaffolding covering the façade.

Langdon's thoughts were a blur as they raced toward the edifice. He stared up at the church in wonder. Could a murder really be about to take place inside? He wished Olivetti would hurry. The gun felt awkward in his pocket.

The church's front stairs were *ventaglio* – a welcoming, curved fan – ironic in this case because they were blocked with scaffolding, construction equipment, and a sign warning: COSTRUZIONE. NON ENTRARE.

Langdon realized that a church closed for renovation meant total privacy for a killer. Not like the Pantheon. No fancy tricks needed here. Only to find a way in.

Vittoria slipped without hesitation between the sawhorses and headed up the staircase.

'Vittoria,' Langdon cautioned. 'If he's still in there . . .'

Vittoria did not seem to hear. She ascended the main portico to the church's sole wooden door. Langdon hurried up the stairs behind her. Before he could say a word she had grasped the handle and pulled. Langdon held his breath. The door did not budge.

'There must be another entrance,' Vittoria said.

'Probably,' Langdon said, exhaling, 'but Olivetti will be here in a minute. It's too dangerous to go in. We should cover the church from out here until—'

Vittoria turned, her eyes blazing. 'If there's another way *in*, there's another way *out*. If this guy disappears, we're *spacciàti*.'

Langdon knew enough Italian to know she was right.

The alley on the right side of the church was pinched and dark, with high walls on both sides. It smelled of urine – a common aroma in a city where bars outnumbered public rest rooms twenty to one.

Langdon and Vittoria hurried into the fetid dimness. They had gone about fifteen yards down when Vittoria tugged Langdon's arm and pointed.

Langdon saw it too. Up ahead was an unassuming wooden door with heavy hinges. Langdon recognized it as the standard *porta sacra* – a private entrance for clergy. Most of these entrances had gone out of use years ago as encroaching buildings and limited real estate relegated side entrances to inconvenient alleyways.

Vittoria hurried to the door. She arrived and stared down at the doorknob, apparently perplexed. Langdon arrived behind her and eyed the peculiar donut-shaped hoop hanging where the doorknob should have been.

'An annulus,' he whispered. Langdon reached out and quietly lifted the ring in his hand. He pulled the ring toward him. The fixture clicked.

Vittoria shifted, looking suddenly uneasy. Quietly, Langdon twisted the ring clockwise. It spun loosely 360 degrees, not engaging. Langdon frowned and tried the other direction with the same result.

Vittoria looked down the remainder of the alley. 'You think there's another entrance?'

Langdon doubted it. Most Renaissance cathedrals were designed as makeshift fortresses in the event a city was stormed. They had as few entrances as possible. 'If there *is* another way in,' he said, 'it's probably recessed in the rear bastion – more of an escape route than an entrance.'

Vittoria was already on the move.

Langdon followed deeper into the alley. The walls shot skyward on both sides of him. Somewhere a bell began ringing eight o'clock . . .

Robert Langdon did not hear Vittoria the first time she called to him. He had slowed at a stained-glass window covered with bars and was trying to peer inside the church.

'Robert!' Her voice was a loud whisper.

Langdon looked up. Vittoria was at the end of the alley. She was pointing around the back of the church and waving to him. Langdon jogged reluctantly toward her. At the base of the rear wall, a stone bulwark jutted out concealing a narrow grotto – a kind of compressed passageway cutting directly into the foundation of the church.

'An entrance?' Vittoria asked.

Langdon nodded. *Actually an exit, but we won't get technical.*

Vittoria knelt and peered into the tunnel. 'Let's check the door. See if it's open.'

Langdon opened his mouth to object, but Vittoria took his hand and pulled him into the opening.

'Wait,' Langdon said.

She turned impatiently toward him.

Langdon sighed. 'I'll go first.'

Vittoria looked surprised. 'More chivalry?'

'Age before beauty.'

'Was that a compliment?'

Langdon smiled and moved past her into the dark. 'Careful on the stairs.'

He inched slowly into the darkness, keeping one hand on the wall. The stone felt sharp on his fingertips. For an instant Langdon recalled the ancient myth of Daedelus, how the boy kept one hand on the wall as he moved through the Minotaur's labyrinth, knowing he was guaranteed to find the end if he never broke contact with the wall. Langdon moved forward, not entirely certain he wanted to find the end.

The tunnel narrowed slightly, and Langdon slowed his pace. He sensed Vittoria close behind him. As the wall curved left, the tunnel opened into a semicircular alcove. Oddly, there was faint light here. In the dimness Langdon saw the outline of a heavy wooden door.

'Oh oh,' he said.

'Locked?'

'It *was.*'

'*Was?*' Vittoria arrived at his side.

Langdon pointed. Lit by a shaft of light coming from within, the door hung ajar . . . its hinges splintered by a wrecking bar still lodged in the wood.

They stood a moment in silence. Then, in the dark, Langdon felt Vittoria's hands on his chest, groping, sliding beneath his jacket.

'Relax, professor,' she said. 'I'm just getting the gun.'

At that moment, inside the Vatican Museums, a task force of Swiss Guards spread out in all directions. The museum was dark, and the guards wore U.S. Marine issue infrared goggles. The goggles made everything appear an eerie shade of green. Every guard wore headphones connected to an antennalike detector that he waved rhythmically in front of him – the same devices they used twice a week to sweep for electronic bugs inside the Vatican. They moved methodically, checking behind statues, inside niches, closets, under furniture. The antennae would sound if they detected even the tiniest magnetic field.

Tonight, however, they were getting no readings at all.

65

The interior of Santa Maria del Popolo was a murky cave in the dimming light. It looked more like a half-finished subway station than a cathedral. The main sanctuary was an obstacle course of torn-up flooring, brick pallets, mounds of dirt, wheelbarrows, and even a rusty backhoe. Mammoth columns rose through the floor, supporting a vaulted roof. In the air, silt drifted lazily in the muted glow of the stained glass. Langdon stood with Vittoria beneath a sprawling Pinturicchio fresco and scanned the gutted shrine.

Nothing moved. Dead silence.

Vittoria held the gun out in front of her with both hands. Langdon checked his watch: 8.04 p.m. *We're crazy to be in here,* he thought. *It's too dangerous.* Still he knew if the killer were inside, the man could leave through any door he wanted, making a one-gun outside stakeout totally fruitless. Catching him inside was the only way . . . that was, if he was even still here. Langdon felt guilt-ridden over the blunder that had cost everyone their chance at the Pantheon. He was in no position to insist on precaution now; *he* was the one who had backed them into this corner.

Vittoria looked harrowed as she scanned the church. 'So,' she whispered. 'Where is this Chigi Chapel?'

Langdon gazed through the dusky ghostliness toward the back of the cathedral and studied the outer walls. Contrary to common perception, Renaissance cathedrals invariably contained *multiple* chapels, huge cathedrals like Notre Dame having dozens. Chapels were less *rooms* than they were *hollows* – semicircular niches holding tombs around a church's perimeter wall.

Bad news, Langdon thought, seeing the four recesses on each side wall. There were eight chapels in all. Although eight was not a particularly overwhelming number, all eight openings were covered with huge sheets of clear polyurethane due to the construction, the translucent curtains apparently intended to keep dust off the tombs inside the alcoves.

'It could be any of those draped recesses,' Langdon said. 'No way to know which is the Chigi without looking inside every one. Could be a good reason to wait for Oliv—'

'Which is the secondary left apse?' she asked.

Langdon studied her, surprised by her command of architectural terminology. 'Secondary left apse?'

Vittoria pointed at the wall behind him. A decorative tile was embedded in the stone. It was engraved with the same symbol they had seen outside – a pyramid beneath a shining star. The grime-covered plaque beside it read:

COAT OF ARMS OF ALEXANDER CHIGI
WHOSE TOMB IS LOCATED IN THE
SECONDARY LEFT APSE OF THIS CATHEDRAL

Langdon nodded. *Chigi's coat of arms was a pyramid and star?* He suddenly found himself wondering if the wealthy patron Chigi had been an Illuminatus. He nodded to Vittoria. 'Nice work, Nancy Drew.'

'What?'

'Never mind. I—'

A piece of metal clattered to the floor only yards away. The clang echoed through the entire church. Langdon pulled Vittoria behind a pillar as she whipped the gun toward the sound and held it there. Silence. They waited. Again there was a sound, this time a rustling. Langdon held his breath. *I never should have let us come in here!* The sound moved closer, an intermittent scuffling, like a man with a limp. Suddenly around the base of the pillar, an object came into view.

'*Figlio di puttana!*' Vittoria cursed under her breath, jumping back. Langdon fell back with her.

Beside the pillar, dragging a half-eaten sandwich in paper, was an enormous rat. The creature paused when it saw them, staring a long moment down the barrel of Vittoria's weapon, and then, apparently unmoved, continued dragging its prize off to the recesses of the church.

'Son of a . . .' Langdon gasped, his heart racing.

Vittoria lowered the gun, quickly regaining her composure. Langdon peered around the side of the column to see a workman's lunchbox splayed on the floor, apparently knocked off a sawhorse by the resourceful rodent.

Langdon scanned the basilica for movement and whispered, 'If this guy's here, he sure as hell heard *that.* You sure you don't want to wait for Olivetti?'

'Secondary left apse,' Vittoria repeated. 'Where is it?'

Reluctantly Langdon turned and tried to get his bearings: Cathedral terminology was like stage directions – totally counterintuitive. He faced the main altar. *Stage center.* Then he pointed with his thumb backward over his shoulder.

They both turned and looked where he was pointing.

It seemed the Chigi Chapel was located in the third of four recessed alcoves to their right. The good news was that Langdon and Vittoria were on the correct *side* of the church. The bad news was that they were at the wrong *end*. They would have to traverse the length of the cathedral, passing three other chapels, each of them, like the Chigi Chapel, covered with translucent plastic shrouds.

'Wait,' Langdon said. 'I'll go first.'

'Forget it.'

'I'm the one who screwed up at the Pantheon.'

She turned. 'But I'm the one with the gun.'

In her eyes Langdon could see what she was really thinking . . . *I'm the one who lost my father. I'm the one who helped build a weapon of mass destruction. This guy's kneecaps are mine . . .*

Langdon sensed the futility and let her go. He moved beside her, cautiously, down the east side of the basilica. As they passed the first shrouded alcove, Langdon felt taut, like a contestant on some surreal game show. *I'll take curtain number three,* he thought.

The church was quiet, the thick stone walls blocking out all hints of the outside world. As they hurried past one chapel after the other, pale humanoid forms wavered like ghosts behind the rustling plastic. *Carved marble,* Langdon told himself, hoping he was right. It was 8.06 p.m. Had the killer been punctual and slipped out before Langdon and Vittoria had entered? Or was he still here? Langdon was unsure which scenario he preferred.

They passed the second apse, ominous in the slowly darkening cathedral. Night seemed to be falling quickly now, accentuated by the musty tint of the stained-glass windows. As they pressed on, the plastic curtain beside them billowed suddenly, as if caught in a draft. Langdon wondered if someone somewhere had opened a door.

Vittoria slowed as the third niche loomed before them. She held the gun before her, motioning with her head to the stele beside the apse. Carved in the granite block were two words:

CAPELLA CHIGI

Langdon nodded. Without a sound they moved to the corner of the opening, positioning themselves behind a wide pillar. Vittoria leveled the gun around a corner at the plastic. Then she signaled for Langdon to pull back the shroud.

A good time to start praying, he thought. Reluctantly, he reached over her shoulder. As carefully as possible, he began to pull the plastic aside. It moved an inch and then crinkled loudly. They both froze. Silence. After a moment, moving in slow motion, Vittoria leaned forward and peered through the narrow slit. Langdon looked over her shoulder.

For a moment, neither one of them breathed.

'Empty,' Vittoria finally said, lowering the gun. 'We're too late.'

Langdon did not hear. He was in awe, transported for an instant to another world. In his life, he had never imagined a chapel that looked like this. Finished entirely in chestnut marble, the Chigi Chapel was breathtaking. Langdon's trained eye devoured it in gulps. It was as *earthly* a chapel as Langdon could fathom, almost as if Galileo and the Illuminati had designed it themselves.

Overhead, the domed cupola shone with a field of illuminated stars and the seven astronomical planets. Below that the twelve signs of the zodiac – pagan, earthly symbols rooted in astronomy. The zodiac was also tied directly to Earth, Air, Fire, Water . . . the quadrants representing power, intellect, ardor, emotion. *Earth is for power*, Langdon recalled.

Farther down the wall, Langdon saw tributes to the Earth's four temporal seasons – *primavera, estate, autunno, invérno*. But far more incredible than any of this were the two huge structures dominating the room. Langdon stared at them in silent wonder. *It can't be*, he thought. *It just can't be!* But it was. On either side of the chapel, in perfect symmetry, were two ten-foot-high marble pyramids.

'I don't see a cardinal,' Vittoria whispered. 'Or an assassin.' She pulled aside the plastic and stepped in.

Langdon's eyes were transfixed on the pyramids. *What are pyramids doing inside a Christian chapel?* And incredibly, there was more. Dead center of each pyramid, embedded in their anterior façades, were gold medallions . . . medallions like few Langdon had ever seen . . . perfect *ellipses*. The burnished disks glimmered in the setting sun as it sifted through the cupola. *Galileo's ellipses? Pyramids? A cupola of stars?* The room had more Illuminati significance than any room Langdon could have fabricated in his mind.

'Robert,' Vittoria blurted, her voice cracking. 'Look!'

Langdon wheeled, reality returning as his eyes dropped to where she was pointing. 'Bloody hell!' he shouted, jumping backward.

Sneering up at them from the floor was the image of a skeleton – an intricately detailed, marble mosaic depicting 'death in flight.' The skeleton was carrying a tablet portraying the same pyramid and stars they had seen outside. It was not the image, however, that had turned Langdon's blood cold. It was the fact that the mosaic was mounted on a circular stone – a *cupermento* – that had been lifted out of the floor like a manhole cover and was now sitting off to one side of a dark opening in the floor.

'Demon's hole,' Langdon gasped. He had been so taken with the ceiling he had not even seen it. Tentatively he moved toward the pit. The stench coming up was overwhelming.

Vittoria put a hand over her mouth. '*Che puzza.*'

'Effluvium,' Langdon said. 'Vapors from decaying bone.' He breathed through his sleeve as he leaned out over the hole, peering down. Blackness. 'I can't see a thing.'

'You think anybody's down there?'

'No way to know.'

Vittoria motioned to the far side of the hole where a rotting, wooden ladder descended into the depths.

Langdon shook his head. 'Like hell.'

'Maybe there's a flashlight outside in those tools.' She sounded eager for an excuse to escape the smell. 'I'll look.'

'Careful!' Langdon warned. 'We don't know for sure that the Hassassin—'

But Vittoria was already gone.

One strong-willed woman, Langdon thought.

As he turned back to the pit, he felt light-headed from the fumes. Holding his breath, he dropped his head below the rim and peered deep into the darkness. Slowly, as his eyes adjusted, he began to see faint shapes below. The pit appeared to open into a small chamber. *Demon's hole.* He wondered how many generations of Chigis had been unceremoniously dumped in. Langdon closed his eyes and waited, forcing his pupils to dilate so he could see better in the dark. When he opened his eyes again, a pale muted figure hovered below in the darkness. Langdon shivered but fought instinct to pull out. *Am I seeing things? Is that a body?* The figure faded. Langdon closed his eyes again and waited, longer this time, so his eyes would pick up the faintest light.

Dizziness started to set in, and his thoughts wandered in the blackness. *Just a few more seconds.* He wasn't sure if it was breathing the fumes or holding his head at a low inclination, but Langdon was definitely starting to feel squeamish. When he finally opened his eyes again, the image before him was totally inexplicable.

He was now staring at a crypt bathed in an eerie bluish light. A faint hissing sound reverberated in his ears. Light flickered on the steep walls of the shaft. Suddenly, a long shadow materialized over him. Startled, Langdon scrambled up.

'Look out!' someone exclaimed behind him.

Before Langdon could turn, he felt a sharp pain on the back of his neck. He spun to see Vittoria twisting a lit blowtorch away from him, the hissing flame throwing blue light around the chapel.

Langdon grabbed his neck. 'What the hell are you doing?'

'I was giving you some light,' she said. 'You backed right into me.'

Langdon glared at the portable blowtorch in her hand.

'Best I could do,' she said. 'No flashlights.'

Langdon rubbed his neck. 'I didn't hear you come in.'

Vittoria handed him the torch, wincing again at the stench of the crypt. 'You think those fumes are combustible?'

'Let's hope not.'

He took the torch and moved slowly toward the hole. Cautiously, he advanced to the rim and pointed the flame down into the hole, lighting the side wall. As he directed the light, his eyes traced the outline of the wall downward. The crypt was circular and about twenty feet across. Thirty feet down, the glow found the floor. The ground was dark and mottled. Earthy. Then Langdon saw the body.

His instinct was to recoil. 'He's here,' Langdon said, forcing himself not to turn away. The figure was a pallid outline against the earthen floor. 'I think he's been stripped naked.' Langdon flashed on the nude corpse.

'Is it one of the cardinals?'

Langdon had no idea, but he couldn't imagine who the hell else it would be. He stared down at the pale blob. Unmoving. Lifeless. *And yet* . . . Langdon hesitated. There was something very strange about the way the figure was positioned. He seemed to be . . .

Langdon called out. 'Hello?'

'You think he's alive?'

There was no response from below.

'He's not moving,' Langdon said. 'But he looks . . .' *No, impossible.*

'He looks *what?*' Vittoria was peering over the edge now too.

Langdon squinted into the darkness. 'He looks like he's standing up.'

Vittoria held her breath and lowered her face over the edge for a better look. After a moment, she pulled back. 'You're right. He's standing up! Maybe he's alive and needs help!' She called into the hole. 'Hello?! *Mi puó sentire?*'

There was no echo off the mossy interior. Only silence.

Vittoria headed for the rickety ladder. 'I'm going down.'

Langdon caught her arm. 'No. It's dangerous. I'll go.'

This time Vittoria didn't argue.

66

Chinita Macri was mad. She sat in the passenger's seat of the BBC van as it idled at a corner on Via Tomacelli. Gunther Glick was checking his map of Rome, apparently lost. As she had feared, his mystery caller had phoned back, this time with information.

'Piazza del Popolo,' Glick insisted. 'That's what we're looking for. There's a church there. And inside is proof.'

'Proof.' Chinita stopped polishing the lens in her hand and turned to him. 'Proof that a cardinal has been murdered?'

'That's what he said.'

'You believe everything you hear?' Chinita wished, as she often did, that *she* was the one in charge. Videographers, however, were at the whim of the crazy reporters for whom they shot footage. If Gunther Glick wanted to follow a feeble phone tip, Macri was his dog on a leash.

She looked at him, sitting there in the driver's seat, his jaw set intently. The man's parents, she decided, must have been frustrated comedians to have given him a name like Gunther Glick. No wonder the guy felt like he had something to prove. Nonetheless, despite his unfortunate appellative and annoying eagerness to make a mark, Glick was sweet . . . charming in a pasty, *Briddish*, unstrung sort of way. Like Hugh Grant on lithium.

'Shouldn't we be back at St Peter's?' Macri said as patiently as possible. 'We can check this mystery church out later. Conclave started an hour ago. What if the cardinals come to a decision while we're gone?'

Glick did not seem to hear. 'I think we go to the right, here.' He tilted the map and studied it again. 'Yes, if I take a right . . . and then an immediate left.' He began to pull out onto the narrow street before them.

'Look out!' Macri yelled. She was a video technician, and her eyes were sharp. Fortunately, Glick was pretty fast too. He slammed on the brakes and avoided entering the intersection just as a line of four Alfa Romeos appeared out of nowhere and tore by in a blur. Once past, the cars skidded, decelerating, and cut sharply left one block ahead, taking the exact route Glick had intended to take.

'Maniacs!' Macri shouted.

Glick looked shaken. 'Did you see that?'

'Yeah, I saw that! They almost killed us!'

'No, I mean the cars,' Glick said, his voice suddenly excited. 'They were all the same.'

'So they were maniacs with no imagination.'

'The cars were also full.'

'So what?'

'Four identical cars, *all* with four passengers?'

'You ever heard of carpooling?'

'In Italy?' Glick checked the intersection. 'They haven't even heard of unleaded gas.' He hit the accelerator and peeled out after the cars.

Macri was thrown back in her seat. 'What the hell are you doing?'

Glick accelerated down the street and hung a left after the Alfa Romeos. 'Something tells me you and I are not the only ones going to church right now.'

67

The descent was slow.

Langdon dropped rung by rung down the creaking ladder ... deeper and deeper beneath the floor of the Chigi Chapel. *Into the Demon's hole*, he thought. He was facing the side wall, his back to the chamber, and he wondered how many more dark, cramped spaces one day could provide. The ladder groaned with every step, and the pungent smell of rotting flesh and dampness was almost asphyxiating. Langdon wondered where the hell Olivetti was.

Vittoria's outline was still visible above, holding the blowtorch inside the hole, lighting Langdon's way. As he lowered himself deeper into the darkness, the bluish glow from above got fainter. The only thing that got stronger was the stench.

Twelve rungs down, it happened. Langdon's foot hit a spot that was slippery with decay, and he faltered. Lunging forward, he caught the ladder with his forearms to avoid plummeting to the bottom. Cursing the bruises now throbbing on his arms, he dragged his body back onto the ladder and began his descent again.

Three rungs deeper, he almost fell again, but this time it was not a rung that caused the mishap. It was a bolt of fear. He had descended past a hollowed niche in the wall before him and suddenly found himself face to face with a collection of skulls. As he caught his breath and looked around him, he realized the wall at this level was honeycombed with shelflike openings – burial niches – all filled with skeletons. In the phosphorescent light, it made for an eerie collection of empty sockets and decaying rib cages flickering around him.

Skeletons by firelight, he grimaced wryly, realizing he had quite coincidentally endured a similar evening just last month. *An evening of bones and flames.* The New York Museum of Archeology's candlelight benefit dinner – salmon flambé in the shadow of a brontosaurus skeleton. He had attended at the invitation of Rebecca Strauss – one-time fashion model now art critic from the *Times*, a whirlwind of black velvet, cigarettes, and not-so-subtly enhanced breasts. She'd called him twice since. Langdon had not returned her calls. *Most ungentlemanly*, he chided, wondering how long Rebecca Strauss would last in a stink-pit like this.

Langdon was relieved to feel the final rung give way to the spongy earth at the bottom. The ground beneath his shoes felt damp. Assuring himself the walls were not going to close in on him, he turned into the crypt. It was circular, about twenty feet across. Breathing through his sleeve again, Langdon turned his eyes to the body. In the gloom, the image was hazy. A white, fleshy outline. Facing the other direction. Motionless. Silent.

Advancing through the murkiness of the crypt, Langdon tried to make sense of what he was looking at. The man had his back to Langdon, and Langdon could not see his face, but he *did* indeed seem to be standing.

'Hello?' Langdon choked through his sleeve. Nothing. As he drew nearer, he realized the man was very short. *Too short . . .*

'What's happening?' Vittoria called from above, shifting the light.

Langdon did not answer. He was now close enough to see it all. With a tremor of repulsion, he understood. The chamber seemed to contract around him. Emerging like a demon from the earthen floor was an old man . . . or at least half of him. He was buried up to his waist in the earth. Standing upright with half of him below ground. Stripped naked. His hands tied behind his back with a red cardinal's sash. He was propped limply upward, spine arched backward like some sort of hideous punching bag. The man's head lay backward, eyes toward the heavens as if pleading for help from God himself.

'Is he dead?' Vittoria called.

Langdon moved toward the body. *I hope so, for his sake.* As he drew to within a few feet, he looked down at the upturned eyes. They bulged out-ward, blue and bloodshot. Langdon leaned down to listen for breath but immediately recoiled. 'For Christ's sake!'

'What!'

Langdon almost gagged. 'He's dead all right. I just saw the cause of death.' The sight was gruesome. The man's mouth had been jammed open and packed solid with dirt. 'Somebody stuffed a fistful of dirt down his throat. He suffocated.'

'Dirt?' Vittoria said. 'As in . . . *earth?*'

Langdon did a double take. *Earth.* He had almost forgotten. *The brands. Earth, Air, Fire, Water.* The killer had threatened to brand each victim with one of the ancient elements of science. The first element was *Earth. From Santi's earthly tomb.* Dizzy from the fumes, Langdon circled to the front of the body. As he did, the symbologist within him loudly reasserted the artistic challenge of creating the mythical ambigram. *Earth? How?* And yet, an instant later, it was before him. Centuries of Illuminati legend whirled in his mind. The marking on the cardinal's chest was charred and oozing. The flesh was seared black. *La lingua pura . . .*

Langdon stared at the brand as the room began to spin.

'Earth,' he whispered, tilting his head to see the symbol upside down.
'Earth.'

Then, in a wave of horror, he had one final cognition. *There are three
more.*

68

Despite the soft glow of candlelight in the Sistine Chapel, Cardinal Mortati was on edge. Conclave had officially begun. And it had begun in a most inauspicious fashion.

Half an hour ago, at the appointed hour, Camerlengo Carlo Ventresca had entered the chapel. He walked to the front altar and gave opening prayer. Then, he unfolded his hands and spoke to them in a tone as direct as anything Mortati had ever heard from the altar of the Sistine.

'You are well aware,' the camerlengo said, 'that our four *preferiti* are not present in conclave at this moment. I ask, in the name of his late Holiness, that you proceed as you must . . . with faith and purpose. May you have only God before your eyes.' Then he turned to go.

'But,' one cardinal blurted out, 'where *are* they?'

The camerlengo paused. 'That I cannot honestly say.'

'When will they return?'

'That I cannot honestly say.'

'Are they okay?'

'That I cannot honestly say.'

'*Will* they return?'

There was a long pause.

'Have faith,' the camerlengo said. Then he walked out of the room.

The doors to the Sistine Chapel had been sealed, as was the custom, with two heavy chains on the outside. Four Swiss Guards stood watch in the hallway beyond. Mortati knew the only way the doors could be opened now, prior to electing a Pope, was if someone inside fell deathly ill, or if the *preferiti* arrived. Mortati prayed it would be the latter, although from the knot in his stomach he was not so sure.

Proceed as we must, Mortati decided, taking his lead from the resolve in the camerlengo's voice. So he had called for a vote. What else could he do?

It had taken thirty minutes to complete the preparatory rituals leading up to this first vote. Mortati had waited patiently at the main altar as each cardinal, in order of seniority, had approached and performed the specific balloting procedure.

Now, at last, the final cardinal had arrived at the altar and was kneeling before him.

'I call as my witness,' the cardinal declared, exactly as those before him, 'Christ the Lord, who will be my judge that my vote is given to the one who before God I think should be elected.'

The cardinal stood up. He held his ballot high over his head for everyone to see. Then he lowered the ballot to the altar, where a plate sat atop a large chalice. He placed the ballot on the plate. Next he picked up the plate and used it to drop the ballot into the chalice. Use of the plate was to ensure no one secretly dropped multiple ballots.

After he had submitted his ballot, he replaced the plate over the chalice, bowed to the cross, and returned to his seat.

The final ballot had been cast.

Now it was time for Mortati to go to work.

Leaving the plate on top of the chalice, Mortati shook the ballots to mix them. Then he removed the plate and extracted a ballot at random. He unfolded it. The ballot was exactly two inches wide. He read aloud for everyone to hear.

'*Eligo in summum pontificem . . .*' he declared, reading the text that was embossed at the top of every ballot. *I elect as Supreme Pontiff . . .* Then he announced the nominee's name that had been written beneath it. After he read the name, he raised a threaded needle and pierced the ballot through the word *Eligo*, carefully sliding the ballot onto the thread. Then he made note of the vote in a logbook.

Next, he repeated the entire procedure. He chose a ballot from the chalice, read it aloud, threaded it onto the line, and made note in his log. Almost immediately, Mortati sensed this first vote would be failed. No consensus. After only seven ballots, already seven different cardinals had been named. As was normal, the handwriting on each ballot was disguised by block printing or flamboyant script. The concealment was ironic in this case because the cardinals were obviously submitting votes for themselves. This apparent conceit, Mortati knew, had nothing to do with self-centered ambition. It was a holding pattern. A defensive maneuver. A stall tactic to ensure no cardinal received enough votes to win . . . and another vote would be forced.

The cardinals were waiting for their *preferiti . . .*

When the last of the ballots had been tallied, Mortati declared the vote 'failed.'

He took the thread carrying all the ballots and tied the ends together to create a ring. Then he laid the ring of ballots on a silver tray. He added the proper chemicals and carried the tray to a small chimney behind him. Here he lit the ballots. As the ballots burned, the chemicals he'd added created

216

black smoke. The smoke flowed up a pipe to a hole in the roof where it rose above the chapel for all to see. Cardinal Mortati had just sent his first communication to the outside world.

One balloting. No Pope.

69

Nearly asphyxiated by fumes, Langdon struggled up the ladder toward the light at the top of the pit. Above him he heard voices, but nothing making sense. His head was spinning with images of the branded cardinal.

Earth . . . Earth . . .

As he pushed upward, his vision narrowed and he feared consciousness would slip away. Two rungs from the top, his balance faltered. He lunged upward trying to find the lip, but it was too far. He lost his grip on the ladder and almost tumbled backward into the dark. There was a sharp pain under his arms, and suddenly Langdon was airborne, legs swinging wildly out over the chasm.

The strong hands of two Swiss Guards hooked him under the armpits and dragged him skyward. A moment later Langdon's head emerged from the Demon's hole, choking and gasping for air. The guards dragged him over the lip of the opening, across the floor, and laid him down, back against the cold marble floor.

For a moment, Langdon was unsure where he was. Overhead he saw stars .. orbiting planets. Hazy figures raced past him. People were shouting. He tried to sit up. He was lying at the base of a stone pyramid. The familiar bite of an angry tongue echoed inside the chapel, and then Langdon knew.

Olivetti was screaming at Vittoria. 'Why the hell didn't you figure that out in the first place?'

Vittoria was trying to explain the situation.

Olivetti cut her off midsentence and turned to bark orders to his men. 'Get that body out of there! Search the rest of the building!'

Langdon tried to sit up. The Chigi Chapel was packed with Swiss Guards. The plastic curtain over the chapel opening had been torn off the entryway, and fresh air filled Langdon's lungs. As his senses slowly returned, Langdon saw Vittoria coming toward him. She knelt down, her face like an angel.

'You okay?' Vittoria took his arm and felt his pulse. Her hands were tender on his skin.

'Thanks.' Langdon sat up fully. 'Olivetti's mad.'

Vittoria nodded. 'He has a right to be. We blew it.'

'You mean *I* blew it.'

'So redeem yourself. Get him next time.'

Next time? Langdon thought it was a cruel comment. *There is no next time! We missed our shot!*

Vittoria checked Langdon's watch. 'Mickey says we've got forty minutes. Get your head together and help me find the next marker.'

'I told you, Vittoria, the sculptures are gone. The Path of Illumination is—' Langdon halted.

Vittoria smiled softly.

Suddenly Langdon was staggering to his feet. He turned dizzying circles, staring at the artwork around him. *Pyramids, stars, planets, ellipses.* Suddenly everything came back. *This is the first altar of science! Not the Pantheon!* It dawned on him now how perfectly Illuminati the chapel was, far more subtle and selective than the world famous Pantheon. The Chigi was an out of the way alcove, a literal hole-in-the-wall, a tribute to a great patron of science, decorated with earthly symbology. *Perfect.*

Langdon steadied himself against the wall and gazed up at the enormous pyramid sculptures. Vittoria was dead right. If *this* chapel was the first altar of science, it might still contain the Illuminati sculpture that served as the first marker. Langdon felt an electrifying rush of hope to realize there was still a chance. If the marker were indeed here, and they could follow it to the next altar of science, they might have another chance to catch the killer.

Vittoria moved closer. 'I found out who the unknown Illuminati sculptor was.'

Langdon's head whipped around. 'You *what?*'

'Now we just need to figure out which sculpture in here is the—'

'Wait a minute! You *know* who the Illuminati sculptor was?' He had spent years trying to find that information.

Vittoria smiled. 'It was Bernini.' She paused. '*The* Bernini.'

Langdon immediately knew she was mistaken. Bernini was an impossibility. Gianlorenzo Bernini was the second most famous sculptor of all time, his fame eclipsed only by Michelangelo himself. During the 1600s Bernini created more sculptures than any other artist. Unfortunately, the man they were looking for was supposedly an unknown, a nobody.

Vittoria frowned. 'You don't look excited.'

'Bernini is impossible.'

'Why? Bernini was a contemporary of Galileo. He was a brilliant sculptor.'

'He was a very famous man and a Catholic.'

'Yes,' Vittoria said. 'Exactly like Galileo.'

'No,' Langdon argued. '*Nothing* like Galileo. Galileo was a thorn in the Vatican's side. Bernini was the Vatican's wonder boy. The church *loved* Bernini. He was elected the Vatican's overall artistic authority. He practically lived inside Vatican City his entire life!'

'A perfect cover. Illuminati infiltration.'

Langdon felt flustered. 'Vittoria, the Illuminati members referred to their secret artist as *il maestro ignoto* – the unknown master.'

'Yes, unknown to *them*. Think of the secrecy of the Masons – only the upper-echelon members knew the whole truth. Galileo could have kept Bernini's true identity secret from most members . . . for Bernini's own safety. That way, the Vatican would never find out.'

Langdon was unconvinced but had to admit Vittoria's logic made strange sense. The Illuminati were famous for keeping secret information compartmentalized, only revealing the truth to upper-level members. It was the cornerstone of their ability to stay secret . . . very few knew the whole story.

'And Bernini's affiliation with the Illuminati,' Vittoria added with a smile, 'explains why he designed those two pyramids.'

Langdon turned to the huge sculpted pyramids and shook his head. 'Bernini was a *religious* sculptor. There's no way he carved those pyramids.'

Vittoria shrugged. 'Tell that to the sign behind you.'

Langdon turned to the plaque:

ART OF THE CHIGI CHAPEL
While the architecture is Raphael's,
all interior adornments are those of Gianlorenzo Bernini.

Langdon read the plaque twice, and still he was not convinced. Gianlorenzo Bernini was celebrated for his intricate, holy sculptures of the Virgin Mary, angels, prophets, Popes. What was he doing carving *pyramids*?

Langdon looked up at the towering monuments and felt totally disoriented. Two pyramids, each with a shining, elliptical medallion. They were about as un-Christian as sculpture could get. The pyramids, the stars above, the signs of the Zodiac. *All interior adornments are those of Gianlorenzo Bernini.* If that were true, Langdon realized, it meant Vittoria *had* to be right. By default, Bernini was the Illuminati's unknown master; nobody else had contributed artwork to this chapel! The implications came almost too fast for Langdon to process.

Bernini was an Illuminatus.
Bernini designed the Illuminati ambigrams.
Bernini laid out the path of Illumination.

Langdon could barely speak. Could it be that here in this tiny Chigi Chapel, the world-renowned Bernini had placed a sculpture that pointed across Rome toward the next altar of science?

'Bernini,' he said. 'I never would have guessed.'

'Who other than a famous Vatican artist would have had the clout to put his artwork in specific Catholic chapels around Rome and create the Path of Illumination? Certainly not an unknown.'

Langdon considered it. He looked at the pyramids, wondering if one of them could somehow be the marker. *Maybe both of them?* 'The pyramids face opposite directions,' Langdon said, not sure what to make of them. 'They are also identical, so I don't know which . . .'

'I don't think the pyramids are what we're looking for.'

'But they're the only sculptures here.'

Vittoria cut him off by pointing toward Olivetti and some of his guards who were gathered near the demon's hole.

Langdon followed the line of her hand to the far wall. At first he saw nothing. Then someone moved and he caught a glimpse. White marble. An arm. A torso. And then a sculpted face. Partially hidden in its niche. Two life-size human figures intertwined. Langdon's pulse accelerated. He had been so taken with the pyramids and demon's hole, he had not even seen this sculpture. He moved across the room, through the crowd. As he drew near, Langdon recognized the work was pure Bernini – the intensity of the artistic composition, the intricate faces and flowing clothing, all from the purest white marble Vatican money could buy. It was not until he was almost directly in front of it that Langdon recognized the sculpture itself. He stared up at the two faces and gasped.

'Who are they?' Vittoria urged, arriving behind him.

Langdon stood astonished. '*Habakkuk and the Angel*,' he said, his voice almost inaudible. The piece was a fairly well-known Bernini work that was included in some art history texts. Langdon had forgotten it was here.

'Habakkuk?'

'Yes. The prophet who predicted the annihilation of the earth.'

Vittoria looked uneasy. 'You think this is the marker?'

Langdon nodded in amazement. Never in his life had he been so sure of anything. This was the first Illuminati marker. No doubt. Although Langdon had fully expected the sculpture to somehow 'point' to the next altar of science, he did not expect it to be *literal*. Both the angel and Habakkuk had their arms outstretched and were pointing into the distance.

Langdon found himself suddenly smiling. 'Not too subtle, is it?'

Vittoria looked excited but confused. 'I see them pointing, but they are contradicting each other. The angel is pointing one way, and the prophet the other.'

Langdon chuckled. It was true. Although both figures were pointing into the distance, they were pointing in totally opposite directions. Langdon, however, had already solved that problem. With a burst of energy he headed for the door.

'Where are you going?' Vittoria called.

'Outside the building!' Langdon's legs felt light again as he ran toward the door. 'I need to see what direction that sculpture is pointing!'

'Wait! How do you know *which* finger to follow?'

'The poem,' he called over his shoulder. 'The last line!'

' "Let angels guide you on your lofty quest?" ' She gazed upward at the outstretched finger of the angel. Her eyes misted unexpectedly. 'Well I'll be damned!'

70

Gunther Glick and Chinita Macri sat parked in the BBC van in the shadows at the far end of Piazza del Popolo. They had arrived shortly after the four Alfa Romeos, just in time to witness an inconceivable chain of events. Chinita still had no idea what it all meant, but she'd made sure the camera was rolling.

As soon as they'd arrived, Chinita and Glick had seen a veritable army of young men pour out of the Alfa Romeos and surround the church. Some had weapons drawn. One of them, a stiff older man, led a team up the front steps of the church. The soldiers drew guns and blew the locks off the front doors. Macri heard nothing and figured they must have had silencers. Then the soldiers entered.

Chinita had recommended they sit tight and film from the shadows. After all, guns were guns, and they had a clear view of the action from the van. Glick had not argued. Now, across the piazza, men moved in and out of the church. They yelled to each other. Chinita adjusted her camera to follow a team as they searched the surrounding area. All of them, though dressed in civilian clothes, seemed to move with military precision. 'Who do you think they are?' she asked.

'Hell if I know.' Glick looked riveted. 'You getting all this?'

'Every frame.'

Glick sounded smug. 'Still think we should go back to Pope-Watch?'

Chinita wasn't sure what to say. There was obviously something going on here, but she had been in journalism long enough to know that there was often a very dull explanation for interesting events. 'This could be nothing,' she said. 'These guys could have gotten the same tip you got and are just checking it out. Could be a false alarm.'

Glick grabbed her arm. 'Over there! Focus.' He pointed back to the church.

Chinita swung the camera back to the top of the stairs. 'Hello there,' she said, training on the man now emerging from the church.

'Who's the dapper?'

Chinita moved in for a close-up. 'Haven't seen him before.' She tightened in on the man's face and smiled. 'But I wouldn't mind seeing him again.'

Robert Langdon dashed down the stairs outside the church and into the middle of the piazza. It was getting dark now, the springtime sun setting late in southern Rome. The sun had dropped below the surrounding buildings, and shadows streaked the square.

'Okay, Bernini,' he said aloud to himself. 'Where the hell is your angel pointing?'

He turned and examined the orientation of the church from which he had just come. He pictured the Chigi Chapel inside, and the sculpture of the angel inside that. Without hesitation he turned due west, into the glow of the impending sunset. Time was evaporating.

'Southwest,' he said, scowling at the shops and apartments blocking his view. 'The next marker is out there.'

Racking his brain, Langdon pictured page after page of Italian art history. Although very familiar with Bernini's work, Langdon knew the sculptor had been far too prolific for any nonspecialist to know all of it. Still, considering the relative fame of the first marker – *Habakkuk and the Angel* – Langdon hoped the second marker was a work he might know from memory.

Earth, Air, Fire, Water, he thought. *Earth* they had found – inside the Chapel of the Earth – Habakkuk, the prophet who predicted the earth's annihilation.

Air is next. Langdon urged himself to think. *A Bernini sculpture that has something to do with Air!* He was drawing a total blank. Still he felt energized. *I'm on the path of Illumination! It is still intact!*

Looking southwest, Langdon strained to see a spire or cathedral tower jutting up over the obstacles. He saw nothing. He needed a map. If they could figure out what churches were southwest of here, maybe one of them would spark Langdon's memory. *Air*, he pressed. *Air. Bernini. Sculpture. Air. Think!*

Langdon turned and headed back up the cathedral stairs. He was met beneath the scaffolding by Vittoria and Olivetti.

'Southwest,' Langdon said, panting. 'The next church is southwest of here.'

Olivetti's whisper was cold. 'You sure this time?'

Langdon didn't bite. 'We need a map. One that shows all the churches in Rome.'

The commander studied him a moment, his expression never changing.

Langdon checked his watch. 'We only have half an hour.'

Olivetti moved past Langdon down the stairs toward his car, parked directly in front of the cathedral. Langdon hoped he was going for a map.

Vittoria looked excited. 'So the angel's pointing southwest? No idea which churches are southwest?'

'I can't see past the damn buildings.' Langdon turned and faced the square again. 'And I don't know Rome's churches well enou—' He stopped.

Vittoria looked startled. 'What?'

Langdon looked out at the piazza again. Having ascended the church stairs, he was now higher, and his view was better. He still couldn't see anything, but he realized he was moving in the right direction. His eyes climbed the tower of rickety scaffolding above him. It rose six stories, almost to the top of the church's rose window, far higher than the other buildings in the square. He knew in an instant where he was headed.

Across the square, Chinita Macri and Gunther Glick sat glued to the windshield of the BBC van.

'You getting this?' Gunther asked.

Macri tightened her shot on the man now climbing the scaffolding. 'He's a little well dressed to be playing Spiderman if you ask me.'

'And who's Ms Spidey?'

Chinita glanced at the attractive woman beneath the scaffolding. 'Bet you'd like to find out.'

'Think I should call editorial?'

'Not yet. Let's watch. Better to have something in the can before we admit we abandoned conclave.'

'You think somebody really killed one of the old farts in there?'

Chinita clucked. 'You're *definitely* going to hell.'

'And I'll be taking the Pulitzer with me.'

71

The scaffolding seemed less stable the higher Langdon climbed. His view of Rome, however, got better with every step. He continued upward.

He was breathing harder than he expected when he reached the upper tier. He pulled himself onto the last platform, brushed off the plaster, and stood up. The height did not bother him at all. In fact, it was invigorating.

The view was staggering. Like an ocean on fire, the red-tiled rooftops of Rome spread out before him, glowing in the scarlet sunset. From that spot, for the first time in his life, Langdon saw beyond the pollution and traffic of Rome to its ancient roots – *Città di Dio* – The city of God.

Squinting into the sunset, Langdon scanned the rooftops for a church steeple or bell tower. But as he looked farther and farther toward the horizon, he saw nothing. *There are hundreds of churches in Rome*, he thought. *There must be one southwest of here! If the church is even visible*, he reminded himself. *Hell, if the church is even still standing!*

Forcing his eyes to trace the line slowly, he attempted the search again. He knew, of course, that not all churches would have visible spires, especially smaller, out-of-the-way sanctuaries. Not to mention, Rome had changed dramatically since the 1600s when churches were by law the tallest buildings allowed. Now, as Langdon looked out, he saw apartment buildings, high-rises, TV towers.

For the second time, Langdon's eye reached the horizon without seeing anything. Not one single spire. In the distance, on the very edge of Rome, Michelangelo's massive dome blotted the setting sun. St Peter's Basilica. Vatican City. Langdon found himself wondering how the cardinals were faring, and if the Swiss Guards' search had turned up the antimatter. Something told him it hadn't . . . and wouldn't.

The poem was rattling through his head again. He considered it, carefully, line by line. *From Santi's earthly tomb with demon's hole.* They had found Santi's tomb. *'Cross Rome the mystic elements unfold.* The mystic elements were Earth, Air, Fire, Water. *The path of light is laid, the sacred test.* The path of Illumination formed by Bernini's sculptures. *Let angels guide you on your lofty quest.*

The angel was pointing southwest . . .

'Front stairs!' Glick exclaimed, pointing wildly through the windshield of the BBC van. 'Something's going on!'

Macri dropped her shot back down to the main entrance. Something was definitely going on. At the bottom of the stairs, the military-looking man had pulled one of the Alfa Romeos close to the stairs and opened the trunk. Now he was scanning the square as if checking for onlookers. For a moment, Macri thought the man had spotted them, but his eyes kept moving. Apparently satisfied, he pulled out a walkie-talkie and spoke into it.

Almost instantly, it seemed an army emerged from the church. Like an American football team breaking from a huddle, the soldiers formed a straight line across the top of the stairs. Moving like a human wall, they began to descend. Behind them, almost entirely hidden by the wall, four soldiers seemed to be carrying something. Something heavy. Awkward.

Glick leaned forward on the dashboard. 'Are they stealing something from the church?'

Chinita tightened her shot even more, using the telephoto to probe the wall of men, looking for an opening. *One split second*, she willed. *A single frame. That's all I need.* But the men moved as one. *Come on!* Macri stayed with them, and it paid off. When the soldiers tried to lift the object into the trunk, Macri found her opening. Ironically, it was the older man who faltered. Only for an instant, but long enough. Macri had her frame. Actually, it was more like ten frames.

'Call editorial,' Chinita said. 'We've got a dead body.'

Far away, at CERN, Maximilian Kohler maneuvered his wheelchair into Leonardo Vetra's study. With mechanical efficiency, he began sifting through Vetra's files. Not finding what he was after, Kohler moved to Vetra's bedroom. The top drawer of his bedside table was locked. Kohler pried it open with a knife from the kitchen.

Inside Kohler found exactly what he was looking for.

72

Langdon swung off the scaffolding and dropped back to the ground. He brushed the plaster dust from his clothes. Vittoria was there to greet him.

'No luck?' she said.

He shook his head.

'They put the cardinal in the trunk.'

Langdon looked over to the parked car where Olivetti and a group of soldiers now had a map spread out on the hood. 'Are they looking south-west?'

She nodded. 'No churches. From here the first one you hit is St Peter's.'

Langdon grunted. At least they were in agreement. He moved toward Olivetti. The soldiers parted to let him through.

Olivetti looked up. 'Nothing. But this doesn't show every last church. Just the big ones. About fifty of them.'

'Where are we?' Langdon asked.

Olivetti pointed to Piazza del Popolo and traced a straight line exactly southwest. The line missed, by a substantial margin, the cluster of black squares indicating Rome's major churches. Unfortunately, Rome's major churches were also Rome's older churches . . . those that would have been around in the 1600s.

'I've got some decisions to make,' Olivetti said. 'Are you *certain* of the direction?'

Langdon pictured the angel's outstretched finger, the urgency rising in him again. 'Yes, sir. Positive.'

Olivetti shrugged and traced the straight line again. The path intersected the Queen Margherita Bridge, Via Cola di Riezo, and passed through Piazza del Risorgimento, hitting no churches at all until it deadended abruptly at the center of St Peter's Square.

'What's wrong with St Peter's?' one of the soldiers said. He had a deep scar under his left eye. 'It's a church.'

Langdon shook his head. 'Needs to be a public place. Hardly seems public at the moment.'

'But the line goes through St Peter's *Square*,' Vittoria added, looking over Langdon's shoulder. 'The square is public.'

Langdon had already considered it. 'No statues, though.'

'Isn't there a monolith in the middle?'

She was right. There was an Egyptian monolith in St Peter's Square. Langdon looked out at the monolith in the piazza in front of them. *The lofty pyramid.* An odd coincidence, he thought. He shook it off. 'The Vatican's monolith is not by Bernini. It was brought in by Caligula. And it has nothing to do with *Air.*' There was another problem as well. 'Besides, the poem says the elements are spread across *Rome.* St Peter's Square is in Vatican City. Not Rome.'

'Depends who you ask,' a guard interjected.

Langdon looked up. 'What?'

'Always a bone of contention. Most maps show St Peter's Square as part of Vatican City, but because it's *outside* the walled city, Roman officials for centuries have claimed it as part of Rome.'

'You're kidding,' Langdon said. He had never known that.

'I only mention it,' the guard continued, 'because Commander Olivetti and Ms Vetra were asking about a sculpture that had to do with Air.'

Langdon was wide-eyed. 'And you know of one in St Peter's Square?'

'Not exactly. It's not really a sculpture. Probably not relevant.'

'Let's hear it,' Olivetti pressed.

The guard shrugged. 'The only reason I know about it is because I'm usually on piazza duty. I know every corner of St Peter's Square.'

'The sculpture,' Langdon urged. 'What does it look like?' Langdon was starting to wonder if the Illuminati could really have been gutsy enough to position their second marker right outside St Peter's Church.

'I patrol past it every day,' the guard said. 'It's in the center, directly where that line is pointing. That's what made me think of it. As I said, it's not really a sculpture. It's more of a . . . block.'

Olivetti looked mad. 'A block?'

'Yes, sir. A marble block embedded in the square. At the base of the monolith. But the block is not a rectangle. It's an ellipse. And the block is carved with the image of a billowing gust of wind.' He paused. '*Air,* I suppose, if you wanted to get scientific about it.'

Langdon stared at the young soldier in amazement. 'A relief!' he exclaimed suddenly.

Everyone looked at him.

'*Relief,*' Langdon said, 'is the other half of sculpture!' *Sculpture is the art of shaping figures in the round and also in relief.* He had written the definition on chalkboards for years. Reliefs were essentially two-dimensional sculptures, like Abraham Lincoln's profile on the penny. Bernini's Chigi Chapel medallions were another perfect example.

'*Bassorilievo?*' the guard asked, using the Italian art term.

'Yes! *Bas-relief!*' Langdon rapped his knuckles on the hood. 'I wasn't thinking in those terms! That tile you're talking about in St Peter's Square is called the *West Ponente* – the West Wind. It's also known as *Respiro di Dio.*'

'Breath of God?'

'Yes! *Air!* And it was carved and put there by the original architect!'

Vittoria looked confused. 'But I thought Michelangelo designed St Peter's.'

'Yes, the *basilica!*' Langdon exclaimed, triumph in his voice. 'But St Peter's *Square* was designed by Bernini!'

As the caravan of Alfa Romeos tore out of Piazza del Popolo, everyone was in too much of a hurry to notice the BBC van pulling out behind them.

73

Gunther Glick floored the BBC van's accelerator and swerved through traffic as he tailed the four speeding Alfa Romeos across the Tiber River on Ponte Margherita. Normally Glick would have made an effort to maintain an inconspicuous distance, but today he could barely keep up. These guys were flying.

Macri sat in her work area in the back of the van finishing a phone call with London. She hung up and yelled to Glick over the sound of the traffic. 'You want the good news or bad news?'

Glick frowned. Nothing was ever simple when dealing with the home office. 'Bad news.'

'Editorial is burned we abandoned our post.'

'Surprise.'

'They also think your tipster is a fraud.'

'Of course.'

'And the boss just warned me that you're a few crumpets short of a proper tea.'

Glick scowled. 'Great. And the good news?'

'They agreed to look at the footage we just shot.'

Glick felt his scowl soften into a grin. *I guess we'll see who's short of a few crumpets.* 'So fire it off.'

'Can't transmit until we stop and get a fixed cell read.'

Glick gunned the van onto Via Cola di Rienzo. 'Can't stop now.' He tailed the Alfa Romeos through a hard left swerve around Piazza Risorgimento.

Macri held on to her computer gear in back as everything slid. 'Break my transmitter,' she warned, 'and we'll have to *walk* this footage to London.'

'Sit tight, love. Something tells me we're almost there.'

Macri looked up. 'Where?'

Glick gazed out at the familiar dome now looming directly in front of them. He smiled. 'Right back where we started.'

The four Alfa Romeos slipped deftly into traffic surrounding St Peter's Square. They split up and spread out along the piazza perimeter, quietly unloading men at select points. The debarking guards moved into the throng of tourists and media vans on the edge of the square and instantly became invisible. Some of the guards entered the forest of pillars encompassing the colonnade. They too seemed to evaporate into the surroundings. As Langdon watched through the windshield, he sensed a noose tightening around St Peter's.

In addition to the men Olivetti had just dispatched, the commander had radioed ahead to the Vatican and sent additional undercover guards to the center where Bernini's *West Ponente* was located. As Langdon looked out at the wide-open spaces of St Peter's Square, a familiar question nagged. *How does the Illuminati assassin plan to get away with this? How will he get a cardinal through all these people and kill him in plain view?* Langdon checked his Mickey Mouse watch. It was 8.54 P.M. Six minutes.

In the front seat, Olivetti turned and faced Langdon and Vittoria. 'I want you two right on top of this Bernini brick or block or whatever the hell it is. Same drill. You're tourists. Use the phone if you see anything.'

Before Langdon could respond, Vittoria had his hand and was pulling him out of the car.

The springtime sun was setting behind St Peter's Basilica, and a massive shadow spread, engulfing the piazza. Langdon felt an ominous chill as he and Vittoria moved into the cool, black umbra. Snaking through the crowd, Langdon found himself searching every face they passed, wondering if the killer was among them. Vittoria's hand felt warm.

As they crossed the open expanse of St Peter's Square, Langdon sensed Bernini's sprawling piazza having the exact effect the artist had been commissioned to create – that of 'humbling all those who entered.' Langdon certainly felt humbled at the moment. *Humbled and hungry*, he realized, surprised such a mundane thought could enter his head at a moment like this.

'To the obelisk?' Vittoria asked.

Langdon nodded, arching left across the piazza.

'Time?' Vittoria asked, walking briskly, but casually.

'Five of.'

Vittoria said nothing, but Langdon felt her grip tighten. He was still carrying the gun. He hoped Vittoria would not decide she needed it. He could not imagine her whipping out a weapon in St Peter's Square and blowing away the kneecaps of some killer while the global media looked on. Then again, an incident like that would be nothing compared to the branding and murder of a cardinal out here.

Air, Langdon thought. *The second element of science.* He tried to picture the brand. The method of murder. Again he scanned the sprawling expanse of granite beneath his feet – St Peter's Square – an open desert surrounded by Swiss Guard. If the Hassassin really dared attempt this, Langdon could not imagine how he would escape.

In the center of the piazza rose Caligula's 350-ton Egyptian obelisk. It stretched eighty-one feet skyward to the pyramidal apex onto which was affixed a hollow iron cross. Sufficiently high to catch the last of the evening sun, the cross shone as if magic . . . purportedly containing relics of the cross on which Christ was crucified.

Two fountains flanked the obelisk in perfect symmetry. Art historians knew the fountains marked the exact geometric focal points of Bernini's elliptical piazza, but it was an architectural oddity Langdon had never really considered until today. It seemed Rome was suddenly filled with ellipses, pyramids, and startling geometry.

As they neared the obelisk, Vittoria slowed. She exhaled heavily, as if coaxing Langdon to relax along with her. Langdon made the effort, lowering his shoulders and loosening his clenched jaw.

Somewhere around the obelisk, boldly positioned outside the largest church in the world, was the second altar of science – Bernini's *West Ponente* – an elliptical block in St Peter's Square.

Gunther Glick watched from the shadows of the pillars surrounding St Peter's Square. On any other day the man in the tweed jacket and the woman in khaki shorts would not have interested him in the least. They appeared to be nothing but tourists enjoying the square. But today was not any other day. Today had been a day of phone tips, corpses, unmarked cars racing through Rome, and men in tweed jackets climbing scaffolding in search of God only knew what. Glick would stay with them.

He looked out across the square and saw Macri. She was exactly where he had told her to go, on the far side of the couple, hovering on their flank. Macri carried her video camera casually, but despite her imitation of a bored member of the press, she stood out more than Glick would have liked. No other reporters were in this far corner of the square, and the acronym 'BBC' stenciled on her camera was drawing some looks from tourists.

The tape Macri had shot earlier of the naked body dumped in the trunk was playing at this very moment on the VCR transmitter back in the van. Glick knew the images were sailing over his head right now en route to London. He wondered what editorial would say.

He wished he and Macri had reached the body sooner, before the army of plainclothed soldiers had intervened. The same army, he knew, had now fanned out and surrounded this piazza. Something big was about to happen.

The media is the right arm of anarchy, the killer had said. Glick wondered if he had missed his chance for a big scoop. He looked out at the other media vans in the distance and watched Macri tailing the mysterious couple across the piazza. Something told Glick he was still in the game . . .

74

Langdon saw what he was looking for a good ten yards before they reached it. Through the scattered tourists, the white marble ellipse of Bernini's *West Ponente* stood out against the gray granite cubes that made up the rest of the piazza. Vittoria apparently saw it too. Her hand tensed.

'Relax,' Langdon whispered. 'Do your piranha thing.'

Vittoria loosened her grip.

As they drew nearer, everything seemed forbiddingly normal. Tourists wandered, nuns chatted along the perimeter of the piazza, a girl fed pigeons at the base of the obelisk.

Langdon refrained from checking his watch. He knew it was almost time.

The elliptical stone arrived beneath their feet, and Langdon and Vittoria slowed to a stop – not overeagerly – just two tourists pausing dutifully at a point of mild interest.

'*West Ponente*,' Vittoria said, reading the inscription on the stone.

Langdon gazed down at the marble relief and felt suddenly naïve. Not in his art books, not in his numerous trips to Rome, not *ever* had *West Ponente's* significance jumped out at him.

Not until now.

The relief was elliptical, about three feet long, and carved with a rudimentary face – a depiction of the West Wind as an angel–like countenance. Gusting from the angel's mouth, Bernini had drawn a powerful breath of air blowing outward away from the Vatican . . . *the breath of God*. This was Bernini's tribute to the second element . . . Air . . . an ethereal zephyr blown from angel's lips. As Langdon stared, he realized the significance of the relief went deeper still. Bernini had carved the air in *five* distinct gusts . . . five! What was more, flanking the medallion were *two* shining stars. Langdon thought of Galileo. *Two stars, five gusts, ellipses, symmetry* . . . He felt hollow. His head hurt.

Vittoria began walking again almost immediately, leading Langdon away from the relief. 'I think someone's following us,' she said.

Langdon looked up. 'Where?'

Vittoria moved a good thirty yards before speaking. She pointed up at the Vatican as if showing Langdon something on the dome. 'The same person has been behind us all the way across the square.' Casually, Vittoria glanced over her shoulder. 'Still on us. Keep moving.'

'You think it's the Hassassin?'

Vittoria shook her head. 'Not unless the Illuminati hires women with BBC cameras.'

When the bells of St Peter's began their deafening clamor, both Langdon and Vittoria jumped. It was time. They had circled away from *West Ponente* in an attempt to lose the reporter but were now moving back toward the relief.

Despite the clanging bells, the area seemed perfectly calm. Tourists wandered. A homeless drunk dozed awkwardly at the base of the obelisk. A little girl fed pigeons. Langdon wondered if the reporter had scared the killer off. *Doubtful,* he decided, recalling the killer's promise. *I will make your cardinals media luminaries.*

As the echo of the ninth bell faded away, a peaceful silence descended across the square.

Then . . . the little girl began to scream.

75

Langdon was the first to reach the screaming girl.

The terrified youngster stood frozen, pointing at the base of the obelisk where a shabby, decrepit drunk sat slumped on the stairs. The man was a miserable sight . . . apparently one of Rome's homeless. His gray hair hung in greasy strands in front of his face, and his entire body was wrapped in some sort of dirty cloth. The girl kept screaming as she scampered off into the crowd.

Langdon felt an upsurge of dread as he dashed toward the invalid. There was a dark, widening stain spreading across the man's rags. Fresh, flowing blood.

Then, it was as if everything happened at once.

The old man seemed to crumple in the middle, tottering forward. Langdon lunged, but he was too late. The man pitched forward, toppled off the stairs, and hit the pavement face down. Motionless.

Langdon dropped to his knees. Vittoria arrived beside him. A crowd was gathering.

Vittoria put her fingers on the man's throat from behind. 'There's a pulse,' she declared. 'Roll him.'

Langdon was already in motion. Grasping the man's shoulders, he rolled the body. As he did, the loose rags seemed to slough away like dead flesh. The man flopped limp onto his back. Dead center of his naked chest was a wide area of charred flesh.

Vittoria gasped and pulled back.

Langdon felt paralyzed, pinned somewhere between nausea and awe. The symbol had a terrifying simplicity to it.

'Air,' Vittoria choked. 'It's . . . him.'

Swiss Guards appeared from out of nowhere, shouting orders, racing after an unseen assassin.

Nearby, a tourist explained that only minutes ago, a dark-skinned man had been kind enough to help this poor, wheezing, homeless man across the square . . . even sitting a moment on the stairs with the invalid before disappearing back into the crowd.

Vittoria ripped the rest of the rags off the man's abdomen. He had two deep puncture wounds, one on either side of the brand, just below his rib cage. She cocked the man's head back and began to administer mouth to mouth. Langdon was not prepared for what happened next. As Vittoria blew, the wounds on either side of the man's midsection hissed and sprayed blood into the air like blowholes on a whale. The salty liquid hit Langdon in the face.

Vittoria stopped short, looking horrified. 'His lungs . . .' she stammered. 'They're . . . punctured.'

Langdon wiped his eyes as he looked down at the two perforations. The holes gurgled. The cardinal's lungs were destroyed. He was gone.

Vittoria covered the body as the Swiss Guards moved in.

Langdon stood, disoriented. As he did, he saw her. The woman who had been following them earlier was crouched nearby. Her BBC video camera was shouldered, aimed, and running. She and Langdon locked eyes, and he knew she'd gotten it all. Then, like a cat, she bolted.

76

Chinita Macri was on the run. She had the story of her life.

Her video camera felt like an anchor as she lumbered across St Peter's Square, pushing through the gathering crowd. Everyone seemed to be moving in the opposite direction than her ... *toward* the commotion. Macri was trying to get as far away as possible. The man in the tweed jacket had seen her, and now she sensed others were after her, men she could not see, closing in from all sides.

Macri was still aghast from the images she had just recorded. She wondered if the dead man was really who she feared he was. Glick's mysterious phone contact suddenly seemed a little less crazy.

As she hurried in the direction of the BBC van, a young man with a decidedly militaristic air emerged from the crowd before her. Their eyes met, and they both stopped. Like lightning, he raised a walkie-talkie and spoke into it. Then he moved toward her. Macri wheeled and doubled back into the crowd, her heart pounding.

As she stumbled through the mass of arms and legs, she removed the spent video cassette from her camera. *Cellulose gold,* she thought, tucking the tape under her belt flush to her backside and letting her coat tails cover it. For once she was glad she carried some extra weight. *Glick, where the hell are you!*

Another soldier appeared to her left, closing in. Macri knew she had little time. She banked into the crowd again. Yanking a blank cartridge from her case, she slapped it into the camera. Then she prayed.

She was thirty yards from the BBC van when the two men materialized directly in front of her, arms folded. She was going nowhere.

'Film,' one snapped. 'Now.'

Macri recoiled, wrapping her arms protectively around her camera. 'No chance.'

One of the men pulled aside his jacket, revealing a sidearm.

'So shoot me,' Macri said, amazed by the boldness of her voice.

'Film,' the first one repeated.

Where the devil is Glick? Macri stamped her foot and yelled as loudly as possible, 'I am a professional videographer with the BBC! By Article 12 of the Free Press Act, this film is property of the British Broadcasting Corporation!'

The men did not flinch. The one with the gun took a step toward her. 'I am a lieutenant with the Swiss Guard, and by the Holy Doctrine governing the property on which you are now standing, you are subject to search and seizure.'

A crowd had started to gather now around them.

Macri yelled, 'I will not under any circumstances give you the film in this camera without speaking to my editor in London. I suggest you—'

The guards ended it. One yanked the camera out of her hands. The other forcibly grabbed her by the arm and twisted her in the direction of the Vatican. '*Grazie*,' he said, leading her through a jostling crowd.

Macri prayed they would not search her and find the tape. If she could somehow protect the film long enough to—

Suddenly, the unthinkable happened. Someone in the crowd was groping under her coat. Macri felt the video yanked away from her. She wheeled, but swallowed her words. Behind her, a breathless Gunther Glick gave her a wink and dissolved back into the crowd.

77

Robert Langdon staggered into the private bathroom adjoining the Office of the Pope. He dabbed the blood from his face and lips. The blood was not his own. It was that of Cardinal Lamassé, who had just died horribly in the crowded square outside the Vatican. *Virgin sacrifices on the altars of science.* So far, the Hassassin had made good on his threat.

Langdon felt powerless as he gazed into the mirror. His eyes were drawn, and stubble had begun to darken his cheeks. The room around him was immaculate and lavish – black marble with gold fixtures, cotton towels, and scented hand soaps.

Langdon tried to rid his mind of the bloody brand he had just seen. Air. The image stuck. He had witnessed three ambigrams since waking up this morning . . . and he knew there were two more coming.

Outside the door, it sounded as if Olivetti, the camerlengo, and Captain Rocher were debating what to do next. Apparently, the antimatter search had turned up nothing so far. Either the guards had missed the canister, or the intruder had gotten deeper inside the Vatican than Commander Olivetti had been willing to entertain.

Langdon dried his hands and face. Then he turned and looked for a urinal. No urinal. Just a bowl. He lifted the lid.

As he stood there, tension ebbing from his body, a giddy wave of exhaustion shuddered through his core. The emotions knotting his chest were so many, so incongruous. He was fatigued, running on no food or sleep, walking the Path of Illumination, traumatized by two brutal murders. Langdon felt a deepening horror over the possible outcome of this drama.

Think, he told himself. His mind was blank.

As he flushed, an unexpected realization hit him. *This is the Pope's toilet,* he thought. *I just took a leak in the Pope's toilet.* He had to chuckle. *The Holy Throne.*

78

In London, a BBC technician ejected a video cassette from a satellite receiver unit and dashed across the control room floor. She burst into the office of the editor-in-chief, slammed the video into his VCR, and pressed play.

As the tape rolled, she told him about the conversation she had just had with Gunther Glick in Vatican City. In addition, BBC photo archives had just given her a positive ID on the victim in St Peter's Square.

When the editor-in-chief emerged from his office, he was ringing a cow-bell. Everything in editorial stopped.

'Live in five!' the man boomed. 'On-air talent to prep! Media coordinators, I want your contacts on-line! We've got a story we're selling! And we've got film!'

The market coordinators grabbed their Rolodexes.

'Film specs!' one of them yelled.

'Thirty-second trim,' the chief replied.

'Content?'

'Live homicide.'

The coordinators looked encouraged. 'Usage and licensing price?'

'A million U.S. per.'

Heads shot up. 'What!'

'You heard me! I want top of the food chain. CNN, MSNBC, then the big three! Offer a dial-in preview. Give them five minutes to piggyback before BBC runs it.'

'What the hell happened?' someone demanded. 'The prime minister get skinned alive?'

The chief shook his head. 'Better.'

At that exact instant, somewhere in Rome, the Hassassin enjoyed a fleeting moment of repose in a comfortable chair. He admired the legendary chamber around him. *I am sitting in the Church of Illumination*, he thought. *The Illuminati lair.* He could not believe it was still here after all of these centuries.

Dutifully, he dialed the BBC reporter to whom he had spoken earlier. It was time. The world had yet to hear the most shocking news of all.

79

Vittoria Vetra sipped a glass of water and nibbled absently at some tea scones just set out by one of the Swiss Guards. She knew she should eat, but she had no appetite. The Office of the Pope was bustling now, echoing with tense conversations. Captain Rocher, Commander Olivetti, and half a dozen guards assessed the damage and debated the next move.

Robert Langdon stood nearby staring out at St Peter's Square. He looked dejected. Vittoria walked over. 'Ideas?'

He shook his head.

'Scone?'

His mood seemed to brighten at the sight of food. 'Hell yes. Thanks.' He ate voraciously.

The conversation behind them went quiet suddenly when two Swiss Guards escorted Camerlengo Ventresca through the door. If the chamberlain had looked drained before, Vittoria thought, now he looked empty.

'What happened?' the camerlengo said to Olivetti. From the look on the camerlengo's face, he appeared to have already been told the worst of it.

Olivetti's official update sounded like a battlefield casualty report. He gave the facts with flat efficacy. 'Cardinal Ebner was found dead in the church of Santa Maria del Popolo just after eight o'clock. He had been suffocated and branded with the ambigrammatic word "Earth." Cardinal Lamassé was murdered in St Peter's Square ten minutes ago. He died of perforations to the chest. He was branded with the word "Air," also ambigrammatic. The killer escaped in both instances.'

The camerlengo crossed the room and sat heavily behind the Pope's desk. He bowed his head.

'Cardinals Guidera and Baggia, however, are still alive.'

The camerlengo's head shot up, his expression pained. 'This is our consolation? Two cardinals have been murdered, commander. And the other two will obviously not be alive much longer unless you find them.'

'We will find them,' Olivetti assured. 'I am encouraged.'

'Encouraged? We've had nothing but failure.'

'Untrue. We've lost two battles, signore, but we're winning the war. The Illuminati had intended to turn this evening into a media circus. So far we

243

have thwarted their plan. Both cardinals' bodies have been recovered without incident. In addition,' Olivetti continued, 'Captain Rocher tells me he is making excellent headway on the antimatter search.'

Captain Rocher stepped forward in his red beret. Vittoria thought he looked more human somehow than the other guards – stern but not so rigid. Rocher's voice was emotional and crystalline, like a violin. 'I am hopeful we will have the canister for you within an hour, signore.'

'Captain,' the camerlengo said, 'excuse me if I seem less than hopeful, but I was under the impression that a search of Vatican City would take far more time than we have.'

'A *full* search, yes. However, after assessing the situation, I am confident the antimatter canister is located in one of our white zones – those Vatican sectors accessible to public tours – the museums and St Peter's Basilica, for example. We have already killed power in those zones and are conducting our scan.'

'You intend to search only a small *percentage* of Vatican City?'

'Yes, signore. It is highly unlikely that an intruder gained access to the inner zones of Vatican City. The fact that the missing security camera was stolen from a public access area – a stairwell in one of the museums – clearly implies that the intruder had limited access. Therefore he would only have been able to *relocate* the camera and antimatter in another public access area. It is these areas on which we are focusing our search.'

'But the intruder kidnapped four cardinals. That certainly implies deeper infiltration than we thought.'

'Not necessarily. We must remember that the cardinals spent much of today in the Vatican museums and St Peter's Basilica, enjoying those areas without the crowds. It is probable that the missing cardinals were taken in one of these areas.'

'But how were they removed from our walls?'

'We are still assessing that.'

'I see.' The camerlengo exhaled and stood up. He walked over to Olivetti. 'Commander, I would like to hear your contingency plan for evacuation.'

'We are still formalizing that, signore. In the meantime, I am faithful Captain Rocher will find the canister.'

Rocher clicked his boots as if in appreciation of the vote of confidence. 'My men have already scanned two-thirds of the white zones. Confidence is high.'

The camerlengo did not appear to share that confidence.

At that moment the guard with a scar beneath one eye came through the door carrying a clipboard and a map. He strode toward Langdon. 'Mr Langdon? I have the information you requested on the *West Ponente*.'

Langdon swallowed his scone. 'Good. Let's have a look.'

The others kept talking while Vittoria joined Robert and the guard as they spread out the map on the Pope's desk.

The soldier pointed to St Peter's Square. 'This is where we are. The central line of *West Ponente's* breath points due east, directly away from Vatican City.' The guard traced a line with his finger from St Peter's Square across the Tiber River and up into the heart of old Rome. 'As you can see, the line passes through almost all of Rome. There are about twenty Catholic churches that fall near this line.'

Langdon slumped. '*Twenty?*'

'Maybe more.'

'Do any of the churches fall *directly* on the line?'

'Some look closer than others,' the guard said, 'but translating the exact bearing of the *West Ponente* onto a map leaves margin for error.'

Langdon looked out at St Peter's Square a moment. Then he scowled, stroking his chin. 'How about *fire*? Any of them have Bernini artwork that has to do with fire?'

Silence.

'How about obelisks?' he demanded. 'Are any of the churches located near obelisks?'

The guard began checking the map.

Vittoria saw a glimmer of hope in Langdon's eyes and realized what he was thinking. *He's right!* The first two markers had been located on or near piazzas that contained obelisks! Maybe obelisks were a theme? Soaring pyramids marking the Illuminati path? The more Vittoria thought about it, the more perfect it seemed . . . four towering beacons rising over Rome to mark the altars of science.

'It's a long shot,' Langdon said, 'but I know that many of Rome's obelisks were erected or moved during Bernini's reign. He was no doubt involved in their placement.'

'Or,' Vittoria added, 'Bernini could have placed his markers *near* existing obelisks.'

Langdon nodded. 'True.'

'Bad news,' the guard said. 'No obelisks on the line.' He traced his finger across the map. 'None even remotely close. Nothing.'

Langdon sighed.

Vittoria's shoulders slumped. She'd thought it was a promising idea. Apparently, this was not going to be as easy as they'd hoped. She tried to stay positive. 'Robert, think. You must know of a Bernini statue relating to *fire*. Anything at all.'

'Believe me, I've been thinking. Bernini was incredibly prolific. Hundreds of works. I was hoping *West Ponente* would point to a single church. Something that would ring a bell.'

'*Fuòco*,' she pressed. '*Fire*. No Bernini titles jump out?'

Langdon shrugged. 'There's his famous sketches of *Fireworks*, but they're not sculpture, and they're in Leipzig, Germany.'

Vittoria frowned. 'And you're sure the *breath* is what indicates the direction?'

'You saw the relief, Vittoria. The design was totally symmetrical. The only indication of bearing was the breath.'

Vittoria knew he was right.

'Not to mention,' he added, 'because the *West Ponente* signifies *Air*, following the *breath* seems symbolically appropriate.'

Vittoria nodded. *So we follow the breath. But where?*

Olivetti came over. 'What have you got?'

'Too many churches,' the soldier said. 'Two dozen or so. I suppose we could put four men on each church—'

'Forget it,' Olivetti said. 'We missed this guy twice when we knew exactly where he was going to be. A mass stakeout means leaving Vatican City unprotected and canceling the search.'

'We need a reference book,' Vittoria said. 'An index of Bernini's work. If we can scan titles, maybe something will jump out.'

'I don't know,' Langdon said. 'If it's a work Bernini created specifically for the Illuminati, it may be very obscure. It probably won't be listed in a book.'

Vittoria refused to believe it. 'The other two sculptures were fairly well-known. You'd heard of them both.'

Langdon shrugged. 'Yeah.'

'If we scan titles for references to the word "fire," maybe we'll find a statue that's listed as being in the right direction.'

Langdon seemed convinced it was worth a shot. He turned to Olivetti. 'I need a list of all Bernini's work. You guys probably don't have a coffee-table Bernini book around here, do you?'

'Coffee-table book?' Olivetti seemed unfamiliar with the term.

'Never mind. Any list. How about the Vatican Museum? They must have Bernini references.'

The guard with the scar frowned. 'Power in the museum is out, and the records room is enormous. Without the staff there to help—'

'The Bernini work in question,' Olivetti interrupted. 'Would it have been created while Bernini was employed here at the Vatican?'

'Almost definitely,' Langdon said. 'He was here almost his entire career. And certainly during the time period of the Galileo conflict.'

Olivetti nodded. 'Then there's another reference.'

Vittoria felt a flicker of optimism. 'Where?'

The commander did not reply. He took his guard aside and spoke in hushed tones. The guard seemed uncertain but nodded obediently. When Olivetti was finished talking, the guard turned to Langdon.

'This way please, Mr Langdon. It's nine-fifteen. We'll have to hurry.'

Langdon and the guard headed for the door.

Vittoria started after them. 'I'll help.'

Olivetti caught her by the arm. 'No, Ms Vetra. I need a word with you.' His grasp was authoritative.

Langdon and the guard left. Olivetti's face was wooden as he took

Vittoria aside. But whatever it was Olivetti had intended to say to her, he never got the chance. His walkie-talkie crackled loudly. '*Comandante?*'

Everyone in the room turned.

The voice on the transmitter was grim. 'I think you better turn on the television.'

80

When Langdon had left the Vatican Secret Archives only two hours ago, he had never imagined he would see them again. Now, winded from having jogged the entire way with his Swiss Guard escort, Langdon found himself back at the archives once again.

His escort, the guard with the scar, now led Langdon through the rows of translucent cubicles. The silence of the archives felt somehow more forbidding now, and Langdon was thankful when the guard broke it.

'Over here, I think,' he said, escorting Langdon to the back of the chamber where a series of smaller vaults lined the wall. The guard scanned the titles on the vaults and motioned to one of them. 'Yes, here it is. Right where the commander said it would be.'

Langdon read the title. ATTIVI VATICANI. Vatican assets? He scanned the list of contents. Real estate . . . currency . . . Vatican Bank . . . antiquities . . . The list went on.

'Paperwork of all Vatican assets,' the guard said.

Langdon looked at the cubicle. *Jesus.* Even in the dark, he could tell it was packed.

'My commander said that whatever Bernini created while under Vatican patronage would be listed here as an asset.'

Langdon nodded, realizing the commander's instincts just might pay off. In Bernini's day, everything an artist created while under the patronage of the Pope became, by law, property of the Vatican. It was more like feudalism than patronage, but top artists lived well and seldom complained. 'Including works placed in churches *outside* Vatican City?'

The soldier gave him an odd look. 'Of course. All Catholic churches in Rome are property of the Vatican.'

Langdon looked at the list in his hand. It contained the names of the twenty or so churches that were located on a direct line with *West Ponente's* breath. The third altar of science was one of them, and Langdon hoped he had time to figure out which it was. Under other circumstances, he would gladly have explored each church in person. Today, however, he had about twenty minutes to find what he was looking for – the one church containing a Bernini tribute to *fire.*

Langdon walked to the vault's electronic revolving door. The guard did not follow. Langdon sensed an uncertain hesitation. He smiled. 'The air's fine. Thin, but breathable.'

'My orders are to escort you here and then return immediately to the security center.'

'You're *leaving?*'

'Yes. The Swiss Guard are not allowed inside the archives. I am breaching protocol by escorting you this far. The commander reminded me of that.'

'Breaching protocol?' *Do you have any idea what is going on here tonight?* 'Whose side is your damn commander on!'

All friendliness disappeared from the guard's face. The scar under his eye twitched. The guard stared, looking suddenly a lot like Olivetti himself.

'I apologize,' Langdon said, regretting the comment. 'It's just ... I could use some help.'

The guard did not blink. 'I am trained to follow orders. Not debate them. When you find what you are looking for, contact the commander immediately.'

Langdon was flustered. 'But where will he be?'

The guard removed his walkie-talkie and set it on a nearby table. 'Channel one.' Then he disappeared into the dark.

81

The television in the Office of the Pope was an oversized Hitachi hidden in a recessed cabinet opposite his desk. The doors to the cabinet were now open, and everyone gathered around. Vittoria moved in close. As the screen warmed up, a young female reporter came into view. She was a doe-eyed brunette.

'For MSNBC news,' she announced, 'this is Kelly Horan-Jones, live from Vatican City.' The image behind her was a night shot of St Peter's Basilica with all its lights blazing.

'You're not *live*,' Rocher snapped. 'That's stock footage! The lights in the basilica are *out*.'

Olivetti silenced him with a hiss.

The reporter continued, sounding tense. 'Shocking developments in the Vatican elections this evening. We have reports that two members of the College of Cardinals have been brutally murdered in Rome.'

Olivetti swore under his breath.

As the reporter continued, a guard appeared at the door, breathless. 'Commander, the central switchboard reports every line lit. They're requesting our official position on—'

'Disconnect it,' Olivetti said, never taking his eyes from the TV.

The guard looked uncertain. 'But, commander—'

'Go!'

The guard ran off.

Vittoria sensed the camerlengo had wanted to say something but had stopped himself. Instead, the man stared long and hard at Olivetti before turning back to the television.

MSNBC was now running tape. The Swiss Guards carried the body of Cardinal Ebner down the stairs outside Santa Maria del Popolo and lifted him into an Alfa Romeo. The tape froze and zoomed in as the cardinal's naked body became visible just before they deposited him in the trunk of the car.

'Who the hell shot this footage?' Olivetti demanded.

The MSNBC reporter kept talking. 'This is believed to be the body of Cardinal Ebner of Frankfurt, Germany. The men removing his body from the church are believed to be Vatican Swiss Guard.' The reporter looked like she was making every effort to appear appropriately moved. They closed in on her face, and she became even more somber. 'At this time, MSNBC would like to issue our viewers a discretionary warning. The images we are about to show are exceptionally vivid and may not be suitable for all audiences.'

Vittoria grunted at the station's feigned concern for viewer sensibility, recognizing the warning as exactly what it was – the ultimate media 'teaser line.' Nobody ever changed channels after a promise like that.

The reporter drove it home. 'Again, this footage may be shocking to some viewers.'

'What footage?' Olivetti demanded. 'You just showed—'

The shot that filled the screen was of a couple in St Peter's Square, moving through the crowd. Vittoria instantly recognized the two people as Robert and herself. In the corner of the screen was a text overlay: COURTESY OF THE BBC. A bell was tolling.

'Oh, no,' Vittoria said aloud. 'Oh . . . no.'

The camerlengo looked confused. He turned to Olivetti. 'I thought you said you confiscated this tape!'

Suddenly, on television, a child was screaming. The image panned to find a little girl pointing at what appeared to be a bloody homeless man. Robert Langdon entered abruptly into the frame, trying to help the little girl. The shot tightened.

Everyone in the Pope's office stared in horrified silence as the drama unfolded before them. The cardinal's body fell face first onto the pavement. Vittoria appeared and called orders. There was blood. A brand. A ghastly, failed attempt to administer CPR.

'This astonishing footage,' the reporter was saying, 'was shot only minutes ago outside the Vatican. Our sources tell us this is the body of Cardinal Lamassé from France. How he came to be dressed this way and why he was not in conclave remain a mystery. So far, the Vatican has refused to comment.' The tape began to roll again.

'Refused comment?' Rocher said. 'Give us a damn minute!'

The reporter was still talking, her eyebrows furrowing with intensity. 'Although MSNBC has yet to confirm a motive for the attack, our sources tell us that responsibility for the murders has been claimed by a group calling themselves the Illuminati.'

Olivetti exploded. '*What!*'

'. . . find out more about the Illuminati by visiting our website at—'

'*Non è possibile!*' Olivetti declared. He switched channels.

This station had a Hispanic male reporter. '—a satanic cult known as the Illuminati, who some historians believe—'

Olivetti began pressing the remote wildly. Every channel was in the middle of a live update. Most were in English.

'—Swiss Guards removing a body from a church earlier this evening. The body is believed to be that of Cardinal—'

'—lights in the basilica and museums are extinguished leaving speculation—'

'—will be speaking with conspiracy theorist Tyler Tingley, about this shocking resurgence—'

'—rumors of two more assassinations planned for later this evening—'

'—questioning now whether papal hopeful Cardinal Baggia is among the missing—'

Vittoria turned away. Everything was happening so fast. Outside the window, in the settling dark, the raw magnetism of human tragedy seemed to be sucking people toward Vatican City. The crowd in the square thickened almost by the instant. Pedestrians streamed toward them while a new batch of media personnel unloaded vans and staked their claim in St Peter's Square.

Olivetti set down the remote control and turned to the camerlengo. 'Signore, I cannot imagine how this could happen. We took the tape that was in that camera!'

The camerlengo looked momentarily too stunned to speak.

Nobody said a word. The Swiss Guards stood rigid at attention.

'It appears,' the camerlengo said finally, sounding too devastated to be angry, 'that we have not contained this crisis as well as I was led to believe.' He looked out the window at the gathering masses. 'I need to make an address.'

Olivetti shook his head. 'No, signore. That is exactly what the Illuminati want you to do – confirm them, empower them. We must remain silent.'

'And these people?' The camerlengo pointed out the window. 'There will be tens of thousands shortly. Then hundreds of thousands. Continuing this charade only puts them in danger. I need to warn them. Then we need to evacuate our College of Cardinals.'

'There is still time. Let Captain Rocher find the antimatter.'

The camerlengo turned. 'Are you attempting to give me an order?'

'No, I am giving you advice. If you are concerned about the people outside, we can announce a gas leak and clear the area, but admitting we are hostage is dangerous.'

'Commander, I will only say this once. I will not use this office as a pulpit to lie to the world. If I announce anything at all, it will be the truth.'

'The truth? That Vatican City is threatened to be destroyed by satanic terrorists? It only weakens our position.'

The camerlengo glared. 'How much weaker could our position be?'

Rocher shouted suddenly, grabbing the remote and increasing the volume on the television. Everyone turned.

On air, the woman from MSNBC now looked genuinely unnerved. Superimposed beside her was a photo of the late Pope. '. . . breaking information. This just in from the BBC . . .' She glanced off camera as if

252

to confirm she was really supposed to make this announcement. Apparently getting confirmation, she turned and grimly faced the viewers. 'The Illuminati have just claimed responsibility for . . .' She hesitated. 'They have claimed responsibility for the death of the Pope fifteen days ago.'

The camerlengo's jaw fell.

Rocher dropped the remote control.

Vittoria could barely process the information.

'By Vatican law,' the woman continued, 'no formal autopsy is ever performed on a Pope, so the Illuminati claim of murder cannot be confirmed. Nonetheless, the Illuminati hold that the cause of the late Pope's death was not a *stroke* as the Vatican reported, but *poisoning*.'

The room went totally silent again.

Olivetti erupted. 'Madness! A bold-faced lie!'

Rocher began flipping channels again. The bulletin seemed to spread like a plague from station to station. Everyone had the same story. Headlines competed for optimal sensationalism.

MURDER AT THE VATICAN
POPE POISONED
SATAN TOUCHES HOUSE OF GOD

The camerlengo looked away. 'God help us.'

As Rocher flipped, he passed a BBC station. '—tipped me off about the killing at Santa Maria de Popolo—'

'Wait!' the camerlengo said. 'Back.'

Rocher went back. On screen, a prim-looking man sat at a BBC news desk. Superimposed over his shoulder was a still snapshot of an odd-looking man with a red beard. Underneath his photo, it said: GUNTHER GLICK – LIVE IN VATICAN CITY. Reporter Glick was apparently reporting by phone, the connection scratchy '. . . my videographer got the footage of the cardinal being removed from the Chigi Chapel.'

'Let me reiterate for our viewers,' the anchorman in London was saying, 'BBC reporter Gunther Glick is the man who first broke this story. He has been in phone contact twice now with the alleged Illuminati assassin. Gunther, you say the assassin phoned only moments ago to pass along a message from the Illuminati?'

'He did.'

'And their message was that the Illuminati were somehow *responsible* for the Pope's death?' The anchorman sounded incredulous.

'Correct. The caller told me that the Pope's death was *not* a stroke, as the Vatican had thought, but rather that the Pope had been poisoned by the Illuminati.'

Everyone in the Pope's office froze.

'Poisoned?' the anchorman demanded. 'But . . . but *how*!'

'They gave no specifics,' Glick replied, 'except to say that they killed him with a drug known as . . .' – there was a rustling of papers on the line – 'something known as Heparin.'

The camerlengo, Olivetti, and Rocher all exchanged confused looks.

'Heparin?' Rocher demanded, looking unnerved. 'But isn't that . . . ?'

The camerlengo blanched. 'The Pope's medication.'

Vittoria was stunned. 'The Pope was on Heparin?'

'He had thrombophlebitis,' the camerlengo said. 'He took an injection once a day.'

Rocher looked flabbergasted. 'But Heparin isn't a *poison*. Why would the Illuminati claim—'

'Heparin is lethal in the wrong dosages,' Vittoria offered. 'It's a powerful anticoagulant. An overdose would cause massive internal bleeding and brain hemorrhages.'

Olivetti eyed her suspiciously. 'How would you know that?'

'Marine biologists use it on sea mammals in captivity to prevent blood clotting from decreased activity. Animals have died from improper administration of the drug.' She paused. 'A Heparin overdose in a human would cause symptoms easily mistaken for a stroke . . . especially in the absence of a proper autopsy.'

The camerlengo now looked deeply troubled.

'Signore,' Olivetti said, 'this is obviously an Illuminati ploy for publicity. Someone overdosing the Pope would be impossible. Nobody had access. And even if we take the bait and try to refute their claim, how could we? Papal law prohibits autopsy. Even *with* an autopsy, we would learn nothing. We would find traces of Heparin in his body from his daily injections.'

'True.' The camerlengo's voice sharpened. 'And yet something else troubles me. No one on the outside *knew* His Holiness was taking this medication.'

There was a silence.

'If he overdosed with Heparin,' Vittoria said, 'his body would show signs.'

Olivetti spun toward her. 'Ms Vetra, in case you didn't hear me, papal autopsies are prohibited by Vatican Law. We are not about to defile His Holiness's body by cutting him open just because an enemy makes a taunting claim!'

Vittoria felt shamed. 'I was not implying . . .' She had not meant to seem disrespectful. 'I certainly was not suggesting you exhume the Pope . . .' She hesitated, though. Something Robert told her in the Chigi passed like a ghost through her mind. He had mentioned that papal sarcophagi were above ground and never cemented shut, a throwback to the days of the pharaohs when sealing and burying a casket was believed to trap the deceased's soul inside. *Gravity* had become the mortar of choice, with coffin lids often weighing hundreds of pounds. *Technically*, she realized, *it would be possible to*—

254

'What *sort* of signs?' the camerlengo said suddenly.

Vittoria felt her heart flutter with fear. 'Overdoses can cause bleeding of the oral mucosa.'

'Oral what?'

'The victim's gums would bleed. Post mortem, the blood congeals and turns the inside of the mouth black.' Vittoria had once seen a photo taken at an aquarium in London where a pair of killer whales had been mistakenly overdosed by their trainer. The whales floated lifeless in the tank, their mouths hanging open and their tongues black as soot.

The camerlengo made no reply. He turned and stared out the window.

Rocher's voice had lost its optimism. 'Signore, if this claim about poisoning is true . . .'

'It's not true,' Olivetti declared. 'Access to the Pope by an outsider is utterly impossible.'

'*If* this claim is true,' Rocher repeated, 'and our Holy Father *was* poisoned, then that has profound implications for our antimatter search. The alleged assassination implies a much deeper infiltration of Vatican City than we had imagined. Searching the white zones may be inadequate. If we are compromised to such a deep extent, we may not find the canister in time.'

Olivetti leveled his captain with a cold stare. 'Captain, I will tell you what is going to happen.'

'No,' the camerlengo said, turning suddenly. 'I will tell *you* what is going to happen.' He looked directly at Olivetti. 'This has gone far enough. In twenty minutes I will be making a decision whether or not to cancel conclave and evacuate Vatican City. My decision will be final. Is that clear?'

Olivetti did not blink. Nor did he respond.

The camerlengo spoke forcefully now, as though tapping a hidden reserve of power. 'Captain Rocher, you will complete your search of the white zones and report directly to me when you are finished.'

Rocher nodded, throwing Olivetti an uneasy glance.

The camerlengo then singled out two guards. 'I want the BBC reporter, Mr Glick, in this office immediately. If the Illuminati have been communicating with him, he may be able to help us. Go.'

The two soldiers disappeared.

Now the camerlengo turned and addressed the remaining guards. 'Gentlemen, I will not permit any more loss of life this evening. By ten o'clock you will locate the remaining two cardinals and capture the monster responsible for these murders. Do I make myself understood?'

'But, signore,' Olivetti argued, 'we have no idea where—'

'Mr Langdon is working on that. He seems capable. I have faith.'

With that, the camerlengo strode for the door, a new determination in his step. On his way out, he pointed to three guards. 'You three, come with me. Now.'

The guards followed.

In the doorway, the camerlengo stopped. He turned to Vittoria. 'Ms Vetra. You too. Please come with me.'

Vittoria hesitated. 'Where are we going?'

He headed out the door. 'To see an old friend.'

82

At CERN, secretary Sylvie Baudeloque was hungry, wishing she could go home. To her dismay, Kohler had apparently survived his trip to the infirmary; he had phoned and demanded – not asked, *demanded* – that Sylvie stay late this evening. No explanation.

Over the years, Sylvie had programmed herself to ignore Kohler's bizarre mood swings and eccentricities – his silent treatments, his unnerving propensity to secretly film meetings with his wheelchair's porta-video. She secretly hoped one day he would shoot himself during his weekly visit to CERN's recreational pistol range, but apparently he was a pretty good shot.

Now, sitting alone at her desk, Sylvie heard her stomach growling. Kohler had not yet returned, nor had he given her any additional work for the evening. *To hell with sitting here bored and starving*, she decided. She left Kohler a note and headed for the staff dining commons to grab a quick bite.

She never made it.

As she passed CERN's recreational '*suites de loisir*' – a long hallway of lounges with televisions – she noticed the rooms were overflowing with employees who had apparently abandoned dinner to watch the news. Something big was going on. Sylvie entered the first suite. It was packed with byte-heads – wild young computer programmers. When she saw the headlines on the TV, she gasped.

TERROR AT THE VATICAN

Sylvie listened to the report, unable to believe her ears. Some ancient brotherhood killing cardinals? What did that prove? Their hatred? Their dominance? Their ignorance?

And yet, incredibly, the mood in this suite seemed anything but somber.

Two young techies ran by waving T-shirts that bore a picture of Bill Gates and the message: AND THE *GEEK* SHALL INHERIT THE EARTH!

'Illuminati!' one shouted. 'I told you these guys were real!'

'Incredible! I thought it was just a game!'

'They killed the Pope, man! The *Pope*!'

'Jeez! I wonder how many points you get for *that*?'

They ran off laughing.

Sylvie stood in stunned amazement. As a Catholic working among scientists, she occasionally endured the antireligious whisperings, but the party these kids seemed to be having was all-out euphoria over the church's loss. How could they be so callous? Why the hatred?

For Sylvie, the church had always been an innocuous entity . . . a place of fellowship and introspection . . . sometimes just a place to sing out loud without people staring at her. The church recorded the benchmarks of her life – funerals, weddings, baptisms, holidays – and it asked for nothing in return. Even the monetary dues were voluntary. Her children emerged from Sunday School every week uplifted, filled with ideas about helping others and being kinder. What could possibly be wrong with *that*?

It never ceased to amaze her that so many of CERN's so-called 'brilliant minds' failed to comprehend the importance of the church. Did they really believe quarks and mesons inspired the average human being? Or that *equations* could replace someone's need for faith in the divine?

Dazed, Sylvie moved down the hallway past the other lounges. All the TV rooms were packed. She began wondering now about the call Kohler had gotten from the Vatican earlier. Coincidence? Perhaps. The Vatican called CERN from time to time as a 'courtesy' before issuing scathing statements condemning CERN's research – most recently for CERN's breakthroughs in nanotechnology, a field the church denounced because of its implications for genetic engineering. CERN never cared. Invariably, within minutes after a Vatican salvo, Kohler's phone would ring off the hook with tech-investment companies wanting to license the new discovery. 'No such thing as bad press,' Kohler would always say.

Sylvie wondered if she should page Kohler, wherever the hell he was, and tell him to turn on the news. Did he care? Had he heard? Of course he'd heard. He was probably videotaping the entire report with his freaky little camcorder, smiling for the first time in a year.

As Sylvie continued down the hall, she finally found a lounge where the mood was subdued . . . almost melancholy. Here the scientists watching the report were some of CERN's oldest and most respected. They did not even look up as Sylvie slipped in and took a seat.

On the other side of CERN, in Leonardo Vetra's frigid apartment, Maximilian Kohler had finished reading the leather-bound journal he'd taken from Vetra's bedside table. Now he was watching the television reports. After a few minutes, he replaced Vetra's journal, turned off the television, and left the apartment.

*

Far away, in Vatican City, Cardinal Mortati carried another tray of ballots to the Sistine Chapel chimney. He burned them, and the smoke was black.

Two ballotings. No Pope.

83

Flashlights were no match for the voluminous blackness of St Peter's Basilica. The void overhead pressed down like a starless night, and Vittoria felt the emptiness spread out around her like a desolate ocean. She stayed close as the Swiss Guards and the camerlengo pushed on. High above, a dove cooed and fluttered away.

As if sensing her discomfort, the camerlengo dropped back and laid a hand on her shoulder. A tangible strength transferred in the touch, as if the man were magically infusing her with the calm she needed to do what they were about to do.

What are we about to do? she thought. *This is madness!*

And yet, Vittoria knew, for all its impiety and inevitable horror, the task at hand was inescapable. The grave decisions facing the camerlengo required information . . . information entombed in a sarcophagus in the Vatican Grottoes. She wondered what they would find. *Did the Illuminati murder the Pope? Did their power really reach so far? Am I really about to perform the first papal autopsy?*

Vittoria found it ironic that she felt more apprehensive in this unlit church than she would swimming at night with barracuda. Nature was her refuge. She understood nature. But it was matters of man and spirit that left her mystified. Killer fish gathering in the dark conjured images of the press gathering outside. TV footage of branded bodies reminded her of her father's corpse . . . and the killer's harsh laugh. The killer was out there somewhere. Vittoria felt the anger drowning her fear.

As they circled past a pillar – thicker in girth than any redwood she could imagine – Vittoria saw an orange glow up ahead. The light seemed to emanate from beneath the floor in the center of the basilica. As they came closer, she realized what she was seeing. It was the famous sunken sanctuary beneath the main altar – the sumptuous underground chamber that held the Vatican's most sacred relics. As they drew even with the gate surrounding the hollow, Vittoria gazed down at the golden coffer surrounded by scores of glowing oil lamps.

'St Peter's bones?' she asked, knowing full well that they were. Everyone who came to St Peter's knew what was in the golden casket.

'Actually, no,' the camerlengo said. 'A common misconception. That's not a reliquary The box holds *palliums* – woven sashes that the Pope gives to newly elected cardinals.'

'But I thought—'

'As does everyone. The guidebooks label this as St Peter's tomb, but his true grave is two stories beneath us, buried in the earth. The Vatican excavated it in the forties. Nobody is allowed down there.'

Vittoria was shocked. As they moved away from the glowing recession into the darkness again, she thought of the stories she'd heard of pilgrims traveling thousands of miles to look at that golden box, thinking they were in the presence of St Peter. 'Shouldn't the Vatican tell people?'

'We all benefit from a sense of contact with divinity . . . even if it is only imagined.'

Vittoria, as a scientist, could not argue the logic. She had read countless studies of the placebo effect – aspirins curing cancer in people who *believed* they were using a miracle drug. What was *faith*, after all?

'Change,' the camerlengo said, 'is not something we do well within Vatican City. Admitting our past faults, modernization, are things we historically eschew. His Holiness was trying to change that.' He paused. 'Reaching to the modern world. Searching for new paths to God.'

Vittoria nodded in the dark. 'Like science?'

'To be honest, science seems irrelevant.'

'Irrelevant?' Vittoria could think of a lot of words to describe science, but in the modern world 'irrelevant' did not seem like one of them.

'Science can heal, or science can kill. It depends on the soul of the man using the science. It is the soul that interests me.'

'When did you hear your call?'

'Before I was born.'

Vittoria looked at him.

'I'm sorry, that always seems like a strange question. What I mean is that I've always known I would serve God. From the moment I could first think. It wasn't until I was a young man, though, in the military, that I truly understood my purpose.'

Vittoria was surprised. 'You were in the military?'

'Two years. I refused to fire a weapon, so they made me fly instead. Medevac helicopters. In fact, I still fly from time to time.'

Vittoria tried to picture the young priest flying a helicopter. Oddly, she could see him perfectly behind the controls. Camerlengo Ventresca possessed a grit that seemed to accentuate his conviction rather than cloud it. 'Did you ever fly the Pope?'

'Heavens no. We left that precious cargo to the professionals. His Holiness let me take the helicopter to our retreat in Gandolfo sometimes.' He paused, looking at her. 'Ms Vetra, thank you for your help here today. I am very sorry about your father. Truly.'

'Thank you.'

'I never knew my father. He died before I was born. I lost my mother when I was ten.'

Vittoria looked up. 'You were orphaned?' She felt a sudden kinship.

'I survived an accident. An accident that took my mother.'

'Who took care of you?'

'God,' the camerlengo said. 'He quite literally sent me another father. A bishop from Palermo appeared at my hospital bed and took me in. At the time I was not surprised. I had sensed God's watchful hand over me even as a boy. The bishop's appearance simply confirmed what I had already suspected, that God had somehow chosen me to serve him.'

'You believed God chose you?'

'I did. And I do.' There was no trace of conceit in the camerlengo's voice, only gratitude. 'I worked under the bishop's tutelage for many years. He eventually became a cardinal. Still, he never forgot me. He is the father I remember.' A beam of a flashlight caught the camerlengo's face, and Vittoria sensed a loneliness in his eyes.

The group arrived beneath a towering pillar, and their lights converged on an opening in the floor. Vittoria looked down at the staircase descending into the void and suddenly wanted to turn back. The guards were already helping the camerlengo onto the stairs. They helped her next.

'What became of him?' she asked, descending, trying to keep her voice steady. 'The cardinal who took you in?'

'He left the College of Cardinals for another position.'

Vittoria was surprised.

'And then, I'm sorry to say, he passed on.'

'*Le mie condoglianze*,' Vittoria said. 'Recently?'

The camerlengo turned, shadows accentuating the pain on his face. 'Exactly fifteen days ago. We are going to see him right now.'

84

The dark lights glowed hot inside the archival vault. This vault was much smaller than the previous one Langdon had been in. *Less air. Less time.* He wished he'd asked Olivetti to turn on the recirculating fans.

Langdon quickly located the section of assets containing the ledgers cataloging *Belle Arti.* The section was impossible to miss. It occupied almost eight full stacks. The Catholic church owned millions of individual pieces worldwide.

Langdon scanned the shelves searching for Gianlorenzo Bernini. He began his search about midway down the first stack, at about the spot he thought the *B*'s would begin. After a moment of panic fearing the ledger was missing, he realized, to his greater dismay, that the ledgers were not arranged alphabetically. *Why am I not surprised?*

It was not until Langdon circled back to the beginning of the collection and climbed a rolling ladder to the top shelf that he understood the vault's organization. Perched precariously on the upper stacks he found the fattest ledgers of all – those belonging to the masters of the Renaissance – Michelangelo, Raphael, da Vinci, Botticelli. Langdon now realized, appropriate to a vault called 'Vatican Assets,' the ledgers were arranged by the overall monetary *value* of each artist's collection. Sandwiched between Raphael and Michelangelo, Langdon found the ledger marked Bernini. It was over five inches thick.

Already short of breath and struggling with the cumbersome volume, Langdon descended the ladder. Then, like a kid with a comic book, he spread himself out on the floor and opened the cover.

The book was cloth-bound and very solid. The ledger was handwritten in Italian. Each page cataloged a single work, including a short description, date, location, cost of materials, and sometimes a rough sketch of the piece. Langdon fanned through the pages . . . over eight hundred in all. Bernini had been a busy man.

As a young student of art, Langdon had wondered how single artists could create so *much* work in their lifetimes. Later he learned, much to his disappointment, that famous artists actually created very little of their own work. They ran studios where they trained young artists to carry out their designs. Sculptors like Bernini created miniatures in clay and hired others to enlarge them into marble. Langdon knew that if Bernini had been required to *personally* complete all of his commissions, he would still be working today.

'Index,' he said aloud, trying to ward off the mental cobwebs. He flipped to the back of the book, intending to look under the letter *F* for titles containing the word *fuòco* – fire – but the *F*'s were not together. Langdon swore under his breath. *What the hell do these people have against alphabetizing?*

The entries had apparently been logged chronologically, one by one, as Bernini created each new work. Everything was listed by date. No help at all.

As Langdon stared at the list, another disheartening thought occurred to him. The title of the sculpture he was looking for might not even contain the word *Fire*. The previous two works – *Habakkuk and the Angel* and *West Ponente* – had not contained specific references to *Earth* or *Air*.

He spent a minute or two flipping randomly through the ledger in hopes that an illustration might jump out at him. Nothing did. He saw dozens of obscure works he had never heard of, but he also saw plenty he recognized ... *Daniel and the Lion*, *Apollo and Daphne*, as well as a half dozen fountains. When he saw the fountains, his thoughts skipped momentarily ahead. Water. He wondered if the fourth altar of science was a fountain. A fountain seemed a perfect tribute to water. Langdon hoped they could catch the killer before he had to consider *Water* – Bernini had carved dozens of fountains in Rome, most of them in front of churches.

Langdon turned back to the matter at hand. *Fire.* As he looked through the book, Vittoria's words encouraged him. *You were familiar with the first two sculptures ... you probably know this one too.* As he turned to the index again, he scanned for titles he knew. Some were familiar, but none jumped out. Langdon now realized he would never complete his search before passing out, so he decided, against his better judgment, that he would have to take the book outside the vault. *It's only a ledger*, he told himself. *It's not like I'm removing an original Galilean folio.* Langdon recalled the folio in his breast pocket and reminded himself to return it before leaving.

Hurrying now, he reached down to lift the volume, but as he did, he saw something that gave him pause. Although there were numerous notations throughout the index, the one that had just caught his eye seemed odd.

The note indicated that the famous Bernini sculpture, *The Ecstasy of St Teresa*, shortly after its unveiling, had been moved from its original location inside the Vatican. This in itself was not what had caught Langdon's eye. He was already familiar with the sculpture's checkered past. Though some thought it a masterpiece, Pope Urban VIII had rejected *The Ecstasy of St Teresa* as too sexually explicit for the Vatican. He had banished it to some obscure chapel across town. What had caught Langdon's eye was that the work had apparently been placed in one of the five churches on his list.

What was more, the note indicated it had been moved there *per suggeri-mento del artista.*

By suggestion of the artist? Langdon was confused. It made no sense that Bernini had suggested his masterpiece be hidden in some obscure location. All artists wanted their work displayed prominently, not in some remote— Langdon hesitated. *Unless . . .*

He was fearful even to entertain the notion. Was it possible? Had Bernini intentionally created a work so explicit that it forced the Vatican to hide it in some out-of-the-way spot? A location perhaps that Bernini himself could suggest? Maybe a remote church on a direct line with *West Ponente's* breath?

As Langdon's excitement mounted, his vague familiarity with the statue intervened, insisting the work had nothing to do with *fire*. The sculpture, as anyone who had seen it could attest, was anything but scientific – *porno-graphic* maybe, but certainly not scientific. An English critic had once condemned *The Ecstasy of St Teresa* as 'the most unfit ornament ever to be placed in a Christian Church.' Langdon certainly understood the con-troversy. Though brilliantly rendered, the statue depicted St Teresa on her back in the throes of a toe-curling orgasm. Hardly Vatican fare.

Langdon hurriedly flipped to the ledger's description of the work. When he saw the sketch, he felt an instantaneous and unexpected tingle of hope. In the sketch, St Teresa did indeed appear to be enjoying herself, but there was another figure in the statue who Langdon had forgotten was there.

An angel.

The sordid legend suddenly came back . . .

St Teresa was a nun sainted after she claimed an angel had paid her a blissful visit in her sleep. Critics later decided her encounter had probably been more sexual than spiritual. Scrawled at the bottom of the ledger, Langdon saw a familiar excerpt. St Teresa's own words left little to the imagination:

> . . . his great golden spear . . . filled with fire . . . plunged into me sev-eral times . . . penetrated to my entrails . . . a sweetness so extreme that one could not possibly wish it to stop.

Langdon smiled. *If that's not a metaphor for some serious sex, I don't know what is.* He was smiling also because of the ledger's description of the work. Although the paragraph was in Italian, the word *fuòco* appeared a half dozen times:

> . . . angel's spear tipped with point of *fire* . . .
> . . . angel's head emanating rays of *fire* . . .
> . . . woman inflamed by passion's *fire* . . .

Langdon was not entirely convinced until he glanced up at the sketch again. The angel's fiery spear was raised like a beacon, pointing the way. *Let angels guide you on your lofty quest.* Even the *type* of angel Bernini had selected seemed significant. *It's a seraph*, Langdon realized. *Seraph literally means 'the fiery one.'*

Robert Langdon was not a man who had ever looked for confirmation from above, but when he read the name of the church where the sculpture now resided, he decided he might become a believer after all.

Santa Maria della Vittoria.

Vittoria, he thought, grinning. *Perfect.*

Staggering to his feet, Langdon felt a rush of dizziness. He glanced up the ladder, wondering if he should replace the book. *The hell with it*, he thought. *Father Jaqui can do it.* He closed the book and left it neatly at the bottom of the shelf.

As he made his way toward the glowing button on the vault's electronic exit, he was breathing in shallow gasps. Nonetheless, he felt rejuvenated by his good fortune.

His good fortune, however, ran out before he reached the exit.

Without warning, the vault let out a pained sigh. The lights dimmed, and the exit button went dead. Then, like an enormous expiring beast, the archival complex went totally black. Someone had just killed power.

85

The Holy Vatican Grottoes are located beneath the main floor of St Peter's Basilica. They are the burial place of deceased Popes.

Vittoria reached the bottom of the spiral staircase and entered the grotto. The darkened tunnel reminded her of CERN's Large Hadron Collider – black and cold. Lit now only by the flashlights of the Swiss Guards, the tunnel carried a distinctly incorporeal feel. On both sides, hollow niches lined the walls. Recessed in the alcoves, as far as the lights let them see, the hulking shadows of sarcophagi loomed.

An iciness raked her flesh. *It's the cold*, she told herself, knowing that was only partially true. She had the sense they were being watched, not by anyone in the flesh, but by specters in the dark. On top of each tomb, in full papal vestments, lay life-sized semblances of each Pope, shown in death, arms folded across their chests. The prostrate bodies seemed to emerge from within the tombs, pressing upward against the marble lids as if trying to escape their mortal restraints. The flashlight procession moved on, and the papal silhouettes rose and fell against the walls, stretching and vanishing in a macabre shadowbox dance.

A silence had fallen across the group, and Vittoria couldn't tell whether it was one of respect or apprehension. She sensed both. The camerlengo moved with his eyes closed, as if he knew every step by heart. Vittoria suspected he had made this eerie promenade many times since the Pope's death . . . perhaps to pray at his tomb for guidance.

I worked under the cardinal's tutelage for many years, the camerlengo had said. *He was like a father to me.* Vittoria recalled the camerlengo speaking those words in reference to the cardinal who had 'saved' him from the army. Now, however, Vittoria understood the rest of the story. That very cardinal who had taken the camerlengo under his wing had apparently later risen to the papacy and brought with him his young protégé to serve as chamberlain.

That explains a lot, Vittoria thought. She had always possessed a well-tuned perception for others' inner emotions, and something about the camerlengo had been nagging her all day since meeting him, she had sensed an anguish more soulful and private than the overwhelming crisis he now faced. Behind his pious calm, she saw a man tormented by personal demons. Now she knew her instincts had been correct. Not only was he facing the most devastating threat in Vatican history, but he was doing it without his mentor and friend . . . flying solo.

The guards slowed now, as if unsure where exactly in the darkness the most recent Pope was buried. The camerlengo continued assuredly and stopped before a marble tomb that seemed to glisten brighter than the others. Lying atop was a carved figure of the late Pope. When Vittoria recognized his face from television, a shot of fear gripped her. *What are we doing?*

'I realize we do not have much time,' the camerlengo said. 'I still ask we take a moment of prayer.'

The Swiss Guard all bowed their heads where they were standing. Vittoria followed suit, her heart pounding in the silence. The camerlengo knelt before the tomb and prayed in Italian. As Vittoria listened to his words, an unexpected grief surfaced as tears . . . tears for her own mentor . . . her own holy father. The camerlengo's words seemed as appropriate for her father as they did for the Pope.

'Supreme father, counselor, friend.' The camerlengo's voice echoed dully around the ring. 'You told me when I was young that the voice in my heart was that of God. You told me I must follow it no matter what painful places it leads. I hear that voice now, asking of me impossible tasks. Give me strength. Bestow on me forgiveness. What I do . . . I do in the name of everything you believe. Amen.'

'Amen,' the guards whispered.

Amen, Father. Vittoria wiped her eyes.

The camerlengo stood slowly and stepped away from the tomb. 'Push the covering aside.'

The Swiss Guards hesitated. 'Signore,' one said, 'by law we are at your command.' He paused. 'We will do as you say . . .'

The camerlengo seemed to read the young man's mind. 'Someday I will ask your forgiveness for placing you in this position. Today I ask for your obedience. Vatican laws are established to protect this church. It is in that very spirit that I command you to break them now.'

There was a moment of silence and then the lead guard gave the order. The three men set down their flashlights on the floor, and their shadows leapt overhead. Lit now from beneath, the men advanced toward the tomb. Bracing their hands against the marble covering near the head of the tomb, they planted their feet and prepared to push. On signal, they all thrust, straining against the enormous slab. When the lid did not move at all, Vittoria found herself almost hoping it was too heavy. She was suddenly fearful of what they would find inside.

The men pushed harder, and still the stone did not move.

'*Ancóra*,' the camerlengo said, rolling up the sleeves of his cassock and preparing to push along with them. '*Ora!*' Everyone heaved.

Vittoria was about to offer her own help, but just then, the lid began to slide. The men dug in again, and with an almost primal growl of stone on stone, the lid rotated off the top of the tomb and came to rest at an angle – the Pope's carved head now pushed back into the niche and his feet extended out into the hallway.

Everyone stepped back.

Tentatively, a guard bent and retrieved his flashlight. Then he aimed it into the tomb. The beam seemed to tremble a moment, and then the guard held it steady. The other guards gathered one by one. Even in the darkness Vittoria sensed them recoil. In succession, they crossed themselves.

The camerlengo shuddered when he looked into the tomb, his shoulders dropping like weights. He stood a long moment before turning away.

Vittoria had feared the corpse's mouth might be clenched tight with *rigor mortis* and that she would have to suggest breaking the jaw to see the tongue. She now saw it would be unnecessary. The cheeks had collapsed, and the Pope's mouth gaped wide.

His tongue was black as death.

86

No light. No sound.

The Secret Archives were black.

Fear, Langdon now realized, was an intense motivator. Short of breath, he fumbled through the blackness toward the revolving door. He found the button on the wall and rammed his palm against it. Nothing happened. He tried again. The door was dead.

Spinning blind, he called out, but his voice emerged strangled. The peril of his predicament suddenly closed in around him. His lungs strained for oxygen as the adrenaline doubled his heart rate. He felt like someone had just punched him in the gut.

When he threw his weight into the door, for an instant he thought he felt the door start to turn. He pushed again, seeing stars. Now he realized it was the entire room turning, not the door. Staggering away, Langdon tripped over the base of a rolling ladder and fell hard. He tore his knee against the edge of a book stack. Swearing, he got up and groped for the ladder.

He found it. He had hoped it would be heavy wood or iron, but it was aluminum. He grabbed the ladder and held it like a battering ram. Then he ran through the dark at the glass wall. It was closer than he thought. The ladder hit head-on, bouncing off. From the feeble sound of the collision, Langdon knew he was going to need a hell of a lot more than an aluminum ladder to break this glass.

When he flashed on the semiautomatic, his hopes surged and then instantly fell. The weapon was gone. Olivetti had relieved him of it in the Pope's office, saying he did not want loaded weapons around with the camerlengo present. It made sense at the time.

Langdon called out again, making less sound than the last time.

Next he remembered the walkie-talkie the guard had left on the table outside the vault. *Why the hell didn't I bring it in!* As the purple stars began to dance before his eyes, Langdon forced himself to think. *You've been trapped before*, he told himself. *You survived worse. You were just a kid and you figured it out.* The crushing darkness came flooding in. *Think!*

Langdon lowered himself onto the floor. He rolled over on his back and laid his hands at his sides. The first step was to gain control.

Relax. Conserve.

No longer fighting gravity to pump blood, Langdon's heart began to slow. It was a trick swimmers used to re-oxygenate their blood between tightly scheduled races.

There is plenty of air in here, he told himself. *Plenty. Now think.* He waited, half-expecting the lights to come back on at any moment. They did not. As he lay there, able to breathe better now, an eerie resignation came across him. He felt peaceful. He fought it.

You will move, damn it! But where . . .

On Langdon's wrist, Mickey Mouse glowed happily as if enjoying the dark: 9.33 p.m. Half an hour until *Fire.* Langdon thought it felt a whole hell of a lot later. His mind, instead of coming up with a plan for escape, was suddenly demanding an explanation. *Who turned off the power? Was Rocher expanding his search? Wouldn't Olivetti have warned Rocher that I'm in here!* Langdon knew at this point it made no difference.

Opening his mouth wide and tipping back his head, Langdon pulled the deepest breaths he could manage. Each breath burned a little less than the last. His head cleared. He reeled his thoughts in and forced the gears into motion.

Glass walls, he told himself. *But damn thick glass.*

He wondered if any of the books in here were stored in heavy, steel, fire-proof file cabinets. Langdon had seen them from time to time in other archives but had seen none here. Besides, finding one in the dark could prove time-consuming. Not that he could lift one anyway, particularly in his present state.

How about the examination table? Langdon knew this vault, like the other, had an examination table in the center of the stacks. *So what!* He knew he couldn't lift it. Not to mention, even if he could drag it, he wouldn't get it far. The stacks were closely packed, the aisles between them far too narrow.

The aisles are too narrow . . .

Suddenly, Langdon knew.

With a burst of confidence, he jumped to his feet far too fast. Swaying in the fog of a head rush, he reached out in the dark for support. His hand found a stack. Waiting a moment, he forced himself to conserve. He would need all of his strength to do this.

Positioning himself against the book stack like a football player against a training sled, he planted his feet and pushed. *If I can somehow tip the shelf.* But it barely moved. He realigned and pushed again. His feet slipped backward on the floor. The stack creaked but did not move.

He needed leverage.

Finding the glass wall again, he placed one hand on it to guide him as he raced in the dark toward the far end of the vault. The back wall loomed suddenly, and he collided with it, crushing his shoulder. Cursing, Langdon circled the shelf and grabbed the stack at about eye level. Then, propping one leg on the glass behind him and another on the lower shelves, he started to climb. Books fell around him, fluttering into the darkness. He didn't care. Instinct for survival had long since overridden archival decorum. He sensed his equilibrium was hampered by the total darkness and closed his eyes, coaxing his brain to ignore visual input. He moved faster now. The air felt leaner the higher he went. He scrambled toward the upper shelves, stepping on books, trying to gain purchase, heaving himself upward. Then, like a rock climber conquering a rock face, Langdon grasped the top shelf. Stretching his legs out behind him, he walked his feet up the glass wall until he was almost horizontal.

Now or never, Robert, a voice urged. *Just like the leg press in the Harvard gym.*

With dizzying exertion, he planted his feet against the wall behind him, braced his arms and chest against the stack, and pushed. Nothing happened.

Fighting for air, he repositioned and tried again, extending his legs. Ever so slightly, the stack moved. He pushed again, and the stack rocked forward an inch or so and then back. Langdon took advantage of the motion, inhaling what felt like an oxygenless breath and heaving again. The shelf rocked farther.

Like a swing set, he told himself. *Keep the rhythm. A little more.*

Langdon rocked the shelf, extending his legs farther with each push. His quadriceps burned now, and he blocked the pain. The pendulum was in motion. *Three more pushes*, he urged himself.

It only took two.

There was an instant of weightless uncertainty. Then, with a thundering of books sliding off the shelves, Langdon and the shelf were falling forward.

Halfway to the ground, the shelf hit the stack next to it. Langdon hung on, throwing his weight forward, urging the second shelf to topple. There was a moment of motionless panic, and then, creaking under the weight, the second stack began to tip. Langdon was falling again.

Like enormous dominoes, the stacks began to topple, one after another. Metal on metal, books tumbling everywhere. Langdon held on as his inclined stack bounced downward like a ratchet on a jack. He wondered how many stacks there were in all. How much would they weigh? The glass at the far end was thick . . .

Langdon's stack had fallen almost to the horizontal when he heard what he was waiting for – a different kind of collision. Far off. At the end of the vault. The sharp smack of metal on glass. The vault around him shook, and Langdon knew the final stack, weighted down by the others, had hit the glass hard. The sound that followed was the most unwelcome sound Langdon had ever heard.

Silence.

There was no crashing of glass, only the resounding thud as the wall accepted the weight of the stacks now propped against it. He lay wide-eyed on the pile of books. Somewhere in the distance there was a creaking. Langdon would have held his breath to listen, but he had none left to hold.

One second. Two . . .

Then, as he teetered on the brink of unconsciousness, Langdon heard a distant yielding . . . a ripple spidering outward through the glass. Suddenly, like a cannon, the glass exploded. The stack beneath Langdon collapsed to the floor.

Like welcome rain on a desert, shards of glass tinkled downward in the dark. With a great sucking hiss, the air gushed in.

Thirty seconds later, in the Vatican Grottoes, Vittoria was standing before a corpse when the electronic squawk of a walkie-talkie broke the silence. The voice blaring out sounded short of breath. 'This is Robert Langdon! Can anyone hear me?'

Vittoria looked up. *Robert!* She could not believe how much she suddenly wished he were there.

The guards exchanged puzzled looks. One took a radio off his belt. 'Mr Langdon? You are on channel three. The commander is waiting to hear from you on channel one.'

'I know he's on channel one, damn it! I don't want to speak to him. I want the camerlengo. Now! Somebody find him for me.'

In the obscurity of the Secret Archives, Langdon stood amidst shattered glass and tried to catch his breath. He felt a warm liquid on his left hand and knew he was bleeding. The camerlengo's voice spoke at once, startling Langdon.

'This is Camerlengo Ventresca. What's going on?'

Langdon pressed the button, his heart still pounding. 'I think somebody just tried to kill me!'

There was a silence on the line.

Langdon tried to calm himself. 'I also know where the next killing is going to be.'

The voice that came back was not the camerlengo's. It was Commander Olivetti's: 'Mr Langdon. Do not speak another word.'

87

Langdon's watch, now smeared with blood, read 9.41 p.m. as he ran across the Courtyard of the Belvedere and approached the fountain outside the Swiss Guard security center. His hand had stopped bleeding and now felt worse than it looked. As he arrived, it seemed everyone convened at once – Olivetti, Rocher, the camerlengo, Vittoria, and a handful of guards.

Vittoria hurried toward him immediately. 'Robert, you're hurt.'

Before Langdon could answer, Olivetti was before him. 'Mr Langdon, I'm relieved you're okay. I'm sorry about the crossed signals in the archives.'

'Crossed signals?' Langdon demanded. 'You knew damn well—'

'It was my fault,' Rocher said, stepping forward, sounding contrite. 'I had no idea you were in the archives. Portions of our white zones are cross-wired with that building. We were extending our search. I'm the one who killed power. If I had known . . .'

'Robert,' Vittoria said, taking his wounded hand in hers and looking it over, 'the Pope was poisoned. The Illuminati killed him.'

Langdon heard the words, but they barely registered. He was saturated. All he could feel was the warmth of Vittoria's hands.

The camerlengo pulled a silk handkerchief from his cassock and handed it to Langdon so he could clean himself. The man said nothing. His green eyes seemed filled with a new fire.

'Robert,' Vittoria pressed, 'you said you found where the next cardinal is going to be killed?'

Langdon felt flighty. 'I do, it's at the—'

'No,' Olivetti interrupted. 'Mr Langdon, when I asked you not to speak another word on the walkie-talkie, it was for a reason.' He turned to the handful of assembled Swiss Guards. 'Excuse us, gentlemen.'

The soldiers disappeared into the security center. No indignity. Only compliance.

Olivetti turned back to the remaining group. 'As much as it pains me to say this, the murder of our Pope is an act that could only have been accomplished with help from within these walls. For the good of all, we can trust no one. Including our guards.' He seemed to be suffering as he spoke the words.

Rocher looked anxious. 'Inside collusion implies—'

'Yes,' Olivetti said. 'The integrity of your search is compromised. And yet it is a gamble we must take. Keep looking.'

Rocher looked like he was about to say something, thought better of it, and left.

The camerlengo inhaled deeply. He had not said a word yet, and Langdon sensed a new rigor in the man, as if a turning point had been reached.

'Commander?' The camerlengo's tone was impermeable. 'I am going to break conclave.'

Olivetti pursed his lips, looking dour. 'I advise against it. We still have two hours and twenty minutes.'

'A heartbeat.'

Olivetti's tone was now challenging. 'What do you intend to do? Evacuate the cardinals single-handedly?'

'I intend to save this church with whatever power God has given me. How I proceed is no longer your concern.'

Olivetti straightened. 'Whatever you intend to do . . .' He paused. 'I do not have the authority to restrain you. Particularly in light of my apparent failure as head of security. I ask only that you wait. Wait twenty minutes . . . until after ten o'clock. If Mr Langdon's information is correct, I may still have a chance to catch this assassin. There is still a chance to preserve protocol and decorum.'

'Decorum?' The camerlengo let out a choked laugh. 'We have long since passed propriety, commander. In case you hadn't noticed, this is war.'

A guard emerged from the security center and called out to the camerlengo, 'Signore, I just got word we have detained the BBC reporter, Mr Glick.'

The camerlengo nodded. 'Have both he and his camerawoman meet me outside the Sistine Chapel.'

Olivetti's eyes widened. 'What are you doing?'

'Twenty minutes, commander. That's all I'm giving you.' Then he was gone.

When Olivetti's Alfa Romeo tore out of Vatican City, this time there was no line of unmarked cars following him. In the back seat, Vittoria bandaged Langdon's hand with a first-aid kit she'd found in the glove box.

Olivetti stared straight ahead. 'Okay Mr Langdon. Where are we going?'

88

Even with its siren now affixed and blaring, Olivetti's Alfa Romeo seemed to go unnoticed as it rocketed across the bridge into the heart of old Rome. All the traffic was moving in the other direction, toward the Vatican, as if the Holy See had suddenly become the hottest entertainment in Rome.

Langdon sat in the back seat, the questions whipping through his mind. He wondered about the killer, if they would catch him this time, if he would tell them what they needed to know, if it was already too late. How long before the camerlengo told the crowd in St Peter's Square they were in danger? The incident in the vault still nagged. *A mistake.*

Olivetti never touched the brakes as he snaked the howling Alfa Romeo toward the Church of Santa Maria della Vittoria. Langdon knew on any other day his knuckles would have been white. At the moment, however, he felt anesthetized. Only the throbbing in his hand reminded him where he was.

Overhead, the siren wailed. *Nothing like telling him we're coming,* Langdon thought. And yet they were making incredible time. He guessed Olivetti would kill the siren as they drew nearer.

Now with a moment to sit and reflect, Langdon felt a tinge of amazement as the news of the Pope's murder finally registered in his mind. The thought was inconceivable, and yet somehow it seemed a perfectly logical event. Infiltration had always been the Illuminati powerbase – rearrangements of power from within. And it was not as if Popes had never been murdered. Countless rumors of treachery abounded, although with no autopsy, none was ever confirmed. Until recently. Academics not long ago had gotten permission to X-ray the tomb of Pope Celestine V, who had allegedly died at the hands of his overeager successor, Boniface VIII. The researchers had hoped the X-ray might reveal some small hint of foul play – a broken bone perhaps. Incredibly, the X-ray had revealed a ten-inch nail driven into the Pope's skull.

Langdon now recalled a series of news clippings fellow Illuminati buffs had sent him years ago. At first he had thought the clippings were a prank, so he'd gone to the Harvard microfiche collection to confirm the articles were authentic. Incredibly, they were. He now kept them on his bulletin board as examples of how even respectable news organizations sometimes got carried away with Illuminati paranoia. Suddenly, the media's suspicions seemed a lot less paranoid. Langdon could see the articles clearly in his mind . . .

THE BRITISH BROADCASTING CORPORATION
June 14, 1998

Pope John Paul I, who died in 1978, fell victim to a plot by the P2 Masonic Lodge . . . The secret society P2 decided to murder John Paul I when it saw he was determined to dismiss the American Archbishop Paul Marcinkus as President of the Vatican Bank. The Bank had been implicated in shady financial deals with the Masonic Lodge . . .

THE NEW YORK TIMES
August 24, 1998

Why was the late John Paul I wearing his day shirt in bed? Why was it torn? The questions don't stop there. No medical investigations were made. Cardinal Villot forbade an autopsy on the grounds that no Pope was ever given a postmortem. And John Paul's medicines mysteriously vanished from his bedside, as did his glasses, slippers and his last will and testament.

LONDON DAILY MAIL
August 27, 1998

. . . a plot including a powerful, ruthless and illegal Masonic lodge with tentacles stretching into the Vatican.

The cellular in Vittoria's pocket rang, thankfully erasing the memories from Langdon's mind.

Vittoria answered, looking confused as to who might be calling her. Even from a few feet away, Langdon recognized the laserlike voice on the phone.

'Vittoria? This is Maximilian Kohler. Have you found the antimatter yet?'

'Max? You're okay?'

'I saw the news. There was no mention of CERN or the antimatter. This is good. What is happening?'

'We haven't located the canister yet. The situation is complex. Robert Langdon has been quite an asset. We have a lead on catching the man assassinating cardinals. Right now we are headed—'

'Ms Vetra,' Olivetti interrupted. 'You've said enough.'

She covered the receiver, clearly annoyed. 'Commander, this is the president of CERN. Certainly he has a right to—'

'He has a right,' Olivetti snapped, 'to be here handling this situation. You're on an open cellular line. You've said enough.'

Vittoria took a deep breath. 'Max?'

'I may have some information for you,' Max said. 'About your father . . . I may know who he told about the antimatter.'

Vittoria's expression clouded. 'Max, my father said he told no one.'

'I'm afraid, Vittoria, your father *did* tell someone. I need to check some security records. I will be in touch soon.' The line went dead.

Vittoria looked waxen as she returned the phone to her pocket.

'You okay?' Langdon asked.

Vittoria nodded, her trembling fingers revealing the lie.

'The church is near Piazza Barberini,' Olivetti said, killing the siren and checking his watch. 'We have nine minutes.'

When Langdon had first realized the location of the third marker, the position of the church had rung some distant bell for him. *Piazza Barberini*. Something about the name was familiar . . . something he could not place. Now Langdon realized what it was. The piazza was the sight of a controversial subway stop. Twenty years ago, construction of the subway terminal had created a stir among art historians who feared digging beneath Piazza Barberini might topple the multiton obelisk that stood in the center. City planners had removed the obelisk and replaced it with a small fountain called the *Triton*.

In Bernini's day, Langdon now realized, *Piazza Barberini had contained an obelisk!* Whatever doubts Langdon had felt that this was the location of the third marker now totally evaporated.

A block from the piazza, Olivetti turned into an alley, gunned the car halfway down, and skidded to a stop. He pulled off his suit jacket, rolled up his sleeves, and loaded his weapon.

'We can't risk your being recognized,' he said. 'You two were on television. I want you across the piazza, out of sight, watching the front entrance. I'm going in the back.' He produced a familiar pistol and handed it to Langdon. 'Just in case.'

Langdon frowned. It was the second time today he had been handed the gun. He slid it into his breast pocket. As he did, he realized he was still carrying the folio from *Diagramma*. He couldn't believe he had forgotten to leave it behind. He pictured the Vatican Curator collapsing in spasms of outrage at the thought of this priceless artifact being packed around Rome like some tourist map. Then Langdon thought of the mess of shattered glass and strewn documents that he'd left behind in the archives. The curator had other problems. *If the archives even survive the night . . .*

Olivetti got out of the car and motioned back up the alley. 'The piazza is that way. Keep your eyes open and don't let yourselves be seen.' He tapped the phone on his belt. 'Ms Vetra, let's retest our auto dial.'

Vittoria removed her phone and hit the auto dial number she and Olivetti had programmed at the Pantheon. Olivetti's phone vibrated in silent-ring mode on his belt.

The commander nodded. 'Good. If you see anything, I want to know.' He cocked his weapon. 'I'll be inside waiting. This heathen is mine.'

At that moment, very nearby, another cellular phone was ringing.

The Hassassin answered. 'Speak.'

'It is I,' the voice said. 'Janus.'

The Hassassin smiled. 'Hello, master.'

'Your position may be known. Someone is coming to stop you.'

'They are too late. I have already made the arrangements here.'

'Good. Make sure you escape alive. There is work yet to be done.'

'Those who stand in my way will die.'

'Those who stand in your way are knowledgeable.'

'You speak of an American scholar?'

'You are aware of him?'

The Hassassin chuckled. 'Cool-tempered but naïve. He spoke to me on the phone earlier. He is with a female who seems quite the opposite.' The killer felt a stirring of arousal as he recalled the fiery temperament of Leonardo Vetra's daughter.

There was a momentary silence on the line, the first hesitation the Hassassin had ever sensed from his Illuminati master. Finally, Janus spoke. 'Eliminate them if need be.'

The killer smiled. 'Consider it done.' He felt a warm anticipation spreading through his body. *Although the woman I may keep as a prize.*

89

War had broken out in St Peter's Square.

The piazza had exploded into a frenzy of aggression. Media trucks skidded into place like assault vehicles claiming beachheads. Reporters unfurled high-tech electronics like soldiers arming for battle. All around the perimeter of the square, networks jockeyed for position as they raced to erect the newest weapon in media wars – flat-screen displays.

Flat-screen displays were enormous video screens that could be assembled on top of trucks or portable scaffolding. The screens served as a kind of billboard advertisement for the network, broadcasting that network's coverage and corporate logo like a drive-in movie. If a screen were well-situated – in front of the action, for example – a competing network could not shoot the story without including an advertisement for their competitor.

The square was quickly becoming not only a multimedia extravaganza, but a frenzied public vigil. Onlookers poured in from all directions. Open space in the usually limitless square was fast becoming a valuable commodity. People clustered around the towering flat-screen displays, listening to live reports in stunned excitement.

Only a hundred yards away, inside the thick walls of St Peter's Basilica, the world was serene. Lieutenant Chartrand and three other guards moved through the darkness. Wearing their infrared goggles, they fanned out across the nave, swinging their detectors before them. The search of Vatican City's public access areas so far had yielded nothing.

'Better remove your goggles up here,' the senior guard said.

Chartrand was already doing it. They were nearing the Niche of the Palliums – the sunken area in the center of the basilica. It was lit by ninety-nine oil lamps, and the amplified infrared would have seared their eyes.

Chartrand enjoyed being out of the heavy goggles, and he stretched his neck as they descended into the sunken niche to scan the area. The room was beautiful . . . golden and glowing. He had not been down here yet.

It seemed every day since Chartrand had arrived in Vatican City he had learned some new Vatican mystery. These oil lamps were one of them. There were exactly ninety-nine lamps burning at all times. It was tradition.

The clergy vigilantly refilled the lamps with sacred oils such that no lamp ever burned out. It was said they would burn until the end of time.

Or at least until midnight, Chartrand thought, feeling his mouth go dry again.

Chartrand swung his detector over the oil lamps. Nothing hidden in here. He was not surprised; the canister, according to the video feed, was hidden in a *dark* area.

As he moved across the niche, he came to a bulkhead grate covering a hole in the floor. The hole led to a steep and narrow stairway that went straight down. He had heard stories about what lay down there. Thankfully they would not have to descend. Rocher's orders were clear. *Search only the public access areas; ignore the white zones.*

'What's that smell?' he asked, turning away from the grate. The niche smelled intoxicatingly sweet.

'Fumes from the lamps,' one of them replied.

Chartrand was surprised. 'Smells more like cologne than kerosene.'

'It's not kerosene. These lamps are close to the papal altar, so they take a special, ambiental mixture – ethanol, sugar, butane, and perfume.'

'*Butane?*' Chartrand eyed the lamps uneasily.

The guard nodded. 'Don't spill any. Smells like heaven, but burns like hell.'

The guards had completed searching the Niche of the Palliums and were moving across the basilica again when their walkie-talkies went off.

It was an update. The guards listened in shock.

Apparently there were troubling new developments, which could not be shared on-air, but the camerlengo had decided to break tradition and enter conclave to address the cardinals. Never before in history had this been done. Then again, Chartrand realized, never before in history had the Vatican been sitting on what amounted to some sort of neoteric nuclear warhead.

Chartrand felt comforted to know the camerlengo was taking control. The camerlengo was the person inside Vatican City for whom Chartrand held the most respect. Some of the guards thought of the camerlengo as a *beato* – a religious zealot whose love of God bordered on obsession – but even they agreed . . . when it came to fighting the enemies of God, the camerlengo was the one man who would stand up and play hardball.

The Swiss Guards had seen a lot of the camerlengo this week in preparation for conclave, and everyone had commented that the man seemed a bit rough around the edges, his verdant eyes a bit more intense than usual. Not surprisingly, they had all commented; not only was the camerlengo responsible for planning the sacred conclave, but he had to do it immediately on the heels of the loss of his mentor, the Pope.

Chartrand had only been at the Vatican a few months when he heard the story of the bomb that blew up the camerlengo's mother before the kid's very eyes. *A bomb in church . . . and now it's happening all over again.* Sadly, the authorities never caught the bastards who planted the bomb . . . probably some anti-Christian hate group they said, and the case faded away. No wonder the camerlengo despised apathy.

A couple months back, on a peaceful afternoon inside Vatican City, Chartrand had bumped into the camerlengo coming across the grounds. The camerlengo had apparently recognized Chartrand as a new guard and invited him to accompany him on a stroll. They had talked about nothing in particular, and the camerlengo made Chartrand feel immediately at home.

'Father,' Chartrand said, 'may I ask you a strange question?'

The camerlengo smiled. 'Only if I may give you a strange answer.'

Chartrand laughed. 'I have asked every priest I know, and I still don't understand.'

'What troubles you?' The camerlengo led the way in short, quick strides, his frock kicking out in front of him as he walked. His black, crepe-sole shoes seemed befitting, Chartrand thought, like reflections of the man's essence . . . modern but humble, and showing signs of wear.

Chartrand took a deep breath. 'I don't understand this *omnipotent-benevolent* thing.'

The camerlengo smiled. 'You've been reading Scripture.'

'I try.'

'You are confused because the Bible describes God as an omnipotent and benevolent deity.'

'Exactly.'

'Omnipotent-benevolent simply means that God is all-powerful *and* well-meaning.'

'I understand the concept. It's just . . . there seems to be a contradiction.'

'Yes. The contradiction is pain. Man's starvation, war, sickness . . .'

'Exactly!' Chartrand knew the camerlengo would understand. 'Terrible things happen in this world. Human tragedy seems like proof that God could not possibly be *both* all-powerful and well-meaning. If He *loves* us and has the *power* to change our situation, He would prevent our pain, wouldn't He?'

The camerlengo frowned. 'Would He?'

Chartrand felt uneasy. Had he overstepped his bounds? Was this one of those religious questions you just didn't ask? 'Well . . . if God loves us, and He can protect us, He would *have* to. It seems He is either omnipotent and uncaring, or benevolent and powerless to help.'

'Do you have children, Lieutenant?'

Chartrand flushed. 'No, signore.'

'Imagine you had an eight-year-old son . . . would you love him?'

'Of course.'

'Would you do everything in your power to prevent pain in his life?'

282

'Of course.'

'Would you let him skateboard?'

Chartrand did a double take. The camerlengo always seemed oddly 'in touch' for a clergyman. 'Yeah, I guess,' Chartrand said. 'Sure, I'd let him skateboard, but I'd tell him to be careful.'

'So as this child's father, you would give him some basic, good advice and then let him go off and make his own mistakes?'

'I wouldn't run behind him and mollycoddle him if that's what you mean.'

'But what if he fell and skinned his knee?'

'He would learn to be more careful.'

The camerlengo smiled. 'So although you have the *power* to interfere and prevent your child's pain, you would *choose* to show your love by letting him learn his own lessons?'

'Of course. Pain is part of growing up. It's how we learn.'

The camerlengo nodded. 'Exactly.'

90

Langdon and Vittoria observed Piazza Barberini from the shadows of a small alleyway on the western corner. The church was opposite them, a hazy cupola emerging from a faint cluster of buildings across the square. The night had brought with it a welcome cool, and Langdon was surprised to find the square deserted. Above them, through open windows, blaring televisions reminded Langdon where everyone had disappeared to.

'. . . no comment yet from the Vatican . . . Illuminati murders of two cardinals . . . satanic presence in Rome . . . speculation about further infiltration . . .'

The news had spread like Nero's fire. Rome sat riveted, as did the rest of the world. Langdon wondered if they would really be able to stop this runaway train. As he scanned the piazza and waited, Langdon realized that despite the encroachment of modern buildings, the piazza still looked remarkably elliptical. High above, like some sort of modern shrine to a bygone hero, an enormous neon sign blinked on the roof of a luxurious hotel. Vittoria had already pointed it out to Langdon. The sign seemed eerily befitting.

HOTEL BERNINI

'Five of ten,' Vittoria said, cat eyes darting around the square. No sooner had she spoken the words than she grabbed Langdon's arm and pulled him back into the shadows. She motioned into the center of the square.

Langdon followed her gaze. When he saw it, he stiffened.

Crossing in front of them, beneath a street lamp, two dark figures appeared. Both were cloaked, their heads covered with dark *mantles*, the traditional black covering of Catholic widows. Langdon would have guessed they were women, but he couldn't be sure in the dark. One looked elderly and moved as if in pain, hunched over. The other, larger and stronger, was helping.

'Give me the gun,' Vittoria said.

'You can't just—'

Fluid as a cat, Vittoria was in and out of his pocket once again. The gun glinted in her hand. Then, in absolute silence, as if her feet never touched the cobblestone, she was circling left in the shadows, arching across the square to approach the couple from the rear. Langdon stood transfixed as Vittoria disappeared. Then, swearing to himself, he hurried after her.

The couple was moving slowly, and it was only a matter of half a minute before Langdon and Vittoria were positioned behind them, closing in from the rear. Vittoria concealed the gun beneath casually crossed arms in front of her, out of sight but accessible in a flash. She seemed to float faster and faster as the gap lessened, and Langdon battled to keep up. When his shoes scuffed a stone and sent it skittering, Vittoria shot him a sideways glare. But the couple did not seem to hear. They were talking.

At thirty feet, Langdon could start to hear voices. No words. Just faint murmurings. Beside him, Vittoria moved faster with every step. Her arms loosened before her, the gun starting to peek out. Twenty feet. The voices were clearer – one much louder than the other. Angry. Ranting. Langdon sensed it was the voice of an old woman. Gruff. Androgynous. He strained to hear what she was saying, but another voice cut the night.

'*Mi scusi!*' Vittoria's friendly tone lit the square like a torch.

Langdon tensed as the cloaked couple stopped short and began to turn. Vittoria kept striding toward them, even faster now, on a collision course. They would have no time to react. Langdon realized his own feet had stopped moving. From behind, he saw Vittoria's arms loosening, her hand coming free, the gun swinging forward. Then, over her shoulder, he saw a face, lit now in the street lamp. The panic surged to his legs, and he lunged forward. 'Vittoria no!'

Vittoria, however, seemed to exist a split second ahead of him. In a motion as swift as it was casual, Vittoria's arms were raised again, the gun disappearing as she clutched herself like a woman on a chilly night. Langdon stumbled to her side, almost colliding with the cloaked couple before them.

'*Buona sera,*' Vittoria blurted, her voice startled with retreat.

Langdon exhaled in relief. Two elderly women stood before them scowling out from beneath their mantles. One was so old she could barely stand. The other was helping her. Both clutched rosaries. They seemed confused by the sudden interruption.

Vittoria smiled, although she looked shaken. '*Dov'è la chiesa Santa Maria della Vittoria?* Where is the Church of—'

The two women motioned in unison to a bulky silhouette of a building on an inclined street from the direction they had come. '*È là.*'

'*Grazie,*' Langdon said, putting his hands on Vittoria's shoulders and gently pulling her back. He couldn't believe they'd almost attacked a pair of old ladies.

'*Non si può entrare,*' one woman warned. '*È stata chiusa presto.*'

'Closed early?' Vittoria looked surprised. '*Perchè?*'

Both women explained at once. They sounded irate. Langdon understood only parts of the grumbling Italian. Apparently, the women had been inside the church fifteen minutes ago praying for the Vatican in its time of need, when some man had appeared and told them the church was closing early.

'*Conoscete chi è quest'uomo?*' Vittoria demanded, sounding tense. 'Did you know the man?'

The women shook their heads. The man was a *straniero maleducato*, they explained, and he had forcibly made everyone inside leave, even the young priest and janitor, who said they were calling the police. But the intruder had only laughed, telling them to be sure the police brought cameras.

Cameras? Langdon wondered.

The women clucked angrily and called the man a *bar-àrabo*. Then, grumbling, they continued on their way.

'Bar-àrabo?' Langdon asked Vittoria. 'A barbarian?'

Vittoria looked suddenly taut. 'Not quite. *Bar-àrabo* is derogatory wordplay. It means *Àrabo* . . . Arab.'

Langdon felt a shiver and turned toward the outline of the church. As he did, his eyes glimpsed something in the church's stained-glass windows. The image shot dread through his body.

Unaware, Vittoria removed her cell phone and pressed the auto dial. 'I'm warning Olivetti.'

Speechless, Langdon reached out and touched her arm. With a tremulous hand, he pointed to the church.

Vittoria let out a gasp.

Inside the building, glowing like evil eyes through the stained-glass windows . . . shone the growing flash of flames.

91

Langdon and Vittoria dashed to the main entrance of the church of Santa Maria della Vittoria and found the wooden door locked. Vittoria fired three shots from Olivetti's semi-automatic into the ancient bolt, and it shattered.

The church had no anteroom, so the entirety of the sanctuary spread out in one gasping sweep as Langdon and Vittoria threw open the main door. The scene before them was so unexpected, so bizarre, that Langdon had to close his eyes and reopen them before his mind could take it all in.

The church was lavish baroque . . . gilded walls and altars. Dead center of the sanctuary, beneath the main cupola, wooden pews had been stacked high and were now ablaze in some sort of epic funeral pyre. A bonfire shooting high into the dome. As Langdon's eyes followed the inferno upward, the true horror of the scene descended like a bird of prey.

High overhead, from the left and right sides of the ceiling, hung two incensor cables – lines used for swinging frankincense vessels above the congregation. These lines, however, carried no incensors now. Nor were they swinging. They had been used for something else . . .

Suspended from the cables was a human being. A naked man. Each wrist had been connected to an opposing cable, and he had been hoisted almost to the point of being torn apart. His arms were outstretched in a spread-eagle as if he were nailed to some sort of invisible crucifix hovering within the house of God.

Langdon felt paralyzed as he stared upward. A moment later, he witnessed the final abomination. The old man was alive, and he raised his head. A pair of terrified eyes gazed down in a silent plea for help. On the man's chest was a scorched emblem. He had been branded. Langdon could not see it clearly, but he had little doubt what the marking said. As the flames climbed higher, lapping at the man's feet, the victim let out a cry of pain, his body trembling.

As if ignited by some unseen force, Langdon felt his body suddenly in motion, dashing down the main aisle toward the conflagration. His lungs filled with smoke as he closed in. Ten feet from the inferno, at a full sprint, Langdon hit a wall of heat. The skin on his face singed, and he fell back, shielding his eyes and landing hard on the marble floor. Staggering upright, he pressed forward again, hands raised in protection.

Instantly he knew. The fire was far too hot.

Moving back again, he scanned the chapel walls. *A heavy tapestry*, he thought. *If I can somehow smother the . . .* But he knew a tapestry was not to be found. *This is a baroque chapel, Robert, not some damn German castle! Think!* He forced his eyes back to the suspended man.

High above, smoke and flames swirled in the cupola. The incensor cables stretched outward from the man's wrists, rising to the ceiling where they passed through pulleys, and descended again to metal cleats on either side of the church. Langdon looked over at one of the cleats. It was high on the wall, but he knew if he could get to it and loosen one of the lines, the tension would slacken and the man would swing wide of the fire.

A sudden surge of flames crackled higher, and Langdon heard a piercing scream from above. The skin on the man's feet was starting to blister. The cardinal was being roasted alive. Langdon fixed his sights on the cleat and ran for it.

In the rear of the church, Vittoria clutched the back of a pew, trying to gather her senses. The image overhead was horrid. She forced her eyes away. *Do something!* She wondered where Olivetti was. Had he seen the Hassassin? Had he caught him? Where were they now? Vittoria moved forward to help Langdon, but as she did, a sound stopped her.

The crackling of the flames was getting louder by the instant, but a second sound also cut the air. A metallic vibration. Nearby. The repetitive pulse seemed to emanate from the end of the pews to her left. It was a stark rattle, like the ringing of a phone, but stony and hard. She clutched the gun firmly and moved down the row of pews. The sound grew louder. On. Off. A recurrent vibration.

As she approached the end of the aisle, she sensed the sound was coming from the floor just around the corner at the end of the pews. As she moved forward, gun outstretched in her right hand, she realized she was also holding something in her left hand – her cell phone. In her panic she had forgotten that outside she had used it to dial the commander . . . setting off his phone's silent vibration feature as a warning. Vittoria raised her phone to her ear. It was still ringing. The commander had never answered. Suddenly, with rising fear, Vittoria sensed she knew what was making the sound. She stepped forward, trembling.

The entire church seemed to sink beneath her feet as her eyes met the lifeless form on the floor. No stream of liquid flowed from the body. No signs of violence tattooed the flesh. There was only the fearful geometry of the commander's head . . . torqued backward, twisted 180 degrees in the wrong direction. Vittoria fought the images of her own father's mangled body.

The phone on the commander's belt lay against the floor, vibrating over and over against the cold marble. Vittoria hung up her own phone, and the ringing stopped. In the silence, Vittoria heard a new sound. A breathing in the dark directly behind her.

She started to spin, gun raised, but she knew she was too late. A laser beam of heat screamed from the top of her skull to the soles of her feet as the killer's elbow crashed down on the back of her neck.

'Now you are mine,' a voice said.

Then, everything went black.

Across the sanctuary, on the left lateral wall, Langdon balanced atop a pew and scraped upward on the wall trying to reach the cleat. The cable was still six feet above his head. Cleats like these were common in churches and were placed high to prevent tampering. Langdon knew priests used wooden ladders called *piuòli* to access the cleats. The killer had obviously used the church's ladder to hoist his victim. *So where the hell is the ladder now!* Langdon looked down, searching the floor around him. He had a faint recollection of seeing a ladder in here somewhere. *But where?* A moment later his heart sank. He realized where he had seen it. He turned toward the raging fire. Sure enough, the ladder was high atop the blaze, engulfed in flames.

Filled now with desperation, Langdon scanned the entire church from his raised platform, looking for anything at all that could help him reach the cleat. As his eyes probed the church, he had a sudden realization.

Where the hell is Vittoria? She had disappeared. *Did she go for help?* Langdon screamed out her name, but there was no response. *And where is Olivetti!*

There was a howl of pain from above, and Langdon sensed he was already too late. As his eyes went skyward again and saw the slowly roasting victim, Langdon had thoughts for only one thing. *Water. Lots of it. Put out the fire. At least lower the flames.* 'I need water, damn it!' he yelled out loud.

'That's next,' a voice growled from the back of the church.

Langdon wheeled, almost falling off the pews.

Striding up the side aisle directly toward him came a dark monster of a man. Even in the glow of the fire, his eyes burned black. Langdon recognized the gun in his hand as the one from his own jacket pocket . . . the one Vittoria had been carrying when they came in.

The sudden wave of panic that rose in Langdon was a frenzy of disjunct fears. His initial instinct was for Vittoria. What had this animal done to her? Was she hurt? Or *worse*? In the same instant, Langdon realized the man overhead was screaming louder. The cardinal would die. Helping him now was impossible. Then, as the Hassassin leveled the gun at Langdon's chest, Langdon's panic turned inward, his senses on overload. He reacted on instinct as the shot went off. Launching off the bench, Langdon sailed arms first over the sea of church pews.

289

When he hit the pews, he hit harder than he had imagined, immediately rolling to the floor. The marble cushioned his fall with all the grace of cold steel. Footsteps closed to his right. Langdon turned his body toward the front of the church and began scrambling for his life beneath the pews.

High above the chapel floor, Cardinal Guidera endured his last torturous moments of consciousness. As he looked down the length of his naked body, he saw the skin on his legs begin to blister and peel away. *I am in hell,* he decided. *God, why hast thou forsaken me?* He knew this must be hell because he was looking at the brand on his chest upside down . . . and yet, as if by the devil's magic, the word made perfect sense.

92

Three ballotings. No Pope.

Inside the Sistine Chapel, Cardinal Mortati had begun praying for a miracle. *Send us the candidates!* The delay had gone on long enough. A *single* missing candidate, Mortati could understand. But all four? It left no options. Under these conditions, achieving a two-thirds majority would take an act of God Himself.

When the bolts on the outer door began to grind open, Mortati and the entire College of Cardinals wheeled in unison toward the entrance. Mortati knew this unsealing could mean only one thing. By law, the chapel door could only be unsealed for two reasons – to remove the very ill, or to admit late cardinals.

The preferiti are coming!

Mortati's heart soared. Conclave had been saved.

But when the door opened, the gasp that echoed through the chapel was not one of joy. Mortati stared in incredulous shock as the man walked in. For the first time in Vatican history, a *camerlengo* had just crossed the sacred threshold of conclave *after* sealing the doors.

What is he thinking!

The camerlengo strode to the altar and turned to address the thunder-struck audience. 'Signori,' he said, 'I have waited as long as I can. There is something you have a right to know.'

93

Langdon had no idea where he was going. Reflex was his only compass, driving him away from danger. His elbows and knees burned as he clambered beneath the pews. Still he clawed on. Somewhere a voice was telling him to move left. *If you can get to the main aisle, you can dash for the exit.* He knew it was impossible. *There's a wall of flames blocking the main aisle!* His mind hunting for options, Langdon scrambled blindly on. The footsteps closed faster now to his right.

When it happened, Langdon was unprepared. He had guessed he had another ten feet of pews until he reached the front of the church. He had guessed wrong. Without warning, the cover above him ran out. He froze for an instant, half exposed at the front of the church. Rising in the recess to his left, gargantuan from this vantage point, was the very thing that had brought him here. He had entirely forgotten. Bernini's *Ecstasy of St Teresa* rose up like some sort of pornographic still life . . . the saint on her back, arched in pleasure, mouth open in a moan, and over her, an angel pointing his spear of fire.

A bullet exploded in the pew over Langdon's head. He felt his body rise like a sprinter out of a gate. Fueled only by adrenaline, and barely conscious of his actions, he was suddenly running, hunched, head down, pounding across the front of the church to his right. As the bullets erupted behind him, Langdon dove yet again, sliding out of control across the marble floor before crashing in a heap against the railing of a niche on the right-hand wall.

It was then that he saw her. A crumpled heap near the back of the church. *Vittoria!* Her bare legs were twisted beneath her, but Langdon sensed somehow that she was breathing. He had no time to help her.

Immediately, the killer rounded the pews on the far left of the church and bore relentlessly down. Langdon knew in a heartbeat it was over. The killer raised the weapon, and Langdon did the only thing he could do. He rolled his body over the banister into the niche. As he hit the floor on the other side, the marble columns of the balustrade exploded in a storm of bullets.

Langdon felt like a cornered animal as he scrambled deeper into the semicircular niche. Rising before him, the niche's sole contents seemed ironically apropos – a single sarcophagus. *Mine perhaps*, Langdon thought. Even the casket itself seemed fitting. It was a *scàtola* – a small, unadorned, marble box. Burial on a budget. The casket was raised off the floor on two marble blocks, and Langdon eyed the opening beneath it, wondering if he could slide through.

Footsteps echoed behind him.

With no other option in sight, Langdon pressed himself to the floor and slithered toward the casket. Grabbing the two marble supports, one with each hand, he pulled like a breaststroker, dragging his torso into the opening beneath the tomb. The gun went off.

Accompanying the roar of the gun, Langdon felt a sensation he had never felt in his life . . . a bullet sailing past his flesh. There was a hiss of wind, like the backlash of a whip, as the bullet just missed him and exploded in the marble with a puff of dust. Blood surging, Langdon heaved his body the rest of the way beneath the casket. Scrambling across the marble floor, he pulled himself out from beneath the casket and to the other side.

Dead end.

Langdon was now face to face with the rear wall of the niche. He had no doubt that this tiny space behind the tomb would become his grave. *And soon*, he realized, as he saw the barrel of the gun appear in the opening beneath the sarcophagus. The Hassassin held the weapon parallel with the floor, pointing directly at Langdon's midsection.

Impossible to miss.

Langdon felt a trace of self-preservation grip his unconscious mind. He twisted his body onto his stomach, parallel with the casket. Face down, he planted his hands flat on the floor, the glass cut from the archives pinching open with a stab. Ignoring the pain, he pushed. Driving his body upward in an awkward push-up, Langdon arched his stomach off the floor just as the gun went off. He could feel the shock wave of the bullets as they sailed beneath him and pulverized the porous travertine behind. Closing his eyes and straining against exhaustion, Langdon prayed for the thunder to stop.

And then it did.

The roar of gunfire was replaced with the cold click of an empty chamber.

Langdon opened his eyes slowly, almost fearful his eyelids would make a sound. Fighting the trembling pain, he held his position, arched like a cat. He didn't even dare breathe. His eardrums numbed by gunfire, Langdon listened for any hint of the killer's departure. Silence. He thought of Vittoria and ached to help her.

The sound that followed was deafening. Barely human. A guttural bellow of exertion.

The sarcophagus over Langdon's head suddenly seemed to rise on its side. Langdon collapsed on the floor as hundreds of pounds teetered toward him. Gravity overcame friction, and the lid was the first to go, sliding off the tomb and crashing to the floor beside him. The casket came next, rolling off its supports and toppling upside down toward Langdon.

As the box rolled, Langdon knew he would either be entombed in the hollow beneath it or crushed by one of the edges. Pulling in his legs and head, Langdon compacted his body and yanked his arms to his sides. Then he closed his eyes and awaited the sickening crush.

When it came, the entire floor shook beneath him. The upper rim landed only millimeters from the top of his head, rattling his teeth in their sockets. His right arm, which Langdon had been certain would be crushed, miraculously still felt intact. He opened his eyes to see a shaft of light. The right rim of the casket had not fallen all the way to the floor and was still propped partially on its supports. Directly overhead, though, Langdon found himself staring quite literally into the face of death.

The original occupant of the tomb was suspended above him, having adhered, as decaying bodies often did, to the bottom of the casket. The skeleton hovered a moment, like a tentative lover, and then with a sticky crackling, it succumbed to gravity and peeled away. The carcass rushed down to embrace him, raining putrid bones and dust into Langdon's eyes and mouth.

Before Langdon could react, a blind arm was slithering through the opening beneath the casket, sifting through the carcass like a hungry python. It groped until it found Langdon's neck and clamped down. Langdon tried to fight back against the iron fist now crushing his larynx, but he found his left sleeve pinched beneath the edge of the coffin. He had only one arm free, and the fight was a losing battle.

Langdon's legs bent in the only open space he had, his feet searching for the casket floor above him. He found it. Coiling, he planted his feet. Then, as the hand around his neck squeezed tighter, Langdon closed his eyes and extended his legs like a ram. The casket shifted, ever so slightly, but enough.

With a raw grinding, the sarcophagus slid off the supports and landed on the floor. The casket rim crashed onto the killer's arm, and there was a muffled scream of pain. The hand released Langdon's neck, twisting and jerking away into the dark. When the killer finally pulled his arm free, the casket fell with a conclusive thud against the flat marble floor.

Complete darkness. Again.

And silence.

There was no frustrated pounding outside the overturned sarcophagus. No prying to get in. Nothing. As Langdon lay in the dark amidst a pile of bones, he fought the closing darkness and turned his thoughts to her.

Vittoria. Are you alive?

If Langdon had known the truth – the horror to which Vittoria would soon awake – he would have wished for her sake that she were dead.

94

Sitting in the Sistine Chapel among his stunned colleagues, Cardinal Mortati tried to comprehend the words he was hearing. Before him, lit only by the candlelight, the camerlengo had just told a tale of such hatred and treachery that Mortati found himself trembling. The camerlengo spoke of kidnapped cardinals, branded cardinals, *murdered* cardinals. He spoke of the ancient Illuminati – a name that dredged up forgotten fears – and of their resurgence and vow of revenge against the church. With pain in his voice, the camerlengo spoke of his late Pope . . . the victim of an Illuminati poisoning. And finally, his words almost a whisper, he spoke of a deadly new technology, antimatter, which in less than two hours threatened to destroy all of Vatican City.

When he was through, it was as if Satan himself had sucked the air from the room. Nobody could move. The camerlengo's words hung in the darkness.

The only sound Mortati could now hear was the anomalous hum of a television camera in back – an electronic presence no conclave in history had ever endured – but a presence demanded by the camerlengo. To the utter astonishment of the cardinals, the camerlengo had entered the Sistine Chapel with two BBC reporters – a man and a woman – and announced that they would be transmitting his solemn statement, *live* to the world.

Now, speaking directly to the camera, the camerlengo stepped forward. 'To the Illuminati,' he said, his voice deepening, 'and to those of science, let me say this.' He paused. 'You have won the war.'

The silence spread now to the deepest corners of the chapel. Mortati could hear the desperate thumping of his own heart.

'The wheels have been in motion for a long time,' the camerlengo said. 'Your victory has been inevitable. Never before has it been as obvious as it is at this moment. Science is the new God.'

What is he saying! Mortati thought. *Has he gone mad? The entire world is hearing this!*

'Medicine, electronic communications, space travel, genetic manipulation . . . these are the miracles about which we now tell our children. These are the miracles we herald as proof that science will bring us the answers. The ancient stories of immaculate conceptions, burning bushes, and parting seas are no longer relevant. God has become obsolete. Science has won the battle. We concede.'

A rustle of confusion and bewilderment swept through the chapel.

'But science's victory,' the camerlengo added, his voice intensifying, 'has cost every one of us. And it has cost us deeply.'

Silence.

'Science may have alleviated the miseries of disease and drudgery and provided an array of gadgetry for our entertainment and convenience, but it has left us in a world without wonder. Our sunsets have been reduced to wavelengths and frequencies. The complexities of the universe have been shredded into mathematical equations. Even our self-worth as human beings has been destroyed. Science proclaims that Planet Earth and its inhabitants are a meaningless speck in the grand scheme. A cosmic accident.' He paused. 'Even the technology that promises to unite us, divides us. Each of us is now electronically connected to the globe, and yet we feel utterly alone. We are bombarded with violence, division, fracture, and betrayal. Skepticism has become a virtue. Cynicism and demand for proof has become enlightened thought. Is it any wonder that humans now feel more depressed and defeated than they have at any point in human history? Does science hold *anything* sacred? Science looks for answers by probing our unborn fetuses. Science even presumes to rearrange our own DNA. It shatters God's world into smaller and smaller pieces in quest of meaning . . . and all it finds is more questions.'

Mortati watched in awe. The camerlengo was almost hypnotic now. He had a physical strength in his movements and voice that Mortati had never witnessed on a Vatican altar. The man's voice was wrought with conviction and sadness.

'The ancient war between science and religion is over,' the camerlengo said. 'You have won. But you have not won fairly You have not won by providing answers. You have won by so radically reorienting our society that the truths we once saw as signposts now seem inapplicable. Religion cannot keep up. Scientific growth is exponential. It feeds on itself like a virus. Every new breakthrough opens doors for new breakthroughs. Mankind took thousands of years to progress from the wheel to the car. Yet only decades from the car into space. Now we measure scientific progress in weeks. We are spinning out of control. The rift between us grows deeper and deeper, and as religion is left behind, people find themselves in a spiritual void. We cry out for meaning. And believe me, we *do* cry out. We see UFOs, engage in channeling, spirit contact, out-of-body experiences, mindquests – all these eccentric ideas have a scientific veneer, but they are unashamedly irrational. They are the desperate cry of the modern soul, lonely and tormented, crippled by its own enlightenment and its inability to accept meaning in anything removed from technology.'

Mortati could feel himself leaning forward in his seat. He and the other cardinals and people around the world were hanging on this priest's every utterance. The camerlengo spoke with no rhetoric or vitriol. No references to scripture or Jesus Christ. He spoke in modern terms, unadorned and pure. Somehow, as though the words were flowing from God himself, he spoke the modern language . . . delivering the ancient message. In that moment, Mortati saw one of the reasons the late Pope held this young man so dear. In a world of apathy, cynicism, and technological deification, men like the camerlengo, realists who could speak to our souls like this man just had, were the church's only hope.

The camerlengo was talking more forcefully now. 'Science, you say, will save us. Science, I say, has destroyed us. Since the days of Galileo, the church has tried to slow the relentless march of science, sometimes with misguided means, but always with benevolent intention. Even so, the temptations are too great for man to resist. I warn you, look around yourselves. The promises of science have not been kept. Promises of efficiency and simplicity have bred nothing but pollution and chaos. We are a fractured and frantic species . . . moving down a path of destruction.'

The camerlengo paused a long moment and then sharpened his eyes on the camera.

'Who is this God science? Who is the God who offers his people power but no moral framework to tell you how to use that power? What kind of God gives a child *fire* but does not warn the child of its dangers? The language of science comes with no signposts about good and bad. Science textbooks tell us how to create a nuclear reaction, and yet they contain no chapter asking us if it is a good or a bad idea.

'To science, I say this. The church is tired. We are exhausted from trying to be your signposts. Our resources are drying up from our campaign to be the voice of balance as you plow blindly on in your quest for smaller chips and larger profits. We ask not why you will not govern yourselves, but how can you? Your world moves so fast that if you stop even for an instant to consider the implications of your actions, someone more efficient will whip past you in a blur. So you move on. You proliferate weapons of mass destruction, but it is the Pope who travels the world beseeching leaders to use restraint. You clone living creatures, but it is the church reminding us to consider the moral implications of our actions. You encourage people to interact on phones, video screens, and computers, but it is the church who opens its doors and reminds us to commune in person as we were meant to do. You even murder unborn babies in the name of research that will save lives. Again, it is the church who points out the fallacy of this reasoning.

'And all the while, you proclaim the church is ignorant. But who is more ignorant? The man who cannot define lightning, or the man who does not respect its awesome power? This church is reaching out to you. Reaching out to everyone. And yet the more we reach, the more you push us away.

Show me *proof* there is a God, you say. I say use your telescopes to look to the heavens, and tell me how there could *not* be a God!' The camerlengo had tears in his eyes now. 'You ask what does God look like. I say, where did that question come from? The answers are one and the same. Do you not see God in your science? How can you miss Him! You proclaim that even the slightest change in the force of gravity or the weight of an atom would have rendered our universe a lifeless mist rather than our magnificent sea of heavenly bodies, and yet you fail to see God's hand in *this*? Is it really so much easier to believe that we simply chose the right card from a deck of billions? Have we become so spiritually bankrupt that we would rather believe in mathematical impossibility than in a power greater than us?

'Whether or not you believe in God,' the camerlengo said, his voice deepening with deliberation, 'you must believe this. When we as a species abandon our trust in the power greater than us, we abandon our sense of accountability. Faith . . . *all* faiths . . . are admonitions that there is something we cannot understand, something to which we are accountable . . . With faith we are accountable to each other, to ourselves, and to a higher truth. Religion is flawed, but only because *man* is flawed. If the outside world could see this church as I do . . . looking beyond the ritual of these walls . . . they would see a modern miracle . . . a brotherhood of imperfect, simple souls wanting only to be a voice of compassion in a world spinning out of control.'

The camerlengo motioned out over the College of Cardinals, and the BBC camerawoman instinctively followed, panning the crowd.

'Are we obsolete?' the camerlengo asked. 'Are these men dinosaurs? Am I? Does the world really need a voice for the poor, the weak, the oppressed, the unborn child? Do we really need souls like these who, though imperfect, spend their lives imploring each of us to read the signposts of morality and not lose our way?'

Mortati now realized that the camerlengo, whether consciously or not, was making a brilliant move. By showing the cardinals, he was personalizing the church. Vatican City was no longer a building, it was *people* – people like the camerlengo who had spent their lives in the service of goodness.

'Tonight we are perched on a precipice,' the camerlengo said. 'None of us can afford to be apathetic. Whether you see this evil as Satan, corruption, or immorality . . . the dark force is alive and growing every day. Do not ignore it.' The camerlengo lowered his voice to a whisper, and the camera moved in. 'The force, though mighty, is not invincible. Goodness can prevail. Listen to your hearts. Listen to God. Together we can step back from this abyss.'

Now Mortati understood. This was the reason. Conclave had been violated, but this was the only way. It was a dramatic and desperate plea for help. The camerlengo was speaking to both his enemy and his friends now. He was entreating anyone, friend or foe, to see the light and stop this madness. Certainly someone listening would realize the insanity of this plot and come forward.

The camerlengo knelt at the altar. 'Pray with me.'

The College of Cardinals dropped to their knees to join him in prayer. Outside in St Peter's Square and around the globe . . . a stunned world knelt with them.

95

The Hassassin arranged his unconscious trophy in the rear of the van and took a moment to admire her sprawled body. She was not as beautiful as the women he bought, and yet she had an animal strength that excited him. Her body was radiant, dewy with perspiration. She smelled of musk.

As the Hassassin stood there savoring his prize, he ignored the throb in his arm. The bruise from the falling sarcophagus, although painful, was insignificant . . . well worth the compensation that lay before him. He took consolation in knowing the American who had done this to him was probably dead by now.

Gazing down at his incapacitated prisoner, the Hassassin visualized what lay ahead. He ran a palm up beneath her shirt. Her breasts felt perfect beneath her bra. *Yes*, he smiled. *You are more than worthy.* Fighting the urge to take her right there, he closed the door and drove off into the night.

There was no need to alert the press about *this* killing . . . the flames would do that for him.

At CERN, Sylvie sat stunned by the camerlengo's address. Never before had she felt so proud to be a Catholic and so ashamed to work at CERN. As she left the recreational wing, the mood in every single viewing room was dazed and somber. When she got back to Kohler's office, all seven phone lines were ringing. Media inquiries were never routed to Kohler's office, so the incoming calls could only be one thing.

Geld. Money calls.

Antimatter technology already had some takers.

Inside the Vatican, Gunther Glick was walking on air as he followed the camerlengo from the Sistine Chapel. Glick and Macri had just made *the* live transmission of the decade. And what a transmission it had been. The camerlengo had been spellbinding.

Now out in the hallway, the camerlengo turned to Glick and Macri. 'I have asked the Swiss Guard to assemble photos for you – photos of the branded cardinals as well as one of His late Holiness. I must warn you, these are not pleasant pictures. Ghastly burns. Blackened tongues. But I would like you to broadcast them to the world.'

Glick decided it must be perpetual Christmas inside Vatican City. *He wants me to broadcast an exclusive photo of the dead Pope?* 'Are you sure?' Glick asked, trying to keep the excitement from his voice.

The camerlengo nodded. 'The Swiss Guard will also provide you a live video feed of the antimatter canister as it counts down.'

Glick stared. *Christmas. Christmas. Christmas!*

'The Illuminati are about to find out,' the camerlengo declared, 'that they have grossly overplayed their hand.'

96

Like a recurring theme in some demonic symphony, the suffocating darkness had returned.

No light. No air. No exit.

Langdon lay trapped beneath the overturned sarcophagus and felt his mind careening dangerously close to the brink. Trying to drive his thoughts in any direction other than the crushing space around him, Langdon urged his mind toward some logical process . . . mathematics, music, anything. But there was no room for calming thoughts. *I can't move! I can't breathe!*

The pinched sleeve of his jacket had thankfully come free when the casket fell, leaving Langdon now with two mobile arms. Even so, as he pressed upward on the ceiling of his tiny cell, he found it immovable. Oddly, he wished his sleeve were still caught. *At least it might create a crack for some air.*

As Langdon pushed against the roof above, his sleeve fell back to reveal the faint glow of an old friend. Mickey. The greenish cartoon face seemed mocking now.

Langdon probed the blackness for any other sign of light, but the casket rim was flush against the floor. Goddamn Italian perfectionists, he cursed, now imperiled by the same artistic excellence he taught his students to revere . . . impeccable edges, faultless parallels, and of course, use only of the most seamless and resilient *Carrara* marble.

Precision can be suffocating.

'Lift the damn thing,' he said aloud, pressing harder through the tangle of bones. The box shifted slightly. Setting his jaw, he heaved again. The box felt like a boulder, but this time it raised a quarter of an inch. A fleeting glimmer of light surrounded him, and then the casket thudded back down. Langdon lay panting in the dark. He tried to use his legs to lift as he had before, but now that the sarcophagus had fallen flat, there was no room even to straighten his knees.

As the claustrophobic panic closed in, Langdon was overcome by images of the sarcophagus shrinking around him. Squeezed by delirium, he fought the illusion with every logical shred of intellect he had.

'Sarcophagus,' he stated aloud, with as much academic sterility as he could muster. But even erudition seemed to be his enemy today. *Sarcophagus is from the Greek 'sarx' meaning 'flesh', and 'phagein' meaning 'to eat.' I'm trapped in a box literally designed to 'eat flesh.'*

Images of flesh eaten from bone only served as a grim reminder that Langdon lay covered in human remains. The notion brought nausea and chills. But it also brought an idea.

Fumbling blindly around the coffin, Langdon found a shard of bone. A rib maybe? He didn't care. All he wanted was a wedge. If he could lift the box, even a crack, and slide the bone fragment beneath the rim, then maybe enough air could . . .

Reaching across his body and wedging the tapered end of the bone into the crack between the floor and the coffin, Langdon reached up with his other hand and heaved skyward. The box did not move. Not even slightly. He tried again. For a moment, it seemed to tremble slightly, but that was all.

With the fetid stench and lack of oxygen choking the strength from his body, Langdon realized he only had time for one more effort. He also knew he would need both arms.

Regrouping, he placed the tapered edge of the bone against the crack, and shifting his body, he wedged the bone against his shoulder, pinning it in place. Careful not to dislodge it, he raised both hands above him. As the stifling confine began to smother him, he felt a welling of intensified panic. It was the second time today he had been trapped with no air. Hollering aloud, Langdon thrust upward in one explosive motion. The casket jostled off the floor for an instant. But long enough. The bone shard he had braced against his shoulder slipped outward into the widening crack. When the casket fell again, the bone shattered. But this time Langdon could see the casket was propped up. A tiny slit of light showed beneath the rim.

Exhausted, Langdon collapsed. Hoping the strangling sensation in his throat would pass, he waited. But it only worsened as the seconds passed. Whatever air was coming through the slit seemed imperceptible. Langdon wondered if it would be enough to keep him alive. And if so, for how long? If he passed out, who would know he was even in there?

With arms like lead, Langdon raised his watch again: 10.12 p.m. Fighting trembling fingers, he fumbled with the watch and made his final play. He twisted one of the tiny dials and pressed a button.

As consciousness faded, and the walls squeezed closer, Langdon felt the old fears sweep over him. He tried to imagine, as he had so many times, that he was in an open field. The image he conjured, however, was no help. The nightmare that had haunted him since his youth came crashing back . . .

The flowers here are like paintings, *the child thought, laughing as he ran across the meadow. He wished his parents had come along. But his parents were busy pitching camp.*

'Don't explore too far,' his mother had said.

He had pretended not to hear as he bounded off into the woods.

Now, traversing this glorious field, the boy came across a pile of fieldstones. He figured it must be the foundation of an old homestead. He would not go near it. He knew better. Besides, his eyes had been drawn to something else – a brilliant lady's slipper – the rarest and most beautiful flower in New Hampshire. He had only ever seen them in books.

Excited, the boy moved toward the flower. He knelt down. The ground beneath him felt mulchy and hollow. He realized his flower had found an extra fertile spot. It was growing from a patch of rotting wood.

Thrilled by the thought of taking home his prize, the boy reached out . . . fingers extending toward the stem.

He never reached it.

With a sickening crack, the earth gave way.

In the three seconds of dizzying terror as he fell, the boy knew he would die. Plummeting downward, he braced for the bone-crushing collision. When it came, there was no pain. Only softness.

And cold.

He hit the deep liquid face first, plunging into a narrow blackness. Spinning disoriented somersaults, he groped the sheer walls that enclosed him on all sides. Somehow, as if by instinct, he sputtered to the surface.

Light.

Faint. Above him. Miles above him, it seemed.

His arms clawed at the water, searching the walls of the hollow for something to grab onto. Only smooth stone. He had fallen through an abandoned well covering. He screamed for help, but his cries reverberated in the tight shaft. He called out again and again. Above him, the tattered hole grew dim.

Night fell.

Time seemed to contort in the darkness. Numbness set in as he treaded water in the depths of the chasm, calling, crying out. He was tormented by visions of the walls collapsing in, burying him alive. His arms ached with fatigue. A few times he thought he heard voices. He shouted out, but his own voice was muted . . . like a dream.

As the night wore on, the shaft deepened. The walls inched quietly inward. The boy pressed out against the enclosure, pushing it away. Exhausted, he wanted to give up. And yet he felt the water buoy him, cooling his burning fears until he was numb.

When the rescue team arrived, they found the boy barely conscious. He had been treading water for five hours. Two days later, the Boston Globe ran a front-page story called 'The Little Swimmer That Could.'

97

The Hassassin smiled as he pulled his van into the mammoth stone structure overlooking the Tiber River. He carried his prize up and up . . .
spiraling higher in the stone tunnel, grateful his load was slender.

He arrived at the door.

The Church of Illumination, he gloated. *The ancient Illuminati meeting
room. Who would have imagined it to be here?*

Inside, he placed her on a plush divan. Then he expertly bound her arms
behind her back and tied her feet. He knew that what he longed for would
have to wait until his final task was finished. *Water.*

Still, he thought, he had a moment for indulgence. Kneeling beside her,
he ran his hand along her thigh. It was smooth. Higher. His dark fingers
snaked beneath the cuff of her shorts. Higher.

He stopped. *Patience*, he told himself, feeling aroused. *There is work to be
done.*

He walked for a moment out onto the chamber's high stone balcony. The
evening breeze slowly cooled his ardor. Far below the Tiber raged. He
raised his eyes to the dome of St Peter's, three quarters of a mile away,
naked under the glare of hundreds of press lights.

'Your final hour,' he said aloud, picturing the thousands of Muslims
slaughtered during the Crusades. 'At midnight you will meet your
God.'

Behind him, the woman stirred. The Hassassin turned. He considered
letting her wake up. Seeing terror in a woman's eyes was his ultimate
aphrodisiac.

He opted for prudence. It would be better if she remained unconscious
while he was gone. Although she was tied and would never escape, the
Hassassin did not want to return and find her exhausted from struggling.
I want your strength preserved . . . for me.

Lifting her head slightly, he placed his palm beneath her neck and found
the hollow directly beneath her skull. The crown/meridian pressure point
was one he had used countless times. With crushing force, he drove his
thumb into the soft cartilage and felt it depress. The woman slumped
instantly. *Twenty minutes*, he thought. She would be a tantalizing end to a

perfect day. After she had served him and died doing it, he would stand on the balcony and watch the midnight Vatican fireworks.

Leaving his prize unconscious on the couch, the Hassassin went downstairs into a torchlit dungeon. The final task. He walked to the table and revered the sacred, metal forms that had been left there for him.

Water. It was his last.

Removing a torch from the wall as he had done three times already, he began heating the end. When the end of the object was white hot, he carried it to the cell.

Inside, a single man stood in silence. Old and alone.

'Cardinal Baggia,' the killer hissed. 'Have you prayed yet?'

The Italian's eyes were fearless. 'Only for your soul.'

98

The six *pompieri* firemen who responded to the fire at the Church of Santa Maria Della Vittoria extinguished the bonfire with blasts of Halon gas. Water was cheaper, but the steam it created would have ruined the frescoes in the chapel, and the Vatican paid Roman *pompieri* a healthy stipend for swift and prudent service in all Vatican-owned buildings.

Pompieri, by the nature of their work, witnessed tragedy almost daily, but the execution in this church was something none of them would ever forget. Part crucifixion, part hanging, part burning at the stake, the scene was something dredged from a Gothic nightmare.

Unfortunately, the press, as usual, had arrived before the fire department. They'd shot plenty of video before the *pompieri* cleared the church. When the firemen finally cut the victim down and laid him on the floor, there was no doubt who the man was.

'*Cardinale Guidera,*' one whispered. '*Di Barcellona.*'

The victim was nude. The lower half of his body was crimson-black, blood oozing through gaping cracks in his thighs. His shinbones were exposed. One fireman vomited. Another went outside to breathe.

The true horror, though, was the symbol seared on the cardinal's chest. The squad chief circled the corpse in awestruck dread. *Lavoro del diavolo*, he said to himself. *Satan himself did this*. He crossed himself for the first time since childhood.

'*Un' altro corpo!*' someone yelled. One of the firemen had found another body.

The second victim was a man the chief recognized immediately. The austere commander of the Swiss Guard was a man for whom few public law enforcement officials had any affection. The chief called the Vatican, but all the circuits were busy. He knew it didn't matter. The Swiss Guard would hear about this on television in a matter of minutes.

As the chief surveyed the damage, trying to recreate what possibly could have gone on here, he saw a niche riddled with bullet holes. A coffin had been rolled off its supports and fallen upside down in an apparent struggle. It was a mess. *That's for the police and Holy See to deal with*, the chief thought, turning away.

As he turned, though, he stopped. Coming from the coffin he heard a sound. It was not a sound any fireman ever liked to hear.

'*Bomba!*' he cried out. '*Tutti fuori!*'

When the bomb squad rolled the coffin over, they discovered the source of the electronic beeping. They stared, confused.

'*Mèdico!*' one finally screamed. '*Mèdico!*'

99

'Any word from Olivetti?' the camerlengo asked, looking drained as Rocher escorted him back from the Sistine Chapel to the Pope's office.

'No, signore. I am fearing the worst.'

When they reached the Pope's office, the camerlengo's voice was heavy. 'Captain, there is nothing more I can do here tonight. I fear I have done too much already. I am going into this office to pray. I do not wish to be disturbed. The rest is in God's hands.'

'Yes, signore.'

'The hour is late, Captain. Find that canister.'

'Our search continues.' Rocher hesitated. 'The weapon proves to be too well hidden.'

The camerlengo winced, as if he could not think of it. 'Yes. At exactly 11.15 p.m., if the church is still in peril, I want you to evacuate the cardinals. I am putting their safety in your hands. I ask only one thing. Let these men proceed from this place with dignity. Let them exit into St Peter's Square and stand side by side with the rest of the world. I do not want the last image of this church to be frightened old men sneaking out a back door.'

'Very good, signore. And you? Shall I come for you at 11.15 as well?'

'There will be no need.'

'Signore?'

'I will leave when the spirit moves me.'

Rocher wondered if the camerlengo intended to go down with the ship.

The camerlengo opened the door to the Pope's office and entered. 'Actually . . .' he said, turning. 'There is one thing.'

'Signore?'

'There seems to be a chill in this office tonight. I am trembling.'

'The electric heat is out. Let me lay you a fire.'

The camerlengo smiled tiredly. 'Thank you. Thank you, very much.'

Rocher exited the Pope's office where he had left the camerlengo praying by firelight in front of a small statue of the Blessed Mother Mary. It was an eerie sight. A black shadow kneeling in the flickering glow. As Rocher headed down the hall, a guard appeared, running toward him. Even by candlelight Rocher recognized Lieutenant Chartrand. Young, green, and eager.

'Captain,' Chartrand called, holding out a cellular phone. 'I think the camerlengo's address may have worked. We've got a caller here who says he has information that can help us. He phoned on one of the Vatican's private extensions. I have no idea how he got the number.'

Rocher stopped. 'What?'

'He will only speak to the ranking officer.'

'Any word from Olivetti?'

'No, sir.'

He took the receiver. 'This is Captain Rocher. I am ranking officer here.'

'Rocher,' the voice said. 'I will explain to you who I am. Then I will tell you what you are going to do next.'

When the caller stopped talking and hung up, Rocher stood stunned. He now knew from whom he was taking orders.

Back at CERN, Sylvie Baudeloque was frantically trying to keep track of all the licensing inquiries coming in on Kohler's voice mail. When the private line on the director's desk began to ring, Sylvie jumped. Nobody had that number. She answered.

'Yes?'

'Ms Baudeloque? This is Director Kohler. Contact my pilot. My jet is to be ready in five minutes.'

100

Robert Langdon had no idea where he was or how long he had been unconscious when he opened his eyes and found himself staring up at the underside of a baroque, frescoed cupola. Smoke drifted overhead. Something was covering his mouth. An oxygen mask. He pulled it off. There was a terrible smell in the room – like burning flesh.

Langdon winced at the pounding in his head. He tried to sit up. A man in white was kneeling beside him.

'*Riposati!*' the man said, easing Langdon onto his back again. '*Sono il paramédico.*'

Langdon succumbed, his head spiraling like the smoke overhead. *What the hell happened?* Wispy feelings of panic sifted through his mind.

'*Sórcio salvatore,*' the paramedic said. 'Mouse . . . savior.'

Langdon felt even more lost. *Mouse savior?*

The man motioned to the Mickey Mouse watch on Langdon's wrist. Langdon's thoughts began to clear. He remembered setting the alarm. As he stared absently at the watch face, Langdon also noted the hour. 10.28 p.m.

He sat bolt upright.

Then, it all came back.

Langdon stood near the main altar with the fire chief and a few of his men. They had been rattling him with questions. Langdon wasn't listening. He had questions of his own. His whole body ached, but he knew he needed to act immediately.

A *pompiero* approached Langdon across the church. 'I checked again, sir. The only bodies we found are Cardinal Guidera and the Swiss Guard commander. There's no sign of a woman here.'

'*Grazie,*' Langdon said, unsure whether he was relieved or horrified. He knew he had seen Vittoria unconscious on the floor. Now she was gone. The only explanation he came up with was not a comforting one. The killer had not been subtle on the phone. *A woman of spirit. I am aroused. Perhaps before this night is over, I will find you. And when I do . . .*

Langdon looked around. 'Where is the Swiss Guard?'

'Still no contact. Vatican lines are jammed.'

Langdon felt overwhelmed and alone. Olivetti was dead. The cardinal was dead. Vittoria was missing. A half hour of his life had disappeared in a blink.

Outside, Langdon could hear the press swarming. He suspected footage of the third cardinal's horrific death would no doubt air soon, if it hadn't already. Langdon hoped the camerlengo had long since assumed the worst and taken action. *Evacuate the damn Vatican! Enough games! We lose!*

Langdon suddenly realized that all of the catalysts that had been driving him – helping to save Vatican City, rescuing the four cardinals, coming face to face with the brotherhood he had studied for years – all of these things had evaporated from his mind. The war was lost. A new compulsion had ignited within him. It was simple. Stark. Primal.

Find Vittoria.

He felt an unexpected emptiness inside. Langdon had often heard that intense situations could unite two people in ways that decades together often did not. He now believed it. In Vittoria's absence he felt something he had not felt in years. Loneliness. The pain gave him strength.

Pushing all else from his mind, Langdon mustered his concentration. He prayed that the Hassassin would take care of business before pleasure. Otherwise, Langdon knew he was already too late. *No*, he told himself, *you have time*. Vittoria's captor still had work to do. He had to surface one last time before disappearing forever.

The last altar of science, Langdon thought. The killer had one final task. *Earth. Air. Fire. Water.*

He looked at his watch. Thirty minutes. Langdon moved past the firemen toward Bernini's *Ecstasy of St Teresa*. This time, as he stared at Bernini's marker, Langdon had no doubt what he was looking for.

Let angels guide you on your lofty quest . . .

Directly over the recumbent saint, against a backdrop of gilded flame, hovered Bernini's angel. The angel's hand clutched a pointed spear of fire. Langdon's eyes followed the direction of the shaft, arching toward the right side of the church. His eyes hit the wall. He scanned the spot where the spear was pointing. There was nothing there. Langdon knew, of course, the spear was pointing far beyond the wall, into the night, somewhere across Rome.

'What direction is that?' Langdon asked, turning and addressing the chief with a newfound determination.

'Direction?' The chief glanced where Langdon was pointing. He sounded confused. 'I don't know . . . west, I think.'

'What churches are in that direction?'

The chief's puzzlement seemed to deepen. 'Dozens. Why?'

Langdon frowned. Of course there were dozens. 'I need a city map. Right away.'

The chief sent someone running out to the fire truck for a map.

Langdon turned back to the statue. *Earth . . . Air . . . Fire . . . VITTORIA.* *The final marker is Water,* he told himself. *Bernini's Water.* It was in a church out there somewhere. A needle in a haystack. He spurred his mind through all the Bernini works he could recall. *I need a tribute to Water!*

Langdon flashed on Bernini's statue of *Triton* – the Greek God of the sea. Then he realized it was located in the square outside this very church, in entirely the wrong direction. He forced himself to think. *What figure would Bernini have carved as a glorification of water? Neptune and Tritone?* Unfortunately that statue was in London's Victoria & Albert Museum.

'Signore?' A fireman ran in with a map.

Langdon thanked him and spread it out on the altar. He immediately realized he had asked the right people; the fire department's map of Rome was as detailed as any Langdon had ever seen. 'Where are we now?'

The man pointed. 'Next to Piazza Barberini.'

Langdon looked at the angel's spear again to get his bearings. The chief had estimated correctly. According to the map, the spear was pointing west. Langdon traced a line from his current location west across the map. Almost instantly his hopes began to sink. It seemed that with every inch his finger traveled, he passed yet another building marked by a tiny black cross. *Churches.* The city was riddled with them. Finally, Langdon's finger ran out of churches and trailed off into the suburbs of Rome. He exhaled and stepped back from the map. *Damn.*

Surveying the whole of Rome, Langdon's eyes touched down on the three churches where the first three cardinals had been killed. *The Chigi Chapel . . . St Peter's . . . here . . .*

Seeing them all laid out before him now, Langdon noted an oddity in their locations. Somehow he had imagined the churches would be scattered randomly across Rome. But they most definitely were not. Improbably, the three churches seemed to be separated systematically, in an enormous city-wide triangle. Langdon double-checked. He was not imagining things. '*Penna,*' he said suddenly, without looking up.

Someone handed him a ballpoint pen.

Langdon circled the three churches. His pulse quickened. He triple-checked his markings. *A symmetrical triangle!*

Langdon's first thought was for the Great Seal on the one-dollar bill – the triangle containing the all-seeing eye. But it didn't make sense. He had marked only *three* points. There were supposed to be four in all.

So where the hell is Water? Langdon knew that anywhere he placed the fourth point, the triangle would be destroyed. The only option to retain the symmetry was to place the fourth marker inside the triangle, at the center. He looked at the spot on the map. Nothing. The idea bothered him anyway. The four elements of science were considered *equal.* Water was not special; Water would not be at the *center* of the others.

Still, his instinct told him the systematic arrangement could not possibly be accidental. *I'm not yet seeing the whole picture.* There was only one alternative. The four points did not make a triangle; they made some other shape.

Langdon looked at the map. *A square, perhaps?* Although a square made no symbolic sense, squares were symmetrical at least. Langdon put his finger on the map at one of the points that would turn the triangle into a square. He saw immediately that a perfect square was impossible. The angles of the original triangle were oblique and created more of a distorted quadrilateral.

As he studied the other possible points around the triangle, something unexpected happened. He noticed that the line he had drawn earlier to indicate the direction of the angel's spear passed perfectly through one of the possibilities. Stupefied, Langdon circled that point. He was now looking at four ink marks on the map, arranged in somewhat of an awkward, kitelike diamond.

He frowned. Diamonds were not an Illuminati symbol either. He paused. *Then again . . .*

For an instant Langdon flashed on the famed Illuminati Diamond. The thought, of course, was ridiculous. He dismissed it. Besides, this diamond was oblong – like a kite – hardly an example of the flawless symmetry for which the Illuminati Diamond was revered.

When he leaned in to examine where he had placed the final mark, Langdon was surprised to find that the fourth point lay dead center of Rome's famed Piazza Navona. He knew the piazza contained a major church, but he had already traced his finger through that piazza and considered the church there. To the best of his knowledge it contained no Bernini works. The church was called Saint Agnes in Agony, named for St Agnes, a ravishing teenage virgin banished to a life of sexual slavery for refusing to renounce her faith.

There must be something in that church! Langdon racked his brain, picturing the inside of the church. He could think of no Bernini works at all inside, much less anything to do with *water*. The arrangement on the map was bothering him too. A diamond. It was far too accurate to be coincidence, but it was not accurate enough to make any sense. *A kite?* Langdon wondered if he had chosen the wrong point. *What am I missing!*

The answer took another thirty seconds to hit him, but when it did, Langdon felt an exhilaration like nothing he had ever experienced in his academic career.

The Illuminati genius, it seemed, would never cease.

The shape he was looking at was not intended as a diamond at all. The four points only formed a diamond because Langdon had connected *adjacent* points. *The Illuminati believe in opposites!* Connecting opposite vertices with his pen, Langdon's fingers were trembling. There before him on the map was a giant cruciform. *It's a cross!* The four elements of science unfolded before his eyes . . . sprawled across Rome in an enormous, city-wide cross.

As he stared in wonder, a line of poetry rang in his mind . . . like an old friend with a new face.

'Cross Rome the mystic elements unfold . . .

'Cross Rome . . .

The fog began to clear. Langdon saw that the answer had been in front of him all night! The Illuminati poem had been telling him *how* the altars were laid out. A cross!

'Cross Rome the mystic elements unfold!

It was cunning wordplay. Langdon had originally read the word *'Cross* as an abbreviation of *Across*. He assumed it was poetic license intended to retain the meter of the poem. But it was so much more than that! Another hidden clue.

The cruciform on the map, Langdon realized, was the ultimate Illuminati duality. It was a religious symbol formed by elements of science. Galileo's path of Illumination was a tribute to both science *and* God!

The rest of the puzzle fell into place almost immediately.

Piazza Navona.

Dead center of Piazza Navona, outside the church of St Agnes in Agony, Bernini had forged one of his most celebrated sculptures. Everyone who came to Rome went to see it.

The Fountain of the Four Rivers!

A flawless tribute to water, Bernini's *Fountain of the Four Rivers* glorified the four major rivers of the Old World – The Nile, Ganges, Danube, and Rio Plata.

Water, Langdon thought. *The final marker.* It was perfect.

And even more perfect, Langdon realized, the cherry on the cake, was that high atop Bernini's fountain stood a towering obelisk.

Leaving confused firemen in his wake, Langdon ran across the church in the direction of Olivetti's lifeless body.

10.31 p.m., he thought. *Plenty of time.* It was the first instant all day that Langdon felt ahead of the game.

Kneeling beside Olivetti, out of sight behind some pews, Langdon discreetly took possession of the commander's semiautomatic and walkie-talkie. Langdon knew he would call for help, but this was not the place to do it. The final altar of science needed to remain a secret for now. The media and fire department racing with sirens blaring to Piazza Navona would be no help at all.

Without a word, Langdon slipped out the door and skirted the press, who were now entering the church in droves. He crossed Piazza Barberini. In the shadows he turned on the walkie-talkie. He tried to hail Vatican City but heard nothing but static. He was either out of range or the transmitter needed some kind of authorization code. Langdon adjusted the complex dials and buttons to no avail. Abruptly, he realized his plan to get help was not going to work. He spun, looking for a pay phone. None. Vatican circuits were jammed anyway.

He was alone.

Feeling his initial surge of confidence decay, Langdon stood a moment and took stock of his pitiful state – covered in bone dust, cut, deliriously exhausted, and hungry.

Langdon glanced back at the church. Smoke spiraled over the cupola, lit by the media lights and fire trucks. He wondered if he should go back and get help. Instinct warned him however that extra help, especially untrained help, would be nothing but a liability. *If the Hassassin sees us coming . . .* He thought of Vittoria and knew this would be his final chance to face her captor.

Piazza Navona, he thought, knowing he could get there in plenty of time and stake it out. He scanned the area for a taxi, but the streets were almost entirely deserted. Even the taxi drivers, it seemed, had dropped everything to find a television. Piazza Navona was only about a mile away but Langdon had no intention of wasting precious energy on foot. He glanced back at the church, wondering if he could borrow a vehicle from someone.

A fire truck? A press van? Be serious.

Sensing options and minutes slipping away, Langdon made his decision. Pulling the gun from his pocket, he committed an act so out of character that he suspected his soul must now be possessed. Running over to a lone Citroën sedan idling at a stoplight, Langdon pointed the weapon through the driver's open window. '*Fuori!*' he yelled.

The trembling man got out.

Langdon jumped behind the wheel and hit the gas.

101

Gunther Glick sat on a bench in a holding tank inside the office of the Swiss Guard. He prayed to every god he could think of. *Please let this NOT be a dream.* It had been the scoop of his life. The scoop of anyone's life. Every reporter on earth wished he were Glick right now. *You are awake*, he told himself *And you are a star. Dan Rather is crying right now.*

Macri was beside him, looking a little bit stunned. Glick didn't blame her. In addition to exclusively broadcasting the camerlengo's address, she and Glick had provided the world with gruesome photos of the cardinals and of the Pope – *that tongue!* – as well as a live video feed of the antimatter canister counting down. *Incredible!*

Of course, all of that had been at the camerlengo's behest, so that was not the reason Glick and Macri were now locked in a Swiss Guard holding tank. It had been Glick's daring addendum to their coverage that the guards had not appreciated. Glick knew the conversation on which he had just reported was not intended for his ears, but this was his moment in the sun. *Another Glick scoop!*

'The 11th Hour Samaritan?' Macri groaned on the bench beside him, clearly unimpressed.

Glick smiled. 'Brilliant, wasn't it?'

'Brilliantly dumb.'

She's just jealous, Glick knew. Shortly after the camerlengo's address, Glick had again, by chance, been in the right place at the right time. He'd overheard Rocher giving new orders to his men. Apparently Rocher had received a phone call from a mysterious individual who Rocher claimed had critical information regarding the current crisis. Rocher was talking as if this man could help them and was advising his guards to prepare for the guest's arrival.

Although the information was clearly private, Glick had acted as any dedicated reporter would – without honor. He'd found a dark corner, ordered Macri to fire up her remote camera, and he'd reported the news.

'Shocking new developments in God's city,' he had announced, squinting his eyes for added intensity. Then he'd gone on to say that a mystery guest was coming to Vatican City to save the day. *The 11th Hour Samaritan*,

Glick had called him – a perfect name for the faceless man appearing at the last moment to do a good deed. The other networks had picked up the catchy sound bite, and Glick was yet again immortalized.

I'm brilliant, he mused. *Peter Jennings just jumped off a bridge.*

Of course Glick had not stopped there. While he had the world's attention, he had thrown in a little of his own conspiracy theory for good measure.

Brilliant. Utterly brilliant.

'You screwed us,' Macri said. 'You totally blew it.'

'What do you mean? I was great!'

Macri stared disbelievingly. 'Former President George Bush? An Illuminatus?'

Glick smiled. How much more obvious could it be? George Bush was a well-documented, 33rd-degree Mason, *and* he was the head of the CIA when the agency closed their Illuminati investigation for lack of evidence. And all those speeches about 'a thousand points of light' and a 'New World Order' . . . Bush was obviously Illuminati.

'And that bit about CERN?' Macri chided. 'You are going to have a very big line of lawyers outside your door tomorrow.'

'CERN? Oh come on! It's so obvious! Think about it! The Illuminati disappear off the face of the earth in the 1950s at about the same time CERN is *founded*. CERN is a haven for the most enlightened people on earth. Tons of private funding. They build a weapon that can destroy the church, and oops! . . . they *lose* it!'

'So you tell the world that CERN is the new home base of the Illuminati?'

'Obviously! Brotherhoods don't just disappear. The Illuminati had to go *somewhere*. CERN is a perfect place for them to hide. I'm not saying everyone at CERN is Illuminati. It's probably like a huge Masonic lodge, where most people are innocent, but the upper echelons—'

'Have you ever heard of slander, Glick? Liability?'

'Have you ever heard of real journalism!'

'Journalism? You were pulling bullshit out of thin air! I should have turned off the camera! And what the hell was that crap about CERN's corporate logo? Satanic symbology? Have you lost your mind?'

Glick smiled. Macri's jealousy was definitely showing. The CERN logo had been the most brilliant coup of all. Ever since the camerlengo's address, all the networks were talking about CERN and antimatter. Some stations were showing the CERN corporate logo as a backdrop. The logo seemed standard enough – two intersecting circles representing two particle accelerators, and five tangential lines representing particle injection tubes. The whole world was staring at this logo, but it had been Glick, a bit of a symbologist himself, who had first seen the Illuminati symbology hidden in it.

'You're not a symbologist,' Macri chided, 'you're just one lucky-ass reporter. You should have left the symbology to the Harvard guy.'

'The Harvard guy missed it,' Glick said.

The Illuminati significance in this logo is so obvious!

He was beaming inside. Although CERN had lots of accelerators, their logo showed only two. *Two is the Illuminati number of duality.* Although most accelerators had only one injection tube, the logo showed five. *Five is the number of the Illuminati pentagram.* Then had come the coup – the most brilliant point of all. Glick pointed out that the logo contained a large numeral '6' – clearly formed by one of the lines and circles – and when the logo was rotated, another six appeared . . . and then another. The logo contained three sixes! 666! The devil's number! The mark of the beast!

Glick was a genius.

Macri looked ready to slug him.

The jealousy would pass, Glick knew, his mind now wandering to another thought. If CERN was Illuminati headquarters, was CERN where the Illuminati kept their infamous Illuminati Diamond? Glick had read about it on the Internet – '*a flawless diamond, born of the ancient elements with such perfection that all those who saw it could only stand in wonder.*'

Glick wondered if the secret whereabouts of the Illuminati Diamond might be yet another mystery he could unveil tonight.

102

Piazza Navona. *Fountain of the Four Rivers.*

Nights in Rome, like those in the desert, can be surprisingly cool, even after a warm day. Langdon was huddled now on the fringes of Piazza Navona, pulling his jacket around him. Like the distant white noise of traffic, a cacophony of news reports echoed across the city. He checked his watch. Fifteen minutes. He was grateful for a few moments of rest.

The piazza was deserted. Bernini's masterful fountain sizzled before him with a fearful sorcery. The foaming pool sent a magical mist upward, lit from beneath by underwater floodlights. Langdon sensed a cool electricity in the air.

The fountain's most arresting quality was its height. The central core alone was over twenty feet tall – a rugged mountain of travertine marble riddled with caves and grottoes through which the water churned. The entire mound was draped with pagan figures. Atop this stood an obelisk that climbed another forty feet. Langdon let his eyes climb. On the obelisk's tip, a faint shadow blotted the sky, a lone pigeon perched silently.

A cross, Langdon thought, still amazed by the arrangement of the markers across Rome. Bernini's *Fountain of the Four Rivers* was the last altar of science. Only hours ago Langdon had been standing in the Pantheon convinced the Path of Illumination had been broken and he would never get this far. It had been a foolish blunder. In fact, the entire path was intact. *Earth, Air, Fire, Water.* And Langdon had followed it . . . from beginning to end.

Not quite to the end, he reminded himself. The path had *five* stops, not four. This fourth marker fountain somehow pointed to the ultimate destiny – the Illuminati's sacred lair – the Church of Illumination. Langdon wondered if the lair were still standing. He wondered if that was where the Hassassin had taken Vittoria.

Langdon found his eyes probing the figures in the fountain, looking for any clue as to the direction of the lair. *Let angels guide you on your lofty quest.* Almost immediately though, he was overcome by an unsettling awareness. This fountain contained no angels whatsoever. It certainly contained none Langdon could see from where he was standing . . . and none he had ever seen in the past. *The Fountain of the Four Rivers* was a pagan work. The carvings were all profane – humans, animals, even an awkward armadillo. An angel here would stick out like a sore thumb.

Is this the wrong place? He considered the cruciform arrangement of the four obelisks. He clenched his fists. *This fountain is perfect.*

It was only 10.46 p.m. when a black van emerged from the alleyway on the far side of the piazza. Langdon would not have given it a second look except that the van drove with no headlights. Like a shark patrolling a moonlit bay the vehicle circled the perimeter of the piazza.

Langdon hunkered lower, crouched in the shadows beside the huge stairway leading up to the Church of St Agnes in Agony. He gazed out at the piazza, his pulse climbing.

After making two complete circuits, the van banked inward toward Bernini's fountain. It pulled abreast of the basin, moving laterally along the rim until its side was flush with the fountain. Then it parked, its sliding door positioned only inches above the churning water.

Mist billowed.

Langdon felt an uneasy premonition. Had the Hassassin arrived early? Had he come in a van? Langdon had imagined the killer escorting his last victim across the piazza on foot, like he had at St Peter's, giving Langdon an open shot. But if the Hassassin had arrived in a van, the rules had just changed.

Suddenly, the van's side door slid open.

On the floor of the van, contorted in agony, lay a naked man. The man was wrapped in yards of heavy chains. He thrashed against the iron links, but the chains were too heavy. One of the links bisected the man's mouth like a horse's bit, stifling his cries for help. It was then that Langdon saw the second figure, moving around behind the prisoner in the dark, as though making final preparations.

Langdon knew he had only seconds to act.

Taking the gun, he slipped off his jacket and dropped it on the ground. He didn't want the added encumbrance of a tweed jacket, nor did he have any intention of taking Galileo's *Diagramma* anywhere near the water. The document would stay here where it was safe and dry.

Langdon scrambled to his right. Circling the perimeter of the fountain, he positioned himself directly opposite the van. The fountain's massive centerpiece obscured his view. Standing, he ran directly toward the basin. He hoped the thundering water was drowning his footsteps. When he reached the fountain, he climbed over the rim and dropped into the foaming pool.

The water was waist deep and like ice. Langdon grit his teeth and plowed through the water. The bottom was slippery, made doubly treacherous by a stratum of coins thrown for good luck. Langdon sensed he would need more than good luck. As the mist rose all around him, he wondered if it was the cold or the fear that was causing the gun in his hand to shake.

He reached the interior of the fountain and circled back to his left. He waded hard, clinging to the cover of the marble forms. Hiding himself behind the huge carved form of a horse, Langdon peered out. The van was only fifteen feet away. The Hassassin was crouched on the floor of the van, hands planted on the cardinal's chain-clad body, preparing to roll him out the open door into the fountain.

Waist-deep in water, Robert Langdon raised his gun and stepped out of the mist, feeling like some sort of aquatic cowboy making a final stand. 'Don't move.' His voice was steadier than the gun.

The Hassassin looked up. For a moment he seemed confused, as though he had seen a ghost. Then his lips curled into an evil smile. He raised his arms in submission. 'And so it goes.'

'Get out of the van.'

'You look wet.'

'You're early.'

'I am eager to return to my prize.'

Langdon leveled the gun. 'I won't hesitate to shoot.'

'You've already hesitated.'

Langdon felt his finger tighten on the trigger. The cardinal lay motionless now. He looked exhausted, moribund. 'Untie him.'

'Forget him. You've come for the woman. Do not pretend otherwise.'

Langdon fought the urge to end it right there. 'Where is she?'

'Somewhere safe. Awaiting my return.'

She's alive. Langdon felt a ray of hope. 'At the Church of Illumination?'

The killer smiled. 'You will never find its location.'

Langdon was incredulous. *The lair is still standing.* He aimed the gun. 'Where?'

'The location has remained secret for centuries. Even to me it was only revealed recently. I would die before I break that trust.'

'I can find it without you.'

'An arrogant thought.'

Langdon motioned to the fountain. 'I've come this far.'

'So have many. The final step is the hardest.'

Langdon stepped closer, his footing tentative beneath the water. The Hassassin looked remarkably calm, squatting there in the back of the van with his arms raised over his head. Langdon aimed at his chest, wondering if he should simply shoot and be done with it. *No. He knows where Vittoria is. He knows where the antimatter is. I need information!*

From the darkness of the van the Hassassin gazed out at his aggressor and couldn't help but feel an amused pity. The American was brave, that he had proven. But he was also untrained. That he had also proven. Valor without expertise was suicide. There were rules of survival. Ancient rules. And the American was breaking all of them.

You had the advantage – the element of surprise. You squandered it.

The American was indecisive . . . hoping for backup most likely . . . or perhaps a slip of the tongue that would reveal critical information.

Never interrogate before you disable your prey. A cornered enemy is a deadly enemy.

The American was talking again. Probing. Maneuvering.

The killer almost laughed aloud. *This is not one of your Hollywood movies . . . there will be no long discussions at gunpoint before the final shoot-out. This is the end. Now.*

Without breaking eye contact, the killer inched his hands across the ceiling of the van until he found what he was looking for. Staring dead ahead, he grasped it.

Then he made his play.

The motion was utterly unexpected. For an instant, Langdon thought the laws of physics had ceased to exist. The killer seemed to hang weightless in the air as his legs shot out from beneath him, his boots driving into the cardinal's side and launching the chain-laden body out the door. The cardinal splashed down, sending up a sheet of spray.

Water dousing his face, Langdon realized too late what had happened. The killer had grasped one of the van's roll bars and used it to swing outward. Now the Hassassin was sailing toward him, feet-first through the spray.

Langdon pulled the trigger, and the silencer spat. The bullet exploded through the toe of the Hassassin's left boot. Instantly Langdon felt the soles of the Hassassin's boots connect with his chest, driving him back with a crushing kick.

The two men splashed down in a spray of blood and water.

As the icy liquid engulfed Langdon's body, his first cognition was pain. Survival instinct came next. He realized he was no longer holding his weapon. It had been knocked away. Diving deep, he groped along the slimy bottom. His hand gripped metal. A handful of coins. He dropped them. Opening his eyes, Langdon scanned the glowing basin. The water churned around him like a frigid Jacuzzi.

Despite the instinct to breathe, fear kept him on the bottom. Always moving. He did not know from where the next assault would come. He needed to find the gun! His hands groped desperately in front of him.

You have the advantage, he told himself. *You are in your element.* Even in a soaked turtleneck Langdon was an agile swimmer. *Water is your element.*

When Langdon's fingers found metal a second time, he was certain his luck had changed. The object in his hand was no handful of coins. He gripped it and tried to pull it toward him, but when he did, he found himself gliding through the water. The object was stationary.

Langdon realized even before he coasted over the cardinal's writhing body that he had grasped part of the metal chain that was weighing the man down. Langdon hovered a moment, immobilized by the sight of the terrified face staring up at him from the floor of the fountain.

Jolted by the life in the man's eyes, Langdon reached down and grabbed the chains, trying to heave him toward the surface. The body came slowly . . . like an anchor. Langdon pulled harder. When the cardinal's head broke the surface, the old man gasped a few sucking, desperate breaths. Then, violently, his body rolled, causing Langdon to lose his grip on the slippery chains. Like a stone, Baggia went down again and disappeared beneath the foaming water.

Langdon dove, eyes wide in the liquid murkiness. He found the cardinal. This time, when Langdon grabbed on, the chains across Baggia's chest shifted . . . parting to reveal a further wickedness . . . a word stamped in seared flesh.

An instant later, two boots strode into view. One was gushing blood.

103

As a water polo player, Robert Langdon had endured more than his fair share of underwater battles. The competitive savagery that raged beneath the surface of a water polo pool, away from the eyes of the referees, could rival even the ugliest wrestling match. Langdon had been kicked, scratched, held, and even bitten once by a frustrated defenseman from whom Langdon had continuously twisted away.

Now, though, thrashing in the frigid water of Bernini's fountain, Langdon knew he was a long way from the Harvard pool. He was fighting not for a game, but for his life. This was the second time they had battled. No referees here. No rematches. The arms driving his face toward the bottom of the basin thrust with a force that left no doubt that it intended to kill.

Langdon instinctively spun like a torpedo. *Break the hold!* But the grip torqued him back, his attacker enjoying an advantage no water polo defenseman ever had – two feet on solid ground. Langdon contorted, trying to get his own feet beneath him. The Hassassin seemed to be favoring one arm . . . but nonetheless, his grip held firm.

It was then that Langdon knew he was not coming up. He did the only thing he could think of to do. He stopped trying to surface. *If you can't go north, go east.* Marshalling the last of his strength, Langdon dolphin-kicked his legs and pulled his arms beneath him in an awkward butterfly stroke. His body lurched forward.

The sudden switch in direction seemed to take the Hassassin off guard. Langdon's lateral motion dragged his captor's arms sideways, compromising his balance. The man's grip faltered, and Langdon kicked again. The sensation felt like a towline had snapped. Suddenly Langdon was free. Blowing the stale air from his lungs, Langdon clawed for the surface. A single breath was all he got. With crashing force the Hassassin was on top of him again, palms on his shoulders, all of his weight bearing down. Langdon scrambled to plant his feet beneath him but the Hassassin's leg swung out, cutting Langdon down.

He went under again.

Langdon's muscles burned as he twisted beneath the water. This time his maneuvers were in vain. Through the bubbling water, Langdon scanned the bottom, looking for the gun. Everything was blurred. The bubbles were denser here. A blinding light flashed in his face as the killer wrestled him deeper, toward a submerged spotlight bolted on the floor of the fountain. Langdon reached out, grabbing the canister. It was hot. Langdon tried to pull himself free, but the contraption was mounted on hinges and pivoted in his hand. His leverage was instantly lost.

The Hassassin drove him deeper still.

It was then Langdon saw it. Poking out from under the coins directly beneath his face. A narrow, black cylinder. *The silencer of Olivetti's gun!* Langdon reached out, but as his fingers wrapped around the cylinder, he did not feel metal, he felt plastic. When he pulled, the flexible rubber hose came flopping toward him like a flimsy snake. It was about two feet long with a jet of bubbles surging from the end. Langdon had not found the gun at all. It was one of the fountain's many harmless *spumanti* . . . bubble makers.

Only a few feet away Cardinal Baggia felt his soul straining to leave his body. Although he had prepared for this moment his entire life, he had never imagined the end would be like this. His physical shell was in agony . . . burned, bruised, and held underwater by an immovable weight. He reminded himself that this suffering was nothing compared to what Jesus had endured.

He died for my sins . . .

Baggia could hear the thrashing of a battle raging nearby. He could not bear the thought of it. His captor was about to extinguish yet another life . . . the man with kind eyes, the man who had tried to help.

As the pain mounted, Baggia lay on his back and stared up through the water at the black sky above him. For a moment he thought he saw stars.

It was time.

Releasing all fear and doubt, Baggia opened his mouth and expelled what he knew would be his final breath. He watched his spirit gurgle heavenward in a burst of transparent bubbles. Then, reflexively, he gasped. The water poured in like icy daggers to his sides. The pain lasted only a few seconds.

Then . . . peace.

The Hassassin ignored the burning in his foot and focused on the drowning American, whom he now held pinned beneath him in the churning water. *Finish it fully.* He tightened his grip, knowing *this* time Robert Langdon would not survive. As he predicted, his victim's struggling became weaker and weaker.

Suddenly Langdon's body went rigid. He began to shake wildly.

Yes, the Hassassin mused. *The rigors. When the water first hits the lungs.* The rigors, he knew, would last about five seconds.

They lasted six.

Then, exactly as the Hassassin expected, his victim went suddenly flaccid. Like a great deflating balloon, Robert Langdon fell limp. It was over. The Hassassin held him down for another thirty seconds to let the water flood all of his pulmonary tissue. Gradually, he felt Langdon's body sink, on its own accord, to the bottom. Finally, the Hassassin let go. The media would find a double surprise in the *Fountain of the Four Rivers*.

'*Tabban!*' the Hassassin swore, clambering out of the fountain and looking at his bleeding toe. The tip of his boot was shredded, and the front of his big toe had been sheared off. Angry at his own carelessness, he tore the cuff from his pant leg and rammed the fabric into the toe of his boot. Pain shot up his leg. '*Ibn al-kalb!*' He clenched his fists and rammed the cloth deeper. The bleeding slowed until it was only a trickle.

Turning his thoughts from pain to pleasure, the Hassassin got into his van. His work in Rome was done. He knew exactly what would soothe his discomfort. Vittoria Vetra was bound and waiting. The Hassassin, even cold and wet, felt himself stiffen.

I have earned my reward.

Across town Vittoria awoke in pain. She was on her back. All of her muscles felt like stone. Tight. Brittle. Her arms hurt. When she tried to move, she felt spasms in her shoulders. It took her a moment to comprehend her hands were tied behind her back. Her initial reaction was confusion. *Am I dreaming?* But when she tried to lift her head, the pain at the base of her skull informed her of her wakefulness.

Confusion transforming to fear, she scanned her surroundings. She was in a crude, stone room – large and well-furnished, lit by torches. Some kind of ancient meeting hall. Old-fashioned benches sat in a circle nearby.

Vittoria felt a breeze, cold now on her skin. Nearby, a set of double doors stood open, beyond them a balcony. Through the slits in the balustrade, Vittoria could have sworn she saw the Vatican.

104

Robert Langdon lay on a bed of coins at the bottom of the *Fountain of the Four Rivers*. His mouth was still wrapped around the plastic hose. The air being pumped through the *spumanti* tube to froth the fountain had been polluted by the pump, and his throat burned. He was not complaining, though. He was alive.

He was not sure how accurate his imitation of a drowning man had been, but having been around water his entire life, Langdon had certainly heard accounts. He had done his best. Near the end, he had even blown all the air from his lungs and stopped breathing so that his muscle mass would carry his body to the floor.

Thankfully, the Hassassin had bought it and let go.

Now, resting on the bottom of the fountain, Langdon had waited as long as he could wait. He was about to start choking. He wondered if the Hassassin was still out there. Taking an acrid breath from the tube, Langdon let go and swam across the bottom of the fountain until he found the smooth swell of the central core. Silently, he followed it upward, sur-facing out of sight, in the shadows beneath the huge marble figures.

The van was gone.

That was all Langdon needed to see. Pulling a long breath of fresh air back into his lungs, he scrambled back toward where Cardinal Baggia had gone down. Langdon knew the man would be unconscious now, and chances of revival were slim, but he had to try. When Langdon found the body, he planted his feet on either side, reached down, and grabbed the chains wrapped around the cardinal. Then Langdon pulled. When the car-dinal broke water, Langdon could see the eyes were already rolled upward, bulging. Not a good sign. There was no breath or pulse.

Knowing he could never get the body up and over the fountain rim, Langdon lugged Cardinal Baggia through the water and into the hollow beneath the central mound of marble. Here the water became shallow and there was an inclined ledge. Langdon dragged the naked body up onto the ledge as far as he could. Not far.

Then he went to work. Compressing the cardinal's chain-clad chest, Langdon pumped the water from his lungs. Then he began CPR.

Counting carefully. Deliberately. Resisting the instinct to blow too hard and too fast. For three minutes Langdon tried to revive the old man. After five minutes, Langdon knew it was over.

Il preferito. The man who would be Pope. Lying dead before him.

Somehow, even now, prostrate in the shadows on the semisubmerged ledge, Cardinal Baggia retained an air of quiet dignity. The water lapped softly across his chest, seeming almost remorseful . . . as if asking forgiveness for being the man's ultimate killer . . . as if trying to cleanse the scalded wound that bore its name.

Gently, Langdon ran a hand across the man's face and closed his upturned eyes. As he did, he felt an exhausted shudder of tears well from within. It startled him. Then, for the first time in years, Langdon cried.

105

The fog of weary emotion lifted slowly as Langdon waded away from the dead cardinal, back into deep water. Depleted and alone in the fountain, Langdon half-expected to collapse. But instead, he felt a new compulsion rising within him. Undeniable. Frantic. He sensed his muscles hardening with an unexpected grit. His mind, as though ignoring the pain in his heart, forced aside the past and brought into focus the single, desperate task ahead.

Find the Illuminati lair. Help Vittoria.

Turning now to the mountainous core of Bernini's fountain, Langdon summoned hope and launched himself into his quest for the final Illuminati marker. He knew somewhere on this gnarled mass of figures was a clue that pointed to the lair. As Langdon scanned the fountain, though, his hope withered quickly. The words of the *segno* seemed to gurgle mockingly all around him. *Let angels guide you on your lofty quest.* Langdon glared at the carved forms before him. *The fountain is pagan! It has no damn angels anywhere!*

When Langdon completed his fruitless search of the core, his eyes instinctively climbed the towering stone pillar. *Four markers*, he thought, *spread across Rome in a giant cross.*

Scanning the hieroglyphics covering the obelisk, he wondered if perhaps there were a clue hidden in the Egyptian symbology. He immediately dismissed the idea. The hieroglyphs predated Bernini by centuries, and hieroglyphs had not even been decipherable until the Rosetta Stone was discovered. Still, Langdon ventured, maybe Bernini had carved an additional symbol? One that would go unnoticed among all the hieroglyphs?

Feeling a shimmer of hope, Langdon circumnavigated the fountain one more time and studied all four façades of the obelisk. It took him two minutes, and when he reached the end of the final face, his hopes sank. Nothing in the hieroglyphs stood out as any kind of addition. Certainly no angels.

Langdon checked his watch. It was eleven on the dot. He couldn't tell whether time was flying or crawling. Images of Vittoria and the Hassassin started to swirl hauntingly as Langdon clambered his way around the fountain, the frustration mounting as he frantically completed yet another fruitless circle. Beaten and exhausted, Langdon felt ready to collapse. He threw back his head to scream into the night.

The sound jammed in his throat.

Langdon was staring straight up the obelisk. The object perched at the very top was one he had seen earlier and ignored. Now, however, it stopped him short. It was not an angel. Far from it. In fact, he had not even perceived it as *part* of Bernini's fountain. He thought it was a living creature, another one of the city's scavengers perched on a lofty tower.

A pigeon.

Langdon squinted skyward at the object, his vision blurred by the glowing mist around him. It was a pigeon, wasn't it? He could clearly see the head and beak silhouetted against a cluster of stars. And yet the bird had not budged since Langdon's arrival, even with the battle below. The bird sat now exactly as it had been when Langdon entered the square. It was perched high atop the obelisk, gazing calmly westward.

Langdon stared at it a moment and then plunged his hand into the fountain and grabbed a fistful of coins. He hurled the coins skyward. They clattered across the upper levels of the granite obelisk. The bird did not budge. He tried again. This time, one of the coins hit the mark. A faint sound of metal on metal clanged across the square.

The damned pigeon was bronze.

You're looking for an angel, not a pigeon, a voice reminded him. But it was too late. Langdon had made the connection. He realized the bird was not a pigeon at all.

It was a dove.

Barely aware of his own actions, Langdon splashed toward the center of the fountain and began scrambling up the travertine mountain, clambering over huge arms and heads, pulling himself higher. Halfway to the base of the obelisk, he emerged from the mist and could see the head of the bird more clearly.

There was no doubt. It was a dove. The bird's deceptively dark color was the result of Rome's pollution tarnishing the original bronze. Then the significance hit him. He had seen a pair of doves earlier today at the Pantheon. A *pair* of doves carried no meaning. This dove, however, was alone.

The lone dove is the pagan symbol for the Angel of Peace.

The truth almost lifted Langdon the rest of the way to the obelisk. Bernini had chosen the *pagan* symbol for the angel so he could disguise it in a pagan fountain. *Let angels guide you on your lofty quest. The dove is the angel!* Langdon could think of no more lofty perch for the Illuminati's final marker than atop this obelisk.

The bird was looking west. Langdon tried to follow its gaze, but he could not see over the buildings. He climbed higher. A quote from St Gregory of Nyssa emerged from his memory most unexpectedly. *As the soul becomes enlightened . . . it takes the beautiful shape of the dove.*

Langdon rose heavenward. Toward the dove. He was almost flying now. He reached the platform from which the obelisk rose and could climb no higher. With one look around, though, he knew he didn't have to. All of Rome spread out before him. The view was stunning.

To his left, the chaotic media lights surrounding St Peter's. To his right, the smoking cupola of Santa Maria della Vittoria. In front of him in the distance, Piazza del Popolo. Beneath him, the fourth and final point. A giant cross of obelisks.

Trembling, Langdon looked to the dove overhead. He turned and faced the proper direction, and then he lowered his eyes to the skyline.

In an instant he saw it.

So obvious. So clear. So deviously simple.

Staring at it now, Langdon could not believe the Illuminati lair had stayed hidden for so many years. The entire city seemed to fade away as he looked out at the monstrous stone structure across the river in front of him. The building was as famous as any in Rome. It stood on the banks of the Tiber River diagonally adjacent to the Vatican. The building's geometry was stark – a circular castle, within a square fortress, and then, outside its walls, surrounding the entire structure, a park in the shape of a *pentagram.*

The ancient stone ramparts before him were dramatically lit by soft floodlights. High atop the castle stood the mammoth bronze angel. The angel pointed his sword downward at the exact center of the castle. And as if that were not enough, leading solely and directly to the castle's main entrance stood the famous Bridge of Angels . . . a dramatic approachway adorned by twelve towering angels carved by none other than Bernini himself.

In a final breathtaking revelation, Langdon realized Bernini's city-wide cross of obelisks marked the fortress in perfect Illuminati fashion; the cross's central arm passed *directly* through the center of the castle's bridge, dividing it into two equal halves.

Langdon retrieved his tweed coat, holding it away from his dripping body. Then he jumped into the stolen sedan and rammed his soggy shoe into the accelerator, speeding off into the night.

106

It was 11.07 p.m. Langdon's car raced through the Roman night. Speeding down Lungotevere Tor Di Nona, parallel with the river, Langdon could now see his destination rising like a mountain to his right.

Castel Sant' Angelo. Castle of the Angel.

Without warning, the turnoff to the narrow Bridge of Angels – Ponte Sant' Angelo – appeared suddenly. Langdon slammed on his brakes and swerved. He turned in time, but the bridge was barricaded. He skidded ten feet and collided with a series of short cement pillars blocking his way. Langdon lurched forward as the vehicle stalled, wheezing and shuddering. He had forgotten the Bridge of Angels, in order to preserve it, was now zoned pedestrians only.

Shaken, Langdon staggered from the crumpled car, wishing now he had chosen one of the other routes. He felt chilled, shivering from the fountain. He donned his Harris tweed over his damp shirt, grateful for Harris's trademark double lining. The *Diagramma* folio would remain dry. Before him, across the bridge, the stone fortress rose like a mountain. Aching and depleted, Langdon broke into a loping run.

On both sides of him now, like a gauntlet of escorts, a procession of Bernini angels whipped past, funneling him toward his final destination. *Let angels guide you on your lofty quest.* The castle seemed to rise as he advanced, an unscalable peak, more intimidating to him even than St Peter's. He sprinted toward the bastion, running on fumes, gazing upward at the citadel's circular core as it shot skyward to a gargantuan, sword-wielding angel.

The castle appeared deserted.

Langdon knew through the centuries the building had been used by the Vatican as a tomb, a fortress, a papal hideout, a prison for enemies of the church, and a museum. Apparently, the castle had other tenants as well – the Illuminati. Somehow it made eerie sense. Although the castle was property of the Vatican, it was used only sporadically, and Bernini had made numerous renovations to it over the years. The building was now rumored to be honeycombed with secret entries, passageways, and hidden chambers. Langdon had little doubt that the angel and surrounding pentagonal park were Bernini's doing as well.

Arriving at the castle's elephantine double doors, Langdon shoved them hard. Not surprisingly, they were immovable. Two iron knockers hung at eye level. Langdon didn't bother. He stepped back, his eyes climbing the sheer outer wall. These ramparts had fended off armies of Berbers, heathens, and Moors. Somehow he sensed his chances of breaking in were slim.

Vittoria, Langdon thought. *Are you in there?*

Langdon hurried around the outer wall. *There must be another entrance!*

Rounding the second bulwark to the west, Langdon arrived breathless in a small parking area off Lungotere Angelo. On this wall he found a second castle entrance, a drawbridge-type ingress, raised and sealed shut. Langdon gazed upward again.

The only lights on the castle were exterior floods illuminating the façade. All the tiny windows inside seemed black. Langdon's eyes climbed higher. At the very peak of the central tower, a hundred feet above, directly beneath the angel's sword, a single balcony protruded. The marble parapet seemed to shimmer slightly, as if the room beyond it were aglow with torchlight. Langdon paused, his soaked body shivering suddenly. A shadow? He waited, straining. Then he saw it again. His spine prickled. *Someone is up there!*

'Vittoria!' he called out, unable to help himself, but his voice was swallowed by the raging Tiber behind him. He wheeled in circles, wondering where the hell the Swiss Guard were. Had they even heard his transmission?

Across the lot a large media truck was parked. Langdon ran toward it. A paunchy man in headphones sat in the cabin adjusting levers. Langdon rapped on the side of the truck. The man jumped, saw Langdon's dripping clothes, and yanked off his headset.

'What's the worry, mate?' His accent was Australian.

'I need your phone.' Langdon was frenzied.

The man shrugged. 'No dial tone. Been trying all night. Circuits are packed.'

Langdon swore aloud. 'Have you seen anyone go in there?' He pointed to the drawbridge.

'Actually, yeah. A black van's been going in and out all night.'

Langdon felt a brick hit the bottom of his stomach.

'Lucky bastard,' the Aussie said, gazing up at the tower, and then frowning at his obstructed view of the Vatican. 'I bet the view from up there is perfect. I couldn't get through the traffic in St Peter's, so I'm shooting from here.'

Langdon wasn't listening. He was looking for options.

'What do you say?' the Australian said. 'This 11th Hour Samaritan for real?'

Langdon turned. 'The what?'

'You didn't hear? The Captain of the Swiss Guard got a call from somebody who claims to have some primo info. The guy's flying in right now. All I know is if he saves the day . . . there go the ratings!' The man laughed.

Langdon was suddenly confused. A good Samaritan flying in to help? Did the person somehow know where the antimatter was? Then why didn't he just *tell* the Swiss Guard? Why was he coming in person? Something was odd, but Langdon didn't have time to figure out what.

'Hey,' the Aussie said, studying Langdon more closely. 'Ain't you that guy I saw on TV? Trying to save that cardinal in St Peter's Square?'

Langdon did not answer. His eyes had suddenly locked on a contraption attached to the top of the truck – a satellite dish on a collapsible appendage. Langdon looked at the castle again. The outer rampart was fifty feet tall. The inner fortress climbed farther still. A shelled defense. The top was impossibly high from here, but maybe if he could clear the first wall . . .

Langdon spun to the newsman and pointed to the satellite arm. 'How high does that go?'

'Huh?' The man looked confused. 'Fifteen meters. Why?'

'Move the truck. Park next to the wall. I need help.'

'What are you talking about?'

Langdon explained.

The Aussie's eyes went wide. 'Are you insane? That's a two–hundred–thousand–dollar telescoping extension. Not a ladder!'

'You want ratings? I've got information that will make your day.' Langdon was desperate.

'Information worth two hundred grand?'

Langdon told him what he would reveal in exchange for the favor.

Ninety seconds later, Robert Langdon was gripping the top of the satellite arm wavering in the breeze fifty feet off the ground. Leaning out, he grabbed the top of the first bulwark, dragged himself onto the wall, and dropped onto the castle's lower bastion.

'Now keep your bargain!' the Aussie called up. 'Where is he?'

Langdon felt guilt-ridden for revealing this information, but a deal was a deal. Besides, the Hassassin would probably call the press anyway. 'Piazza Navona,' Langdon shouted. 'He's in the fountain.'

The Aussie lowered his satellite dish and peeled out after the scoop of his career.

In a stone chamber high above the city, the Hassassin removed his soaking boots and bandaged his wounded toe. There was pain, but not so much that he couldn't enjoy himself.

He turned to his prize.

She was in the corner of the room, on her back on a rudimentary divan, hands tied behind her, mouth gagged. The Hassassin moved toward her. She was awake now. This pleased him. Surprisingly, in her eyes he saw fire instead of fear.

The fear will come.

107

Robert Langdon dashed around the outer bulwark of the castle, grateful for the glow of the floodlights. As he circled the wall, the courtyard beneath him looked like a museum of ancient warfare – catapults, stacks of marble cannonballs, and an arsenal of fearful contraptions. Parts of the castle were open to tourists during the day, and the courtyard had been partially restored to its original state.

Langdon's eyes crossed the courtyard to the central core of the fortress. The circular citadel shot skyward 107 feet to the bronze angel above. The balcony at the top still glowed from within. Langdon wanted to call out but knew better. He would have to find a way in.

He checked his watch.

11.12 p.m.

Dashing down the stone ramp that hugged the inside of the wall, Langdon descended to the courtyard. Back on ground level, he ran through shadows, clockwise around the fort. He passed three porticos, but all of them were permanently sealed. *How did the Hassassin get in?* Langdon pushed on. He passed two modern entrances, but they were padlocked from the outside. *Not here.* He kept running.

Langdon had circled almost the entire building when he saw a gravel drive cutting across the courtyard in front of him. At one end, on the outer wall of the castle, he saw the back of the gated drawbridge leading back outside. At the other end, the drive disappeared into the fortress. The drive seemed to enter a kind of tunnel – a gaping entry in the central core. *Il traforo!* Langdon had read about this castle's *traforo*, a giant spiral ramp that circled up inside the fort, used by commanders on horseback to ride from top to bottom rapidly. *The Hassassin drove up!* The gate blocking the tunnel was raised, ushering Langdon in. He felt almost exuberant as he ran toward the tunnel. But as he reached the opening, his excitement disappeared.

The tunnel spiraled *down*.

The wrong way. This section of the *traforo* apparently descended to the dungeons, not to the top.

Standing at the mouth of a dark bore that seemed to twist endlessly deeper into the earth, Langdon hesitated, looking up again at the balcony. He could swear he saw motion up there. *Decide!* With no other options, he dashed down into the tunnel.

High overhead, the Hassassin stood over his prey. He ran a hand across her arm. Her skin was like cream. The anticipation of exploring her bodily treasures was inebriating. How many ways could he violate her?

The Hassassin knew he deserved this woman. He had served Janus well. She was a spoil of war, and when he was finished with her, he would pull her from the divan and force her to her knees. She would service him again. *The ultimate submission.* Then, at the moment of his own climax, he would slit her throat.

Ghayat assa'adah, they called it. *The ultimate pleasure.*

Afterward, basking in his glory, he would stand on the balcony and savor the culmination of the Illuminati triumph . . . a revenge desired by so many for so long.

The tunnel grew darker. Langdon descended.

After one complete turn into the earth, the light was all but gone. The tunnel leveled out, and Langdon slowed, sensing by the echo of his footfalls that he had just entered a larger chamber. Before him in the murkiness, he thought he saw glimmers of light . . . fuzzy reflections in the ambient gleam. He moved forward, reaching out his hand. He found smooth surfaces. Chrome and glass. It was a vehicle. He groped the surface, found a door, and opened it.

The vehicle's interior dome-light flashed on. He stepped back and recognized the black van immediately. Feeling a surge of loathing, he stared a moment, then he dove in, rooting around in hopes of finding a weapon to replace the one he'd lost in the fountain. He found none. He did, however, find Vittoria's cell phone. It was shattered and useless. The sight of it filled Langdon with fear. He prayed he was not too late.

He reached up and turned on the van's headlights. The room around him blazed into existence, harsh shadows in a simple chamber. Langdon guessed the room was once used for horses and ammunition. It was also a dead end.

No exit. *I came the wrong way!*

At the end of his rope, Langdon jumped from the van and scanned the walls around him. No doorways. No gates. He thought of the angel over the tunnel entrance and wondered if it had been a coincidence. *No!* He thought of the killer's words at the fountain. *She is in the Church of Illumination . . . awaiting my return.* Langdon had come too far to fail now. His heart was pounding. Frustration and hatred were starting to cripple his senses.

When he saw the blood on the floor, Langdon's first thought was for Vittoria. But as his eyes followed the stains, he realized they were bloody footprints. The strides were long. The splotches of blood were only on the left foot. *The Hassassin!*

Langdon followed the footprints toward the corner of the room, his sprawling shadow growing fainter. He felt more and more puzzled with every step. The bloody prints looked as though they walked directly into the corner of the room and then disappeared.

When Langdon arrived in the corner, he could not believe his eyes. The granite block in the floor here was not a square like the others. He was looking at another signpost. The block was carved into a perfect pentagram, arranged with the tip pointing into the corner. Ingeniously concealed by overlapping walls, a narrow slit in the stone served as an exit. Langdon slid through. He was in a passage. In front of him were the remains of a wooden barrier that had once been blocking this tunnel.

Beyond it there was light.

Langdon was running now. He clambered over the wood and headed for the light. The passage quickly opened into another, larger chamber. Here a single torch flickered on the wall. Langdon was in a section of the castle that had no electricity . . . a section no tourists would ever see. The room would have been frightful in daylight, but the torch made it even more gruesome.

La prigione.

There were a dozen tiny jail cells, the iron bars on most eroded away. One of the larger cells, however, remained intact, and on the floor Langdon saw something that almost stopped his heart. Black robes and red sashes. *This is where he held the cardinals!*

Near the cell was an iron doorway in the wall. The door was ajar and beyond it Langdon could see some sort of passage. He ran toward it. But Langdon stopped before he got there. The trail of blood did not enter the passage. When Langdon saw the words carved over the archway, he knew why.

Il Passetto.

He was stunned. He had heard of this tunnel many times, never knowing where exactly the entrance was. *Il Passetto* – The Little Passage – was a slender, three-quarter-mile tunnel built between Castle St Angelo and the Vatican. It had been used by various Popes to escape to safety during sieges of the Vatican . . . as well as by a few less pious Popes to secretly visit mistresses or oversee the torture of their enemies. Nowadays both ends of the tunnel were supposedly sealed with impenetrable locks whose keys were kept in some Vatican vault. Langdon suddenly feared he knew how the Illuminati had been moving in and out of the Vatican. He found himself wondering *who* on the inside had betrayed the church and coughed up the keys. *Olivetti? One of the Swiss Guard?* None of it mattered anymore.

The blood on the floor led to the opposite end of the prison. Langdon followed. Here, a rusty gate hung draped with chains. The lock had been removed and the gate stood ajar. Beyond the gate was a steep ascension of spiral stairs. The floor here was also marked with a pentagramal block. Langdon stared at the block, trembling, wondering if Bernini himself had held the chisel that had shaped these chunks. Overhead, the archway was adorned with a tiny carved cherub. This was it.

The trail of blood curved up the stairs.

Before ascending, Langdon knew he needed a weapon, any weapon. He found a four-foot section of iron bar near one of the cells. It had a sharp, splintered end. Although absurdly heavy, it was the best he could do. He hoped the element of surprise, combined with the Hassassin's wound, would be enough to tip the scales in his advantage. Most of all, though, he hoped he was not too late.

The staircase's spiral treads were worn and twisted steeply upward. Langdon ascended, listening for sounds. None. As he climbed, the light from the prison area faded away. He ascended into the total darkness, keeping one hand on the wall. Higher. In the blackness, Langdon sensed the ghost of Galileo, climbing these very stairs, eager to share his visions of heaven with other men of science and faith.

Langdon was still in a state of shock over the location of the lair. The Illuminati meeting hall was in a building owned by the Vatican. No doubt while the Vatican guards were out searching basements and homes of well-known scientists, the Illuminati were meeting *here* . . . right under the Vatican's nose. It suddenly seemed so perfect. Bernini, as head architect of renovations here, would have had unlimited access to this structure . . . remodeling it to his own specifications with no questions asked. How many secret entries had Bernini added? How many subtle embellishments pointing the way?

The Church of Illumination. Langdon knew he was close.

As the stairs began narrowing, Langdon felt the passage closing around him. The shadows of history were whispering in the dark, but he moved on. When he saw the horizontal shaft of light before him, he realized he was standing a few steps beneath a landing, where the glow of torchlight spilled out beneath the threshold of a door in front of him. Silently he moved up.

Langdon had no idea where in the castle he was right now, but he knew he had climbed far enough to be near the peak. He pictured the mammoth angel atop the castle and suspected it was directly overhead.

Watch over me, angel, he thought, gripping the bar. Then, silently, he reached for the door.

On the divan, Vittoria's arms ached. When she had first awoken to find them tied behind her back, she'd thought she might be able to relax and work her hands free. But time had run out. The beast had returned. Now he was standing over her, his chest bare and powerful, scarred from battles he had endured. His eyes looked like two black slits as he stared down at her body. Vittoria sensed he was imagining the deeds he was about to perform. Slowly, as if to taunt her, the Hassassin removed his soaking belt and dropped it on the floor.

Vittoria felt a loathing horror. She closed her eyes. When she opened them again, the Hassassin had produced a switchblade knife. He snapped it open directly in front of her face.

Vittoria saw her own terrified reflection in the steel.

The Hassassin turned the blade over and ran the back of it across her belly. The icy metal gave her chills. With a contemptuous stare, he slipped the blade below the waistline of her shorts. She inhaled. He moved back and forth, slowly, dangerously . . . lower. Then he leaned forward, his hot breath whispering in her ear.

'This blade cut out your father's eye.'

Vittoria knew in that instant that she was capable of killing.

The Hassassin turned the blade again and began sawing upward through the fabric of her khaki shorts. Suddenly, he stopped, looking up. Someone was in the room.

'Get away from her,' a deep voice growled from the doorway.

Vittoria could not see who had spoken, but she recognized the voice. *Robert! He's alive!*

The Hassassin looked as if he had seen a ghost. 'Mr Langdon, you must have a guardian angel.'

108

In the split second it took Langdon to take in his surroundings, he realized he was in a sacred place. The embellishments in the oblong room, though old and faded, were replete with familiar symbology. Pentagram tiles. Planet frescoes. Doves. Pyramids.

The Church of Illumination. Simple and pure. He had arrived.

Directly in front of him, framed in the opening of the balcony, stood the Hassassin. He was bare chested, standing over Vittoria, who lay bound but very much alive. Langdon felt a wave of relief to see her. For an instant, their eyes met, and a torrent of emotions flowed – gratitude, desperation, and regret.

'So we meet yet again,' the Hassassin said. He looked at the bar in Langdon's hand and laughed out loud. 'And this time you come for me with *that?*'

'Untie her.'

The Hassassin put the knife to Vittoria's throat. 'I will kill her.'

Langdon had no doubt the Hassassin was capable of such an act. He forced a calm into his voice. 'I imagine she would welcome it . . . considering the alternative.'

The Hassassin smiled at the insult. 'You're right. She has much to offer. It would be a waste.'

Langdon stepped forward, grasping the rusted bar, and aimed the splintered end directly at the Hassassin. The cut on his hand bit sharply. 'Let her go.'

The Hassassin seemed for a moment to be considering it. Exhaling, he dropped his shoulders. It was a clear motion of surrender, and yet at that exact instant the Hassassin's arm seemed to accelerate unexpectedly. There was a blur of dark muscle, and a blade suddenly came tearing through the air toward Langdon's chest.

Whether it was instinct or exhaustion that buckled Langdon's knees at that moment, he didn't know, but the knife sailed past his left ear and clattered to the floor behind him. The Hassassin seemed unfazed. He smiled at Langdon, who was kneeling now, holding the metal bar. The killer stepped away from Vittoria and moved toward Langdon like a stalking lion.

As Langdon scrambled to his feet, lifting the bar again, his wet turtleneck and pants felt suddenly more restrictive. The Hassassin, half-clothed, seemed to move much faster, the wound on his foot apparently not slowing him at all. Langdon sensed this was a man accustomed to pain. For the first time in his life, Langdon wished he were holding a very big gun.

The Hassassin circled slowly, as if enjoying himself, always just out of reach, moving toward the knife on the floor. Langdon cut him off. Then the killer moved back toward Vittoria. Again Langdon cut him off.

'There's still time,' Langdon ventured. 'Tell me where the canister is. The Vatican will pay more than the Illuminati ever could.'

'You are naïve.'

Langdon jabbed with the bar. The Hassassin dodged. He navigated around a bench, holding the weapon in front of him, trying to corner the Hassassin in the oval room. *This damn room has no corners!* Oddly, the Hassassin did not seem interested in attacking or fleeing. He was simply playing Langdon's game. Coolly waiting.

Waiting for what? The killer kept circling, a master at positioning himself. It was like an endless game of chess. The weapon in Langdon's hand was getting heavy, and he suddenly sensed he knew what the Hassassin was waiting for. *He's tiring me out.* It was working, too. Langdon was hit by a surge of weariness, the adrenaline alone no longer enough to keep him alert. He knew he had to make a move.

The Hassassin seemed to read Langdon's mind, shifting again, as if intentionally leading Langdon toward a table in the middle of the room. Langdon could tell there was something on the table. Something glinted in the torchlight. *A weapon?* Langdon kept his eyes focused on the Hassassin and maneuvered himself closer to the table. When the Hassassin cast a long, guileless glance at the table, Langdon tried to fight the obvious bait. But instinct overruled. He stole a glance. The damage was done.

It was not a weapon at all. The sight momentarily riveted him.

On the table lay a rudimentary copper chest, crusted with ancient patina. The chest was a pentagon. The lid lay open. Arranged inside in five padded compartments were five brands. The brands were forged of iron – large embossing tools with stout handles of wood. Langdon had no doubt what they said.

ILLUMINATI, EARTH, AIR, FIRE, WATER.

Langdon snapped his head back up, fearing the Hassassin would lunge. He did not. The killer was waiting, almost as if he were refreshed by the game. Langdon fought to recover his focus, locking eyes again with his quarry, thrusting with the pipe. But the image of the box hung in his mind. Although the brands themselves were mesmerizing – artifacts few Illuminati scholars even believed existed – Langdon suddenly realized there had been something *else* about the box that had ignited a wave of foreboding within. As the Hassassin maneuvered again, Langdon stole another glance downward.

My God!

In the chest, the five brands sat in compartments around the outer edge. But in the *center*, there was another compartment. This partition was empty, but it clearly was intended to hold another brand . . . a brand much larger than the others, and perfectly square.

The attack was a blur.

The Hassassin swooped toward him like a bird of prey. Langdon, his concentration having been masterfully diverted, tried to counter, but the pipe felt like a tree trunk in his hands. His parry was too slow. The Hassassin dodged. As Langdon tried to retract the bar, the Hassassin's hands shot out and grabbed it. The man's grip was strong, his injured arm seeming no longer to affect him. Violently, the two men struggled. Langdon felt the bar ripped away, and a searing pain shot through his palm. An instant later, Langdon was staring into the splintered point of the weapon. The hunter had become the hunted.

Langdon felt like he'd been hit by a cyclone. The Hassassin circled, smiling now, backing Langdon against the wall. 'What is your American *adàgio?*' he chided. 'Something about curiosity and the cat?'

Langdon could barely focus. He cursed his carelessness as the Hassassin moved in. Nothing was making sense. *A sixth Illuminati brand?* In frustration he blurted, 'I've never read anything about a *sixth* Illuminati brand!'

'I think you probably have.' The killer chuckled as he herded Langdon around the oval wall.

Langdon was lost. He most certainly had not. There were *five* Illuminati brands. He backed up, searching the room for any weapon at all.

'A perfect union of the ancient elements,' the Hassassin said. 'The final brand is the most brilliant of all. I'm afraid you will never see it, though.'

Langdon sensed he would not be seeing much of anything in a moment. He kept backing up, searching the room for an option. 'And you've seen this final brand?' Langdon demanded, trying to buy time.

'Someday perhaps they will honor me. As I prove myself.' He jabbed at Langdon, as if enjoying a game.

Langdon slid backward again. He had the feeling the Hassassin was directing him around the wall toward some unseen destination. *Where?* Langdon could not afford to look behind him. 'The brand?' he demanded. 'Where is it?'

'Not here. Janus is apparently the only one who holds it.'

'Janus?' Langdon did not recognize the name.

'The Illuminati leader. He is arriving shortly.'

'The Illuminati leader is coming *here?*'

'To perform the final branding.'

Langdon shot a frightened glance to Vittoria. She looked strangely calm, her eyes closed to the world around her, her lungs pulling slowly . . . deeply. Was she the final victim? Was *he?*

'Such conceit,' the Hassassin sneered, watching Langdon's eyes. 'The two of you are nothing. You will die, of course, that is for certain. But the final victim of whom I speak is a truly dangerous enemy.'

Langdon tried to make sense of the Hassassin's words. A dangerous enemy? The top cardinals were all dead. The Pope was dead. The Illuminati had wiped them all out. Langdon found the answer in the vacuum of the Hassassin's eyes.

The camerlengo.

Camerlengo Ventresca was the one man who had been a beacon of hope for the world through this entire tribulation. The camerlengo had done more to condemn the Illuminati tonight than decades of conspiracy theorists. Apparently he would pay the price. He was the Illuminati's final target.

'You'll never get to him,' Langdon challenged.

'Not I,' the Hassassin replied, forcing Langdon farther back around the wall. 'That honor is reserved for Janus himself.'

'The Illuminati leader *himself* intends to brand the camerlengo?'

'Power has its privileges.'

'But no one could possibly get into Vatican City right now!'

The Hassassin looked smug. 'Not unless he had an appointment.'

Langdon was confused. The only person expected at the Vatican right now was the person the press was calling the 11th Hour Samaritan – the person Rocher said had information that could save—

Langdon stopped short. *Good God!*

The Hassassin smirked, clearly enjoying Langdon's sickening cognition. 'I too wondered how Janus would gain entrance. Then in the van I heard the radio – a report about an 11th hour Samaritan.' He smiled. 'The Vatican will welcome Janus with open arms.'

Langdon almost stumbled backward. *Janus is the Samaritan!* It was an unthinkable deception. The Illuminati leader would get a royal escort directly to the camerlengo's chambers. *But how did Janus fool Rocher? Or was Rocher somehow involved?* Langdon felt a chill. Ever since he had almost suffocated in the secret archives, Langdon had not entirely trusted Rocher.

The Hassassin jabbed suddenly, nicking Langdon in the side.

Langdon jumped back, his temper flaring. 'Janus will never get out alive!'

The Hassassin shrugged. 'Some causes are worth dying for.'

Langdon sensed the killer was serious. Janus coming to Vatican City on a *suicide* mission? A question of honor? For an instant, Langdon's mind took in the entire terrifying cycle. The Illuminati plot had come full circle. The priest whom the Illuminati had inadvertently brought to power by killing the Pope had emerged as a worthy adversary. In a final act of defiance, the Illuminati leader would destroy him.

Suddenly, Langdon felt the wall behind him disappear. There was a rush of cool air, and he staggered backward into the night. *The balcony!* He now realized what the Hassassin had in mind.

Langdon immediately sensed the precipice behind him – a hundred-foot drop to the courtyard below. He had seen it on his way in. The Hassassin wasted no time. With a violent surge, he lunged. The spear sliced toward Langdon's midsection. Langdon skidded back, and the point came up short, catching only his shirt. Again the point came at him. Langdon slid farther back, feeling the banister right behind him. Certain the next jab would kill him, Langdon attempted the absurd. Spinning to one side, he reached out and grabbed the shaft, sending a jolt of pain through his palm. Langdon held on.

The Hassassin seemed unfazed. They strained for a moment against one another, face to face, the Hassassin's breath fetid in Langdon's nostrils. The bar began to slip. The Hassassin was too strong. In a final act of desperation, Langdon stretched out his leg, dangerously off balance as he tried to ram his foot down on the Hassassin's injured toe. But the man was a professional and adjusted to protect his weakness.

Langdon had just played his final card. And he knew he had lost the hand.

The Hassassin's arms exploded upward, driving Langdon back against the railing. Langdon sensed nothing but empty space behind him as the railing hit just beneath his buttocks. The Hassassin held the bar crosswise and drove it into Langdon's chest. Langdon's back arched over the chasm.

'*Ma'assalamah*,' the Hassassin sneered. 'Good-bye.'

With a merciless glare, the Hassassin gave a final shove. Langdon's center of gravity shifted, and his feet swung up off the floor. With only one hope of survival, Langdon grabbed on to the railing as he went over. His left hand slipped, but his right hand held on. He ended up hanging upside down by his legs and one hand . . . straining to hold on.

Looming over him, the Hassassin raised the bar overhead, preparing to bring it crashing down. As the bar began to accelerate, Langdon saw a vision. Perhaps it was the imminence of death or simply blind fear, but in that moment, he sensed a sudden aura surrounding the Hassassin. A glowing effulgence seemed to swell out of nothing behind him . . . like an incoming fireball.

Halfway through his swing, the Hassassin dropped the bar and screamed in agony.

The iron bar clattered past Langdon out into the night. The Hassassin spun away from him, and Langdon saw a blistering torch burn on the killer's back. Langdon pulled himself up to see Vittoria, eyes flaring, now facing the Hassassin.

Vittoria waved a torch in front of her, the vengeance in her face resplendent in the flames. How she had escaped, Langdon did not know or care. He began scrambling back up over the banister.

The battle would be short. The Hassassin was a deadly match. Screaming with rage, the killer lunged for her. She tried to dodge, but the man was on her, holding the torch and about to wrestle it away. Langdon did not wait. Leaping off the banister, Langdon jabbed his clenched fist into the blistered burn on the Hassassin's back.

The scream seemed to echo all the way to the Vatican.

The Hassassin froze a moment, his back arched in anguish. He let go of the torch, and Vittoria thrust it hard into his face. There was a hiss of flesh as his left eye sizzled. He screamed again, raising his hands to his face.

'Eye for an eye,' Vittoria hissed. This time she swung the torch like a bat, and when it connected, the Hassassin stumbled back against the railing. Langdon and Vittoria went for him at the same instant, both heaving and pushing. The Hassassin's body sailed backward over the banister into the night. There was no scream. The only sound was the crack of his spine as he landed spread-eagle on a pile of cannonballs far below.

Langdon turned and stared at Vittoria in bewilderment. Slackened ropes hung off her midsection and shoulders. Her eyes blazed like an inferno.

'Houdini knew yoga.'

109

Meanwhile, in St Peter's Square, the wall of Swiss Guards yelled orders and fanned outward, trying to push the crowds back to a safer distance. It was no use. The crowd was too dense and seemed far more interested in the Vatican's impending doom than in their own safety. The towering media screens in the square were now transmitting a live countdown of the anti-matter canister – a direct feed from the Swiss Guard security monitor – compliments of the camerlengo. Unfortunately, the image of the canister counting down was doing nothing to repel the crowds. The people in the square apparently looked at the tiny droplet of liquid suspended in the canister and decided it was not as menacing as they had thought. They could also see the countdown clock now – a little under forty-five minutes until detonation. Plenty of time to stay and watch.

Nonetheless, the Swiss Guards unanimously agreed that the camerlengo's bold decision to address the world with the truth and then provide the media with actual *visuals* of Illuminati treachery had been a savvy maneuver. The Illuminati had no doubt expected the Vatican to be their usual reticent selves in the face of adversity. Not tonight. Camerlengo Carlo Ventresca had proven himself a commanding foe.

Inside the Sistine Chapel, Cardinal Mortati was getting restless. It was past 11.15 p.m. Many of the cardinals were continuing to pray, but others had clustered around the exit, clearly unsettled by the hour. Some of the cardinals began pounding on the door with their fists.

Outside the door Lieutenant Chartrand heard the pounding and didn't know what to do. He checked his watch. It was time. Captain Rocher had given strict orders that the cardinals were not to be let out until he gave the word. The pounding on the door became more intense, and Chartrand felt uneasy. He wondered if the captain had simply forgotten. The captain had been acting very erratic since his mysterious phone call.

Chartrand pulled out his walkie-talkie. 'Captain? Chartrand here. It is past time. Should I open the Sistine?'

'That door stays shut. I believe I already gave you that order.'

'Yes, sir, I just—'

'Our guest is arriving shortly. Take a few men upstairs, and guard the door of the Pope's office. The camerlengo is not to go *anywhere*.'

'I'm sorry, sir?'

'What is it that you don't understand, Lieutenant?'

'Nothing, sir. I am on my way.'

Upstairs in the Office of the Pope, the camerlengo stared in quiet meditation at the fire. *Give me strength, God. Bring us a miracle.* He poked at the coals, wondering if he would survive the night.

110

Eleven-twenty-three p.m.

Vittoria stood trembling on the balcony of Castle St Angelo, staring out across Rome, her eyes moist with tears. She wanted badly to embrace Robert Langdon, but she could not. Her body felt anesthetized. Readjusting. Taking stock. The man who had killed her father lay far below, dead, and she had almost been a victim as well.

When Langdon's hand touched her shoulder, the infusion of warmth seemed to magically shatter the ice. Her body shuddered back to life. The fog lifted, and she turned. Robert looked like hell – wet and matted – he had obviously been through purgatory to come rescue her.

'Thank you . . .' she whispered.

Langdon gave an exhausted smile and reminded her that it was *she* who deserved thanks – her ability to practically dislocate her shoulders had just saved them both. Vittoria wiped her eyes. She could have stood there forever with him, but the reprieve was short-lived.

'We need to get out of here,' Langdon said.

Vittoria's mind was elsewhere. She was staring out toward the Vatican. The world's smallest country looked unsettlingly close, glowing white under a barrage of media lights. To her shock, much of St Peter's Square was still packed with people! The Swiss Guard had apparently been able to clear only about a hundred and fifty feet back – the area directly in front of the basilica – less than one-third of the square. The shell of congestion encompassing the square was compacted now, those at the safer distances pressing for a closer look, trapping the others inside. *They are too close!* Vittoria thought. *Much too close!*

'I'm going back in,' Langdon said flatly.

Vittoria turned, incredulous. 'Into the *Vatican?*'

Langdon told her about the Samaritan, and how it was a ploy. The Illuminati leader, a man named Janus, was actually coming himself to brand the camerlengo. A final Illuminati act of domination.

'Nobody in Vatican City knows,' Langdon said. 'I have no way to contact them, and this guy is arriving any minute. I have to warn the guards before they let him in.'

'But you'll never get through the crowd!'

Langdon's voice was confident. 'There's a way. Trust me.'

Vittoria sensed once again that the historian knew something she did not. 'I'm coming.'

'No. Why risk both—'

'I have to find a way to get those people out of there! They're in incredible dange—'

Just then, the balcony they were standing on began to shake. A deafening rumble shook the whole castle. Then a white light from the direction of St Peter's blinded them. Vittoria had only one thought. *Oh my God! The antimatter annihilated early!*

But instead of an explosion, a huge cheer went up from the crowd. Vittoria squinted into the light. It was a barrage of media lights from the square, now trained, it seemed, on them! Everyone was turned their way, hollering and pointing. The rumble grew louder. The air in the square seemed suddenly joyous.

Langdon looked baffled. 'What the devil—'

The sky overhead roared.

Emerging from behind the tower, without warning, came the papal helicopter. It thundered fifty feet above them, on a beeline for Vatican City. As it passed overhead, radiant in the media lights, the castle trembled. The lights followed the helicopter as it passed by, and Langdon and Vittoria were suddenly again in the dark.

Vittoria had the uneasy feeling they were too late as they watched the mammoth machine slow to a stop over St Peter's Square. Kicking up a cloud of dust, the chopper dropped onto the open portion of the square between the crowd and the basilica, touching down at the bottom of the basilica's staircase.

'Talk about an entrance,' Vittoria said. Against the white marble, she could see a tiny speck of a person emerge from the Vatican and move toward the chopper. She would never have recognized the figure except for the bright red beret on his head. 'Red carpet greeting. That's Rocher.'

Langdon pounded his fist on the banister. 'Somebody's got to warn them!' He turned to go.

Vittoria caught his arm. 'Wait!' She had just seen something else, something her eyes refused to believe. Fingers trembling, she pointed toward the chopper. Even from this distance, there was no mistaking. Descending the gangplank was another figure . . . a figure who moved so uniquely that it could only be one man. Although the figure was seated, he accelerated across the open square with effortless control and startling speed.

A king on an electric throne.

It was Maximilian Kohler.

111

Kohler was sickened by the opulence of the Hallway of the Belvedere. The gold leaf in the ceiling alone probably could have funded a year's worth of cancer research. Rocher led Kohler up a handicapped ramp on a circuitous route into the Apostolic Palace.

'No elevator?' Kohler demanded.

'No power.' Rocher motioned to the candles burning around them in the darkened building. 'Part of our search tactic.'

'Tactics which no doubt failed.'

Rocher nodded.

Kohler broke into another coughing fit and knew it might be one of his last. It was not an entirely unwelcome thought.

When they reached the top floor and started down the hallway toward the Pope's office, four Swiss Guards ran toward them, looking troubled. 'Captain, what are you doing up here? I thought this man had information that—'

'He will only speak to the camerlengo.'

The guards recoiled, looking suspicious.

'Tell the camerlengo,' Rocher said forcefully, 'that the director of CERN, Maximilian Kohler, is here to see him. Immediately.'

'Yes, sir!' One of the guards ran off in the direction of the camerlengo's office. The others stood their ground. They studied Rocher, looking uneasy. 'Just one moment, captain. We will announce your guest.'

Kohler, however, did not stop. He turned sharply and maneuvered his chair around the sentinels.

The guards spun and broke into a jog beside him. '*Fermati!* Sir! Stop!'

Kohler felt repugnance for them. Not even the most elite security force in the world was immune to the pity everyone felt for cripples. Had Kohler been a healthy man, the guards would have tackled him. *Cripples are powerless*, Kohler thought. *Or so the world believes.*

Kohler knew he had very little time to accomplish what he had come for. He also knew he might die here tonight. He was surprised how little he cared. Death was a price he was ready to pay. He had endured too much in his life to have his work destroyed by someone like Camerlengo Ventresca.

'*Signore!*' the guards shouted, running ahead and forming a line across the hallway '*You must stop!*' One of them pulled a sidearm and aimed it at Kohler.

Kohler stopped.

Rocher stepped in, looking contrite. 'Mr Kohler, please. It will only be a moment. No one enters the Office of the Pope unannounced.'

Kohler could see in Rocher's eyes that he had no choice but to wait. *Fine*, Kohler thought. *We wait.*

The guards, cruelly it seemed, had stopped Kohler next to a full-length gilded mirror. The sight of his own twisted form repulsed Kohler. The ancient rage brimmed yet again to the surface. It empowered him. He was among the enemy now. *These* were the people who had robbed him of his dignity. These were the people. Because of *them* he had never felt the touch of a woman . . . had never stood tall to accept an award. *What truth do these people possess? What proof, damn it! A book of ancient fables? Promises of miracles to come? Science creates miracles every day!*

Kohler stared a moment into his own stony eyes. *Tonight I may die at the hands of religion*, he thought. *But it will not be the first time.*

For a moment, he was eleven years old again, lying in his bed in his parents' Frankfurt mansion. The sheets beneath him were Europe's finest linen, but they were soaked with sweat. Young Max felt like he was on fire, the pain wracking his body unimaginable. Kneeling beside his bed, where they had been for two days, were his mother and father. They were praying.

In the shadows stood three of Frankfurt's best doctors.

'I urge you to reconsider!' one of the doctors said. 'Look at the boy! His fever is increasing. He is in terrible pain. And danger!'

But Max knew his mother's reply before she even said it. '*Gott wird ihn beschuetzen.*'

Yes, Max thought. *God will protect me.* The conviction in his mother's voice gave him strength. *God will protect me.*

An hour later, Max felt like his whole body was being crushed beneath a car. He could not even breathe to cry.

'Your son is in great suffering,' another doctor said. 'Let me at least ease his pain. I have in my bag a simple injection of—'

'*Ruhe, bitte!*' Max's father silenced the doctor without even opening his eyes. He simply kept praying.

'Father, please!' Max wanted to scream. 'Let them stop the pain!' But his words were lost in a spasm of coughing.

An hour later, the pain had worsened.

'Your son could become paralyzed,' one of the doctors scolded. 'Or even die! We have medicines that will help!'

Frau and Herr Kohler would not allow it. They did not believe in medicine. Who were they to interfere with God's master plan? They prayed harder. After all, God had blessed them with this boy, why would God take the child away? His mother whispered to Max to be strong. She explained that God was testing him . . . like the Bible story of Abraham . . . a test of his faith.

Max tried to have faith, but the pain was excruciating.

'I cannot watch this!' one of the doctors finally said, running from the room.

By dawn, Max was barely conscious. Every muscle in his body spasmed in agony. *Where is Jesus?* he wondered. *Doesn't he love me?* Max felt the life slipping from his body.

His mother had fallen asleep at the bedside, her hands still clasped over him. Max's father stood across the room at the window staring out at the dawn. He seemed to be in a trance. Max could hear the low mumble of his ceaseless prayers for mercy.

It was then that Max sensed the figure hovering over him. *An angel?* Max could barely see. His eyes were swollen shut. The figure whispered in his ear, but it was not the voice of an angel. Max recognized it as one of the doctors . . . the one who had sat in the corner for two days, never leaving, begging Max's parents to let him administer some new drug from England.

'I will never forgive myself,' the doctor whispered, 'if I do not do this.' Then the doctor gently took Max's frail arm. 'I wish I had done it sooner.'

Max felt a tiny prick in his arm – barely discernible through the pain.

Then the doctor quietly packed his things. Before he left, he put a hand on Max's forehead. 'This will save your life. I have great faith in the power of medicine.'

Within minutes, Max felt as if some sort of magic spirit were flowing through his veins. The warmth spread through his body numbing his pain. Finally, for the first time in days, Max slept.

When the fever broke, his mother and father proclaimed a miracle of God. But when it became evident that their son was crippled, they became despondent. They wheeled their son into the church and begged the priest for counseling.

'It was only by the grace of God,' the priest told them, 'that this boy survived.'

Max listened, saying nothing.

'But our son cannot walk!' Frau Kohler was weeping.

The priest nodded sadly. 'Yes. It seems God has punished him for not having enough faith.'

'Mr Kohler?' It was the Swiss Guard who had run ahead. 'The camerlengo says he will grant you audience.'

Kohler grunted, accelerating again down the hall.

'He is surprised by your visit,' the guard said.

'I'm sure.' Kohler rolled on. 'I would like to see him alone.'

'Impossible,' the guard said. 'No one—'

'Lieutenant,' Rocher barked. 'The meeting will be as Mr Kohler wishes.'

The guard stared in obvious disbelief.

Outside the door to the Pope's office, Rocher allowed his guards to take standard precautions before letting Kohler in. Their handheld metal detector was rendered worthless by the myriad of electronic devices on Kohler's wheelchair. The guards frisked him but were obviously too ashamed of his disability to do it properly. They never found the revolver affixed beneath his chair. Nor did they relieve him of the other object . . . the one that Kohler knew would bring unforgettable closure to this evening's chain of events.

When Kohler entered the Pope's office, Camerlengo Ventresca was alone, kneeling in prayer beside a dying fire. He did not open his eyes.

'Mr Kohler,' the camerlengo said. 'Have you come to make me a martyr?'

112

All the while, the narrow tunnel called *Il Passetto* stretched out before Langdon and Vittoria as they dashed toward Vatican City. The torch in Langdon's hand threw only enough light to see a few yards ahead. The walls were close on either side, and the ceiling low. The air smelled dank. Langdon raced on into the darkness with Vittoria close at his heels.

The tunnel inclined steeply as it left the Castle St Angelo, proceeding upward into the underside of a stone bastion that looked like a Roman aqueduct. There, the tunnel leveled out and began its secret course toward Vatican City.

As Langdon ran, his thoughts turned over and over in a kaleidoscope of confounding images – Kohler, Janus, the Hassassin, Rocher . . . a sixth brand? *I'm sure you've heard about the sixth brand,* the killer had said. *The most brilliant of all.* Langdon was quite certain he had *not.* Even in conspiracy theory lore, Langdon could think of no references to any sixth brand. Real or imagined. There were rumors of a gold bullion and a flawless Illuminati Diamond but never any mention of a sixth brand.

'Kohler can't be Janus!' Vittoria declared as they ran down the interior of the dike. 'It's impossible!'

Impossible was one word Langdon had stopped using tonight. 'I don't know,' Langdon yelled as they ran. 'Kohler has a serious grudge, and he also has some serious influence.'

'This crisis has made CERN look like monsters! Max would *never* do anything to damage CERN's reputation!'

On one count, Langdon knew CERN had taken a public beating tonight, all because of the Illuminati's insistence on making this a public spectacle. And yet, he wondered how much CERN had *really* been damaged. Criticism from the church was nothing new for CERN. In fact, the more Langdon thought about it, the more he wondered if this crisis might actually *benefit* CERN. If publicity were the game, then antimatter was the jackpot winner tonight. The entire planet was talking about it.

'You know what promoter P. T. Barnum said,' Langdon called over his shoulder. '"I don't care what you say about me, just spell my name right!" I bet people are already secretly lining up to license antimatter technology. And after they see its true power at midnight tonight . . .'

'Illogical,' Vittoria said. 'Publicizing scientific breakthroughs is not about showing destructive power! This is *terrible* for antimatter, trust me!'

Langdon's torch was fading now. 'Then maybe it's all much simpler than that. Maybe Kohler gambled that the Vatican would keep the antimatter a secret – refusing to empower the Illuminati by confirming the weapon's existence. Kohler expected the Vatican to be their usual tight-lipped selves about the threat, but the camerlengo changed the rules.'

Vittoria was silent as they dashed down the tunnel.

Suddenly the scenario was making more sense to Langdon. 'Yes! Kohler never counted on the camerlengo's reaction. The camerlengo broke the Vatican tradition of secrecy and went public about the crisis. He was dead honest. He put the antimatter on TV, for God's sake. It was a brilliant response, and Kohler never expected it. And the irony of the whole thing is that the Illuminati attack backfired. It inadvertently produced a new church leader in the camerlengo. And now Kohler is coming to kill him!'

'Max is a bastard,' Vittoria declared, 'but he is not a murderer. And he would *never* have been involved in my father's assassination.'

In Langdon's mind, it was Kohler's voice that answered. *Leonardo was considered dangerous by many purists at CERN. Fusing science and God is the ultimate scientific blasphemy.* 'Maybe Kohler found out about the antimatter project weeks ago and didn't like the religious implications.'

'So he *killed* my father over it? Ridiculous! Besides, Max Kohler would never have *known* the project existed.'

'While you were gone, maybe your father broke down and consulted Kohler, asking for guidance. You yourself said your father was concerned about the moral implications of creating such a deadly substance.'

'Asking moral guidance from Maximilian Kohler?' Vittoria snorted. 'I don't think so!'

The tunnel banked slightly westward. The faster they ran, the dimmer Langdon's torch became. He began to fear what the place would look like if the light went out. Black.

'Besides,' Vittoria argued, 'why would Kohler have bothered to call you in this morning and ask for help if *he* is behind the whole thing?'

Langdon had already considered it. 'By calling me, Kohler covered his bases. He made sure no one would accuse him of nonaction in the face of crisis. He probably never expected us to get this far.'

The thought of being *used* by Kohler incensed Langdon. Langdon's involvement had given the Illuminati a level of credibility. His credentials and publications had been quoted all night by the media, and as ridiculous as it was, the presence of a Harvard professor in Vatican City had somehow raised the whole emergency beyond the scope of paranoid delusion and convinced skeptics around the world that the Illuminati brotherhood was not only a historical fact, but a force to be reckoned with.

'That BBC reporter,' Langdon said, 'thinks CERN is the new Illuminati lair.'

'What!' Vittoria stumbled behind him. She pulled herself up and ran on. 'He *said* that!?'

'On air. He likened CERN to the Masonic lodges – an innocent organization unknowingly harboring the Illuminati brotherhood within.'

'My God, this is going to destroy CERN.'

Langdon was not so sure. Either way, the theory suddenly seemed less far-fetched. CERN was the ultimate scientific haven. It was home to scientists from over a dozen countries. They seemed to have endless private funding. And Maximilian Kohler was their director.

Kohler is Janus.

'If Kohler's not involved,' Langdon challenged, 'then what is he doing here?'

'Probably trying to stop this madness. Show support. Maybe he really is acting as the Samaritan! He could have found out who knew about the antimatter project and has come to share information.'

'The killer said he was coming to brand the camerlengo.'

'Listen to yourself! It would be a suicide mission. Max would never get out alive.'

Langdon considered it. *Maybe that was the point.*

The outline of a steel gate loomed ahead, blocking their progress down the tunnel. Langdon's heart almost stopped. When they approached, however, they found the ancient lock hanging open. The gate swung freely.

Langdon breathed a sigh of relief, realizing as he had suspected, that the ancient tunnel was in use. Recently. As in today. He now had little doubt that four terrified cardinals had been secreted through here earlier.

They ran on. Langdon could now hear the sounds of chaos to his left. It was St Peter's Square. They were getting close.

They hit another gate, this one heavier. It too was unlocked. The sound of St Peter's Square faded behind them now, and Langdon sensed they had passed through the outer wall of Vatican City. He wondered where inside the Vatican this ancient passage would conclude. *In the gardens? In the basilica? In the papal residence?*

Then, without warning, the tunnel ended.

The cumbrous door blocking their way was a thick wall of riveted iron. Even by the last flickers of his torch, Langdon could see that the portal was perfectly smooth – no handles, no knobs, no keyholes, no hinges. No entry.

He felt a surge of panic. In architect-speak, this rare kind of door was called a *senza chiave* – a one-way portal, used for security, and only operable from one side – the *other* side. Langdon's hope dimmed to black . . . along with the torch in his hand.

He looked at his watch. Mickey glowed.

11.29 p.m.

With a scream of frustration, Langdon swung the torch and started pounding on the door.

113

Something was wrong.

Lieutenant Chartrand stood outside the Pope's office and sensed in the uneasy stance of the soldier standing with him that they shared the same anxiety. The private meeting they were shielding, Rocher had said, could save the Vatican from destruction. So Chartrand wondered why his protective instincts were tingling. And why was Rocher acting so strangely?

Something definitely was awry.

Captain Rocher stood to Chartrand's right, staring dead ahead, his sharp gaze uncharacteristically distant. Chartrand barely recognized the captain. Rocher had not been himself in the last hour. His decisions made no sense.

Someone should be present inside this meeting! Chartrand thought. He had heard Maximilian Kohler bolt the door after he entered. *Why had Rocher permitted this?*

But there was so much more bothering Chartrand. *The cardinals.* The cardinals were still locked in the Sistine Chapel. This was absolute insanity. The camerlengo had wanted them evacuated fifteen minutes ago! Rocher had overruled the decision and not informed the camerlengo. Chartrand had expressed concern, and Rocher had almost taken off his head. Chain of command was never questioned in the Swiss Guard, and Rocher was now top dog.

Half an hour, Rocher thought, discreetly checking his Swiss chronometer in the dim light of the candelabra lighting the hall. *Please hurry.*

Chartrand wished he could hear what was happening on the other side of the doors. Still, he knew there was no one he would rather have handling this crisis than the camerlengo. The man had been tested beyond reason tonight, and he had not flinched. He had confronted the problem head-on . . . truthful, candid, shining like an example to all. Chartrand felt proud right now to be a Catholic. The Illuminati had made a mistake when they challenged Camerlengo Ventresca.

At that moment, however, Chartrand's thoughts were jolted by an unexpected sound. A banging. It was coming from down the hall. The pounding was distant and muffled, but incessant. Rocher looked up. The captain turned to Chartrand and motioned down the hall. Chartrand understood. He turned on his flashlight and took off to investigate.

The banging was more desperate now. Chartrand ran thirty yards down the corridor to an intersection. The noise seemed to be coming from around the corner, beyond the Sala Clementina. Chartrand felt perplexed. There was only one room back there – the Pope's private library. His Holiness's private library had been locked since the Pope's death. Nobody could possibly be in there!

Chartrand hurried down the second corridor, turned another corner, and rushed to the library door. The wooden portico was diminutive, but it stood in the dark like a dour sentinel. The banging was coming from somewhere inside. Chartrand hesitated. He had never been inside the private library. Few had. No one was allowed in without an escort by the Pope himself.

Tentatively, Chartrand reached for the doorknob and turned. As he had imagined, the door was locked. He put his ear to the door. The banging was louder. Then he heard something else. *Voices! Someone calling out!*

He could not make out the words, but he could hear the panic in their shouts. Was someone trapped in the library? Had the Swiss Guard not properly evacuated the building? Chartrand hesitated, wondering if he should go back and consult Rocher. The hell with that. Chartrand had been trained to make decisions, and he would make one now. He pulled out his side arm and fired a single shot into the door latch. The wood exploded, and the door swung open.

Beyond the threshold Chartrand saw nothing but blackness. He shone his flashlight. The room was rectangular – oriental carpets, high oak shelves packed with books, a stitched leather couch, and a marble fireplace. Chartrand had heard stories of this place – three thousand ancient volumes side by side with hundreds of current magazines and periodicals, anything His Holiness requested. The coffee table was covered with journals of science and politics.

The banging was clearer now. Chartrand shone his light across the room toward the sound. On the far wall, beyond the sitting area, was a huge door made of iron. It looked impenetrable as a vault. It had four mammoth locks. The tiny etched letters dead center of the door took Chartrand's breath away.

IL PASSETTO

Chartrand stared. *The Pope's secret escape route!* Chartrand had certainly heard of *Il Passetto*, and he had even heard rumors that it had once had an entrance here in the library, but the tunnel had not been used in ages! *Who could be banging on the other side?*

Chartrand took his flashlight and rapped on the door. There was a muffled exultation from the other side. The banging stopped, and the voices yelled louder. Chartrand could barely make out their words through the barricade.

'. . . Kohler . . . lie . . . camerlengo . . .'

'Who is that?' Chartrand yelled.

'. . . ert Langdon . . . Vittoria Ve . . .'

Chartrand understood enough to be confused. *I thought you were dead!*

'. . . the door,' the voices yelled. 'Open . . . !'

Chartrand looked at the iron barrier and knew he would need dynamite to get through there. 'Impossible!' he yelled. 'Too thick!'

'. . . meeting . . . stop . . . erlengo . . . danger . . .'

Despite his training on the hazards of panic, Chartrand felt a sudden rush of fear at the last few words. Had he understood correctly? Heart pounding, he turned to run back to the office. As he turned, though, he stalled. His gaze had fallen to something on the door . . . something more shocking even than the message coming from beyond it. Emerging from the keyholes of each of the door's massive locks were *keys*. Chartrand stared. The *keys* were here? He blinked in disbelief. The keys to this door were supposed to be in a vault someplace! This passage was never used – not for centuries!

Chartrand dropped his flashlight on the floor. He grabbed the first key and turned. The mechanism was rusted and stiff, but it still worked. Someone had opened it recently. Chartrand worked the next lock. And the next. When the last bolt slid aside, Chartrand pulled. The slab of iron creaked open. He grabbed his light and shone it into the passage.

Robert Langdon and Vittoria Vetra looked like apparitions as they staggered into the library. Both were ragged and tired, but they were very much alive.

'What is this!' Chartrand demanded. 'What's going on! Where did you come from?'

'Where's Max Kohler?' Langdon demanded.

Chartrand pointed. 'In a private meeting with the camer—'

Langdon and Vittoria pushed past him and ran down the darkened hall. Chartrand turned, instinctively raising his gun at their backs. He quickly lowered it and ran after them. Rocher apparently heard them coming, because as they arrived outside the Pope's office, Rocher had spread his legs in a protective stance and was leveling his gun at them. '*Alt!*'

'The camerlengo is in danger!' Langdon yelled, raising his arms in surrender as he slid to a stop. 'Open the door! Max Kohler is going to kill the camerlengo!'

Rocher looked angry.

'Open the door!' Vittoria said. 'Hurry!'

But it was too late.

From inside the Pope's office came a bloodcurdling scream. It was the camerlengo.

114

The confrontation lasted only seconds.

Camerlengo Ventresca was still screaming when Chartrand stepped past Rocher and blew open the door of the Pope's office. The guards dashed in. Langdon and Vittoria ran in behind them.

The scene before them was staggering.

The chamber was lit only by candlelight and a dying fire. Kohler was near the fireplace, standing awkwardly in front of his wheelchair. He brandished a pistol, aimed at the camerlengo, who lay on the floor at his feet, writhing in agony. The camerlengo's cassock was torn open, and his bare chest was seared black. Langdon could not make out the symbol from across the room, but a large, square brand lay on the floor near Kohler. The metal still glowed red.

Two of the Swiss Guards acted without hesitation. They opened fire. The bullets smashed into Kohler's chest, driving him backward. Kohler collapsed into his wheelchair, his chest gurgling blood. His gun went skittering across the floor.

Langdon stood stunned in the doorway.

Vittoria seemed paralyzed. 'Max . . .' she whispered.

The camerlengo, still twisting on the floor, rolled toward Rocher, and with the trancelike terror of the early witch hunts, pointed his index finger at Rocher and yelled a single word. 'ILLUMINATUS!'

'You bastard,' Rocher said, running at him. 'You sanctimonious bas—'

This time it was Chartrand who reacted on instinct, putting three bullets in Rocher's back. The captain fell face first on the tile floor and slid lifeless through his own blood. Chartrand and the guards dashed immediately to the camerlengo, who lay clutching himself, convulsing in pain.

Both guards let out exclamations of horror when they saw the symbol seared on the camerlengo's chest. The second guard saw the brand upside down and immediately staggered backward with fear in his eyes. Chartrand, looking equally overwhelmed by the symbol, pulled the camerlengo's torn cassock up over the burn, shielding it from view.

Langdon felt delirious as he moved across the room. Through a mist of insanity and violence, he tried to make sense of what he was seeing.

A crippled scientist, in a final act of symbolic dominance, had flown into Vatican City and branded the church's highest official. *Some things are worth dying for*, the Hassassin had said. Langdon wondered how a handicapped man could possibly have overpowered the camerlengo. Then again, Kohler had a gun. *It doesn't matter how he did it! Kohler accomplished his mission!*

Langdon moved toward the gruesome scene. The camerlengo was being attended, and Langdon felt himself drawn toward the smoking brand on the floor near Kohler's wheelchair. *The sixth brand?* The closer Langdon got, the more confused he became. The brand seemed to be a perfect square, quite large, and had obviously come from the sacred center compartment of the chest in the Illuminati Lair. *A sixth and final brand*, the Hassassin had said. *The most brilliant of all.*

Langdon knelt beside Kohler and reached for the object. The metal still radiated heat. Grasping the wooden handle, Langdon picked it up. He was not sure what he expected to see, but it most certainly was not this.

Langdon stared a long, confused moment. Nothing was making sense. Why had the guards cried out in horror when they saw this? It was a square of meaningless squiggles. *The most brilliant of all?* It was symmetrical, Langdon could tell as he rotated it in his hand, but it was gibberish.

When he felt a hand on his shoulder, Langdon looked up, expecting Vittoria. The hand, however, was covered with blood. It belonged to Maximilian Kohler, who was reaching out from his wheelchair.

Langdon dropped the brand and staggered to his feet. *Kohler's still alive!*

Slumped in his wheelchair, the dying director was still breathing, albeit barely, sucking in sputtering gasps. Kohler's eyes met Langdon's, and it was the same stony gaze that had greeted Langdon at CERN earlier that day. The eyes looked even harder in death, the loathing and enmity rising to the surface.

The scientist's body quivered, and Langdon sensed he was trying to move. Everyone else in the room was focused on the camerlengo, and Langdon wanted to call out, but he could not react. He was transfixed by the intensity radiating from Kohler in these final seconds of his life. The director, with tremulous effort, lifted his arm and pulled a small device off the arm of his wheelchair. It was the size of a matchbox. He held it out, quivering. For an instant, Langdon feared Kohler had a weapon. But it was something else.

'G-give . . .' Kohler's final words were a gurgling whisper. 'G-give this . . . to the m-media.' Kohler collapsed motionless, and the device fell in his lap.

Shocked, Langdon stared at the device. It was electronic. The words SONY RUVI were printed across the front. Langdon recognized it as one of those new ultraminiature, palm-held camcorders. *The balls on this guy!* he thought. Kohler had apparently recorded some sort of final suicide message he wanted the media to broadcast . . . no doubt some sermon about the importance of science and the evils of religion. Langdon decided he had done enough for this man's cause tonight. Before Chartrand saw Kohler's camcorder, Langdon slipped it into his deepest jacket pocket. *Kohler's final message can rot in hell!*

It was the voice of the camerlengo that broke the silence. He was trying to sit up. 'The cardinals,' he gasped to Chartrand.

'Still in the Sistine Chapel!' Chartrand exclaimed. 'Captain Rocher ordered—'

'Evacuate . . . now. Everyone.'

Chartrand sent one of the other guards running off to let the cardinals out.

The camerlengo grimaced in pain. 'Helicopter . . . out front . . . get me to a hospital.'

115

In St Peter's Square, the Swiss Guard pilot sat in the cockpit of the parked Vatican helicopter and rubbed his temples. The chaos in the square around him was so loud that it drowned out the sound of his idling rotors. This was no solemn candlelight vigil. He was amazed a riot had not broken out yet.

With less than twenty-five minutes left until midnight, the people were still packed together, some praying, some weeping for the church, others screaming obscenities and proclaiming that this was what the church deserved, still others chanting apocalyptic Bible verses.

The pilot's head pounded as the media lights glinted off his windshield. He squinted out at the clamorous masses. Banners waved over the crowd.

ANTIMATTER IS THE ANTICHRIST!
SCIENTIST=SATANIST
WHERE IS YOUR GOD NOW?

The pilot groaned, his headache worsening. He half considered grabbing the windshield's vinyl covering and putting it up so he wouldn't have to watch, but he knew he would be airborne in a matter of minutes. Lieutenant Chartrand had just radioed with terrible news. The camerlengo had been attacked by Maximilian Kohler and seriously injured. Chartrand, the American, and the woman were carrying the camerlengo out now so he could be evacuated to a hospital.

The pilot felt personally responsible for the attack. He reprimanded himself for not acting on his gut. Earlier, when he had picked up Kohler at the airport, he had sensed something in the scientist's dead eyes. He couldn't place it, but he didn't like it. Not that it mattered. Rocher was running the show, and Rocher insisted *this* was the guy. Rocher had apparently been wrong.

A new clamor arose from the crowd, and the pilot looked over to see a line of cardinals processing solemnly out of the Vatican onto St Peter's Square. The cardinals' relief to be leaving ground zero seemed to be quickly overcome by looks of bewilderment at the spectacle now going on outside the church.

The crowd noise intensified yet again. The pilot's head pounded. He needed an aspirin. Maybe three. He didn't like to fly on medication, but a few aspirin would certainly be less debilitating than this raging headache. He reached for the first-aid kit, kept with assorted maps and manuals in a cargo box bolted between the two front seats. When he tried to open the box, though, he found it locked. He looked around for the key and then finally gave up. Tonight was clearly not his lucky night. He went back to massaging his temples.

Inside the darkened basilica, Langdon, Vittoria, and the two guards strained breathlessly toward the main exit. Unable to find anything more suitable, the four of them were transporting the wounded camerlengo on a narrow table, balancing the inert body between them as though on a stretcher. Outside the doors, the faint roar of human chaos was now audible. The camerlengo teetered on the brink of unconsciousness.

Time was running out.

116

It was 11.39 p.m. when Langdon stepped with the others from St Peter's Basilica. The glare that hit his eyes was searing. The media lights shone off the white marble like sunlight off a snowy tundra. Langdon squinted, trying to find refuge behind the façade's enormous columns, but the light came from all directions. In front of him, a collage of massive video screens rose above the crowd.

Standing there atop the magnificent stairs that spilled down to the piazza below, Langdon felt like a reluctant player on the world's biggest stage. Somewhere beyond the glaring lights, Langdon heard an idling helicopter and the roar of a hundred thousand voices. To their left, a procession of cardinals was now evacuating onto the square. They all stopped in apparent distress to see the scene now unfolding on the staircase.

'Careful now,' Chartrand urged, sounding focused as the group began descending the stairs toward the helicopter.

Langdon felt like they were moving underwater. His arms ached from the weight of the camerlengo and the table. He wondered how the moment could get much less dignified. Then he saw the answer. The two BBC reporters had apparently been crossing the open square on their way back to the press area. But now, with the roar of the crowd, they had turned. Glick and Macri were now running back toward them. Macri's camera was raised and rolling. *Here come the vultures*, Langdon thought.

'*Alt!*' Chartrand yelled. 'Get back!'

But the reporters kept coming. Langdon guessed the other networks would take about six seconds to pick up this live BBC feed again. He was wrong. They took two. As if connected by some sort of universal consciousness, every last media screen in the piazza cut away from their countdown clocks and their Vatican experts and began transmitting the same picture – a jiggling action footage swooping up the Vatican stairs. Now, everywhere Langdon looked, he saw the camerlengo's limp body in a Technicolor close-up.

This is wrong! Langdon thought. He wanted to run down the stairs and interfere, but he could not. It wouldn't have helped anyway. Whether it was the roar of the crowd or the cool night air that caused it, Langdon would never know, but at that moment, the inconceivable occurred.

Like a man awakening from a nightmare, the camerlengo's eyes shot open and he sat bolt upright. Taken entirely by surprise, Langdon and the others fumbled with the shifting weight. The front of the table dipped. The camerlengo began to slide. They tried to recover by setting the table down, but it was too late. The camerlengo slid off the front. Incredibly, he did not fall. His feet hit the marble, and he swayed upright. He stood a moment, looking disoriented, and then, before anyone could stop him, he lurched forward, staggering down the stairs toward Macri.

'*No!*' Langdon screamed.

Chartrand rushed forward, trying to reign in the camerlengo. But the camerlengo turned on him, wild-eyed, crazed. 'Leave me!'

Chartrand jumped back.

The scene went from bad to worse. The camerlengo's torn cassock, having been only laid over his chest by Chartrand, began to slip lower. For a moment, Langdon thought the garment might hold, but that moment passed. The cassock let go, sliding off his shoulders down around his waist.

The gasp that went up from the crowd seemed to travel around the globe and back in an instant. Cameras rolled, flashbulbs exploded. On media screens everywhere, the image of the camerlengo's branded chest was projected, towering and in grisly detail. Some screens were even freezing the image and rotating it 180 degrees.

The ultimate Illuminati victory.

Langdon stared at the brand on the screens. Although it was the imprint of the square brand he had held earlier, the symbol *now* made sense. Perfect sense. The marking's awesome power hit Langdon like a train.

Orientation. Langdon had forgotten the first rule of symbology. *When is a square not a square?* He had also forgotten that iron brands, just like rubber stamps, never looked like their imprints. They were in reverse. Langdon had been looking at the brand's *negative*!

As the chaos grew, an old Illuminati quote echoed with new meaning: 'A flawless diamond, born of the ancient elements with such perfection that all those who saw it could only stare in wonder.'

Langdon knew now the myth was true.

Earth, Air, Fire, Water.

The Illuminati Diamond.

117

Robert Langdon had little doubt that the chaos and hysteria coursing through St Peter's Square at this very instant exceeded anything Vatican Hill had ever witnessed. No battle, no crucifixion, no pilgrimage, no mystical vision . . . nothing in the shrine's 2,000-year history could possibly match the scope and drama of this very moment.

As the tragedy unfolded, Langdon felt oddly separate, as if hovering there beside Vittoria at the top of the stairs. The action seemed to distend, as if in a time warp, all the insanity slowing to a crawl . . .

The branded camerlengo . . . raving for the world to see . . .

The Illuminati Diamond . . . unveiled in its diabolical genius . . .

The countdown clock registering the final twenty minutes of Vatican history . . .

The drama, however, had only just begun.

The camerlengo, as if in some sort of post-traumatic trance, seemed suddenly puissant, possessed by demons. He began babbling, whispering to unseen spirits, looking up at the sky and raising his arms to God.

'Speak!' the camerlengo yelled to the heavens. 'Yes, I hear you!'

In that moment, Langdon understood. His heart dropped like a rock.

Vittoria apparently understood too. She went white. 'He's in shock,' she said. 'He's hallucinating. He thinks he's talking to God!'

Somebody's got to stop this, Langdon thought. It was a wretched and embarrassing end. *Get this man to a hospital!*

Below them on the stairs, Chinita Macri was poised and filming, apparently having located her ideal vantage point. The images she filmed appeared instantly across the square behind her on media screens . . . like endless drive-in movies all playing the same grisly tragedy.

The whole scene felt epic. The camerlengo, in his torn cassock, with the scorched brand on his chest, looked like some sort of battered champion who had overcome the rings of hell for this one moment of revelation. He bellowed to the heavens.

'*Ti sento, Dio!* I hear you, God!'

Chartrand backed off, a look of awe on his face.

The hush that fell across the crowd was instant and absolute. For a moment it was as if the silence had fallen across the entire planet . . . everyone in front of their TVs rigid, a communal holding of breath.

The camerlengo stood on the stairs, before the world, and held out his arms. He looked almost Christlike, bare and wounded before the world. He raised his arms to the heavens and, looking up, exclaimed, '*Grazie! Grazie, Dio!*'

The silence of the masses never broke.

'*Grazie, Dio!*' the camerlengo cried out again. Like the sun breaking through a stormy sky, a look of joy spread across his face. '*Grazie, Dio!*'

Thank you, God? Langdon stared in wonder.

The camerlengo was radiant now, his eerie transformation complete. He looked up at the sky, still nodding furiously. He shouted to the heavens, 'Upon this rock I will build my church!'

Langdon knew the words, but he had no idea why the camerlengo could possibly be shouting them.

The camerlengo turned back to the crowd and bellowed again into the night. 'Upon this rock I will build my church!' Then he raised his hands to the sky and laughed out loud. '*Grazie, Dio! Grazie!*'

The man had clearly gone mad.

The world watched, spellbound.

The culmination, however, was something no one expected.

With a final joyous exultation, the camerlengo turned and dashed back into St Peter's Basilica.

118

Eleven forty-two p.m.

The frenzied convoy that plunged back into the basilica to retrieve the camerlengo was not one Langdon had ever imagined he would be part of ... much less leading. But he had been closest to the door and had acted on instinct.

He'll die in here, Langdon thought, sprinting over the threshold into the darkened void. 'Camerlengo! Stop!'

The wall of blackness that hit Langdon was absolute. His pupils were contracted from the glare outside, and his field of vision now extended no farther than a few feet before his face. He skidded to a stop. Somewhere in the blackness ahead, he heard the camerlengo's cassock rustle as the priest ran blindly into the abyss.

Vittoria and the guards arrived immediately. Flashlights came on, but the lights were almost dead now and did not even begin to probe the depths of the basilica before them. The beams swept back and forth, revealing only columns and bare floor. The camerlengo was nowhere to be seen.

'Camerlengo!' Chartrand yelled, fear in his voice. 'Wait! Signore!'

A commotion in the doorway behind them caused everyone to turn. Chinita Macri's large frame lurched through the entry. Her camera was shouldered, and the glowing red light on top revealed that it was still transmitting. Glick was running behind her, microphone in hand, yelling for her to slow down.

Langdon could not believe these two. *This is not the time!*

'Out!' Chartrand snapped. 'This is not for your eyes!'

But Macri and Glick kept coming.

'Chinita!' Glick sounded fearful now. 'This is suicide! I'm not coming!'

Macri ignored him. She threw a switch on her camera. The spotlight on top glared to life, blinding everyone.

Langdon shielded his face and turned away in pain. *Damn it!* When he looked up, though, the church around them was illuminated for thirty yards.

At that moment the camerlengo's voice echoed somewhere in the distance. 'Upon this rock I will build my church!'

Macri wheeled her camera toward the sound. Far off, in the grayness at the end of the spotlight's reach, black fabric billowed, revealing a familiar form running down the main aisle of the basilica.

There was a fleeting instant of hesitation as everyone's eyes took in the bizarre image. Then the dam broke. Chartrand pushed past Langdon and sprinted after the camerlengo. Langdon took off next. Then the guards and Vittoria.

Macri brought up the rear, lighting everyone's way and transmitting the sepulchral chase to the world. An unwilling Glick cursed aloud as he tagged along, fumbling through a terrified blow-by-blow commentary.

The main aisle of St Peter's Basilica, Lieutenant Chartrand had once figured out, was longer than an Olympic soccer field. Tonight, however, it felt like twice that. As the guard sprinted after the camerlengo, he wondered where the man was headed. The camerlengo was clearly in shock, delirious no doubt from his physical trauma and bearing witness to the horrific massacre in the Pope's office.

Somewhere up ahead, beyond the reach of the BBC spotlight, the camerlengo's voice rang out joyously. 'Upon this rock I will build my church!'

Chartrand knew the man was shouting Scripture – Matthew 16:18, if Chartrand recalled correctly. *Upon this rock I will build my church*. It was an almost cruelly inapt inspiration – the church was about to be destroyed. Surely the camerlengo had gone mad.

Or had he?

For a fleeting instant, Chartrand's soul fluttered. Holy visions and divine messages had always seemed like wishful delusions to him – the product of overzealous minds hearing what they wanted to hear – God did not interact *directly*!

A moment later, though, as if the Holy Spirit Himself had descended to persuade Chartrand of His power, Chartrand had a vision.

Fifty yards ahead, in the center of the church, a ghost appeared . . . a diaphanous, glowing outline. The pale shape was that of the half-naked camerlengo. The specter seemed transparent, radiating light. Chartrand staggered to a stop, feeling a knot tighten in his chest. *The camerlengo is glowing!* The body seemed to shine brighter now. Then, it began to sink . . . deeper and deeper, until it disappeared as if by magic into the blackness of the floor.

Langdon had seen the phantom also. For a moment, he too thought he had witnessed a magical vision. But as he passed the stunned Chartrand and ran toward the spot where the camerlengo had disappeared, he realized what had just happened. The camerlengo had arrived at the Niche of the Palliums – the sunken chamber lit by ninety-nine oil lamps. The lamps in the niche shone up from beneath, illuminating him like a ghost. Then, as the camerlengo descended the stairs into the light, he had seemed to disappear beneath the floor.

Langdon arrived breathless at the rim overlooking the sunken room. He peered down the stairs. At the bottom, lit by the golden glow of oil lamps, the camerlengo dashed across the marble chamber toward the set of glass doors that led to the room holding the famous golden box.

What is he doing? Langdon wondered. *Certainly he can't think the golden box—*

The camerlengo yanked open the doors and ran inside. Oddly though, he totally ignored the golden box, rushing right past it. Five feet beyond the box, he dropped to his knees and began struggling to lift an iron grate embedded in the floor.

Langdon watched in horror, now realizing where the camerlengo was headed. *Good God, no!* He dashed down the stairs after him. 'Father! Don't!'

As Langdon opened the glass doors and ran toward the camerlengo, he saw the camerlengo heave on the grate. The hinged, iron bulkhead fell open with a deafening crash, revealing a narrow shaft and a steep stairway that dropped into nothingness. As the camerlengo moved toward the hole, Langdon grabbed his bare shoulders and pulled him back. The man's skin was slippery with sweat, but Langdon held on.

The camerlengo wheeled, obviously startled. 'What are you doing!'

Langdon was surprised when their eyes met. The camerlengo no longer had the glazed look of a man in a trance. His eyes were keen, glistening with a lucid determination. The brand on his chest looked excruciating.

'Father,' Langdon urged, as calmly as possible, 'you can't go down there. We need to evacuate.'

'My son,' the camerlengo said, his voice eerily sane. 'I have just had a message. I know—'

'Camerlengo!' It was Chartrand and the others. They came dashing down the stairs into the room, lit by Macri's camera.

When Chartrand saw the open grate in the floor, his eyes filled with dread. He crossed himself and shot Langdon a thankful look for having stopped the camerlengo. Langdon understood; he had read enough about Vatican architecture to know what lay beneath that grate. It was the most sacred place in all of Christendom. *Terra Santa.* Holy Ground. Some called it the Necropolis. Some called it the Catacombs. According to accounts from the select few clergy who had descended over the years, the Necropolis was a dark maze of subterranean crypts that could swallow a visitor whole if he lost his way. It was not the kind of place through which they wanted to be chasing the camerlengo.

'Signore,' Chartrand pleaded. 'You're in shock. We need to leave this place. You cannot go down there. It's suicide.'

The camerlengo seemed suddenly stoic. He reached out and put a quiet hand on Chartrand's shoulder. 'Thank you for your concern and service. I cannot tell you how. I cannot tell you I understand. But I have had a revelation. I know where the antimatter is.'

Everyone stared.

The camerlengo turned to the group. 'Upon this rock I will build my church. That was the message. The meaning is clear.'

Langdon was still unable to comprehend the camerlengo's conviction that he had spoken to God, much less that he had deciphered the message. *Upon this rock I will build my church?* They were the words spoken by Jesus when he chose Peter as his first apostle. What did they have to do with anything?

Macri moved in for a closer shot. Glick was mute, as if shell-shocked.

The camerlengo spoke quickly now. 'The Illuminati have placed their tool of destruction on the very cornerstone of this church. At the foundation.' He motioned down the stairs. 'On the very rock upon which this church was built. And I know where that rock is.'

Langdon was certain the time had come to overpower the camerlengo and carry him off. As lucid as he seemed, the priest was talking nonsense. *A rock? The cornerstone in the foundation?* The stairway before them didn't lead to the foundation, it led to the Necropolis! 'The quote is a metaphor, Father! There is no actual *rock*!'

The camerlengo looked strangely sad. 'There *is* a rock, my son.' He pointed into the hole. '*Pietro è la pietra.*'

Langdon froze. In an instant it all came clear.

The austere simplicity of it gave him chills. As Langdon stood there with the others, staring down the long staircase, he realized that there was indeed a rock buried in the darkness beneath this church.

Pietro è la pietra. Peter is the rock.

Peter's faith in God was so steadfast that Jesus called Peter 'the rock' – the unwavering disciple on whose shoulders Jesus would build his church. On this very location, Langdon realized – Vatican Hill – Peter had been crucified and buried. The early Christians built a small shrine over his tomb. As Christianity spread, the shrine got bigger, layer upon layer, culminating in this colossal basilica. The entire Catholic faith had been built, quite literally, upon St Peter. The rock.

'The antimatter is on St Peter's tomb,' the camerlengo said, his voice crystalline.

Despite the seemingly supernatural origin of the information, Langdon sensed a stark logic in it. Placing the antimatter on St Peter's tomb seemed painfully obvious now. The Illuminati, in an act of symbolic defiance, had located the antimatter at the core of Christendom, both literally and figuratively. *The ultimate infiltration.*

'And if you all need worldly proof,' the camerlengo said, sounding impatient now, 'I just found that grate unlocked.' He pointed to the open

bulkhead in the floor. 'It is *never* unlocked. Someone has been down there
. . . *recently*.'

Everyone stared into the hole.

An instant later, with deceptive agility, the camerlengo spun, grabbed an oil lamp, and headed for the opening.

119

The stone steps declined steeply into the earth.

I'm going to die down here, Vittoria thought, gripping the heavy rope banister as she bounded down the cramped passageway behind the others. Although Langdon had made a move to stop the camerlengo from entering the shaft, Chartrand had intervened, grabbing Langdon and holding on. Apparently, the young guard was now convinced the camerlengo knew what he was doing.

After a brief scuffle, Langdon had freed himself and pursued the camerlengo with Chartrand close on his heels. Instinctively, Vittoria had dashed after them.

Now she was racing headlong down a precipitous grade where any misplaced step could mean a deadly fall. Far below, she could see the golden glow of the camerlengo's oil lamp. Behind her, Vittoria could hear the BBC reporters hurrying to keep up. The camera spotlight threw gnarled shadows beyond her down the shaft, illuminating Chartrand and Langdon. Vittoria could scarcely believe the world was bearing witness to this insanity. *Turn off the damn camera!* Then again, she knew the light was the only reason any of them could see where they were going.

As the bizarre chase continued, Vittoria's thoughts whipped like a tempest. What could the camerlengo possibly do down here? Even if he found the antimatter? There was no time!

Vittoria was surprised to find her intuition now telling her the camerlengo was probably right. Placing the antimatter three stories beneath the earth seemed an almost noble and merciful choice. Deep underground – much as in Z-lab – an antimatter annihilation would be partially contained. There would be no heat blast, no flying shrapnel to injure onlookers, just a biblical opening of the earth and a towering basilica crumbling into a crater.

Was this Kohler's one act of decency? Sparing lives? Vittoria still could not fathom the director's involvement. She could accept his hatred of religion . . . but this awesome conspiracy seemed beyond him. Was Kohler's loathing really this profound? Destruction of the Vatican? Hiring an assassin? The murders of her father, the Pope, and four cardinals? It seemed unthinkable. And how had Kohler managed all this treachery within the Vatican walls? *Rocher was Kohler's inside man*, Vittoria told herself. *Rocher was an Illuminatus.* No doubt Captain Rocher had keys to everything – the Pope's chambers, *Il Passetto*, the Necropolis, St Peter's tomb, all of it. He could have placed the antimatter on St Peter's tomb – a highly restricted locale – and then commanded his guards not to waste time searching the Vatican's restricted areas. Rocher *knew* nobody would ever find the canister.

But Rocher never counted on the camerlengo's message from above.

The message. This was the leap of faith Vittoria was still struggling to accept. Had God actually *communicated* with the camerlengo? Vittoria's gut said no, and yet hers was the science of entanglement physics – the study of interconnectedness. She witnessed miraculous communications every day – twin sea-turtle eggs separated and placed in labs thousands of miles apart hatching at the same instant . . . acres of jellyfish pulsating in perfect rhythm as if of a single mind. *There are invisible lines of communication everywhere*, she thought.

But between God and man?

Vittoria wished her father were there to give her faith. He had once explained divine communication to her in scientific terms, and he had made her believe. She still remembered the day she had seen him praying and asked him, 'Father, why do you bother to pray? God cannot answer you.'

Leonardo Vetra had looked up from his meditations with a paternal smile. 'My daughter the skeptic. So you don't believe God speaks to man? Let me put it in your language.' He took a model of the human brain down from a shelf and set it in front of her. 'As you probably know, Vittoria, human beings normally use a very small percentage of their brain power. However, if you put them in emotionally charged situations – like physical trauma, extreme joy or fear, deep meditation – all of a sudden their neurons start firing like crazy, resulting in massively enhanced mental clarity.'

'So what?' Vittoria said. 'Just because you think clearly doesn't mean you talk to God.'

'Aha!' Vetra exclaimed. 'And yet remarkable solutions to seemingly impossible problems often occur in these moments of clarity. It's what gurus call higher consciousness. Biologists call it altered states. Psychologists call it super-sentience.' He paused. 'And Christians call it answered prayer.' Smiling broadly, he added, 'Sometimes, divine revelation simply means adjusting your brain to hear what your heart already knows.'

Now, as she dashed down, headlong into the dark, Vittoria sensed perhaps her father was right. Was it so hard to believe that the camerlengo's trauma had put his mind in a state where he had simply 'realized' the antimatter's location?

Each of us is a God, Buddha had said. *Each of us knows all. We need only open our minds to hear our own wisdom.*

It was in that moment of clarity, as Vittoria plunged deeper into the earth, that she felt her own mind open . . . her own wisdom surface. She sensed now without a doubt what the camerlengo's intentions were. Her awareness brought with it a fear like nothing she had ever known.

'Camerlengo, no!' she shouted down the passage. 'You don't understand!' Vittoria pictured the multitudes of people surrounding Vatican City, and her blood ran cold. 'If you bring the antimatter up . . . everyone will *die*!'

Langdon was leaping three steps at a time now, gaining ground. The passage was cramped, but he felt no claustrophobia. His once debilitating fear was overshadowed by a far deeper dread.

'Camerlengo!' Langdon felt himself closing the gap on the lantern's glow. 'You must leave the antimatter where it is! There's no other choice!'

Even as Langdon spoke the words, he could not believe them. Not only had he accepted the camerlengo's divine revelation of the antimatter's location, but he was lobbying for the destruction of St Peter's Basilica – one of the greatest architectural feats on earth . . . as well as all of the art inside.

But the people outside . . . it's the only way.

It seemed a cruel irony that the only way to save the people now was to destroy the church. Langdon figured the Illuminati were amused by the symbolism.

The air coming up from the bottom of the tunnel was cool and dank. Somewhere down here was the sacred *Necropolis* . . . burial place of St Peter and countless other early Christians. Langdon felt a chill, hoping this was not a suicide mission.

Suddenly, the camerlengo's lantern seemed to halt. Langdon closed on him fast.

The end of the stairs loomed abruptly from out of the shadows. A wrought-iron gate with three embossed skulls blocked the bottom of the stairs. The camerlengo was there, pulling the gate open. Langdon leapt, pushing the gate shut, blocking the camerlengo's way. The others came thundering down the stairs, everyone ghostly white in the BBC spotlight . . . especially *Glick*, who was looking more pasty with every step.

Chartrand grabbed Langdon. 'Let the camerlengo pass!'

'No!' Vittoria said from above, breathless. 'We must evacuate right now! You *cannot* take the antimatter out of here! If you bring it up, everyone outside will *die*!'

The camerlengo's voice was remarkably calm. 'All of you . . . we must trust. We have little time.'

'You don't understand,' Vittoria said. 'An explosion at ground level will be much worse than one down here!'

The camerlengo looked at her, his green eyes resplendently sane. 'Who said anything about an explosion at ground level?'

Vittoria stared. 'You're *leaving* it down here?'

The camerlengo's certitude was hypnotic. 'There will be no more death tonight.'

'Father, but—'

'Please . . . some *faith*.' The camerlengo's voice plunged to a compelling hush. 'I am not asking anyone to join me. You are all free to go. All I am asking is that you not interfere with His bidding. Let me do what I have been called to do.' The camerlengo's stare intensified. 'I am to save this church. And I *can*. I swear on my life.'

The silence that followed might as well have been thunder.

120

Eleven fifty-one p.m.

Necropolis literally means *City of the Dead.*

Nothing Robert Langdon had ever read about this place prepared him for the sight of it. The colossal subterranean hollow was filled with crumbling mausoleums, like small houses on the floor of a cave. The air smelled lifeless. An awkward grid of narrow walkways wound between the decaying memorials, most of which were fractured brick with marble platings. Like columns of dust, countless pillars of unexcavated earth rose up, supporting a dirt sky, which hung low over the penumbral hamlet.

City of the dead, Langdon thought, feeling trapped between academic wonder and raw fear. He and the others dashed deeper down the winding passages. *Did I make the wrong choice?*

Chartrand had been the first to fall under the camerlengo's spell, yanking open the gate and declaring his faith in the camerlengo. Glick and Macri, at the camerlengo's suggestion, had nobly agreed to provide light to the quest, although considering what accolades awaited them if they got out of here alive, their motivations were certainly suspect. Vittoria had been the least eager of all, and Langdon had seen in her eyes a wariness that looked, unsettlingly, a lot like female intuition.

It's too late now, he thought, he and Vittoria dashing after the others. *We're committed.*

Vittoria was silent, but Langdon knew they were thinking the same thing. *Nine minutes is not enough time to get the hell out of Vatican City if the camerlengo is wrong.*

As they ran on through the mausoleums, Langdon felt his legs tiring, noting to his surprise that the group was ascending a steady incline. The explanation, when it dawned on him, sent shivers to his core. The topography beneath his feet was that of Christ's time. He was running up the original Vatican Hill! Langdon had heard Vatican scholars claim that St Peter's tomb was near the *top* of Vatican Hill, and he had always wondered how they knew. Now he understood. *The damn hill is still here!*

Langdon felt like he was running through the pages of history.

Somewhere ahead was St Peter's tomb – *the* Christian relic. It was hard to imagine that the original grave had been marked only with a modest shrine. Not any more. As Peter's eminence spread, new shrines were built on top of the old, and now, the homage stretched 440 feet overhead to the top of Michelangelo's dome, the apex positioned directly over the original tomb within a fraction of an inch.

They continued ascending the sinuous passages. Langdon checked his watch. *Eight minutes.* He was beginning to wonder if he and Vittoria would be joining the deceased here permanently.

'Look out!' Glick yelled from behind them. 'Snake holes!'

Langdon saw it in time. A series of small holes riddled the path before them. He leapt, just clearing them.

Vittoria jumped too, barely avoiding the narrow hollows. She looked uneasy as they ran on. '*Snake* holes?'

'*Snack* holes, actually,' Langdon corrected. 'Trust me, you don't want to know.' The holes, he had just realized, were *libation tubes.* The early Christians had believed in the resurrection of the flesh, and they'd used the holes to literally 'feed the dead' by pouring milk and honey into crypts beneath the floor.

The camerlengo felt weak.

He dashed onward, his legs finding strength in his duty to God and man. *Almost there.* He was in incredible pain. *The mind can bring so much more pain than the body.* Still he felt tired. He knew he had precious little time.

'I will save your church, Father. I swear it.'

Despite the BBC lights behind him, for which he was grateful, the camerlengo carried his oil lamp high. *I am a beacon in the darkness. I am the light.* The lamp sloshed as he ran, and for an instant he feared the flammable oil might spill and burn him. He had experienced enough burned flesh for one evening.

As he approached the top of the hill, he was drenched in sweat, barely able to breathe. But when he emerged over the crest, he felt reborn. He staggered onto the flat piece of earth where he had stood many times. Here the path ended. The Necropolis came to an abrupt halt at a wall of earth. A tiny marker read: *Mausoleum S.*

La tomba di San Pietro.

Before him, at waist level, was an opening in the wall. There was no gilded plaque here. No fanfare. Just a simple hole in the wall, beyond which lay a small grotto and a meager, crumbling sarcophagus. The camerlengo gazed into the hole and smiled in exhaustion. He could hear the others coming up the hill behind him. He set down his oil lamp and knelt to pray.

Thank you, God. It is almost over.

*

Outside in the square, surrounded by astounded cardinals, Cardinal Mortati stared up at the media screen and watched the drama unfold in the crypt below. He no longer knew what to believe. Had the entire world just witnessed what *he* had seen? Had God truly spoken to the camerlengo? Was the antimatter really going to appear on St Peter's—

'Look!' A gasp went up from the throngs.

'There!' Everyone was suddenly pointing at the screen. 'It's a miracle!'

Mortati looked up. The camera angle was unsteady, but it was clear enough. The image was unforgettable.

Filmed from behind, the camerlengo was kneeling in prayer on the earthen floor. In front of him was a rough-hewn hole in the wall. Inside the hollow, among the rubble of ancient stone, was a terra cotta casket. Although Mortati had seen the coffin only once in his life, he knew beyond a doubt what it contained.

San Pietro.

Mortati was not naïve enough to think that the shouts of joy and amazement now thundering through the crowd were exaltations from bearing witness to one of Christianity's most sacred relics. St Peter's tomb was not what had people falling to their knees in spontaneous prayer and thanksgiving. It was the object on *top* of his tomb.

The antimatter canister. It was there . . . where it had been all day . . . hiding in the darkness of the Necropolis. Sleek. Relentless. Deadly. The camerlengo's revelation was correct.

Mortati stared in wonder at the transparent cylinder. The globule of liquid still hovered at its core. The grotto around the canister blinked red as the LED counted down into its final five minutes of life.

Also sitting on the tomb, inches away from the canister, was the wireless Swiss Guard security camera that had been pointed at the canister and transmitting all along.

Mortati crossed himself, certain this was the most frightful image he had seen in his entire life. He realized, a moment later, however, that it was about to get worse.

The camerlengo stood suddenly. He grabbed the antimatter in his hands and wheeled toward the others. His face showing total focus. He pushed past the others and began descending the Necropolis the way he had come, running down the hill.

The camera caught Vittoria Vetra, frozen in terror. 'Where are you going! Camerlengo! I thought you said—'

'Have faith!' he exclaimed as he ran off.

Vittoria spun toward Langdon. 'What do we do?'

Robert Langdon tried to stop the camerlengo, but Chartrand was running interference now, apparently trusting the camerlengo's conviction.

The picture coming from the BBC camera was like a roller coaster ride now, winding, twisting. Fleeting freeze-frames of confusion and terror as the chaotic cortège stumbled through the shadows back toward the Necropolis entrance.

Out in the square, Mortati let out a fearful gasp. 'Is he bringing that up *here*?'

On televisions all over the world, larger than life, the camerlengo raced upward out of the Necropolis with the antimatter before him. 'There will be no more death tonight!'

But the camerlengo was wrong.

121

The camerlengo erupted through the doors of St Peter's Basilica at exactly 11.56 p.m. He staggered into the dazzling glare of the world spotlight, carrying the antimatter before him like some sort of numinous offering. Through burning eyes he could see his own form, half-naked and wounded, towering like a giant on the media screens around the square. The roar that went up from the crowd in St Peter's Square was like none the camerlengo had ever heard – crying, screaming, chanting, praying . . . a mix of veneration and terror.

Deliver us from evil, he whispered.

He felt totally depleted from his race out of the Necropolis. It had almost ended in disaster. Robert Langdon and Vittoria Vetra had wanted to intercept him, to throw the canister back into its subterranean hiding place, to run outside for cover. *Blind fools!*

The camerlengo realized now, with fearful clarity, that on any other night, he would never have won the race. Tonight, however, God again had been with him. Robert Langdon, on the verge of overtaking the camerlengo, had been grabbed by Chartrand, ever trusting and dutiful to the camerlengo's demands for faith. The reporters, of course, were spellbound and lugging too much equipment to interfere.

The Lord works in mysterious ways.

The camerlengo could hear the others behind him now . . . see them on the screens, closing in. Mustering the last of his physical strength, he raised the antimatter high over his head. Then, throwing back his bare shoulders in an act of defiance to the Illuminati brand on his chest, he dashed down the stairs.

There was one final act.

Godspeed, he thought. *Godspeed*.

Four minutes . . .

Langdon could barely see as he burst out of the basilica. Again the sea of media lights bore into his retinas. All he could make out was the murky outline of the camerlengo, directly ahead of him, running down the stairs. For an instant, refulgent in his halo of media lights, the camerlengo looked celestial, like some kind of modern deity. His cassock was at his waist like a shroud. His body was scarred and wounded by the hands of his enemies, and still he endured. The camerlengo ran on, standing tall, calling out to the world to have faith, running toward the masses carrying this weapon of destruction.

Langdon ran down the stairs after him. *What is he doing? He will kill them all!*

'Satan's work,' the camerlengo screamed, 'has no place in the House of God!' He ran on toward a now terrified crowd.

'Father!' Langdon screamed, behind him. 'There's nowhere to go!'

'Look to the heavens! We forget to look to the heavens!'

In that moment, as Langdon saw where the camerlengo was headed, the glorious truth came flooding all around him. Although Langdon could not see it on account of the lights, he knew their salvation was directly overhead.

A star-filled Italian sky. The escape route.

The helicopter the camerlengo had summoned to take him to the hospital sat dead ahead, pilot already in the cockpit, blades already humming in neutral. As the camerlengo ran toward it, Langdon felt a sudden overwhelming exhilaration.

The thoughts that tore through Langdon's mind came as a torrent . . .

First he pictured the wide-open expanse of the Mediterranean Sea. How far was it? Five miles? Ten? He knew the beach at *Fiumocino* was only about seven minutes by train. But by helicopter, 200 miles an hour, no stops . . . If they could fly the canister far enough out to sea, and drop it . . . There were other options too, he realized, feeling almost weightless as he ran. *La Cava Romana!* The marble quarries north of the city were less than three miles away. How large were they? Two square miles? Certainly they were deserted at this hour! Dropping the canister *there* . . .

'Everyone back!' the camerlengo yelled. His chest ached as he ran. 'Get away! Now!'

The Swiss Guard standing around the chopper stood slack-jawed as the camerlengo approached them.

'Back!' the priest screamed.

The guards moved back.

With the entire world watching in wonder, the camerlengo ran around the chopper to the pilot's door and yanked it open. 'Out, son! Now!'

The guard jumped out.

The camerlengo looked at the high cockpit seat and knew that in his exhausted state, he would need both hands to pull himself up. He turned to the pilot, trembling beside him, and thrust the canister into his hands. 'Hold this. Hand it back when I'm in.'

As the camerlengo pulled himself up, he could hear Robert Langdon yelling excitedly, running toward the craft. *Now you understand*, the camerlengo thought. *Now you have faith!*

The camerlengo pulled himself up into the cockpit, adjusted a few familiar levers, and then turned back to his window for the canister.

But the guard to whom he had given the canister stood empty-handed. 'He took it!' the guard yelled.

The camerlengo felt his heart seize. 'Who!'

The guard pointed. 'Him!'

Robert Langdon was surprised by how heavy the canister was. He ran to the other side of the chopper and jumped in the rear compartment where he and Vittoria had sat only hours ago. He left the door open and buckled himself in. Then he yelled to the camerlengo in the front seat.

'Fly, Father!'

The camerlengo craned back at Langdon, his face bloodless with dread. 'What are you doing!'

'*You* fly! I'll throw!' Langdon barked. 'There's no time! Just fly the blessed chopper!'

The camerlengo seemed momentarily paralyzed, the media lights glaring through the cockpit darkening the creases in his face. 'I can do this alone,' he whispered. 'I am *supposed* to do this alone.'

Langdon wasn't listening. *Fly!* he heard himself screaming. *Now! I'm here to help you!* Langdon looked down at the canister and felt his breath catch in his throat when he saw the numbers. '*Three* minutes, Father! *Three!*'

The number seemed to stun the camerlengo back to sobriety. Without hesitation, he turned back to the controls. With a grinding roar, the helicopter lifted off.

Through a swirl of dust, Langdon could see Vittoria running toward the chopper. Their eyes met, and then she dropped away like a sinking stone.

122

Inside the chopper, the whine of the engines and the gale from the open door assaulted Langdon's senses with a deafening chaos. He steadied himself against the magnified drag of gravity as the camerlengo accelerated the craft straight up. The glow of St Peter's Square shrank beneath them until it was an amorphous glowing ellipse radiating in a sea of city lights.

The antimatter canister felt like deadweight in Langdon's hands. He held tighter, his palms slick now with sweat and blood. Inside the trap, the globule of antimatter hovered calmly, pulsing red in the glow of the LED countdown clock.

'Two minutes!' Langdon yelled, wondering where the camerlengo intended to drop the canister.

The city lights beneath them spread out in all directions. In the distance to the west, Langdon could see the twinkling delineation of the Mediterranean coast – a jagged border of luminescence beyond which spread an endless dark expanse of nothingness. The sea looked farther now than Langdon had imagined. Moreover, the concentration of lights at the coast was a stark reminder that even far out at sea an explosion might have devastating effects. Langdon had not even considered the effects of a ten-kiloton tidal wave hitting the coast.

When Langdon turned and looked straight ahead through the cockpit window, he was more hopeful. Directly in front of them, the rolling shadows of the Roman foothills loomed in the night. The hills were spotted with lights – the villas of the very wealthy – but a mile or so north, the hills grew dark. There were no lights at all – just a huge pocket of blackness. Nothing.

The quarries! Langdon thought. *La Cava Romana!*

Staring intently at the barren pocket of land, Langdon sensed that it was plenty large enough. It seemed close, too. Much closer than the ocean. Excitement surged through him. This was obviously where the camerlengo planned to take the antimatter! The chopper was pointing directly toward it! The quarries! Oddly, however, as the engines strained louder and the chopper hurtled through the air, Langdon could see that the quarries were not getting any closer. Bewildered, he shot a glance out the side door to get his bearings. What he saw doused his excitement in a wave of panic. Directly beneath them, thousands of feet straight down, glowed the media lights in St Peter's Square.

We're still over the Vatican!

'Camerlengo!' Langdon choked. 'Go forward! We're high *enough*! You've got to start moving forward! We can't drop the canister back over Vatican City!'

The camerlengo did not reply. He appeared to be concentrating on flying the craft.

'We've got less than *two* minutes!' Langdon shouted, holding up the canister. 'I can see them! *La Cava Romana!* A couple of miles north! We don't have—'

'No,' the camerlengo said. 'It's far too dangerous. I'm sorry.' As the chopper continued to claw heavenward, the camerlengo turned and gave Langdon a mournful smile. 'I wish you had not come, my friend. You have made the ultimate sacrifice.'

Langdon looked in the camerlengo's exhausted eyes and suddenly understood. His blood turned to ice. 'But . . . there must be *somewhere* we can go!'

'*Up*,' the camerlengo replied, his voice resigned. 'It's the only guarantee.'

Langdon could barely think. He had entirely misinterpreted the camerlengo's plan. *Look to the heavens!*

Heaven, Langdon now realized, was literally where he was headed. The camerlengo had never intended to drop the antimatter. He was simply getting it as far away from Vatican City as humanly possible.

This was a one-way trip.

123

In St Peter's Square, Vittoria Vetra stared upward. The helicopter was a speck now, the media lights no longer reaching it. Even the pounding of the rotors had faded to a distant hum. It seemed, in that instant, that the entire world was focused upward, silenced in anticipation, necks craned to the heavens . . . all peoples, all faiths . . . all hearts beating as one.

Vittoria's emotions were a cyclone of twisting agonies. As the helicopter disappeared from sight, she pictured Robert's face, rising above her. *What had he been thinking? Didn't he understand?*

Around the square, television cameras probed the darkness, waiting. A sea of faces stared heavenward, united in a silent countdown. The media screens all flickered the same tranquil scene . . . a Roman sky illuminated with brilliant stars. Vittoria felt the tears begin to well.

Behind her on the marble escarpment, 161 cardinals stared up in silent awe. Some folded their hands in prayer. Most stood motionless, transfixed. Some wept. The seconds ticked past.

In homes, bars, businesses, airports, hospitals around the world, souls were joined in universal witness. Men and women locked hands. Others held their children. Time seemed to hover in limbo, souls suspended in unison.

Then, cruelly, the bells of St Peter's began to toll.

Vittoria let the tears come.

Then . . . with the whole world watching . . . time ran out.

The dead silence of the event was the most terrifying of all.

High above Vatican City, a pinpoint of light appeared in the sky. For a fleeting instant, a new heavenly body had been born . . . a speck of light as pure and white as anyone had ever seen.

Then it happened.

A flash. The point billowed, as if feeding on itself, unraveling across the sky in a dilating radius of blinding white. It shot out in all directions, accelerating with incomprehensible speed, gobbling up the dark. As the sphere of light grew, it intensified, like a burgeoning fiend preparing to consume the entire sky. It raced downward, toward them, picking up speed.

Blinded, the multitudes of starkly lit human faces gasped as one, shielding their eyes, crying out in strangled fear.

As the light roared out in all directions, the unimaginable occurred. As if bound by God's own will, the surging radius seemed to hit a wall. It was as if the explosion were contained somehow in a giant glass sphere. The light rebounded inward, sharpening, rippling across itself. The wave appeared to have reached a predetermined diameter and hovered there. For that instant, a perfect and silent sphere of light glowed over Rome. Night had become day.

Then it hit.

The concussion was deep and hollow – a thunderous shock wave from above. It descended on them like the wrath of hell, shaking the granite foundation of Vatican City, knocking the breath out of people's lungs, sending others stumbling backward. The reverberation circled the colonnade, followed by a sudden torrent of warm air. The wind tore through the square, letting out a sepulchral moan as it whistled through the columns and buffeted the walls. Dust swirled overhead as people huddled . . . witnesses to Armageddon.

Then, as fast as it appeared, the sphere imploded, sucking back in on itself, crushing inward to the tiny point of light from which it had come.

124

Never before had so many been so silent.

The faces in St Peter's Square, one by one, averted their eyes from the darkening sky and turned downward, each person in his or her own private moment of wonder. The media lights followed suit, dropping their beams back to earth as if out of reverence for the blackness now settling upon them. It seemed for a moment the entire world was bowing its head in unison.

Cardinal Mortati knelt to pray, and the other cardinals joined him. The Swiss Guard lowered their long swords and stood numb. No one spoke. No one moved. Everywhere, hearts shuddered with spontaneous emotion. Bereavement. Fear. Wonder. Belief. And a dread-filled respect for the new and awesome power they had just witnessed.

Vittoria Vetra stood trembling at the foot of the basilica's sweeping stairs. She closed her eyes. Through the tempest of emotions now coursing through her blood, a single word tolled like a distant bell. Pristine. Cruel. She forced it away. And yet the word echoed. Again she drove it back. The pain was too great. She tried to lose herself in the images that blazed in others' minds . . . antimatter's mind-boggling power . . . the Vatican's deliverance . . . the camerlengo . . . feats of bravery . . . miracles . . . selflessness. And still the word echoed . . . tolling through the chaos with a stinging loneliness.

Robert.

He had come for her at Castle St Angelo.

He had saved her.

And now he had been destroyed by *her* creation.

As Cardinal Mortati prayed, he wondered if he too would hear God's voice as the camerlengo had. *Does one need to believe in miracles to experience them?* Mortati was a modern man in an ancient faith. Miracles had never played a part in his belief. Certainly his faith spoke of miracles . . . bleeding palms, ascensions from the dead, imprints on shrouds . . . and yet, Mortati's rational mind had always justified these accounts as part of the myth. They were simply the result of man's greatest weakness – his *need* for proof.

Miracles were nothing but stories we all clung to because we *wished* they were true.

And yet . . .

Am I so modern that I cannot accept what my eyes have just witnessed? It was a miracle, was it not? Yes! God, with a few whispered words in the camerlengo's ear, had intervened and saved this church. Why was this so hard to believe? What would it say about God if God had done nothing? That the Almighty did not care? That He was powerless to stop it? *A miracle was the only possible response!*

As Mortati knelt in wonder, he prayed for the camerlengo's soul. He gave thanks to the young chamberlain who, even in his youthful years, had opened this old man's eyes to the miracles of unquestioning faith.

Incredibly, though, Mortati never suspected the extent to which his faith was about to be tested . . .

The silence of St Peter's Square broke with a ripple at first. The ripple grew to a murmur. And then, suddenly, to a roar. Without warning, the multitudes were crying out as one.

'Look! Look!'

Mortati opened his eyes and turned to the crowd. Everyone was pointing behind him, toward the front of St Peter's Basilica. Their faces were white. Some fell to their knees. Some fainted. Some burst into uncontrollable sobs.

'Look! Look!'

Mortati turned, bewildered, following their outstretched hands. They were pointing to the uppermost level of the basilica, the rooftop terrace, where huge statues of Christ and his apostles watched over the crowd.

There, on the right of Jesus, arms outstretched to the world . . . stood Camerlengo Carlo Ventresca.

125

Robert Langdon was no longer falling.

There was no more terror. No pain. Not even the sound of the racing wind. There was only the soft sound of lapping water, as though he were comfortably asleep on a beach.

In a paradox of self-awareness, Langdon sensed this was death. He felt glad for it. He allowed the drifting numbness to possess him entirely. He let it carry him wherever it was he would go. His pain and fear had been anesthetized, and he did not wish it back at any price. His final memory had been one that could only have been conjured in hell.

Take me. Please . . .

But the lapping that lulled in him a far-off sense of peace was also pulling him back. It was trying to awaken him from a dream. *No! Let me be!* He did not want to awaken. He sensed demons gathering on the perimeter of his bliss, pounding to shatter his rapture. Fuzzy images swirled. Voices yelled. Wind churned. *No, please!* The more he fought, the more the fury filtered through.

Then, harshly, he was living it all again . . .

The helicopter was in a dizzying dead climb. He was trapped inside. Beyond the open door, the lights of Rome looked farther away with every passing second. His survival instinct told him to jettison the canister right now. Langdon knew it would take less than twenty seconds for the canister to fall half a mile. But it would be falling toward a city of people.

Higher! Higher!

Langdon wondered how high they were now. Small prop planes, he knew, flew at altitudes of about four miles. This helicopter *had* to be at a good fraction of that by now. *Two miles up? Three?* There was still a chance. If they timed the drop perfectly, the canister would fall only partway toward earth, exploding a safe distance over the ground and away from the chopper. Langdon looked out at the city sprawling below them.

'And if you calculate incorrectly?' the camerlengo said.

Langdon turned, startled. The camerlengo was not even looking at him, apparently having read Langdon's thoughts from the ghostly reflection in the windshield. Oddly, the camerlengo was no longer engrossed in his controls. His hands were not even on the throttle. The chopper, it seemed, was now in some sort of autopilot mode, locked in a climb. The camerlengo reached above his head, to the ceiling of the cockpit, fishing behind a cable-housing, where he removed a key, taped there out of view.

Langdon watched in bewilderment as the camerlengo quickly unlocked the metal cargo box bolted between the seats. He removed some sort of large, black, nylon pack. He laid it on the seat next to him. Langdon's thoughts churned. The camerlengo's movements seemed composed, as if he had a solution.

'Give me the canister,' the camerlengo said, his tone serene.

Langdon did not know what to think anymore. He thrust the canister to the camerlengo. 'Ninety seconds!'

What the camerlengo did with the antimatter took Langdon totally by surprise. Holding the canister carefully in his hands, the camerlengo placed it inside the cargo box. Then he closed the heavy lid and used the key to lock it tight.

'What are you doing!' Langdon demanded.

'Leading us from temptation.' The camerlengo threw the key out the open window.

As the key tumbled into the night, Langdon felt his soul falling with it.

The camerlengo then took the nylon pack and slipped his arms through the straps. He fastened a waist clamp around his stomach and cinched it all down like a backpack. He turned to a dumbstruck Robert Langdon.

'I'm sorry,' the camerlengo said. 'It wasn't supposed to happen this way.' Then he opened his door and hurled himself into the night.

The image burned in Langdon's unconscious mind, and with it came the pain. Real pain. Physical pain. Aching. Searing. He begged to be taken, to let it end, but as the water lapped louder in his ears, new images began to flash. His hell had only just begun. He saw bits and pieces. Scattered frames of sheer panic. He lay halfway between death and nightmare, begging for deliverance, but the pictures grew brighter in his mind.

The antimatter canister was locked out of reach. It counted relentlessly downward as the chopper shot upward. *Fifty seconds.* Higher. Higher. Langdon spun wildly in the cabin, trying to make sense of what he had just seen. *Forty-five seconds.* He dug under seats searching for another parachute. *Forty seconds.* There was none! There had to be an option! *Thirty-five seconds.* He raced to the open doorway of the chopper and stood in the raging wind, gazing down at the lights of Rome below. *Thirty-two seconds.*

And then he made the choice.

The unbelievable choice . . .

With no parachute, Robert Langdon had jumped out the door. As the night swallowed his tumbling body, the helicopter seemed to rocket off above him, the sound of its rotors evaporating in the deafening rush of his own free fall.

As he plummeted toward earth, Robert Langdon felt something he had not experienced since his years on the high dive – the inexorable pull of gravity during a dead drop. The faster he fell, the harder the earth seemed to pull, sucking him down. This time, however, the drop was not fifty feet into a pool. The drop was thousands of feet into a city – an endless expanse of pavement and concrete.

Somewhere in the torrent of wind and desperation, Kohler's voice echoed from the grave . . . words he had spoken earlier this morning standing at CERN's free-fall tube. *One square yard of drag will slow a falling body almost twenty per cent.* Twenty per cent, Langdon now realized, was not even close to what one would need to survive a fall like this. Nonetheless, more out of paralysis than hope, he clenched in his hands the sole object he had grabbed from the chopper on his way out the door. It was an odd memento, but it was one that for a fleeting instant had given him hope.

The windshield tarp had been lying in the back of the helicopter. It was a concave rectangle – about four yards by two – like a huge fitted sheet . . . the crudest approximation of a parachute imaginable. It had no harness, only bungie loops at either end for fastening it to the curvature of the windshield. Langdon had grabbed it, slid his hands through the loops, held on, and leapt out into the void.

His last great act of youthful defiance.

No illusions of life beyond this moment.

Langdon fell like a rock. Feet first. Arms raised. His hands gripping the loops. The tarp billowed like a mushroom overhead. The wind tore past him violently.

As he plummeted toward earth, there was a deep explosion somewhere above him. It seemed farther off than he had expected. Almost instantly, the shock wave hit. He felt the breath crushed from his lungs. There was a sudden warmth in the air all around him. He fought to hold on. A wall of heat raced down from above. The top of the tarp began to smolder . . . but held.

Langdon rocketed downward, on the edge of a billowing shroud of light, feeling like a surfer trying to outrun a thousand-foot tidal wave. Then suddenly, the heat receded.

He was falling again through the dark coolness.

For an instant, Langdon felt hope. A moment later, though, that hope faded like the withdrawing heat above. Despite his straining arms assuring him that the tarp was slowing his fall, the wind still tore past his body with deafening velocity. Langdon had no doubt he was still moving too fast to survive the fall. He would be crushed when he hit the ground.

Mathematical figures tumbled through his brain, but he was too numb to make sense of them . . . *one square yard of drag* . . . *20 per cent reduction of speed.* All Langdon could figure was that the tarp over his head was big enough to slow him more than 20 per cent. Unfortunately, though, he could tell from the wind whipping past him that whatever good the tarp was doing was not enough. He was still falling fast . . . there would be no surviving the impact on the waiting sea of concrete.

Beneath him, the lights of Rome spread out in all directions. The city looked like an enormous starlit sky that Langdon was falling into. The perfect expanse of stars was marred only by a dark strip that split the city in two – a wide, unlit ribbon that wound through the dots of light like a fat snake. Langdon stared down at the meandering swatch of black.

Suddenly, like the surging crest of an unexpected wave, hope filled him again.

With almost maniacal vigor, Langdon yanked down hard with his right hand on the canopy. The tarp suddenly flapped louder, billowing, cutting right to find the path of least resistance. Langdon felt himself drifting sideways. He pulled again, harder, ignoring the pain in his palm. The tarp flared, and Langdon sensed his body sliding laterally. Not much. But *some*! He looked beneath him again, to the sinuous serpent of black. It was off to the right, but he was still pretty high. Had he waited too long? He pulled with all his might and accepted somehow that it was now in the hands of God. He focused hard on the widest part of the serpent and . . . for the first time in his life, prayed for a miracle.

The rest was a blur.

The darkness rushing up beneath him . . . the diving instincts coming back . . . the reflexive locking of his spine and pointing of the toes . . . the inflating of his lungs to protect his vital organs . . . the flexing of his legs into a battering ram . . . and finally . . . the thankfulness that the winding Tiber River was raging . . . making its waters frothy and air-filled . . . and three times softer than standing water.

Then there was impact . . . and blackness.

It had been the thundering sound of the flapping canopy that drew the group's eyes away from the fireball in the sky. The sky above Rome had been filled with sights tonight . . . a skyrocketing helicopter, an enormous explosion, and now this strange object that had plummeted into the churning waters of the Tiber River, directly off the shore of the river's tiny island, Isola Tiberina.

Ever since the island had been used to quarantine the sick during the Roman plague of A.D. 1656, it had been thought to have mystic healing properties. For this reason, the island had later become the site for Rome's Hospital Tiberina.

The body was battered when they pulled it onto shore. The man still had a faint pulse, which was amazing, they thought. They wondered if it was Isola Tiberina's mythical reputation for healing that had somehow kept his heart pumping. Minutes later, when the man began coughing and slowly regained consciousness, the group decided the island must indeed be magical.

126

Cardinal Mortati knew there were no words in any language that could have added to the mystery of this moment. The silence of the vision over St Peter's Square sang louder than any chorus of angels.

As he stared up at Camerlengo Ventresca, Mortati felt the paralyzing collision of his heart and mind. The vision seemed real, tangible. And yet ... how could it be? Everyone had seen the camerlengo get in the helicopter. They had all witnessed the ball of light in the sky. And now, somehow, the camerlengo stood high above them on the rooftop terrace. Transported by angels? Reincarnated by the hand of God?

This is impossible ...

Mortati's heart wanted nothing more than to believe, but his mind cried out for reason. And yet all around him, the cardinals stared up, obviously seeing what he was seeing, paralyzed with wonder.

It was the camerlengo. There was no doubt. But he looked different somehow. Divine. As if he had been purified. A spirit? A man? His white flesh shone in the spotlights with an incorporeal weightlessness.

In the square there was crying, cheering, spontaneous applause. A group of nuns fell to their knees and wailed *saetas*. A pulsing grew from in the crowd. Suddenly, the entire square was chanting the camerlengo's name. The cardinals, some with tears rolling down their faces, joined in. Mortati looked around him and tried to comprehend. *Is this really happening?*

Camerlengo Carlo Ventresca stood on the rooftop terrace of St Peter's Basilica and looked down over the multitudes of people staring up at him. Was he awake or dreaming? He felt transformed, otherworldly. He wondered if it was his body or just his spirit that had floated down from heaven toward the soft, darkened expanse of the Vatican City Gardens ... alighting like a silent angel on the deserted lawns, his black parachute shrouded from the madness by the towering shadow of St Peter's Basilica. He wondered if it was his body or his spirit that had possessed the strength to climb the ancient Stairway of Medallions to the rooftop terrace where he now stood.

He felt as light as a ghost.

Although the people below were chanting his name, he knew it was not *him* they were cheering. They were cheering from impulsive joy, the same kind of joy he felt every day of his life as he pondered the Almighty. They were experiencing what each of them had always longed for . . . an assurance of the beyond . . . a substantiation of the power of the Creator.

Camerlengo Ventresca had prayed all his life for this moment, and still, even *he* could not fathom that God had found a way to make it manifest. He wanted to cry out to them. *Your God is a living God! Behold the miracles all around you!*

He stood there a while, numb and yet feeling more than he had ever felt. When, at last, the spirit moved him, he bowed his head and stepped back from the edge.

Alone now, he knelt on the roof, and prayed.

127

The images around him blurred, drifting in and out. Langdon's eyes slowly began to focus. His legs ached, and his body felt like it had been run over by a truck. He was lying on his side on the ground. Something stunk, like bile. He could still hear the incessant sound of lapping water. It no longer sounded peaceful to him. There were other sounds too – talking close around him. He saw blurry white forms. Were they all wearing white? Langdon decided he was either in an asylum or heaven. From the burning in his throat, Langdon decided it could not be heaven.

'*He's finished vomiting*,' one man said in Italian. '*Turn him*.' The voice was firm and professional.

Langdon felt hands slowly rolling him onto his back. His head swam. He tried to sit up, but the hands gently forced him back down. His body submitted. Then Langdon felt someone going through his pockets, removing items.

Then he passed out cold.

Dr Jacobus was not a religious man; the science of medicine had bred that from him long ago. And yet, the events in Vatican City tonight had put his systematic logic to the test. *Now bodies are falling from the sky?*

Dr Jacobus felt the pulse of the bedraggled man they had just pulled from the Tiber River. The doctor decided that God himself had hand-delivered this one to safety. The concussion of hitting the water had knocked the victim unconscious, and if it had not been for Jacobus and his crew standing out on the shore watching the spectacle in the sky, this falling soul would surely have gone unnoticed and drowned.

'*È Americano*,' a nurse said, going through the man's wallet after they pulled him to dry land.

American? Romans often joked that Americans had gotten so abundant in Rome that hamburgers should become the official Italian food. *But Americans falling from the sky?* Jacobus flicked a penlight in the man's eyes, testing his dilation. 'Sir? Can you hear me? Do you know where you are?'

The man was unconscious again. Jacobus was not surprised. The man had vomited a lot of water after Jacobus had performed CPR.

'*Si chiama Robert Langdon*,' the nurse said, reading the man's driver's license.

The group assembled on the dock all stopped short.

'*Impossibile!*' Jacobus declared. Robert Langdon was the man from the television – the American professor who had been helping the Vatican. Jacobus had seen Mr Langdon, only minutes ago, getting into a helicopter in St Peter's Square and flying miles up into the air. Jacobus and the others had run out to the dock to witness the antimatter explosion – a tremendous sphere of light like nothing any of them had ever seen. *How could this be the same man!*

'It's him!' the nurse exclaimed, brushing his soaked hair back. 'And I recognize his tweed coat!'

Suddenly someone was yelling from the hospital entryway. It was one of the patients. She was screaming, going mad, holding her portable radio to the sky and praising God. Apparently Camerlengo Ventresca had just miraculously appeared on the roof of the Vatican.

Dr Jacobus decided, when his shift got off at 8 a.m., he was going straight to church.

The lights over Langdon's head were brighter now, sterile. He was on some kind of examination table. He smelled astringents, strange chemicals. Someone had just given him an injection, and they had removed his clothes.

Definitely not gypsies, he decided in his semiconscious delirium. *Aliens, perhaps?* Yes, he had heard about things like this. Fortunately these beings would not harm him. All they wanted were his—

'Not on your life!' Langdon sat bolt upright, eyes flying open.

'*Attento!*' one of the creatures yelled, steadying him. His badge read Dr Jacobus. He looked remarkably human.

Langdon stammered, 'I . . . thought . . .'

'Easy, Mr Langdon. You're in a hospital.'

The fog began to lift. Langdon felt a wave of relief. He hated hospitals, but they certainly beat aliens harvesting his testicles.

'My name is Dr Jacobus,' the man said. He explained what had just happened. 'You are very lucky to be alive.'

Langdon did not feel lucky. He could barely make sense of his own memories . . . the helicopter . . . the camerlengo. His body ached everywhere. They gave him some water, and he rinsed out his mouth. They placed a new gauze on his palm.

'Where are my clothes?' Langdon asked. He was wearing a paper robe.

One of the nurses motioned to a dripping wad of shredded khaki and tweed on the counter. 'They were soaked. We had to cut them off you.'

Langdon looked at his shredded Harris tweed and frowned.

'You had some Kleenex in your pocket,' the nurse said.

It was then that Langdon saw the ravaged shreds of parchment clinging

402

all over the lining of his jacket. The folio from Galileo's *Diagramma*. The last copy on earth had just dissolved. He was too numb to know how to react. He just stared.

'We saved your personal items.' She held up a plastic bin. 'Wallet, camcorder, and pen. I dried the camcorder off the best I could.'

'I don't own a camcorder.'

The nurse frowned and held out the bin. Langdon looked at the contents. Along with his wallet and pen was a tiny Sony RUVI camcorder. He recalled it now. Kohler had handed it to him and asked him to give it to the media.

'We found it in your pocket. I think you'll need a new one, though.' The nurse flipped open the two-inch screen on the back. 'Your viewer is cracked.' Then she brightened. 'The sound still works, though. Barely.' She held the device up to her ear. 'Keeps playing something over and over.' She listened a moment and then scowled, handing it to Langdon. 'Two guys arguing, I think.'

Puzzled, Langdon took the camcorder and held it to his ear. The voices were pinched and metallic, but they were discernible. One close. One far away. Langdon recognized them both.

Sitting there in his paper gown, Langdon listened in amazement to the conversation. Although he couldn't see what was happening, when he heard the shocking finale, he was thankful he had been spared the visual.

My God!

As the conversation began playing again from the beginning, Langdon lowered the camcorder from his ear and sat in appalled mystification. The antimatter . . . the helicopter . . . Langdon's mind now kicked into gear.

But that means . . .

He wanted to vomit again. With a rising fury of disorientation and rage, Langdon got off the table and stood on shaky legs.

'Mr Langdon!' the doctor said, trying to stop him.

'I need some clothes,' Langdon demanded, feeling the draft on his rear from the backless gown.

'But, you need to rest.'

'I'm checking out. Now. I need some clothes.'

'But, sir, you—'

'Now!'

Everyone exchanged bewildered looks. 'We have no clothes,' the doctor said. 'Perhaps tomorrow a friend could bring you some.'

Langdon drew a slow patient breath and locked eyes with the doctor. 'Dr Jacobus, I am walking out your door right now. I need clothes. I am going to Vatican City. One does not go to Vatican City with one's ass hanging out. Do I make myself clear?'

Dr Jacobus swallowed hard. 'Get this man something to wear.'

When Langdon limped out of Hospital Tiberina, he felt like an overgrown Cub Scout. He was wearing a blue paramedic's jumpsuit that zipped up the front and was adorned with cloth badges that apparently depicted his numerous qualifications.

The woman accompanying him was heavyset and wore a similar suit. The doctor had assured Langdon she would get him to the Vatican in record time.

'*Molto traffico*,' Langdon said, reminding her that the area around the Vatican was packed with cars and people.

The woman looked unconcerned. She pointed proudly to one of her patches. '*Sono conducente di ambulanza.*'

'*Ambulanza?*' That explained it. Langdon felt like he could use an ambulance ride.

The woman led him around the side of the building. On an outcropping over the water was a cement deck where her vehicle sat waiting. When Langdon saw the vehicle he stopped in his tracks. It was an aging medevac chopper. The hull read *Aero-Ambulanza*.

He hung his head.

The woman smiled. 'Fly Vatican City. Very fast.'

128

The College of Cardinals bristled with ebullience and electricity as they streamed back into the Sistine Chapel. In contrast, Mortati felt in himself a rising confusion he thought might lift him off the floor and carry him away. He believed in the ancient miracles of the Scriptures, and yet what he had just *witnessed* in person was something he could not possibly comprehend. After a lifetime of devotion, seventy-nine years, Mortati knew these events should ignite in him a pious exuberance . . . a fervent and living faith. And yet all he felt was a growing spectral unease. Something did not feel right.

'Signore Mortati!' a Swiss Guard yelled, running down the hall.

'We have gone to the roof as you asked. The camerlengo is . . . *flesh*! He is a true man! He is not a spirit! He is exactly as we knew him!'

'Did he *speak* to you?'

'He kneels in silent prayer! We are afraid to touch him!'

Mortati was at a loss. 'Tell him . . . his cardinals await.'

'Signore, because he is a *man* . . .' the guard hesitated.

'What is it?'

'His chest . . . he is burned. Should we bind his wounds? He must be in pain.'

Mortati considered it. Nothing in his lifetime of service to the church had prepared him for this situation. 'He is a man, so serve him as a man. Bathe him. Bind his wounds. Dress him in fresh robes. We await his arrival in the Sistine Chapel.'

The guard ran off.

Mortati headed for the chapel. The rest of the cardinals were inside now. As he walked down the hall, he saw Vittoria Vetra slumped alone on a bench at the foot of the Royal Staircase. He could see the pain and loneliness of her loss and wanted to go to her, but he knew it would have to wait. He had work to do . . . although he had no idea what that work could possibly be.

Mortati entered the chapel. There was a riotous excitement. He closed the door. *God help me.*

*

Hospital Tiberina's twin-rotor *Aero-Ambulanza* circled in behind Vatican City, and Langdon clenched his teeth, swearing to God this was the very last helicopter ride of his life.

After convincing the pilot that the rules governing Vatican airspace were the least of the Vatican's concerns right now, he guided her in, unseen, over the rear wall, and landed them on the Vatican's helipad.

'*Grazie*,' he said, lowering himself painfully onto the ground. She blew him a kiss and quickly took off, disappearing back over the wall and into the night.

Langdon exhaled, trying to clear his head, hoping to make sense of what he was about to do. With the camcorder in hand, he boarded the same golf cart he had ridden earlier that day. It had not been charged, and the battery-meter registered close to empty. Langdon drove without headlights to conserve power.

He also preferred no one see him coming.

At the back of the Sistine Chapel, Cardinal Mortati stood in a daze as he watched the pandemonium before him.

'It was a miracle!' one of the cardinals shouted. 'The work of God!'

'Yes!' others exclaimed. 'God has made His will manifest!'

'The camerlengo will be our Pope!' another shouted. 'He is not a cardinal, but God has sent a miraculous sign!'

'Yes!' someone agreed. 'The laws of conclave are *man*'s laws. God's will is before us! I call for a balloting immediately!'

'A balloting?' Mortati demanded, moving toward them. 'I believe that is *my* job.'

Everyone turned.

Mortati could sense the cardinals studying him. They seemed distant, at a loss, offended by his sobriety. Mortati longed to feel his heart swept up in the miraculous exultation he saw in the faces around him. But he was not. He felt an inexplicable pain in his soul . . . an aching sadness he could not explain. He had vowed to guide these proceedings with purity of soul, and this hesitancy was something he could not deny.

'My friends,' Mortati said, stepping to the altar. His voice did not seem his own. 'I suspect I will struggle for the rest of my days with the meaning of what I have witnessed tonight. And yet, what you are suggesting regarding the camerlengo . . . it cannot possibly be God's will.'

The room fell silent.

'How . . . can you say that?' one of the cardinals finally demanded. 'The camerlengo *saved* the church. God spoke to the camerlengo directly! The man survived death itself! What sign do we need!'

'The camerlengo is coming to us now,' Mortati said. 'Let us wait. Let us hear him before we have a balloting. There may be an explanation.'

'An explanation?'

'As your Great Elector, I have vowed to uphold the laws of conclave. You

406

are no doubt aware that by Holy Law the camerlengo is ineligible for election to the papacy. He is not a cardinal. He is a priest . . . a chamberlain. There is also the question of his inadequate age.' Mortati felt the stares hardening. 'By even allowing a balloting, I would be requesting that you endorse a man who Vatican Law proclaims ineligible. I would be asking each of you to break a sacred oath.'

'But what happened here tonight,' someone stammered, 'it *certainly* transcends our laws!'

'Does it?' Mortati boomed, not even knowing now where his words were coming from. 'Is it God's will that we discard the rules of the church? Is it God's will that we abandon reason and give ourselves over to frenzy?'

'But did you not see what *we* saw?' another challenged angrily. 'How can you presume to question that kind of power!'

Mortati's voice bellowed now with a resonance he had never known. 'I am not questioning God's power! It is *God* who gave us reason and circumspection! It is God we serve by exercising prudence!'

129

In the hallway outside the Sistine Chapel, Vittoria Vetra sat benumbed on a bench at the foot of the Royal Staircase. When she saw the figure coming through the rear door, she wondered if she were seeing another spirit. He was bandaged, limping, and wearing some kind of medical suit.

She stood . . . unable to believe the vision. 'Ro . . . bert?'

He never answered. He strode directly to her and wrapped her in his arms. When he pressed his lips to hers, it was an impulsive, longing kiss filled with thankfulness.

Vittoria felt the tears coming. 'Oh, God . . . oh, thank God . . .'

He kissed her again, more passionately, and she pressed against him, losing herself in his embrace. Their bodies locked, as if they had known each other for years. She forgot the fear and pain. She closed her eyes, weightless in the moment.

'It is God's will!' someone was yelling, his voice echoing in the Sistine Chapel. 'Who but the *chosen* one could have survived that diabolical explosion?'

'Me,' a voice reverberated from the back of the chapel.

Mortati and the others turned in wonder at the bedraggled form coming up the center aisle. 'Mr . . . *Langdon?*'

Without a word, Langdon walked slowly to the front of the chapel. Vittoria Vetra entered too. Then two guards hurried in, pushing a cart with a large television on it. Langdon waited while they plugged it in, facing the cardinals. Then Langdon motioned for the guards to leave. They did, closing the door behind them.

Now it was only Langdon, Vittoria, and the cardinals. Langdon plugged the Sony RUVI's output into the television. Then he pressed PLAY.

The television blared to life.

The scene that materialized before the cardinals revealed the Pope's office. The video had been awkwardly filmed, as if by hidden camera. Off center on the screen the camerlengo stood in the dimness, in front of a fire. Although he appeared to be talking directly to the camera, it quickly became evident that he was speaking to someone else – whoever was making this video. Langdon told them the video was filmed by Maximilian Kohler, the director of CERN. Only an hour ago Kohler had secretly recorded his meeting with the camerlengo by using a tiny camcorder covertly mounted under the arm of his wheelchair.

Mortati and the cardinals watched in bewilderment. Although the conversation was already in progress, Langdon did not bother to rewind. Apparently, whatever Langdon wanted the cardinals to see was coming up . . .

'Leonardo Vetra kept diaries?' the camerlengo was saying. 'I suppose that is good news for CERN. If the diaries contain his processes for creating antimatter—'

'They don't,' Kohler said. 'You will be relieved to know those processes died with Leonardo. However, his diaries spoke of something else. *You.*'

The camerlengo looked troubled. 'I don't understand.'

'They described a meeting Leonardo had last month. With *you.*'

The camerlengo hesitated, then looked toward the door. 'Rocher should not have granted you access without consulting me. How did you get in here?'

'Rocher knows the truth. I called earlier and told him what you have done.'

'What *I* have done? Whatever story you told him, Rocher is a Swiss Guard and far too faithful to this church to believe a bitter scientist over his camerlengo.'

'Actually, he is too faithful *not* to believe. He is so faithful that despite the evidence that one of his loyal guards had betrayed the church, he refused to accept it. All day long he has been searching for another explanation.'

'So you gave him one.'

'The truth. Shocking as it was.'

'If Rocher believed you, he would have arrested me.'

'No. I wouldn't let him. I offered him my silence in exchange for this meeting.'

The camerlengo let out an odd laugh. 'You plan to *blackmail* the church with a story that no one will possibly believe?'

'I have no need of blackmail. I simply want to hear the truth from your lips. Leonardo Vetra was a friend.'

The camerlengo said nothing. He simply stared down at Kohler.

'Try this,' Kohler snapped. 'About a month ago, Leonardo Vetra contacted you requesting an urgent audience with the Pope – an audience you granted because the Pope was an admirer of Leonardo's work and because Leonardo said it was an emergency.'

The camerlengo turned to the fire. He said nothing.

'Leonardo came to the Vatican in great secrecy. He was betraying his daughter's confidence by coming here, a fact that troubled him deeply, but he felt he had no choice. His research had left him deeply conflicted and in need of spiritual guidance from the church. In a private meeting, he told you and the Pope that he had made a scientific discovery with profound religious implications. He had *proved* Genesis was physically possible, and that intense sources of energy – what Vetra called *God* – could duplicate the moment of Creation.'

Silence.

'The Pope was stunned,' Kohler continued. 'He wanted Leonardo to go public. His Holiness thought this discovery might begin to bridge the gap between science and religion – one of the Pope's life dreams. Then Leonardo explained to you the downside – the reason he required the church's guidance. It seemed his Creation experiment, exactly as your Bible predicts, produced everything in pairs. Opposites. Light *and* dark. Vetra found himself, in addition to creating matter, creating *antimatter*. Shall I go on?'

The camerlengo was silent. He bent down and stoked the coals.

'After Leonardo Vetra came here,' Kohler said, '*you* came to CERN to see his work. Leonardo's diaries said you made a personal trip to his lab.'

The camerlengo looked up.

Kohler went on. 'The Pope could not travel without attracting media attention, so he sent *you*. Leonardo gave you a secret tour of his lab. He showed you an antimatter annihilation – the Big Bang – the power of Creation. He also showed you a large specimen he kept locked away as proof that his new process could produce antimatter on a large scale. You were in awe. You returned to Vatican City to report to the Pope what you had witnessed.'

The camerlengo sighed. 'And what is it that troubles you? That I would respect Leonardo's confidentiality by pretending before the world tonight that I knew nothing of antimatter?'

'No! It troubles me that Leonardo Vetra practically *proved* the existence of your God, and you had him murdered!'

The camerlengo turned now, his face revealing nothing.

The only sound was the crackle of the fire.

Suddenly, the camera jiggled, and Kohler's arm appeared in the frame. He leaned forward, seeming to struggle with something affixed beneath his wheelchair. When he sat back down, he held a pistol out before him. The camera angle was a chilling one . . . looking from behind . . . down the length of the outstretched gun . . . directly at the camerlengo.

Kohler said, 'Confess your sins, Father. Now.'

The camerlengo looked startled. 'You will never get out of here alive.'

'Death would be a welcome relief from the misery your faith has put me through since I was a boy.' Kohler held the gun with both hands now. 'I am giving you a choice. Confess your sins . . . or die right now.'

The camerlengo glanced toward the door.

'Rocher is outside,' Kohler challenged. 'He too is prepared to kill you.'

'Rocher is a sworn protector of th—'

'Rocher let me in here. *Armed*. He is sickened by your lies. You have a single option. Confess to me. I have to hear it from your very lips.'

The camerlengo hesitated.

Kohler cocked his gun. 'Do you really doubt I will kill you?'

'No matter what I tell you,' the camerlengo said, 'a man like you will never understand.'

'Try me.'

The camerlengo stood still for a moment, a dominant silhouette in the dim light of the fire. When he spoke, his words echoed with a dignity more suited to the glorious recounting of altruism than that of a confession.

'Since the beginning of time,' the camerlengo said, 'this church has fought the enemies of God. Sometimes with words. Sometimes with swords. And we have always survived.'

The camerlengo radiated conviction.

'But the demons of the past,' he continued, 'were demons of fire and abomination . . . *they* were enemies we could fight – enemies who inspired *fear*. Yet Satan is shrewd. As time passed, he cast off his diabolical countenance for a new face . . . the face of pure reason. Transparent and insidious, but soulless all the same.' The camerlengo's voice flashed sudden anger – an almost maniacal transition. 'Tell me, Mr Kohler! How can the church condemn that which makes logical sense to our minds! How can we decry that which is now the very foundation of our society! Each time the church raises its voice in warning, *you* shout back, calling us ignorant. Paranoid. Controlling! And so your evil grows. Shrouded in a veil of self-righteous intellectualism. It spreads like a cancer. Sanctified by the miracles of its own technology. Deifying itself! Until we no longer suspect you are anything but pure goodness. Science has come to save us from our sickness, hunger, and pain! Behold science – the new God of endless miracles, omnipotent and benevolent! Ignore the weapons and the chaos. Forget the fractured loneliness and endless peril. Science is here!' The camerlengo stepped toward the gun. 'But I have seen Satan's face lurking . . . I have seen the peril . . .'

'What are you talking about! Vetra's science practically *proved* the existence of your God! He was your ally!'

'Ally? Science and religion are not in this together! We do not seek the same God, you and I! Who is your God? One of protons, masses, and particle charges? How does your God *inspire*? How does your God reach into the hearts of man and remind him he is accountable to a greater power! Remind him that he is accountable to his fellow man! Vetra was misguided. His work was not religious, it was *sacrilegious*! Man cannot put God's Creation in a test tube and wave it around for the world to see! This does not glorify God, it *demeans* God!' The camerlengo was clawing at his body now, his voice manic.

'And so you had Leonardo Vetra killed!'

'For the church! For all mankind! The madness of it! Man is not ready to hold the power of Creation in his hands. God in a test tube? A droplet of liquid that can vaporize an entire city? He had to be stopped!' The camerlengo fell abruptly silent. He looked away, back toward the fire. He seemed to be contemplating his options.

Kohler's hands leveled the gun. 'You have confessed. You have no escape.'

The camerlengo laughed sadly. 'Don't you see. Confessing your sins *is* the escape.' He looked toward the door. 'When God is on your side, you have options a man like you could never comprehend.' With his words still hanging in the air, the camerlengo grabbed the neck of his cassock and violently tore it open, revealing his bare chest.

Kohler jolted, obviously startled. 'What are you doing!'

The camerlengo did not reply. He stepped backward, toward the fireplace, and removed an object from the glowing embers.

'Stop!' Kohler demanded, his gun still leveled. 'What are you doing!'

When the camerlengo turned, he was holding a red-hot brand. The Illuminati Diamond. The man's eyes looked wild suddenly. 'I had intended to do this all alone.' His voice seethed with a feral intensity 'But now . . . I see God meant for you to be here. *You* are my salvation.'

Before Kohler could react, the camerlengo closed his eyes, arched his back, and rammed the red hot brand into the center of his own chest. His flesh hissed. '*Mother Mary! Blessed Mother . . . Behold your son!*' He screamed out in agony.

Kohler lurched into the frame now . . . standing awkwardly on his feet, gun wavering wildly before him.

The camerlengo screamed louder, teetering in shock. He threw the brand at Kohler's feet. Then the priest collapsed on the floor, writhing in agony.

What happened next was a blur.

There was a great flurry onscreen as the Swiss Guard burst into the room. The soundtrack exploded with gunfire. Kohler clutched his chest, blown backward, bleeding, falling into his wheelchair.

'No!' Rocher called, trying to stop his guards from firing on Kohler.

The camerlengo, still writhing on the floor, rolled and pointed frantically at Rocher. '*Illuminatus!*'

'You bastard,' Rocher yelled, running at him. 'You sanctimonious bas—'

Chartrand cut him down with three bullets. Rocher slid dead across the floor.

Then the guards ran to the wounded camerlengo, gathering around him. As they huddled, the video caught the face of a dazed Robert Langdon, kneeling beside the wheelchair, looking at the brand. Then, the entire frame began lurching wildly. Kohler had regained consciousness and was

412

detaching the tiny camcorder from its holder under the arm of the wheel-chair. Then he tried to hand the camcorder to Langdon.

'G-give . . .' Kohler gasped. 'G-give this to the m-media.'

Then the screen went blank.

130

The camerlengo began to feel the fog of wonder and adrenaline dissipating. As the Swiss Guard helped him down the Royal Staircase toward the Sistine Chapel, the camerlengo heard singing in St Peter's Square and he knew that mountains had been moved.

Grazie Dio.

He had prayed for strength, and God had given it to him. At moments when he had doubted, God had spoken. *Yours is a Holy mission*, God had said. *I will give you strength.* Even with God's strength, the camerlengo had felt fear, questioning the righteousness of his path.

If not you, God had challenged, *then WHO?*

If not now, then WHEN?

If not this way, then HOW?

Jesus, God reminded him, had saved them all . . . saved them from their own apathy. With two deeds, Jesus had opened their eyes. Horror and Hope. The crucifixion and the resurrection. He had changed the world.

But that was millennia ago. Time had eroded the miracle. People had forgotten. They had turned to false idols – techno-deities and miracles of the mind. *What about miracles of the heart!*

The camerlengo had often prayed to God to show him how to make the people believe again. But God had been silent. It was not until the camerlengo's moment of deepest darkness that God had come to him. *Oh, the horror of that night!*

The camerlengo could still remember lying on the floor in tattered nightclothes, clawing at his own flesh, trying to purge his soul of the pain brought on by a vile truth he had just learned. *It cannot be!* he had screamed. And yet he knew it was. The deception tore at him like the fires of hell. The bishop who had taken him in, the man who had been like a father to him, the clergyman whom the camerlengo had stood beside while he rose to the papacy . . . was a fraud. A common sinner. Lying to the world about a deed so traitorous at its core that the camerlengo doubted even God could forgive it. 'Your *vow*!' the camerlengo had screamed at the Pope. 'You broke your vow to God! *You*, of all men!'

The Pope had tried to explain himself, but the camerlengo could not listen. He had run out, staggering blindly through the hallways, vomiting, tearing at his own skin, until he found himself bloody and alone, lying on the cold earthen floor before St Peter's tomb. *Mother Mary, what do I do?* It was in that moment of pain and betrayal, as the camerlengo lay devastated in the Necropolis, praying for God to take him from this faithless world, that God had come.

The voice in his head resounded like peals of thunder. *'Did you vow to serve your God?'*

'Yes!' the camerlengo cried out.

'Would you die for your God?'

'Yes! Take me now!'

'Would you die for your church?'

'Yes! Please deliver me!'

'But would you die for . . . mankind?'

It was in the silence that followed that the camerlengo felt himself falling into the abyss. He tumbled farther, faster, out of control. And yet he knew the answer. He had always known.

'Yes!' he shouted into the madness. 'I would die for man! Like your son, I would die for them!'

Hours later, the camerlengo still lay shivering on his floor. He saw his mother's face. *God has plans for you*, she was saying. The camerlengo plunged deeper into madness. It was then God had spoken again. This time with silence. But the camerlengo understood. *Restore their faith.*

If not me . . . then who?

If not now . . . then when?

As the guards unbolted the door of the Sistine Chapel, Camerlengo Carlo Ventresca felt the power moving in his veins . . . exactly as it had when he was a boy. God had chosen him. Long ago.

His will be done.

The camerlengo felt reborn. The Swiss Guard had bandaged his chest, bathed him, and dressed him in a fresh white linen robe. They had also given him an injection of morphine for the burn. The camerlengo wished they had not given him painkillers. *Jesus endured his pain for three days before ascending!* He could already feel the drug uprooting his senses . . . a dizzying undertow.

As he walked into the chapel, he was not at all surprised to see the cardinals staring at him in wonder. *They are in awe of God*, he reminded himself. *Not of me, but how God works THROUGH me.* As he moved up the center aisle, he saw bewilderment in every face. And yet, with each new face he passed, he sensed something *else* in their eyes. What was it? The camerlengo had tried to imagine how they would receive him tonight. Joyfully? Reverently? He tried to read their eyes and saw neither emotion.

It was then the camerlengo looked at the altar and saw Robert Langdon.

131

Camerlengo Carlo Ventresca stood in the aisle of the Sistine Chapel. The cardinals were all standing near the front of the church, turned, staring at him. Robert Langdon was on the altar beside a television that was on endless loop, playing a scene the camerlengo recognized but could not imagine how it had come to be. Vittoria Vetra stood beside him, her face drawn.

The camerlengo closed his eyes for a moment, hoping the morphine was making him hallucinate and that when he opened them the scene might be different. But it was not.

They knew

Oddly, he felt no fear. *Show me the way, Father. Give me the words that I can make them see Your vision.*

But the camerlengo heard no reply.

Father, We have come too far together to fail now.

Silence.

They do not understand what We have done.

The camerlengo did not know whose voice he heard in his own mind, but the message was stark.

And the truth shall set you free . . .

And so it was that Camerlengo Carlo Ventresca held his head high as he walked toward the front of the Sistine Chapel. As he moved toward the cardinals, not even the diffused light of the candles could soften the eyes boring into him. *Explain yourself,* the faces said. *Make sense of this madness. Tell us our fears are wrong!*

Truth, the camerlengo told himself. *Only truth.* There were too many secrets in these walls . . . one so dark it had driven him to madness. *But from the madness had come the light.*

'If you could give your own soul to save millions,' the camerlengo said, as he moved down the aisle, '*would* you?'

The faces in the chapel simply stared. No one moved. No one spoke. Beyond the walls, the joyous strains of song could be heard in the square.

The camerlengo walked toward them. 'Which is the greater sin? Killing one's enemy? Or standing idle while your true love is strangled?' *They are singing in St Peter's Square!* The camerlengo stopped for a moment and gazed up at the ceiling of the Sistine. Michelangelo's God was staring down from the darkened vault . . . and He seemed pleased.

'I could no longer stand by,' the camerlengo said. Still, as he drew nearer, he saw no flicker of understanding in anyone's eyes. Didn't they see the radiant simplicity of his deeds? Didn't they see the utter necessity!

It had been so pure.

The Illuminati. Science and Satan as one.

Resurrect the ancient fear. Then crush it.

Horror and Hope. Make them believe again.

Tonight, the power of the Illuminati had been unleashed anew . . . and with glorious consequence. The apathy had evaporated. The fear had shot out across the world like a bolt of lightning, uniting the people. And then God's majesty had vanquished the darkness.

I could not stand idly by!

The inspiration had been God's own – appearing like a beacon in the camerlengo's night of agony *Oh, this faithless world! Someone must deliver them. You. If not you, who? You have been saved for a reason. Show them the old demons. Remind them of their fear. Apathy is death. Without darkness, there is no light. Without evil, there is no good. Make them choose. Dark or light. Where is the fear? Where are the heroes? If not now, when?*

The camerlengo walked up the center aisle directly toward the crowd of standing cardinals. He felt like Moses as the sea of red sashes and caps parted before him, allowing him to pass. On the altar, Robert Langdon switched off the television, took Vittoria's hand, and relinquished the altar. The fact that Robert Langdon had survived, the camerlengo knew, could only have been God's will. God had saved Robert Langdon. The camerlengo wondered why.

The voice that broke the silence was the voice of the only woman in the Sistine Chapel. 'You *killed* my father?' she said, stepping forward.

When the camerlengo turned to Vittoria Vetra, the look on her face was one he could not quite understand – pain yes, but *anger*? Certainly she must understand. Her father's genius was deadly. He had to be stopped. For the good of Mankind.

'He was doing God's work,' Vittoria said.

'God's work is not done in a lab. It is done in the heart.'

'My father's heart was pure! And his research proved—'

'His research proved yet again that man's mind is progressing faster than his soul!' The camerlengo's voice was sharper than he had expected. He lowered his voice. 'If a man as spiritual as your father could create a weapon like the one we saw tonight, imagine what an ordinary man will do with his technology.'

'A man like *you*?'

The camerlengo took a deep breath. Did she not see? Man's morality was not advancing as fast as man's science. Mankind was not spiritually evolved enough for the powers he possessed. *We have never created a weapon we have not used!* And yet he knew that antimatter was nothing – another weapon in man's already burgeoning arsenal. Man could already destroy. Man learned to kill long ago. *And his mother's blood rained down.* Leonardo Vetra's genius was dangerous for another reason.

'For centuries,' the camerlengo said, 'the church has stood by while science picked away at religion bit by bit. Debunking miracles. Training the mind to overcome the heart. Condemning religion as the opiate of the masses. They denounce God as a hallucination – a delusional crutch for those too weak to accept that life is meaningless. I could not stand by while science presumed to harness the power of God Himself! *Proof*, you say? Yes, proof of science's ignorance! What is wrong with the admission that something exists beyond our understanding? The day science substantiates God in a lab is the day people stop needing faith!'

'You mean the day they stop needing the *church*,' Vittoria challenged, moving toward him. 'Doubt is your last shred of control. It is *doubt* that brings souls to you. Our need to know that life has meaning. Man's insecurity and need for an enlightened soul assuring him everything is part of a master plan. But the church is not the only enlightened soul on the planet! We all seek God in different ways. What are you afraid of? That God will show himself somewhere *other* than inside these walls? That people will find him in their own lives and leave your antiquated rituals behind? Religions evolve! The mind finds answers, the heart grapples with new truths. My father was on *your* quest! A parallel path! Why couldn't you see that? God is not some omnipotent authority looking down from above, threatening to throw us into a pit of fire if we disobey. God is the energy that flows through the synapses of our nervous system and the chambers of our hearts! God is in all things!'

'*Except* science,' the camerlengo fired back, his eyes showing only pity. 'Science, by definition, is soulless. Divorced from the heart. Intellectual miracles like antimatter arrive in this world with no ethical instructions attached. This in itself is perilous! But when science heralds its Godless pursuits as the enlightened path? Promising answers to questions whose beauty is that they have no answers?' He shook his head. 'No.'

There was a moment of silence. The camerlengo felt suddenly tired as he returned Vittoria's unbending stare. This was not how it was supposed to be. *Is this God's final test?*

It was Mortati who broke the spell. 'The *preferiti*,' he said in a horrified whisper. 'Baggia and the others. Please tell me you did not . . .'

The camerlengo turned to him, surprised by the pain in his voice. Certainly *Mortati* could understand. Headlines carried science's miracles every day. How long had it been for religion? Centuries? Religion needed a miracle! Something to awaken a sleeping world. Bring them back to the path of righteousness. Restore faith. The *preferiti* were not leaders anyway, they were transformers – liberals prepared to embrace the new world and

418

abandon the old ways! This was the only way. A new leader. Young. Powerful. Vibrant. Miraculous. The *preferiti* served the church far more effectively in death than they ever could alive. Horror and Hope. *Offer four souls to save millions.* The world would remember them forever as martyrs. The church would raise glorious tribute to their names. *How many thousands have died for the glory of God? They are only four.*

'The *preferiti*,' Mortati repeated.

'I shared their pain,' the camerlengo defended, motioning to his chest. 'And I too would die for God, but my work is only just begun. They are singing in St Peter's Square!'

The camerlengo saw the horror in Mortati's eyes and again felt confused. Was it the morphine? Mortati was looking at him as if the camerlengo himself had killed these men with his bare hands. *I would do even that for God*, the camerlengo thought, and yet he had not. The deeds had been carried out by the Hassassin – a heathen soul tricked into thinking he was doing the work of the Illuminati. *I am Janus*, the camerlengo had told him. *I will prove my power.* And he had. The Hassassin's hatred had made him God's pawn.

'Listen to the singing,' the camerlengo said, smiling, his own heart rejoicing. 'Nothing unites hearts like the presence of evil. Burn a church and the community rises up, holding hands, singing hymns of defiance as they rebuild. Look how they flock tonight. Fear has brought them home. Forge modern demons for modern man. Apathy is dead. Show them the face of evil – Satanists lurking among us – running our governments, our banks, our schools, threatening to obliterate the very House of God with their misguided science. Depravity runs deep. Man must be vigilant. Seek the goodness. *Become* the goodness!'

In the silence, the camerlengo hoped they now understood. The Illuminati had not resurfaced. The Illuminati were long deceased. Only their myth was alive. The camerlengo had resurrected the Illuminati as a reminder. Those who knew the Illuminati history relived their evil. Those who did not, had learned of it and were amazed how blind they had been. The ancient demons had been resurrected to awaken an indifferent world.

'But . . . the brands?' Mortati's voice was stiff with outrage.

The camerlengo did not answer. Mortati had no way of knowing, but the brands had been confiscated by the Vatican over a century ago. They had been locked away, forgotten and dust covered, in the Papal Vault – the Pope's private reliquary, deep within his Borgia apartments. The Papal Vault contained those items the church deemed too dangerous for anyone's eyes except the Pope's.

Why did they hide that which inspired fear? Fear brought people to God!

The vault's key was passed down from Pope to Pope. Camerlengo Carlo Ventresca had purloined the key and ventured inside; the myth of what the vault contained was bewitching – including the original manuscript for the fourteen unpublished books of the Bible known as the *Apocrypha* and the location of the tomb of the Virgin Mary. In addition to these, the camerlengo had found the Illuminati Collection – all the secrets the church had uncovered after banishing the group from Rome ... their contemptible Path of Illumination ... the cunning deceit of the Vatican's head artist, Bernini ... Europe's top scientists mocking religion as they secretly assembled in the Vatican's own Castle St Angelo. The collection included a pentagon box containing iron brands, one of them the mythical Illuminati Diamond. This was a part of Vatican history the ancients thought best forgotten. The camerlengo, however, had disagreed.

'But the *antimatter*...' Vittoria demanded. 'You risked destroying the Vatican!'

'There is no risk when God is at your side,' the camerlengo said. 'This cause was His.'

'You're insane!' she seethed.

'Millions were saved.'

'People were *killed*!'

'Souls were saved.'

'Tell that to my father and Max Kohler!'

'CERN's arrogance needed to be revealed. A droplet of liquid that can vaporize a half mile? And you call me mad?' The camerlengo felt a rage rising in him. Did they think his was a simple charge? 'Those who *believe* undergo great tests for God! God asked Abraham to sacrifice his child! God commanded Jesus to endure crucifixion! And so we hang the symbol of the crucifix before our eyes – bloody, painful, agonizing – to remind us of evil's power! To keep our hearts vigilant! The scars on Jesus' body are a living reminder of the powers of darkness! My scars are a living reminder! Evil lives, but the power of God will overcome!'

His shouts echoed off the back wall of the Sistine Chapel and then a profound silence fell. Time seemed to stop. Michelangelo's *Last Judgment* rose ominously behind him ... Jesus casting sinners into hell. Tears brimmed in Mortati's eyes.

'What have you done, Carlo?' Mortati asked in a whisper. He closed his eyes, and a tear rolled. 'His *Holiness*?'

A collective sigh of pain went up, as if everyone in the room had forgotten until that very moment. The Pope. Poisoned.

'A vile liar,' the camerlengo said.

Mortati looked shattered. 'What do you mean? He was honest! He ... loved you.'

'And I him.' *Oh, how I loved him! But the deceit! The broken vows to God!*

The camerlengo knew they did not understand right now, but they *would*. When he told them, they would see! His Holiness was the most nefarious deceiver the church had ever seen. The camerlengo still remembered that terrible night. He had returned from his trip to CERN with news of Vetra's *Genesis* and of antimatter's horrific power. The camerlengo was certain the Pope would see the perils, but the Holy Father saw only

420

hope in Vetra's breakthrough. He even suggested the Vatican *fund* Vetra's work as a gesture of goodwill toward spiritually based scientific research.

Madness! The church investing in research that threatened to make the church obsolete? Work that spawned weapons of mass destruction? The bomb that had killed his mother . . .

'But . . . you can't!' the camerlengo had exclaimed.

'I owe a deep debt to science,' the Pope had replied. 'Something I have hidden my entire life. Science gave me a gift when I was a young man. A gift I have never forgotten.'

'I don't understand. What does science have to offer a man of *God*?'

'It is complicated,' the Pope had said. 'I will need time to make you understand. But first, there is a simple fact about me that you must know. I have kept it hidden all these years. I believe it is time I told you.'

Then the Pope had told him the astonishing truth.

132

The camerlengo lay curled in a ball on the dirt floor in front of St Peter's tomb. The Necropolis was cold, but it helped clot the blood flowing from the wounds he had torn at his own flesh. His Holiness would not find him here. Nobody would find him here . . .

'It is complicated,' the Pope's voice echoed in his mind. 'I will need time to make you understand . . .'

But the camerlengo knew no amount of time could make him understand.

Liar! I believed in you! GOD believed in you!

With a single sentence, the Pope had brought the camerlengo's world crashing down around him. Everything the camerlengo had ever believed about his mentor was shattered before his eyes. The truth drilled into the camerlengo's heart with such force that he staggered backward out of the Pope's office and vomited in the hallway.

'Wait!' the Pope had cried, chasing after him. 'Please let me explain!'

But the camerlengo ran off. How could His Holiness expect him to endure any more? Oh, the wretched depravity of it! What if someone else found out? Imagine the desecration to the church! Did the Pope's holy vows mean nothing?

The madness came quickly, screaming in his ears, until he awoke before St Peter's tomb. It was then that God came to him with an awesome fierceness.

YOURS IS A VENGEFUL GOD!

Together, they made their plans. Together they would protect the church. Together they would restore faith to this faithless world. Evil was everywhere. And yet the world had become immune! Together they would unveil the darkness for the world to see . . . and God would overcome! Horror and Hope. Then the world would believe!

God's first test had been less horrible than the camerlengo imagined. Sneaking into the Papal bed chambers . . . filling his syringe . . . covering the deceiver's mouth as his body spasmed into death. In the moonlight, the camerlengo could see in the Pope's wild eyes there was something he wanted to say.

But it was too late.

The Pope had said enough.

133

'The Pope fathered a child.'

Inside the Sistine Chapel, the camerlengo stood unwavering as he spoke. Five solitary words of astonishing disclosure. The entire assembly seemed to recoil in unison. The cardinals' accusing miens evaporated into aghast stares, as if every soul in the room were praying the camerlengo was wrong.

The Pope fathered a child.

Langdon felt the shock wave hit him too. Vittoria's hand, tight in his, jolted, while Langdon's mind, already numb with unanswered questions, wrestled to find a center of gravity.

The camerlengo's utterance seemed like it would hang forever in the air above them. Even in the camerlengo's frenzied eyes, Langdon could see pure conviction. Langdon wanted to disengage, tell himself he was lost in some grotesque nightmare, soon to wake up in a world that made sense.

'This must be a lie!' one of the cardinals yelled.

'I will not believe it!' another protested. 'His Holiness was as devout a man as ever lived!'

It was Mortati who spoke next, his voice thin with devastation. 'My friends. What the camerlengo says is true.' Every cardinal in the chapel spun as though Mortati had just shouted an obscenity. 'The Pope indeed fathered a child.'

The cardinals blanched with dread.

The camerlengo looked stunned. 'You *knew*? But . . . how could you possibly know this?'

Mortati sighed. 'When His Holiness was elected . . . *I* was the Devil's Advocate.'

There was a communal gasp.

Langdon understood. This meant the information was probably true. The infamous 'Devil's Advocate' was *the* authority when it came to scandalous information inside the Vatican. Skeletons in a Pope's closet were dangerous, and prior to elections, secret inquiries into a candidate's background were carried out by a lone cardinal who served as the 'Devil's Advocate' – that individual responsible for unearthing reasons why the eligible cardinals should *not* become Pope. The Devil's Advocate was appointed in advance by the reigning Pope in preparation for his own death. The Devil's Advocate was never supposed to reveal his identity. *Ever.*

'*I* was the Devil's Advocate,' Mortati repeated. 'That is how I found out.'

Mouths dropped. Apparently tonight was a night when all the rules were going out the window.

The camerlengo felt his heart filling with rage. 'And you . . . told *no one?*'

'I confronted His Holiness,' Mortati said. 'And he confessed. He explained the entire story and asked only that I let my heart guide my decision as to whether or not to reveal his secret.'

'And your heart told you to *bury* the information?'

'He was the runaway favorite for the papacy. People loved him. The scandal would have hurt the church deeply.'

'But he fathered a *child*! He broke his sacred vow of celibacy!' The camerlengo was screaming now. He could hear his mother's voice. *A promise to God is the most important promise of all. Never break a promise to God.* 'The Pope broke his vow!'

Mortati looked delirious with angst. 'Carlo, his love . . . was *chaste*. He had broken no vow. He didn't explain it to you?'

'Explain what?' The camerlengo remembered running out of the Pope's office while the Pope was calling to him. *Let me explain!*

Slowly, sadly, Mortati let the tale unfold. Many years ago, the Pope, when he was still just a priest, had fallen in love with a young nun. Both of them had taken vows of celibacy and never even considered breaking their covenant with God. Still, as they fell deeper in love, although they could resist the temptations of the flesh, they both found themselves longing for something they never expected – to participate in God's ultimate miracle of creation – a child. *Their* child. The yearning, especially in her, became overwhelming. Still, God came first. A year later, when the frustration had reached almost unbearable proportions, she came to him in a whirl of excitement. She had just read an article about a new miracle of science – a process by which two people, without ever having sexual relations, could have a child. She sensed this was a sign from God. The priest could see the happiness in her eyes and agreed. A year later she had a child through the miracle of artificial insemination . . .

'This cannot . . . be true,' the camerlengo said, panicked, hoping it was the morphine washing over his senses. Certainly he was hearing things.

Mortati now had tears in his eyes. 'Carlo, this is why His Holiness has always had an affection for the sciences. He felt he owed a debt to science. Science let him experience the joys of fatherhood without breaking his vow of celibacy. His Holiness told me he had no regrets except one – that his advancing stature in the church prohibited him from being with the woman he loved and seeing his infant grow up.'

Camerlengo Carlo Ventresca felt the madness setting in again. He wanted to claw at his flesh. *How could I have known?*

'The Pope committed no sin, Carlo. He was chaste.'

'But . . .' The camerlengo searched his anguished mind for any kind of rationale. 'Think of the jeopardy . . . of his deeds.' His voice felt weak. 'What if this whore of his came forward? Or, heaven forbid, his *child?* Imagine the shame the church would endure.'

Mortati's voice was tremulous. 'The child has *already* come forward.'

Everything stopped.

'Carlo . . .?' Mortati crumbled. 'His Holiness's child . . . is *you.*'

At that moment, the camerlengo could feel the fire of faith dim in his heart. He stood trembling on the altar, framed by Michelangelo's towering *Last Judgment.* He knew he had just glimpsed hell itself. He opened his mouth to speak, but his lips wavered, soundless.

'Don't you see?' Mortati choked. '*That* is why His Holiness came to you in the hospital in Palermo when you were a boy. *That* is why he took you in and raised you. The nun he loved was Maria . . . your mother. She left the nunnery to raise you, but she never abandoned her strict devotion to God. When the Pope heard she had died in an explosion and that you, his son, had miraculously survived . . . he swore to God he would never leave you alone again. Carlo, your parents were both virgins. They kept their vows to God. And still they found a way to bring you into the world. You were their miraculous child.'

The camerlengo covered his ears, trying to block out the words. He stood paralyzed on the altar. Then, with his world yanked from beneath him, he fell violently to his knees and let out a wail of anguish.

Seconds. Minutes. Hours.

Time seemed to have lost all meaning inside the four walls of the chapel. Vittoria felt herself slowly breaking free of the paralysis that seemed to have gripped them all. She let go of Langdon's hand and began moving through the crowd of cardinals. The chapel door seemed miles away and she felt like she was moving underwater . . . slow motion.

As she maneuvered through the robes, her motion seemed to pull others from their trance. Some of the cardinals began to pray. Others wept. Some turned to watch her go, their blank expressions turning slowly to a foreboding cognition as she moved toward the door. She had almost reached the back of the crowd when a hand caught her arm. The touch was frail but resolute. She turned, face to face with a wizened cardinal. His visage was clouded by fear.

'No,' the man whispered. 'You cannot.'

Vittoria stared, incredulous.

Another cardinal was at her side now. 'We must think before we act.'

And another. 'The pain this could cause . . .'

Vittoria was surrounded. She looked at them all, stunned. 'But these deeds here today, tonight . . . certainly the world should know the truth.'

'My heart agrees,' the wizened cardinal said, still holding her arm, 'and yet it is a path from which there is no return. We must consider the shattered hopes. The cynicism. How could the people *ever* trust again?'

Suddenly, more cardinals seemed to be blocking her way. There was a wall of black robes before her. 'Listen to the people in the square,' one said. 'What will this do to their hearts? We must exercise prudence.'

'We need time to think and pray,' another said. 'We must act with foresight. The repercussions of this . . .'

'He killed my father!' Vittoria said. 'He killed his *own* father!'

'I'm certain he will pay for his sins,' the cardinal holding her arm said sadly.

Vittoria was certain too, and she intended to *ensure* he paid. She tried to push toward the door again, but the cardinals huddled closer, their faces frightened.

'What are you going to do?' she exclaimed. '*Kill* me?'

The old men blanched, and Vittoria immediately regretted her words. She could see these men were gentle souls. They had seen enough violence tonight. They meant no threat. They were simply trapped. Scared. Trying to get their bearings.

'I want . . .' the wizened cardinal said, '. . . to do what is right.'

'Then you will let her out,' a deep voice declared behind her. The words were calm but absolute. Robert Langdon arrived at her side, and she felt his hand take hers. 'Ms Vetra and I are leaving this chapel. Right now.'

Faltering, hesitant, the cardinals began to step aside.

'Wait!' It was Mortati. He moved toward them now, down the center aisle, leaving the camerlengo alone and defeated on the altar. Mortati looked older all of a sudden, wearied beyond his years. His motion was burdened with shame. He arrived, putting a hand on Langdon's shoulder and one on Vittoria's as well. Vittoria felt sincerity in his touch. The man's eyes were more tearful now.

'*Of course* you are free to go,' Mortati said. 'Of course.' The man paused, his grief almost tangible. 'I ask only this . . .' He stared down at his feet a long moment then back up at Vittoria and Langdon. 'Let *me* do it. I will go into the square right now and find a way. I will tell them. I don't know how . . . but I will find a way. The church's confession should come from within. Our failures should be our own to expose.'

Mortati turned sadly back toward the altar. 'Carlo, you have brought this church to a disastrous juncture.' He paused, looking around. The altar was bare.

There was a rustle of cloth down the side aisle, and the door clicked shut.

The camerlengo was gone.

134

Camerlengo Ventresca's white robe billowed as he moved down the hallway away from the Sistine Chapel. The Swiss Guards had seemed perplexed when he emerged all alone from the chapel and told them he needed a moment of solitude. But they had obeyed, letting him go.

Now as he rounded the corner and left their sight, the camerlengo felt a maelstrom of emotions like nothing he thought possible in human experience. He had poisoned the man he called 'Holy Father,' the man who addressed him as 'my son.' The camerlengo had always believed the words 'father' and 'son' were religious tradition, but now he knew the diabolical truth – the words had been *literal*.

Like that fateful night weeks ago, the camerlengo now felt himself reeling madly through the darkness.

It was raining the morning the Vatican staff banged on the camerlengo's door, awakening him from a fitful sleep. The Pope, they said, was not answering his door or his phone. The clergy were frightened. The camerlengo was the only one who could enter the Pope's chambers unannounced.

The camerlengo entered alone to find the Pope, as he was the night before, twisted and dead in his bed. His Holiness's face looked like that of Satan. His tongue black like death. The Devil himself had been sleeping in the Pope's bed.

The camerlengo felt no remorse. God had spoken.

Nobody would see the treachery . . . not yet. That would come later.

He announced the terrible news – His Holiness was dead of a stroke. Then the camerlengo prepared for conclave.

Mother Maria's voice was whispering in his ear. 'Never break a promise to God.'

'I hear you, Mother,' he replied. 'It is a faithless world. They need to be brought back to the path of righteousness. Horror and Hope. It is the only way.'

'Yes,' she said. 'If not you . . . then who? Who will lead the church out of darkness?'

Certainly not one of the *preferiti*. They were old . . . walking death . . . liberals who would follow the Pope, endorsing science in his memory, seeking modern followers by abandoning the ancient ways. Old men desperately behind the times, pathetically pretending they were not. They would fail, of course. The church's strength was its tradition, not its transience. The whole world was transitory. The church did not need to change, it simply needed to remind the world it was relevant! Evil lives! God will overcome!

The church needed a leader. Old men do not inspire! Jesus inspired! Young, vibrant, powerful . . . *MIRACULOUS*.

'Enjoy your tea,' the camerlengo told the four *preferiti*, leaving them in the Pope's private library before conclave. 'Your guide will be here soon.'

The *preferiti* thanked him, all abuzz that they had been offered a chance to enter the famed Passetto. Most uncommon! The camerlengo, before leaving them, had unlocked the door to the Passetto, and exactly on schedule, the door had opened, and a foreign-looking priest with a torch had ushered the excited *preferiti* in.

The men had never come out.

They will be the Horror. I will be the Hope.

No . . . I am the horror.

The camerlengo staggered now through the darkness of St Peter's Basilica. Somehow, through the insanity and guilt, through the images of his father, through the pain and revelation, even through the pull of the morphine . . . he had found a brilliant clarity. A sense of destiny. *I know my purpose*, he thought, awed by the lucidity of it.

From the beginning, nothing tonight had gone exactly as he had planned. Unforeseen obstacles had presented themselves, but the camerlengo had adapted, making bold adjustments. Still, he had never imagined tonight would end this way, and yet now he saw the preordained majesty of it.

It could end no other way.

Oh, what terror he had felt in the Sistine Chapel, wondering if God had forsaken him! *Oh, what deeds He had ordained!* He had fallen to his knees, awash with doubt, his ears straining for the voice of God but hearing only silence. He had begged for a sign. Guidance. Direction. Was this God's will? The church destroyed by scandal and abomination? No! *God* was the one who had willed the camerlengo to act! *Hadn't He?*

Then he had seen it. Sitting on the altar. A sign. Divine communication – something ordinary seen in an extraordinary light. The crucifix. Humble, wooden. Jesus on the cross. In that moment, it had all come clear . . . the camerlengo was not alone. He would never be alone.

This was His will . . . His meaning.

God had always asked great sacrifice of those he loved most. Why had the camerlengo been so slow to understand? Was he too fearful? Too humble? It made no difference. God had found a way. The camerlengo even understood now why Robert Langdon had been saved. It was to bring the truth. To compel this ending.

This was the sole path to the church's salvation!

The camerlengo felt like he was floating as he descended into the Niche of the Palliums. The surge of morphine seemed relentless now, but he knew God was guiding him.

In the distance, he could hear the cardinals clamoring in confusion as they poured from the chapel, yelling commands to the Swiss Guard.

But they would never find him. Not in time.

The camerlengo felt himself drawn . . . faster . . . descending the stairs into the sunken area where the ninety-nine oil lamps shone brightly. God was returning him to Holy Ground. The camerlengo moved toward the grate covering the hole that led down to the Necropolis. The Necropolis is where this night would end. In the sacred darkness below. He lifted an oil lamp, preparing to descend.

But as he moved across the Niche, the camerlengo paused. Something about this felt wrong. How did this serve God? A solitary and silent end? *Jesus* had suffered before the eyes of the entire world. Surely this could not be God's will! The camerlengo listened for the voice of his God, but heard only the blurring buzz of drugs.

'*Carlo.*' It was his mother. '*God has plans for you.*'

Bewildered, the camerlengo kept moving.

Then, without warning, God arrived.

The camerlengo stopped short, staring. The light of the ninety-nine oil lanterns had thrown the camerlengo's shadow on the marble wall beside him. Giant and fearful. A hazy form surrounded by golden light. With flames flickering all around him, the camerlengo looked like an angel ascending to heaven. He stood a moment, raising his arms to his sides, watching his own image. Then he turned, looking back up the stairs.

God's meaning was clear.

Three minutes had passed in the chaotic hallways outside the Sistine Chapel, and still nobody could locate the camerlengo. It was as if the man had been swallowed up by the night. Mortati was about to demand a full-scale search of Vatican City when a roar of jubilation erupted outside in St Peter's Square. The spontaneous celebration of the crowd was tumultuous. The cardinals all exchanged startled looks.

Mortati closed his eyes. 'God help us.'

For the second time that evening, the College of Cardinals flooded onto St Peter's Square. Langdon and Vittoria were swept up in the jostling crowd of cardinals, and they too emerged into the night air. The media lights and cameras were all pivoted toward the basilica. And there, having just stepped onto the sacred Papal Balcony located in the exact center of the towering façade, Camerlengo Carlo Ventresca stood with his arms raised to the heavens. Even far away, he looked like purity incarnate. A figurine. Dressed in white. Flooded with light.

The energy in the square seemed to grow like a cresting wave, and all at once the Swiss Guard barriers gave way. The masses streamed toward the basilica in a euphoric torrent of humanity. The onslaught rushed forward – people crying, singing, media cameras flashing. Pandemonium. As the people flooded in around the front of the basilica, the chaos intensified, until it seemed nothing could stop it.

And then something did.

High above, the camerlengo made the smallest of gestures. He folded his hands before him. Then he bowed his head in silent prayer. One by one, then dozens by dozens, then hundreds by hundreds, the people bowed their heads along with him.

The square fell silent . . . as if a spell had been cast.

In his mind, swirling and distant now, the camerlengo's prayers were a torrent of hopes and sorrows . . . *forgive me, Father . . . Mother . . . full of grace . . . you are the church . . . may you understand this sacrifice of your only begotten son.*

Oh, my Jesus . . . save us from the fires of hell . . . take all souls to heaven, especially those most in need of thy mercy . . .

The camerlengo did not open his eyes to see the throngs below him, the television cameras, the whole world watching. He could feel it in his soul. Even in his anguish, the unity of the moment was intoxicating. It was as if a connective web had shot out in all directions around the globe. In front of televisions, at home, and in cars, the world prayed as one. Like synapses of a giant heart all firing in tandem, the people reached for God, in dozens of languages, in hundreds of countries. The words they whispered were newborn and yet as familiar to them as their own voices . . . ancient truths . . . imprinted on the soul.

The consonance felt eternal.

As the silence lifted, the joyous strains of singing began to rise again.

He knew the moment had come.

Most Holy Trinity, I offer Thee the most precious Body, Blood, Soul . . . in reparation for the outrages, sacrileges, and indifferences . . .

The camerlengo already felt the physical pain setting in. It was spreading across his skin like a plague, making him want to claw at his flesh like he had weeks ago when God had first come to him. *Do not forget what pain Jesus endured.* He could taste the fumes now in his throat. Not even the morphine could dull the bite.

My work here is done.

The Horror was his. The Hope was theirs.

In the Niche of the Palliums, the camerlengo had followed God's will and anointed his body. His hair. His face. His linen robe. His flesh. He was soaking now with the sacred, vitreous oils from the lamps. They smelled sweet like his mother, but they burned. *His* would be a merciful ascension. Miraculous and swift. And he would leave behind not scandal . . . but a new strength and wonder.

He slipped his hand into the pocket of his robe and fingered the small, golden lighter he had brought with him from the Pallium *incendiario.*

He whispered a verse from Judgments. *And when the flame went up toward heaven, the angel of the Lord ascended in the flame.*

He positioned his thumb.

They were singing in St Peter's Square . . .

The vision the world witnessed no one would ever forget.

High above on the balcony, like a soul tearing free of its corporeal restrains, a luminous pyre of flame erupted from the camerlengo's center. The fire shot upward, engulfing his entire body instantly. He did not scream. He raised his arms over his head and looked toward heaven. The conflagration roared around him, entirely shrouding his body in a column of light. It raged for what seemed like an eternity, the whole world bearing witness. The light flared brighter and brighter. Then, gradually, the flames dissipated. The camerlengo was gone. Whether he had collapsed behind the balustrade or evaporated into thin air was impossible to tell. All that was left was a cloud of smoke spiraling skyward over Vatican City.

135

Dawn came late to Rome.

An early rainstorm had washed the crowds from St Peter's Square. The media stayed on, huddling under umbrellas and in vans, commentating on the evening's events. Across the world, churches overflowed. It was a time of reflection and discussion . . . in all religions. Questions abounded, and yet the answers seemed only to bring deeper questions. Thus far, the Vatican had remained silent, issuing no statement whatsoever.

Deep in the Vatican Grottoes, Cardinal Mortati knelt alone before the open sarcophagus. He reached in and closed the old man's blackened mouth. His Holiness looked peaceful now. In quiet repose for eternity.

At Mortati's feet was a golden urn, heavy with ashes. Mortati had gathered the ashes himself and brought them here. 'A chance for forgiveness,' he said to His Holiness, laying the urn inside the sarcophagus at the Pope's side. 'No love is greater than that of a father for His son.' Mortati tucked the urn out of sight beneath the papal robes. He knew this sacred grotto was reserved exclusively for the relics of Popes, but somehow Mortati sensed this was appropriate.

'Signore?' someone said, entering the grottoes. It was Lieutenant Chartrand. He was accompanied by three Swiss Guards. 'They are ready for you in conclave.'

Mortati nodded. 'In a moment.' He gazed one last time into the sarcophagus before him, and then stood up. He turned to the guards. 'It is time for His Holiness to have the peace he has earned.'

The guards came forward and with enormous effort slid the lid of the Pope's sarcophagus back into place. It thundered shut with finality.

Mortati was alone as he crossed the Borgia Courtyard toward the Sistine Chapel. A damp breeze tossed his robe. A fellow cardinal emerged from the Apostolic Palace and strode beside him.

'May I have the honor of escorting you to conclave, signore?'

'The honor is mine.'

'Signore,' the cardinal said, looking troubled. 'The college owes you an apology for last night. We were blinded by—'

'Please,' Mortati replied. 'Our minds sometimes see what our hearts wish were true.'

The cardinal was silent a long time. Finally he spoke. 'Have you been told? You are no longer our Great Elector.'

Mortati smiled. 'Yes. I thank God for small blessings.'

'The college insisted you be eligible.'

'It seems charity is not dead in the church.'

'You are a wise man. You would lead us well.'

'I am an old man. I would lead you briefly.'

They both laughed.

As they reached the end of the Borgia Courtyard, the cardinal hesitated. He turned to Mortati with a troubled mystification, as if the precarious awe of the night before had slipped back into his heart.

'Were you aware,' the cardinal whispered, 'that we found no remains on the balcony?'

Mortati smiled. 'Perhaps the rain washed them away.'

The man looked to the stormy heavens. 'Yes, perhaps . . .'

136

The midmorning sky still hung heavy with clouds as the Sistine Chapel's chimney gave up its first faint puffs of white smoke. The pearly wisps curled upward toward the firmament and slowly dissipated.

Far below, in St Peter's Square, reporter Gunther Glick watched in reflective silence. *The final chapter* . . .

Chinita Macri approached him from behind and hoisted her camera onto her shoulder. 'It's time,' she said.

Glick nodded dolefully. He turned toward her, smoothed his hair, and took a deep breath. *My last transmission*, he thought. A small crowd had gathered around them to watch.

'Live in sixty seconds,' Macri announced.

Glick glanced over his shoulder at the roof of the Sistine Chapel behind him. 'Can you get the smoke?'

Macri patiently nodded. 'I know how to frame a shot, Gunther.'

Glick felt dumb. Of course she did. Macri's performance behind the camera last night had probably won her the Pulitzer. *His* performance, on the other hand . . . he didn't want to think about it. He was sure the BBC would let him go; no doubt they would have legal troubles from numerous powerful entities . . . CERN and George Bush among them.

'You look good,' Chinita patronized, looking out from behind her camera now with a hint of concern. 'I wonder if I might offer you . . .' She hesitated, holding her tongue.

'Some *advice*?'

Macri sighed. 'I was only going to say that there's no need to go out with a bang.'

'I know,' he said. 'You want a straight wrap.'

'The straightest in history. I'm trusting you.'

Glick smiled. *A straight wrap? Is she crazy?* A story like last night's deserved so much more. A twist. A final bombshell. An unforeseen revelation of shocking truth.

Fortunately, Glick had just the ticket waiting in the wings . . .

*

'You're on in . . . five . . . four . . . three . . .'

As Chinita Macri looked through her camera, she sensed a sly glint in Glick's eye. *I was insane to let him do this*, she thought. *What was I thinking?*

But the moment for second thoughts had passed. They were on.

'Live from Vatican City,' Glick announced on cue, 'this is Gunther Glick reporting.' He gave the camera a solemn stare as the white smoke rose behind him from the Sistine Chapel. 'Ladies and gentlemen, it is now *official*. Cardinal Saverio Mortati, a seventy-nine-year-old progressive, has just been elected the next Pope of Vatican City. Although an unlikely candidate, Mortati was chosen by an unprecedented *unanimous* vote by the College of Cardinals.'

As Macri watched him, she began to breathe easier. Glick seemed surprisingly professional today. Even austere. For the first time in his life, Glick actually looked and sounded somewhat like a newsman.

'And as we reported earlier,' Glick added, his voice intensifying perfectly, 'the Vatican has yet to offer *any* statement whatsoever regarding the miraculous events of last night.'

Good. Chinita's nervousness waned some more. *So far, so good.*

Glick's expression grew sorrowful now. 'And though last night was a night of wonder, it was also a night of tragedy. Four cardinals perished in yesterday's conflict, along with Commander Olivetti and Captain Rocher of the Swiss Guard, both in the line of duty. Other casualties include Leonardo Vetra, the renowned CERN physicist and pioneer of antimatter technology, as well as Maximilian Kohler, the director of CERN, who apparently came to Vatican City in an effort to help but reportedly passed away in the process. No official report has been issued yet on Mr Kohler's death, but conjecture is that he died due to complications brought on by a long-time illness.'

Macri nodded. The report was going perfectly. Just as they discussed.

'And in the wake of the explosion in the sky over the Vatican last night, CERN's antimatter technology has become *the* hot topic among scientists, sparking excitement and controversy. A statement read by Mr Kohler's assistant in Geneva, Sylvie Baudeloque, announced this morning that CERN's board of directors, although enthusiastic about antimatter's potential, are suspending all research and licensing until further inquiries into its safety can be examined.'

Excellent, Macri thought. *Home stretch.*

'Notably absent from our screens tonight,' Glick reported, 'is the face of Robert Langdon, the Harvard professor who came to Vatican City yesterday to lend his expertise during this Illuminati crisis. Although originally thought to have perished in the antimatter blast, we now have reports that Langdon was spotted in St Peter's Square *after* the explosion. How he got there is still speculation, although a spokesman from Hospital Tiberina claims that Mr Langdon fell out of the sky into the Tiber River shortly after midnight, was treated, and released.' Glick arched his eyebrows at the camera. 'And if *that* is true . . . it was indeed a night of miracles.'

Perfect ending! Macri felt herself smiling broadly. *Flawless wrap! Now sign off!*

But Glick did not sign off. Instead, he paused a moment and then stepped toward the camera. He had a mysterious smile. 'But before we sign off . . .'

No!

'. . . I would like to invite a guest to join me.'

Chinita's hands froze on the camera. *A guest? What the hell is he doing? What guest! Sign off!* But she knew it was too late. Glick had committed.

'The man I am about to introduce,' Glick said, 'is an American . . . a renowned scholar.'

Chinita hesitated. She held her breath as Glick turned to the small crowd around them and motioned for his guest to step forward. Macri said a silent prayer. *Please tell me he somehow located Robert Langdon . . . and not some Illuminati-conspiracy nutcase.*

But as Glick's guest stepped out, Macri's heart sank. It was not Robert Langdon at all. It was a bald man in blue jeans and a flannel shirt. He had a cane and thick glasses. Macri felt terror. *Nutcase!*

'May I introduce,' Glick announced, 'the renowned Vatican scholar from De Paul University in Chicago. Dr Joseph Vanek.'

Macri now hesitated as the man joined Glick on camera. This was no conspiracy buff; Macri had actually *heard* of this guy.

'Dr Vanek,' Glick said. 'You have some rather startling information to share with us regarding last night's conclave.'

'I do indeed,' Vanek said. 'After a night of such surprises, it is hard to imagine there are any surprises left . . . and yet . . .' He paused.

Glick smiled. 'And yet, there is a strange twist to all this.'

Vanek nodded. 'Yes. As perplexing as this will sound, I believe the College of Cardinals unknowingly elected *two* Popes this weekend.'

Macri almost dropped the camera.

Glick gave a shrewd smile. 'Two Popes, you say?'

The scholar nodded. 'Yes. I should first say that I have spent my life studying the laws of papal election. Conclave judicature is extremely complex, and much of it is now forgotten or ignored as obsolete. Even the Great Elector is probably not aware of what I am about to reveal. Nonetheless . . . according to the ancient forgotten laws put forth in the *Romano Pontifici Eligendo, Numero 63* . . . balloting is not the *only* method by which a Pope can be elected. There is another, more *divine* method. It is called "Acclamation by Adoration."' He paused. 'And it happened last night.'

Glick gave his guest a riveted look. 'Please, go on.'

'As you may recall,' the scholar continued, 'last night, when Camerlengo Carlo Ventresca was standing on the roof of the basilica, all of the cardinals below began calling out his name in unison.'

'Yes, I recall.'

'With that image in mind, allow me to read verbatim from the ancient electoral laws.' The man pulled some papers from his pocket, cleared his throat, and began to read. ' "Election by Adoration occurs when . . . all the cardinals, as if by inspiration of the Holy Spirit, freely and spontaneously, unanimously and aloud, proclaim one individual's name." '

Glick smiled. 'So you're saying that last night, when the cardinals chanted Carlo Ventresca's name together, they actually *elected* him Pope?'

'They did indeed. Furthermore, the law states that Election by Adoration supersedes the cardinal eligibility requirement and permits *any* clergyman – ordained priest, bishop, or cardinal – to be elected. So, as you can see, the camerlengo was perfectly qualified for papal election by this procedure.' Dr Vanek looked directly into the camera now. 'The facts are these . . . Carlo Ventresca was elected Pope last night. He reigned for just under seventeen minutes. And had he not ascended miraculously into a pillar of fire, he would now be buried in the Vatican Grottoes along with the other Popes.'

'Thank you, doctor.' Glick turned to Macri with a mischievous wink. 'Most illuminating . . .'

137

High atop the steps of the Roman Coliseum, Vittoria laughed and called down to him. 'Robert, hurry up! I knew I should have married a younger man!' Her smile was magic.

He struggled to keep up, but his legs felt like stone. 'Wait,' he begged. 'Please . . .'

There was a pounding in his head.

Robert Langdon awoke with a start.

Darkness.

He lay still for a long time in the foreign softness of the bed, unable to figure out where he was. The pillows were goose down, oversized and wonderful. The air smelled of potpourri. Across the room, two glass doors stood open to a lavish balcony, where a light breeze played beneath a glistening cloud-swept moon. Langdon tried to remember how he had gotten here . . . and where *here* was.

Surreal wisps of memory sifted back into his consciousness . . .

A pyre of mystical fire . . . an angel materializing from out of the crowd . . . her soft hand taking his and leading him into the night . . . guiding his exhausted, battered body through the streets . . . leading him here . . . to this suite . . . propping him half-sleeping in a scalding hot shower . . . leading him to this bed . . . and watching over him as he fell asleep like the dead.

In the dimness now, Langdon could see a second bed. The sheets were tousled, but the bed was empty. From one of the adjoining rooms, he could hear the faint, steady stream of a shower.

As he gazed at Vittoria's bed, he saw a boldly embroidered seal on her pillowcase. It read: HOTEL BERNINI. Langdon had to smile. Vittoria had chosen well. Old World luxury overlooking Bernini's Triton Fountain . . . there was no more fitting hotel in all of Rome.

As Langdon lay there, he heard a pounding and realized what had awoken him. Someone was knocking at the door. It grew louder.

Confused, Langdon got up. *Nobody knows we're here*, he thought, feeling a trace of uneasiness. Donning a luxuriant Hotel Bernini robe, he walked out of the bedroom into the suite's foyer. He stood a moment at the heavy oak door, and then pulled it open.

A powerful man adorned in lavish purple and yellow regalia stared down at him. 'I am Lieutenant Chartrand,' the man said. 'Vatican Swiss Guard.'

Langdon knew full well who he was. 'How . . . how did you find us?'

'I saw you leave the square last night. I followed you. I'm relieved you're still here.'

Langdon felt a sudden anxiety, wondering if the cardinals had sent Chartrand to escort Langdon and Vittoria back to Vatican City. After all, the two of them were the only two people beyond the College of Cardinals who knew the *truth*. They were a liability.

'His Holiness asked me to give this to you,' Chartrand said, handing over an envelope sealed with the Vatican signet. Langdon opened the envelope and read the handwritten note.

Mr Langdon and Ms Vetra,

> *Although it is my profound desire to request your discretion in the matters of the past 24 hours, I cannot possibly presume to ask more of you than you have already given. I therefore humbly retreat hoping only that you let your hearts guide you in this matter. The world seems a better place today . . . maybe the questions are more powerful than the answers.*
>
> *My door is always open,*

His Holiness, Saverio Mortati

Langdon read the message twice. The College of Cardinals had obviously chosen a noble and munificent leader.

Before Langdon could say anything, Chartrand produced a small package. 'A token of thanks from His Holiness.'

Langdon took the package. It was heavy, wrapped in brown paper.

'By his decree,' Chartrand said, 'this artifact is on indefinite loan to you from the sacred Papal Vault. His Holiness asks only that in your last will and testament you ensure it finds its way home.'

Langdon opened the package and was struck speechless. It was the brand. *The Illuminati Diamond.*

Chartrand smiled. 'May peace be with you.' He turned to go.

'Thank . . . you,' Langdon managed, his hands trembling around the precious gift.

The guard hesitated in the hall. 'Mr Langdon, may I ask you something?'

'Of course.'

'My fellow guards and I are curious. Those last few minutes . . . what *happened* up there in the helicopter?'

Langdon felt a rush of anxiety. He knew this moment was coming – the moment of truth. He and Vittoria had talked about it last night as they

440

stole away from St Peter's Square. And they had made their decision. Even before the Pope's note.

Vittoria's father had dreamed his antimatter discovery would bring about a spiritual awakening. Last night's events were no doubt not what he had intended, but the undeniable fact remained . . . at this moment, around the world, people were considering God in ways they never had before. How long the magic would last, Langdon and Vittoria had no idea, but they knew they could never shatter the wonderment with scandal and doubt. *The Lord works in strange ways*, Langdon told himself, wondering wryly if maybe . . . just maybe . . . yesterday had been God's will after all.

'Mr Langdon?' Chartrand repeated. 'I was asking about the helicopter?'

Langdon gave a sad smile. 'Yes, I know . . .' He felt the words flow not from his mind but from his heart. 'Perhaps it was the shock of the fall . . . but my memory . . . it seems . . . it's all a blur . . .'

Chartrand slumped. 'You remember *nothing*?'

Langdon sighed. 'I fear it will remain a mystery forever.'

When Robert Langdon returned to the bedroom, the vision awaiting him stopped him in his tracks. Vittoria stood on the balcony, her back to the railing, her eyes gazing deeply at him. She looked like a heavenly apparition . . . a radiant silhouette with the moon behind her. She could have been a Roman goddess, enshrouded in her white terrycloth robe, the drawstring cinched tight, accentuating her slender curves. Behind her, a pale mist hung like a halo over Bernini's Triton Fountain.

Langdon felt wildly drawn to her . . . more than to any woman in his life. Quietly, he laid the Illuminati Diamond and the Pope's letter on his bedside table. There would be time to explain all of that later. He went to her on the balcony.

Vittoria looked happy to see him. 'You're awake,' she said, in a coy whisper. '*Finally.*'

Langdon smiled. 'Long day.'

She ran a hand through her luxuriant hair, the neck of her robe falling open slightly. 'And now . . . I suppose you want your reward.'

The comment took Langdon off guard. 'I'm . . . sorry?'

'We're adults, Robert. You can admit it. You feel a longing. I see it in your eyes. A deep, carnal hunger.' She smiled. 'I feel it too. And that craving is about to be satisfied.'

'It is?' He felt emboldened and took a step toward her.

'*Completely.*' She held up a room-service menu. 'I ordered everything they've got.'

The feast was sumptuous. They dined together by moonlight . . . sitting on their balcony . . . savoring *frisée*, truffles, and risotto. They sipped *Dolcetto* wine and talked late into the night.

Langdon did not need to be a symbologist to read the signs Vittoria was sending him. During dessert of boysenberry cream with *savoiardi* and steaming *Romcaffè*, Vittoria pressed her bare legs against his beneath the table and fixed him with a sultry stare. She seemed to be willing him to set down his fork and carry her off in his arms.

But Langdon did nothing. He remained the perfect gentleman. *Two can play at this game*, he thought, hiding a roguish smile.

When all the food was eaten, Langdon retired to the edge of his bed where he sat alone, turning the Illuminati Diamond over and over in his hands, making repeated comments about the miracle of its symmetry. Vittoria stared at him, her confusion growing to an obvious frustration.

'You find that ambigram terribly interesting, don't you?' she demanded.

Langdon nodded. 'Mesmerizing.'

'Would you say it's the most interesting thing in this room?'

Langdon scratched his head, making a show of pondering it. 'Well, there is *one* thing that interests me more.'

She smiled and took a step toward him. 'That being?'

'How you disproved that Einstein theory using tuna fish.'

Vittoria threw up her hands. '*Dio mio!* Enough with the tuna fish! Don't play with me, I'm warning you.'

Langdon grinned. 'Maybe for your *next* experiment, you could study flounders and prove the earth is flat.'

Vittoria was steaming now, but the first faint hints of an exasperated smile appeared on her lips. 'For your information, professor, my next experiment will make scientific history. I plan to prove neutrinos have mass.'

'Neutrinos have *mass*?' Langdon shot her a stunned look. 'I didn't even know they were Catholic!'

With one fluid motion, she was on him, pinning him down. 'I hope you believe in life after death, Robert Langdon.' Vittoria was laughing as she straddled him, her hands holding him down, her eyes ablaze with a mischievous fire.

'Actually,' he choked, laughing harder now, 'I've always had trouble picturing anything beyond this world.'

'Really? So you've never had a religious experience? A perfect moment of glorious rapture?'

Langdon shook his head. 'No, and I seriously doubt I'm the kind of man who could ever *have* a religious experience.'

Vittoria slipped off her robe. 'You've never been to bed with a yoga master, have you?'

THE DA VINCI CODE

For Blythe . . . again.
More than ever.

Acknowledgements

First and foremost, to my friend and editor, Jason Kaufman, for working so hard on this project and for truly understanding what this book is all about. And to the incomparable Heide Lange – tireless champion of The Da Vinci Code, agent extraordinaire and trusted friend.

I cannot fully express my gratitude to the exceptional team at Doubleday, for their generosity, faith and superb guidance. Thank you especially to Bill Thomas and Steve Rubin, who believed in this book from the start. My thanks also to the initial core of early in-house supporters, headed by Michael Palgon, Suzanne Herz, Janelle Moburg, Jackie Everly and Adrienne Sparks, as well as to the talented people of Doubleday's sales force.

My sincere appreciation to the entire team at Transworld Publishers in London, with special thanks to Bill Scott-Kerr and Judith Welsh. My thanks as well to Abner Stein for bringing us all together.

For their generous assistance in the research of the book, I would like to acknowledge the Louvre Museum, the French Ministry of Culture, Project Gutenberg, Bibliothèque Nationale, the Gnostic Society Library, the Department of Paintings Study and Documentation Service at the Louvre, Catholic World News, Royal Observatory Greenwich, London Record Society, the Muniment Collection at Westminster Abbey, John Pike and the Federation of American Scientists, and the five members of Opus Dei (three active, two former) who recounted their stories, both positive and negative, regarding their experiences inside Opus Dei.

My gratitude also to Water Street Bookstore for tracking down so many of my research books, my father Richard Brown for his assistance with Phi and the Divine Proportion, Michael Windsor, Stan Planton, Sylvie Baudeloque, Peter McGuigan, Margie Wachtel, Andre Vernet, Ken Kelleher at Anchorball Web Media, Cara Sottak, Karyn Popham, Esther Sung, Miriam Abramowitz, William Tunstall-Pedoe, Simon Edwards and Griffin Wooden Brown.

And finally, in a novel drawing so heavily on the sacred feminine, I would be remiss if I did not mention the two extraordinary women who have touched my life. First, my mother, Connie Brown – fellow scribe, nurturer, musician and role model. And my wife, Blythe – art historian, painter, front-line editor and without a doubt the most astonishingly talented woman I have ever known.

FACT:

The Priory of Sion – a European secret society founded in 1099 – is a real organization.

In 1975 Paris's Bibliothèque Nationale discovered parchments known as *Les Dossiers Secrets*, identifying numerous members of the Priory of Sion, including Sir Isaac Newton, Sandro Botticelli, Victor Hugo and Leonardo da Vinci.

The Vatican prelature known as Opus Dei is a deeply devout Catholic sect that has been the topic of recent controversy due to reports of brainwashing, coercion and a dangerous practice known as 'corporal mortification'. Opus Dei has just completed construction of a $47 million National Headquarters at 243 Lexington Avenue in New York City.

All descriptions of artwork, architecture, documents and secret rituals in this novel are accurate.

Prologue

Renowned curator Jacques Saunière staggered through the vaulted archway of the museum's Grand Gallery. He lunged for the nearest painting he could see, a Caravaggio. Grabbing the gilded frame, the seventy-six-year-old man heaved the masterpiece toward himself until it tore from the wall and Saunière collapsed backward in a heap beneath the canvas.

As he had anticipated, a thundering iron gate fell nearby, barricading the entrance to the suite. The parquet floor shook. Far off, an alarm began to ring.

The curator lay a moment, gasping for breath, taking stock. *I am still alive.* He crawled out from under the canvas and scanned the cavernous space for somewhere to hide.

A voice spoke, chillingly close. 'Do not move.'

On his hands and knees, the curator froze, turning his head slowly.

Only fifteen feet away, outside the sealed gate, the mountainous silhouette of his attacker stared through the iron bars. He was broad and tall, with ghost-pale skin and thinning white hair. His irises were pink with dark red pupils. The albino drew a pistol from his coat and aimed the barrel through the bars, directly at the curator. 'You should not have run.' His accent was not easy to place. 'Now tell me where it is.'

'I told you already,' the curator stammered, kneeling defenceless on the floor of the gallery. 'I have no idea what you are talking about!'

'You are lying.' The man stared at him, perfectly immobile except for the glint in his ghostly eyes. 'You and your brethren possess something that is not yours.'

The curator felt a surge of adrenaline. *How could he possibly know this?*

'Tonight the rightful guardians will be restored. Tell me where it is hidden, and you will live.' The man levelled his gun at the curator's head. 'Is it a secret you will die for?'

Saunière could not breathe.

The man tilted his head, peering down the barrel of his gun.

Saunière held up his hands in defence. 'Wait,' he said slowly. 'I will tell you what you need to know.' The curator spoke his next words carefully. The lie he told was one he had rehearsed many times . . . each time praying he would never have to use it.

When the curator had finished speaking, his assailant smiled smugly. 'Yes. This is exactly what the others told me.'

Saunière recoiled. *The others?*

'I found them, too,' the huge man taunted. 'All three of them. They confirmed what you have just said.'

It cannot be! The curator's true identity, along with the identities of his three *sénéchaux*, was almost as sacred as the ancient secret they protected. Saunière now realized his *sénéchaux*, following strict procedure, had told the same lie before their own deaths. It was part of the protocol.

The attacker aimed his gun again. 'When you are gone, I will be the only one who knows the truth.'

The truth. In an instant, the curator grasped the true horror of the situation. *If I die, the truth will be lost for ever.* Instinctively, he tried to scramble for cover.

The gun roared, and the curator felt a searing heat as the bullet lodged in his stomach. He fell forward . . . struggling against the pain. Slowly, Saunière rolled over and stared back through the bars at his attacker.

The man was now taking dead aim at Saunière's head.

Saunière closed his eyes, his thoughts a swirling tempest of fear and regret.

The click of an empty chamber echoed through the corridor.

The curator's eyes flew open.

The man glanced down at his weapon, looking almost amused. He reached for a second clip, but then seemed to reconsider, smirking calmly at Saunière's gut. 'My work here is done.'

The curator looked down and saw the bullet hole in his white linen shirt. It was framed by a small circle of blood a few inches below his breastbone. *My stomach.* Almost cruelly, the bullet had missed his heart. As a veteran of *la Guerre d'Algérie*, the curator had witnessed this horribly drawn-out death before. For fifteen minutes, he would survive as his stomach acids seeped into his chest cavity, slowly poisoning him from within.

'Pain is good, monsieur,' the man said.

Then he was gone.

Alone now, Jacques Saunière turned his gaze again to the iron gate. He was trapped, and the doors could not be reopened for at least twenty minutes. By the time anyone got to him, he would be dead. Even so, the fear that now gripped him was a fear far greater than that of his own death.

I must pass on the secret.

Staggering to his feet, he pictured his three murdered brethren. He thought of the generations who had come before them . . . of the mission with which they had all been entrusted.

An unbroken chain of knowledge.

Suddenly, now, despite all the precautions . . . despite all the fail-safes . . . Jacques Saunière was the only remaining link, the sole guardian of one of the most powerful secrets ever kept.

Shivering, he pulled himself to his feet.

I must find some way. . .

He was trapped inside the Grand Gallery, and there existed only one person on earth to whom he could pass the torch. Saunière gazed up at the walls of his opulent prison. A collection of the world's most famous paintings seemed to smile down on him like old friends.

Wincing in pain, he summoned all of his faculties and strength. The desperate task before him, he knew, would require every remaining second of his life.

1

Robert Langdon awoke slowly.

A telephone was ringing in the darkness – a tinny, unfamiliar ring. He fumbled for the bedside lamp and turned it on. Squinting at his surroundings he saw a plush Renaissance bedroom with Louis XVI furniture, hand-frescoed walls, and a colossal mahogany four-poster bed.

Where the hell am I?

The jacquard bathrobe hanging on his bedpost bore the monogram: *HOTEL RITZ PARIS.*

Slowly, the fog began to lift.

Langdon picked up the receiver. 'Hello?'

'Monsieur Langdon?' a man's voice said. 'I hope I have not awoken you?'

Dazed, Langdon looked at the bedside clock. It was 12:32 A.M. He had been asleep only an hour, but he felt like the dead.

'This is the concierge, monsieur. I apologize for this intrusion, but you have a visitor. He insists it is urgent.'

Langdon still felt fuzzy. *A visitor?* His eyes focused now on a crumpled flyer on his bedside table.

THE AMERICAN UNIVERSITY OF PARIS
proudly presents
AN EVENING WITH ROBERT LANGDON
PROFESSOR OF RELIGIOUS SYMBOLOGY, HARVARD UNIVERSITY

Langdon groaned. Tonight's lecture – a slide show about pagan symbolism hidden in the stones of Chartres Cathedral – had probably ruffled some conservative feathers in the audience. Most likely, some religious scholar had trailed him home to pick a fight.

'I'm sorry,' Langdon said, 'but I'm very tired and—'

'*Mais, monsieur,*' the concierge pressed, lowering his voice to an urgent whisper. 'Your guest is an important man.'

Langdon had little doubt. His books on religious paintings and cult symbology had made him a reluctant celebrity in the art world, and last year Langdon's visibility had increased a hundredfold after his involvement in a widely publicized incident at the Vatican. Since then, the stream of self-important historians and art buffs arriving at his door had seemed never-ending.

'If you would be so kind,' Langdon said, doing his best to remain polite, 'could you take the man's name and number, and tell him I'll try to call him before I leave Paris on Tuesday? Thank you.' He hung up before the concierge could protest.

Sitting up now, Langdon frowned at his bedside *Guest Relations Handbook*, whose cover boasted: SLEEP LIKE A BABY IN THE CITY OF LIGHTS. SLUMBER AT THE PARIS RITZ. He turned and gazed tiredly into the full-length mirror across the room. The man staring back at him was a stranger – tousled and weary.

You need a vacation, Robert.

The past year had taken a heavy toll on him, but he didn't appreciate seeing proof in the mirror. His usually sharp blue eyes looked hazy and drawn tonight. A dark stubble was shrouding his strong jaw and dimpled chin. Around his temples, the grey highlights were advancing, making their way deeper into his thicket of coarse black hair. Although his female colleagues insisted the grey only accentuated his bookish appeal, Langdon knew better.

If Boston Magazine *could see me now.*

Last month, much to Langdon's embarrassment, *Boston Magazine* had listed him as one of that city's top ten most intriguing people – a dubious honour that made him the brunt of endless ribbing by his Harvard colleagues. Tonight, three thousand miles from home, the accolade had resurfaced to haunt him at the lecture he had given.

'Ladies and gentlemen . . .' the hostess had announced to a full house at the American University of Paris's Pavillon Dauphine, 'Our guest tonight needs no introduction. He is the author of numerous books: *The Symbology of Secret Sects*, *The Art of the Illuminati*, *The Lost Language of Ideograms*, and when I say he wrote the book on *Religious Iconology*, I mean that quite literally. Many of you use his textbooks in class.'

The students in the crowd nodded enthusiastically.

'I had planned to introduce him tonight by sharing his impressive curriculum vitae. However . . .' She glanced playfully at Langdon, who was seated onstage. 'An audience member has just handed me a far more, shall we say . . . *intriguing* introduction.'

She held up a copy of *Boston Magazine*.

Langdon cringed. *Where the hell did she get that?*

The hostess began reading choice excerpts from the inane article, and Langdon felt himself sinking lower and lower in his chair. Thirty seconds later, the crowd was grinning, and the woman showed no signs of letting up. 'And Mr Langdon's refusal to speak publicly about his unusual role in last year's Vatican conclave certainly wins him points on our intrigue-o-meter.' The hostess goaded the crowd. 'Would you like to hear more?'

The crowd applauded.

Somebody stop her, Langdon pleaded as she dived into the article again.

'Although Professor Langdon might not be considered hunk-handsome like some of our younger awardees, this forty-something academic has more than his share of scholarly allure. His captivating presence is punctuated by an unusually low, baritone speaking voice, which his female students describe as "chocolate for the ears".'

The hall erupted in laughter.

Langdon forced an awkward smile. He knew what came next – some ridiculous line about 'Harrison Ford in Harris tweed' – and because this evening he had figured it was finally safe again to wear his Harris tweed and Burberry turtleneck, he decided to take action.

'Thank you, Monique,' Langdon said, standing prematurely and edging her away from the podium. '*Boston Magazine* clearly has a gift for fiction.' He turned to the audience with an embarrassed sigh. 'And if I find which one of you provided that article, I'll have the consulate deport you.'

The crowd laughed.

'Well, folks, as you all know, I'm here tonight to talk about the power of symbols . . .'

The ringing of Langdon's hotel phone once again broke the silence.

Groaning in disbelief, he picked up. 'Yes?'

As expected, it was the concierge. 'Mr Langdon, again my apologies. I am calling to inform you that your guest is now en route to your room. I thought I should alert you.'

Langdon was wide awake now. 'You sent someone to my *room?*'

'I apologize, monsieur, but a man like this . . . I cannot presume the authority to stop him.'

'Who exactly *is* he?'

But the concierge was gone.

Almost immediately, a heavy fist pounded on Langdon's door.

Uncertain, Langdon slid off the bed, feeling his toes sink deep into the savonnerie carpet. He donned the hotel bathrobe and moved toward the door. 'Who is it?'

'Mr Langdon? I need to speak with you.' The man's English was accented – a sharp, authoritative bark. 'My name is Lieutenant Jérôme Collet. Direction Centrale Police Judiciaire.'

Langdon paused. *The Judicial Police?* The DCPJ was the rough equivalent of the US FBI.

Leaving the security chain in place, Langdon opened the door a few inches. The face staring back at him was thin and washed out. The man was exceptionally lean, dressed in an official-looking blue uniform.

'May I come in?' the agent asked.

Langdon hesitated, feeling uncertain as the stranger's sallow eyes studied him. 'What is this all about?'

'My *capitaine* requires your expertise in a private matter.'

'Now?' Langdon managed. 'It's after midnight.'

'Am I correct that you were scheduled to meet with the curator of the Louvre this evening?'

Langdon felt a sudden surge of uneasiness. He and the revered curator Jacques Saunière had been slated to meet for drinks after Langdon's lecture tonight, but Saunière had never shown up. 'Yes. How did you know that?'

'We found your name in his daily planner.'

'I trust nothing is wrong?'

The agent gave a dire sigh and slid a Polaroid snapshot through the narrow opening in the door.

When Langdon saw the photo, his entire body went rigid.

'This photo was taken less than an hour ago. Inside the Louvre.'

As Langdon stared at the bizarre image, his initial revulsion and shock gave way to a sudden upwelling of anger. 'Who would do this!'

'We had hoped that you might help us answer that very question, considering your knowledge in symbology and your plans to meet him.'

Langdon stared at the picture, his horror now laced with fear. The image was gruesome and profoundly strange, bringing with it an unsettling sense of déjà vu. A little over a year ago, Langdon had received a photograph of a corpse and a similar request for help. Twenty-four hours later, he had almost lost his life inside Vatican City. This photo was entirely different, and yet something about the scenario felt disquietingly familiar.

The agent checked his watch. 'My *capitaine* is waiting, sir.'

Langdon barely heard him. His eyes were still riveted on the picture. 'This symbol here, and the way his body is so oddly . . .'

'Positioned?' the agent offered.

Langdon nodded, feeling a chill as he looked up. 'I can't imagine who would do this to someone.'

The agent looked grim. 'You don't understand, Mr Langdon. What you see in this photograph . . .' He paused. 'Monsieur Saunière did that to himself.'

2

One mile away, the hulking albino named Silas limped through the front gate of the luxurious residence on Rue La Bruyère. The spiked *cilice* belt that he wore around his thigh cut into his flesh, and yet his soul sang with satisfaction of service to the Lord.

Pain is good.

His red eyes scanned the lobby as he entered the residence. Empty. He climbed the stairs quietly, not wanting to awaken any of his fellow numeraries. His bedroom door was open; locks were forbidden here. He entered, closing the door behind him.

The room was spartan – hardwood floors, a pine dresser, a canvas mat in the corner that served as his bed. He was a visitor here this week, and yet for many years he had been blessed with a similar sanctuary in New York City.

The Lord has provided me shelter and purpose in my life.

Tonight, at last, Silas felt he had begun to repay his debt. Hurrying to the dresser, he found the cell phone hidden in his bottom drawer and placed a call.

'Yes?' a male voice answered.

'Teacher, I have returned.'

'Speak,' the voice commanded, sounding pleased to hear from him.

'All four are gone. The three *sénéchaux* . . . and the *Grand Master* himself.'

There was a momentary pause, as if for prayer. 'Then I assume you have the information?'

'All four concurred. Independently.'

'And you believed them?'

'Their agreement was too great for coincidence.'

An excited breath. 'Excellent. I had feared the brotherhood's reputation for secrecy might prevail.'

'The prospect of death is strong motivation.'

'So, my pupil, tell me what I must know.'

Silas knew the information he had gleaned from his victims would come as a shock. 'Teacher, all four confirmed the existence of the *clef de voûte* . . . the legendary *keystone*.'

He heard a quick intake of breath over the phone and could feel the Teacher's excitement. 'The *keystone*. Exactly as we suspected.'

According to lore, the brotherhood had created a map of stone – a *clef de voûte* . . . or *keystone* – an engraved tablet that revealed the final resting place of the brotherhood's greatest secret . . . information so powerful that its protection was the reason for the brotherhood's very existence.

'When we possess the keystone,' the Teacher said, 'we will be only one step away.'

'We are closer than you think. The keystone is here in Paris.'

'Paris? Incredible. It is almost too easy.'

Silas relayed the earlier events of the evening . . . how all four of his victims, moments before death, had desperately tried to buy back their godless lives by telling their secret. Each had told Silas the exact same thing – that the keystone was ingeniously hidden at a precise location inside one of Paris's ancient churches – the Eglise de Saint-Sulpice.

'Inside a house of the Lord,' the Teacher exclaimed. 'How they mock us!'

'As they have for centuries.'

The Teacher fell silent, as if letting the triumph of this moment settle over him. Finally, he spoke. 'You have done a great service to God. We have waited centuries for this. You must retrieve the stone for me. Immediately. Tonight. You understand the stakes.'

Silas knew the stakes were incalculable, and yet what the Teacher was now commanding seemed impossible. 'But the church, it is a fortress. Especially at night. How will I enter?'

With the confident tone of a man of enormous influence, the Teacher explained what was to be done.

When Silas hung up the phone, his skin tingled with anticipation.

One hour, he told himself, grateful that the Teacher had given him time to carry out the necessary penance before entering a house of God. *I must purge my soul of today's sins*. The sins committed today had been holy in purpose. Acts of war against the enemies of God had been committed for centuries. Forgiveness was assured.

Even so, Silas knew, absolution required sacrifice.

Pulling his shades, he stripped naked and knelt in the centre of his room. Looking down, he examined the spiked *cilice* belt clamped around his thigh. All true followers of *The Way* wore this device – a leather strap, studded with sharp metal barbs that cut into the flesh as a perpetual reminder of Christ's suffering. The pain caused by the device also helped counteract the desires of the flesh.

Although Silas already had worn his *cilice* today longer than the requisite two hours, he knew today was no ordinary day. Grasping the buckle, he cinched it one notch tighter, wincing as the barbs dug deeper into his flesh. Exhaling slowly, he savored the cleansing ritual of his pain.

Pain is good, Silas whispered, repeating the sacred mantra of Father Josemaría Escrivá – the Teacher of all Teachers. Although Escrivá had died in 1975, his wisdom lived on, his words still whispered by thousands of faithful servants around the globe as they knelt on the floor and performed the sacred practice known as 'corporal mortification'.

Silas turned his attention now to a heavy knotted rope coiled neatly on the floor beside him. *The Discipline*. The knots were caked with dried blood. Eager for the purifying effects of his own agony, Silas said a quick prayer. Then, gripping one end of the rope, he closed his eyes and swung it hard over his shoulder, feeling the knots slap against his back. He whipped it over his shoulder again, slashing at his flesh. Again and again, he lashed.

Castigo corpus meum.

Finally, he felt the blood begin to flow.

459

3

The crisp April air whipped through the open window of the Citroën ZX as it skimmed south past the Opera House and crossed Place Vendôme. In the passenger seat, Robert Langdon felt the city tear past him as he tried to clear his thoughts. His quick shower and shave had left him looking reasonably presentable but had done little to ease his anxiety. The frightening image of the curator's body remained locked in his mind.

Jacques Saunière is dead.

Langdon could not help but feel a deep sense of loss at the curator's death. Despite Saunière's reputation for being reclusive, his recognition for dedication to the arts made him an easy man to revere. His books on the secret codes hidden in the paintings of Poussin and Teniers were some of Langdon's favourite classroom texts. Tonight's meeting had been one Langdon was very much looking forward to, and he was disappointed when the curator had not turned up.

Again the image of the curator's body flashed in his mind. *Jacques Saunière did that to himself?* Langdon turned and looked out of the window, forcing the picture from his mind.

Outside, the city was just now winding down – street vendors wheeling carts of candied *amandes*, waiters carrying bags of garbage to the curb, a pair of late-night lovers cuddling to stay warm in a breeze scented with jasmine blossom. The Citroën navigated the chaos with authority, its dissonant two-tone siren parting the traffic like a knife.

'*Le capitaine* was pleased to discover you were still in Paris tonight,' the agent said, speaking for the first time since they'd left the hotel. 'A fortunate coincidence.'

Langdon was feeling anything but fortunate, and coincidence was a concept he did not entirely trust. As someone who had spent his life exploring the hidden interconnectivity of disparate emblems and ideologies, Langdon viewed the world as a web of profoundly intertwined histories and events. *The connections may be invisible,* he often preached to his symbology classes at Harvard, *but they are always there, buried just beneath the surface.*

'I assume,' Langdon said, 'that the American University of Paris told you where I was staying?'

The driver shook his head. 'Interpol.'

Interpol, Langdon thought. *Of course.* He had forgotten that the seemingly innocuous request of all European hotels to see a passport at check-in was more than a quaint formality – it was the law. On any given night, all across Europe, Interpol officials could pinpoint exactly who was sleeping where. Finding Langdon at the Ritz had probably taken all of five seconds.

As the Citroën accelerated southward across the city, the illuminated profile of the Eiffel Tower appeared, shooting skyward in the distance to the right. Seeing it, Langdon thought of Vittoria, recalling their playful promise a year ago that every six months they would meet again at a different romantic spot on the globe. The Eiffel Tower, Langdon suspected, would have made their list. Sadly, he last kissed Vittoria in a noisy airport in Rome more than a year ago.

'Did you mount her?' the agent asked, looking over.

Langdon glanced up, certain he had misunderstood. 'I beg your pardon?'

'She is lovely, no?' The agent motioned through the windshield toward the Eiffel Tower. 'Have you mounted her?'

Langdon rolled his eyes. 'No, I haven't climbed the tower.'

'She is the symbol of France. I think she is perfect.'

Langdon nodded absently. Symbologists often remarked that France – a country renowned for machismo, womanizing and diminutive insecure leaders like Napoleon and Pepin the Short – could not have chosen a more apt national emblem than a thousand-foot phallus.

When they reached the intersection at Rue de Rivoli, the traffic light was red, but the Citroën didn't slow. The agent gunned the sedan across the junction and sped onto a wooded section of Rue Castiglione, which served as the northern entrance to the famed Tuileries Gardens – Paris's own version of Central Park. Most tourists mistranslated Jardins des Tuileries as relating to the thousands of tulips that bloomed here, but *Tuileries* was actually a literal reference to something far less romantic. This park had once been an enormous, polluted excavation pit from which Parisian contractors mined clay to manufacture the city's famous red roofing tiles – or *tuiles.*

As they entered the deserted park, the agent reached under the dash and turned off the blaring siren. Langdon exhaled, savouring the sudden quiet. Outside the car, the pale wash of halogen headlights skimmed over the crushed gravel parkway, the rugged whir of the tyres intoning a hypnotic rhythm. Langdon had always considered the Tuileries to be sacred ground. These were the gardens in which Claude Monet had experimented with form and colour, and literally inspired the birth of the Impressionist movement. Tonight, however, this place held a strange aura of foreboding.

The Citroën swerved left now, angling west down the park's central boulevard. Curling around a circular pond, the driver cut across a desolate avenue out into a wide quadrangle beyond. Langdon could now see the end of the Tuileries Gardens, marked by a giant stone archway.

Arc du Carrousel.

Despite the orgiastic rituals once held at the Arc du Carrousel, art aficionados revered this place for another reason entirely. From the esplanade at the end of the Tuileries, four of the finest art museums in the world could be seen . . . one at each point of the compass.

Out of the right-hand window, south across the Seine and Quai Voltaire, Langdon could see the dramatically lit façade of the old train station – now the esteemed Musée d'Orsay. Glancing left, he could make out the top of the ultramodern Pompidou Centre, which housed the Museum of Modern Art. Behind him to the west, Langdon knew the ancient obelisk of Ramses rose above the trees, marking the Musée du Jeu de Paume.

But it was straight ahead, to the east, through the archway, that Langdon could now see the monolithic Renaissance palace that had become the most famous art museum in the world.

Musée du Louvre.

Langdon felt a familiar tinge of wonder as his eyes made a futile attempt to absorb the entire mass of the edifice. Across a staggeringly expansive plaza, the imposing façade of the Louvre rose like a citadel against the Paris sky. Shaped like an enormous horseshoe, the Louvre was the longest building in Europe, stretching farther than three Eiffel Towers laid end to end. Not even the million square feet of open plaza between the museum wings could challenge the majesty of the façade's breadth. Langdon had once walked the Louvre's entire perimeter, an astonishing three-mile journey.

Despite the estimated five weeks it would take a visitor to properly appreciate the 65,300 pieces of art in this building, most tourists chose an abbreviated experience Langdon referred to as 'Louvre Lite' – a full sprint through the museum to see the three most famous objects: the *Mona Lisa*, *Venus de Milo* and *Winged Victory*. Art Buchwald had once boasted he'd seen all three masterpieces in five minutes and fifty-six seconds.

The driver pulled out a handheld walkie-talkie and spoke in rapid-fire French. '*Monsieur Langdon est arrivé. Deux minutes.*'

An indecipherable confirmation came crackling back.

The agent stowed the device, turning now to Langdon. 'You will meet the *capitaine* at the main entrance.'

The driver ignored the signs prohibiting auto traffic on the plaza, revved the engine, and gunned the Citroën up over the curb. The Louvre's main entrance was visible now, rising boldly in the distance, encircled by seven triangular pools from which spouted illuminated fountains.

La Pyramide.

The new entrance to the Paris Louvre had become almost as famous as the museum itself. The controversial, neomodern glass pyramid designed by Chinese-born American architect I. M. Pei still evoked scorn from traditionalists who felt it destroyed the dignity of the Renaissance courtyard. Goethe had described architecture as frozen music, and Pei's critics described this pyramid as fingernails on a chalkboard. Progressive admirers, though, hailed Pei's seventy-one-foot-tall transparent pyramid as a dazzling synergy of ancient structure and modern method – a symbolic link between the old and new – helping usher the Louvre into the next millennium.

'Do you like our pyramid?' the agent asked.

Langdon frowned. The French, it seemed, loved to ask Americans this. It was a loaded question, of course. Admitting you liked the pyramid made you a tasteless American, and expressing dislike was an insult to the French.

'Mitterrand was a bold man,' Langdon replied, splitting the difference. The late French president who had commissioned the pyramid was said to have suffered from a 'Pharaoh complex'. Singlehandedly responsible for filling Paris with Egyptian obelisks, art and artefacts, François Mitterrand had an affinity for Egyptian culture that was so all-consuming that the French still referred to him as the Sphinx.

'What is the captain's name?' Langdon asked, changing topics.

'Bezu Fache,' the driver said, approaching the pyramid's main entrance. 'We call him *le Taureau*.'

Langdon glanced over at him, wondering if every Frenchman had a mysterious animal epithet. 'You call your captain *the Bull*?'

The man arched his eyebrows. 'Your French is better than you admit, Monsieur Langdon.'

My French stinks, Langdon thought, *but my zodiac iconography is pretty good*. Taurus was always the bull. Astrology was a symbolic constant all over the world.

The agent pulled the car to a stop and pointed between two fountains to a large door in the side of the pyramid. 'There is the entrance. Good luck, monsieur.'

'You're not coming?'

'My orders are to leave you here. I have other business to attend to.'

Langdon heaved a sigh and climbed out. *It's your circus.*

The agent revved his engine and sped off.

As Langdon stood alone and watched the departing rearlights, he realized he could easily reconsider, exit the courtyard, grab a taxi, and head home to bed. Something told him it was probably a lousy idea.

As he moved toward the mist of the fountains, Langdon had the uneasy sense he was crossing an imaginary threshold into another world. The dreamlike quality of the evening was settling around him again. Twenty minutes ago he had been asleep in his hotel room. Now he was standing in front of a transparent pyramid built by the Sphinx, waiting for a policeman they called the Bull.

I'm trapped in a Salvador Dalí painting, he thought.

Langdon strode to the main entrance – an enormous revolving door. The foyer beyond was dimly lit and deserted.

Do I knock?

Langdon wondered if any of Harvard's revered Egyptologists had ever knocked on the front door of a pyramid and expected an answer. He raised his hand to bang on the glass, but out of the darkness below, a figure appeared, striding up the curving staircase. The man was stocky and dark, almost Neanderthal, dressed in a dark double-breasted suit that strained to cover his wide shoulders. He advanced with unmistakable authority on squat, powerful legs. He was speaking on his cell phone but finished the call as he arrived. He motioned for Langdon to enter.

'I am Bezu Fache,' he announced as Langdon pushed through the revolving door. 'Captain of the Central Directorate Judicial Police.' His tone was fitting – a guttural rumble . . . like a gathering storm.

Langdon held out his hand to shake. 'Robert Langdon.'

Fache's enormous palm wrapped around Langdon's with crushing force.

'I saw the photo,' Langdon said. 'Your agent said Jacques Saunière *himself* did—'

'Mr Langdon,' Fache's ebony eyes locked on. 'What you see in the photo is only the beginning of what Saunière did.'

4

Captain Bezu Fache carried himself like an angry ox, with his wide shoulders thrown back and his chin tucked hard into his chest. His dark hair was slicked back with oil, accentuating an arrow-like widow's peak that divided his jutting brow and preceded him like the prow of a battleship. As he advanced, his dark eyes seemed to scorch the earth before him, radiating a fiery clarity that forecast his reputation for unblinking severity in all matters.

Langdon followed the captain down the famous marble staircase into the sunken atrium beneath the glass pyramid. As they descended, they passed between two armed Judicial Police guards with machine guns. The message was clear: Nobody goes in or out tonight without the blessing of Captain Fache.

Descending below ground level, Langdon fought a rising trepidation. Fache's presence was anything but welcoming, and the Louvre itself had an almost sepulchral aura at this hour. The staircase, like the aisle of a dark cinema, was illuminated by subtle tread-lighting embedded in each step. Langdon could hear his own footsteps reverberating off the glass overhead. As he glanced up, he could see the faint illuminated wisps of mist from the fountains fading away outside the transparent roof.

'Do you approve?' Fache asked, nodding upward with his broad chin.

Langdon sighed, too tired to play games. 'Yes, your pyramid is magnificent.'

Fache grunted. 'A scar on the face of Paris.'

Strike one. Langdon sensed his host was a hard man to please. He wondered if Fache had any idea that this pyramid, at President Mitterrand's explicit demand, had been constructed of exactly 666 panes of glass – a bizarre request that had always been a hot topic among conspiracy buffs who claimed 666 was the number of Satan.

Langdon decided not to bring it up.

As they dropped farther into the subterranean foyer, the yawning space slowly emerged from the shadows. Built fifty-seven feet beneath ground level, the Louvre's newly constructed 70,000-square-foot lobby spread out like an endless grotto. Constructed in warm ochre marble to be compatible with the honey-coloured stone of the Louvre façade above, the subterranean hall was usually vibrant with sunlight and tourists. Tonight, however, the lobby was barren and dark, giving the entire space a cold and crypt-like atmosphere.

'And the museum's regular security staff?' Langdon asked.

'*En quarantaine*,' Fache replied, sounding as if Langdon were questioning the integrity of Fache's team. 'Obviously, someone gained entry tonight who should not have. All Louvre night wardens are in the Sully Wing being questioned. My own agents have taken over museum security for the evening.'

Langdon nodded, moving quickly to keep pace with Fache.

'How well did you know Jacques Saunière?' the captain asked.

'Actually, not at all. We'd never met.'

Fache looked surprised. 'Your first meeting was to be tonight?'

'Yes. We'd planned to meet at the American University reception following my lecture, but he never showed up.'

Fache scribbled some notes in a little book. As they walked, Langdon caught a glimpse of the Louvre's lesser-known pyramid – *La Pyramide Inversée* – a huge inverted skylight that hung from the ceiling like a stalactite in an adjoining section of the entresol. Fache guided Langdon up a short set of stairs to the mouth of an arched tunnel, over which a sign read: DENON. The Denon Wing was the most famous of the Louvre's three main sections.

'Who requested tonight's meeting?' Fache asked suddenly. 'You or he?'

The question seemed odd. 'Mr Saunière did,' Langdon replied as they entered the tunnel. 'His secretary contacted me a few weeks ago via e-mail. She said the curator had heard I would be lecturing in Paris this month and wanted to discuss something with me while I was here.'

'Discuss what?'

'I don't know. Art, I imagine. We share similar interests.'

Fache looked sceptical. 'You have *no* idea what your meeting was about?'

Langdon did not. He'd been curious at the time but had not felt comfortable demanding specifics. The venerated Jacques Saunière had a renowned penchant for privacy and granted very few meetings; Langdon was grateful simply for the opportunity to meet him.

'Mr Langdon, can you at least *guess* what our murder victim might have wanted to discuss with you on the night he was killed? It might be helpful.'

The pointedness of the question made Langdon uncomfortable. 'I really can't imagine. I didn't ask. I felt honoured to have been contacted at all. I'm an admirer of Mr Saunière's work. I use his texts often in my classes.'

Fache made note of that fact in his book.

The two men were now halfway up the Denon Wing's entry tunnel, and Langdon could see the twin ascending escalators at the far end, both motionless.

'So you shared interests with him?' Fache asked.

'Yes. In fact, I've spent much of the last year writing the draft for a book that deals with Mr Saunière's primary area of expertise. I was looking forward to picking his brain.'

Fache glanced up. 'Pardon?'

The idiom apparently didn't translate. 'I was looking forward to learning his thoughts on the topic.'

'I see. And what is the topic?'

Langdon hesitated, uncertain exactly how to put it. 'Essentially, the manuscript is about the iconography of goddess worship – the concept of female sanctity and the art and symbols associated with it.'

Fache ran a meaty hand across his hair. 'And Saunière was knowledgeable about this?'

'Nobody more so.'

'I see.'

Langdon sensed Fache did not see at all. Jacques Saunière was considered the premiere goddess iconographer on earth. Not only did Saunière have a personal passion for relics relating to fertility, goddess cults, Wicca and the sacred feminine, but during his twenty-year tenure as curator, Saunière had helped the Louvre amass the largest collection of goddess art on earth – labrys axes from the priestesses' oldest Greek shrine in Delphi, gold caducei wands, hundreds of Tjet ankhs resembling small standing angels, sistrum rattles used in ancient Egypt to dispel evil spirits, and an astonishing array of statues depicting Horus being nursed by the goddess Isis.

'Perhaps Jacques Saunière knew of your manuscript?' Fache offered. 'And he called the meeting to offer his help on your book.'

Langdon shook his head. 'Actually, nobody yet knows about my manuscript. It's still in draft form, and I haven't shown it to anyone except my editor.'

Fache fell silent.

Langdon did not add the *reason* he hadn't yet shown the manuscript to anyone else. The three-hundred-page draft – tentatively titled *Symbols of the Lost Sacred Feminine* – proposed some very unconventional interpretations of established religious iconography which would certainly be controversial.

Now, as Langdon approached the stationary escalators, he paused, realizing Fache was no longer beside him. Turning, Langdon saw Fache standing several yards back at a service elevator.

'We'll take the elevator,' Fache said as the lift doors opened. 'As I'm sure you're aware, the gallery is quite a distance on foot.'

Although Langdon knew the elevator would expedite the long, two-storey climb to the Denon Wing, he remained motionless.

'Is something wrong?' Fache was holding the door, looking impatient.

Langdon exhaled, turning a longing glance back up the open-air escalator. *Nothing's wrong at all*, he lied to himself, trudging back toward the elevator. As a boy, Langdon had fallen down an abandoned well shaft and almost died treading water in the narrow space for hours before being rescued. Since then, he'd suffered a haunting phobia of enclosed spaces – elevators, subways, squash courts. *The elevator is a perfectly safe machine*, Langdon continually told himself, never believing it. *It's a tiny metal box hanging in an enclosed shaft!* Holding his breath, he stepped into the lift, feeling the familiar tingle of adrenaline as the doors slid shut.

Two floors. Ten seconds.

'You and Mr Saunière,' Fache said as the lift began to move, 'you never spoke at all? Never corresponded? Never sent each other anything in the mail?'

Another odd question. Langdon shook his head. 'No. Never.'

Fache cocked his head, as if making a mental note of that fact. Saying nothing, he stared dead ahead at the chrome doors.

As they ascended, Langdon tried to focus on anything other than the four walls around him. In the reflection of the shiny elevator door, he saw the captain's tie clip – a silver crucifix with thirteen embedded pieces of black onyx. Langdon found it vaguely surprising. The symbol was known as a *crux gemmata* – a cross bearing thirteen gems – a Christian ideogram for Christ and His twelve apostles. Somehow Langdon had not expected the captain of the French police to broadcast his religion so openly. Then again, this was France; Christianity was not a religion here so much as a birthright.

'It's a *crux gemmata*,' Fache said suddenly.

Startled, Langdon glanced up to find Fache's eyes on him in the reflection.

The elevator jolted to a stop, and the doors opened.

Langdon stepped quickly out into the hallway, eager for the wide-open space afforded by the famous high ceilings of the Louvre galleries. The world into which he stepped, however, was nothing like he expected.

Surprised, Langdon stopped short.

Fache glanced over. 'I gather, Mr Langdon, you have never seen the Louvre after hours?'

I guess not, Langdon thought, trying to get his bearings.

Usually impeccably illuminated, the Louvre galleries were startlingly dark tonight. Instead of the customary flat-white light flowing down from above, a muted red glow seemed to emanate upward from the baseboards – intermittent patches of red light spilling out onto the tile floors.

As Langdon gazed down the murky corridor, he realized he should have anticipated this scene. Virtually all major galleries employed red service lighting at night – strategically placed, low-level, noninvasive lights that enabled staff members to navigate hallways and yet kept the paintings in relative darkness to slow the fading effects of overexposure to light. Tonight, the museum possessed an almost oppressive quality. Long shadows encroached everywhere, and the usually soaring vaulted ceilings appeared as a low, black void.

'This way,' Fache said, turning sharply right and setting out through a series of interconnected galleries.

Langdon followed, his vision slowly adjusting to the dark. All around, large-format oils began to materialize like photos developing before him in an enormous darkroom . . . their eyes following as he moved through the rooms. He could taste the familiar tang of museum air – an arid, deionized essence that carried a faint hint of carbon – the product of industrial, coal-filter dehumidifiers that ran around the clock to counteract the corrosive carbon dioxide exhaled by visitors.

Mounted high on the walls, the visible security cameras sent a clear message to visitors: *We see you. Do not touch anything.*

'Any of them real?' Langdon asked, motioning to the cameras.

Fache shook his head. 'Of course not.'

Langdon was not surprised. Video surveillance in museums this size was cost-prohibitive and ineffective. With acres of galleries to watch over, the Louvre would require several hundred technicians simply to monitor the feeds. Most large museums now used 'containment security'. *Forget keeping thieves out. Keep them in.* Containment was activated after hours, and if an intruder removed a piece of artwork, compartmentalized exits would seal around that gallery, and the thief would find himself behind bars even before the police arrived.

The sound of voices echoed down the marble corridor up ahead. The noise seemed to be coming from a large recessed alcove that lay ahead on the right. A bright light spilled out into the hallway.

'Office of the curator,' the captain said.

As he and Fache drew nearer the alcove, Langdon peered down a short hallway, into Saunière's luxurious study – warm wood, Old Master paintings and an enormous antique desk on which stood a two-foot-tall model of a knight in full armour. A handful of police agents bustled about the room, talking on phones and taking notes. One of them was seated at Saunière's desk, typing into a laptop. Apparently, the curator's private office had become DCPJ's makeshift command post for the evening.

'*Messieurs,*' Fache called out, and the men turned. '*Ne nous dérangez pas sous aucun prétexte. Entendu?*'

Everyone inside the office nodded their understanding.

Langdon had hung enough NE PAS DERANGER signs on hotel room doors to catch the gist of the captain's orders. Fache and Langdon were not to be disturbed under any circumstances.

Leaving the small congregation of agents behind, Fache led Langdon farther down the darkened hallway. Thirty yards ahead loomed the gateway to the Louvre's most popular section – *la Grande Galerie* – a seemingly endless corridor that housed the Louvre's most valuable Italian masterpieces. Langdon had already discerned that *this* was where Saunière's body lay; the Grand Gallery's famous parquet floor had been unmistakable in the Polaroid.

As they approached, Langdon saw the entrance was blocked by an enormous steel grate that looked like something used by medieval castles to keep out marauding armies.

'Containment security,' Fache said, as they neared the grate.

Even in the darkness, the barricade looked as if it could have restrained a tank. Arriving outside, Langdon peered through the bars into the dimly lit caverns of the Grand Gallery.

'After you, Mr Langdon,' Fache said.

Langdon turned. *After me, where?*

Fache motioned toward the floor at the base of the grate.

Langdon looked down. In the darkness, he hadn't noticed. The barricade was raised about two feet, providing an awkward clearance underneath.

'This area is still off limits to Louvre security,' Fache said. 'My team from *Police Technique et Scientifique* has just finished their investigation.' He motioned to the opening. 'Please slide under.'

Langdon stared at the narrow crawl space at his feet and then up at the massive iron grate. *He's kidding, right?* The barricade looked like a guillotine waiting to crush intruders.

Fache grumbled something in French and checked his watch. Then he dropped to his knees and slithered his bulky frame underneath the grate. On the other side, he stood up and looked back through the bars at Langdon.

Langdon sighed. Placing his palms flat on the polished parquet, he lay on his stomach and pulled himself forward. As he slid underneath, the nape of his Harris tweed snagged on the bottom of the grate, and he cracked the back of his head on the iron.

Very suave, Robert, he thought, fumbling and then finally pulling himself through. As he stood up, Langdon was beginning to suspect it was going to be a very long night.

5

Murray Hill Place – the new Opus Dei World Headquarters and conference centre – is located at 243 Lexington Avenue in New York City. With a price tag of just over $47 million, the 133,000-square-foot tower is clad in red brick and Indiana limestone. Designed by May & Pinska, the building contains over one hundred bedrooms, six dining rooms, libraries, living rooms, meeting rooms and offices. The second, eighth and sixteenth floors contain chapels, ornamented with millwork and marble. The seventeenth floor is entirely residential. Men enter the building through the main doors on Lexington Avenue. Women enter through a side street and are 'acoustically and visually separated' from the men at all times within the building.

Earlier this evening, within the sanctuary of his penthouse apartment, Bishop Manuel Aringarosa had packed a small travel bag and dressed in a traditional black cassock. Normally, he would have wrapped a purple cincture around his waist, but tonight he would be travelling among the public, and he preferred not to draw attention to his high office. Only those with a keen eye would notice his 14-carat gold bishop's ring with purple amethyst, large diamonds and hand-tooled mitre-crozier appliqué. Throwing the travel bag over his shoulder, he said a silent prayer and left his apartment, descending to the lobby where his driver was waiting to take him to the airport.

Now, sitting aboard a commercial airliner bound for Rome, Aringarosa gazed out of the window at the dark Atlantic. The sun had already set, but Aringarosa knew his own star was on the rise. *Tonight the battle will be won*, he thought, amazed that only months ago he had felt powerless against the hands that threatened to destroy his empire.

As president-general of Opus Dei, Bishop Aringarosa had spent the last decade of his life spreading the message of 'God's Work' – literally, *Opus Dei*. The congregation, founded in 1928 by the Spanish priest Josemaría Escrivá, promoted a return to conservative Catholic values and encouraged its members to make sweeping sacrifices in their own lives in order to do the Work of God.

Opus Dei's traditionalist philosophy initially had taken root in Spain before Franco's regime, but with the 1934 publication of Josemaría

Escrivá's spiritual book *The Way* – 999 points of meditation for doing God's Work in one's own life – Escrivá's message exploded across the world. Now, with over four million copies of *The Way* in circulation in forty-two languages, Opus Dei was a global force. Its residence halls, teaching centres and even universities could be found in almost every major metropolis on earth. Opus Dei was the fastest-growing and most financially secure Catholic organization in the world. Unfortunately, Aringarosa had learned, in an age of religious cynicism, cults and televangelists, Opus Dei's escalating wealth and power were a magnet for suspicion.

'Many call Opus Dei a brainwashing cult,' reporters often challenged. 'Others call you an ultraconservative Christian secret society. Which are you?'

'Opus Dei is neither,' the bishop would patiently reply. 'We are a Catholic Church. We are a congregation of Catholics who have chosen as our priority to follow Catholic doctrine as rigorously as we can in our own daily lives.'

'Does God's Work necessarily include vows of chastity, tithing and atonement for sins through self-flagellation and the *cilice*?'

'You are describing only a small portion of the Opus Dei population,' Aringarosa said. 'There are many levels of involvement. Thousands of Opus Dei members are married, have families and do God's Work in their own communities. Others choose lives of asceticism within our cloistered residence halls. These choices are personal, but everyone in Opus Dei shares the goal of bettering the world by doing the Work of God. Surely this is an admirable quest.'

Reason seldom worked, though. The media always gravitated toward scandal, and Opus Dei, like most large organizations, had within its membership a few misguided souls who cast a shadow over the entire group.

Two months ago, an Opus Dei group at a midwestern university had been caught drugging new recruits with mescaline in an effort to induce a euphoric state that neophytes would perceive as a religious experience. Another university student had used his barbed *cilice* belt more often than the recommended two hours a day and had given himself a near lethal infection. In Boston not long ago, a disillusioned young investment banker had signed over his entire life savings to Opus Dei before attempting suicide.

Misguided sheep, Aringarosa thought, his heart going out to them.

Of course, the ultimate embarrassment had been the widely publicized trial of FBI spy Robert Hanssen, who, in addition to being a prominent member of Opus Dei, had turned out to be a sexual deviant, his trial uncovering evidence that he had rigged hidden video cameras in his own bedroom so his friends could watch him having sex with his wife. 'Hardly the pastime of a devout Catholic,' the judge had noted.

Sadly, all of these events had helped spawn the new watch group known as the Opus Dei Awareness Network (ODAN). The group's popular website – *www.odan.org* – relayed frightening stories from former Opus Dei members who warned of the dangers of joining. The media was now referring to Opus Dei as 'God's Mafia' and 'the Cult of Christ'.

We fear what we do not understand, Aringarosa thought, wondering if these critics had any idea how many lives Opus Dei had enriched. The group enjoyed the full endorsement and blessing of the Vatican. *Opus Dei is a personal prelature of the Pope himself.*

Recently, however, Opus Dei had found itself threatened by a force infinitely more powerful than the media . . . an unexpected foe from which Aringarosa could not possibly hide. Five months ago, the kaleidoscope of power had been shaken, and Aringarosa was still reeling from the blow.

'They know not the war they have begun,' Aringarosa whispered to himself, staring out of the plane's window at the darkness of the ocean below. For an instant, his eyes refocused, lingering on the reflection of his awkward face – dark and oblong, dominated by a flat, crooked nose that had been shattered by a fist in Spain when he was a young missionary. The physical flaw barely registered now. Aringarosa's was a world of the soul, not of the flesh.

As the jet passed over the coast of Portugal, the cell phone in Aringarosa's cassock began vibrating in silent ring mode. Despite airline regulations prohibiting the use of cell phones during flights, Aringarosa knew this was a call he could not miss. Only one man possessed this number, the man who had mailed Aringarosa the phone.

Excited, the bishop answered quietly. 'Yes?'

'Silas has located the keystone,' the caller said. 'It is in Paris. Within the Church of Saint-Sulpice.'

Bishop Aringarosa smiled. 'Then we are close.'

'We can obtain it immediately. But we need your influence.'

'Of course. Tell me what to do.'

When Aringarosa switched off the phone, his heart was pounding. He gazed once again into the void of night, feeling dwarfed by the events he had put into motion.

Five hundred miles away, the albino named Silas stood over a small basin of water and dabbed the blood from his back, watching the patterns of red spinning in the water. *Purge me with hyssop and I shall be clean,* he prayed, quoting Psalms. *Wash me, and I shall be whiter than snow.*

Silas was feeling an aroused anticipation that he had not felt since his previous life. It both surprised and electrified him. For the last decade, he had been following *The Way,* cleansing himself of sins . . . rebuilding his life . . . erasing the violence in his past. Tonight, however, it had all come rushing back. The hatred he had fought so hard to bury had been summoned. He had been startled how quickly his past had resurfaced. And with it, of course, had come his skills. Rusty but serviceable.

Jesus' message is one of peace . . . of nonviolence . . . of love. This was the message Silas had been taught from the beginning, and the message he held in his heart. And yet *this* was the message the enemies of Christ now threatened to destroy. *Those who threaten God with force will be met with force. Immovable and steadfast.*

For two millennia, Christian soldiers had defended their faith against those who tried to displace it. Tonight, Silas had been called to battle.

Drying his wounds, he donned his ankle-length, hooded robe. It was plain, made of dark wool, accentuating the whiteness of his skin and hair. Tightening the rope-tie around his waist, he raised the hood over his head and allowed his red eyes to admire his reflection in the mirror. *The wheels are in motion.*

6

Having squeezed beneath the security gate, Robert Langdon now stood just inside the entrance to the Grand Gallery. He was staring into the mouth of a long, deep canyon. On either side of the gallery, stark walls rose thirty feet, evaporating into the darkness above. The reddish glow of the service lighting sifted upward, casting an unnatural smoulder across a staggering collection of Da Vincis, Titians and Caravaggios that hung suspended from ceiling cables. Still lifes, religious scenes and landscapes accompanied portraits of nobility and politicians.

Although the Grand Gallery housed the Louvre's most famous Italian art, many visitors felt the wing's most stunning offering was actually its famous parquet floor. Laid out in a dazzling geometric design of diagonal oak slats, the floor produced an ephemeral optical illusion – a multi-dimensional network that gave visitors the sense they were floating through the gallery on a surface that changed with every step.

As Langdon's gaze began to trace the inlay, his eyes stopped short on an unexpected object lying on the floor just a few yards to his left, surrounded by police tape. He spun toward Fache. 'Is that . . . a *Caravaggio* on the floor?'

Fache nodded without even looking.

The painting, Langdon guessed, was worth upward of two million dollars, and yet it was lying on the floor like a discarded poster. 'What the devil is it doing on the floor!'

Fache glowered, clearly unmoved. 'This is a crime scene, Mr Langdon. We have touched nothing. That canvas was pulled from the wall by the curator. It was how he activated the security system.'

Langdon looked back at the gate, trying to picture what had happened.

'The curator was attacked in his office, fled into the Grand Gallery, and activated the security gate by pulling that painting from the wall. The gate fell immediately, sealing off all access. This is the only door in or out of this gallery.'

Langdon felt confused. 'So the curator actually captured his attacker inside the Grand Gallery?'

Fache shook his head. 'The security gate *separated* Saunière from his attacker. The killer was locked out there in the hallway and shot Saunière through this gate.' Fache pointed toward an orange tag hanging from one of the bars on the gate under which they had just passed. 'The PTS team found flashback residue from a gun. He fired through the bars. Saunière died in here alone.'

Langdon pictured the photograph of Saunière's body. *They said he did that to himself.* Langdon looked out at the enormous corridor before them. 'So where is his body?'

Fache straightened his cruciform tie clip and began to walk. 'As you probably know, the Grand Gallery is quite long.'

The exact length, if Langdon recalled correctly, was around fifteen hundred feet, the length of three Washington Monuments laid end to end. Equally breathtaking was the corridor's width, which easily could have accommodated a pair of side-by-side passenger trains. The centre of the hallway was dotted by the occasional statue or colossal porcelain urn, which served as a tasteful divider and kept the flow of traffic moving down one wall and up the other.

Fache was silent now, striding briskly up the right side of the corridor with his gaze dead ahead. Langdon felt almost disrespectful to be racing past so many masterpieces without pausing for so much as a glance.

Not that I could see anything in this lighting, he thought.

The muted crimson lighting unfortunately conjured memories of Langdon's last experience in noninvasive lighting in the Vatican Secret Archives. This was tonight's second unsettling parallel with his near-death in Rome. He flashed on Vittoria again. She had been absent from his dreams for months. Langdon could not believe Rome had been only a year ago; it felt like decades. *Another life.* His last correspondence from Vittoria had been in December – a postcard saying she was headed to the Java Sea to continue her research in entanglement physics . . . something about using satellites to track manta ray migrations. Langdon had never harboured delusions that a woman like Vittoria Vetra could have been happy living with him on a college campus, but their encounter in Rome had unlocked in him a longing he never imagined he could feel. His lifelong affinity for bachelorhood and the simple freedoms it allowed had been shaken somehow . . . replaced by an unexpected emptiness that seemed to have grown over the past year.

They continued walking briskly, yet Langdon still saw no corpse. 'Jacques Saunière went this *far?*'

'Mr Saunière suffered a bullet wound to his stomach. He died very slowly. Perhaps over fifteen or twenty minutes. He was obviously a man of great personal strength.'

Langdon turned, appalled. 'Security took *fifteen* minutes to get here?'

'Of course not. Louvre security responded immediately to the alarm and found the Grand Gallery sealed. Through the gate, they could hear someone moving around at the far end of the corridor, but they could not see who it was. They shouted, but they got no answer. Assuming it could only be a criminal, they followed protocol and called in the Judicial Police. We took up positions within fifteen minutes. When we arrived, we raised the barricade enough to slip underneath, and I sent a dozen armed agents inside. They swept the length of the gallery to corner the intruder.'

'And?'

'They found no one inside. Except . . .' He pointed farther down the hall. 'Him.'

Langdon lifted his gaze and followed Fache's outstretched finger. At first he thought Fache was pointing to a large marble statue in the middle of the hallway. As they continued, though, Langdon began to see past the statue. Thirty yards down the hall, a single spotlight on a portable pole stand shone down on the floor, creating a stark island of white light in the dark crimson gallery. In the centre of the light, like an insect under a microscope, the corpse of the curator lay naked on the parquet floor.

'You saw the photograph,' Fache said, 'so this should be of no surprise.'

Langdon felt a deep chill as they approached the body. Before him was one of the strangest images he had ever seen.

The pallid corpse of Jacques Saunière lay on the parquet floor exactly as it appeared in the photograph. As Langdon stood over the body and squinted in the harsh light, he reminded himself to his amazement that Saunière had spent his last minutes of life arranging his own body in this strange fashion.

Saunière looked remarkably fit for a man of his years . . . and all of his musculature was in plain view. He had stripped off every shred of clothing, placed it neatly on the floor, and laid down on his back in the centre of the wide corridor, perfectly aligned with the long axis of the room. His arms and legs were sprawled outward in a wide spread- eagle, like those of a child making a snow angel . . . or, perhaps more appropriately, like a man being drawn and quartered by some invisible force.

Just below Saunière's breastbone, a bloody smear marked the spot where the bullet had pierced his flesh. The wound had bled surprisingly little, leaving only a small pool of blackened blood.

Saunière's left index finger was also bloody, apparently having been dipped into the wound to create the most unsettling aspect of his own macabre deathbed; using his own blood as ink, and employing his own naked abdomen as a canvas, Saunière had drawn a simple symbol on his flesh – five straight lines that intersected to form a five-pointed star.

The pentacle.

The bloody star, centred on Saunière's navel, gave his corpse a distinctly ghoulish aura. The photo Langdon had seen was chilling enough, but now, witnessing the scene in person, Langdon felt a deepening uneasiness.

He did this to himself.

'Mr Langdon?' Fache's dark eyes settled on him again.

'It's a pentacle,' Langdon offered, his voice feeling hollow in the huge space. 'One of the oldest symbols on earth. Used over four thousand years before Christ.'

'And what does it mean?'

Langdon always hesitated when he got this question. Telling someone what a symbol 'meant' was like telling them how a song should make them feel – it was different for all people. A white Ku Klux Klan headpiece conjured images of hatred and racism in the United States, and yet the same costume carried a meaning of religious faith in Spain.

'Symbols carry different meanings in different settings,' Langdon said. 'Primarily, the pentacle is a pagan religious symbol.'

Fache nodded. 'Devil worship.'

'No,' Langdon corrected, immediately realizing his choice of vocabulary should have been clearer.

Nowadays, the term *pagan* had become almost synonymous with devil worship – a gross misconception. The word's roots actually reached back to the Latin *paganus*, meaning country-dwellers. 'Pagans' were literally unindoctrinated country-folk who clung to the old, rural religions of Nature worship. In fact, so strong was the Church's fear of those who lived in the rural *villes* that the once innocuous word for 'villager' – *vilain* – came to mean a wicked soul.

'The pentacle,' Langdon clarified, 'is a pre-Christian symbol that relates to Nature worship. The ancients envisioned their world in two halves – masculine and feminine. Their gods and goddesses worked to keep a balance of power. Yin and yang. When male and female were balanced, there was harmony in the world. When they were unbalanced, there was chaos.' Langdon motioned to Saunière's stomach. 'This pentacle is representative of the *female* half of all things – a concept religious historians call the "sacred feminine" or the "divine goddess". Saunière, of all people, would know this.'

'Saunière drew a *goddess* symbol on his stomach?'

Langdon had to admit, it seemed odd. 'In its most specific interpretation, the pentacle symbolizes Venus – the goddess of female sexual love and beauty.'

Fache eyed the naked man, and grunted.

'Early religion was based on the divine order of Nature. The goddess Venus and the planet Venus were one and the same. The goddess had a place in the nighttime sky and was known by many names – Venus, the Eastern Star, Ishtar, Astarte – all of them powerful female concepts with ties to Nature and Mother Earth.'

Fache looked more troubled now, as if he somehow preferred the idea of devil worship.

Langdon decided not to share the pentacle's most astonishing property – the *graphic* origin of its ties to Venus. As a young astronomy student, Langdon had been stunned to learn the planet Venus traced a *perfect* pentacle across the ecliptic sky every eight years. So astonished were the ancients to observe this phenomenon, that Venus and her pentacle became symbols of perfection, beauty, and the cyclic qualities of sexual love. As a tribute to the magic of Venus, the Greeks used her eight-year cycle to organize their Olympic games. Nowadays, few people realized that the four-year schedule of modern Olympics still followed the half-cycles of Venus. Even fewer people knew that the five-pointed star had almost become the official Olympic seal but was modified at the last moment – its five points exchanged for five intersecting rings to better reflect the games' spirit of inclusion and harmony.

'Mr Langdon,' Fache said abruptly. 'Obviously, the pentacle must *also* relate to the devil. Your American horror films make that point clearly.'

Langdon frowned. *Thank you, Hollywood.* The five-pointed star was now a virtual cliché in Satanic serial killer films, usually scrawled on the wall of some Satanist's apartment along with other alleged demonic symbology. Langdon was always frustrated when he saw the symbol in this context; the pentacle's true origins were actually quite godly.

'I assure you,' Langdon said, 'despite what you see in the movies, the pentacle's demonic interpretation is historically inaccurate. The original feminine meaning is correct, but the symbolism of the pentacle has been distorted over the millennia. In this case, through bloodshed.'

'I'm not sure I follow.'

Langdon glanced at Fache's crucifix, uncertain how to phrase his next point. 'The Church, sir. Symbols are very resilient, but the pen-tacle was altered by the early Roman Catholic Church. As part of the Vatican's campaign to eradicate pagan religions and convert the masses to Christianity, the Church launched a smear campaign against the pagan gods and goddesses, recasting their divine symbols as evil.'

'Go on.'

'This is very common in times of turmoil,' Langdon continued. 'A newly emerging power will take over the existing symbols and degrade them over time in an attempt to erase their meaning. In the battle between the pagan symbols and Christian symbols, the pagans lost; Poseidon's trident became the devil's pitchfork, the wise crone's pointed hat became the symbol of a witch, and Venus's pentacle became a sign of the devil.' Langdon paused. 'Unfortunately, the United States military has also perverted the pentacle; it's now our foremost symbol of war. We paint it on all our fighter jets and hang it on the shoulders of all our generals.' *So much for the goddess of love and beauty.*

'Interesting.' Fache nodded toward the spread-eagle corpse. 'And the positioning of the body? What do you make of that?'

Langdon shrugged. 'The position simply reinforces the reference to the pentacle and sacred feminine.'

Fache's expression clouded. 'I beg your pardon?'

'Replication. Repeating a symbol is the simplest way to strengthen its meaning. Jacques Saunière positioned himself in the shape of a five-pointed star.' *If one pentacle is good, two is better.*

Fache's eyes followed the five points of Saunière's arms, legs, and head as he again ran a hand across his slick hair. 'Interesting analysis.' He paused. 'And the *nudity?*' He grumbled as he spoke the word, sounding repulsed by the sight of an aging male body. 'Why did he remove his clothing?'

Damned good question, Langdon thought. He'd been wondering the same thing ever since he first saw the Polaroid. His best guess was that a naked human form was yet another endorsement of Venus – the goddess of human sexuality. Although modern culture had erased much of Venus's association with the male/female physical union, a sharp etymological eye could still spot a vestige of Venus's original meaning in the word 'venereal'. Langdon decided not to go there.

'Mr Fache, I obviously can't tell you why Mr Saunière drew that symbol on himself or placed himself in this way, but I *can* tell you that a man like Jacques Saunière would consider the pentacle a sign of the female deity. The correlation between this symbol and the sacred feminine is widely known by art historians and symbologists.'

'Fine. And the use of his own blood as ink?'

'Obviously he had nothing else to write with.'

Fache was silent a moment. 'Actually, I believe he used blood such that the police would follow certain forensic procedures.'

'I'm sorry?'

'Look at his left hand.'

Langdon's eyes traced the length of the curator's pale arm to his left hand but saw nothing. Uncertain, he circled the corpse and crouched down, now noting with surprise that the curator was clutching a large, felt-tipped marker.

'Saunière was holding it when we found him,' Fache said, leaving Langdon and moving several yards to a portable table covered with investigation tools, cables and assorted electronic gear. 'As I told you,' he said, rummaging around the table, 'we have touched nothing. Are you familiar with this kind of pen?'

Langdon knelt down farther to see the pen's label.

STYLO DE LUMIERE NOIRE.

He glanced up in surprise.

The black-light pen or watermark stylus was a specialized felt-tipped marker originally designed by museums, restorers and forgery police to place invisible marks on items. The stylus wrote in a noncorrosive, alcohol-based fluorescent ink that was visible only under black light. Nowadays, museum maintenance staffs carried these markers on their daily rounds to place invisible 'tick marks' on the frames of paintings that needed restoration.

As Langdon stood up, Fache walked over to the spotlight and turned it off. The gallery plunged into sudden darkness.

Momentarily blinded, Langdon felt a rising uncertainty. Fache's silhouette appeared, illuminated in bright purple. He approached carrying a portable light source, which shrouded him in a violet haze.

'As you may know,' Fache said, his eyes luminescing in the violet glow, 'police use black-light illumination to search crime scenes for blood and other forensic evidence. So you can imagine our surprise . . .' Abruptly, he pointed the light down at the corpse.

Langdon looked down and jumped back in shock.

His heart pounded as he took in the bizarre sight now glowing before him on the parquet floor. Scrawled in luminescent handwriting, the curator's final words glowed purple beside his corpse. As Langdon stared at the shimmering text, he felt the fog that had surrounded this entire night growing thicker.

Langdon read the message again and looked up at Fache. 'What the hell does this mean!'

Fache's eyes shone white. '*That*, monsieur, is precisely the question you are here to answer.'

Not far away, inside Saunière's office, Lieutenant Collet had returned to the Louvre and was huddled over an audio console set up on the curator's enormous desk. With the exception of the eerie, robot-like doll of a medieval knight that seemed to be staring at him from the corner of Saunière's desk, Collet was comfortable. He adjusted his AKG headphones and checked the input levels on the hard-disk recording system. All systems were go. The microphones were functioning flawlessly, and the audio feed was crystal clear.

Le moment de vérité, he mused.

Smiling, he closed his eyes and settled in to enjoy the rest of the conversation now being taped inside the Grand Gallery.

7

The modest dwelling within the Church of Saint-Sulpice was located on the second floor of the church itself, to the left of the choir balcony. A two-room suite with a stone floor and minimal furnishings, it had been home to Sister Sandrine Bieil for over a decade. The nearby convent was her formal residence, if anyone asked, but she preferred the quiet of the church and had made herself quite comfortable upstairs with a bed, phone and hot plate.

As the church's *conservatrice d'affaires*, Sister Sandrine was responsible for overseeing all nonreligious aspects of church operations – general maintenance, hiring support staff and guides, securing the building after hours, and ordering supplies like communion wine and wafers.

Tonight, asleep in her small bed, she awoke to the shrill of her telephone. Tiredly, she lifted the receiver.

'*Soeur Sandrine. Eglise Saint-Sulpice.*'

'Hello, Sister,' the man said in French.

Sister Sandrine sat up. *What time is it?* Although she recognized her boss's voice, in fifteen years she had never been awoken by him. The abbé was a deeply pious man who went home to bed immediately after mass.

'I apologize if I have awoken you, Sister,' the abbé said, his own voice sounding groggy and on edge. 'I have a favour to ask of you. I just received a call from an influential American bishop. Perhaps you know him? Manuel Aringarosa?'

'The head of Opus Dei?' *Of course I know of him. Who in the Church doesn't?* Aringarosa's conservative prelature had grown powerful in recent years. Their ascension to grace was jump-started in 1982 when Pope John Paul II unexpectedly elevated them to a 'personal prelature of the Pope', officially sanctioning all of their practices. Suspiciously, Opus Dei's elevation occurred the same year the wealthy sect allegedly had transferred almost one billion dollars into the Vatican's Institute for Religious Works – commonly known as the Vatican Bank – bailing it out of an embarrassing bankruptcy. In a second manoeuvre that raised eyebrows, the Pope placed the founder of Opus Dei on the 'fast track' for sainthood, accelerating an often century-long waiting period for canonization to a mere twenty years.

Sister Sandrine could not help but feel that Opus Dei's good standing in Rome was suspect, but one did not argue with the Holy See.

'Bishop Aringarosa called to ask me a favour,' the abbé told her, his voice nervous. 'One of his numeraries is in Paris tonight. . . .'

As Sister Sandrine listened to the odd request, she felt a deepening confusion. 'I'm sorry, you say this visiting Opus Dei numerary cannot wait until morning?'

'I'm afraid not. His plane leaves very early. He has always dreamed of seeing Saint-Sulpice.'

'But the church is far more interesting by day. The sun's rays through the oculus, the graduated shadows on the gnomon, *this* is what makes Saint-Sulpice unique.'

'Sister, I agree, and yet I would consider it a personal favour if you could let him in tonight. He can be there at . . . say one o'clock? That's in twenty minutes.'

Sister Sandrine frowned. 'Of course. It would be my pleasure.'

The abbé thanked her and hung up.

Puzzled, Sister Sandrine remained a moment in the warmth of her bed, trying to shake off the cobwebs of sleep. Her sixty-year-old body did not awake as fast as it used to, although tonight's phone call had certainly roused her senses. Opus Dei had always made her uneasy. Beyond the prelature's adherence to the arcane ritual of corporal mortification, their views on women were medieval at best. She had been shocked to learn that female numeraries were forced to clean the men's residence halls for no pay while the men were at mass; women slept on hardwood floors, while the men had straw mats; and women were forced to endure additional requirements of corporal mortification . . . all as added penance for original sin. It seemed Eve's bite from the apple of knowledge was a debt women were doomed to pay for eternity. Sadly, while most of the Catholic Church was gradually moving in the right direction with respect to women's rights, Opus Dei threatened to reverse the progress. Even so, Sister Sandrine had her orders.

Swinging her legs off the bed, she stood slowly, chilled by the cold stone on the soles of her bare feet. As the chill rose through her flesh, she felt an unexpected apprehension.

Women's intuition?

A follower of God, Sister Sandrine had learned to find peace in the calming voices of her own soul. Tonight, however, those voices were as silent as the empty church around her.

8

Langdon couldn't tear his eyes from the glowing purple text scrawled across the parquet floor. Jacques Saunière's final communication seemed as unlikely a departing message as any Langdon could imagine.

The message read:

13-3-2-21-1-1-8-5
O, Draconian devil!
Oh, lame saint!

Although Langdon had not the slightest idea what it meant, he did understand Fache's instinct that the pentacle had something to do with devil worship.

O, Draconian devil!

Saunière had left a literal reference to the devil. Equally as bizarre was the series of numbers. 'Part of it looks like a numeric cipher.'

'Yes,' Fache said. 'Our cryptographers are already working on it. We believe these numbers may be the key to who killed him. Maybe a telephone exchange or some kind of social identification. Do the numbers have any symbolic meaning to you?'

Langdon looked again at the digits, sensing it would take him hours to extract any symbolic meaning. *If Saunière had even intended any.* To Langdon, the numbers looked totally random. He was accustomed to symbolic progressions that made some semblance of sense, but everything here – the pentacle, the text, the numbers – seemed disparate at the most fundamental level.

'You alleged earlier,' Fache said, 'that Saunière's actions here were all in an effort to send some sort of message . . . goddess worship or something in that vein? How does this message fit in?'

Langdon knew the question was rhetorical. This bizarre communiqué obviously did not fit Langdon's scenario of goddess worship at all.

O, Draconian devil? Oh, lame saint?

Fache said, 'This text appears to be an accusation of some sort. Wouldn't you agree?'

Langdon tried to imagine the curator's final minutes trapped alone in the Grand Gallery, knowing he was about to die. It seemed logical. 'An accusation against his murderer makes sense, I suppose.'

'My job, of course, is to put a name to that person. Let me ask you this, Mr Langdon. To your eye, beyond the numbers, what about this message is most strange?'

Most strange? A dying man had barricaded himself in the gallery, drawn a pentacle on himself, and scrawled a mysterious accusation on the floor. What about the scenario *wasn't* strange?

'The word "Draconian"?' he ventured, offering the first thing that came to mind. Langdon was fairly certain that a reference to Draco – the ruthless seventh-century BC politician – was an unlikely dying thought. ' 'Draconian devil' seems an odd choice of vocabulary.'

'*Draconian?*' Fache's tone came with a tinge of impatience now. 'Saunière's choice of vocabulary hardly seems the primary issue here.'

Langdon wasn't sure what issue Fache had in mind, but he was starting to suspect that Draco and Fache would have got along well.

'Saunière was a Frenchman,' Fache said flatly. 'He lived in Paris. And yet he chose to write this message . . .'

'In English,' Langdon said, now realizing the captain's meaning.

Fache nodded. '*Précisément.* Any idea why?'

Langdon knew Saunière spoke impeccable English, and yet the reason he had chosen English as the language in which to write his final words escaped Langdon. He shrugged.

Fache motioned back to the pentacle on Saunière's abdomen. 'Nothing to do with devil worship? Are you still certain?'

Langdon was certain of nothing any more. 'The symbology and text don't seem to coincide. I'm sorry I can't be of more help.'

'Perhaps this will clarify.' Fache backed away from the body and raised the black light again, letting the beam spread out in a wider angle. 'And now?'

To Langdon's amazement, a rudimentary circle glowed around the curator's body. Saunière had apparently laid down and swung the pen around himself in several long arcs, essentially inscribing himself inside a circle.

In a flash, the meaning became clear.

'*The Vitruvian Man,*' Langdon gasped. Saunière had created a life-sized replica of Leonardo da Vinci's most famous sketch.

Considered the most anatomically correct drawing of its day, Da Vinci's *The Vitruvian Man* had become a modern-day icon of culture, appearing on posters, mouse pads and T-shirts around the world. The celebrated sketch consisted of a perfect circle in which was inscribed a nude male . . . his arms and legs outstretched in a naked spread-eagle.

Da Vinci. Langdon felt a shiver of amazement. The clarity of Saunière's intentions could not be denied. In his final moments of life, the curator had stripped off his clothing and arranged his body in a clear image of Leonardo da Vinci's *Vitruvian Man.*

The circle had been the missing critical element. A feminine symbol of protection, the circle around the naked man's body completed Da Vinci's intended message – male and female harmony. The question now, though, was *why* Saunière would imitate a famous drawing.

'Mr Langdon,' Fache said, 'certainly a man like yourself is aware that Leonardo da Vinci had a tendency toward the darker arts.'

Langdon was surprised by Fache's knowledge of Da Vinci, and it certainly went a long way toward explaining the captain's suspicions about devil worship. Da Vinci had always been an awkward subject for historians, especially in the Christian tradition. Despite the visionary's genius, he was a flamboyant homosexual and worshipper of Nature's divine order, both of which placed him in a perpetual state of sin against God. Moreover, the artist's eerie eccentricities projected an admittedly demonic aura: Da Vinci exhumed corpses to study human anatomy; he kept mysterious journals in illegible reverse handwriting; he believed he possessed the alchemic power to turn lead into gold and even cheat God by creating an elixir to postpone death; and his inventions included horrific, never-before-imagined weapons of war and torture.

Misunderstanding breeds distrust, Langdon thought.

Even Da Vinci's enormous output of breathtaking Christian art only furthered the artist's reputation for spiritual hypocrisy. Accepting hundreds of lucrative Vatican commissions, Da Vinci painted Christian themes not as an expression of his own beliefs but rather as a commercial venture – a means of funding a lavish lifestyle. Unfortunately, Da Vinci was a prankster who often amused himself by quietly gnawing at the hand that fed him. He incorporated in many of his Christian paintings hidden symbolism that was anything but Christian – tributes to his own beliefs and a subtle thumbing of his nose at the Church. Langdon had even given a lecture once at the National Gallery in London entitled: 'The Secret Life of Leonardo: Pagan Symbolism in Christian Art.'

'I understand your concerns,' Langdon now said, 'but Da Vinci never really practised any dark arts. He was an exceptionally spiritual man, albeit one in constant conflict with the Church.' As Langdon said this, an odd thought popped into his mind. He glanced down at the message on the floor again. *O, Draconian devil! Oh, lame saint!*

'Yes?' Fache said.

Langdon weighed his words carefully. 'I was just thinking that Saunière shared a lot of spiritual ideologies with Da Vinci, including a concern over the Church's elimination of the sacred feminine from modern religion. Maybe, by imitating a famous Da Vinci drawing, Saunière was simply echoing some of their shared frustrations with the modern Church's demonization of the goddess.'

Fache's eyes hardened. 'You think Saunière is calling the Church a lame saint and a Draconian devil?'

Langdon had to admit it seemed far-fetched, and yet the pentacle

486

seemed to endorse the idea on some level. 'All I am saying is that Mr Saunière dedicated his life to studying the history of the goddess, and nothing has done more to erase that history than the Catholic Church. It seems reasonable that Saunière might have chosen to express his disappointment in his final good-bye.'

'Disappointment?' Fache demanded, sounding hostile now. 'This message sounds more *enraged* than disappointed, wouldn't you say?'

Langdon was reaching the end of his patience. 'Captain, you asked for my instincts as to what Saunière is trying to say here, and that's what I'm giving you.'

'That this is an indictment of the Church?' Fache's jaw tightened as he spoke through clenched teeth. 'Mr Langdon, I have seen a lot of death in my work, and let me tell you something. When a man is murdered by another man, I do not believe his final thoughts are to write an obscure spiritual statement that no one will understand. I believe he is thinking of one thing only.' Fache's whispery voice sliced the air. '*La vengeance.* I believe Saunière wrote this note to tell us who killed him.'

Langdon stared. 'But that makes no sense whatsoever.'

'No?'

'No,' he fired back, tired and frustrated. 'You told me Saunière was attacked in his office by someone he had apparently invited in.'

'Yes.'

'So it seems reasonable to conclude that the curator *knew* his attacker.'

Fache nodded. 'Go on.'

'So if Saunière *knew* the person who killed him, what kind of indictment is this?' He pointed at the floor. 'Numeric codes? Lame saints? Draconian devils? Pentacles on his stomach? It's all too cryptic.'

Fache frowned as if the idea had never occurred to him. 'You have a point.'

'Considering the circumstances,' Langdon said, 'I would assume that if Saunière wanted to tell you who killed him, he would have written down somebody's *name*.'

As Langdon spoke those words, a smug smile crossed Fache's lips for the first time all night. '*Précisément,*' Fache said. '*Précisément.*'

I am witnessing the work of a master, mused Lieutenant Collet as he tweaked his audio gear and listened to Fache's voice coming through the headphones. The *agent supérieur* knew it was moments like these that had lifted the captain to the pinnacle of French law enforcement.

Fache will do what no one else dares.

The delicate art of *cajoler* was a lost skill in modern law enforcement, one that required exceptional poise under pressure. Few men possessed the necessary sangfroid for this kind of operation, but Fache seemed born for it. His restraint and patience bordered on the robotic.

Fache's sole emotion this evening seemed to be one of intense resolve, as if this arrest were somehow personal to him. Fache's briefing of his agents an hour ago had been unusually succinct and assured. *I know who murdered Jacques Saunière,* Fache had said. *You know what to do. No mistakes tonight.*

And so far, no mistakes had been made.

Collet was not yet privy to the evidence that had cemented Fache's certainty of their suspect's guilt, but he knew better than to question the instincts of the Bull. Fache's intuition seemed almost supernatural at times. *God whispers in his ear,* one agent had insisted after a particularly impressive display of Fache's sixth sense. Collet had to admit, if there was a God, Bezu Fache would be on His A-list. The captain attended mass and confession with zealous regularity – far more than the requisite holiday attendance fulfilled by other officials in the name of good public relations. When the Pope visited Paris a few years back, Fache had used all his muscle to obtain the honour of an audience. A photo of Fache with the Pope now hung in his office. *The Papal Bull,* the agents secretly called it.

Collet found it ironic that one of Fache's rare popular public stances in recent years had been his outspoken reaction to the Catholic paedophilia scandal. *These priests should be hanged twice!* Fache had declared. *Once for their crimes against children. And once for shaming the good name of the Catholic Church.* Collet had the odd sense it was the latter that angered Fache more.

Turning now to his laptop computer, Collet attended to the other half of his responsibilities here tonight – the GPS tracking system. The image onscreen revealed a detailed floor plan of the Denon Wing, a structural schematic uploaded from the Louvre Security Office. Letting his eyes trace the maze of galleries and hallways, Collet found what he was looking for.

Deep in the heart of the Grand Gallery blinked a tiny red dot.

La marque.

Fache was keeping his prey on a very tight leash tonight. Wisely so. Robert Langdon had proven himself one cool customer.

9

To ensure his conversation with Mr Langdon would not be interrupted, Bezu Fache had turned off his cellular phone. Unfortunately, it was an expensive model equipped with a two-way radio feature, which, contrary to his orders, was now being used by one of his agents to page him.

'*Capitaine?*' The phone crackled like a walkie-talkie.

Fache felt his teeth clench in rage. He could imagine nothing important enough that Collet would interrupt this *surveillance cachée* – especially at this critical juncture.

He gave Langdon a calm look of apology. 'One moment please.' He pulled the phone from his belt and pressed the radio transmission button. '*Oui?*'

'*Capitaine, un agent du Département de Cryptographie est arrivé.*'

Fache's anger stalled momentarily. *A cryptographer?* Despite the lousy timing, this was probably good news. Fache, after finding Saunière's cryptic text on the floor, had uploaded photographs of the entire crime scene to the Cryptography Department in hopes someone there could tell him what the hell Saunière was trying to say. If a code breaker had now arrived, it most likely meant someone had decrypted Saunière's message.

'I'm busy at the moment,' Fache radioed back, leaving no doubt in his tone that a line had been crossed. 'Ask the cryptographer to wait at the command post. I'll speak to him when I'm done.'

'*Her,*' the voice corrected. 'It's Agent Neveu.'

Fache was becoming less amused with this call every passing moment. Sophie Neveu was one of DCPJ's biggest mistakes. A young Parisian *déchiffreuse* who had studied cryptography in England at the Royal Holloway, Sophie Neveu had been foisted on Fache two years ago as part of the ministry's attempt to incorporate more women into the police force. The ministry's ongoing foray into political correctness, Fache argued, was weakening the department. Women not only lacked the physicality necessary for police work, but their mere presence posed a dangerous distraction to the men in the field. As Fache had feared, Sophie Neveu was proving far more distracting than most.

At thirty-two years old, she had a dogged determination that bordered on obstinate. Her eager espousal of Britain's new cryptologic methodology continually exasperated the veteran French cryptographers above her. And by far the most troubling to Fache was the inescapable universal truth that in an office of middle-aged men, an attractive young woman always drew eyes away from the work at hand.

The man on the radio said, 'Agent Neveu insisted on speaking to you immediately, Captain. I tried to stop her, but she's on her way into the gallery.'

Fache recoiled in disbelief. 'Unacceptable! I made it very clear—'

For a moment, Robert Langdon thought Bezu Fache was suffering a stroke. The captain was mid-sentence when his jaw stopped moving and his eyes bulged. His blistering gaze seemed fixated on something over Langdon's shoulder. Before Langdon could turn to see what it was, he heard a woman's voice chime out behind him.

'*Excusez-moi, messieurs.*'

Langdon turned to see a young woman approaching. She was moving down the corridor toward them with long, fluid strides . . . a haunting certainty to her gait. Dressed casually in a knee-length, cream-coloured Irish sweater over black leggings, she was attractive and looked to be about thirty. Her thick burgundy hair fell unstyled to her shoulders, framing the warmth of her face. Unlike the waifish, cookie-cutter blondes that adorned Harvard dorm room walls, this woman was healthy with an unembellished beauty and genuineness that radiated a striking personal confidence.

To Langdon's surprise, the woman walked directly up to him and extended a polite hand. 'Monsieur Langdon, I am Agent Neveu from DCPJ's Cryptology Department.' Her words curved richly around her muted Anglo–Franco accent. 'It is a pleasure to meet you.'

Langdon took her soft palm in his and felt himself momentarily fixed in her strong gaze. Her eyes were olive-green – incisive and clear.

Fache drew a seething inhalation, clearly preparing to launch into a reprimand.

'Captain,' she said, turning quickly and beating him to the punch, 'please excuse the interruption, but—'

'*Ce n'est pas le moment!*' Fache sputtered.

'I tried to phone you.' Sophie continued in English, as if out of courtesy to Langdon. 'But your cell phone was turned off.'

'I turned it off for a reason,' Fache hissed. 'I am speaking to Mr Langdon.'

'I've deciphered the numeric code,' she said flatly.

Langdon felt a pulse of excitement. *She broke the code?*

Fache looked uncertain how to respond.

'Before I explain,' Sophie said, 'I have an urgent message for Mr Langdon.'

Fache's expression turned to one of deepening concern. 'For Mr Langdon?'

She nodded, turning back to Langdon. 'You need to contact the US Embassy, Mr Langdon. They have a message for you from the States.'

Langdon reacted with surprise, his excitement over the code giving way to a sudden ripple of concern. *A message from the States?* He tried to imagine who could be trying to reach him. Only a few of his colleagues knew he was in Paris.

Fache's broad jaw had tightened with the news. 'The US Embassy?' he demanded, sounding suspicious. 'How would they know to find Mr Langdon *here?*'

Sophie shrugged. 'Apparently they called Mr Langdon's hotel, and the concierge told them Mr Langdon had been collected by a DCPJ agent.'

Fache looked troubled. 'And the embassy contacted DCPJ *Cryptography?*'

'No, sir,' Sophie said, her voice firm. 'When I called the DCPJ switchboard in an attempt to contact you, they had a message waiting for Mr Langdon and asked me to pass it along if I got through to you.'

Fache's brow furrowed in apparent confusion. He opened his mouth to speak, but Sophie had already turned back to Langdon.

'Mr Langdon,' she declared, pulling a small slip of paper from her pocket, 'this is the number for your embassy's messaging service. They asked that you phone in as soon as possible.' She handed him the paper with an intent gaze. 'While I explain the code to Captain Fache, you need to make this call.'

Langdon studied the slip. It had a Paris phone number and extension on it. 'Thank you,' he said, feeling worried now. 'Where do I find a phone?'

Sophie began to pull a cell phone from her sweater pocket, but Fache waved her off. He now looked like Mount Vesuvius about to erupt. Without taking his eyes off Sophie, he produced his own cell phone and held it out. 'This line is secure, Mr Langdon. You may use it.'

Langdon felt mystified by Fache's anger with the young woman. Feeling uneasy, he accepted the captain's phone. Fache immediately marched Sophie several steps away and began chastising her in hushed tones. Disliking the captain more and more, Langdon turned away from the odd confrontation and switched on the cell phone. Checking the slip of paper Sophie had given him, Langdon dialled the number.

The line began to ring.

One ring . . . two rings . . . three rings . . .

Finally the call connected.

Langdon expected to hear an embassy operator, but he found himself instead listening to an answering machine. Oddly, the voice on the tape was familiar. It was that of Sophie Neveu.

'*Bonjour, vous êtes bien chez Sophie Neveu,*' the woman's voice said. '*Je suis absente pour le moment, mais . . .*'

Confused, Langdon turned back toward Sophie. 'I'm sorry, Ms Neveu? I think you may have given me—'

'No, that's the right number,' Sophie interjected quickly, as if anticipating Langdon's confusion. 'The embassy has an automated message system. You have to dial an access code to pick up your messages.'

Langdon stared. 'But—'

'It's the three-digit code on the paper I gave you.'

Langdon opened his mouth to explain the bizarre error, but Sophie flashed him a silencing glare that lasted only an instant. Her green eyes sent a crystal-clear message.

Don't ask questions. Just do it.

Bewildered, Langdon punched in the extension on the slip of paper: 454.

Sophie's outgoing message immediately cut off, and Langdon heard an electronic voice announce in French: 'You have *one* new message.' Apparently, 454 was Sophie's remote access code for picking up her messages while away from home.

I'm picking up this woman's messages?

Langdon could hear the tape rewinding now. Finally, it stopped, and the machine engaged. Langdon listened as the message began to play. Again, the voice on the line was Sophie's.

'Mr Langdon,' the message began in a fearful whisper. 'Do *not* react to this message. Just listen calmly. You are in danger right now. Follow my directions very closely.'

10

Silas sat behind the wheel of the black Audi the Teacher had arranged for him and gazed out at the great Church of Saint-Sulpice. Lit from beneath by banks of floodlights, the church's two bell towers rose like stalwart sentinels above the building's long body. On either flank, a shadowy row of sleek buttresses jutted out like the ribs of a beautiful beast.

The heathens used a house of God to conceal their keystone. Again the brotherhood had confirmed their legendary reputation for illusion and deceit. Silas was looking forward to finding the keystone and giving it to the Teacher so they could recover what the brotherhood had long ago stolen from the faithful.

How powerful that will make Opus Dei.

Parking the Audi on the deserted Place Saint-Sulpice, Silas exhaled, telling himself to clear his mind for the task at hand. His broad back still ached from the corporal mortification he had endured earlier today, and yet the pain was inconsequential compared with the anguish of his life before Opus Dei had saved him.

Still, the memories haunted his soul.

Release your hatred, Silas commanded himself. *Forgive those who trespassed against you.*

Looking up at the stone towers of Saint-Sulpice, Silas fought that familiar undertow . . . that force that often dragged his mind back in time, locking him once again in the prison that had been his world as a young man. The memories of purgatory came as they always did, like a tempest to his senses . . . the reek of rotting cabbage, the stench of death, human urine and faeces. The cries of hopelessness against the howling wind of the Pyrenees and the soft sobs of forgotten men.

Andorra, he thought, feeling his muscles tighten.

Incredibly, it was in that barren and forsaken suzerain between Spain and France, shivering in his stone cell, wanting only to die, that Silas had been saved.

He had not realized it at the time.

The light came long after the thunder.

His name was not Silas then, although he didn't recall the name his parents had given him. He had left home when he was seven. His drunken father, a burly dockworker, enraged by the arrival of an albino son, beat his mother regularly, blaming her for the boy's embarrassing condition. When the boy tried to defend her, he too was badly beaten.

One night, there was a horrific fight, and his mother never got up. The boy stood over his lifeless mother and felt an unbearable upwelling of guilt for permitting it to happen.

This is my fault!

As if some kind of demon were controlling his body, the boy walked to the kitchen and grasped a butcher's knife. Hypnotically, he moved to the bedroom where his father lay on the bed in a drunken stupor. Without a word, the boy stabbed him in the back. His father cried out in pain and tried to roll over, but his son stabbed him again, over and over until the apartment fell quiet.

The boy fled home but found the streets of Marseilles equally unfriendly. His strange appearance made him an outcast among the other young runaways, and he was forced to live alone in the basement of a dilapidated factory, eating stolen fruit and raw fish from the dock. His only companions were tattered magazines he found in the trash, and he taught himself to read them. Over time, he grew strong. When he was twelve, another drifter – a girl twice his age – mocked him on the streets and attempted to steal his food. The girl found herself pummeled to within inches of her life. When the authorities pulled the boy off her, they gave him an ultimatum – leave Marseilles or go to juvenile prison.

The boy moved down the coast to Toulon. Over time, the looks of pity on the streets turned to looks of fear. The boy had grown to a powerful young man. When people passed by, he could hear them whispering to one another. *A ghost,* they would say, their eyes wide with fright as they stared at his white skin. *A ghost with the eyes of a devil!*

And he felt like a ghost . . . transparent . . . floating from seaport to seaport.

People seemed to look right through him.

At eighteen, in a port town, while attempting to steal a case of cured ham from a cargo ship, he was caught by a pair of crewmen. The two sailors who began to beat him smelled of beer, just as his father had. The memories of fear and hatred surfaced like a monster from the deep. The young man broke the first sailor's neck with his bare hands, and only the arrival of the police saved the second sailor from a similar fate.

Two months later, in shackles, he arrived at a prison in Andorra.

You are as white as a ghost, the inmates ridiculed as the guards marched him in, naked and cold. *Mira el espectro! Perhaps the ghost will pass right through these walls!*

Over the course of twelve years, his flesh and soul withered until he knew he had become transparent.

I am a ghost.

I am weightless.

Yo soy un espectro . . . pálido como un fantasma . . . caminando este mundo a solas.

One night the ghost awoke to the screams of other inmates. He didn't know what invisible force was shaking the floor on which he slept, nor what mighty hand was trembling the mortar of his stone cell, but as he jumped to his feet, a large boulder toppled onto the very spot where he had been sleeping. Looking up to see where the stone had come from, he saw a hole in the trembling wall, and beyond it, a vision he had not seen in over ten years. The moon.

Even while the earth still shook, the ghost found himself scrambling through a narrow tunnel, staggering out into an expansive vista, and tumbling down a barren mountainside into the woods. He ran all night, always downward, delirious with hunger and exhaustion.

Skirting the edges of consciousness, he found himself at dawn in a clearing where train tracks cut a swath across the forest. Following the rails, he moved on as if dreaming. Seeing an empty freight car, he crawled in for shelter and rest. When he awoke the train was moving. *How long? How far?* A pain was growing in his gut. *Am I dying?* He slept again. This time he awoke to someone yelling, beating him, throwing him out of the freight car. Bloody, he wandered the outskirts of a small village looking in vain for food. Finally, his body too weak to take another step, he lay down by the side of the road and slipped into unconsciousness.

The light came slowly, and the ghost wondered how long he had been dead. *A day? Three days?* It didn't matter. His bed was soft like a cloud, and the air around him smelled sweet with candles. Jesus was there, staring down at him. *I am here,* Jesus said. *The stone has been rolled aside, and you are born again.*

He slept and awoke. Fog shrouded his thoughts. He had never believed in heaven, and yet Jesus was watching over him. Food appeared beside his bed, and the ghost ate it, almost able to feel the flesh materializing on his bones. He slept again. When he awoke, Jesus was still smiling down, speaking. *You are saved, my son. Blessed are those who follow my path.*

Again, he slept.

It was a scream of anguish that startled the ghost from his slumber. His body leapt out of bed, staggered down a hallway toward the sounds of shouting. He entered a kitchen and saw a large man beating a smaller man. Without knowing why, the ghost grabbed the large man and hurled him backward against a wall. The man fled, leaving the ghost standing over the body of a young man in priest's robes. The priest had a badly shattered nose. Lifting the bloody priest, the ghost carried him to a couch.

'Thank you, my friend,' the priest said in awkward French. 'The offertory money is tempting for thieves. You speak French in your sleep. Do you also speak Spanish?'

The ghost shook his head.

'What is your name?' he continued in broken French.

The ghost could not remember the name his parents had given him. All he heard were the taunting gibes of the prison guards.

The priest smiled. '*No hay problema*. My name is Manuel Aringarosa. I am a missionary from Madrid. I was sent here to build a church for the Obra de Dios.'

'Where am I?' His voice sounded hollow.

'Oviedo. In the north of Spain.'

'How did I get here?'

'Someone left you on my doorstep. You were ill. I fed you. You've been here many days.'

The ghost studied his young caretaker. Years had passed since anyone had shown any kindness. 'Thank you, Father.'

The priest touched his bloody lip. 'It is I who am thankful, my friend.'

When the ghost awoke in the morning, his world felt clearer. He gazed up at the crucifix on the wall above his bed. Although it no longer spoke to him, he felt a comforting aura in its presence. Sitting up, he was surprised to find a newspaper clipping on his bedside table. The article was in French, a week old. When he read the story, he was filled with fear. It told of an earthquake in the mountains that had destroyed a prison and freed many dangerous criminals.

His heart began pounding. *The priest knows who I am!* The emotion he felt was one he had not felt for some time. Shame. Guilt. It was accompanied by the fear of being caught. He jumped from his bed. *Where do I run?*

'The Book of Acts,' a voice said from the door.

The ghost turned, frightened.

The young priest was smiling as he entered. His nose was awkwardly bandaged, and he was holding out an old Bible. 'I found one in French for you. The chapter is marked.'

Uncertain, the ghost took the Bible and looked at the chapter the priest had marked.

Acts 16.

The verses told of a prisoner named Silas who lay naked and beaten in his cell, singing hymns to God. When the ghost reached Verse 26, he gasped in shock.

'*. . . And suddenly, there was a great earthquake, so that the foundations of the prison were shaken, and all the doors fell open.*'

His eyes shot up at the priest.

The priest smiled warmly. 'From now on, my friend, if you have no other name, I shall call you Silas.'

The ghost nodded blankly. *Silas.* He had been given flesh. *My name is Silas.*

'It's time for breakfast,' the priest said. 'You will need your strength if you are to help me build this church.'

*

Twenty thousand feet above the Mediterranean, Alitalia flight 1618 bounced in turbulence, causing passengers to shift nervously. Bishop Aringarosa barely noticed. His thoughts were with the future of Opus Dei. Eager to know how plans in Paris were progressing, he wished he could phone Silas. But he could not. The Teacher had seen to that.

'It is for your own safety,' the Teacher had explained, speaking in English with a French accent. 'I am familiar enough with electronic communications to know they can be intercepted. The results could be disastrous for you.'

Aringarosa knew he was right. The Teacher seemed an exceptionally careful man. He had not revealed his own identity to Aringarosa, and yet he had proven himself a man well worth obeying. After all, he had somehow obtained very secret information. *The names of the brotherhood's four top members!* This had been one of the coups that convinced the bishop the Teacher was truly capable of delivering the astonishing prize he claimed he could unearth.

'Bishop,' the Teacher had told him, 'I have made all the arrangements. For my plan to succeed, you must allow Silas to answer *only* to me for several days. The two of you will not speak. I will communicate with him through secure channels.'

'You will treat him with respect?'

'A man of faith deserves the highest.'

'Excellent. Then I understand. Silas and I shall not speak until this is over.'

'I do this to protect your identity, Silas's identity, and my investment.'

'Your investment?'

'Bishop, if your own eagerness to keep abreast of progress puts you in jail, then you will be unable to pay me my fee.'

The bishop smiled. 'A fine point. Our desires are in accord. Godspeed.'

Twenty million euros, the bishop thought, now gazing out the plane's window. The sum was approximately the same number of US dollars. *A pittance for something so powerful.*

He felt a renewed confidence that the Teacher and Silas would not fail. Money and faith were powerful motivators.

11

'*Une plaisanterie numérique?*' Bezu Fache was livid, glaring at Sophie Neveu in disbelief. *A numeric joke?* 'Your professional assessment of Saunière's code is that it is some kind of mathematical prank?'

Fache was in utter incomprehension of this woman's gall. Not only had she just barged in on Fache without permission, but she was now trying to convince him that Saunière, in his final moments of life, had been inspired to leave a mathematical gag?

'This code,' Sophie explained in rapid French, 'is simplistic to the point of absurdity. Jacques Saunière must have known we would see through it immediately.' She pulled a scrap of paper from her sweater pocket and handed it to Fache. 'Here is the decryption.'

Fache looked at the card.

$$1-1-2-3-5-8-13-21$$

'This is it?' he snapped. 'All you did was put the numbers in increasing order!'

Sophie actually had the nerve to give a satisfied smile. 'Exactly.'

Fache's tone lowered to a guttural rumble. 'Agent Neveu, I have no idea where the hell you're going with this, but I suggest you get there fast.' He shot an anxious glance at Langdon, who stood nearby with the phone pressed to his ear, apparently still listening to his phone message from the US Embassy. From Langdon's ashen expression, Fache sensed the news was bad.

'Captain,' Sophie said, her tone dangerously defiant, 'the sequence of numbers you have in your hand happens to be one of the most famous mathematical progressions in history.'

Fache was not aware there even existed a mathematical progression that qualified as famous, and he certainly didn't appreciate Sophie's off-hand tone.

'This is the Fibonacci sequence,' she declared, nodding toward the piece of paper in Fache's hand. 'A progression in which each term is equal to the sum of the two preceding terms.'

Fache studied the numbers. Each term was indeed the sum of the two previous, and yet Fache could not imagine what the relevance of all this was to Saunière's death.

'Mathematician Leonardo Fibonacci created this succession of numbers in the thirteenth century. Obviously there can be no coincidence that *all* of the numbers Saunière wrote on the floor belong to Fibonacci's famous sequence.'

Fache stared at the young woman for several moments. 'Fine, if there is no coincidence, would you tell me *why* Jacques Saunière chose to do this. What is he saying? What does this *mean?*'

She shrugged. 'Absolutely nothing. That's the point. It's a simplistic cryptographic joke. Like taking the words of a famous poem and shuffling them at random to see if anyone recognizes what all the words have in common.'

Fache took a menacing step forward, placing his face only inches from Sophie's. 'I certainly hope you have a much more satisfying explanation than *that.*'

Sophie's soft features grew surprisingly stern as she leaned in. 'Captain, considering what you have at stake here tonight, I thought you might appreciate knowing that Jacques Saunière might be playing games with you. Apparently not. I'll inform the director of Cryptography you no longer need our services.'

With that, she turned on her heel, and marched off the way she had come.

Stunned, Fache watched her disappear into the darkness. *Is she out of her mind?* Sophie Neveu had just redefined *le suicide professionnel.*

Fache turned to Langdon, who was still on the phone, looking more concerned than before, listening intently to his phone message. *The US Embassy.* Bezu Fache despised many things . . . but few drew more wrath than the US Embassy.

Fache and the ambassador locked horns regularly over shared affairs of state – their most common battleground being law enforcement for visiting Americans. Almost daily, DCPJ arrested American exchange students in possession of drugs, US businessmen for soliciting underage prostitutes, American tourists for shoplifting or destruction of property. Legally, the US Embassy could intervene and extradite guilty citizens back to the United States, where they received nothing more than a slap on the wrist.

And the embassy invariably did just that.

L'émasculation de la Police Judiciaire, Fache called it. *Paris Match* had run a cartoon recently depicting Fache as a police dog, trying to bite an American criminal, but unable to reach because it was chained to the US Embassy.

Not tonight, Fache told himself. *There is far too much at stake.*

By the time Robert Langdon hung up the phone, he looked ill.

'Is everything all right?' Fache asked.

Weakly, Langdon shook his head.

Bad news from home, Fache sensed, noticing Langdon was sweating slightly as Fache took back his cell phone.

'An accident,' Langdon stammered, looking at Fache with a strange expression. 'A friend . . .' He hesitated. 'I'll need to fly home first thing in the morning.'

Fache had no doubt the shock on Langdon's face was genuine, and yet he sensed another emotion there too, as if a distant fear were suddenly simmering in the American's eyes. 'I'm sorry to hear that,' Fache said, watching Langdon closely. 'Would you like to sit down?' He motioned toward one of the viewing benches in the gallery.

Langdon nodded absently and took a few steps toward the bench. He paused, looking more confused with every moment. 'Actually, I think I'd like to use the toilet.'

Fache frowned inwardly at the delay. 'The toilet. Of course. Let's take a break for a few minutes.' He motioned back down the long hallway in the direction they had come from. 'The toilets are back toward the curator's office.'

Langdon hesitated, pointing in the other direction toward the far end of the Grand Gallery corridor. 'I believe there's a much closer toilet at the end.'

Fache realized Langdon was right. They were two thirds of the way down, and the Grand Gallery dead-ended at a pair of toilets. 'Shall I accompany you?'

Langdon shook his head, already moving deeper into the gallery. 'Not necessary. I think I'd like a few minutes alone.'

Fache was not wild about the idea of Langdon wandering alone down the remaining length of corridor, but he took comfort in knowing the Grand Gallery was a dead end whose only exit was at the other end – the gate under which they had entered. Although French fire regulations required several emergency stairwells for a space this large, those stairwells had been sealed automatically when Saunière tripped the security system. Granted, that system had now been reset, unlocking the stairwells, but it didn't matter – the external doors, if opened, would set off fire alarms and were guarded outside by DCPJ agents. Langdon could not possibly leave without Fache knowing about it.

'I need to return to Mr Saunière's office for a moment,' Fache said. 'Please come and find me directly, Mr Langdon. There is more we need to discuss.'

Langdon gave a quiet wave as he disappeared into the darkness.

Turning, Fache marched angrily in the opposite direction. Arriving at the gate, he slid under, exited the Grand Gallery, marched down the hall, and stormed into the command centre at Saunière's office.

'Who gave the approval to let Sophie Neveu into this building!' Fache bellowed.

Collet was the first to answer. 'She told the guards outside she'd broken the code.'

Fache looked around. 'Is she gone?'

'She's not with you?'

'She left.' Fache glanced out at the darkened hallway. Apparently Sophie had been in no mood to stop by and chat with the other officers on her way out.

For a moment, Fache considered radioing the guards in the entresol and telling them to stop Sophie and drag her back up here before she could leave the premises. He thought better of it. That was only his pride talking . . . wanting the last word. He'd had enough distractions tonight.

Deal with Agent Neveu later, he told himself, already looking forward to firing her.

Pushing Sophie from his mind, Fache stared for a moment at the miniature knight standing on Saunière's desk. Then he turned back to Collet. 'Do you have him?'

Collet gave a curt nod and spun the laptop toward Fache. The red dot was clearly visible on the floor plan overlay, blinking methodically in a room marked TOILETTES PUBLIQUES.

'Good,' Fache said, lighting a cigarette and stalking into the hall. 'I've got a phone call to make. Be damned sure the toilet is the only place Langdon goes.'

12

Robert Langdon felt light-headed as he trudged toward the end of the Grand Gallery. Sophie's phone message played over and over in his mind. At the end of the corridor, illuminated signs bearing the international stick-figure symbols for toilets guided him through a maze-like series of dividers displaying Italian drawings and hiding the toilets from sight.

Finding the men's room door, Langdon entered and turned on the lights.

The room was empty.

Walking to the sink, he splashed cold water on his face and tried to wake up. Harsh fluorescent lights glared off the stark tiles, and the room smelled of ammonia. As he towelled off, the door creaked open behind him. He spun.

Sophie Neveu entered, her green eyes flashing fear. 'Thank God you came. We don't have much time.'

Langdon stood beside the sinks, staring in bewilderment at DCPJ cryptographer Sophie Neveu. Only minutes ago, Langdon had listened to her phone message, thinking the newly arrived cryptographer must be insane. And yet, the more he listened, the more he sensed Sophie Neveu was speaking in earnest. *Do not react to this message. Just listen calmly. You are in danger right now. Follow my directions very closely.* Filled with uncertainty, Langdon had decided to do exactly as Sophie advised. He told Fache that the phone message was regarding an injured friend back home. Then he had asked to use the toilet at the end of the Grand Gallery.

Sophie stood before him now, still catching her breath after doubling back to the toilets. In the fluorescent lights, Langdon was surprised to see that her strong air actually radiated from unexpectedly soft features. Only her gaze was sharp, and the juxtaposition conjured images of a multi-layered Renoir portrait . . . veiled but distinct, with a boldness that somehow retained its shroud of mystery.

'I wanted to warn you, Mr Langdon . . .' Sophie began, still catching her breath, 'that you are *sous surveillance cachée*. Under a guarded observation.' As she spoke, her accented English resonated off the tiled walls, giving her voice a hollow quality.

'But . . . why?' Langdon demanded. Sophie had already given him an explanation on the phone, but he wanted to hear it from her lips.

'Because,' she said, stepping toward him, 'Fache's primary suspect in this murder is *you*.'

Langdon was braced for the words, and yet they still sounded utterly ridiculous. According to Sophie, Langdon had been called to the Louvre tonight not as a symbologist but rather as a *suspect* and was currently the unwitting target of one of DCPJ's favourite interrogation methods – *surveillance cachée* – a deft deception in which the police calmly invited a suspect to a crime scene and interviewed him in hopes he would get nervous and mistakenly incriminate himself.

'Look in your jacket's left pocket,' Sophie said. 'You'll find proof they are watching you.'

Langdon felt his apprehension rising. *Look in my pocket?* It sounded like some kind of cheap magic trick.

'Just look.'

Bewildered, Langdon reached his hand into his tweed jacket's left pocket – one he never used. Feeling around inside, he found nothing. *What the devil did you expect?* He began wondering if Sophie might just be insane after all. Then his fingers brushed something unexpected. Small and hard. Pinching the tiny object between his fingers, Langdon pulled it out and stared in astonishment. It was a metallic, button-shaped disk, about the size of a watch battery. He had never seen it before. 'What the . . . ?'

'GPS tracking dot,' Sophie said. 'Continuously transmits its location to a Global Positioning System satellite that DCPJ can monitor. We use them to monitor people's locations. It's accurate within two feet anywhere on the globe. They have you on an electronic leash. The agent who picked you up at the hotel slipped it inside your pocket before you left your room.'

Langdon flashed back to the hotel room . . . his quick shower, getting dressed, the DCPJ agent politely holding out Langdon's tweed coat as they left the room. *It's cool outside, Mr Langdon,* the agent had said. *Spring in Paris is not all your song boasts.* Langdon had thanked him and donned the jacket.

Sophie's olive gaze was keen. 'I didn't tell you about the tracking dot earlier because I didn't want you checking your pocket in front of Fache. He can't know you've found it.'

Langdon had no idea how to respond.

'They tagged you with GPS because they thought you might run.' She paused. 'In fact, they *hoped* you would run; it would make their case stronger.'

'Why would I run!' Langdon demanded. 'I'm innocent!'

'Fache feels otherwise.'

Angrily, Langdon stalked toward the trash receptacle to dispose of the tracking dot.

'No!' Sophie grabbed his arm and stopped him. 'Leave it in your pocket.

If you throw it out, the signal will stop moving, and they'll know you found the dot. The only reason Fache left you alone is because he can monitor where you are. If he thinks you've discovered what he's doing . . .' Sophie did not finish the thought. Instead, she pried the metallic disk from Langdon's hand and slid it back into the pocket of his tweed coat. 'The dot stays with you. At least for the moment.'

Langdon felt lost. 'How the hell could Fache actually believe I killed Jacques Saunière!'

'He has some fairly persuasive reasons to suspect you.' Sophie's expression was grim. 'There is a piece of evidence here that you have not yet seen. Fache has kept it carefully hidden from you.'

Langdon could only stare.

'Do you recall the three lines of text that Saunière wrote on the floor?'

Langdon nodded. The numbers and words were imprinted on Langdon's mind.

Sophie's voice dropped to a whisper now. 'Unfortunately, what you saw was not the entire message. There was a *fourth* line that Fache photographed and then wiped clean before you arrived.'

Although Langdon knew the soluble ink of a watermark stylus could easily be wiped away, he could not imagine why Fache would erase evidence.

'The last line of the message,' Sophie said, 'was something Fache did not want you to know about.' She paused. 'At least not until he was done with you.'

Sophie produced a computer printout of a photo from her sweater pocket and began unfolding it. 'Fache uploaded images of the crime scene to the Cryptology Department earlier tonight in hopes we could figure out what Saunière's message was trying to say. This is a photo of the complete message.' She handed the page to Langdon.

Bewildered, Langdon looked at the image. The close-up photo revealed the glowing message on the parquet floor. The final line hit Langdon like a kick in the gut.

13-3-2-21-1-1-8-5
O, Draconian devil!
Oh, lame saint!
P.S. Find Robert Langdon

13

For several seconds, Langdon stared in wonder at the photograph of Saunière's postscript. *P.S. Find Robert Langdon.* He felt as if the floor were tilting beneath his feet. *Saunière left a postscript with my name on it?* In his wildest dreams, Langdon could not fathom why.

'Now do you understand,' Sophie said, her eyes urgent, 'why Fache ordered you here tonight, and why you are his primary suspect?'

The only thing Langdon understood at the moment was why Fache had looked so smug when Langdon suggested Saunière would have accused his killer by name.

Find Robert Langdon.

'Why would Saunière write this?' Langdon demanded, his confusion now giving way to anger. 'Why would I want to kill Jacques Saunière?'

'Fache has yet to uncover a motive, but he has been recording his entire conversation with you tonight in hopes you might reveal one.'

Langdon opened his mouth, but still no words came.

'He's fitted with a miniature microphone,' Sophie explained. 'It's connected to a transmitter in his pocket that radios the signal back to the command post.'

'This is impossible,' Langdon stammered. 'I have an alibi. I went directly back to my hotel after my lecture. You can ask the hotel desk.'

'Fache already did. His report shows you retrieving your room key from the concierge at about ten-thirty. Unfortunately, the time of the murder was closer to eleven. You easily could have left your hotel room unseen.'

'This is insanity! Fache has no evidence!'

Sophie's eyes widened as if to say: *No evidence?* 'Mr Langdon, your name is written on the floor beside the body, and Saunière's date book says you were with him at approximately the time of the murder.' She paused. 'Fache has more than enough evidence to take you into custody for questioning.'

Langdon suddenly sensed that he needed a lawyer. 'I didn't do this.'

Sophie sighed. 'This is not American television, Mr Langdon. In France, the laws protect the police, not criminals. Unfortunately, in this case, there is also the media consideration. Jacques Saunière was a very prominent and well-loved figure in Paris, and his murder will be news in the morning. Fache will be under immediate pressure to make a statement, and he looks a lot better having a suspect in custody already. Whether or not you are guilty, you most certainly will be held by DCPJ until they can figure out what really happened.'

Langdon felt like a caged animal. 'Why are you telling me all this?'

'Because, Mr Langdon, I believe you are innocent.' Sophie looked away for a moment and then back into his eyes. 'And also because it is partially *my* fault that you're in trouble.'

'I'm sorry? It's *your* fault Saunière is trying to frame me?'

'Saunière wasn't trying to frame you. It was a mistake. That message on the floor was meant for me.'

Langdon needed a minute to process that one. 'I beg your pardon?'

'That message wasn't for the police. He wrote it for *me*. I think he was forced to do everything in such a hurry that he just didn't realize how it would look to the police.' She paused. 'The numbered code is meaningless. Saunière wrote it to make sure the investigation included cryptographers, ensuring that *I* would know as soon as possible what had happened to him.'

Langdon felt himself losing touch fast. Whether or not Sophie Neveu had lost her mind was at this point up for grabs, but at least Langdon now understood why she was trying to help him. *P.S. Find Robert Langdon.* She apparently believed the curator had left her a cryptic postscript telling her to find Langdon. 'But why do you think his message was for you?'

'*The Vitruvian Man,*' she said flatly. 'That particular sketch has always been my favourite Da Vinci work. Tonight he used it to catch my attention.'

'Hold on. You're saying the curator *knew* your favourite piece of art?'

She nodded. 'I'm sorry. This is all coming out of order. Jacques Saunière and I . . .'

Sophie's voice caught, and Langdon heard a sudden melancholy there, a painful past, simmering just below the surface. Sophie and Jacques Saunière apparently had some kind of special relationship. Langdon studied the beautiful young woman before him, well aware that aging men in France often took young mistresses. Even so, Sophie Neveu as a 'kept woman' somehow didn't seem to fit.

'We had a falling-out ten years ago,' Sophie said, her voice a whisper now. 'We've barely spoken since. Tonight, when Crypto got the call that he had been murdered, and I saw the images of his body and text on the floor, I realized he was trying to send me a message.'

'Because of *The Vitruvian Man?*'

'Yes. And the letters P.S.'

'*Post Script?*'

She shook her head. 'P.S. are my initials.'

'But your name is Sophie Neveu.'

She looked away. 'P.S. is the nickname he called me when I lived with him.' She blushed. 'It stood for *Princesse Sophie.*'

Langdon had no response.

'Silly, I know,' she said. 'But it was years ago. When I was a little girl.'

'You knew him when you were a little *girl?*'

'Quite well,' she said, her eyes welling now with emotion. 'Jacques Saunière was my grandfather.'

14

'Where's Langdon?' Fache demanded, exhaling the last of a cigarette as he paced back into the command post.

'Still in the men's room, sir.' Lieutenant Collet had been expecting the question.

Fache grumbled, 'Taking his time, I see.'

The captain eyed the GPS dot over Collet's shoulder, and Collet could almost hear the wheels turning. Fache was fighting the urge to go and check on Langdon. Ideally, the subject of an observation was allowed the most time and freedom possible, lulling him into a false sense of security. Langdon needed to return of his own volition. Still, it had been almost ten minutes.

Too long.

'Any chance Langdon is onto us?' Fache asked.

Collet shook his head. 'We're still seeing small movements inside the men's room, so the GPS dot is obviously still on him. Perhaps he feels ill? If he had found the dot, he would have removed it and tried to run.'

Fache checked his watch. 'Fine.'

Still Fache seemed preoccupied. All evening, Collet had sensed an atypical intensity in his captain. Usually detached and cool under pressure, Fache tonight seemed emotionally engaged, as if this were somehow a personal matter for him.

Not surprising, Collet thought. *Fache needs this arrest desperately.* Recently the Board of Ministers and the media had become more openly critical of Fache's aggressive tactics, his clashes with powerful foreign embassies, and his gross overbudgeting on new technologies. Tonight, a high-tech, high-profile arrest of an American would go a long way to silence Fache's critics, helping him secure the job a few more years until he could retire with the lucrative pension. *God knows he needs the pension,* Collet thought. Fache's zeal for technology had hurt him both professionally and personally. Fache was rumoured to have invested his entire savings in the technology craze a few years back and lost his shirt. *And Fache is a man who wears only the finest shirts.*

Tonight, there was still plenty of time. Sophie Neveu's odd interruption, though unfortunate, had been only a minor wrinkle. She was gone now, and Fache still had cards to play. He had yet to inform Langdon that his name had been scrawled on the floor by the victim. *P.S. Find Robert Langdon.* The American's reaction to that little bit of evidence would be telling indeed.

'Captain?' one of the DCPJ agents now called from across the office. 'I think you had better take this call.' He was holding out a telephone receiver, looking concerned.

'Who is it?' Fache said.

The agent frowned. 'It's the director of our Cryptography Department.'

'And?'

'It's about Sophie Neveu, sir. Something is not quite right.'

15

It was time.

Silas felt strong as he stepped from the black Audi, the nighttime breeze rustling his loose-fitting robe. *The winds of change are in the air.* He knew the task before him would require more finesse than force, and he left his handgun in the car. The thirteen-round Heckler Koch USP 40 had been provided by the Teacher.

A weapon of death has no place in a house of God.

The plaza before the great church was deserted at this hour, the only visible souls on the far side of Place Saint-Sulpice a couple of teenage hookers showing their wares to the late night tourist traffic. Their nubile bodies sent a familiar longing to Silas's loins. His thigh flexed instinctively, causing the barbed *cilice* belt to cut painfully into his flesh.

The lust evaporated instantly. For ten years now, Silas had faithfully denied himself all sexual indulgence, even self-administered. It was *The Way*. He knew he had sacrificed much to follow Opus Dei, but he had received much more in return. A vow of celibacy and the relinquishment of all personal assets hardly seemed a sacrifice. Considering the poverty from which he had come and the sexual horrors he had endured in prison, celibacy was a welcome change.

Now, having returned to France for the first time since being arrested and shipped to prison in Andorra, Silas could feel his homeland testing him, dragging violent memories from his redeemed soul. *You have been reborn,* he reminded himself. His service to God today had required the sin of murder, and it was a sacrifice Silas knew he would have to hold silently in his heart for all eternity.

The measure of your faith is the measure of the pain you can endure, the Teacher had told him. Silas was no stranger to pain and felt eager to prove himself to the Teacher, the one who had assured him his actions were ordained by a higher power.

'*Hago la obra de Dios,*' Silas whispered, moving now toward the church entrance.

Pausing in the shadow of the massive doorway, he took a deep breath. It was not until this instant that he truly realized what he was about to do, and what awaited him inside.

The keystone. It will lead us to our final goal.

He raised his ghost-white fist and banged three times on the door.

Moments later, the bolts of the enormous wooden portal began to move.

16

Sophie wondered how long it would take Fache to figure out she had not left the building. Seeing that Langdon was clearly overwhelmed, Sophie questioned whether she had done the right thing by cornering him here in the men's room.

What else was I supposed to do?

She pictured her grandfather's body, naked and spread-eagled on the floor. There was a time when he had meant the world to her, yet tonight, Sophie was surprised to feel almost no sadness for the man. Jacques Saunière was a stranger to her now. Their relationship had evaporated in a single instant one March night when she was twenty-two. *Ten years ago.* Sophie had come home a few days early from graduate university in England and mistakenly witnessed her grandfather engaged in something Sophie was obviously not supposed to see. It was an image she barely could believe to this day.

If I hadn't seen it with my own eyes . . .

Too ashamed and stunned to endure her grandfather's pained attempts to explain, Sophie immediately moved out on her own, taking money she had saved, and getting a small flat with some roommates. She vowed never to speak to anyone about what she had seen. Her grandfather tried desperately to reach her, sending cards and letters, begging Sophie to meet him so he could explain. *Explain how!?* Sophie never responded except once – to forbid him ever to call her or try to meet her in public. She was afraid his explanation would be more terrifying than the incident itself.

Incredibly, Saunière had never given up on her, and Sophie now possessed a decade's worth of correspondence unopened in a dresser drawer. To her grandfather's credit, he had never once disobeyed her request and phoned her.

Until this afternoon.

'Sophie?' His voice had sounded startlingly old on her answering machine. 'I have abided by your wishes for so long . . . and it pains me to call, but I must speak to you. Something terrible has happened.'

Standing in the kitchen of her Paris flat, Sophie felt a chill to hear him again after all these years. His gentle voice brought back a flood of fond childhood memories.

'Sophie, please listen.' He was speaking English to her, as he always did when she was a little girl. *Practise French at school. Practise English at home.* 'You cannot be mad for ever. Have you not read the letters that I've sent all these years? Do you not yet understand?' He paused. 'We must speak at once. Please grant your grandfather this one wish. Call me at the Louvre. Right away. I believe you and I are in grave danger.'

Sophie stared at the answering machine. *Danger?* What was he talking about?

'Princess . . .' Her grandfather's voice cracked with an emotion Sophie could not place. 'I know I've kept things from you, and I know it has cost me your love. But it was for your own safety. Now you must know the truth. Please, I must tell you the truth about your family.'

Sophie suddenly could hear her own heart. *My family?* Sophie's parents had died when she was only four. Their car went off a bridge into fast-moving water. Her grandmother and younger brother had also been in the car, and Sophie's entire family had been erased in an instant. She had a box of newspaper clippings to confirm it.

His words had sent an unexpected surge of longing through her bones. *My family!* In that fleeting instant, Sophie saw images from the dream that had awoken her countless times when she was a little girl: *My family is alive! They are coming home!* But, as in her dream, the pictures evaporated into oblivion.

Your family is dead, Sophie. They are not coming home.

'Sophie . . .' her grandfather said on the machine. 'I have been waiting for years to tell you. Waiting for the right moment, but now time has run out. Call me at the Louvre. As soon as you get this. I'll wait here all night. I fear we both may be in danger. There's so much you need to know.'

The message ended.

In the silence, Sophie stood trembling for what felt like minutes. As she considered her grandfather's message, only one possibility made sense, and his true intent dawned.

It was bait.

Obviously, her grandfather wanted desperately to see her. He was trying anything. Her disgust for the man deepened. Sophie wondered if maybe he had fallen terminally ill and had decided to attempt any ploy he could think of to get Sophie to visit him one last time. If so, he had chosen wisely.

My family.

Now, standing in the darkness of the Louvre men's room, Sophie could hear the echoes of this afternoon's phone message. *Sophie, we both may be in danger. Call me.*

She had not called him. Nor had she planned to. Now, however, her scepticism had been deeply challenged. Her grandfather lay murdered inside his own museum. And he had written a code on the floor.

A code for *her*. Of this, she was certain.

Despite not understanding the meaning of his message, Sophie was certain its cryptic nature was additional proof that the words were intended for her. Sophie's passion and aptitude for cryptography were a product of growing up with Jacques Saunière – a fanatic himself for codes, word games and puzzles. *How many Sundays did we spend doing the cryptograms and crosswords in the newspaper?*

At the age of twelve, Sophie could finish the *Le Monde* crossword without any help, and her grandfather graduated her to crosswords in English, mathematical puzzles and substitution ciphers. Sophie devoured them all. Eventually she turned her passion into a profession by becoming a code-breaker for the Judicial Police.

Tonight, the cryptographer in Sophie was forced to respect the efficiency with which her grandfather had used a simple code to unite two total strangers – Sophie Neveu and Robert Langdon.

The question was *why?*

Unfortunately, from the bewildered look in Langdon's eyes, Sophie sensed the American had no more idea than she did why her grand-father had thrown them together.

She pressed again. 'You and my grandfather had planned to meet tonight. What about?'

Langdon looked truly perplexed. 'His secretary set the meeting and didn't offer any specific reason, and I didn't ask. I assumed he'd heard I would be lecturing on the pagan iconography of French cathedrals, was interested in the topic, and thought it would be fun to meet for drinks after the talk.'

Sophie didn't buy it. The connection was flimsy. Her grandfather knew more about pagan iconography than anyone else on earth. Moreover, he was an exceptionally private man, not someone prone to chatting with random American professors unless there were an important reason.

Sophie took a deep breath and probed further. 'My grandfather called me this afternoon and told me he and I were in grave danger. Does *that* mean anything to you?'

Langdon's blue eyes now clouded with concern. 'No, but considering what just happened . . .'

Sophie nodded. Considering tonight's events, she would be a fool not to be frightened. Feeling drained, she walked to the small plate-glass window at the far end of the bathroom and gazed out in silence through the mesh of alarm tape embedded in the glass. They were high up – forty feet at least.

Sighing, she raised her eyes and gazed out at Paris's dazzling landscape. On her left, across the Seine, the illuminated Eiffel Tower. Straight ahead, the Arc de Triomphe. And to the right, high atop the sloping rise of Montmartre, the graceful arabesque dome of Sacré-Coeur, its polished stone glowing white like a resplendent sanctuary.

Here at the westernmost tip of the Denon Wing, the north-south thoroughfare of Place du Carrousel ran almost flush with the building with only a narrow sidewalk separating it from the Louvre's outer wall. Far below, the usual caravan of the city's nighttime delivery trucks sat idling, waiting for the signals to change, their running lights seeming to twinkle mockingly up at Sophie.

'I don't know what to say,' Langdon said, coming up behind her. 'Your grandfather is obviously trying to tell us something. I'm sorry I'm so little help.'

Sophie turned from the window, sensing a sincere regret in Langdon's deep voice. Even with all the trouble around him, he obviously wanted to help her. *The teacher in him,* she thought, having read DCPJ's workup on their suspect. This was an academic who clearly despised not understanding.

We have that in common, she thought.

As a codebreaker, Sophie made her living extracting meaning from seemingly senseless data. Tonight, her best guess was that Robert Langdon, whether he knew it or not, possessed information that she desperately needed. *Princesse Sophie, Find Robert Langdon.* How much clearer could her grandfather's message be? Sophie needed more time with Langdon. Time to think. Time to sort out this mystery together. Unfortunately, time was running out.

Gazing up at Langdon, Sophie made the only play she could think of. 'Bezu Fache will be taking you into custody at any minute. I can get you out of this museum. But we need to act now.'

Langdon's eyes went wide. 'You want me to *run?*'

'It's the smartest thing you could do. If you let Fache take you into custody now, you'll spend weeks in a French jail while DCPJ and the US Embassy fight over which courts try your case. But if we get you out of here, and make it to your embassy, then your government will protect your rights while you and I prove you had nothing to do with this murder.'

Langdon looked not even vaguely convinced. 'Forget it! Fache has armed guards on every single exit! Even if we escape without being shot, running away only makes me look guilty. You need to tell Fache that the message on the floor was for *you,* and that my name is not there as an accusation.'

'I *will* do that,' Sophie said, speaking hurriedly, 'but after you're safely inside the US Embassy. It's only about a mile from here, and my car is parked just outside the museum. Dealing with Fache from here is too much of a gamble. Don't you see? Fache has made it his mission tonight to prove you are guilty. The only reason he postponed your arrest was to run this observance in hopes you did something that made his case stronger.'

'Exactly. Like *running!*'

The cell phone in Sophie's sweater pocket suddenly began ringing. *Fache probably.* She reached in her sweater and turned off the phone.

'Mr Langdon,' she said hurriedly, 'I need to ask you one last question.' *And your entire future may depend on it.* 'The writing on the floor is obviously not proof of your guilt, and yet Fache told our team he is *certain* you are his man. Can you think of any other reason he might be convinced you're guilty?'

Langdon was silent for several seconds. 'None whatsoever.'

Sophie sighed. *Which means Fache is lying.* Why, Sophie could not begin to imagine, but that was hardly the issue at this point. The fact remained that Bezu Fache was determined to put Robert Langdon behind bars tonight, at any cost. Sophie needed Langdon for herself, and it was this dilemma that left Sophie only one logical conclusion.

I need to get Langdon to the US Embassy.

Turning toward the window, Sophie gazed through the alarm mesh embedded in the plate glass, down the dizzying forty feet to the pavement below. A leap from this height would leave Langdon with a couple of broken legs. At best.

Nonetheless, Sophie made her decision.

Robert Langdon was about to escape the Louvre, whether he wanted to or not.

17

'What do you mean she's not answering?' Fache looked incredulous. 'You're calling her cell phone, right? I know she's carrying it.'

Collet had been trying to reach Sophie now for several minutes. 'Maybe her batteries are dead. Or her ringer's off.'

Fache had looked distressed ever since talking to the director of Cryptography on the phone. After hanging up, he had marched over to Collet and demanded he get Agent Neveu on the line. Now Collet had failed, and Fache was pacing like a caged lion.

'Why did Crypto call?' Collet now ventured.

Fache turned. 'To tell us they found no references to Draconian devils and lame saints.'

'That's all?'

'No, also to tell us that they had just identified the numerics as Fibonacci numbers, but they suspected the series was meaningless.'

Collet was confused. 'But they already sent Agent Neveu to tell us that.'

Fache shook his head. 'They didn't send Neveu.'

'What?'

'According to the director, at my orders he paged his entire team to look at the images I'd wired him. When Agent Neveu arrived, she took one look at the photos of Saunière and the code and left the office without a word. The director said he didn't question her behaviour because she was understandably upset by the photos.'

'Upset? She's never seen a picture of a dead body?'

Fache was silent a moment. 'I was not aware of this, and it seems neither was the director until a co-worker informed him, but apparently Sophie Neveu is Jacques Saunière's granddaughter.'

Collet was speechless.

'The director said she never once mentioned Saunière to him, and he assumed it was because she probably didn't want preferential treatment for having a famous grandfather.'

No wonder she was upset by the pictures. Collet could barely conceive of the unfortunate coincidence that called in a young woman to decipher a code written by a dead family member. Still, her actions made no sense.

'But she obviously recognized the numbers as Fibonacci numbers because she came here and *told* us. I don't understand why she would leave the office without telling anyone she had figured it out.'

Collet could think of only one scenario to explain the troubling developments: Saunière had written a numeric code on the floor in hopes Fache would involve cryptographers in the investigation, and therefore involve his own granddaughter. As for the rest of the message, was Saunière communicating in some way with his granddaughter? If so, what did the message tell her? And how did Langdon fit in?

Before Collet could ponder it any further, the silence of the deserted museum was shattered by an alarm. The bell sounded like it was coming from inside the Grand Gallery.

'*Alarme!*' one of the agents yelled, eyeing his feed from the Louvre security centre. '*Grande Galerie! Toilettes Messieurs!*'

Fache wheeled to Collet. 'Where's Langdon?'

'Still in the men's room!' Collet pointed to the blinking red dot on his laptop schematic. 'He must have broken the window!' Collet knew Langdon wouldn't get far. Although Paris fire codes required windows above fifteen meters in public buildings be breakable in case of fire, exiting a Louvre second-storey window without the help of a hook and ladder would be suicide. Furthermore, there were no trees or grass on the western end of the Denon Wing to cushion a fall. Directly beneath that toilet window, the two-lane Place du Carrousel ran within a few feet of the outer wall. 'My God,' Collet exclaimed, eyeing the screen. 'Langdon's moving to the window ledge!'

But Fache was already in motion. Yanking his Manurhin MR-93 revolver from his shoulder holster, the captain dashed out of the office.

Collet watched the screen in bewilderment as the blinking dot arrived at the window ledge and then did something utterly unexpected. The dot moved *outside* the perimeter of the building.

What's going on? he wondered. *Is Langdon out on a ledge or —*

'*Jesus!*' Collet jumped to his feet as the dot shot farther outside the wall. The signal seemed to shudder for a moment, and then the blinking dot came to an abrupt stop about ten yards outside the perimeter of the building.

Fumbling with the controls, Collet called up a Paris street map and recalibrated the GPS. Zooming in, he could now see the exact location of the signal.

It was no longer moving.

It lay at a dead stop in the middle of Place du Carrousel.

Langdon had jumped.

18

Fache sprinted down the Grand Gallery as Collet's radio blared over the distant sound of the alarm.

'He jumped!' Collet was yelling. 'I'm showing the signal out on Place du Carrousel! Outside the toilet window! And it's not moving at all! Jesus, I think Langdon has just committed suicide!'

Fache heard the words, but they made no sense. He kept running. The hallway seemed never-ending. As he sprinted past Saunière's body, he set his sights on the partitions at the far end of the Denon Wing. The alarm was getting louder now.

'Wait!' Collet's voice blared again over the radio. 'He's moving! My God, he's alive. Langdon's moving!'

Fache kept running, cursing the length of the hallway with every step.

'Langdon's moving faster!' Collet was still yelling on the radio. 'He's running down Carrousel. Wait . . . he's picking up speed. He's moving too fast!'

Arriving at the partitions, Fache snaked his way through them, saw the toilets door, and ran for it.

The walkie-talkie was barely audible now over the alarm. 'He must be in a car! I think he's in a car! I can't—'

Collet's words were swallowed by the alarm as Fache finally burst into the men's room with his gun drawn. Wincing against the piercing shrill, he scanned the area.

The stalls were empty. The washroom deserted. Fache's eyes moved immediately to the shattered window at the far end of the room. He ran to the opening and looked over the edge. Langdon was nowhere to be seen. Fache could not imagine anyone risking a stunt like this. Certainly if he had dropped that far, he would be badly injured.

The alarm cut off finally, and Collet's voice became audible again over the walkie-talkie.

'. . . moving south . . . faster . . . crossing the Seine on Pont du Carrousel!'

Fache turned to his left. The only vehicle on Pont du Carrousel was an enormous twin-bed Trailor delivery truck moving southward away from

519

the Louvre. The truck's open-air bed was covered with a vinyl tarp, roughly resembling a giant hammock. Fache felt a shiver of apprehension. That truck, only moments ago, had probably been stopped at a red light directly beneath the toilets window.

An insane risk, Fache told himself. Langdon had no way of knowing what the truck was carrying beneath that tarp. What if the truck were carrying steel? Or cement? Or even garbage? A forty-foot leap? It was madness.

'The dot is turning!' Collet called. 'He's turning right on Pont des Saints-Pères!'

Sure enough, the Trailor truck that had crossed the bridge was slowing down and making a right turn onto Pont des Saints-Pères. *So be it,* Fache thought. Amazed, he watched the truck disappear around the corner. Collet was already radioing the agents outside, pulling them off the Louvre perimeter and sending them to their patrol cars in pursuit, all the while broadcasting the truck's changing location like some kind of bizarre play-by-play.

It's over, Fache knew. His men would have the truck surrounded within minutes. Langdon was not going anywhere.

Stowing his weapon, Fache exited the toilets and radioed Collet. 'Bring my car round. I want to be there when we make the arrest.'

As Fache jogged back down the length of the Grand Gallery, he wondered if Langdon had even survived the fall.

Not that it mattered.

Langdon ran. Guilty as charged.

Only fifteen yards from the toilets, Langdon and Sophie stood in the darkness of the Grand Gallery, their backs pressed to one of the large partitions that hid the toilets from the gallery. They had barely managed to hide themselves before Fache had darted past them, gun drawn, and disappeared into the toilets.

The last sixty seconds had been a blur.

Langdon had been standing inside the men's room refusing to run from a crime he didn't commit, when Sophie began eyeing the plate-glass window and examining the alarm mesh running through it. Then she peered downward into the street, as if measuring the drop.

'With a little aim, you can get out of here,' she said.

Aim? Uneasy, he peered out of the window.

Up the street, an enormous twin-bed eighteen-wheeler was headed for the stoplight beneath the window. Stretched across the truck's massive cargo bay was a blue vinyl tarp, loosely covering the truck's load. Langdon hoped Sophie was not thinking what she seemed to be thinking.

'Sophie, there's no way I'm jump—'

'Take out the tracking dot.'

Bewildered, Langdon fumbled in his pocket until he found the tiny metallic disk. Sophie took it from him and strode immediately to the sink. She grabbed a thick bar of soap, placed the tracking dot on top of it, and used her thumb to push the disk down hard into the bar. As the disk sank into the soft surface, she pinched the hole closed, firmly embedding the device in the bar.

Handing the bar to Langdon, Sophie retrieved a heavy, cylindrical trash can from under the sinks. Before Langdon could protest, Sophie ran at the window, holding the can before her like a battering ram. Driving the bottom of the trash can into the centre of the window, she shattered the glass.

Alarms erupted overhead at earsplitting decibel levels.

'Give me the soap!' Sophie yelled, barely audible over the alarm.

Langdon thrust the bar into her hand.

Palming the soap, she peered out of the shattered window at the eighteen-wheeler idling below. The target was very big – an expansive, stationary tarp – and it was less than ten feet from the side of the building. As the traffic lights prepared to change, Sophie took a deep breath and lobbed the bar of soap out into the night.

The soap plummeted downward toward the truck, landing on the edge of the tarp, and sliding downward into the cargo bay just as the traffic light turned green.

'Congratulations,' Sophie said, dragging him toward the door. 'You just escaped from the Louvre.'

Fleeing the men's room, they moved into the shadows just as Fache rushed past.

Now, with the fire alarm silenced, Langdon could hear the sounds of DCPJ sirens tearing away from the Louvre. *A police exodus.* Fache had hurried off as well, leaving the Grand Gallery deserted.

'There's an emergency stairwell about fifty metres back into the Grand Gallery,' Sophie said. 'Now that the guards are leaving the perimeter, we can get out of here.'

Langdon decided not to say another word all evening. Sophie Neveu was clearly a hell of a lot smarter than he was.

19

The Church of Saint-Sulpice, it is said, has the most eccentric history of any building in Paris. Built over the ruins of an ancient temple to the Egyptian goddess Isis, the church possesses an architectural footprint matching that of Notre Dame to within inches. The sanctuary has played host to the baptisms of the Marquis de Sade and Baudelaire, as well as the marriage of Victor Hugo. The attached seminary has a well-documented history of unorthodoxy and was once the clandestine meeting hall for numerous secret societies.

Tonight, the cavernous nave of Saint-Sulpice was as silent as a tomb, the only hint of life the faint smell of incense from mass earlier that evening. Silas sensed an uneasiness in Sister Sandrine's demeanour as she led him into the sanctuary. He was not surprised by this. Silas was accustomed to people being uncomfortable with his appearance.

'You're an American,' she said.

'French by birth,' Silas responded. 'I had my calling in Spain, and I now study in the United States.'

Sister Sandrine nodded. She was a small woman with quiet eyes. 'And you have *never* seen Saint-Sulpice?'

'I realize this is almost a sin in itself.'

'She is more beautiful by day.'

'I am certain. Nonetheless, I am grateful that you would provide me this opportunity tonight.'

'The abbé requested it. You obviously have powerful friends.'

You have no idea, Silas thought.

As he followed Sister Sandrine down the main aisle, Silas was surprised by the austerity of the sanctuary. Unlike Notre Dame with its colourful frescos, gilded altar-work, and warm wood, Saint-Sulpice was stark and cold, conveying an almost barren quality reminiscent of the ascetic cathedrals of Spain. The lack of decor made the interior look even more expansive, and as Silas gazed up into the soaring ribbed vault of the ceiling, he imagined he was standing beneath the hull of an enormous overturned ship.

A fitting image, he thought. The brotherhood's ship was about to be capsized for ever. Feeling eager to get to work, Silas wished Sister Sandrine would leave him. She was a small woman whom Silas could incapacitate easily, but he had vowed not to use force unless absolutely necessary. *She is a woman of the cloth, and it is not her fault the brotherhood chose her church as a hiding place for their keystone. She should not be punished for the sins of others.*

'I am embarrassed, Sister, that you were awoken on my behalf.'

'Not at all. You are in Paris a short time. You should not miss Saint-Sulpice. Are your interests in the church more architectural or historical?'

'Actually, Sister, my interests are spiritual.'

She gave a pleasant laugh. 'That goes without saying. I simply wondered where to begin your tour.'

Silas felt his eyes focus on the altar. 'A tour is unnecessary. You have been more than kind. I can show myself around.'

'It is no trouble,' she said. 'After all, I am awake.'

Silas stopped walking. They had reached the front pew now, and the altar was only fifteen yards away. He turned his massive body fully toward the small woman, and he could sense her recoil as she gazed up into his red eyes. 'If it does not seem too rude, Sister, I am not accustomed to simply walking into a house of God and taking a tour. Would you mind if I took some time alone to pray before I look around?'

Sister Sandrine hesitated. 'Oh, of course. I shall wait in the rear of the church for you.'

Silas put a soft but heavy hand on her shoulder and peered down. 'Sister, I feel guilty already for having awoken you. To ask you to stay awake is too much. Please, you should return to bed. I can enjoy your sanctuary and then let myself out.'

She looked uneasy. 'Are you sure you won't feel abandoned?'

'Not at all. Prayer is a solitary joy.'

'As you wish.'

Silas took his hand from her shoulder. 'Sleep well, Sister. May the peace of the Lord be with you.'

'And also with you.' Sister Sandrine headed for the stairs. 'Please be sure the door closes tightly on your way out.'

'I will be sure of it.' Silas watched her climb out of sight. Then he turned and knelt in the front pew, feeling the *cilice* cut into his leg.

Dear God, I offer up to you this work I do today. . . .

Crouching in the shadows of the choir balcony high above the altar, Sister Sandrine peered silently through the balustrade at the cloaked monk kneeling alone. The sudden dread in her soul made it hard to stay still. For a fleeting instant, she wondered if this mysterious visitor could be the enemy they had warned her about, and if tonight she would have to carry out the orders she had been holding all these years. She decided to stay there in the darkness and watch his every move.

20

Emerging from the shadows, Langdon and Sophie moved stealthily up the deserted Grand Gallery corridor toward the emergency exit stairwell.

As he moved, Langdon felt like he was trying to assemble a jigsaw puzzle in the dark. The newest aspect of this mystery was a deeply troubling one: *The captain of the Judicial Police is trying to frame me for murder.*

'Do you think,' he whispered, 'that maybe *Fache* wrote that message on the floor?'

Sophie didn't even turn. 'Impossible.'

Langdon wasn't so sure. 'He seems pretty intent on making me look guilty. Maybe he thought writing my name on the floor would help his case?'

'The Fibonacci sequence? The P.S.? All the Da Vinci and goddess symbolism? That *had* to be my grandfather.'

Langdon knew she was right. The symbolism of the clues meshed too perfectly – the pentacle, *The Vitruvian Man*, Da Vinci, the goddess, and even the Fibonacci sequence. *A coherent symbolic set*, as iconographers would call it. All inextricably tied.

'And his phone call to me this afternoon,' Sophie added. 'He said he had to tell me something. I'm certain his message at the Louvre was his final effort to tell me something important, something he thought you could help me understand.'

Langdon frowned. *O, Draconian devil! Oh, lame saint!* He wished he could comprehend the message, both for Sophie's well-being and for his own. Things had definitely got worse since he first laid eyes on the cryptic words. His fake leap out of the bathroom window was not going to help Langdon's popularity with Fache one bit. Somehow he doubted the captain of the French police would see the humour in chasing down and arresting a bar of soap.

'The doorway isn't much farther,' Sophie said.

'Do you think there's a possibility that the *numbers* in your grandfather's message hold the key to understanding the other lines?' Langdon had once worked on a series of Baconian manuscripts that contained epigraphical ciphers in which certain lines of code were clues as to how to decipher the other lines.

'I've been thinking about the numbers all night. Sums, quotients, products. I don't see anything. Mathematically, they're arranged at random. Cryptographic gibberish.'

'And yet they're all part of the Fibonacci sequence. That can't be coincidence.'

'It's not. Using Fibonacci numbers was my grandfather's way of waving another flag at me – like writing the message in English, or arranging himself like my favourite piece of art, or drawing a pentacle on himself. All of it was to catch my attention.'

'The pentacle has meaning to you?'

'Yes. I didn't get a chance to tell you, but the pentacle was a special symbol between my grandfather and me when I was growing up. We used to play Tarot cards for fun, and my indicator card *always* turned out to be from the suit of pentacles. I'm sure he stacked the deck, but pentacles got to be our little joke.'

Langdon felt a chill. *They played Tarot?* The medieval Italian card game was so replete with hidden heretical symbolism that Langdon had dedicated an entire chapter in his new manuscript to the Tarot. The game's twenty-two cards bore names like *The Female Pope, The Empress,* and *The Star.* Originally, Tarot had been devised as a secret means to pass along ideologies banned by the Church. Now, Tarot's mystical qualities were passed on by modern fortune-tellers.

The Tarot indicator suit for feminine divinity is pentacles, Langdon thought, realizing that if Saunière had been stacking his granddaughter's deck for fun, pentacles was an apropos inside joke.

They arrived at the emergency stairwell, and Sophie carefully pulled open the door. No alarm sounded. Only the doors to the outside were wired. Sophie led Langdon down a tight set of switchback stairs toward the ground level, picking up speed as they went.

'Your grandfather,' Langdon said, hurrying behind her, 'when he told you about the pentacle, did he mention goddess worship or any resentment of the Catholic Church?'

Sophie shook her head. 'I was more interested in the mathematics of it – the Divine Proportion, PHI, Fibonacci sequences, that sort of thing.'

Langdon was surprised. 'Your grandfather taught you about the number PHI?'

'Of course. The Divine Proportion.' Her expression turned sheepish. 'In fact, he used to joke that I was half divine . . . you know, because of the letters in my name.'

Langdon considered it a moment and then groaned.

s-o-PHI-e.

Still descending, Langdon refocused on *PHI.* He was starting to realize that Saunière's clues were even more consistent than he had first imagined.

Da Vinci . . . Fibonacci numbers . . . the pentacle.

Incredibly, all of these things were connected by a single concept so fundamental to art history that Langdon often spent several class periods on the topic.

PHI.

He felt himself suddenly reeling back to Harvard, standing in front of his 'Symbolism in Art' class, writing his favourite number on the chalkboard.

1.618

Langdon turned to face his sea of eager students. 'Who can tell me what this number is?'

A long-legged maths major at the back raised his hand. 'That's the number PHI.' He pronounced it *fee*.

'Nice job, Stettner,' Langdon said. 'Everyone, meet PHI.'

'Not to be confused with PI,' Stettner added, grinning. 'As we mathematicians like to say: PHI is one *H* of a lot cooler than PI!'

Langdon laughed, but nobody else seemed to get the joke.

Stettner slumped.

'This number PHI,' Langdon continued, 'one–point–six–one–eight, is a very important number in art. Who can tell me why?'

Stettner tried to redeem himself. 'Because it's so pretty?'

Everyone laughed.

'Actually,' Langdon said, 'Stettner's right again. PHI is generally considered the most beautiful number in the universe.'

The laughter abruptly stopped, and Stettner gloated.

As Langdon loaded his slide projector, he explained that the number PHI was derived from the Fibonacci sequence – a progression famous not only because the sum of adjacent terms equalled the next term, but because the *quotients* of adjacent terms possessed the astonishing property of approaching the number 1.618 – PHI!

Despite PHI's seemingly mystical mathematical origins, Langdon explained, the truly mind–boggling aspect of PHI was its role as a fundamental building block in nature. Plants, animals and even human beings all possessed dimensional properties that adhered with eerie exactitude to the ratio of PHI to 1.

'PHI's ubiquity in nature,' Langdon said, killing the lights, 'clearly exceeds coincidence, and so the ancients assumed the number PHI must have been preordained by the Creator of the universe. Early scientists heralded one–point–six–one–eight as the *Divine Proportion*.'

'Hold on,' said a young woman in the front row. 'I'm a bio major and I've never seen this Divine Proportion in nature.'

'No?' Langdon grinned. 'Ever study the relationship between females and males in a honeybee community?'

'Sure. The female bees always outnumber the male bees.'

'Correct. And did you know that if you divide the number of female bees by the number of male bees in any beehive in the world, you always get the same number?'

'You do?'

'Yup. PHI.'

The girl gaped. 'NO WAY!'

'Way!' Langdon fired back, smiling as he projected a slide of a spiral seashell. 'Recognize this?'

'It's a nautilus,' the bio major said. 'A cephalopod mollusc that pumps gas into its chambered shell to adjust its buoyancy.'

'Correct. And can you guess what the ratio is of each spiral's diameter to the next?'

The girl looked uncertain as she eyed the concentric arcs of the nautilus spiral.

Langdon nodded. 'PHI. The Divine Proportion. One-point-six-one-eight to one.'

The girl looked amazed.

Langdon advanced to the next slide – a close-up of a sunflower's seed head. 'Sunflower seeds grow in opposing spirals. Can you guess the ratio of each rotation's diameter to the next?'

'PHI?' everyone said.

'Bingo.' Langdon began racing through slides now – spiralled pinecone petals, leaf arrangement on plant stalks, insect segmentation – all displaying astonishing obedience to the Divine Proportion.

'This is amazing!' someone cried out.

'Yeah,' someone else said, 'but what does it have to do with *art?*'

'Aha!' Langdon said. 'Glad you asked.' He pulled up another slide – a pale yellow parchment displaying Leonardo da Vinci's famous male nude – *The Vitruvian Man* – named for Marcus Vitruvius, the brilliant Roman architect who praised the Divine Proportion in his text *De Architectura*.

'Nobody understood better than Da Vinci the divine structure of the human body. Da Vinci actually *exhumed* corpses to measure the exact proportions of human bone structure. He was the first to show that the human body is literally made of building blocks whose proportional ratios *always* equal PHI.'

Everyone in class gave him a dubious look.

'Don't believe me?' Langdon challenged. 'Next time you're in the shower, take a tape measure.'

A couple of football players snickered.

'Not just you insecure jocks,' Langdon prompted. '*All* of you. Guys and girls. Try it. Measure the distance from the tip of your head to the floor. Then divide that by the distance from your belly button to the floor. Guess what number you get.'

'Not PHI!' one of the jocks blurted out in disbelief.

'Yes, PHI,' Langdon replied. 'One-point-six-one-eight. Want another example? Measure the distance from your shoulder to your fingertips, and then divide it by the distance from your elbow to your fingertips. PHI again. Another? Hip to floor divided by knee to floor. PHI again. Finger joints. Toes. Spinal divisions. PHI. PHI. PHI. My friends, each of you is a walking tribute to the Divine Proportion.'

Even in the darkness, Langdon could see they were all astounded. He felt a familiar warmth inside. This is why he taught. 'My friends, as you can see, the chaos of the world has an underlying order. When the ancients discovered PHI, they were certain they had stumbled across God's building block for the world, and they worshipped Nature because of that. And one can understand why. God's hand is evident in Nature, and even to this day there exist pagan, Mother Earth–revering religions. Many of us celebrate Nature the way the pagans did, and don't even know it. May Day is a perfect example, the celebration of spring . . . the earth coming back to life to produce her bounty. The mysterious magic inherent in the Divine Proportion was written at the beginning of time. Man is simply playing by Nature's rules, and because *art* is man's attempt to imitate the beauty of the Creator's hand, you can imagine we might be seeing a lot of instances of the Divine Proportion in art this semester.'

Over the next half hour, Langdon showed them slides of artwork by Michelangelo, Albrecht Dürer, Da Vinci, and many others, demonstrating each artist's intentional and rigorous adherence to the Divine Proportion in the layout of his compositions. Langdon unveiled PHI in the architectural dimensions of the Greek Parthenon, the pyramids of Egypt, and even the United Nations Building in New York. PHI appeared in the organizational structures of Mozart's sonatas, Beethoven's Fifth Symphony, as well as the works of Bartók, Debussy, and Schubert. The number PHI, Langdon told them, was even used by Stradivarius to calculate the exact placement of the f-holes in the construction of his famous violins.

'In closing,' Langdon said, walking to the chalkboard, 'we return to *symbols*.' He drew five intersecting lines that formed a five-pointed star. 'This symbol is one of the most powerful images you will see this term. Formally known as a pentagram – or *pentacle*, as the ancients called it – this symbol is considered both divine and magical by many cultures. Can anyone tell me why that might be?'

Stettner, the maths major, raised his hand. 'Because if you draw a pentagram, the lines automatically divide themselves into segments according to the Divine Proportion.'

Langdon gave the kid a proud nod. 'Nice job. Yes, the ratios of line segments in a pentacle *all* equal PHI, making this symbol the *ultimate* expression of the Divine Proportion. For this reason, the five-pointed star has always been the symbol for beauty and perfection associated with the goddess and the sacred feminine.'

The girls in class beamed.

'One note, folks. We've only touched on Da Vinci today, but we'll be seeing a lot more of him this semester. Leonardo was a well-documented devotee of the ancient ways of the goddess. Tomorrow, I'll show you his fresco *The Last Supper,* which is one of the most astonishing tributes to the sacred feminine you will ever see.'

'You're kidding, right?' somebody said. 'I thought *The Last Supper* was about Jesus!'

Langdon winked. 'There are symbols hidden in places you would never imagine.'

'Come on,' Sophie whispered. 'What's wrong? We're almost there. Hurry!'

Langdon glanced up, feeling himself return from faraway thoughts. He realized he was standing at a dead stop on the stairs, paralysed by sudden revelation.

O, Draconian devil! Oh, lame saint!

Sophie was looking back at him.

It can't be that simple, Langdon thought.

But he knew of course that it was.

There in the bowels of the Louvre . . . with images of PHI and Da Vinci swirling through his mind, Robert Langdon suddenly and unexpectedly deciphered Saunière's code.

'O, Draconian devil!' he said. 'Oh, lame saint! It's the simplest kind of code!'

Sophie was stopped on the stairs below him, staring up in confusion. *A code?* She had been pondering the words all night and had not seen a code. Especially a simple one.

'You said it yourself.' Langdon's voice reverberated with excitement. 'Fibonacci numbers only have meaning in their proper order. Otherwise they're mathematical gibberish.'

Sophie had no idea what he was talking about. *The Fibonacci numbers?* She was certain they had been intended as nothing more than a means to get the Cryptography Department involved tonight. *They have another purpose?* She plunged her hand into her pocket and pulled out the printout, studying her grandfather's message again.

13-3-2-21-1-1-8-5

O, Draconian devil!

Oh, lame saint!

What about the numbers?

'The scrambled Fibonacci sequence is a clue,' Langdon said, taking the printout. 'The numbers are a hint as to how to decipher the rest of the message. He wrote the sequence out of order to tell us to apply the same concept to the text. O, Draconian devil? Oh, lame saint? Those lines mean nothing. They are simply *letters* written out of order.'

Sophie needed only an instant to process Langdon's implication, and it seemed laughably simple. 'You think this message is . . . *une anagramme?*' She stared at him. 'Like a word jumble from a newspaper?'

Langdon could see the scepticism on Sophie's face and certainly understood. Few people realized that anagrams, despite being a trite modern amusement, had a rich history of sacred symbolism.

The mystical teachings of the Kabbala drew heavily on anagrams – rearranging the letters of Hebrew words to derive new meanings. French kings throughout the Renaissance were so convinced that anagrams held magic power that they appointed royal anagrammatists to help them make better decisions by analysing words in important documents. The Romans actually referred to the study of anagrams as *ars magna* – 'the great art'.

Langdon looked up at Sophie, locking eyes with her now. 'Your grandfather's meaning was right in front of us all along, and he left us more than enough clues to see it.'

Without another word, Langdon pulled a pen from his jacket pocket and rearranged the letters in each line.

O, Draconian devil!
Oh, lame saint!

was a perfect anagram of . . .

Leonardo da Vinci!
The Mona Lisa!

21

The Mona Lisa.

For an instant, standing in the exit stairwell, Sophie forgot all about trying to leave the Louvre.

Her shock over the anagram was matched only by her embarrassment at not having deciphered the message herself. Sophie's expertise in complex cryptanalysis had caused her to overlook simplistic word games, and yet she knew she should have seen it. After all, she was no stranger to anagrams – especially in English.

When she was young, often her grandfather would use anagram games to hone her English spelling. Once he had written the English word 'planets' and told Sophie that an astonishing ninety-two *other* English words of varying lengths could be formed using those same letters. Sophie had spent three days with an English dictionary until she found them all.

'I can't imagine,' Langdon said, staring at the printout, 'how your grandfather created such an intricate anagram in the minutes before he died.'

Sophie knew the explanation, and the realization made her feel even worse. *I should have seen this!* She now recalled that her grandfather – a wordplay aficionado and art lover – had entertained himself as a young man by creating anagrams of famous works of art. In fact, one of his anagrams had got him in trouble once when Sophie was a little girl. While being interviewed by an American art magazine, Saunière had expressed his distaste for the modernist Cubist movement by noting that Picasso's masterpiece *Les Demoiselles d'Avignon* was a perfect anagram of *vile meaningless doodles*. Picasso fans were not amused.

'My grandfather probably created this *Mona Lisa* anagram long ago,' Sophie said, glancing up at Langdon. *And tonight he was forced to use it as a makeshift code.* Her grandfather's voice had called out from beyond with chilling precision.

Leonardo da Vinci!

The Mona Lisa!

Why his final words to her referenced the famous painting, Sophie had no idea, but she could think of only one possibility. A disturbing one.

Those were not his final words. . . .

Was she supposed to visit the *Mona Lisa?* Had her grandfather left her a message there? The idea seemed perfectly plausible. After all, the famous painting hung in the Salle des Etats – a private viewing chamber accessible only from the Grand Gallery. In fact, Sophie now realized, the doors that opened into the chamber were situated only twenty metres from where her grandfather had been found dead.

He easily could have visited the Mona Lisa *before he died.*

Sophie gazed back up the emergency stairwell and felt torn. She knew she should usher Langdon from the museum immediately, and yet instinct urged her to the contrary. As Sophie recalled her first childhood visit to the Denon Wing, she realized that if her grandfather had a secret to tell her, few places on earth made a more apt rendezvous than Da Vinci's *Mona Lisa*.

'She's just a little bit farther,' her grandfather had whispered, clutching Sophie's tiny hand as he led her through the deserted museum after hours.

Sophie was six years old. She felt small and insignificant as she gazed up at the enormous ceilings and down at the dizzying floor. The empty museum frightened her, although she was not about to let her grandfather know that. She set her jaw firmly and let go of his hand.

'Up ahead is the Salle des Etats,' her grandfather said as they approached the Louvre's most famous room. Despite her grandfather's obvious excitement, Sophie wanted to go home. She had seen pictures of the *Mona Lisa* in books and didn't like it at all. She couldn't understand why everyone made such a fuss.

'*C'est ennuyeux,*' Sophie grumbled.

'Boring,' he corrected. 'French at school. English at home.'

'*Le Louvre, c'est pas chez moi!*' she challenged.

He gave her a tired laugh. 'Right you are. Then let's speak English just for fun.'

Sophie pouted and kept walking. As they entered the Salle des Etats, her eyes scanned the narrow room and settled on the obvious spot of honour – the centre of the right-hand wall, where a lone portrait hung behind a protective Plexiglas wall. Her grandfather paused in the doorway and motioned toward the painting.

'Go ahead, Sophie. Not many people get a chance to visit her alone.'

Swallowing her apprehension, Sophie moved slowly across the room. After everything she'd heard about the *Mona Lisa,* she felt as if she were approaching royalty. Arriving in front of the protective Plexiglas, Sophie held her breath and looked up, taking it in all at once.

Sophie was not sure what she had expected to feel, but it most certainly was not this. No jolt of amazement. No instant of wonder. The famous face looked as it did in books. She stood in silence for what felt like for ever, waiting for something to happen.

'So what do you think?' her grandfather whispered, arriving behind her. 'Beautiful, yes?'

'She's too little.'

Saunière smiled. 'You're little and you're beautiful.'

I am not beautiful, she thought. Sophie hated her red hair and freckles, and she was bigger than all the boys in her class. She looked back at the *Mona Lisa* and shook her head. 'She's even worse than in the books. Her face is . . . *brumeux.*'

'Foggy,' her grandfather tutored.

'Foggy,' Sophie repeated, knowing the conversation would not continue until she repeated her new vocabulary word.

'That's called the *sfumato* style of painting,' he told her, 'and it's very hard to do. Leonardo da Vinci was better at it than anyone.'

Sophie still didn't like the painting. 'She looks like she knows something . . . like when kids at school have a secret.'

Her grandfather laughed. 'That's part of why she is so famous. People like to guess why she is smiling.'

'Do *you* know why she's smiling?'

'Maybe.' Her grandfather winked. 'Someday I'll tell you all about it.'

Sophie stamped her foot. 'I told you I don't like secrets!'

'Princess,' he smiled. 'Life is filled with secrets. You can't learn them all at once.'

'I'm going back up,' Sophie declared, her voice hollow in the stairwell.

'To the *Mona Lisa*?' Langdon recoiled. '*Now?*'

Sophie considered the risk. 'I'm not a murder suspect. I'll take my chances. I need to understand what my grandfather was trying to tell me.'

'What about the embassy?'

Sophie felt guilty turning Langdon into a fugitive only to abandon him, but she saw no other option. She pointed down the stairs to a metal door. 'Go through that door, and follow the illuminated exit signs. My grandfather used to bring me down here. The signs will lead you to a security turnstile. It's monodirectional and opens out.' She handed Langdon her car keys. 'Mine is the red SmartCar in the employee lot. Directly outside this bulkhead. Do you know how to get to the embassy?'

Langdon nodded, eyeing the keys in his hand.

'Listen,' Sophie said, her voice softening. 'I think my grandfather may have left me a message at the *Mona Lisa* – some kind of clue as to who killed him. Or why I'm in danger.' *Or what happened to my family.* 'I have to go and see.'

'But if he wanted to tell you why you were in danger, why wouldn't he simply write it on the floor where he died? Why this complicated word game?'

'Whatever my grandfather was trying to tell me, I don't think he wanted anyone else to hear it. Not even the police.' Clearly, her grandfather had done everything in his power to send a confidential transmission directly to *her*. He had written it in code, included her secret initials, and told her to find Robert Langdon – a wise command, considering the American symbologist had deciphered his code. 'As strange as it may sound,' Sophie said, 'I think he wants me to get to the *Mona Lisa* before anyone else does.'

'I'll come.'

'No! We don't know how long the Grand Gallery will stay empty. *You* have to go.'

Langdon seemed hesitant, as if his own academic curiosity were threatening to override sound judgment and drag him back into Fache's hands.

'Go. Now.' Sophie gave him a grateful smile. 'I'll see you at the embassy, Mr Langdon.'

Langdon looked displeased. 'I'll meet you there on *one* condition,' he replied, his voice stern.

She paused, startled. 'What's that?'

'That you stop calling me *Mr* Langdon.'

Sophie detected the faint hint of a lopsided grin growing across Langdon's face, and she felt herself smile back. 'Good luck, Robert.'

When Langdon reached the landing at the bottom of the stairs, the unmistakable smell of linseed oil and plaster dust assaulted his nostrils. Ahead, an illuminated SORTIE/EXIT displayed an arrow pointing down a long corridor.

Langdon stepped into the hallway.

To the right gaped a murky restoration studio out of which peered an army of statues in various states of repair. To the left, Langdon saw a suite of studios that resembled Harvard art classrooms – rows of easels, paintings, palettes, framing tools – an art assembly line.

As he moved down the hallway, Langdon wondered if at any moment he might awake with a start in his bed in Cambridge. The entire evening had felt like a bizarre dream. *I'm about to dash out of the Louvre . . . a fugitive.*

Saunière's clever anagrammatic message was still on his mind, and Langdon wondered what Sophie would find at the *Mona Lisa* . . . if anything. She had seemed certain her grandfather meant for her to visit the famous painting one more time. As plausible an interpretation as this seemed, Langdon felt haunted now by a troubling paradox.

P.S. Find Robert Langdon.

Saunière had written Langdon's name on the floor, commanding Sophie to find him. But why? Merely so Langdon could help her break an anagram?

It seemed quite unlikely.

After all, Saunière had no reason to think Langdon was especially skilled at anagrams. *We've never even met.* More important, Sophie had stated flat out that *she* should have broken the anagram on her own. It had been Sophie who spotted the Fibonacci sequence, and, no doubt, Sophie who, if given a little more time, would have deciphered the message with no help from Langdon.

Sophie was supposed to break that anagram on her own. Langdon was suddenly feeling more certain about this, and yet the conclusion left an obvious gaping lapse in the logic of Saunière's actions.

Why me? Langdon wondered, heading down the hall. *Why was Saunière's dying wish that his estranged granddaughter find me? What is it that Saunière thinks I know?*

With an unexpected jolt, Langdon stopped short. Eyes wide, he dug in his pocket and yanked out the computer printout. He stared at the last line of Saunière's message.

P.S. Find Robert Langdon.

He fixated on two letters.

P.S.

In that instant, Langdon felt Saunière's puzzling mix of symbolism fall into stark focus. Like a peal of thunder, a career's worth of symbology and history came crashing down around him. Everything Jacques Saunière had done tonight suddenly made perfect sense.

Langdon's thoughts raced as he tried to assemble the implications of what this all meant. Wheeling, he stared back in the direction from which he had come.

Is there time?

He knew it didn't matter.

Without hesitation, Langdon broke into a sprint back toward the stairs.

22

Kneeling in the first pew, Silas pretended to pray as he scanned the layout of the sanctuary. Saint-Sulpice, like most churches, had been built in the shape of a giant Roman cross. Its long central section – the nave – led directly to the main altar, where it was transversely intersected by a shorter section, known as the transept. The intersection of nave and transept occurred directly beneath the main cupola and was considered the heart of the church . . . her most sacred and mystical point.

Not tonight, Silas thought. *Saint-Sulpice hides her secrets elsewhere.*

Turning his head to the right, he gazed into the south transept, toward the open area of floor beyond the end of the pews, to the object his victims had described.

There it is.

Embedded in the grey granite floor, a thin polished strip of brass glistened in the stone . . . a golden line slanting across the church's floor. The line bore graduated markings, like a ruler. It was a gnomon, Silas had been told, a pagan astronomical device like a sundial. Tourists, scientists, historians and pagans from around the world came to Saint-Sulpice to gaze upon this famous line.

The Rose Line.

Slowly, Silas let his eyes trace the path of the brass strip as it made its way across the floor from his right to left, slanting in front of him at an awkward angle, entirely at odds with the symmetry of the church. Slicing across the main altar itself, the line looked to Silas like a slash wound across a beautiful face. The strip cleaved the communion rail in two and then crossed the entire width of the church, finally reaching the corner of the north transept, where it arrived at the base of a most unexpected structure.

A colossal Egyptian obelisk.

Here, the glistening Rose Line took a ninety-degree *vertical* turn and continued directly up the face of the obelisk itself, ascending thirty-three feet to the very tip of the pyramidical apex, where it finally ceased.

The Rose Line, Silas thought. *The brotherhood hid the keystone at the Rose Line.*

Earlier tonight, when Silas told the Teacher that the Priory keystone was

536

hidden inside Saint-Sulpice, the Teacher had sounded doubtful. But when Silas added that the brothers had all given him a precise location, with relation to a brass line running through Saint-Sulpice, the Teacher had gasped with revelation. 'You speak of the Rose Line!'

The Teacher quickly told Silas of Saint-Sulpice's famed architectural oddity – a strip of brass that segmented the sanctuary on a perfect north-south axis. It was an ancient sundial of sorts, a vestige of the pagan temple that had once stood on this very spot. The sun's rays, shining through the oculus on the south wall, moved farther down the line every day, indicating the passage of time, from solstice to solstice.

The north-south stripe had been known as the Rose Line. For centuries, the symbol of the Rose had been associated with maps and guiding souls in the proper direction. The Compass Rose – drawn on almost every map – indicated North, East, South and West. Originally known as the Wind Rose, it denoted the directions of the thirty-two winds, blowing from the directions of eight major winds, eight half-winds, and sixteen quarter-winds. When diagrammed inside a circle, these thirty-two points of the compass perfectly resembled a traditional thirty-two petal rose bloom. To this day, the fundamental navigational tool was still known as a Compass Rose, its northernmost direction still marked by an arrowhead . . . or, more commonly, the symbol of the fleur-de-lis.

On a globe, a Rose Line – also called a meridian or longitude – was any imaginary line drawn from the North Pole to the South Pole. There were, of course, an infinite number of Rose Lines because every point on the globe could have a longitude drawn through it connecting north and south poles. The question for early navigators was *which* of these lines would be called *the* Rose Line – the zero longitude – the line from which all other longitudes on earth would be measured.

Today that line was in Greenwich, England.

But it had not always been.

Long before the establishment of Greenwich as the prime meridian, the zero longitude of the entire world had passed directly through Paris, and through the Church of Saint-Sulpice. The brass marker in Saint-Sulpice was a memorial to the world's first prime meridian, and although Greenwich had stripped Paris of the honour in 1888, the original Rose Line was still visible today.

'And so the legend is true,' the Teacher had told Silas. 'The Priory keystone has been said to lie "beneath the Sign of the Rose".'

Now, still on his knees in a pew, Silas glanced around the church and listened to make sure no one was there. For a moment, he thought he heard a rustling in the choir balcony. He turned and gazed up for several seconds. Nothing.

I am alone.

Standing now, he faced the altar and genuflected three times. Then he turned left and followed the brass line due north toward the obelisk.

At that moment, at Leonardo da Vinci International Airport in Rome, the jolt of tyres hitting the runway startled Bishop Aringarosa from his slumber.

I drifted off, he thought, impressed he was relaxed enough to sleep.

'*Benvenuto a Roma,*' the intercom announced.

Sitting up, Aringarosa straightened his black cassock and allowed himself a rare smile. This was one trip he had been happy to make. *I have been on the defensive for too long.* Tonight, however, the rules had changed. Only five months ago, Aringarosa had feared for the future of the Faith. Now, as if by the will of God, the solution had presented itself.

Divine intervention.

If all went as planned tonight in Paris, Aringarosa would soon be in possession of something that would make him the most powerful man in Christendom.

23

Sophie arrived breathless outside the large wooden doors of the Salle des Etats – the room that housed the *Mona Lisa*. Before entering, she gazed reluctantly farther down the hall, twenty yards or so, to the spot where her grandfather's body still lay under the spotlight.

The remorse that gripped her was powerful and sudden, a deep sadness laced with guilt. The man had reached out to her so many times over the past ten years, and yet Sophie had remained immovable – leaving his letters and packages unopened in a bottom drawer and denying his efforts to see her. *He lied to me! Kept appalling secrets! What was I supposed to do?* And so she had blocked him out. Completely.

Now her grandfather was dead, and he was talking to her from the grave. *The Mona Lisa.*

She reached for the huge wooden doors, and pushed. The entryway yawned open. Sophie stood on the threshold a moment, scanning the large rectangular chamber beyond. It too was bathed in a soft red light. The Salle des Etats was one of this museum's rare *culs-de-sac* – a dead end and the only room off the middle of the Grand Gallery. This door, the chamber's sole point of entry, faced a dominating fifteen-foot Botticelli on the far wall. Beneath it, centred on the parquet floor, an immense octagonal viewing divan served as a welcome respite for thousands of visitors to rest their legs while they admired the Louvre's most valuable asset.

Even before Sophie entered, though, she knew she was missing something. *A black light.* She gazed down the hall at her grandfather under the lights in the distance, surrounded by electronic gear. If he had written anything in here, he almost certainly would have written it with the watermark stylus.

Taking a deep breath, Sophie hurried down to the well-lit crime scene. Unable to look at her grandfather, she focused solely on the PTS tools. Finding a small ultraviolet penlight, she slipped it in the pocket of her sweater and hurried back up the hallway toward the open doors of the Salle des Etats.

Sophie turned the corner and stepped over the threshold. Her entrance, however, was met by an unexpected sound of muffled footsteps racing toward her from inside the chamber. *There's someone in here!* A ghostly figure emerged suddenly from out of the reddish haze. Sophie jumped back.

'There you are!' Langdon's hoarse whisper cut the air as his silhouette slid to a stop in front of her.

Her relief was only momentary. 'Robert, I told you to get out of here! If Fache—'

'Where were you?'

'I had to get the black light,' she whispered, holding it up. 'If my grandfather left me a message—'

'Sophie, listen.' Langdon caught his breath as his blue eyes held her firmly. 'The letters P.S. . . . do they mean anything else to you? Anything at all?'

Afraid their voices might echo down the hall, Sophie pulled him into the Salle des Etats and closed the enormous twin doors silently, sealing them inside. 'I told you, the initials mean Princess Sophie.'

'I know, but did you ever see them anywhere *else?* Did your grandfather ever use P.S. in any other way? As a monogram, or maybe on stationery or a personal item?'

The question startled her. *How would Robert know that?* Sophie had indeed seen the initials P.S. once before, in a kind of monogram. It was the day before her ninth birthday. She was secretly combing the house, searching for hidden birthday presents. Even then, she could not bear secrets kept from her. *What did Grand-père get for me this year?* She dug through cupboards and drawers. *Did he get me the doll I wanted? Where would he hide it?*

Finding nothing in the entire house, Sophie mustered the courage to sneak into her grandfather's bedroom. The room was off-limits to her, but her grandfather was downstairs asleep on the couch.

I'll just take a fast peek!

Tiptoeing across the creaky wood floor to his closet, Sophie peered on the shelves behind his clothing. Nothing. Next she looked under the bed. Still nothing. Moving to his bureau, she opened the drawers and one by one began pawing carefully through them. *There must be something for me here!* As she reached the bottom drawer, she still had not found any hint of a doll. Dejected, she opened the final drawer and pulled aside some black clothes she had never seen him wear. She was about to close the drawer when her eyes caught a glint of gold in the back of the drawer. It looked like a pocket watch chain, but she knew he didn't wear one. Her heart raced as she realized what it must be.

A necklace!

Sophie carefully pulled the chain from the drawer. To her surprise, on the end was a brilliant gold key. Heavy and shimmering. Spellbound, she held it up. It looked like no key she had ever seen. Most keys were flat with jagged teeth, but this one had a triangular column with little pockmarks all

540

over it. Its large golden head was in the shape of a cross, but not a normal cross. This was an even-armed one, like a plus sign. Embossed in the middle of the cross was a strange symbol – two letters intertwined with some kind of flowery design.

'P.S.,' she whispered, scowling as she read the letters. *Whatever could this be?*

'Sophie?' her grandfather spoke from the doorway.

Startled, she spun, dropping the key on the floor with a loud clang. She stared down at the key, afraid to look up at her grandfather's face. 'I . . . was looking for my birthday present,' she said, hanging her head, knowing she had betrayed his trust.

For what seemed like an eternity, her grandfather stood silently in the doorway. Finally, he let out a long troubled breath. 'Pick up the key, Sophie.'

Sophie retrieved the key.

Her grandfather walked in. 'Sophie, you need to respect other people's privacy.' Gently, he knelt down and took the key from her. 'This key is very special. If you had lost it . . .'

Her grandfather's quiet voice made Sophie feel even worse. 'I'm sorry, *Grand-père*. I really am.' She paused. 'I thought it was a necklace for my birthday.'

He gazed at her for several seconds. 'I'll say this once more, Sophie, because it's important. You need to learn to respect other people's privacy.'

'Yes, *Grand-père*.'

'We'll talk about this some other time. Right now, the garden needs to be weeded.'

Sophie hurried outside to do her chores.

The next morning, Sophie received no birthday present from her grandfather. She hadn't expected one, not after what she had done. But he didn't even wish her happy birthday all day. Sadly, she trudged up to bed that night. As she climbed in, though, she found a note card lying on her pillow. On the card was written a simple riddle. Even before she solved the riddle, she was smiling. *I know what this is!* Her grandfather had done this for her last Christmas morning.

A treasure hunt!

Eagerly, she pored over the riddle until she solved it. The solution pointed her to another part of the house, where she found another card and another riddle. She solved this one too, racing on to the next card. Running wildly, she darted back and forth across the house, from clue to clue, until at last she found a clue that directed her back to her own bedroom. Sophie dashed up the stairs, rushed into her room, and stopped in her tracks. There in the middle of the room sat a shining red bicycle with a ribbon tied to the handlebars. Sophie shrieked with delight.

'I know you asked for a doll,' her grandfather said, smiling in the corner. 'I thought you might like this even better.'

The next day, her grandfather taught her to ride, running beside her down the walkway. When Sophie steered out over the thick lawn and lost her balance, they both went tumbling onto the grass, rolling and laughing.

'*Grand-père*,' Sophie said, hugging him. 'I'm really sorry about the key.'

'I know, sweetie. You're forgiven. I can't possibly stay mad at you. Grandfathers and granddaughters always forgive each other.'

Sophie knew she shouldn't ask, but she couldn't help it. 'What does it open? I never saw a key like that. It was very pretty.'

Her grandfather was silent a long moment, and Sophie could see he was uncertain how to answer. *Grand-père never lies.* 'It opens a box,' he finally said. 'Where I keep many secrets.'

Sophie pouted. 'I hate secrets!'

'I know, but these are important secrets. And someday, you'll learn to appreciate them as much as I do.'

'I saw letters on the key, and a flower.'

'Yes, that's my favourite flower. It's called a fleur-de-lis. We have them in the garden. The white ones. In English we call that kind of flower a lily.'

'I know those! They're *my* favourite too!'

'Then I'll make a deal with you.' Her grandfather's eyebrows raised the way they always did when he was about to give her a challenge. 'If you can keep my key a secret, and *never* talk about it ever again, to me or anybody, then someday I will give it to you.'

Sophie couldn't believe her ears. 'You *will?*'

'I promise. When the time comes, the key will be yours. It has your name on it.'

Sophie scowled. 'No it doesn't. It said P.S. My name isn't P.S.!'

Her grandfather lowered his voice and looked around as if to make sure no one was listening. 'Okay, Sophie, if you *must* know, P.S. is a code. It's your secret initials.'

Her eyes went wide. 'I have secret initials?'

'Of course. Granddaughters *always* have secret initials that only their grandfathers know.'

'P.S.?'

He tickled her. '*Princesse Sophie.*'

She giggled. 'I'm not a princess!'

He winked. 'You are to me.'

From that day on, they never again spoke of the key. And she became his Princess Sophie.

Inside the Salle des Etats, Sophie stood in silence and endured the sharp pang of loss.

'The initials,' Langdon whispered, eyeing her strangely. 'Have you seen them?'

Sophie sensed her grandfather's voice whispering in the corridors of the museum. *Never speak of this key, Sophie. To me or to anyone.* She knew she had failed him in forgiveness, and she wondered if she could break his trust again. *P.S. Find Robert Langdon.* Her grandfather wanted Langdon to help. Sophie nodded. 'Yes, I saw the initials P.S. once. When I was very young.'

'Where?'

Sophie hesitated. 'On something very important to him.'

Langdon locked eyes with her. 'Sophie, this is crucial. Can you tell me if the initials appeared with a symbol? A fleur-de-lis?'

Sophie felt herself staggering backward in amazement. 'But . . . how could you possibly know that!'

Langdon exhaled and lowered his voice. 'I'm fairly certain your grand-father was a member of a secret society. A very old covert brotherhood.'

Sophie felt a knot tighten in her stomach. She was certain of it too. For ten years she had tried to forget the incident that had confirmed that hor-rifying fact for her. She had witnessed something unthinkable. *Unforgivable.*

'The fleur-de-lis,' Langdon said, 'combined with the initials P.S., that is the brotherhood's official device. Their coat of arms. Their logo.'

'How do you know this?' Sophie was praying Langdon was not going to tell her that he *himself* was a member.

'I've written about this group,' he said, his voice tremulous with excite-ment. 'Researching the symbols of secret societies is a specialty of mine. They call themselves the *Prieuré de Sion* – the Priory of Sion. They're based here in France and attract powerful members from all over Europe. In fact, they are one of the oldest surviving secret societies on earth.'

Sophie had never heard of them.

Langdon was talking in rapid bursts now. 'The Priory's membership has included some of history's most cultured individuals: men like Botticelli, Sir Isaac Newton, Victor Hugo.' He paused, his voice brimming now with academic zeal. 'And, Leonardo da Vinci.'

Sophie stared. 'Da Vinci was in a secret society?'

'Da Vinci presided over the Priory between 1510 and 1519 as the broth-erhood's Grand Master, which might help explain your grand-father's passion for Leonardo's work. The two men share a historical fraternal bond. And it all fits perfectly with their fascination for goddess iconology, paganism, feminine deities and contempt for the Church. The Priory has a well-documented history of reverence for the sacred feminine.'

'You're telling me this group is a pagan goddess worship cult?'

'More like *the* pagan goddess worship cult. But more important, they are known as the guardians of an ancient secret. One that made them immea-surably powerful.'

Despite the total conviction in Langdon's eyes, Sophie's gut reaction was one of stark disbelief. *A secret pagan cult? Once headed by Leonardo da Vinci?* It all sounded utterly absurd. And yet, even as she dismissed it, she felt her mind reeling back ten years – to the night she had mistakenly surprised her grandfather and witnessed what she still could not accept. *Could that explain – ?*

'The identities of living Priory members are kept extremely secret,' Langdon said, 'but the P.S. and fleur-de-lis that you saw as a child are proof. It could *only* have been related to the Priory.'

Sophie realized now that Langdon knew far more about her grandfather than she had previously imagined. This American obviously had volumes to share with her, but this was not the place. 'I can't afford to let them catch you, Robert. There's a lot we need to discuss. You need to go!'

Langdon heard only the faint murmur of her voice. He wasn't going anywhere. He was lost in another place now. A place where ancient secrets rose to the surface. A place where forgotten histories emerged from the shadows.

Slowly, as if moving underwater, Langdon turned his head and gazed through the reddish haze toward the *Mona Lisa*.

The fleur-de-lis . . . the flower of Lisa . . . the Mona Lisa.

It was all intertwined, a silent symphony echoing the deepest secrets of the Priory of Sion and Leonardo da Vinci.

A few miles away, on the riverbank beyond Les Invalides, the bewildered driver of a twin-bed Trailor truck stood at gunpoint and watched as the captain of the Judicial Police let out a guttural roar of rage and heaved a bar of soap out into the turgid waters of the Seine.

24

Silas gazed upward at the Saint-Sulpice obelisk, taking in the length of the massive marble shaft. His sinews felt taut with exhilaration. He glanced around the church one more time to make sure he was alone. Then he knelt at the base of the structure, not out of reverence, but out of necessity.

The keystone is hidden beneath the Rose Line.

At the base of the Sulpice obelisk.

All the brothers had concurred.

On his knees now, Silas ran his hands across the stone floor. He saw no cracks or markings to indicate a movable tile, so he began rapping softly with his knuckles on the floor. Following the brass line closer to the obelisk, he knocked on each tile adjacent to the brass line. Finally, one of them echoed strangely.

There's a hollow area beneath the floor!

Silas smiled. His victims had spoken the truth.

Standing, he searched the sanctuary for something with which to break the floor tile.

High above Silas, in the balcony, Sister Sandrine stifled a gasp. Her darkest fears had just been confirmed. This visitor was not who he seemed. The mysterious Opus Dei monk had come to Saint-Sulpice for another purpose.

A secret purpose.

You are not the only one with secrets, she thought.

Sister Sandrine Bieil was more than the keeper of this church. She was a sentry. And tonight, the ancient wheels had been set in motion. The arrival of this stranger at the base of the obelisk was a signal from the brotherhood.

It was a silent call of distress.

25

The US Embassy in Paris is a compact complex on Avenue Gabriel, just north of the Champs-Elysées. The three-acre compound is considered US soil, meaning all those who stand on it are subject to the same laws and protections as they would encounter standing inthe United States.

The embassy's night operator was reading *Time* magazine's International Edition when the sound of her phone interrupted.

'US Embassy,' she answered.

'Good evening.' The caller spoke English accented with French. 'I need some assistance.' Despite the politeness of the man's words, his tone sounded gruff and official. 'I was told you had a phone message for me on your automated system. The name is Langdon. Unfortunately, I have forgotten my three-digit access code. If you could help me, I would be most grateful.'

The operator paused, confused. 'I'm sorry, sir. Your message must be quite old. That system was removed two years ago for security precautions. Moreover, all the access codes were *five*-digit. Who told you we had a message for you?'

'You have *no* automated phone system?'

'No, sir. Any message for you would be handwritten in our services department. What was your name again?'

But the man had hung up.

Bezu Fache felt dumbstruck as he paced the banks of the Seine. He was certain he had seen Langdon dial a local number, enter a three-digit code, and then listen to a recording. *But if Langdon didn't phone the embassy, then who the hell did he call?*

It was at that moment, eyeing his cellular phone, that Fache realized the answers were in the palm of his hand. *Langdon used my phone to place that call.*

Keying into the cell phone's menu, Fache pulled up the list of recently dialled numbers and found the call Langdon had placed.

A Paris exchange, followed by the three-digit code 454.

Redialling the phone number, Fache waited as the line began ringing.

Finally a woman's voice answered. '*Bonjour, vous êtes bien chez Sophie Neveu,*' the recording announced. '*Je suis absente pour le moment, mais . . .*'

Fache's blood was boiling as he typed the numbers 4 . . . 5 . . . 4.

26

Despite her monumental reputation, the *Mona Lisa* was a mere thirty-one inches by twenty-one inches – smaller even than the posters of her sold in the Louvre gift shop. She hung on the northwest wall of the Salle des Etats behind a two-inch-thick pane of protective Plexiglas. Painted on a poplar wood panel, her ethereal, mist-filled atmosphere was attributed to Da Vinci's mastery of the *sfumato* style, in which forms appear to evaporate into one another.

Since taking up residence in the Louvre, the *Mona Lisa* – or *La Jaconde* as they call her in France – had been stolen twice, most recently in 1911, when she disappeared from the Louvre's '*salle impénétrable*' – Le Salon Carré. Parisians wept in the streets and wrote newspaper articles begging the thieves for the painting's return. Two years later, the *Mona Lisa* was discovered hidden in the false bottom of a trunk in a Florence hotel room.

Langdon, now having made it clear to Sophie that he had no intention of leaving, moved with her across the Salle des Etats. The *Mona Lisa* was still twenty yards ahead when Sophie turned on the black light, and the bluish crescent of penlight fanned out on the floor in front of them. She swung the beam back and forth across the floor like a minesweeper, searching for any hint of luminescent ink.

Walking beside her, Langdon was already feeling the tingle of anticipation that accompanied his face-to-face reunions with great works of art. He strained to see beyond the cocoon of purplish light emanating from the black light in Sophie's hand. To the left, the room's octagonal viewing divan emerged, looking like a dark island on the empty sea of parquet.

Langdon could now begin to see the panel of dark glass on the wall. Behind it, he knew, in the confines of her own private cell, hung the most celebrated painting in the world.

The *Mona Lisa*'s status as the most famous piece of art in the world, Langdon knew, had nothing to do with her enigmatic smile. Nor was it due to the mysterious interpretations attributed her by many art historians and conspiracy buffs. Quite simply, the *Mona Lisa* was famous because Leonardo da Vinci claimed she was his finest accomplishment. He carried the painting with him whenever he travelled and, if asked why, would reply that he found it hard to part with his most sublime expression of female beauty.

Even so, many art historians suspected Da Vinci's reverence for the *Mona Lisa* had nothing to do with its artistic mastery. In actuality, the painting was a surprisingly ordinary *sfumato* portrait. Da Vinci's veneration for this work, many claimed, stemmed from something far deeper: a hidden message in the layers of paint. The *Mona Lisa* was, in fact, one of the world's most documented inside jokes. The painting's well-documented collage of double entendres and playful allusions had been revealed in most art history tomes, and yet, incredibly, the public at large still considered her smile a great mystery.

No mystery at all, Langdon thought, moving forward and watching as the faint outline of the painting began to take shape. *No mystery at all.*

Most recently Langdon had shared the *Mona Lisa*'s secret with a rather unlikely group – a dozen inmates at the Essex County Penitentiary. Langdon's jail seminar was part of a Harvard outreach programme attempting to bring education into the prison system – *Culture for Convicts,* as Langdon's colleagues liked to call it.

Standing at an overhead projector in a darkened penitentiary library, Langdon had shared the *Mona Lisa*'s secret with the prisoners attending class, men whom he found surprisingly engaged – rough, but sharp. 'You may notice,' Langdon told them, walking up to the projected image of the *Mona Lisa* on the library wall, 'that the background behind her face is uneven.' Langdon motioned to the glaring discrepancy. 'Da Vinci painted the horizon line on the left significantly lower than the right.'

'He screwed it up?' one of the inmates asked.

Langdon chuckled. 'No. Da Vinci didn't do that too often. Actually, this is a little trick Da Vinci played. By lowering the countryside on the left, Da Vinci made Mona Lisa look much larger from the left side than from the right side. A little Da Vinci inside joke. Historically, the concepts of male and female have assigned sides – left is female, and right is male. Because Da Vinci was a big fan of feminine principles, he made Mona Lisa look more majestic from the *left* than the right.'

'I heard he was a fag,' said a small man with a goatee.

Langdon winced. 'Historians don't generally put it quite that way, but yes, Da Vinci was a homosexual.'

'Is that why he was into that whole feminine thing?'

'Actually, Da Vinci was in tune with the *balance* between male and female. He believed that a human soul could not be enlightened unless it had both male and female elements.'

'You mean like chicks with dicks?' someone called.

This elicited a hearty round of laughs. Langdon considered offering an etymological sidebar about the word *hermaphrodite* and its ties to Hermes and Aphrodite, but something told him it would be lost on this crowd.

'Hey, Mr Langford,' a muscle-bound man said. 'Is it true that the *Mona Lisa* is a picture of Da Vinci in drag? I heard that was true.'

'It's quite possible,' Langdon said. 'Da Vinci was a prankster, and computerized analysis of the *Mona Lisa* and Da Vinci's self-portraits confirm some startling points of congruency in their faces. Whatever Da Vinci was up to,' Langdon said, 'his Mona Lisa is neither male nor female. It carries a subtle message of androgyny. It is a fusing of both.'

'You sure that's not just some Harvard bullshit way of saying Mona Lisa is one ugly chick.'

Now Langdon laughed. 'You may be right. But actually Da Vinci left a big clue that the painting was supposed to be androgynous. Has anyone here ever heard of an Egyptian god named Amon?'

'Hell yes!' the big guy said. 'God of masculine fertility!'

Langdon was stunned.

'It says so on every box of Amon condoms.' The muscular man gave a wide grin. 'It's got a guy with a ram's head on the front and says he's the Egyptian god of fertility.'

Langdon was not familiar with the brand name, but he was glad to hear the prophylactic manufacturers had got their hieroglyphs right. 'Well done. Amon is indeed represented as a man with a ram's head, and his promiscuity and curved horns are related to our modern sexual slang "horny".'

'No shit!'

'No shit,' Langdon said. 'And do you know who Amon's counterpart was? The Egyptian *goddess* of fertility?'

The question met with several seconds of silence.

'It was Isis,' Langdon told them, grabbing a grease pen. 'So we have the male god, Amon.' He wrote it down. 'And the female goddess, Isis, whose ancient pictogram was once called L'ISA.'

Langdon finished writing and stepped back from the projector.

AMON L'ISA

'Ring any bells?' he asked.

'Mona Lisa . . . holy crap,' somebody gasped.

Langdon nodded. 'Gentlemen, not only does the face of Mona Lisa look androgynous, but her name is an anagram of the divine union of male and female. And *that,* my friends, is Da Vinci's little secret, and the reason for Mona Lisa's knowing smile.'

'My grandfather was here,' Sophie said, dropping suddenly to her knees, now only ten feet from the *Mona Lisa*. She pointed the black light tentatively to a spot on the parquet floor.

At first Langdon saw nothing. Then, as he knelt beside her, he saw a tiny droplet of dried liquid that was luminescing. *Ink?* Suddenly he recalled what black lights were actually used for. *Blood*. His senses tingled. Sophie was right. Jacques Saunière had indeed paid a visit to the *Mona Lisa* before he died.

'He wouldn't have come here without a reason,' Sophie whispered, standing up. 'I know he left a message for me here.' Quickly striding the final few steps to the *Mona Lisa*, she illuminated the floor directly in front of the painting. She waved the light back and forth across the bare parquet.

'There's nothing here!'

At that moment, Langdon saw a faint purple glimmer on the protective glass before the *Mona Lisa*. Reaching down, he took Sophie's wrist and slowly moved the light up to the painting itself.

They both froze.

On the glass, six words glowed in purple, scrawled directly across the *Mona Lisa*'s face.

27

Seated at Saunière's desk, Lieutenant Collet pressed the phone to his ear in disbelief. *Did I hear Fache correctly?* 'A bar of soap? But how could Langdon have known about the GPS dot?'

'Sophie Neveu,' Fache replied. 'She told him.'

'What! Why?'

'Damned good question, but I just heard a recording that confirms she tipped him off.'

Collet was speechless. *What was Neveu thinking?* Fache had proof that Sophie had interfered with a DCPJ sting operation? Sophie Neveu was not only going to be fired, she was also going to jail. 'But, Captain . . . then where is Langdon *now?*'

'Have any fire alarms gone off there?'

'No, sir.'

'And no one has come out under the Grand Gallery gate?'

'No. We've got a Louvre security officer on the gate. Just as you requested.'

'Okay, Langdon must still be inside the Grand Gallery.'

'Inside? But what is he doing?'

'Is the Louvre security guard armed?'

'Yes, sir. He's a senior warden.'

'Send him in,' Fache commanded. 'I can't get my men back to the perimeter for a few minutes, and I don't want Langdon breaking for an exit.' Fache paused. 'And you'd better tell the guard Agent Neveu is probably in there with him.'

'Agent Neveu left, I thought.'

'Did you actually *see* her leave?'

'No, sir, but—'

'Well, nobody on the perimeter saw her leave either. They only saw her go in.'

Collet was flabbergasted by Sophie Neveu's bravado. *She's still inside the building?*

'Handle it,' Fache ordered. 'I want Langdon and Neveu at gunpoint by the time I get back.'

As the Trailor truck drove off, Captain Fache rounded up his men. Robert Langdon had proven an elusive quarry tonight, and with Agent Neveu now helping him, he might be far harder to corner than expected.

Fache decided not to take any chances.

Hedging his bets, he ordered half of his men back to the Louvre perimeter. The other half he sent to guard the only location in Paris where Robert Langdon could find safe harbour.

28

Inside the Salle des Etats, Langdon stared in astonishment at the six words glowing on the Plexiglas. The text seemed to hover in space, casting a jagged shadow across Mona Lisa's mysterious smile.

'The Priory,' Langdon whispered. 'This proves your grandfather was a member!'

Sophie looked at him in confusion. 'You *understand* this?'

'It's flawless,' Langdon said, nodding as his thoughts churned. 'It's a proclamation of one of the Priory's most fundamental philosophies!'

Sophie looked baffled in the glow of the message scrawled across the *Mona Lisa*'s face.

So dark the con of man

'Sophie,' Langdon said, 'the Priory's tradition of perpetuating goddess worship is based on a belief that powerful men in the early Christian Church "conned" the world by propagating lies that devalued the female and tipped the scales in favour of the masculine.'

Sophie remained silent, staring at the words.

'The Priory believes that Constantine and his male successors successfully converted the world from matriarchal paganism to patriarchal Christianity by waging a campaign of propaganda that demonized the sacred feminine, obliterating the goddess from modern religion for ever.'

Sophie's expression remained uncertain. 'My grandfather sent me to this spot to find this. He must be trying to tell me more than *that*.'

Langdon understood her meaning. *She thinks this is another code.* Whether a hidden meaning existed here or not, Langdon could not immediately say. His mind was still grappling with the bold clarity of Saunière's outward message.

So dark the con of man, he thought. *So dark indeed.*

Nobody could deny the enormous good the modern Church did in today's troubled world, and yet the Church had a deceitful and violent history. Their brutal crusade to 'reeducate' the pagan and feminine-worshipping religions spanned three centuries, employing methods as inspired as they were horrific.

The Catholic Inquisition published the book that arguably could be called the most blood-soaked publication in human history. *Malleus Maleficarum* – or *The Witches' Hammer* – indoctrinated the world to 'the dangers of freethinking women' and instructed the clergy how to locate, torture and destroy them. Those deemed 'witches' by the Church included all female scholars, priestesses, gypsies, mystics, nature lovers, herb gatherers and any women 'suspiciously attuned to the natural world'. Midwives also were killed for their heretical practice of using medical knowledge to ease the pain of childbirth – a suffering, the Church claimed, that was God's rightful punishment for Eve's partaking of the Apple of Knowledge, thus giving birth to the idea of Original Sin. During three hundred years of witch hunts, the Church burned at the stake an astounding five *million* women.

The propaganda and bloodshed had worked.

Today's world was living proof.

Women, once celebrated as an essential half of spiritual enlightenment, had been banished from the temples of the world. There were no female Orthodox rabbis, Catholic priests, nor Islamic clerics. The once hallowed act of Hieros Gamos – the natural sexual union between man and woman through which each became spiritually whole – had been recast as a shameful act. Holy men who had once required sexual union with their female counterparts to commune with God now feared their natural sexual urges as the work of the devil, collaborating with his favourite accomplice . . . *woman*.

Not even the feminine association with the *left-hand* side could escape the Church's defamation. In France and Italy, the words for 'left' – *gauche* and *sinistra* – came to have deeply negative overtones, while their right-hand counterparts rang of *right*eousness, dexterity, and correctness. To this day, radical thought was considered *left* wing, irrational thought was *left* brain, and anything evil, *sinister*.

The days of the goddess were over. The pendulum had swung. Mother Earth had become a *man's* world, and the gods of destruction and war were taking their toll. The male ego had spent two millennia running unchecked by its female counterpart. The Priory of Sion believed that it was this obliteration of the sacred feminine in modern life that had caused what the Hopi Native Americans called *koyanisquatsi* – 'life out of balance' – an unstable situation marked by testosterone-fuelled wars, a plethora of misogynistic societies and a growing disrespect for Mother Earth.

'Robert!' Sophie said, her whisper yanking him back. 'Someone's coming!'

He heard the approaching footsteps out in the hallway.

'Over here!' Sophie extinguished the black light and seemed to evaporate before Langdon's eyes.

For an instant he felt totally blind. *Over where!* As his vision cleared he saw Sophie's silhouette racing toward the centre of the room and ducking out of sight behind the octagonal viewing bench. He was about to dash after her when a booming voice stopped him cold.

'*Arretez!*' a man commanded from the doorway.

The Louvre security agent advanced through the entrance to the Salle des Etats, his pistol outstretched, taking deadly aim at Langdon's chest.

Langdon felt his arms raise instinctively for the ceiling.

'*Couchez-vous!*' the guard commanded. '*Lie down!*'

Langdon was face first on the floor in a matter of seconds. The guard hurried over and kicked his legs apart, spreading Langdon out.

'*Mauvaise idée, Monsieur Langdon,*' he said, pressing the gun hard into Langdon's back. '*Mauvaise idée.*'

Face down on the parquet floor with his arms and legs spread wide, Langdon found little humour in the irony of his position. *The Vitruvian Man*, he thought. *Face down.*

29

Inside Saint-Sulpice, Silas carried the heavy iron votive candle holder from the altar back toward the obelisk. The shaft would do nicely as a battering ram. Eyeing the grey marble panel that covered the apparent hollow in the floor, he realized he could not possibly shatter the covering without making considerable noise.

Iron on marble. It would echo off the vaulted ceilings.

Would the nun hear him? She should be asleep by now. Even so, it was a chance Silas preferred not to take. Looking around for a cloth to wrap around the tip of the iron pole, he saw nothing except the altar's linen mantle, which he refused to defile. *My cloak,* he thought. Knowing he was alone in the great church, Silas untied his cloak and slipped it off his body. As he removed it, he felt a sting as the wool fibers stuck to the fresh wounds on his back.

Naked now, except for his loin swaddle, Silas wrapped his cloak over the end of the iron rod. Then, aiming at the centre of the floor tile, he drove the tip into it. A muffled thud. The stone did not break. He drove the pole into it again. Again a dull thud, but this time accompanied by a crack. On the third swing, the covering finally shattered, and stone shards fell into a hollow area beneath the floor.

A compartment!

Quickly pulling the remaining pieces from the opening, Silas gazed into the void. His blood pounded as he knelt down before it. Raising his pale bare arm, he reached inside.

At first he felt nothing. The floor of the compartment was bare, smooth stone. Then, feeling deeper, reaching his arm in under the Rose Line, he touched something! A thick stone tablet. Getting his fingers around the edge, he gripped it and gently lifted the tablet out. As he stood and examined his find, he realized he was holding a rough-hewn stone slab with engraved words. He felt for an instant like a modern-day Moses.

As Silas read the words on the tablet, he felt surprise. He had expected the keystone to be a map, or a complex series of directions, perhaps even encoded. The keystone, however, bore the simplest of inscriptions.

Job 38:11

A Bible verse? Silas was stunned with the devilish simplicity. The secret location of that which they sought was revealed in a Bible verse? The brotherhood stopped at nothing to mock the righteous!

Job. Chapter thirty-eight. Verse eleven.

Although Silas did not recall the exact contents of verse eleven by heart, he knew the Book of Job told the story of a man whose faith in God survived repeated tests. *Appropriate,* he thought, barely able to contain his excitement.

Looking over his shoulder, he gazed down the shimmering Rose Line and couldn't help but smile. There atop the main altar, propped open on a gilded book stand, sat an enormous leather-bound Bible.

Up in the balcony, Sister Sandrine was shaking. Moments ago, she had been about to flee and carry out her orders, when the man below suddenly removed his cloak. When she saw his alabaster-white flesh, she was overcome with a horrified bewilderment. His broad, pale back was soaked with blood-red slashes. Even from here she could see the wounds were fresh.

This man has been mercilessly whipped!

She also saw the bloody *cilice* around his thigh, the wound beneath it dripping. *What kind of God would want a body punished this way?* The rituals of Opus Dei, Sister Sandrine knew, were not something she would ever understand. But that was hardly her concern at this instant. *Opus Dei is searching for the keystone.* How they knew of it, Sister Sandrine could not imagine, although she knew she did not have time to think.

The bloody monk was now quietly donning his cloak again, clutching his prize as he moved toward the altar, toward the Bible.

In breathless silence, Sister Sandrine left the balcony and raced down the hall to her quarters. Getting on her hands and knees, she reached beneath her wooden bed frame and retrieved the sealed envelope she had hidden there years ago.

Tearing it open, she found four Paris phone numbers.

Trembling, she began to dial.

Downstairs, Silas laid the stone tablet on the altar and turned his eager hands to the leather Bible. His long white fingers were sweating now as he turned the pages. Flipping through the Old Testament, he found the Book of Job. He located chapter thirty-eight. As he ran his finger down the column of text, he anticipated the words he was about to read.

They will lead The Way!

Finding verse number eleven, Silas read the text. It was only seven words. Confused, he read it again, sensing something had gone terribly wrong. The verse simply read:

HITHERTO SHALT THOU COME, BUT NO FURTHER.

30

Security warden Claude Grouard simmered with rage as he stood over his prostrate captive in front of the *Mona Lisa*. *This bastard killed Jacques Saunière!* Saunière had been like a well-loved father to Grouard and his security team.

Grouard wanted nothing more than to pull the trigger and bury a bullet in Robert Langdon's back. As senior warden, Grouard was one of the few guards who actually carried a loaded weapon. He reminded himself, however, that killing Langdon would be a generous fate compared to the misery about to be communicated by Bezu Fache and the French prison system.

Grouard yanked his walkie-talkie off his belt and attempted to radio for backup. All he heard was static. The additional electronic security in this chamber always wrought havoc with the guards' communications. *I have to move to the doorway.* Still aiming his weapon at Langdon, Grouard began backing slowly toward the entrance. On his third step, he spied something that made him stop short.

What the hell is that!

An inexplicable mirage was materializing near the centre of the room. A silhouette. There was someone else in the room? A woman was moving through the darkness, walking briskly toward the far left wall. In front of her, a purplish beam of light swung back and forth across the floor, as if she were searching for something with a coloured flashlight.

'*Qui est là?*' Grouard demanded, feeling his adrenaline spike for a second time in the last thirty seconds. He suddenly didn't know where to aim his gun or what direction to move.

'PTS,' the woman replied calmly, still scanning the floor with her light.

Police Technique et Scientifique. Grouard was sweating now. *I thought all the agents were gone!* He now recognized the purple light as ultraviolet, consistent with a PTS team, and yet he could not understand why DCPJ would be looking for evidence in here.

'*Votre nom!*' Grouard yelled, instinct telling him something was amiss. '*Répondez!*'

'*C'est moi,*' the voice responded in calm French. '*Sophie Neveu.*'

Somewhere in the distant recesses of Grouard's mind, the name registered.

Sophie Neveu? That was the name of Saunière's granddaughter, wasn't it? She used to come in here as a little kid, but that was years ago. *This couldn't possibly be her!* And even if it were Sophie Neveu, that was hardly a reason to trust her; Grouard had heard the rumours of the painful falling-out between Saunière and his granddaughter.

'You know me,' the woman called. 'And Robert Langdon did not kill my grandfather. Believe me.'

Warden Grouard was not about to take *that* on faith. *I need backup!* Trying his walkie-talkie again, he got only static. The entrance was still a good twenty yards behind him, and Grouard began backing up slowly, choosing to leave his gun trained on the man on the floor. As Grouard inched backward, he could see the woman across the room raising her UV light and scrutinizing a large painting that hung on the far side of the Salle des Etats, directly opposite the *Mona Lisa.*

Grouard gasped, realizing which painting it was.

What in the name of God is she doing?

Across the room, Sophie Neveu felt a cold sweat breaking across her forehead. Langdon was still spread-eagled on the floor. *Hold on, Robert. Almost there.* Knowing the guard would never actually shoot either of them, Sophie now turned her attention back to the matter at hand, scanning the entire area around one masterpiece in particular – another Da Vinci. But the UV light revealed nothing out of the ordinary. Not on the floor, on the walls, or even on the canvas itself.

There must be something here!

Sophie felt totally certain she had deciphered her grandfather's intentions correctly.

What else could he possibly intend?

The masterpiece she was examining was a five-foot-tall canvas. The bizarre scene Da Vinci had painted included an awkwardly posed Virgin Mary sitting with Baby Jesus, John the Baptist and the Angel Uriel on a perilous outcropping of rocks. When Sophie was a little girl, no trip to the *Mona Lisa* had been complete without her grandfather dragging her across the room to see this second painting.

Grand-père, I'm here! But I don't see it!

Behind her, Sophie could hear the guard trying to radio again for help. *Think!*

She pictured the message scrawled on the protective glass of the *Mona Lisa. So dark the con of man.* The painting before her had no protective glass on which to write a message, and Sophie knew her grandfather would never have defaced this masterpiece by writing on the painting itself. She paused. *At least not on the front.* Her eyes shot upward, climbing the long cables that dangled from the ceiling to support the canvas.

Could that be it? Grabbing the left side of the carved wood frame, she pulled it toward her. The painting was large and the backing flexed as she swung it away from the wall. Sophie slipped her head and shoulders in behind the painting and raised the black light to inspect the back.

It took only seconds to realize her instinct had been wrong. The back of the painting was pale and blank. There was no purple text here, only the mottled brown backside of aging canvas and –

Wait.

Sophie's eyes locked on an incongruous glint of lustrous metal lodged near the bottom edge of the frame's wooden armature. The object was small, partially wedged in the slit where the canvas met the frame. A shimmering gold chain dangled off it.

To Sophie's utter amazement, the chain was affixed to a familiar gold key. The broad, sculpted head was in the shape of a cross and bore an engraved seal she had not seen since she was nine years old. A fleur-de-lis with the initials P.S. In that instant, Sophie felt the ghost of her grandfather whispering in her ear. *When the time comes, the key will be yours.* A tightness gripped her throat as she realized that her grandfather, even in death, had kept his promise. *This key opens a box,* his voice was saying, *where I keep many secrets.*

Sophie now realized that the entire purpose of tonight's word game had been this key. Her grandfather had it with him when he was killed. Not wanting it to fall into the hands of the police, he hid it behind this painting. Then he devised an ingenious treasure hunt to ensure only Sophie would find it.

'*Au secours!*' the guard's voice yelled.

Sophie snatched the key from behind the painting and slipped it deep in her pocket along with the UV penlight. Peering out from behind the canvas, she could see the guard was still trying desperately to raise someone on the walkie-talkie. He was backing toward the entrance, still aiming the gun firmly at Langdon.

'*Au secours!*' he shouted again into his radio.

Static.

He can't transmit, Sophie realized, recalling that tourists with cell phones often got frustrated in here when they tried to call home to brag about seeing the *Mona Lisa.* The extra surveillance wiring in the walls made it virtually impossible to get a carrier unless you stepped out into the hall. The guard was backing quickly toward the exit now, and Sophie knew she had to act immediately.

Gazing up at the large painting behind which she was partially ensconced, Sophie realized that Leonardo da Vinci, for the second time tonight, was there to help.

Another few metres, Grouard told himself, keeping his gun levelled.

'*Arrêtez! Ou je la détruis!*' the woman's voice echoed across the room.

Grouard glanced over and stopped in his tracks. '*Mon dieu, non!*'

Through the reddish haze, he could see that the woman had actually lifted the large painting off its cables and propped it on the floor in front of her. At five feet tall, the canvas almost entirely hid her body. Grouard's first thought was to wonder why the painting's trip wires hadn't set off alarms, but of course the artwork cable sensors had yet to be reset tonight. *What is she doing!*

When he saw it, his blood went cold.

The canvas started to bulge in the middle, the fragile outlines of the Virgin Mary, Baby Jesus and John the Baptist beginning to distort.

'*Non!*' Grouard screamed, frozen in horror as he watched the priceless Da Vinci stretching. The woman was pushing her knee into the centre of the canvas from behind! '*NON!*'

Grouard wheeled and aimed his gun at her but instantly realized it was an empty threat. The canvas was only fabric, but it was utterly impenetrable – a six-million-dollar piece of body armour.

I can't put a bullet through a Da Vinci!

'Set down your gun and radio,' the woman said in calm French, 'or I'll put my knee through this painting. I think you know how my grandfather would feel about that.'

Grouard felt dizzy. 'Please . . . no. That's *Madonna of the Rocks!*' He dropped his gun and radio, raising his hands over his head.

'Thank you,' the woman said. 'Now do exactly as I tell you, and everything will work out fine.'

Moments later, Langdon's pulse was still thundering as he ran beside Sophie down the emergency stairwell toward the ground level. Neither of them had said a word since leaving the trembling Louvre guard lying in the Salle des Etats. The guard's pistol was now clutched tightly in Langdon's hands, and he couldn't wait to get rid of it. The weapon felt heavy and dangerously foreign.

Taking the stairs two at a time, Langdon wondered if Sophie had any idea how valuable a painting she had almost ruined. Her choice in art seemed eerily pertinent to tonight's adventure. The Da Vinci she had grabbed, much like the *Mona Lisa,* was notorious among art historians for its plethora of hidden pagan symbolism.

'You chose a valuable hostage,' he said as they ran.

'*Madonna of the Rocks,*' she replied. 'But I didn't choose it, my grandfather did. He left me a little something behind the painting.'

Langdon shot her a startled look. 'What!? But how did you know which painting? Why *Madonna of the Rocks?*'

'So dark the con of man.' She flashed a triumphant smile. 'I missed the first two anagrams, Robert. I wasn't about to miss the third.'

31

'They're dead!' Sister Sandrine stammered into the telephone in her Saint-Sulpice residence. She was leaving a message on an answering machine. 'Please pick up! They're all dead!'

The first three phone numbers on the list had produced terrifying results – a hysterical widow, a detective working late at a murder scene, and a sombre priest consoling a bereaved family. All three contacts were dead. And now, as she called the fourth and final number – the number she was not supposed to call unless the first three could not be reached – she got an answering machine. The outgoing message offered no name but simply asked the caller to leave a message.

'The floor panel has been broken!' she pleaded as she left the message. 'The other three are dead!'

Sister Sandrine did not know the identities of the four men she protected, but the private phone numbers stashed beneath her bed were for use on only one condition.

If that floor panel is ever broken, the faceless messenger had told her, *it means the upper echelon has been breached. One of us has been mortally threatened and been forced to tell a desperate lie. Call the numbers. Warn the others. Do not fail us in this.*

It was a silent alarm. Foolproof in its simplicity. The plan had amazed her when she first heard it. If the identity of one brother was compromised, he could tell a lie that would start in motion a mechanism to warn the others. Tonight, however, it seemed that more than one had been compromised.

'Please answer,' she whispered in fear. 'Where are you?'

'Hang up the phone,' a deep voice said from the doorway.

Turning in terror, she saw the massive monk. He was clutching the heavy iron candle stand. Shaking, she set the phone back in the cradle.

'They are dead,' the monk said. 'All four of them. And they have played me for a fool. Tell me where the keystone is.'

'I don't know!' Sister Sandrine said truthfully. 'That secret is guarded by others.' *Others who are dead!*

The man advanced, his white fists gripping the iron stand. 'You are a sister of the Church, and yet you serve *them*?'

'Jesus had but one true message,' Sister Sandrine said defiantly. 'I cannot see that message in Opus Dei.'

A sudden explosion of rage erupted behind the monk's eyes. He lunged, lashing out with the candle stand like a club. As Sister Sandrine fell, her last feeling was an overwhelming sense of foreboding.

All four are dead.

The precious truth is lost for ever.

32

The security alarm on the west end of the Denon Wing sent the pigeons in the nearby Tuileries Gardens scattering as Langdon and Sophie dashed out of the bulkhead into the Paris night. As they ran across the plaza to Sophie's car, Langdon could hear police sirens wailing in the distance.

'That's it there,' Sophie called, pointing to a red snub-nosed two-seater parked on the plaza.

She's kidding, right? The vehicle was easily the smallest car Langdon had ever seen.

'SmartCar,' she said. 'A hundred kilometres to the litre.'

Langdon had barely thrown himself into the passenger seat before Sophie gunned the SmartCar up and over a curb onto a gravel divider. He gripped the dash as the car shot out across a sidewalk and bounced back down into the small rotary at Carrousel du Louvre.

For an instant, Sophie seemed to consider taking the shortcut across the rotary by ploughing straight ahead, through the median's perimeter hedge, and bisecting the large circle of grass in the centre.

'No!' Langdon shouted, knowing the hedges around Carrousel du Louvre were there to hide the perilous chasm in the centre – *La Pyramide Inversée* – the upside-down pyramid skylight he had seen earlier from inside the museum. It was large enough to swallow their SmartCar in a single gulp. Fortunately, Sophie decided on the more conventional route, jamming the wheel hard to the right, circling properly until she exited, cut left, and swung into the northbound lane, accelerating toward Rue de Rivoli.

The two-tone police sirens blared louder behind them, and Langdon could see the lights now in his side view mirror. The SmartCar engine whined in protest as Sophie urged it faster away from the Louvre. Fifty yards ahead, the traffic light at Rivoli turned red. Sophie cursed under her breath and kept racing toward it. Langdon felt his muscles tighten.

'Sophie?'

Slowing only slightly as they reached the intersection, Sophie flicked her headlights and stole a quick glance both ways before flooring the accelerator again and carving a sharp left turn through the empty intersection onto Rivoli.

As they straightened out, Langdon turned in his seat, craning his neck to look out the rear window toward the Louvre. The police did not seem to be chasing them. The sea of blue lights was assembling at the museum.

His heartbeat finally slowing, Langdon turned back round. 'That was interesting.'

Sophie didn't seem to hear. Her eyes remained fixed ahead. The embassy was only about half a mile away, and Langdon settled into his seat.

So dark the con of man.

Sophie's quick thinking had been impressive.

Madonna of the Rocks.

Sophie had said her grandfather left her something behind the painting. *A final message?* Langdon could not help but marvel over Saunière's brilliant hiding place; *Madonna of the Rocks* was yet another fitting link in the evening's chain of interconnected symbolism. Saunière, it seemed, at every turn, was reinforcing his fondness for the dark and mischievous side of Leonardo da Vinci.

Da Vinci's original commission for *Madonna of the Rocks* had come from an organization known as the Confraternity of the Immaculate Conception, which needed a painting for the centrepiece of an altar triptych in their church of San Francesco in Milan. The nuns gave Leonardo specific dimensions, and the desired theme for the painting – the Virgin Mary, baby John the Baptist, Uriel and Baby Jesus sheltering in a cave. Although Da Vinci did as they requested, when he delivered the work, the group reacted with horror. He had filled the painting with explosive and disturbing details.

The painting showed a blue-robed Virgin Mary sitting with her arm around an infant child, presumably Baby Jesus. Opposite Mary sat Uriel, also with an infant, presumably baby John the Baptist. Oddly, though, rather than the usual Jesus-blessing-John scenario, it was baby *John* who was blessing Jesus . . . and Jesus was submitting to his authority! More troubling still, Mary was holding one hand high above the head of infant John and making a decidedly threatening gesture – her fingers looking like eagle's talons, gripping an invisible head. Finally, the most obvious and frightening image: Just below Mary's curled fingers, Uriel was making a cutting gesture with his hand – as if slicing the neck of the invisible head gripped by Mary's claw-like hand.

Langdon's students were always amused to learn that Da Vinci eventually mollified the confraternity by painting them a second, 'watered-down' version of *Madonna of the Rocks* in which everyone was arranged in a more orthodox manner. The second version now hung in London's National Gallery under the name *Virgin of the Rocks*, although Langdon still preferred the Louvre's more intriguing original.

As Sophie gunned the car up Champs-Elysées, Langdon said, 'The painting. What was behind it?'

Her eyes remained on the road. 'I'll show you once we're safely inside the embassy.'

'You'll *show* it to me?' Langdon was surprised. 'He left you a physical object?'

Sophie gave a curt nod. 'Embossed with a fleur-de-lis and the initials P.S.'

Langdon couldn't believe his ears.

We're going to make it, Sophie thought as she swung the SmartCar's wheel to the right, cutting sharply past the luxurious Hôtel de Crillon into Paris's tree-lined diplomatic neighbourhood. The embassy was less than a mile away now. She was finally feeling like she could breathe normally again.

Even as she drove, Sophie's mind remained locked on the key in her pocket, her memories of seeing it many years ago, the gold head shaped as an equal-armed cross, the triangular shaft, the indentations, the embossed flowery seal, and the letters P.S.

Although the key barely had entered Sophie's thoughts through the years, her work in the intelligence community had taught her plenty about security, and now the key's peculiar tooling no longer looked so mystifying. *A laser-tooled varying matrix. Impossible to duplicate.* Rather than teeth that moved tumblers, this key's complex series of laser-burned pockmarks was examined by an electric eye. If the eye determined that the hexagonal pockmarks were correctly spaced, arranged, and rotated, then the lock would open.

Sophie could not begin to imagine what a key like this opened, but she sensed Robert would be able to tell her. After all, he had described the key's embossed seal without ever seeing it. The cruciform on top implied the key belonged to some kind of Christian organization, and yet Sophie knew of no churches that used laser-tooled varying matrix keys.

Besides, my grandfather was no Christian. . . .

Sophie had witnessed proof of that ten years ago. Ironically, it had been another *key* – a far more normal one – that had revealed his true nature to her.

The afternoon had been warm when she landed at Charles de Gaulle Airport and hailed a taxi home. *Grand-père will be so surprised to see me,* she thought. Returning from graduate school in Britain for spring break a few days early, Sophie couldn't wait to see him and tell him all about the encryption methods she was studying.

When she arrived at their Paris home, however, her grandfather was not there. Disappointed, she knew he had not been expecting her and was probably working at the Louvre. *But it's Saturday afternoon,* she realized. He seldom worked on weekends. On weekends, he usually—

Grinning, Sophie ran out to the garage. Sure enough, his car was gone.

It was the weekend. Jacques Saunière despised city driving and owned a car for one destination only – his vacation château in Normandy, west of Paris. Sophie, after months in the congestion of London, was eager for the smells of nature and to start her vacation right away. It was still early evening, and she decided to leave immediately and surprise him. Borrowing a friend's car, Sophie drove west, winding into the deserted moon-swept hills near Creully. She arrived just after ten o'clock, turning down the long private driveway toward her grandfather's retreat. The access road was over a mile long, and she was halfway down it before she could start to see the house through the trees – a mammoth, old stone château nestled in the woods on the side of a hill.

Sophie had half expected to find her grandfather asleep at this hour and was excited to see the house twinkling with lights. Her delight turned to surprise, however, when she arrived to find the driveway filled with parked cars – Mercedeses, BMWs, Audis and a Rolls-Royce.

Sophie stared a moment and then burst out laughing. *My grand-père, the famous recluse!* Jacques Saunière, it seemed, was far less reclusive than he liked to pretend. Clearly he was hosting a party while Sophie was away at school, and from the looks of the automobiles, some of Paris's most influential people were in attendance.

Eager to surprise him, she hurried to the front door. When she got there, though, she found it locked. She knocked. Nobody answered. Puzzled, she walked around and tried the back door. It too was locked. No answer.

Confused, she stood a moment and listened. The only sound she heard was the cool Normandy air letting out a low moan as it swirled through the valley.

No music.

No voices.

Nothing.

In the silence of the woods, Sophie hurried to the side of the house and clambered up on a woodpile, pressing her face to the living room window. What she saw inside made no sense at all.

'Nobody's here!'

The entire first floor looked deserted.

Where are all the people?

Heart racing, Sophie ran to the woodshed and got the spare key her grandfather kept hidden under the kindling box. She ran to the front door and let herself in. As she stepped into the deserted foyer, the control panel for the security system started blinking red – a warning that the entrant had ten seconds to type the proper code before the security alarms went off.

He has the alarm on during a party?

Sophie quickly typed the code and deactivated the system.

Entering, she found the entire house uninhabited. Upstairs too. As she descended again to the deserted living room, she stood a moment in the silence, wondering what could possibly be happening.

It was then that Sophie heard it.

Muffled voices. And they seemed to be coming from underneath her. Sophie could not imagine. Crouching, she put her ear to the floor and listened. Yes, the sound was definitely coming from below. The voices seemed to be singing, or . . . *chanting*? She was frightened. Almost more eerie than the sound itself was the realization that this house did not even have a basement.

At least none I've ever seen.

Turning now and scanning the living room, Sophie's eyes fell to the only object in the entire house that seemed out of place – her grandfather's favourite antique, a sprawling Aubusson tapestry. It usually hung on the east wall beside the fireplace, but tonight it had been pulled aside on its brass rod, exposing the wall behind it.

Walking toward the bare wooden wall, Sophie sensed the chanting getting louder. Hesitant, she leaned her ear against the wood. The voices were clearer now. People were definitely chanting . . . intoning words Sophie could not discern.

The space behind this wall is hollow!

Feeling around the edge of the panels, Sophie found a recessed finger-hold. It was discreetly crafted. *A sliding door.* Heart pounding, she placed her finger in the slot and pulled it. With noiseless precision, the heavy wall slid sideways. From out of the darkness beyond, the voices echoed up.

Sophie slipped through the door and found herself on a rough-hewn stone staircase that spiralled downward. She'd been coming to this house since she was a child and yet had no idea this staircase even existed!

As she descended, the air grew cooler. The voices clearer. She heard men and women now. Her line of sight was limited by the spiral of the staircase, but the last step was now rounding into view. Beyond it, she could see a small patch of the basement floor – stone, illuminated by the flickering orange blaze of firelight.

Holding her breath, Sophie inched down another few steps and crouched down to look. It took her several seconds to process what she was seeing.

The room was a grotto – a coarse chamber that appeared to have been hollowed from the granite of the hillside. The only light came from torches on the walls. In the glow of the flames, thirty or so people stood in a circle in the centre of the room.

I'm dreaming, Sophie told herself. *A dream. What else could this be?*

Everyone in the room was wearing a mask. The women were dressed in white gossamer gowns and golden shoes. Their masks were white, and in their hands they carried golden orbs. The men wore long black tunics, and their masks were black. They looked like pieces in a giant chess set. Everyone in the circle rocked back and forth and chanted in reverence to something on the floor before them . . . something Sophie could not see.

The chanting grew steady again. Accelerating. Thundering now. Faster. The participants took a step inward and knelt. In that instant, Sophie could finally see what they all were witnessing. Even as she staggered back in horror, she felt the image searing itself into her memory for ever. Overtaken by nausea, Sophie spun, clutching at the stone walls as she clambered back up the stairs. Pulling the door closed, she fled the deserted house, and drove in a tearful stupor back to Paris.

That night, with her life shattered by disillusionment and betrayal, she packed her belongings and left her home. On the dining room table, she left a note.

I WAS THERE. DON'T TRY TO FIND ME.

Beside the note, she laid the old spare key from the château's woodshed.

'Sophie!' Langdon's voice intruded. 'Stop! *Stop!*'

Emerging from the memory, Sophie slammed on the brakes, skidding to a halt. 'What? What happened?!'

Langdon pointed down the long street before them.

When she saw it, Sophie's blood went cold. A hundred yards ahead, the intersection was blocked by a couple of DCPJ police cars, parked askew, their purpose obvious. *They've sealed off Avenue Gabriel!*

Langdon gave a grim sigh. 'I take it the embassy is off-limits this evening?'

Down the street, the two DCPJ officers who stood beside their cars were now staring in their direction, apparently curious about the headlights that had halted so abruptly up the street from them.

Okay, Sophie, turn around very slowly.

Putting the SmartCar in reverse, she performed a composed three-point turn and reversed her direction. As she drove away, she heard the sound of squealing tyres behind them. Sirens blared to life.

Cursing, Sophie slammed down the accelerator.

33

Sophie's SmartCar tore through the diplomatic quarter, weaving past embassies and consulates, finally racing out a side street and taking a right turn back onto the massive thoroughfare of Champs-Elysées.

Langdon sat white-knuckled in the passenger seat, twisted backward, scanning behind them for any signs of the police. He suddenly wished he had not decided to run. *You didn't,* he reminded himself. Sophie had made the decision for him when she threw the GPS dot out of the men's room window. Now, as they sped away from the embassy, serpentining through sparse traffic on Champs-Elysées, Langdon felt his options deteriorating. Although Sophie seemed to have lost the police, at least for the moment, Langdon doubted their luck would hold for long.

Behind the wheel Sophie was fishing in her sweater pocket. She removed a small metal object and held it out for him. 'Robert, you'd better have a look at this. This is what my grandfather left me behind *Madonna of the Rocks.*'

Feeling a shiver of anticipation, Langdon took the object and examined it. It was heavy and shaped like a cruciform. His first instinct was that he was holding a funeral *pieu* – a miniature version of a memorial spike designed to be stuck into the ground at a gravesite. But then he noted the shaft protruding from the cruciform was prismatic and triangular. The shaft was also pockmarked with hundreds of tiny hexagons that appeared to be finely tooled and scattered at random.

'It's a laser-cut key,' Sophie told him. 'Those hexagons are read by an electric eye.'

A key? Langdon had never seen anything like it.

'Look at the other side,' she said, changing lanes and sailing through an intersection.

When Langdon turned the key, he felt his jaw drop. There, intricately embossed on the centre of the cross, was a stylized fleur-de-lis with the initials P.S.! 'Sophie,' he said, 'this is the seal I told you about! The official device of the Priory of Sion.'

She nodded. 'As I told you, I saw the key a long time ago. He told me never to speak of it again.'

Langdon's eyes were still riveted on the embossed key. Its high-tech tooling and age-old symbolism exuded an eerie fusion of ancient and modern worlds.

'He told me the key opened a box where he kept many secrets.'

Langdon felt a chill to imagine what kind of secrets a man like Jacques Saunière might keep. What an ancient brotherhood was doing with a futuristic key, Langdon had no idea. The Priory existed for the sole purpose of protecting a secret. A secret of incredible power. *Could this key have something to do with it?* The thought was overwhelming. 'Do you know what it opens?'

Sophie looked disappointed. 'I was hoping *you* knew.'

Langdon remained silent as he turned the cruciform in his hand, examining it.

'It looks Christian,' Sophie pressed.

Langdon was not so sure about that. The head of this key was not the traditional long-stemmed Christian cross but rather was a *square* cross – with four arms of equal length – which predated Christianity by fifteen hundred years. This kind of cross carried none of the Christian connotations of crucifixion associated with the longer-stemmed Latin cross, originated by Romans as a torture device. Langdon was always surprised how few Christians who gazed upon 'the crucifix' realized their symbol's violent history was reflected in its very name: 'cross' and 'crucifix' came from the Latin verb *cruciare* – to torture.

'Sophie,' he said, 'all I can tell you is that equal-armed crosses like this one are considered *peaceful* crosses. Their square configurations make them impractical for use in crucifixion, and their balanced vertical and horizontal elements convey a natural union of male and female, making them symbolically consistent with Priory philosophy.'

She gave him a weary look. 'You have no idea, do you?'

Langdon frowned. 'Not a clue.'

'Okay, we have to get off the road.' Sophie checked her rearview mirror. 'We need a safe place to figure out what that key opens.'

Langdon thought longingly of his comfortable room at the Ritz. Obviously, that was not an option. 'How about my hosts at the American University of Paris?'

'Too obvious. Fache will check with them.'

'You must know people. You live here.'

'Fache will run my phone and e-mail records, talk to my coworkers. My contacts are compromised, and finding a hotel is no good because they all require identification.'

Langdon wondered again if he might have been better off taking his chances letting Fache arrest him at the Louvre. 'Let's call the embassy. I can explain the situation and have the embassy send someone to meet us somewhere.'

'Meet us?' Sophie turned and stared at him as if he were crazy. 'Robert, you're dreaming. Your embassy has no jurisdiction except on their own property. Sending someone to retrieve us would be considered aiding a fugitive of the French government. It won't happen. If you walk into your embassy and request temporary asylum, that's one thing, but asking them to take action against French law enforcement in the field?' She shook her head. 'Call your embassy right now, and they are going to tell you to avoid further damage and turn yourself over to Fache. Then they'll promise to pursue diplomatic channels to get you a fair trial.' She gazed up the line of elegant storefronts on Champs-Elysées. 'How much cash do you have?'

Langdon checked his wallet. 'A hundred dollars. A few euros. Why?'

'Credit cards?'

'Of course.'

As Sophie accelerated, Langdon sensed she was formulating a plan. Dead ahead, at the end of Champs-Elysées, stood the Arc de Triomphe – Napoleon's 164-foot-tall tribute to his own military potency – encircled by France's largest rotary, a nine-lane behemoth.

Sophie's eyes were on the rearview mirror again as they approached the rotary. 'We lost them for the time being,' she said, 'but we won't last another five minutes if we stay in this car.'

So steal a different one, Langdon mused, *now that we're criminals*. 'What are you going to do?'

Sophie gunned the SmartCar into the rotary. 'Trust me.'

Langdon made no response. Trust had not got him very far this evening. Pulling back the sleeve of his jacket, he checked his watch – a vintage, collector's-edition Mickey Mouse wristwatch that had been a gift from his parents on his tenth birthday. Although its juvenile dial often drew odd looks, Langdon had never owned any other watch; Disney animations had been his first introduction to the magic of form and colour, and Mickey now served as Langdon's daily reminder to stay young at heart. At the moment, however, Mickey's arms were skewed at an awkward angle, indicating an equally awkward hour.

2:51 A.M.

'Interesting watch,' Sophie said, glancing at his wrist and manoeuvring the SmartCar around the wide, counterclockwise rotary.

'Long story,' he said, pulling his sleeve back down.

'I imagine it would have to be.' She gave him a quick smile and exited the rotary, heading due north, away from the city centre. Barely making two green lights, she reached the third intersection and took a hard right onto Boulevard Malesherbes. They'd left the rich, tree-lined streets of the diplomatic neighbourhood and plunged into a darker industrial neighbourhood. Sophie took a quick left, and a moment later, Langdon realized where they were.

Gare Saint-Lazare.

Ahead of them, the glass-roofed train terminal resembled the awkward offspring of an airplane hangar and a greenhouse. European train stations never slept. Even at this hour, a half-dozen taxis idled near the main entrance. Vendors manned carts of sandwiches and mineral water while grungy kids in backpacks emerged from the station rubbing their eyes, looking around as if trying to remember what city they were in now. Up ahead on the street, a couple of city policemen stood on the curb giving directions to some confused tourists.

Sophie pulled her SmartCar in behind the line of taxis and parked in a red zone despite plenty of legal parking across the street. Before Langdon could ask what was going on, she was out of the car. She hurried to the window of the taxi in front of them and began speaking to the driver.

As Langdon got out of the SmartCar, he saw Sophie hand the taxi driver a big wad of cash. The taxi driver nodded and then, to Langdon's bewilderment, sped off without them.

'What happened?' Langdon demanded, joining Sophie on the curb as the taxi disappeared.

Sophie was already heading for the train station entrance. 'Come on. We're buying two tickets on the next train out of Paris.'

Langdon hurried along beside her. What had begun as a one-mile dash to the US Embassy had now become a full-fledged evacuation from Paris. Langdon was liking this idea less and less.

34

The driver who collected Bishop Aringarosa from Leonardo da Vinci International Airport pulled up in a small, unimpressive black Fiat sedan. Aringarosa recalled a day when all Vatican transports were big luxury cars that sported grille-plate medallions and flags emblazoned with the seal of the Holy See. *Those days are gone.* Vatican cars were now less ostentatious and almost always unmarked. The Vatican claimed this was to cut costs to better serve their dioceses, but Aringarosa suspected it was more of a security measure. The world had gone mad, and in many parts of Europe, advertising your love of Jesus Christ was like painting a bull's-eye on the roof of your car.

Bundling his black cassock around himself, Aringarosa climbed into the back seat and settled in for the long drive to Castel Gandolfo. It would be the same ride he had taken five months ago.

Last year's trip to Rome, he sighed. *The longest night of my life.*

Five months ago, the Vatican had phoned to request Aringarosa's immediate presence in Rome. They offered no explanation. *Your tickets are at the airport.* The Holy See worked hard to retain a veil of mystery, even for its highest clergy.

The mysterious summons, Aringarosa suspected, was probably a photo opportunity for the Pope and other Vatican officials to piggyback on Opus Dei's recent public success – the completion of their World Headquarters in New York City. *Architectural Digest* had called Opus Dei's building 'a shining beacon of Catholicism sublimely integrated with the modern landscape', and lately the Vatican seemed to be drawn to anything and everything that included the word 'modern'.

Aringarosa had no choice but to accept the invitation, albeit reluctantly. Not a fan of the current papal administration, Aringarosa, like most conservative clergy, had watched with grave concern as the new Pope settled into his first year in office. An unprecedented liberal, His Holiness had secured the papacy through one of the most controversial and unusual conclaves in Vatican history. Now, rather than being humbled by his unexpected rise to power, the Holy Father had wasted no time flexing all the muscle associated with the highest office in Christendom. Drawing on an unsettling tide of liberal support within the College of Cardinals, the Pope was now declaring his papal mission to be 'rejuvenation of Vatican doctrine and updating Catholicism into the third millennium'.

The translation, Aringarosa feared, was that the man was actually arrogant enough to think he could rewrite God's laws and win back the hearts of those who felt the demands of true Catholicism had become too inconvenient in a modern world.

Aringarosa had been using all of his political sway – substantial considering the size of the Opus Dei constituency and their bankroll – to persuade the Pope and his advisers that softening the Church's laws was not only faithless and cowardly, but political suicide. He reminded them that previous tempering of Church law – the Vatican II fiasco – had left a devastating legacy: Church attendance was now lower than ever, donations were drying up, and there were not even enough Catholic priests to preside over their churches.

People need structure and direction from the Church, Aringarosa insisted, *not coddling and indulgence!*

On that night, months ago, as the Fiat had left the airport, Aringarosa was surprised to find himself heading not toward Vatican City but rather eastward up a sinuous mountain road. 'Where are we going?' he had demanded of his driver.

'Alban Hills,' the man replied. 'Your meeting is at Castel Gandolfo.'

The Pope's summer residence? Aringarosa had never been, nor had he ever desired to see it. In addition to being the Pope's summer vacation home, the sixteenth-century citadel housed the Specula Vaticana – the Vatican Observatory – one of the most advanced astronomical observatories in Europe. Aringarosa had never been comfortable with the Vatican's historical need to dabble in science. What was the rationale for fusing science and faith? Unbiased science could not possibly be performed by a man who possessed faith in God. Nor did faith have any need for physical confirmation of its beliefs.

Nonetheless, there it is, he thought as Castel Gandolfo came into view, rising against a star-filled November sky. From the access road, Gandolfo resembled a great stone monster pondering a suicidal leap. Perched at the very edge of a cliff, the castle leaned out over the cradle of Italian civilization – the valley where the Curiazi and Orazi clans fought long before the founding of Rome.

Even in silhouette, Gandolfo was a sight to behold – an impressive example of tiered, defensive architecture, echoing the potency of this dramatic cliffside setting. Sadly, Aringarosa now saw, the Vatican had ruined the building by constructing two huge aluminium telescope domes atop the roof, leaving this once dignified edifice looking like a proud warrior wearing a couple of party hats.

When Aringarosa got out of the car, a young Jesuit priest hurried out and greeted him. 'Bishop, welcome. I am Father Mangano. An astronomer here.'

Good for you. Aringarosa grumbled his hello and followed his host into the castle's foyer – a wide-open space whose decor was a graceless blend of Renaissance art and astronomy images. Following his escort up the wide travertine marble staircase, Aringarosa saw signs for conference centres, science lecture halls and tourist information services. It amazed him to think the Vatican was failing at every turn to provide coherent, stringent guidelines for spiritual growth and yet somehow still found time to give astrophysics lectures to tourists.

'Tell me,' Aringarosa said to the young priest, 'when did the tail start wagging the dog?'

The priest gave him an odd look. 'Sir?'

Aringarosa waved it off, deciding not to launch into that particular offensive again this evening. *The Vatican has gone mad.* Like a lazy parent who found it easier to acquiesce to the whims of a spoiled child than to stand firm and teach values, the Church just kept softening at every turn, trying to reinvent itself to accommodate a culture gone astray.

The top floor's corridor was wide, lushly appointed, and led in only one direction – toward a huge set of oak doors with a brass sign.

BIBLIOTECA ASTRONOMICA

Aringarosa had heard of this place – the Vatican's Astronomy Library – rumoured to contain more than twenty-five thousand volumes, including rare works of Copernicus, Galileo, Kepler, Newton and Secchi. Allegedly, it was also the place in which the Pope's highest officers held private meetings . . . those meetings they preferred not to hold within the walls of Vatican City.

Approaching the door, Bishop Aringarosa would never have imagined the shocking news he was about to receive inside, or the deadly chain of events it would put into motion. It was not until an hour later, as he staggered from the meeting, that the devastating implications settled in. *Six months from now!* he had thought. *God help us!*

Now, seated in the Fiat, Bishop Aringarosa realized his fists were clenched just thinking about that first meeting. He released his grip and forced a slow inhalation, relaxing his muscles.

Everything will be fine, he told himself as the Fiat wound higher into the mountains. Still, he wished his cell phone would ring. *Why hasn't the Teacher called me? Silas should have the keystone by now.*

Trying to ease his nerves, the bishop meditated on the purple amethyst in his ring. Feeling the textures of the mitre-crozier appliqué and the facets of the diamonds, he reminded himself that this ring was a symbol of power far less than that which he would soon attain.

35

The inside of Gare du Nord looked like every other train station in Europe, a gaping indoor-outdoor cavern dotted with the usual suspects – homeless men holding cardboard signs, collections of bleary-eyed college kids sleeping on backpacks and zoning out to their portable MP3 players, and clusters of blue-clad baggage porters smoking cigarettes.

Sophie raised her eyes to the enormous departure board overhead. The black and white tabs reshuffled, ruffling downward as the information refreshed. When the update was finished, Langdon eyed the offerings. The topmost listing read:

LILLE – RAPIDE – 3:06

'I wish it left sooner,' Sophie said, 'but Lille will have to do.'

Sooner? Langdon checked his watch 2:59 A.M. The train left in seven minutes and they didn't even have tickets yet.

Sophie guided Langdon toward the ticket window and said, 'Buy us two tickets with your credit card.'

'I thought credit card usage could be traced by—'

'Exactly.'

Langdon decided to stop trying to keep ahead of Sophie Neveu. Using his Visa card, he purchased two tickets to Lille and handed them to Sophie.

Sophie guided him out toward the tracks, where a familiar tone chimed overhead and a P.A. announcer gave the final boarding call for Lille. Sixteen separate tracks spread out before them. In the distance to the right, at quay three, the train to Lille was belching and wheezing in preparation for departure, but Sophie already had her arm through Langdon's and was guiding him in the exact opposite direction. They hurried through a side lobby, past an all-night café, and finally out a side door onto a quiet street on the west side of the station.

A lone taxi sat idling by the doorway.

The driver saw Sophie and flicked his lights.

Sophie jumped in the back seat. Langdon got in after her.

As the taxi pulled away from the station, Sophie took out their newly purchased train tickets and tore them up.

Langdon sighed. *Seventy dollars well spent.*

It was not until their taxi had settled into a monotonous northbound hum on Rue de Clichy that Langdon felt they'd actually escaped. Out the window to his right, he could see Montmartre and the beautiful dome of Sacré-Coeur. The image was interrupted by the flash of police lights sailing past them in the opposite direction.

Langdon and Sophie ducked down as the sirens faded.

Sophie had told the cab driver simply to head out of the city, and from her firmly set jaw, Langdon sensed she was trying to figure out their next move.

Langdon examined the cruciform key again, holding it to the window, bringing it close to his eyes in an effort to find any markings on it that might indicate where the key had been made. In the intermittent glow of passing streetlights, he saw no markings except the Priory seal.

'It doesn't make sense,' he finally said.

'Which part?'

'That your grandfather would go to so much trouble to give you a key that you wouldn't know what to do with.'

'I agree.'

'Are you sure he didn't write anything else on the back of the painting?'

'I searched the whole area. This is all there was. This key, wedged behind the painting. I saw the Priory seal, stuck the key in my pocket, then we left.'

Langdon frowned, peering now at the blunt end of the triangular shaft. Nothing. Squinting, he brought the key close to his eyes and examined the rim of the head. Nothing there either. 'I think this key was cleaned recently.'

'Why?'

'It smells like rubbing alcohol.'

She turned. 'I'm sorry?'

'It smells like somebody polished it with a cleaner.' Langdon held the key to his nose and sniffed. 'It's stronger on the other side.' He flipped it over. 'Yes, it's alcohol-based, like it's been buffed with a cleaner or—' Langdon stopped.

'What?'

He angled the key to the light and looked at the smooth surface on the broad arm of the cross. It seemed to shimmer in places . . . like it was wet. 'How well did you look at the back of this key before you put it in your pocket?'

'What? Not well. I was in a hurry.'

Langdon turned to her. 'Do you still have the black light?'

Sophie reached in her pocket and produced the UV penlight. Langdon took it and switched it on, shining the beam on the back of the key.

The back luminesced instantly. There was writing there. In penmanship that was hurried but legible.

'Well,' Langdon said, smiling. 'I guess we know what the alcohol smell was.'

Sophie stared in amazement at the purple writing on the back of the key.

24 Rue Haxo

An address! My grandfather wrote down an address!
'Where is this?' Langdon asked.

Sophie had no idea. Facing front again, she leaned forward and excitedly asked the driver, '*Connaissez-vous la Rue Haxo?*'

The driver thought a moment and then nodded. He told Sophie it was out near the tennis stadium on the western outskirts of Paris. She asked him to take them there immediately.

'Fastest route is through Bois de Boulogne,' the driver told her in French. 'Is that okay?'

Sophie frowned. She could think of far less scandalous routes, but tonight she was not going to be picky. 'Oui.' *We can shock the visiting American.*

Sophie looked back at the key and wondered what they would possibly find at 24 Rue Haxo. *A church? Some kind of Priory headquarters?*

Her mind filled again with images of the secret ritual she had witnessed in the basement grotto ten years ago, and she heaved a long sigh. 'Robert, I have a lot of things to tell you.' She paused, locking eyes with him as the taxi raced westward. 'But first I want you to tell me everything you know about this Priory of Sion.'

36

Outside the Salle des Etats, Bezu Fache was fuming as Louvre warden Grouard explained how Sophie and Langdon had disarmed him. *Why didn't you just shoot the blessed painting!*

'Captain?' Lieutenant Collet loped toward them from the direction of the command post. 'Captain, I just heard. They located Agent Neveu's car.'

'Did she make the embassy?'

'No. Train station. Bought two tickets. Train just left.'

Fache waved off warden Grouard and led Collet to a nearby alcove, addressing him in hushed tones. 'What was the destination?'

'Lille.'

'Probably a decoy.' Fache exhaled, formulating a plan. 'Okay, alert the next station, have the train stopped and searched, just in case. Leave her car where it is and put plainclothes on watch in case they try to come back to it. Send men to search the streets around the station in case they fled on foot. Are buses running from the station?'

'Not at this hour, sir. Only the taxi queue.'

'Good. Question the drivers. See if they saw anything. Then contact the taxi company dispatcher with descriptions. I'm calling Interpol.'

Collet looked surprised. 'You're putting this on the *wire?*'

Fache regretted the potential embarrassment, but he saw no other choice.

Close the net fast, and close it tight.

The first hour was critical. Fugitives were predictable the first hour after escape. They always needed the same thing. *Travel. Lodging. Cash.* The Holy Trinity. Interpol had the power to make all three disappear in the blink of an eye. By broadcast-faxing photos of Langdon and Sophie to Paris travel authorities, hotels and banks, Interpol would leave no options – no way to leave the city, no place to hide, and no way to withdraw cash without being recognized. Usually, fugitives panicked on the street and did something stupid. Stole a car. Robbed a store. Used a bank card in desperation. Whatever mistake they committed, they quickly made their whereabouts known to local authorities.

'Only *Langdon,* right?' Collet said. 'You're not flagging Sophie Neveu. She's our own agent.'

'Of course I'm flagging her!' Fache snapped. 'What good is flagging Langdon if she can do all his dirty work? I plan to run Neveu's employment file – friends, family, personal contacts – anyone she might turn to for help. I don't know what she thinks she's doing out there, but it's going to cost her one hell of a lot more than her job!'

'Do you want me on the phones or in the field?'

'Field. Get over to the train station and coordinate the team. You've got the reins, but don't make a move without talking to me.'

'Yes, sir.' Collet ran out.

Fache felt rigid as he stood in the alcove. Outside the window, the glass pyramid shone, its reflection rippling in the windswept pools. *They slipped through my fingers.* He told himself to relax.

Even a trained field agent would be lucky to withstand the pressure that Interpol was about to apply.

A female cryptologist and a schoolteacher?

They wouldn't last till dawn.

37

The heavily forested park known as the Bois de Boulogne was called many things, but the Parisian cognoscenti knew it as 'the Garden of Earthly Delights'. The epithet, despite sounding flattering, was quite to the contrary. Anyone who had seen the lurid Bosch painting of the same name understood the jab; the painting, like the forest, was dark and twisted, a purgatory for freaks and fetishists. At night, the forest's winding lanes were lined with hundreds of glistening bodies for hire, earthly delights to satisfy one's deepest unspoken desires – male, female, and everything in between.

As Langdon gathered his thoughts to tell Sophie about the Priory of Sion, their taxi passed through the wooded entrance to the park and began heading west on the cobblestone crossfare. Langdon was having trouble concentrating as a scattering of the park's nocturnal residents were already emerging from the shadows and flaunting their wares in the glare of the headlights. Ahead, two topless teenage girls shot smouldering gazes into the taxi. Beyond them, a well-oiled black man in a G-string turned and flexed his buttocks. Beside him, a gorgeous blond woman lifted her miniskirt to reveal that she was not, in fact, a woman.

Heaven help me! Langdon turned his gaze back inside the cab and took a deep breath.

'Tell me about the Priory of Sion,' Sophie said.

Langdon nodded, unable to imagine a less congruous backdrop for the legend he was about to tell. He wondered where to begin. The brotherhood's history spanned more than a millennium . . . an astonishing chronicle of secrets, blackmail, betrayal and even brutal torture at the hands of an angry Pope.

'The Priory of Sion,' he began, 'was founded in Jerusalem in 1099 by a French king named Godefroi de Bouillon, immediately after he had conquered the city.'

Sophie nodded, her eyes riveted on him.

'King Godefroi was allegedly the possessor of a powerful secret – a secret that had been in his family since the time of Christ. Fearing his secret might be lost when he died, he founded a secret brotherhood – the Priory of Sion – and charged them with protecting his secret by quietly passing it on from generation to generation. During their years in Jerusalem, the Priory learned of a stash of hidden documents buried beneath the ruins of Herod's temple, which had been built on top of the earlier ruins of Solomon's temple. These documents, they believed, corroborated Godefroi's powerful secret and were so explosive in nature that the Church would stop at nothing to get them.'

Sophie looked uncertain.

'The Priory vowed that no matter how long it took, these documents must be recovered from the rubble beneath the temple and protected for ever, so the truth would never die. In order to retrieve the documents from within the ruins, the Priory created a military arm – a group of nine knights called the Order of the Poor Knights of Christ and the Temple of Solomon.' Langdon paused. 'More commonly known as the Knights Templar.'

Sophie glanced up with a surprised look of recognition.

Langdon had lectured often enough on the Knights Templar to know that almost everyone on earth had heard of them, at least abstractedly. For academics, the Templars' history was a precarious world where fact, lore and misinformation had become so intertwined that extracting a pristine truth was almost impossible. Nowadays, Langdon hesitated even to mention the Knights Templar while lecturing because it invariably led to a barrage of convoluted inquiries into assorted conspiracy theories.

Sophie already looked troubled. 'You're saying the Knights Templar were founded by the Priory of Sion to retrieve a collection of secret documents? I thought the Templars were created to protect the Holy Land.'

'A common misconception. The idea of protection of pilgrims was the *guise* under which the Templars ran their mission. Their true goal in the Holy Land was to retrieve the documents from beneath the ruins of the temple.'

'And did they find them?'

Langdon grinned. 'Nobody knows for sure, but the one thing on which all academics agree is this: The Knights discovered *something* down there in the ruins . . . something that made them wealthy and powerful beyond anyone's wildest imagination.'

Langdon quickly gave Sophie the standard academic sketch of the accepted Knights Templar history, explaining how the Knights were in the Holy Land during the Second Crusade and told King Baldwin II that they were there to protect Christian pilgrims on the roadways. Although unpaid and sworn to poverty, the Knights told the king they required basic shelter and requested his permission to take up residence in the stables under the ruins of the temple. King Baldwin granted the soldiers' request, and the Knights took up their meagre residence inside the devastated shrine.

The odd choice of lodging, Langdon explained, had been anything but random. The Knights believed the documents the Priory sought were buried deep under the ruins – beneath the Holy of Holies, a sacred chamber where God Himself was believed to reside. Literally, the very centre of the Jewish faith. For almost a decade, the nine Knights lived in the ruins, excavating in total secrecy through solid rock.

Sophie looked over. 'And you said they discovered something?'

'They certainly did,' Langdon said, explaining how it had taken nine years, but the Knights had finally found what they had been searching for. They took the treasure from the temple and travelled to Europe, where their influence seemed to solidify overnight.

Nobody was certain whether the Knights had blackmailed the Vatican or whether the Church simply tried to buy the Knights' silence, but Pope Innocent II immediately issued an unprecedented papal bull that afforded the Knights Templar limitless power and declared them 'a law unto themselves' – an autonomous army independent of all interference from kings and prelates, both religious and political.

With their new carte blanche from the Vatican, the Knights Templar expanded at a staggering rate, both in numbers and political force, amassing vast estates in over a dozen countries. They began extending credit to bankrupt royals and charging interest in return, thereby establishing modern banking and broadening their wealth and influence still further.

By the 1300s, the Vatican sanction had helped the Knights amass so much power that Pope Clement V decided that something had to be done. Working in concert with France's King Philippe IV, the Pope devised an ingeniously planned sting operation to quash the Templars and seize their treasure, thus taking control of the secrets held over the Vatican. In a military manoeuvre worthy of the CIA, Pope Clement issued secret sealed orders to be opened simultaneously by his soldiers all across Europe on Friday, October 13 of 1307.

At dawn on the thirteenth, the documents were unsealed and their appalling contents revealed. Clement's letter claimed that God had visited him in a vision and warned him that the Knights Templar were heretics guilty of devil worship, homosexuality, defiling the cross, sodomy and other blasphemous behaviour. Pope Clement had been asked by God to cleanse the earth by rounding up all the Knights and torturing them until they confessed their crimes against God. Clement's Machiavellian operation came off with clockwork precision. On that day, countless Knights were captured, tortured mercilessly and finally burned at the stake as heretics. Echoes of the tragedy still resonated in modern culture; to this day, Friday the thirteenth was considered unlucky.

Sophie looked confused. 'The Knights Templar were obliterated? I thought fraternities of Templars still exist today?'

'They do, under a variety of names. Despite Clement's false charges and best efforts to eradicate them, the Knights had powerful allies, and some managed to escape the Vatican purges. The Templars' potent treasure trove of documents, which had apparently been their source of power, was Clement's true objective, but it slipped through his fingers. The documents had long since been entrusted to the Templars' shadowy architects, the Priory of Sion, whose veil of secrecy had kept them safely out of range of the Vatican's onslaught. As the Vatican closed in, the Priory smuggled their documents from a Paris preceptory by night onto Templar ships in La Rochelle.'

'Where did the documents go?'

Langdon shrugged. 'That mystery's answer is known only to the Priory of Sion. Because the documents remain the source of constant investigation and speculation even today, they are believed to have been moved and rehidden several times. Current speculation places the documents somewhere in the United Kingdom.'

Sophie looked uneasy.

'For a thousand years,' Langdon continued, 'legends of this secret have been passed on. The entire collection of documents, its power, and the secret it reveals have become known by a single name – Sangreal. Hundreds of books have been written about it, and few mysteries have caused as much interest among historians as the Sangreal.'

'The Sangreal? Does the word have anything to do with the French word *sang* or Spanish *sangre* – meaning "blood"?'

Langdon nodded. Blood was the backbone of the Sangreal, and yet not in the way Sophie probably imagined. 'The legend is complicated, but the important thing to remember is that the Priory guards the proof, and is purportedly awaiting the right moment in history to reveal the truth.'

'What truth? What secret could possibly be that powerful?'

Langdon took a deep breath and gazed out at the underbelly of Paris leering in the shadows. 'Sophie, the word *Sangreal* is an ancient word. It has evolved over the years into another term . . . a more modern name.' He paused. 'When I tell you its modern name, you'll realize you already know a lot about it. In fact, almost everyone on earth has heard the story of the Sangreal.'

Sophie looked skeptical. 'I've never heard of it.'

'Sure you have.' Langdon smiled. 'You're just used to hearing it called by the name "Holy Grail".'

38

Sophie scrutinized Langdon in the back of the taxi. *He's joking.* 'The Holy Grail?'

Langdon nodded, his expression serious. 'Holy Grail is the literal meaning of Sangreal. The phrase derives from the French *Sangraal*, which evolved to Sangreal, and was eventually split into two words, *San Greal.*'

Holy Grail. Sophie was surprised she had not spotted the linguistic ties immediately. Even so, Langdon's claim still made no sense to her. 'I thought the Holy Grail was a *cup*. You just told me the Sangreal is a collection of documents that reveals some dark secret.'

'Yes, but the Sangreal documents are only *half* of the Holy Grail treasure. They are buried with the Grail itself . . . and reveal its true meaning. The documents gave the Knights Templar so much power because the pages revealed the true nature of the Grail.'

The true nature of the Grail? Sophie felt even more lost now. The Holy Grail, she had thought, was the cup that Jesus drank from at the Last Supper and with which Joseph of Arimathea later caught His blood at the crucifixion. 'The Holy Grail is the Cup of Christ,' she said. 'How much simpler could it be?'

'Sophie,' Langdon whispered, leaning toward her now, 'according to the Priory of Sion, the Holy Grail is not a cup at all. They claim the Grail legend – that of a *chalice* – is actually an ingeniously conceived allegory. That is, that the Grail story uses the *chalice* as a metaphor for something else, something far more powerful.' He paused. 'Something that fits perfectly with everything your grandfather has been trying to tell us tonight, including all his symbologic references to the sacred feminine.'

Still unsure, Sophie sensed in Langdon's patient smile that he empathized with her confusion, and yet his eyes remained earnest. 'But if the Holy Grail is not a cup,' she asked, 'what is it?'

Langdon had known this question was coming, and yet he still felt uncertain exactly how to tell her. If he did not present the answer in the proper historical background, Sophie would be left with a vacant air of bewilderment – the exact expression Langdon had seen on his own editor's face a few months ago after Langdon handed him a draft of the manuscript he was working on.

'This manuscript claims *what?*' his editor had choked, setting down his wineglass and staring across his half-eaten power lunch. 'You can't be serious.'

'Serious enough to have spent a year researching it.'

Prominent New York editor Jonas Faukman tugged nervously at his goatee. Faukman no doubt had heard some wild book ideas in his illustrious career, but this one seemed to have left the man flabbergasted.

'Robert,' Faukman finally said, 'don't get me wrong. I love your work, and we've had a great run together. But if I agree to publish an idea like this, I'll have people picketing outside my office for months. Besides, it will kill your reputation. You're a Harvard historian, for God's sake, not a pop schlockmeister looking for a quick buck. Where could you possibly find enough credible evidence to support a theory like this?'

With a quiet smile Langdon pulled a piece of paper from the pocket of his tweed coat and handed it to Faukman. The page listed a bibliography of over fifty titles – books by well-known historians, some contemporary, some centuries old – many of them academic bestsellers. All the book titles suggested the same premise Langdon had just proposed. As Faukman read down the list, he looked like a man who had just discovered the earth was actually flat. 'I *know* some of these authors. They're . . . real historians!'

Langdon grinned. 'As you can see, Jonas, this is not only *my* theory. It's been around for a long time. I'm simply building on it. No book has yet explored the legend of the Holy Grail from a symbologic angle. The iconographic evidence I'm finding to support the theory is, well, staggeringly persuasive.'

Faukman was still staring at the list. 'My God, one of these books was written by Sir Leigh Teabing – a British Royal Historian.'

'Teabing has spent much of his life studying the Holy Grail. I've met with him. He was actually a big part of my inspiration. He's a believer, Jonas, along with all of the others on that list.'

'You're telling me all of these historians actually believe . . .' Faukman swallowed, apparently unable to say the words.

Langdon grinned again. 'The Holy Grail is arguably the most sought-after treasure in human history. The Grail has spawned legends, wars and lifelong quests. Does it make sense that it is merely a cup? If so, then certainly *other* relics should generate similar or greater interest – the Crown of Thorns, the True Cross of the Crucifixion, the Titulus – and yet, they do not. Throughout history, the Holy Grail has been the most special.' Langdon grinned. 'Now you know why.'

Faukman was still shaking his head. 'But with all these books written about it, why isn't this theory more widely known?'

'These books can't possibly compete with centuries of established history, especially when that history is endorsed by the ultimate bestseller of all time.'

Faukman's eyes went wide. 'Don't tell me *Harry Potter* is actually about the Holy Grail.'

'I was referring to the Bible.'

Faukman cringed. 'I knew that.'

'*Laissez-le!*' Sophie's shouts cut the air inside the taxi. 'Put it down!'

Langdon jumped as Sophie leaned forward over the seat and yelled at the taxi driver. Langdon could see the driver was clutching his radio mouthpiece and speaking into it.

Sophie turned now and plunged her hand into the pocket of Langdon's tweed jacket. Before Langdon knew what had happened, she had yanked out the pistol, swung it around, and was pressing it to the back of the driver's head. The driver instantly dropped his radio, raising his one free hand overhead.

'Sophie!' Langdon choked. 'What the hell—'

'*Arrêtez!*' Sophie commanded the driver.

Trembling, the driver obeyed, stopping the car.

It was then that Langdon heard the metallic voice of the taxi company's dispatcher coming from the dashboard. '. . . *qui s'appelle Agent Sophie Neveu . . .*' the radio crackled. '*Et un Américain, Robert Langdon . . .*'

Langdon's muscles turned rigid. *They found us already?*

'*Descendez,*' Sophie demanded.

The trembling driver kept his arms over his head as he got out of his taxi and took several steps backward.

Sophie had rolled down her window and now aimed the gun outside at the bewildered cabbie. 'Robert,' she said quietly, 'take the wheel. You're driving.'

Langdon was not about to argue with a woman wielding a gun. He climbed out of the car and jumped back in behind the wheel. The driver was yelling curses, his arms still raised over his head.

'Robert,' Sophie said from the back seat, 'I trust you've seen enough of our magic forest?'

He nodded. *Plenty.*

'Good. Drive us out of here.'

Langdon looked down at the car's controls and hesitated. *Shit.* He groped for the stick shift and clutch. 'Sophie? Maybe you—'

'Go!' she yelled.

Outside, several hookers were walking over to see what was going on. One woman was placing a call on her cell phone. Langdon depressed the clutch and jostled the stick into what he hoped was first gear. He touched the accelerator, testing the gas.

Langdon popped the clutch. The tyres howled as the taxi leapt forward, fishtailing wildly and sending the gathering crowd diving for cover. The woman with the cell phone leapt into the woods, only narrowly avoiding being run down.

'*Doucement!*' Sophie said, as the car lurched down the road. 'What are you doing?'

'I tried to warn you,' he shouted over the sound of gnashing gears. 'I drive an automatic!'

39

Although the spartan room in the house on Rue La Bruyère had witnessed a lot of suffering, Silas doubted anything could match the anguish now gripping his pale body. *I was deceived. Everything is lost.*

Silas had been tricked. The brothers had lied, choosing death instead of revealing their true secret. Silas did not have the strength to call the Teacher. Not only had Silas killed the only four people who knew where the keystone was hidden, he had killed a nun inside Saint-Sulpice. *She was working against God! She scorned the work of Opus Dei!*

A crime of impulse, the woman's death complicated matters greatly. Bishop Aringarosa had placed the phone call that got Silas into Saint-Sulpice; what would the abbé think when he discovered the nun was dead? Although Silas had placed her back in her bed, the wound on her head was obvious. Silas had attempted to replace the broken tiles in the floor, but that damage too was obvious. They would know someone had been there.

Silas had planned to hide within Opus Dei when his task here was complete. *Bishop Aringarosa will protect me.* Silas could imagine no more blissful existence than a life of meditation and prayer deep within the walls of Opus Dei's headquarters in New York City. He would never again set foot outside. Everything he needed was within that sanctuary. *Nobody will miss me.* Unfortunately, Silas knew, a prominent man like Bishop Aringarosa could not disappear so easily.

I have endangered the bishop. Silas gazed blankly at the floor and pondered taking his own life. After all, it had been Aringarosa who gave Silas life in the first place . . . in that small rectory in Spain, educating him, giving him purpose.

'My friend,' Aringarosa had told him, 'you were born an albino. Do not let others shame you for this. Do you not understand how special this makes you? Were you not aware that Noah himself was an albino?'

'Noah of the Ark?' Silas had never heard this.

Aringarosa was smiling. 'Indeed, Noah of the Ark. An albino. Like you, he had skin white like an angel. Consider this. Noah saved all of life on the planet. You are destined for great things, Silas. The Lord has freed you for a reason. You have your calling. The Lord needs your help to do His work.'

Over time, Silas learned to see himself in a new light. *I am pure. White. Beautiful. Like an angel.*

At the moment, though, in his room at the residence hall, it was his father's disappointed voice that whispered to him from the past.

Tu es un désastre. Un spectre.

Kneeling on the wooden floor, Silas prayed for forgiveness. Then, stripping off his robe, he reached again for the Discipline.

40

Struggling with the gear shift, Langdon managed to manoeuvre the hijacked taxi to the far side of the Bois de Boulogne while stalling only twice. Unfortunately, the inherent humour in the situation was overshadowed by the taxi dispatcher repeatedly hailing their cab over the radio.

'*Voiture cinq-six-trois. Où êtes-vous? Répondez!*'

When Langdon reached the exit of the park, he swallowed his machismo and jammed on the brakes. 'You'd better drive.'

Sophie looked relieved as she jumped behind the wheel. Within seconds she had the car humming smoothly westward along Allée de Longchamp, leaving the Garden of Earthly Delights behind.

'Which way is Rue Haxo?' Langdon asked, watching Sophie edge the speedometer over a hundred kilometers an hour.

Sophie's eyes remained focused on the road. 'The cab driver said it's adjacent to the Roland Garros tennis stadium. I know that area.'

Langdon pulled the heavy key from his pocket again, feeling the weight in his palm. He sensed it was an object of enormous consequence. Quite possibly the key to his own freedom.

Earlier, while telling Sophie about the Knights Templar, Langdon had realized that this key, in addition to having the Priory seal embossed on it, possessed a more subtle tie to the Priory of Sion. The equal-armed cruciform was symbolic of balance and harmony but also of the Knights Templar. Everyone had seen the paintings of Knights Templar wearing white tunics emblazoned with red equal-armed crosses. Granted, the arms of the Templar cross were slightly flared at the ends, but they were still of equal length.

A square cross. Just like the one on this key.

Langdon felt his imagination starting to run wild as he fantasized about what they might find. *The Holy Grail.* He almost laughed out loud at the absurdity of it. The Grail was believed to be somewhere in England, buried in a hidden chamber beneath one of the many Templar churches, where it had been hidden since at least 1500.

The era of Grand Master Da Vinci.

The Priory, in order to keep their powerful documents safe, had been

593

forced to move them many times in the early centuries. Historians now suspected as many as six different Grail relocations since its arrival in Europe from Jerusalem. The last Grail 'sighting' had been in 1447 when numerous eyewitnesses described a fire that had broken out and almost engulfed the documents before they were carried to safety in four huge chests that each required six men to carry. After that, nobody claimed to see the Grail ever again. All that remained were occasional whisperings that it was hidden in Great Britain, the land of King Arthur and the Knights of the Round Table.

Wherever it was, two important facts remained:

Leonardo knew where the Grail resided during his lifetime.

That hiding place had probably not changed to this day.

For this reason, Grail enthusiasts still pored over Da Vinci's art and diaries in hopes of unearthing a hidden clue as to the Grail's current location. Some claimed the mountainous backdrop in *Madonna of the Rocks* matched the topography of a series of cave-ridden hills in Scotland. Others insisted that the suspicious placement of disciples in *The Last Supper* was some kind of code. Still others claimed that X-rays of the *Mona Lisa* revealed she originally had been painted wearing a lapis lazuli pendant of Isis – a detail Da Vinci purportedly later decided to paint over. Langdon had never seen any evidence of the pendant, nor could he imagine how it could possibly reveal the Holy Grail, and yet Grail aficionados still discussed it ad nauseam on Internet bulletin boards and worldwide-web chat rooms.

Everyone loves a conspiracy.

And the conspiracies kept coming. Most recent, of course, had been the earthshaking discovery that Da Vinci's famed *Adoration of the Magi* was hiding a dark secret beneath its layers of paint. Italian art diagnostician Maurizio Seracini had unveiled the unsettling truth, which the *New York Times Magazine* carried prominently in a story titled 'The Leonardo Cover-Up'.

Seracini had revealed beyond any doubt that while the *Adoration*'s grey-green sketched underdrawing was indeed Da Vinci's work, the painting itself was not. The truth was that some anonymous painter had filled in Da Vinci's sketch like a paint-by-numbers years after Da Vinci's death. Far more troubling, however, was what lay *beneath* the impostor's paint. Photographs taken with infrared reflectography and X-ray suggested that this rogue painter, while filling in Da Vinci's sketched study, had made suspicious departures from the underdrawing . . . as if to subvert Da Vinci's true intention. Whatever the true nature of the underdrawing, it had yet to be made public. Even so, embarrassed officials at Florence's Uffizi Gallery immediately banished the painting to a warehouse across the street. Visitors at the gallery's Leonardo Room now found a misleading and unapologetic plaque where the *Adoration* once hung.

In the bizarre underworld of modern Grail seekers, Leonardo da Vinci remained the quest's great enigma. His artwork seemed bursting to tell a secret, and yet whatever it was remained hidden, perhaps beneath a layer of paint, perhaps enciphered in plain view, or perhaps nowhere at all. Maybe Da Vinci's plethora of tantalizing clues was nothing but an empty promise left behind to frustrate the curious and bring a smirk to the face of his knowing Mona Lisa.

'Is it possible,' Sophie asked, drawing Langdon back, 'that the key you're holding unlocks the hiding place of the Holy Grail?'

Langdon's laugh sounded forced, even to him. 'I really can't imagine. Besides, the Grail is believed to be hidden in the United Kingdom somewhere, not France.' He gave her the quick history.

'But the Grail seems the only rational conclusion,' she insisted. 'We have an extremely secure key, stamped with the Priory of Sion seal, delivered to us by a member of the Priory of Sion – a brotherhood which, you just told me, are guardians of the Holy Grail.'

Langdon knew her contention was logical, and yet intuitively he could not possibly accept it. Rumours existed that the Priory had vowed someday to bring the Grail back to France to a final resting place, but certainly no historical evidence existed to suggest that this indeed had happened. Even if the Priory had managed to bring the Grail back to France, the address 24 Rue Haxo near a tennis stadium hardly sounded like a noble final resting place. 'Sophie, I really don't see how this key could have anything to do with the Grail.'

'Because the Grail is supposed to be in England?'

'Not only that. The location of the Holy Grail is one of the best kept secrets in history. Priory members wait decades proving themselves trustworthy before being elevated to the highest echelons of the fraternity and learning where the Grail is. That secret is protected by an intricate system of compartmentalized knowledge, and although the Priory brotherhood is very large, only *four* members at any given time know where the Grail is hidden – the Grand Master and his three *sénéchaux*. The probability of your grandfather being one of those four top people is very slim.'

My grandfather was one of them, Sophie thought, pressing down on the accelerator. She had an image stamped in her memory that confirmed her grandfather's status within the brotherhood beyond any doubt.

'And even if your grandfather *were* in the upper echelon, he would never be allowed to reveal anything to anyone outside the brotherhood. It is inconceivable that he would bring you into the inner circle.'

I've already been there, Sophie thought, picturing the ritual in the basement. She wondered if this were the moment to tell Langdon what she had witnessed that night in the Normandy château. For ten years now, simple shame had kept her from telling a soul. Just thinking about it, she shuddered. Sirens howled somewhere in the distance, and she felt a thickening shroud of fatigue settling over her.

'There!' Langdon said, feeling excited to see the huge complex of the Roland Garros tennis stadium looming ahead.

Sophie snaked her way toward the stadium. After several passes, they located the intersection of Rue Haxo and turned onto it, driving in the direction of the lower numbers. The road became more industrial, lined with businesses.

We need number twenty-four, Langdon told himself, realizing he was secretly scanning the horizon for the spires of a church. *Don't be ridiculous. A forgotten Templar church in this neighborhood?*

'There it is,' Sophie exclaimed, pointing.

Langdon's eyes followed to the structure ahead.

What in the world?

The building was modern. A squat citadel with a giant, neon equal-armed cross emblazoned atop its façade. Beneath the cross were the words:

DEPOSITORY BANK OF ZURICH

Langdon was thankful not to have shared his Templar church hopes with Sophie. A career hazard of symbologists was a tendency to extract hidden meaning from situations that had none. In this case, Langdon had entirely forgotten that the peaceful, equal-armed cross had been adopted as the perfect symbol for the flag of neutral Switzerland.

At least the mystery was solved.

Sophie and Langdon were holding the key to a Swiss bank deposit box.

41

Outside Castel Gandolfo, an updraft of mountain air gushed over the top of the cliff and across the high bluff, sending a chill through Bishop Aringarosa as he stepped from the Fiat. *I should have worn more than this cassock*, he thought, fighting the reflex to shiver. The last thing he needed to appear tonight was weak or fearful.

The castle was dark save the windows at the very top of the building, which glowed ominously. *The library*, Aringarosa thought. *They are awake and waiting*. He ducked his head against the wind and continued on without so much as a glance toward the observatory domes.

The priest who greeted him at the door looked sleepy. He was the same priest who had greeted Aringarosa five months ago, albeit tonight he did so with much less hospitality. 'We were worried about you, Bishop,' the priest said, checking his watch and looking more perturbed than worried.

'My apologies. Airlines are so unreliable these days.'

The priest mumbled something inaudible and then said, 'They are waiting upstairs. I will escort you up.'

The library was a vast square room with dark wood from floor to ceiling. On all sides, towering bookcases groaned with volumes. The floor was amber marble with black basalt trim, a handsome reminder that this building had once been a palace.

'Welcome, Bishop,' a man's voice said from across the room.

Aringarosa tried to see who had spoken, but the lights were ridiculously low – much lower than they had been on his first visit, when everything was ablaze. *The night of stark awakening*. Tonight, these men sat in the shadows, as if they were somehow ashamed of what was about to transpire.

Aringarosa entered slowly, regally even. He could see the shapes of three men at a long table on the far side of the room. The silhouette of the man in the middle was immediately recognizable – the obese Secretarius Vaticana, overlord of all legal matters within Vatican City. The other two were high-ranking Italian cardinals.

Aringarosa crossed the library toward them. 'My humble apologies for the hour. We're on different time zones. You must be tired.'

'Not at all,' the secretarius said, his hands folded on his enormous belly.

'We are grateful you have come so far. The least we can do is be awake to meet you. Can we offer you some coffee or refreshments?'

'I'd prefer we don't pretend this is a social visit. I have another plane to catch. Shall we get to business?'

'Of course,' the secretarius said. 'You have acted more quickly than we imagined.'

'Have I?'

'You still have a month.'

'You made your concerns known five months ago,' Aringarosa said. 'Why should I wait?'

'Indeed. We are very pleased with your expediency.'

Aringarosa's eyes travelled the length of the long table to a large black briefcase. 'Is that what I requested?'

'It is.' The secretarius sounded uneasy. 'Although, I must admit, we are concerned with the request. It seems quite . . .'

'Dangerous,' one of the cardinals finished. 'Are you certain we cannot wire it to you somewhere? The sum is exorbitant.'

Freedom is expensive. 'I have no concerns for my own safety. God is with me.'

The men actually looked doubtful.

'The funds are exactly as I requested?'

The secretarius nodded. 'Large-denomination bearer bonds drawn on the Vatican Bank. Negotiable as cash anywhere in the world.'

Aringarosa walked to the end of the table and opened the briefcase. Inside were two thick stacks of bonds, each embossed with the Vatican seal and the title *PORTATORE*, making the bonds redeemable to whoever was holding them.

The secretarius looked tense. 'I must say, Bishop, all of us would feel less apprehensive if these funds were in *cash*.'

I could not lift that much cash, Aringarosa thought, closing the case. 'Bonds are negotiable as cash. You said so yourself.'

The cardinals exchanged uneasy looks, and finally one said, 'Yes, but these bonds are traceable directly to the Vatican Bank.'

Aringarosa smiled inwardly. That was precisely the reason the Teacher suggested Aringarosa get the money in Vatican Bank bonds. It served as insurance. *We are all in this together now.* 'This is a perfectly legal transaction,' Aringarosa defended. 'Opus Dei is a personal prelature of Vatican City, and His Holiness can disperse monies however he sees fit. No law has been broken here.'

'True, and yet . . .' The secretarius leaned forward and his chair creaked under the burden. 'We have no knowledge of what you intend to do with these funds, and if it is in any way illegal . . .'

'Considering what you are asking of me,' Aringarosa countered, 'what I do with this money is not your concern.'

There was a long silence.

They know I'm right, Aringarosa thought. 'Now, I imagine you have something for me to sign?'

They all jumped, eagerly pushing the paper toward him, as if they wished he would simply leave.

Aringarosa eyed the sheet before him. It bore the papal seal. 'This is identical to the copy you sent me?'

'Exactly.'

Aringarosa was surprised how little emotion he felt as he signed the document. The three men present, however, seemed to sigh in relief.

'Thank you, Bishop,' the secretarius said. 'Your service to the Church will never be forgotten.'

Aringarosa picked up the briefcase, sensing promise and authority in its weight. The four men looked at one another for a moment as if there were something more to say, but apparently there was not. Aringarosa turned and headed for the door.

'Bishop?' one of the cardinals called out as Aringarosa reached the threshold.

Aringarosa paused, turning. 'Yes?'

'Where will you go from here?'

Aringarosa sensed the query was more spiritual than geographical, and yet he had no intention of discussing morality at this hour. 'Paris,' he said, and walked out the door.

42

The Depository Bank of Zurich was a twenty-four-hour *Geldschrank* bank offering the full modern array of anonymous services in the tradition of the Swiss numbered account. Maintaining offices in Zurich, Kuala Lumpur, New York and Paris, the bank had expanded its services in recent years to offer anonymous computer source code escrow services and faceless digitized backup.

The bread and butter of its operation was by far its oldest and simplest offering – the *anonyme Lager* – blind drop services, otherwise known as anonymous safe-deposit boxes. Clients wishing to store anything from stock certificates to valuable paintings could deposit their belongings anonymously, through a series of high-tech veils of privacy, withdrawing items at any time, also in total anonymity.

As Sophie pulled the taxi to a stop in front of their destination, Langdon gazed out at the building's uncompromising architecture and sensed the Depository Bank of Zurich was a firm with little sense of humour. The building was a windowless rectangle that seemed to be forged entirely of dull steel. Resembling an enormous metal brick, the edifice sat back from the road with a fifteen-foot-tall, neon, equilateral cross glowing over its façade.

Switzerland's reputation for secrecy in banking had become one of the country's most lucrative exports. Facilities like this had become controversial in the art community because they provided a perfect place for art thieves to hide stolen goods, for years if necessary, until the heat was off. Because deposits were protected from police inspection by privacy laws and were attached to numbered accounts rather than people's names, thieves could rest easily knowing their stolen goods were safe and could never be traced to them.

Sophie stopped the taxi at an imposing gate that blocked the bank's driveway – a cement-lined ramp that descended beneath the building. A video camera overhead was aimed directly at them, and Langdon had the feeling that this camera, unlike those at the Louvre, was authentic.

Sophie rolled down the window and surveyed the electronic podium on the driver's side. An LCD screen provided directions in seven languages. Topping the list was English.

INSERT KEY.

Sophie took the gold laser-pocked key from her pocket and turned her attention back to the podium. Below the screen was a triangular hole.

'Something tells me it will fit,' Langdon said.

Sophie aligned the key's triangular shaft with the hole and inserted it, sliding it in until the entire shaft had disappeared. This key apparently required no turning. Instantly, the gate began to swing open. Sophie took her foot off the brake and coasted down to a second gate and podium. Behind her, the first gate closed, trapping them like a ship in a lock.

Langdon disliked the constricted sensation. *Let's hope this second gate works too.*

This second podium bore familiar directions.

INSERT KEY.

When Sophie inserted the key, the second gate immediately opened. Moments later they were winding down the ramp into the belly of the structure.

The private garage was small and dim, with spaces for about a dozen cars. At the far end, Langdon spied the building's main entrance. A red carpet stretched across the cement floor, welcoming visitors to a huge door that appeared to be forged of solid metal.

Talk about mixed messages, Langdon thought. *Welcome and keep out.*

Sophie pulled the taxi into a parking space near the entrance and killed the engine. 'You'd better leave the gun here.'

With pleasure, Langdon thought, sliding the pistol under the seat.

Sophie and Langdon got out and walked up the red carpet toward the slab of steel. The door had no handle, but on the wall beside it was another triangular keyhole. No directions were posted this time.

'Keeps out the slow learners,' Langdon said.

Sophie laughed, looking nervous. 'Here we go.' She stuck the key in the hole, and the door swung inward with a low hum. Exchanging glances, Sophie and Langdon entered. The door shut with a thud behind them.

The foyer of the Depository Bank of Zurich employed as imposing a decor as any Langdon had ever seen. Where most banks were content with the usual polished marble and granite, this one had opted for wall-to-wall metal and rivets.

Who's their decorator? Langdon wondered. *Allied Steel?*

Sophie looked equally intimidated as her eyes scanned the lobby.

The grey metal was everywhere – the floor, walls, counters, doors, even the lobby chairs appeared to be fashioned of moulded iron. Nonetheless, the effect was impressive. The message was clear: You are walking into a vault.

A large man behind the counter glanced up as they entered. He turned off the small television he was watching and greeted them with a pleasant smile. Despite his enormous muscles and visible sidearm, his diction chimed with the polished courtesy of a Swiss bellhop.

'*Bonsoir*,' he said. 'How may I help you?'

The dual-language greeting was the newest hospitality trick of the European host. It presumed nothing and opened the door for the guest to reply in whichever language was more comfortable.

Sophie replied with neither. She simply laid the gold key on the counter in front of the man.

The man glanced down and immediately stood straighter. 'Of course. Your elevator is at the end of the hall. I will alert someone that you are on your way.'

Sophie nodded and took her key back. 'Which floor?'

The man gave her an odd look. 'Your key instructs the elevator which floor.'

She smiled. 'Ah, yes.'

The guard watched as the two newcomers made their way to the elevators, inserted their key, boarded the lift, and disappeared. As soon as the door had closed, he grabbed the phone. He was not calling to alert anyone of their arrival; there was no need for that. A vault greeter already had been alerted automatically when the client's key was inserted outside in the entry gate.

Instead, the guard was calling the bank's night manager. As the line rang, the guard switched the television back on and stared at it. The news story he had been watching was just ending. It didn't matter. He got another look at the two faces on the television.

The manager answered. '*Oui?*'

'We have a situation down here.'

'What's happening?' the manager demanded.

'The French police are tracking two fugitives tonight.'

'So?'

'Both of them just walked into our bank.'

The manager cursed quietly. 'Okay. I'll contact Monsieur Vernet immediately.'

The guard then hung up and placed a second call. This one to Interpol.

Langdon was surprised to feel the elevator dropping rather than climbing. He had no idea how many floors they had descended beneath the Depository Bank of Zurich before the door finally opened. He didn't care. He was happy to be out of the elevator.

Displaying impressive alacrity, a host was already standing there to greet them. He was elderly and pleasant, wearing a neatly pressed flannel suit that made him look oddly out of place – an old-world banker in a high-tech world.

'*Bonsoir*,' the man said. 'Good evening. Would you be so kind as to follow me, *s'il vous plaît?*' Without waiting for a response, he spun on his heel and strode briskly down a narrow metal corridor.

Langdon walked with Sophie down a series of corridors, past several large rooms filled with blinking mainframe computers.

'*Voici*,' their host said, arriving at a steel door and opening it for them. 'Here you are.'

Langdon and Sophie stepped into another world. The small room before them looked like a lavish sitting room at a fine hotel. Gone were the metal and rivets, replaced with oriental carpets, dark oak furniture, and cushioned chairs. On the broad desk in the middle of the room, two crystal glasses sat beside an opened bottle of Perrier, its bubbles still fizzing. A pewter pot of coffee steamed beside it.

Clockwork, Langdon thought. *Leave it to the Swiss.*

The man gave a perceptive smile. 'I sense this is your first visit to us?'

Sophie hesitated and then nodded.

'Understood. Keys are often passed on as inheritance, and our first-time users are invariably uncertain of the protocol.' He motioned to the table of drinks. 'This room is yours as long as you care to use it.'

'You say keys are sometimes inherited?' Sophie asked.

'Indeed. Your key is like a Swiss numbered account, which are often willed through generations. On our gold accounts, the shortest safety-deposit box lease is fifty years. Paid in advance. So we see plenty of family turnover.'

Langdon stared. 'Did you say fifty *years?*'

'At a minimum,' their host replied. 'Of course, you can purchase much longer leases, but barring further arrangements, if there is no activity on an account for fifty years, the contents of that safe-deposit box are automatically destroyed. Shall I run through the process of accessing your box?'

Sophie nodded. 'Please.'

Their host swept an arm across the luxurious salon. 'This is your private viewing room. Once I leave the room, you may spend all the time you need in here to review and modify the contents of your safe-deposit box, which arrives . . . over here.' He walked them to the far wall where a wide conveyor belt entered the room in a graceful curve, vaguely resembling a baggage claim carousel. 'You insert your key in that slot there. . . .' The man pointed to a large electronic podium facing the conveyor belt. The podium had a familiar triangular hole. 'Once the computer confirms the markings on your key, you enter your account number, and your safe-deposit box will be retrieved robotically from the vault below for your inspection. When you are finished with your box, you place it back on the conveyor belt, insert your key again, and the process is reversed. Because everything is automated, your privacy is guaranteed, even from the staff of this bank. If you need anything at all, simply press the call button on the table in the centre of the room.'

Sophie was about to ask a question when a telephone rang. The man looked puzzled and embarrassed. 'Excuse me, please.' He walked over to the phone, which was sitting on the table beside the coffee and Perrier.

'*Oui?*' he answered.

His brow furrowed as he listened to the caller. '*Oui . . . oui . . . d'accord.*' He hung up, and gave them an uneasy smile. 'I'm sorry, I must leave you now. Make yourselves at home.' He moved quickly toward the door.

'Excuse me,' Sophie called. 'Could you clarify something before you go? You mentioned that we enter an *account* number?'

The man paused at the door, looking pale. 'But of course. Like most Swiss banks, our safe-deposit boxes are attached to a *number*, not a name. You have a key and a personal account number known only to you. Your key is only half of your identification. Your personal account number is the other half. Otherwise, if you lost your key, anyone could use it.'

Sophie hesitated. 'And if my benefactor gave me no account number?'

The banker's heart pounded. *Then you obviously have no business here!* He gave them a calm smile. 'I will ask someone to help you. He will be in shortly.'

Leaving, the banker closed the door behind him and twisted a heavy lock, sealing them inside.

Across town, Collet was standing in the Gare du Nord train terminal when his phone rang.

It was Fache. 'Interpol got a tip,' he said. 'Forget the train. Langdon and Neveu just walked into the Paris branch of the Depository Bank of Zurich. I want your men over there right away.'

'Any leads yet on what Saunière was trying to tell Agent Neveu and Robert Langdon?'

Fache's tone was cold. 'If you arrest them, Lieutenant Collet, then I can ask them personally.'

Collet took the hint. 'Twenty-four Rue Haxo. Right away, Captain.' He hung up and radioed his men.

43

André Vernet – president of the Paris branch of the Depository Bank of Zurich – lived in a lavish flat above the bank. Despite his plush accommodation, he had always dreamed of owning a riverside apartment on L'Ile Saint-Louis, where he could rub shoulders with the true *cognoscenti*, rather than here, where he simply met the filthy rich.

When I retire, Vernet told himself, *I will fill my cellar with rare Bordeaux, adorn my salon with a Fragonard and perhaps a Boucher, and spend my days hunting for antique furniture and rare books in the Quartier Latin.*

Tonight, Vernet had been awake only six and a half minutes. Even so, as he hurried through the bank's underground corridor, he looked as if his personal tailor and hairdresser had polished him to a fine sheen. Impeccably dressed in a silk suit, Vernet sprayed some breath spray in his mouth and tightened his tie as he walked. No stranger to being awoken to attend to his international clients arriving from different time zones, Vernet modelled his sleep habits after the Masai warriors – the African tribe famous for their ability to rise from the deepest sleep to a state of total battle readiness in a matter of seconds.

Battle ready, Vernet thought, fearing the comparison might be uncharacteristically apt tonight. The arrival of a gold key client always required an extra flurry of attention, but the arrival of a gold key client who was *wanted* by the Judicial Police would be an extremely delicate matter. The bank had enough battles with law enforcement over the privacy rights of their clients without proof that some of them were criminals.

Five minutes, Vernet told himself. *I need these people out of my bank before the police arrive.*

If he moved quickly, this impending disaster could be deftly side-stepped. Vernet could tell the police that the fugitives in question had indeed walked into his bank as reported, but because they were not clients and had no account number, they were turned away. He wished the damned watchman had not called Interpol. Discretion was apparently not part of the vocabulary of a 15-euro-per-hour watchman.

Stopping at the doorway, he took a deep breath and loosened his muscles. Then, forcing a balmy smile, he unlocked the door and swirled into the room like a warm breeze.

'Good evening,' he said, his eyes finding his clients. 'I am André Vernet. How can I be of serv—' The rest of the sentence lodged somewhere beneath his Adam's apple. The woman before him was as unexpected a visitor as Vernet had ever had.

'I'm sorry, do we know each other?' Sophie asked. She did not recognize the banker, but he for a moment looked as if he'd seen a ghost.

'No . . . ,' the bank president fumbled. 'I don't . . . believe so. Our services are anonymous.' He exhaled and forced a calm smile. 'My assistant tells me you have a gold key but no account number? Might I ask how you came by this key?'

'My grandfather gave it to me,' Sophie replied, watching the man closely. His uneasiness seemed more evident now.

'Really? Your grandfather gave you the key but failed to give you the account number?'

'I don't think he had time,' Sophie said. 'He was murdered tonight.'

Her words sent the man staggering backward. 'Jacques Saunière is dead?' he demanded, his eyes filling with horror. 'But . . . how?!'

Now it was Sophie who reeled, numb with shock. 'You *knew* my grandfather?'

Banker André Vernet looked equally astounded, steadying himself by leaning on an end table. 'Jacques and I were dear friends. When did this happen?'

'Earlier this evening. Inside the Louvre.'

Vernet walked to a deep leather chair and sank into it. 'I need to ask you both a very important question.' He glanced up at Langdon and then back to Sophie. 'Did either of you have anything to do with his death?'

'No!' Sophie declared. 'Absolutely not.'

Vernet's face was grim, and he paused, pondering. 'Your pictures are being circulated by Interpol. This is how I recognized you. You're wanted for a murder.'

Sophie slumped. *Fache ran an Interpol broadcast already?* It seemed the captain was more motivated than Sophie had anticipated. She quickly told Vernet who Langdon was and what had happened inside the Louvre tonight.

Vernet looked amazed. 'And as your grandfather was dying, he left you a message telling you to find Mr Langdon?'

'Yes. And this key.' Sophie laid the gold key on the coffee table in front of Vernet, placing the Priory seal face down.

Vernet glanced at the key but made no move to touch it. 'He left you only this key? Nothing else? No slip of paper?'

Sophie knew she had been in a hurry inside the Louvre, but she was certain she had seen nothing else behind *Madonna of the Rocks*. 'No. Just the key.'

Vernet gave a helpless sigh. 'I'm afraid every key is electronically paired with a ten-digit account number that functions as a password. Without that number, your key is worthless.'

Ten digits. Sophie reluctantly calculated the cryptographic odds. *Ten billion possible choices.* Even if she could bring in DCPJ's most powerful parallel processing computers, she still would need weeks to break the code. 'Certainly, monsieur, considering the circumstances, you can help us.'

'I'm sorry. I truly can do nothing. Clients select their own account numbers via a secure terminal, meaning account numbers are known only to the client and computer. This is one way we ensure anonymity. And the safety of our employees.'

Sophie understood. Convenience stores did the same thing. EMPLOYEES DO NOT HAVE KEYS TO THE SAFE. This bank obviously did not want to risk someone stealing a key and then holding an employee hostage for the account number.

Sophie sat down beside Langdon, glanced down at the key and then up at Vernet. 'Do you have any idea what my grandfather is storing in your bank?'

'None whatsoever. That is the definition of a *Geldschrank* bank.'

'Monsieur Vernet,' she pressed, 'our time tonight is short. I am going to be very direct if I may.' She reached out to the gold key and flipped it over, watching the man's eyes as she revealed the Priory of Sion seal. 'Does the symbol on this key mean anything to you?'

Vernet glanced down at the fleur-de-lis seal and made no reaction. 'No, but many of our clients emboss corporate logos or initials onto their keys.'

Sophie sighed, still watching him carefully. 'This seal is the symbol of a secret society known as the Priory of Sion.'

Vernet again showed no reaction. 'I know nothing of this. Your grandfather was a friend, but we spoke mostly of business.' The man adjusted his tie, looking nervous now.

'Monsieur Vernet,' Sophie pressed, her tone firm. 'My grandfather called me tonight and told me he and I were in grave danger. He said he had to give me something. He gave me a key to your bank. Now he is dead. Anything you can tell us would be helpful.'

Vernet broke a sweat. 'We need to get out of the building. I'm afraid the police will arrive shortly. My watchman felt obliged to call Interpol.'

Sophie had feared as much. She took one last shot. 'My grandfather said he needed to tell me the truth about my family. Does that mean anything to you?'

'Mademoiselle, your family died in a car accident when you were young. I'm sorry. I know your grandfather loved you very much. He mentioned to me several times how much it pained him that you two had fallen out of touch.'

Sophie was uncertain how to respond.

Langdon asked, 'Do the contents of this account have anything to do with the Sangreal?'

Vernet gave him an odd look. 'I have no idea what that is.' Just then, Vernet's cell phone rang, and he snatched it off his belt. '*Oui?*' He listened a moment, his expression one of surprise and growing concern. '*La police? Si rapidement?*' He cursed, gave some quick directions in French, and said he would be up to the lobby in a minute.

Hanging up the phone, he turned back to Sophie. 'The police have responded far more quickly than usual. They are arriving as we speak.'

Sophie had no intention of leaving empty-handed. 'Tell them we came and went already. If they want to search the bank, demand a search warrant. That will take them time.'

'Listen,' Vernet said, 'Jacques was a friend, and my bank does not need this kind of press, so for those two reasons, I have no intention of allowing this arrest to be made on my premises. Give me a minute and I will see what I can do to help you leave the bank undetected. Beyond that, I cannot get involved.' He stood up and hurried for the door. 'Stay here. I'll make arrangements and be right back.'

'But the safe-deposit box,' Sophie declared. 'We can't just leave.'

'There's nothing I can do,' Vernet said, hurrying out the door. 'I'm sorry.'

Sophie stared after him a moment, wondering if maybe the account number was buried in one of the countless letters and packages her grandfather had sent her over the years and which she had left unopened.

Langdon stood suddenly, and Sophie sensed an unexpected glimmer of contentment in his eyes.

'Robert? You're smiling.'

'Your grandfather was a genius.'

'I'm sorry?'

'Ten digits?'

Sophie had no idea what he was talking about.

'The account number,' he said, a familiar lopsided grin now crossing his face. 'I'm pretty sure he left it for us after all.'

'Where?'

Langdon produced the printout of the crime scene photo and spread it out on the coffee table. Sophie needed only to read the first line to know Langdon was correct.

13-3-2-21-1-1-8-5

O, Draconian devil!

Oh, lame saint!

P.S. Find Robert Langdon

44

'Ten digits,' Sophie said, her cryptologic senses tingling as she studied the printout.

$$13\text{-}3\text{-}2\text{-}21\text{-}1\text{-}1\text{-}8\text{-}5$$

Grand-père wrote his account number on the Louvre floor!
When Sophie had first seen the scrambled Fibonacci sequence on the parquet, she had assumed its sole purpose was to encourage DCPJ to call in their cryptographers and get Sophie *involved*. Later, she realized the numbers were also a clue as to how to decipher the other lines – *a sequence out of order . . . a numeric anagram*. Now, utterly amazed, she saw the numbers had a more important meaning still. They were almost certainly the final key to opening her grandfather's mysterious safe-deposit box.

'He was the master of double-entendres,' Sophie said, turning to Langdon. 'He loved anything with multiple layers of meaning. Codes within codes.'

Langdon was already moving toward the electronic podium near the conveyor belt. Sophie grabbed the computer printout and followed.

The podium had a keypad similar to that of a bank ATM terminal. The screen displayed the bank's cruciform logo. Beside the keypad was a triangular hole. Sophie wasted no time inserting the shaft of her key into the hole.

The screen refreshed instantly.

ACCOUNT NUMBER:

– – – – – – – – – –

The cursor blinked. Waiting.
Ten digits. Sophie read the numbers off the printout, and Langdon typed them in.

ACCOUNT NUMBER:
1332211185

609

When he had typed the last digit, the screen refreshed again. A message in several languages appeared. English was on top.

```
                        CAUTION:
Before  you  strike  the  enter  key,  please  check
        the  accuracy  of  your  account  number.
For  your  own  security,  if  the  computer  does  not
recognize  your  account  number,  this  system  will
                automatically  shut  down.
```

'*Fonction terminer,*' Sophie said, frowning. 'Looks like we only get one try.' Standard ATM machines allowed users *three* attempts to type a PIN before confiscating their bank card. This was obviously no ordinary cash machine.

'The number looks right,' Langdon confirmed, carefully checking what they had typed and comparing it to the printout. He motioned to the ENTER key. 'Fire away.'

Sophie extended her index finger toward the keypad, but hesitated, an odd thought now hitting her.

'Go ahead,' Langdon urged. 'Vernet will be back soon.'

'No.' She pulled her hand away. 'This isn't the right account number.'

'Of course it is! Ten digits. What else would it be?'

'It's too random.'

Too random? Langdon could not have disagreed more. Every bank advised its customers to choose PINs at random so nobody could guess them. Certainly clients *here* would be advised to choose their account numbers at random.

Sophie deleted everything she had just typed in and looked up at Langdon, her gaze self-assured. 'It's far too coincidental that this supposedly *random* account number could be rearranged to form the Fibonacci sequence.'

Langdon realized she had a point. Earlier, Sophie had rearranged this account number into the Fibonacci sequence. What were the odds of being able to do that?

Sophie was at the keypad again, entering a different number, as if from memory. 'Moreover, with my grandfather's love of symbolism and codes, it seems to follow that he would have chosen an account number that had meaning to him, something he could easily remember.' She finished typing the entry and gave a sly smile. 'Something that appeared random . . . but was *not.*'

Langdon looked at the screen.

```
                ACCOUNT NUMBER:
                1123581321
```

It took him an instant, but when Langdon spotted it, he knew she was right.

The Fibonacci sequence.

1-1-2-3-5-8-13-21

When the Fibonacci sequence was melded into a single ten-digit number, it became virtually unrecognizable. *Easy to remember, and yet seemingly random.* A brilliant ten-digit code that Saunière would never forget. Furthermore, it perfectly explained why the scrambled numbers on the Louvre floor could be rearranged to form the famous progression.

Sophie reached down and pressed the ENTER key.

Nothing happened.

At least nothing they could detect.

At that moment, beneath them, in the bank's cavernous subterranean vault, a robotic claw sprang to life. Sliding on a double-axis transport system attached to the ceiling, the claw headed off in search of the proper coordinates. On the cement floor below, hundreds of identical plastic crates lay aligned on an enormous grid . . . like rows of small coffins in an underground crypt.

Whirring to a stop over the correct spot on the floor, the claw dropped down, an electric eye confirming the bar code on the box. Then, with computer precision, the claw grasped the heavy handle and hoisted the crate vertically. New gears engaged, and the claw transported the box to the far side of the vault, coming to a stop over a stationary conveyor belt.

Gently now, the retrieval arm set down the crate and retracted.

Once the arm was clear, the conveyor belt whirred to life. . . .

Upstairs, Sophie and Langdon exhaled in relief to see the conveyor belt move. Standing beside the belt, they felt like weary travellers at baggage claim awaiting a mysterious piece of luggage whose contents were unknown.

The conveyor belt entered the room on their right through a narrow slit beneath a retractable door. The metal door slid up, and a huge plastic box appeared, emerging from the depths on the inclined conveyor belt. The box was black, heavy moulded plastic, and far larger than she imagined. It looked like an air-freight pet transport crate without any airholes.

The box coasted to a stop directly in front of them.

Langdon and Sophie stood there, silent, staring at the mysterious container.

Like everything else about this bank, this crate was industrial – metal clasps, a bar code sticker on top, and moulded heavy-duty handle. Sophie thought it looked like a giant toolbox.

Wasting no time, Sophie unhooked the two buckles facing her. Then she glanced over at Langdon. Together, they raised the heavy lid and let it fall back.

Stepping forward, they peered down into the crate.

At first glance, Sophie thought the crate was empty. Then she saw something. Sitting at the bottom of the crate. A lone item.

The polished wooden box was about the size of a shoebox and had ornate hinges. The wood was a lustrous deep purple with a strong grain. *Rosewood*, Sophie realized. Her grandfather's favourite. The lid bore a beautiful inlaid design of a rose. She and Langdon exchanged puzzled looks. Sophie leaned in and grabbed the box, lifting it out.

My God, it's heavy!

She carried it gingerly to a large receiving table and set it down. Langdon stood beside her, both of them staring at the small treasure chest her grandfather apparently had sent them to retrieve.

Langdon stared in wonderment at the lid's hand-carved inlay – a five-petal rose. He had seen this type of rose many times. 'The five-petal rose,' he whispered, 'is a Priory symbol for the Holy Grail.'

Sophie turned and looked at him. Langdon could see what she was thinking, and he was thinking it too. The dimensions of the box, the apparent weight of its contents, and a Priory symbol for the Grail all seemed to imply one unfathomable conclusion. *The Cup of Christ is in this wooden box.* Langdon again told himself it was impossible.

'It's a perfect size,' Sophie whispered, 'to hold . . . a chalice.'

It can't be a chalice.

Sophie pulled the box toward her across the table, preparing to open it. As she moved it, though, something unexpected happened. The box let out an odd gurgling sound.

Langdon did a double take. *There's liquid inside?*

Sophie looked equally confused. 'Did you just hear . . . ?'

Langdon nodded, lost. 'Liquid.'

Reaching forward, Sophie slowly unhooked the clasp and raised the lid.

The object inside was unlike anything Langdon had ever seen. One thing was immediately clear to both of them, however. This was definitely *not* the Cup of Christ.

45

'The police are blocking the street,' André Vernet said, walking into the waiting room. 'Getting you out will be difficult.' As he closed the door behind him, Vernet saw the heavy-duty plastic case on the conveyor belt and halted in his tracks. *My God! They accessed Saunière's account?*

Sophie and Langdon were at the table, huddling over what looked to be a large wooden jewelry box. Sophie immediately closed the lid and looked up. 'We had the account number after all,' she said.

Vernet was speechless. This changed everything. He respectfully diverted his eyes from the box and tried to figure out his next move. *I have to get them out of the bank!* But with the police already having set up a road-block, Vernet could imagine only one way to do that. 'Mademoiselle Neveu, if I can get you safely out of the bank, will you be taking the item with you or returning it to the vault before you leave?'

Sophie glanced at Langdon and then back to Vernet. 'We need to take it.'

Vernet nodded. 'Very well. Then whatever the item is, I suggest you wrap it in your jacket as we move through the hallways. I would prefer nobody else see it.'

As Langdon shed his jacket, Vernet hurried over to the conveyor belt, closed the now empty crate, and typed a series of simple commands. The conveyor belt began moving again, carrying the plastic container back down to the vault. Pulling the gold key from the podium, he handed it to Sophie.

'This way please. Hurry.'

When they reached the rear loading dock, Vernet could see the flash of police lights filtering through the underground garage. He frowned. They were probably blocking the ramp. *Am I really going to try to pull this off?* He was sweating now.

Vernet motioned to one of the bank's small armoured trucks. *Transport sûr* was another service offered by the Depository Bank of Zurich. 'Get in the cargo hold,' he said, heaving open the massive rear door and motioning to the glistening steel compartment. 'I'll be right back.'

As Sophie and Langdon climbed in, Vernet hurried across the loading dock to the dock overseer's office, let himself in, collected the keys for the truck, and found a driver's uniform jacket and cap. Shedding his own suit coat and tie, he began to put on the driver's jacket. Reconsidering, he donned a shoulder holster beneath the uniform. On his way out, he grabbed a driver's pistol from the rack, put in a clip, and stuffed it in the holster, buttoning his uniform over it. Returning to the truck, Vernet pulled the driver's cap down low and peered in at Sophie and Langdon, who were standing inside the empty steel box.

'You'll want this on,' Vernet said, reaching inside and flicking a wall switch to illuminate the lone courtesy bulb on the hold's ceiling. 'And you'd better sit down. Not a sound on our way out the gate.'

Sophie and Langdon sat down on the metal floor. Langdon cradled the treasure wadded in his tweed jacket. Swinging the heavy doors closed, Vernet locked them inside. Then he got in behind the wheel and revved the engine.

As the armoured truck lumbered toward the top of the ramp, Vernet could feel the sweat already collecting beneath his driver's cap. He could see there were far more police lights in front than he had imagined. As the truck powered up the ramp, the interior gate swung inward to let him pass. Vernet advanced and waited while the gate behind him closed before pulling forward and tripping the next sensor. The second gate opened, and the exit beckoned.

Except for the police car blocking the top of the ramp.

Vernet dabbed his brow and pulled forward.

A lanky officer stepped out and waved him to a stop a few metres from the roadblock. Four patrol cars were parked out front.

Vernet stopped. Pulling his driver's cap down farther, he effected as rough a façade as his cultured upbringing would allow. Not budging from behind the wheel, he opened the door and gazed down at the agent, whose face was stern and sallow.

'*Qu'est-ce qui se passe?*' Vernet asked, his tone rough.

'*Je suis Jérome Collet,*' the agent said. '*Lieutenant Police Judiciaire.*' He motioned to the truck's cargo hold. '*Qu'est-ce qu'il y a là ô dedans?*'

'Hell if I know,' Vernet replied in crude French. 'I'm only a driver.'

Collet looked unimpressed. 'We're looking for two criminals.'

Vernet laughed. 'Then you came to the right spot. Some of these bastards I drive for have so much money they must be criminals.'

The agent held up a passport picture of Robert Langdon. 'Was this man in your bank tonight?'

Vernet shrugged. 'No clue. I'm a dock rat. They don't let us anywhere near the clients. You need to go in and ask the front desk.'

'Your bank is demanding a search warrant before we can enter.'

Vernet put on a disgusted look. 'Administrators. Don't get me started.'

'Open your truck, please.' Collet motioned toward the cargo hold.

Vernet stared at the agent and forced an obnoxious laugh. 'Open the truck? You think I have keys? You think they trust us? You should see the crap wages I get paid.'

The agent's head tilted to one side, his skepticism evident. 'You're telling me you don't have keys to your own truck?'

Vernet shook his head. 'Not the cargo area. Ignition only. These trucks get sealed by overseers on the loading dock. Then the truck sits in dock while someone drives the cargo keys to the drop-off. Once we get the call that the cargo keys are with the recipient, then I get the okay to drive. Not a second before. I never know what the hell I'm lugging.'

'When was *this* truck sealed?'

'Must have been hours ago. I'm driving all the way up to St. Thurial tonight. Cargo keys are already up there.'

The agent made no response, his eyes probing as if trying to read Vernet's mind.

A drop of sweat was preparing to slide down Vernet's nose. 'You mind?' he said, wiping his nose with his sleeve and motioning to the police car blocking his way. 'I'm on a tight schedule.'

'Do all the drivers wear Rolexes?' the agent asked, pointing to Vernet's wrist.

Vernet glanced down and saw the glistening band of his absurdly expensive watch peeking out from beneath the sleeve of his jacket. *Merde.* 'This piece of shit? Bought it for twenty euro from a Taiwanese street vendor in St Germain des Prés. I'll sell it to you for forty.'

The agent paused and finally stepped aside. 'No thanks. Have a safe trip.'

Vernet did not breathe again until the truck was a good fifty metres down the street. And now he had another problem. His cargo. *Where do I take them?*

46

Silas lay prone on the canvas mat in his room, allowing the lash wounds on his back to clot in the air. Tonight's second session with the Discipline had left him dizzy and weak. He had yet to remove the *cilice* belt, and he could feel the blood trickling down his inner thigh. Still, he could not justify removing the strap.

I have failed the Church.

Far worse, I have failed the bishop.

Tonight was supposed to be Bishop Aringarosa's salvation. Five months ago, the bishop had returned from a meeting at the Vatican Observatory, where he had learned something that left him deeply changed. Depressed for weeks, Aringarosa had finally shared the news with Silas.

'But this is impossible!' Silas had cried out. 'I cannot accept it!'

'It is true,' Aringarosa said. 'Unthinkable, but true. In only six months.'

The bishop's words terrified Silas. He prayed for deliverance, and even in those dark days, his trust in God and *The Way* never wavered. It was only a month later that the clouds parted miraculously and the light of possibility shone through.

Divine intervention, Aringarosa had called it.

The bishop had seemed hopeful for the first time. 'Silas,' he whispered, 'God has bestowed upon us an opportunity to protect *The Way*. Our battle, like all battles, will take sacrifice. Will you be a soldier of God?'

Silas fell to his knees before Bishop Aringarosa – the man who had given him a new life – and he said, 'I am a lamb of God. Shepherd me as your heart commands.'

When Aringarosa described the opportunity that had presented itself, Silas knew it could only be the hand of God at work. *Miraculous fate!* Aringarosa put Silas in contact with the man who had proposed the plan – a man who called himself the Teacher. Although the Teacher and Silas never met face-to-face, each time they spoke by phone, Silas was awed, both by the profundity of the Teacher's faith and by the scope of his power. The Teacher seemed to be a man who knew all, a man with eyes and ears in all places. How the Teacher gathered his information, Silas did not know, but Aringarosa had placed enormous trust in the Teacher, and he had told Silas to do the same. 'Do as the Teacher commands you,' the bishop told Silas. 'And we will be victorious.'

Victorious. Silas now gazed at the bare floor and feared victory had eluded them. The Teacher had been tricked. The keystone was a devious dead end. And with the deception, all hope had vanished.

Silas wished he could call Bishop Aringarosa and warn him, but the Teacher had removed all their lines of direct communication tonight. *For our safety.*

Finally, overcoming enormous trepidation, Silas crawled to his feet and found his robe, which lay on the floor. He dug his cell phone from the pocket. Hanging his head in shame, he dialled.

'Teacher,' he whispered, 'all is lost.' Silas truthfully told the man how he had been tricked.

'You lose your faith too quickly,' the Teacher replied. 'I have just received news. Most unexpected and welcome. The secret lives. Jacques Saunière transferred information before he died. I will call you soon. Our work tonight is not yet done.'

47

Riding inside the dimly lit cargo hold of the armoured truck was like being transported inside a cell for solitary confinement. Langdon fought the all too familiar anxiety that haunted him in confined spaces. *Vernet said he would take us a safe distance out of the city. Where? How far?*

Langdon's legs had got stiff from sitting cross-legged on the metal floor, and he shifted his position, wincing to feel the blood pouring back into his lower body. In his arms, he still clutched the bizarre treasure they had extricated from the bank.

'I think we're on the highway now,' Sophie whispered.

Langdon sensed the same thing. The truck, after an unnerving pause atop the bank ramp, had moved on, snaking left and right for a minute or two, and was now accelerating to what felt like top speed. Beneath them, the bulletproof tyres hummed on smooth pavement. Forcing his attention to the rosewood box in his arms, Langdon laid the precious bundle on the floor, unwrapped his jacket, and extracted the box, pulling it toward him. Sophie shifted her position so they were sitting side by side. Langdon suddenly felt like they were two kids huddled over a Christmas present.

In contrast to the warm colours of the rosewood box, the inlaid rose had been crafted of a pale wood, probably ash, which shone clearly in the dim light. *The Rose.* Entire armies and religions had been built on this symbol, as had secret societies. *The Rosicrucians. The Knights of the Rosy Cross.*

'Go ahead,' Sophie said. 'Open it.'

Langdon took a deep breath. Reaching for the lid, he stole one more admiring glance at the intricate woodwork and then, unhooking the clasp, he opened the lid, revealing the object within.

Langdon had harboured several fantasies about what they might find inside this box, but clearly he had been wrong on every account. Nestled snugly inside the box's heavily padded interior of crimson silk lay an object Langdon could not even begin to comprehend.

Crafted of polished white marble, it was a stone cylinder approximately the dimensions of a tennis ball can. More complicated than a simple column of stone, however, the cylinder appeared to have been assembled in many pieces. Five doughnut-sized disks of marble had been stacked and affixed to one another within a delicate brass framework. It looked like some kind of tubular, multiwheeled kaleidoscope. Each end of the cylinder was affixed with an end cap, also marble, making it impossible to see inside. Having heard liquid within, Langdon assumed the cylinder was hollow.

As mystifying as the construction of the cylinder was, however, it was the engravings around the tube's circumference that drew Langdon's primary focus. Each of the five disks had been carefully carved with the same unlikely series of letters – the entire alphabet. The lettered cylinder reminded Langdon of one of his childhood toys – a rod threaded with lettered tumblers that could be rotated to spell different words.

'Amazing, isn't it?' Sophie whispered.

Langdon glanced up. 'I don't know. What the hell is it?'

Now there was a glint in Sophie's eye. 'My grandfather used to craft these as a hobby. They were invented by Leonardo da Vinci.'

Even in the diffuse light, Sophie could see Langdon's surprise.

'Da Vinci?' he muttered, looking again at the canister.

'Yes. It's called a *cryptex*. According to my grandfather, the blueprints come from one of Da Vinci's secret diaries.'

'What is it for?'

Considering tonight's events, Sophie knew the answer might have some interesting implications. 'It's a vault,' she said. 'For storing secret information.'

Langdon's eyes widened further.

Sophie explained that creating models of Da Vinci's inventions was one of her grandfather's best-loved hobbies. A talented craftsman who spent hours in his wood and metal shop, Jacques Saunière enjoyed imitating master craftsmen – Fabergé, assorted cloisonné artisans, and the less artistic, but far more practical, Leonardo da Vinci.

Even a cursory glance through Da Vinci's journals revealed why the luminary was as notorious for his lack of follow-through as he was famous for his brilliance. Da Vinci had drawn up blueprints for hundreds of inventions he had never built. One of Jacques Saunière's favourite pastimes was bringing Da Vinci's more obscure brainstorms to life – timepieces, water pumps, cryptexes, and even a fully articulated model of a medieval French knight, which now stood proudly on the desk in his office. Designed by Da Vinci in 1495 as an outgrowth of his earliest anatomy and kinesiology studies, the internal mechanism of the robot knight possessed accurate joints and tendons, and was designed to sit up, wave its arms, and move its head via a flexible neck while opening and closing an anatomically correct jaw. This armour-clad knight, Sophie had always believed, was the most beautiful object her grandfather had ever built . . . that was, until she had seen the cryptex in this rosewood box.

'He made me one of these when I was little,' Sophie said. 'But I've never seen one so ornate and large.'

Langdon's eyes had never left the box. 'I've never heard of a cryptex.'

Sophie was not surprised. Most of Leonardo's unbuilt inventions had never been studied or even named. The term *cryptex* possibly had been her grandfather's creation, an apt title for this device that used the science of *cryptology* to protect information written on the contained scroll or *codex*.

Da Vinci had been a cryptology pioneer, Sophie knew, although he was seldom given credit. Sophie's university instructors, while presenting computer encryption methods for securing data, praised modern cryptologists like Zimmerman and Schneier but failed to mention that it was Leonardo who had invented one of the first rudimentary forms of public key encryption centuries ago. Sophie's grandfather, of course, had been the one to tell her all about that.

As their armoured truck roared down the highway, Sophie explained to Langdon that the cryptex had been Da Vinci's solution to the dilemma of sending secure messages over long distances. In an era without telephones or e-mail, anyone wanting to convey private information to someone far away had no option but to write it down and then trust a messenger to carry the letter. Unfortunately, if a messenger suspected the letter might contain valuable information, he could make far more money selling the information to adversaries than he could delivering the letter properly.

Many great minds in history had invented cryptologic solutions to the challenge of data protection: Julius Caesar devised a code-writing scheme called the Caesar Box; Mary, Queen of Scots created a substitution cipher and sent secret communiqués from prison; and the brilliant Arab scientist Abu Yusuf Ismail al-Kindi protected his secrets with an ingeniously conceived polyalphabetic substitution cipher.

Da Vinci, however, eschewed mathematics and cryptology for a *mechanical* solution. The cryptex. A portable container that could safeguard letters, maps, diagrams, anything at all. Once information was sealed inside the cryptex, only the individual with the proper password could access it.

'We require a password,' Sophie said, pointing out the lettered dials. 'A cryptex works much like a bicycle's combination lock. If you align the dials in the proper position, the lock slides open. This cryptex has five lettered dials. When you rotate them to their proper sequence, the tumblers inside align, and the entire cylinder slides apart.'

'And inside?'

'Once the cylinder slides apart, you have access to a hollow central compartment, which can hold a scroll of paper on which is the information you want to keep private.'

Langdon looked incredulous. 'And you say your grandfather built these for you when you were younger?'

'Some smaller ones, yes. A couple of times for my birthday, he gave me a cryptex and told me a riddle. The answer to the riddle was the password to the cryptex, and once I figured it out, I could open it up and find my birthday card.'

'A lot of work for a card.'

'No, the cards always contained another riddle or clue. My grandfather loved creating elaborate treasure hunts around our house, a string of clues that eventually led to my real gift. Each treasure hunt was a test of character and merit, to ensure I earned my rewards. And the tests were never simple.'

Langdon eyed the device again, still looking sceptical. 'But why not just pry it apart? Or smash it? The metal looks delicate, and marble is a soft rock.'

Sophie smiled. 'Because Da Vinci is too smart for that. He designed the cryptex so that if you try to force it open in any way, the information self-destructs. Watch.' Sophie reached into the box and carefully lifted out the cylinder. 'Any information to be inserted is first written on a papyrus scroll.'

'Not vellum?'

Sophie shook her head. 'Papyrus. I know sheep's vellum was more durable and more common in those days, but it had to be papyrus. The thinner the better.'

'Okay.'

'Before the papyrus was inserted into the cryptex's compartment, it was rolled around a delicate glass vial.' She tipped the cryptex, and the liquid inside gurgled. 'A vial of liquid.'

'Liquid *what?*'

Sophie smiled. 'Vinegar.'

Langdon hesitated a moment and then began nodding. 'Brilliant.'

Vinegar and papyrus, Sophie thought. If someone attempted to force open the cryptex, the glass vial would break, and the vinegar would quickly dissolve the papyrus. By the time anyone extracted the secret message, it would be a glob of meaningless pulp.

'As you can see,' Sophie told him, 'the only way to access the information inside is to know the proper five-letter password. And with five dials, each with twenty-six letters, that's twenty-six to the fifth power.' She quickly estimated the permutations. 'Approximately twelve million possibilities.'

'If you say so,' Langdon said, looking like he had approximately twelve million questions running through his head. 'What information do you think is inside?'

'Whatever it is, my grandfather obviously wanted very badly to keep it secret.' She paused, closing the box lid and eyeing the five-petal Rose inlaid on it. Something was bothering her. 'Did you say earlier that the Rose is a symbol for the Grail?'

'Exactly. In Priory symbolism, the Rose and the Grail are synonymous.'

Sophie furrowed her brow. 'That's strange, because my grandfather always told me the Rose meant *secrecy*. He used to hang a rose on his office door at home when he was having a confidential phone call and didn't want me to disturb him. He encouraged me to do the same.' *Sweetie,* her grandfather said, *rather than lock each other out, we can each hang a rose – la fleur des secrets – on our door when we need privacy. This way we learn to respect and trust each other. Hanging a rose is an ancient Roman custom.*

'*Sub rosa,*' Langdon said. 'The Romans hung a rose over meetings to indicate the meeting was confidential. Attendees understood that whatever was said *under the rose* – or *sub rosa* – had to remain a secret.'

Langdon quickly explained that the Rose's overtone of secrecy was not the only reason the Priory used it as a symbol for the Grail. *Rosa rugosa,* one of the oldest species of rose, had five petals and pentagonal symmetry, just like the guiding star of Venus, giving the Rose strong iconographic ties to *womanhood.* In addition, the Rose had close ties to the concept of 'true direction' and navigating one's way. The Compass Rose helped travellers navigate, as did Rose Lines, the longitudinal lines on maps. For this reason, the Rose was a symbol that spoke of the Grail on many levels – secrecy, womanhood and guidance – the feminine chalice and guiding star that led to secret truth.

As Langdon finished his explanation, his expression seemed to tighten suddenly.

'Robert? Are you okay?'

His eyes were riveted to the rosewood box. '*Sub . . . rosa,*' he choked, a fearful bewilderment sweeping across his face. 'It can't be.'

'What?'

Langdon slowly raised his eyes. 'Under the sign of the Rose,' he whispered. 'This cryptex . . . I think I know what it is.'

48

Langdon could scarcely believe his own supposition, and yet, considering *who* had given this stone cylinder to them, *how* he had given it to them, and now, the inlaid Rose on the container, Langdon could formulate only one conclusion.

I am holding the Priory keystone.

The legend was specific.

The keystone is an encoded stone that lies beneath the sign of the Rose.

'Robert?' Sophie was watching him. 'What's going on?'

Langdon needed a moment to gather his thoughts. 'Did your grandfather ever speak to you of something called *la clef de voûte?*'

'The key to the vault?' Sophie translated.

'No, that's the literal translation. *Clef de voûte* is a common architectural term. *Voûte* refers not to a bank vault, but to a *vault* in an archway. Like a *vaulted* ceiling.'

'But vaulted ceilings don't have keys.'

'Actually they do. Every stone archway requires a central, wedge-shaped stone at the top which locks the pieces together and carries all the weight. This stone is, in an architectural sense, the key to the vault. In English we call it a *keystone*.' Langdon watched her eyes for any spark of recognition.

Sophie shrugged, glancing down at the cryptex. 'But this obviously is not a keystone.'

Langdon didn't know where to begin. Keystones as a masonry technique for building stone archways had been one of the best-kept secrets of the early Masonic brotherhood. *The Royal Arch Degree. Architecture. Keystones.* It was all interconnected. The secret knowledge of how to use a wedged keystone to build a vaulted archway was part of the wisdom that had made the Masons such wealthy craftsmen, and it was a secret they guarded carefully. Keystones had always had a tradition of secrecy. And yet, the stone cylinder in the rosewood box was obviously something quite different. The Priory keystone – if this was indeed what they were holding – was not at all what Langdon had imagined.

'The Priory keystone is not my specialty,' Langdon admitted. 'My interest in the Holy Grail is primarily symbologic, so I tend to ignore the plethora of lore regarding how to actually find it.'

Sophie's eyebrows arched. '*Find* the Holy Grail?'

Langdon gave an uneasy nod, speaking his next words carefully. 'Sophie, according to Priory lore, the keystone is an encoded map . . . a map that reveals the hiding place of the Holy Grail.'

Sophie's face went blank. 'And you think this is it?'

Langdon didn't know what to say. Even to him it sounded unbelievable, and yet the keystone was the only logical conclusion he could muster. *An encrypted stone, hidden beneath the sign of the Rose.*

The idea that the cryptex had been designed by Leonardo da Vinci – former Grand Master of the Priory of Sion – shone as another tantalizing indicator that this was indeed the Priory keystone. *A former Grand Master's blueprint . . . brought to life centuries later by another Priory member.* The bond was too palpable to dismiss.

For the last decade, historians had been searching for the keystone in French churches. Grail seekers, familiar with the Priory's history of cryptic double-talk, had concluded *la clef de voûte* was a literal keystone – an architectural wedge – an engraved, encrypted stone, inserted into a vaulted archway in a church. *Beneath the sign of the Rose.* In architecture, there was no shortage of roses. *Rose windows. Rosette reliefs.* And, of course, an abundance of *cinquefoils* – the five-petalled decorative flowers often found at the top of archways, directly over the keystone. The hiding place seemed diabolically simple. The map to the Holy Grail was incorporated high in an archway of some forgotten church, mocking the blind churchgoers who wandered beneath it.

'This cryptex *can't* be the keystone,' Sophie argued. 'It's not old enough. I'm certain my grandfather made this. It can't be part of any ancient Grail legend.'

'Actually,' Langdon replied, feeling a tingle of excitement ripple through him, 'the keystone is believed to have been created by the Priory sometime in the past couple of decades.'

Sophie's eyes flashed disbelief. 'But if this cryptex reveals the hiding place of the Holy Grail, why would my grandfather give it to *me?* I have no idea how to open it or what to do with it. I don't even know what the Holy Grail *is!*'

Langdon realized to his surprise that she was right. He had not yet had a chance to explain to Sophie the true nature of the Holy Grail. That story would have to wait. At the moment, they were focused on the keystone.

If that is indeed what this is. . . .

Against the hum of the bulletproof wheels beneath them, Langdon quickly explained to Sophie everything he had heard about the keystone. Allegedly, for centuries, the Priory's biggest secret – the location of the Holy Grail – was never written down. For security's sake, it was verbally transferred to each new rising *sénéchal* at a clandestine ceremony. However, at some point during the last century, whisperings began to surface that the Priory policy had changed. Perhaps it was on account of new electronic eavesdropping capabilities, but the Priory vowed never again even to *speak* the location of the sacred hiding place.

'But then how could they pass on the secret?' Sophie asked.

'That's where the keystone comes in,' Langdon explained. 'When one of the top four members died, the remaining three would choose from the lower echelons the next candidate to ascend as *sénéchal*. Rather than *telling* the new *sénéchal* where the Grail was hidden, they gave him a test through which he could prove he was worthy.'

Sophie looked unsettled by this, and Langdon suddenly recalled her mentioning how her grandfather used to make treasure hunts for her – *preuves de mérite*. Admittedly, the keystone was a similar concept. Then again, tests like this were extremely common in secret societies. The best known was the Masons', wherein members ascended to higher degrees by proving they could keep a secret and by performing rituals and various tests of merit over many years. The tasks became progressively harder until they culminated in a successful candidate's induction as thirty-second-degree Mason.

'So the keystone is a *preuve de mérite*,' Sophie said. 'If a rising Priory *sénéchal* can open it, he proves himself worthy of the information it holds.'

Langdon nodded. 'I forgot you'd had experience with this sort of thing.'

'Not only with my grandfather. In cryptology, that's called a "self-authorizing language". That is, if you're smart enough to read it, you're permitted to know what is being said.'

Langdon hesitated a moment. 'Sophie, you realize that if this is indeed the keystone, your grandfather's access to it implies he was exceptionally powerful within the Priory of Sion. He would have to have been one of the highest four members.'

Sophie sighed. 'He was powerful in a secret society. I'm certain of it. I can only assume it was the Priory.'

Langdon did a double take. 'You *knew* he was in a secret society?'

'I saw some things I wasn't supposed to see ten years ago. We haven't spoken since.' She paused. 'My grandfather was not only a ranking top member of the group . . . I believe he was *the* top member.'

Langdon could not believe what she had just said. 'Grand Master? But . . . there's no way you could know that!'

'I'd rather not talk about it.' Sophie looked away, her expression as determined as it was pained.

Langdon sat in stunned silence. *Jacques Saunière? Grand Master?* Despite the astonishing repercussions if it were true, Langdon had the eerie sensation it almost made perfect sense. After all, previous Priory Grand Masters had *also* been distinguished public figures with artistic souls. Proof of that fact had been uncovered years ago in Paris's Bibliothèque Nationale in papers that became known as *Les Dossiers Secrets*.

Every Priory historian and Grail buff had read the *Dossiers*. Catalogued under Number 4° lm¹ 249, the *Dossiers Secrets* had been authenticated by many specialists and incontrovertibly confirmed what historians had suspected for a long time: Priory Grand Masters included Leonardo da Vinci, Botticelli, Sir Isaac Newton, Victor Hugo, and, more recently, Jean Cocteau, the famous Parisian artist.

Why not Jacques Saunière?

Langdon's incredulity intensified with the realization that he had been slated to *meet* Saunière tonight. *The Priory Grand Master called a meeting with me. Why? To make artistic small talk?* It suddenly seemed unlikely. After all, if Langdon's instincts were correct, the Grand Master of the Priory of Sion had just transferred the brotherhood's legendary keystone to his granddaughter and simultaneously commanded her to find Robert Langdon.

Inconceivable!

Langdon's imagination could conjure no set of circumstances that would explain Saunière's behaviour. Even if Saunière feared his own death, there were three *sénéchaux* who also possessed the secret and therefore guaranteed the Priory's security. Why would Saunière take such an enormous risk giving his granddaughter the keystone, especially when the two of them didn't get along? And why involve Langdon . . . a total stranger?

A piece of this puzzle is missing, Langdon thought.

The answers were apparently going to have to wait. The sound of the slowing engine caused them both to look up. Gravel crunched beneath the tyres. *Why is he pulling over already?* Langdon wondered. Vernet had told them he would take them well outside the city to safety. The truck decelerated to a crawl and made its way over unexpectedly rough terrain. Sophie shot Langdon an uneasy look, hastily closing the cryptex box and latching it. Langdon slipped his jacket back on.

When the truck came to a stop, the engine remained idling as the locks on the rear doors began to turn. When the doors swung open, Langdon was surprised to see they were parked in a wooded area, well off the road. Vernet stepped into view, a strained look in his eye. In his hand, he held a pistol.

'I'm sorry about this,' he said. 'I really have no choice.'

49

André Vernet looked awkward with a pistol, but his eyes shone with a determination that Langdon sensed would be unwise to test.

'I'm afraid I must insist,' Vernet said, training the weapon on the two of them in the back of the idling truck. 'Set the box down.'

Sophie clutched the box to her chest. 'You said you and my grandfather were friends.'

'I have a duty to protect your grandfather's assets,' Vernet replied. 'And that is exactly what I am doing. Now set the box on the floor.'

'My grandfather entrusted this to me!' Sophie declared.

'Do it,' Vernet commanded, raising the gun.

Sophie set the box at her feet.

Langdon watched the gun barrel swing now in his direction.

'Mr Langdon,' Vernet said, 'you will bring the box over to me. And be aware that I'm asking you because *you* I would not hesitate to shoot.'

Langdon stared at the banker in disbelief. 'Why are you doing this?'

'Why do you imagine?' Vernet snapped, his accented English terse now. 'To protect my client's assets.'

'*We* are your clients now,' Sophie said.

Vernet's visage turned ice-cold, an eerie transformation. 'Mademoiselle Neveu, I don't know *how* you got that key and account number tonight, but it seems obvious that foul play was involved. Had I known the extent of your crimes, I would never have helped you leave the bank.'

'I told you,' Sophie said, 'we had nothing to do with my grandfather's death!'

Vernet looked at Langdon. 'And yet the radio claims you are wanted not only for the murder of Jacques Saunière but for those of three *other* men as well?'

'What!' Langdon was thunderstruck. *Three more murders?* The coincidental number hit him harder than the fact that he was the prime suspect. It seemed too unlikely to be a coincidence. *The three sénéchaux?* Langdon's eyes dropped to the rosewood box. *If the sénéchaux were murdered, Saunière had no options. He had to transfer the keystone to someone.*

'The police can sort that out when I turn you in,' Vernet said. 'I have got my bank involved too far already.'

Sophie glared at Vernet. 'You obviously have no intention of turning us in. You would have driven us back to the bank. And instead you bring us out here and hold us at gunpoint?'

'Your grandfather hired me for one reason – to keep his possessions both safe and private. Whatever this box contains, I have no intention of letting it become a piece of catalogued evidence in a police investigation. Mr Langdon, bring me the box.'

Sophie shook her head. 'Don't do it.'

A gunshot roared, and a bullet tore into the wall above him. The reverberation shook the back of the truck as a spent shell clinked onto the cargo floor.

Shit! Langdon froze.

Vernet spoke more confidently now. 'Mr Langdon, pick up the box.'

Langdon lifted the box.

'Now bring it over to me.' Vernet was taking dead aim, standing on the ground behind the rear bumper, his gun outstretched into the cargo hold now.

Box in hand, Langdon moved across the hold toward the open door.

I've got to do something! Langdon thought. *I'm about to hand over the Priory keystone!* As Langdon moved toward the doorway, his position of higher ground became more pronounced, and he began wondering if he could somehow use it to his advantage. Vernet's gun, though raised, was at Langdon's knee level. *A well-placed kick perhaps?* Unfortunately, as Langdon neared, Vernet seemed to sense the dangerous dynamic developing, and he took several steps back, repositioning himself six feet away. Well out of reach.

Vernet commanded, 'Place the box beside the door.'

Seeing no options, Langdon knelt down and set the rosewood box at the edge of the cargo hold, directly in front of the open doors.

'Now stand up.'

Langdon began to stand up but paused, spying the small, spent pistol shell on the floor beside the truck's precision-crafted doorsill.

'Stand up, and step away from the box.'

Langdon paused a moment longer, eyeing the metal threshold. Then he stood. As he did, he discreetly brushed the shell over the edge onto the narrow ledge that was the door's lower sill. Fully upright now, Langdon stepped backward.

'Return to the back wall and turn around.'

Langdon obeyed.

Vernet could feel his own heart pounding. Aiming the gun with his right hand, he reached now with his left for the wooden box. He discovered that it was far too heavy. *I need two hands.* Turning his eyes back to his captives, he calculated the risk. Both were a good fifteen feet away, at the far end of the cargo hold, facing away from him. Vernet made up his mind. Quickly, he laid down the gun on the bumper, lifted the box with two hands, and set it on the ground, immediately grabbing the gun again and aiming it back into the hold. Neither of his prisoners had moved.

Perfect. Now all that remained was to close and lock the door. Leaving the box on the ground for the moment, he grabbed the metal door and began to heave it closed. As the door swung past him, Vernet reached up to grab the single bolt that needed to be slid into place. The door closed with a thud, and Vernet quickly grabbed the bolt, pulling it to the left. The bolt slid a few inches and crunched to an unexpected halt, not lining up with its sleeve. *What's going on?* Vernet pulled again, but the bolt wouldn't lock. The mechanism was not properly aligned. *The door isn't fully closed!* Feeling a surge of panic, Vernet shoved hard against the outside of the door, but it refused to budge. *Something is blocking it!* Vernet turned to throw his full shoulder into the door, but this time the door exploded outward, striking Vernet in the face and sending him reeling backward onto the ground, his nose shattering in pain. The gun flew as Vernet reached for his face and felt the warm blood running from his nose.

Robert Langdon hit the ground somewhere nearby, and Vernet tried to get up, but he couldn't see. His vision blurred and he fell backward again. Sophie Neveu was shouting. Moments later, Vernet felt a cloud of dirt and exhaust billowing over him. He heard the crunching of tyres on gravel and sat up just in time to see the truck's wide wheelbase fail to navigate a turn. There was a crash as the front bumper clipped a tree. The engine roared, and the tree bent. Finally, it was the bumper that gave, tearing half off. The armoured car lurched away, its front bumper dragging. When the truck reached the paved access road, a shower of sparks lit up the night, trailing the truck as it sped away.

Vernet turned his eyes back to the ground where the truck had been parked. Even in the faint moonlight he could see there was nothing there.

The wooden box was gone.

50

The unmarked Fiat sedan departing from Castel Gandolfo snaked downward through the Alban Hills into the valley below. In the back seat, Bishop Aringarosa smiled, feeling the weight of the bearer bonds in the briefcase on his lap and wondering how long it would be before he and the Teacher could make the exchange.

Twenty million euros.

The sum would buy Aringarosa power far more valuable than that.

As his car sped back toward Rome, Aringarosa again found himself wondering why the Teacher had not yet contacted him. Pulling his cell phone from his cassock pocket, he checked the carrier signal. Extremely faint.

'Cell service is intermittent up here,' the driver said, glancing at him in the rearview mirror. 'In about five minutes, we'll be out of the mountains, and service improves.'

'Thank you.' Aringarosa felt a sudden surge of concern. *No service in the mountains?* Maybe the Teacher had been trying to reach him all this time. Maybe something had gone terribly wrong.

Quickly, Aringarosa checked the phone's voice mail. Nothing. Then again, he realized, the Teacher never would have left a recorded message; he was a man who took enormous care with his communications. Nobody understood better than the Teacher the perils of speaking openly in this modern world. Electronic eavesdropping had played a major role in how he had gathered his astonishing array of secret knowledge.

For this reason, he takes extra precautions.

Unfortunately, the Teacher's protocols for caution included a refusal to give Aringarosa any kind of contact number. *I alone will initiate contact,* the Teacher had informed him. *So keep your phone close.* Now that Aringarosa realized his phone might not have been working properly, he feared what the Teacher might think if he had been repeatedly phoning with no answer.

He'll think something is wrong.

Or that I failed to get the bonds.

The bishop broke a light sweat.

Or worse . . . that I took the money and ran!

51

Even at a modest sixty kilometers an hour, the dangling front bumper of the armoured truck grated against the deserted suburban road with a grinding roar, spraying sparks up onto the hood.

We've got to get off the road, Langdon thought.

He could barely even see where they were headed. The truck's lone working headlight had been knocked off-centre and was casting a skewed sidelong beam into the woods beside the country highway. Apparently the *armour* in this 'armoured truck' referred only to the cargo hold and not the front end.

Sophie sat in the passenger seat, staring blankly at the rosewood box on her lap.

'Are you okay?' Langdon asked.

Sophie looked shaken. 'Do you believe him?'

'About the three additional murders? Absolutely. It answers a lot of questions – the issue of your grandfather's desperation to pass on the keystone, as well as the intensity with which Fache is hunting me.'

'No, I meant about Vernet trying to protect his bank.'

Langdon glanced over. 'As opposed to?'

'Taking the keystone for himself.'

Langdon had not even considered it. 'How would he even know what this box contains?'

'His bank stored it. He knew my grandfather. Maybe he knew things. He might have decided he wanted the Grail for himself.'

Langdon shook his head. Vernet hardly seemed the type. 'In my experience, there are only two reasons people seek the Grail. Either they are naive and believe they are searching for the long-lost Cup of Christ . . .'

'Or?'

'Or they know the truth and are threatened by it. Many groups throughout history have sought to destroy the Grail.'

The silence between them accentuated the sound of the scraping bumper. They had driven a few kilometres now, and as Langdon watched the cascade of sparks coming off the front of the truck, he wondered if it was dangerous. Either way, if they passed another car, it would certainly draw attention. Langdon made up his mind.

'I'm going to see if I can bend this bumper back.'

Pulling onto the shoulder, he brought the truck to a stop.

Silence at last.

As Langdon walked toward the front of the truck, he felt surprisingly alert. Staring into the barrel of yet another gun tonight had given him a second wind. He took a deep breath of nighttime air and tried to get his wits about him. Accompanying the gravity of being a hunted man, Langdon was starting to feel the ponderous weight of responsibility, the prospect that he and Sophie might actually be holding an encrypted set of directions to one of the most enduring mysteries of all time.

As if this burden were not great enough, Langdon now realized that any possibility of finding a way to return the keystone to the Priory had just evaporated. News of the three additional murders had dire implications. *The Priory has been infiltrated. They are compromised.* The brotherhood was obviously being watched, or there was a mole within the ranks. It seemed to explain why Saunière might have transferred the keystone to Sophie and Langdon – people *outside* the brotherhood, people he knew were not compromised. *We can't very well give the keystone back to the brotherhood.* Even if Langdon had any idea how to find a Priory member, chances were good that whoever stepped forward to take the keystone could be the enemy himself. For the moment, at least, it seemed the keystone was in Sophie and Langdon's hands, whether they wanted it or not.

The truck's front end looked worse than Langdon had imagined. The left headlight was gone, and the right one looked like an eyeball dangling from its socket. Langdon straightened it, and it dislodged again. The only good news was that the front bumper had been torn almost clean off. Langdon gave it a hard kick and sensed he might be able to break it off entirely.

As he repeatedly kicked the twisted metal, Langdon recalled his earlier conversation with Sophie. *My grandfather left me a phone message,* Sophie had told him. *He said he needed to tell me the truth about my family.* At the time it had meant nothing, but now, knowing the Priory of Sion was involved, Langdon felt a startling new possibility emerge.

The bumper broke off suddenly with a crash. Langdon paused to catch his breath. At least the truck would no longer look like a Fourth of July sparkler. He grabbed the bumper and began dragging it out of sight into the woods, wondering where they should go next. They had no idea how to open the cryptex, or why Saunière had given it to them. Unfortunately, their survival tonight seemed to depend on getting answers to those very questions.

We need help, Langdon decided. *Professional help.*

In the world of the Holy Grail and the Priory of Sion, that meant only one man. The challenge, of course, would be selling the idea to Sophie.

Inside the armoured car, while Sophie waited for Langdon to return, she could feel the weight of the rosewood box on her lap and resented it. *Why did my grandfather give this to me?* She had not the slightest idea what to do with it.

Think, Sophie! Use your head. Grand-père is trying to tell you something!

Opening the box, she eyed the cryptex's dials. *A proof of merit.* She could feel her grandfather's hand at work. *The keystone is a map that can be followed only by the worthy.* It sounded like her grandfather to the core.

Lifting the cryptex out of the box, Sophie ran her fingers over the dials. *Five letters.* She rotated the dials one by one. The mechanism moved smoothly. She aligned the disks such that her chosen letters lined up between the cryptex's two brass alignment arrows on either end of the cylinder. The dials now spelled a five-letter word that Sophie knew was absurdly obvious.

G-R-A-I-L

Gently, she held the two ends of the cylinder and pulled, applying pressure slowly. The cryptex didn't budge. She heard the vinegar inside gurgle and stopped pulling. Then she tried again.

V-I-N-C-I

Again, no movement.

V-O-U-T-E

Nothing. The cryptex remained locked solid.

Frowning, she replaced it in the rosewood box and closed the lid. Looking outside at Langdon, Sophie felt grateful he was with her tonight. *P.S. Find Robert Langdon.* Her grandfather's rationale for including him was now clear. Sophie was not equipped to understand her grandfather's intentions, and so he had assigned Robert Langdon as her guide. A tutor to oversee her education. Unfortunately for Langdon, he had turned out to be far more than a tutor tonight. He had become the target of Bezu Fache . . . and some unseen force intent on possessing the Holy Grail.

Whatever the Grail turns out to be.

Sophie wondered if finding out was worth her life.

As the armoured truck accelerated again, Langdon was pleased how much more smoothly it drove. 'Do you know how to get to Versailles?'

Sophie eyed him. 'Sightseeing?'

'No, I have a plan. There's a religious historian I know who lives near Versailles. I can't remember exactly where, but we can look it up. I've been to his estate a few times. His name is Leigh Teabing. He's a former British Royal Historian.'

'And he lives in Paris?'

'Teabing's life passion is the Grail. When whisperings of the Priory keystone surfaced about fifteen years ago, he moved to France to search churches in hopes of finding it. He's written some books on the keystone and the Grail. He may be able to help us figure out how to open it and what to do with it.'

Sophie's eyes were wary. 'Can you trust him?'

'Trust him to what? Not steal the information?'

'And not to turn us in.'

'I don't intend to tell him we're wanted by the police. I'm hoping he'll take us in until we can sort all this out.'

'Robert, has it occurred to you that every television in France is probably getting ready to broadcast our pictures? Bezu Fache always uses the media to his advantage. He'll make it impossible for us to move around without being recognized.'

Terrific, Langdon thought. *My French TV debut will be on 'Paris's Most Wanted.'* At least Jonas Faukman would be pleased; every time Langdon made the news, his book sales jumped.

'Is this man a good enough friend?' Sophie asked.

Langdon doubted Teabing was someone who watched television, especially at this hour, but still the question deserved consideration. Instinct told Langdon that Teabing would be totally trustworthy. An ideal safe harbour. Considering the circumstances, Teabing would probably trip over himself to help them as much as possible. Not only did he owe Langdon a favour, but Teabing was a Grail researcher, and Sophie claimed her grandfather was the actual *Grand Master* of the Priory of Sion. If Teabing heard *that,* he would salivate at the thought of helping them figure this out.

'Teabing could be a powerful ally,' Langdon said. *Depending on how much you want to tell him.*

'Fache probably will be offering a monetary reward.'

Langdon laughed. 'Believe me, money is the last thing this guy needs.' Leigh Teabing was wealthy in the way small countries were wealthy. A descendant of Britain's first Duke of Lancaster, Teabing had got his money the old-fashioned way – he'd inherited it. His estate outside Paris was a seventeenth-century palace with two private lakes.

Langdon had first met Teabing several years ago through the British Broadcasting Corporation. Teabing had approached the BBC with a proposal for a historical documentary in which he would expose the explosive history of the Holy Grail to a mainstream television audience. The BBC producers loved Teabing's hot premise, his research, and his credentials, but they had concerns that the concept was so shocking and hard to swallow that the network might end up tarnishing its reputation for quality journalism. At Teabing's suggestion, the BBC solved its credibility fears by soliciting three cameos from respected historians from around the world, all of whom corroborated the stunning nature of the Holy Grail secret with their own research.

Langdon had been among those chosen.

The BBC had flown Langdon to Teabing's Paris estate for the filming. He sat before cameras in Teabing's opulent drawing room and shared his story, admitting his initial scepticism on hearing of the alternative Holy Grail story, then describing how years of research had persuaded him that the story was true. Finally, Langdon offered some of his own research – a series of symbologic connections that strongly supported the seemingly controversial claims.

When the programme aired in Britain, despite its ensemble cast and well-documented evidence, the premise rubbed so hard against the grain of popular Christian thought that it instantly confronted a firestorm of hostility. It never aired in the States, but the repercussions echoed across the Atlantic. Shortly afterward, Langdon received a postcard from an old friend – the Catholic Bishop of Philadelphia. The card simply read: *Et tu, Robert?*

'Robert,' Sophie asked, 'you're *certain* we can trust this man?'

'Absolutely. We're colleagues, he doesn't need money, and I happen to know he despises the French authorities. The French government taxes him at absurd rates because he bought a historic landmark. He'll be in no hurry to cooperate with Fache.'

Sophie stared out at the dark roadway. 'If we go to him, how much do you want to tell him?'

Langdon looked unconcerned. 'Believe me, Leigh Teabing knows more about the Priory of Sion and the Holy Grail than anyone on earth.'

Sophie eyed him. 'More than my grandfather?'

'I meant more than anyone *outside* the brotherhood.'

'How do you know Teabing isn't a member of the brotherhood?'

'Teabing has spent his life trying to broadcast the truth about the Holy Grail. The Priory's oath is to keep its true nature hidden.'

'Sounds to me like a conflict of interest.'

Langdon understood her concerns. Saunière had given the cryptex directly to Sophie, and although she didn't know what it contained or what she was supposed to do with it, she was hesitant to involve a total stranger. Considering the information potentially enclosed, the instinct was probably a good one. 'We don't need to tell Teabing about the keystone immediately. Or at all, even. His house will give us a place to hide and think, and maybe when we talk to him about the Grail, you'll start to have an idea why your grandfather gave this to you.'

'*Us*,' Sophie reminded.

Langdon felt a humble pride and wondered yet again why Saunière had included him.

'Do you know more or less where Mr. Teabing lives?' Sophie asked.

'His estate is called Château Villette.'

Sophie turned with an incredulous look. '*The* Château Villette?'

'That's the one.'

'Nice friends.'

'You know the estate?'

'I've passed it. It's in the castle district. Twenty minutes from here.'

Langdon frowned. 'That far?'

'Yes, which will give you enough time to tell me what the Holy Grail *really* is.'

Langdon paused. 'I'll tell you at Teabing's. He and I specialize in different areas of the legend, so between the two of us, you'll get the full story.' Langdon smiled. 'Besides, the Grail has been Teabing's life, and hearing the story of the Holy Grail from Leigh Teabing will be like hearing the theory of relativity from Einstein himself.'

'Let's hope Leigh doesn't mind late-night visitors.'

'For the record, it's *Sir* Leigh.' Langdon had made that mistake only once. 'Teabing is quite a character. He was knighted by the Queen several years back after composing an extensive history of the House of York.'

Sophie looked over. 'You're kidding, right? We're going to visit a *knight?*'

Langdon gave an awkward smile. 'We're on a Grail quest, Sophie. Who better to help us than a knight?'

52

The sprawling 185-acre estate of Château Villette was located twenty-five minutes northwest of Paris in the environs of Versailles. Designed by François Mansart in 1668 for the Count of Aufflay, it was one of Paris's most significant historical châteaux. Complete with two rectangular lakes and gardens designed by Le Nôtre, Château Villette was more of a modest castle than a mansion. The estate had fondly become known as *la Petite Versailles*.

Langdon brought the armoured truck to a shuddering stop at the foot of the mile-long driveway. Beyond the imposing security gate, Sir Leigh Teabing's residence rose on a meadow in the distance. The sign on the gate was in English: PRIVATE PROPERTY. NO TRESPASSING.

As if to proclaim his home a British Isle unto itself, Teabing had not only posted his signs in English, but he had installed his gate's intercom entry system on the *right-hand* side of the truck – the passenger's side everywhere in Europe except England.

Sophie gave the misplaced intercom an odd look. 'And if someone arrives without a passenger?'

'Don't ask.' Langdon had already been through that with Teabing. 'He prefers things the way they are at home.'

Sophie rolled down her window. 'Robert, you'd better do the talking.'

Langdon shifted his position, leaning out across Sophie to press the intercom button. As he did, an alluring whiff of Sophie's perfume filled his nostrils, and he realized how close they were. He waited there, awkwardly prone, while a telephone began ringing over the small speaker.

Finally, the intercom crackled and an irritated French accent spoke. 'Château Villette. Who is calling?'

'This is Robert Langdon,' Langdon called out, sprawled across Sophie's lap. 'I'm a friend of Sir Leigh Teabing. I need his help.'

'My master is sleeping. As was I. What is your business with him?'

'It is a private matter. One of great interest to him.'

'Then I'm sure he will be pleased to receive you in the morning.'

Langdon shifted his weight. 'It's quite important.'

'As is Sir Leigh's sleep. If you are a friend, then you are aware he is in poor health.'

Sir Leigh Teabing had suffered from polio as a child and now wore leg braces and walked with crutches, but Langdon had found him such a lively and colourful man on his last visit that it hardly seemed an infirmity. 'If you would, please tell him I have uncovered new information about the Grail. Information that cannot wait until morning.'

There was a long pause.

Langdon and Sophie waited, the truck idling loudly.

A full minute passed.

Finally, someone spoke. 'My good man, I daresay you are still on Harvard Standard Time.' The voice was crisp and light.

Langdon grinned, recognizing the thick English accent. 'Leigh, my apologies for waking you at this obscene hour.'

'My manservant tells me that not only are you in Paris, but you speak of the Grail.'

'I thought that might get you out of bed.'

'And so it has.'

'Any chance you'd open the gate for an old friend?'

'Those who seek the truth are more than friends. They are brothers.'

Langdon rolled his eyes at Sophie, well accustomed to Teabing's predilection for dramatic antics.

'Indeed I will open the gate,' Teabing proclaimed, 'but first I must confirm your heart is true. A test of your honour. You will answer three questions.'

Langdon groaned, whispering at Sophie. 'Bear with me here. As I mentioned, he's something of a character.'

'Your first question,' Teabing declared, his tone Herculean. 'Shall I serve you coffee, or tea?'

Langdon knew Teabing's feelings about the American phenomenon of coffee. 'Tea,' he replied. 'Earl Grey.'

'Excellent. Your second question. Milk or sugar?'

Langdon hesitated.

'*Milk,*' Sophie whispered in his ear. 'I think the English take milk.'

'Milk,' Langdon said.

Silence.

'Sugar?'

Teabing made no reply.

Wait! Langdon now recalled the bitter beverage he had been served on his last visit and realized this question was a trick. '*Lemon!*' he declared. 'Earl Grey with *lemon.*'

'Indeed.' Teabing sounded deeply amused now. 'And finally, I must make the most grave of inquiries.' Teabing paused and then spoke in a solemn tone. 'In which year did a Harvard sculler last outrow an Oxford man at Henley?'

Langdon had no idea, but he could imagine only one reason the question had been asked. 'Surely such a travesty has never occurred.'

The gate clicked open. 'Your heart is true, my friend. You may pass.'

53

'Monsieur Vernet!' The night manager of the Depository Bank of Zurich felt relieved to hear the bank president's voice on the phone. 'Where did you go, sir? The police are here, everyone is waiting for you!'

'I have a little problem,' the bank president said, sounding distressed. 'I need your help right away.'

You have more than a little problem, the manager thought. The police had entirely surrounded the bank and were threatening to have the DCPJ captain himself show up with the warrant the bank had demanded. 'How can I help you, sir?'

'Armored truck number three. I need to find it.'

Puzzled, the manager checked his delivery schedule. 'It's here. Downstairs at the loading dock.'

'Actually, no. The truck was stolen by the two individuals the police are tracking.'

'What? How did they drive out?'

'I can't go into the specifics on the phone, but we have a situation here that could potentially be extremely unfortunate for the bank.'

'What do you need me to do, sir?'

'I'd like you to activate the truck's emergency transponder.'

The night manager's eyes moved to the LoJack control box across the room. Like many armoured cars, each of the bank's trucks had been equipped with a radio-controlled homing device, which could be activated remotely from the bank. The manager had only used the emergency system once, after a hijacking, and it had worked flawlessly – locating the truck and transmitting the coordinates to the authorities automatically. Tonight, however, the manager had the impression the president was hoping for a bit more prudence. 'Sir, you are aware that if I activate the LoJack system, the transponder will simultaneously inform the authorities that we have a problem.'

Vernet was silent for several seconds. 'Yes, I know. Do it anyway. Truck number three. I'll hold. I need the exact location of that truck the instant you have it.'

'Right away, sir.'

Thirty seconds later, forty kilometres away, hidden in the undercarriage of the armoured truck, a tiny transponder blinked to life.

54

As Langdon and Sophie drove the armoured truck up the winding, poplar-lined driveway toward the house, Sophie could already feel her muscles relaxing. It was a relief to be off the road, and she could think of few safer places to get their feet under them than this private, gated estate owned by a good-natured foreigner.

They turned into the sweeping circular driveway, and Château Villette came into view on their right. Three storeys tall and at least sixty metres long, the edifice had grey stone facing illuminated by outside spotlights. The coarse façade stood in stark juxtaposition to the immaculately land-scaped gardens and glassy pond.

The inside lights were just now coming on.

Rather than driving to the front door, Langdon pulled into a parking area nestled in the evergreens. 'No reason to risk being spotted from the road,' he said. 'Or having Leigh wonder why we arrived in a wrecked armoured truck.'

Sophie nodded. 'What do we do with the cryptex? We probably should-n't leave it out here, but if Leigh sees it, he'll certainly want to know what it is.'

'Not to worry,' Langdon said, removing his jacket as he stepped out of the car. He wrapped the tweed coat around the box and held the bundle in his arms like a baby.

Sophie looked dubious. 'Subtle.'

'Teabing never answers his own door; he prefers to make an entrance. I'll find somewhere inside to stash this before he joins us.' Langdon paused. 'Actually, I should probably warn you before you meet him. Sir Leigh has a sense of humour that people often find a bit . . . strange.'

Sophie doubted anything tonight would strike her as strange anymore.

The pathway to the main entrance was hand-laid cobblestone. It curved to a door of carved oak and cherry with a brass knocker the size of a grape-fruit. Before Sophie could grasp the knocker, the door swung open from within.

A prim and elegant butler stood before them, making final adjustments on the white tie and tuxedo he had apparently just donned. He looked to be about fifty, with refined features and an austere expression that left little doubt he was unamused by their presence here.

'Sir Leigh will be down presently,' he declared, his accent thick French. 'He is dressing. He prefers not to greet visitors while wearing only a nightshirt. May I take your coat?' He scowled at the bunched-up tweed in Langdon's arms.

'Thank you, I'm fine.'

'Of course you are. Right this way, please.'

The butler guided them through a lush marble foyer into an exquisitely adorned drawing room, softly lit by tassel-draped Victorian lamps. The air inside smelled antediluvian, regal somehow, with traces of pipe tobacco, tea leaves, cooking sherry, and the earthen aroma of stone architecture. Against the far wall, flanked between two glistening suits of chain mail armour, was a rough-hewn fireplace large enough to roast an ox. Walking to the hearth, the butler knelt and touched a match to a pre-laid arrangement of oak logs and kindling. A fire quickly crackled to life.

The man stood, straightening his jacket. 'His master requests that you make yourselves at home.' With that, he departed, leaving Langdon and Sophie alone.

Sophie wondered which of the fireside antiques she was supposed to sit on – the Renaissance velvet divan, the rustic eagle-claw rocker, or the pair of stone pews that looked like they'd been lifted from some Byzantine temple.

Langdon unwrapped the cryptex from his coat, walked to the velvet divan and slid the wooden box deep underneath it, well out of sight. Then, shaking out his jacket, he put it back on, smoothed the lapels, and smiled at Sophie as he sat down directly over the stashed treasure.

The divan it is, Sophie thought, taking a seat beside him.

As she stared into the growing fire, enjoying the warmth, Sophie had the sensation that her grandfather would have loved this room. The dark wood panelling was bedecked with Old Master paintings, one of which Sophie recognized as a Poussin, her grandfather's second-favourite painter. On the mantel above the fireplace, an alabaster bust of Isis watched over the room.

Beneath the Egyptian goddess, inside the fireplace, two stone gargoyles served as andirons, their mouths gaping to reveal their menacing hollow throats. Gargoyles had always terrified Sophie as a child; that was, until her grandfather cured her of the fear by taking her atop Notre Dame Cathedral in a rainstorm. 'Princess, look at these silly creatures,' he had told her, pointing to the gargoyle rainspouts with their mouths gushing water. 'Do you hear that funny sound in their throats?' Sophie nodded, having to smile at the burping sound of the water gurgling through their throats. 'They're *gargling*,' her grandfather told her. '*Gargariser!* And that's where they get the silly name "gargoyles".' Sophie had never again been afraid.

The fond memory caused Sophie a pang of sadness as the harsh reality of the murder gripped her again. *Grand-père is gone.* She pictured the cryptex under the divan and wondered if Leigh Teabing would have any idea how to open it. *Or if we even should ask him.* Sophie's grandfather's final words had instructed her to find Robert Langdon. He had said nothing about involving anyone else. *We needed somewhere to hide,* Sophie said, deciding to trust Robert's judgment.

'Sir Robert!' a voice bellowed somewhere behind them. 'I see you travel with a maiden.'

Langdon stood up. Sophie jumped to her feet as well. The voice had come from the top of a curled staircase that snaked up to the shadows of the second floor. At the top of the stairs, a form moved in the shadows, only his silhouette visible.

'Good evening,' Langdon called up. 'Sir Leigh, may I present Sophie Neveu.'

'An honour.' Teabing moved into the light.

'Thank you for having us,' Sophie said, now seeing the man wore metal leg braces and used crutches. He was coming down one stair at a time. 'I realize it's quite late.'

'It is so late, my dear, it's early.' He laughed. *'Vous n'êtes pas Américaine?'*

Sophie shook her head. *'Parisienne.'*

'Your English is superb.'

'Thank you. I studied at the Royal Holloway.'

'So then, that explains it.' Teabing hobbled lower through the shadows. 'Perhaps Robert told you I schooled just down the road at Oxford.' Teabing fixed Langdon with a devilish smile. 'Of course, I also applied to Harvard as my safety school.'

Their host arrived at the bottom of the stairs, appearing to Sophie no more like a knight than Sir Elton John. Portly and ruby-faced, Sir Leigh Teabing had bushy red hair and jovial hazel eyes that seemed to twinkle as he spoke. He wore pleated trousers and a roomy silk shirt under a paisley waistcoat. Despite the aluminium braces on his legs, he carried himself with a resilient, vertical dignity that seemed more a by-product of noble ancestry than any kind of conscious effort.

Teabing arrived and extended a hand to Langdon. 'Robert, you've lost weight.'

Langdon grinned. 'And you've found some.'

Teabing laughed heartily, patting his rotund belly. 'Touché. My only carnal pleasures these days seem to be culinary.' Turning now to Sophie, he gently took her hand, bowing his head slightly, breathing lightly on her fingers and diverting his eyes. 'M'lady.'

Sophie glanced at Langdon, uncertain whether she'd stepped back in time or into a nuthouse.

The butler who had answered the door now entered carrying a tea service, which he arranged on a table in front of the fireplace.

'This is Rémy Legaludec,' Teabing said, 'my manservant.'

The slender butler gave a stiff nod and disappeared yet again.

'Rémy is *Lyonais*,' Teabing whispered, as if it were an unfortunate disease. 'But he does sauces quite nicely.'

Langdon looked amused. 'I would have thought you'd import an English staff?'

'Good heavens, no! I would not wish an English chef on anyone except the French tax collectors.' He glanced over at Sophie. '*Pardonnez-moi*, Mademoiselle Neveu. Please be assured that my distaste for the French extends only to politics and the soccer pitch. Your government steals my money, and your football squad recently humiliated us.'

Sophie offered an easy smile.

Teabing eyed her a moment and then looked at Langdon. 'Something has happened. You both look shaken.'

Langdon nodded. 'We've had an interesting night, Leigh.'

'No doubt. You arrive on my doorstep unannounced in the middle of the night speaking of the Grail. Tell me, is this indeed about the Grail, or did you simply say that because you know it is the one topic for which I would rouse myself in the middle of the night?'

A little of both, Sophie thought, picturing the cryptex hidden beneath the couch.

'Leigh,' Langdon said, 'we'd like to talk to you about the Priory of Sion.'

Teabing's bushy eyebrows arched with intrigue. 'The keepers. So this is indeed about the Grail. You say you come with information? Something new, Robert?'

'Perhaps. We're not quite sure. We might have a better idea if we could get some information from you first.'

Teabing wagged his finger. 'Ever the wily American. A game of quid pro quo. Very well. I am at your service. What is it I can tell you?'

Langdon sighed. 'I was hoping you would be kind enough to explain to Ms Neveu the true nature of the Holy Grail.'

Teabing looked stunned. 'She doesn't *know?*'

Langdon shook his head.

The smile that grew on Teabing's face was almost obscene. 'Robert, you've brought me a *virgin?*'

Langdon winced, glancing at Sophie. '*Virgin* is the term Grail enthusiasts use to describe anyone who has never heard the true Grail story.'

Teabing turned eagerly to Sophie. 'How much do you know, my dear?'

Sophie quickly outlined what Langdon had explained earlier – the Priory of Sion, the Knights Templar, the Sangreal documents, and the Holy Grail, which many claimed was not a cup . . . but rather something far more powerful.

'That's *all?*' Teabing fired Langdon a scandalous look. 'Robert, I thought you were a gentleman. You've robbed her of the climax!'

'I know, I thought perhaps you and I could . . .' Langdon apparently decided the unseemly metaphor had gone far enough.

Teabing already had Sophie locked in his twinkling gaze. 'You are a Grail virgin, my dear. And trust me, you will never forget your first time.'

55

Seated on the divan beside Langdon, Sophie drank her tea and ate a scone, feeling the welcome effects of caffeine and food. Sir Leigh Teabing was beaming as he awkwardly paced before the open fire, his leg braces clicking on the stone hearth.

'The Holy Grail,' Teabing said, his voice sermonic. 'Most people ask me only *where* it is. I fear that is a question I may never answer.' He turned and looked directly at Sophie. 'However . . . the far more relevant question is this: *What* is the Holy Grail?'

Sophie sensed a rising air of academic anticipation now in both of her male companions.

'To fully understand the Grail,' Teabing continued, 'we must first understand the Bible. How well do you know the New Testament?'

Sophie shrugged. 'Not at all, really. I was brought up by a man who worshipped Leonardo da Vinci.'

Teabing looked both startled and pleased. 'An enlightened soul. Superb! Then you must be aware that Leonardo was one of the keepers of the secret of the Holy Grail. And he hid clues in his art.'

'Robert told me as much, yes.'

'And Da Vinci's views on the New Testament?'

'I have no idea.'

Teabing's eyes turned mirthful as he motioned to the bookshelf across the room. 'Robert, would you mind? On the bottom shelf. *La Storia di Leonardo.*'

Langdon went across the room, found a large art book, and brought it back, setting it down on the table between them. Twisting the book to face Sophie, Teabing flipped open the heavy cover and pointed inside the rear cover to a series of quotations. 'From Da Vinci's notebook on polemics and speculation,' Teabing said, indicating one quote in particular. 'I think you'll find this relevant to our discussion.'

Sophie read the words.

Many have made a trade of delusions
and false miracles, deceiving the stupid multitude.
—LEONARDO DA VINCI

'Here's another,' Teabing said, pointing to a different quote.

Blinding ignorance does mislead us.
O! Wretched mortals, open your eyes!
—LEONARDO DA VINCI

Sophie felt a little chill. 'Da Vinci is talking about the Bible?'

Teabing nodded. 'Leonardo's feelings about the Bible relate directly to the Holy Grail. In fact, Da Vinci painted the true Grail, which I will show you in a moment, but first we must speak of the Bible.' Teabing smiled. 'And everything you need to know about the Bible can be summed up by the great canon doctor Martyn Percy.' Teabing cleared his throat and declared, 'The Bible did not arrive by fax from heaven.'

'I beg your pardon?'

'The Bible is a product of *man*, my dear. Not of God. The Bible did not fall magically from the clouds. Man created it as a historical record of tumultuous times, and it has evolved through countless translations, additions and revisions. History has never had a definitive version of the book.'

'Okay.'

'Jesus Christ was a historical figure of staggering influence, perhaps the most enigmatic and inspirational leader the world has ever seen. As the prophesied Messiah, Jesus toppled kings, inspired millions and founded new philosophies. As a descendant of the lines of King Solomon and King David, Jesus possessed a rightful claim to the throne of the King of the Jews. Understandably, His life was recorded by thousands of followers across the land.' Teabing paused to sip his tea and then placed the cup back on the mantel. 'More than *eighty* gospels were considered for the New Testament, and yet only a relative few were chosen for inclusion – Matthew, Mark, Luke and John among them.

'Who chose which gospels to include?' Sophie asked.

'Aha!' Teabing burst in with enthusiasm. 'The fundamental irony of Christianity! The Bible, as we know it today, was collated by the pagan Roman emperor Constantine the Great.'

'I thought Constantine was a Christian,' Sophie said.

'Hardly,' Teabing scoffed. 'He was a lifelong pagan who was baptized on his deathbed, too weak to protest. In Constantine's day, Rome's official religion was sun worship – the cult of *Sol Invictus,* or the Invincible Sun – and Constantine was its head priest. Unfortunately for him, a growing religious turmoil was gripping Rome. Three centuries after the crucifixion of Jesus Christ, Christ's followers had multiplied exponentially. Christians and pagans began warring, and the conflict grew to such proportions that it threatened to rend Rome in two. Constantine decided something had to be done. In 325 AD, he decided to unify Rome under a single religion. Christianity.'

Sophie was surprised. 'Why would a pagan emperor choose *Christianity* as the official religion?'

Teabing chuckled. 'Constantine was a very good businessman. He could see that Christianity was on the rise, and he simply backed the winning horse. Historians still marvel at the brilliance with which Constantine converted the sun-worshipping pagans to Christianity. By fusing pagan symbols, dates and rituals into the growing Christian tradition, he created a kind of hybrid religion that was acceptable to both parties.'

'Transmogrification,' Langdon said. 'The vestiges of pagan religion in Christian symbology are undeniable. Egyptian sun disks became the halos of Catholic saints. Pictograms of Isis nursing her miraculously conceived son Horus became the blueprint for our modern images of the Virgin Mary nursing Baby Jesus. And virtually all the elements of the Catholic ritual – the mitre, the altar, the doxology and communion, the act of 'God-eating' – were taken directly from earlier pagan mystery religions.'

Teabing groaned. 'Don't get a symbologist started on Christian icons. Nothing in Christianity is original. The pre-Christian God Mithras – called *the Son of God* and *the Light of the World* – was born on December 25, died, was buried in a rock tomb, and then resurrected in three days. By the way, December 25 is also the birthday of Osiris, Adonis and Dionysus. The newborn Krishna was presented with gold, frankincense, and myrrh. Even Christianity's weekly holy day was stolen from the pagans.'

'What do you mean?'

'Originally,' Langdon said, 'Christianity honoured the Jewish Sabbath of Saturday, but Constantine shifted it to coincide with the pagan's veneration day of the sun.' He paused, grinning. 'To this day, most churchgoers attend services on Sunday morning with no idea that they are there on account of the pagan sun god's weekly tribute – *Sun*day.'

Sophie's head was spinning. 'And all of this relates to the Grail?'

'Indeed,' Teabing said. 'Stay with me. During this fusion of religions, Constantine needed to strengthen the new Christian tradition, and held a famous ecumenical gathering known as the Council of Nicaea.'

Sophie had heard of it only insofar as its being the birthplace of the Nicene Creed.

'At this gathering,' Teabing said, 'many aspects of Christianity were debated and voted upon – the date of Easter, the role of the bishops, the administration of sacraments, and, of course, the *divinity* of Jesus.'

'I don't follow. His divinity?'

'My dear,' Teabing declared, 'until *that* moment in history, Jesus was viewed by His followers as a mortal prophet . . . a great and powerful man, but a *man* nonetheless. A mortal.'

'Not the Son of God?'

'Right,' Teabing said. 'Jesus' establishment as "the Son of God" was officially proposed and voted on by the Council of Nicaea.'

'Hold on. You're saying Jesus' divinity was the result of a *vote?*'

'A relatively close vote at that,' Teabing added. 'Nonetheless, establishing Christ's divinity was critical to the further unification of the Roman empire and to the new Vatican power base. By officially endorsing Jesus as the Son of God, Constantine turned Jesus into a deity who existed beyond the scope of the human world, an entity whose power was unchallengeable. This not only precluded further pagan challenges to Christianity, but now the followers of Christ were able to redeem themselves *only* via the established sacred channel – the Roman Catholic Church.'

Sophie glanced at Langdon, and he gave her a soft nod of concurrence.

'It was all about power,' Teabing continued. 'Christ as Messiah was critical to the functioning of Church and state. Many scholars claim that the early Church literally *stole* Jesus from His original followers, hijacking His human message, shrouding it in an impenetrable cloak of divinity, and using it to expand their own power. I've written several books on the topic.'

'And I assume devout Christians send you hate mail on a daily basis?'

'Why would they?' Teabing countered. 'The vast majority of educated Christians know the history of their faith. Jesus was indeed a great and powerful man. Constantine's underhanded political manoeuvres don't diminish the majesty of Christ's life. Nobody is saying Christ was a fraud, or denying that He walked the earth and inspired millions to better lives. All we are saying is that Constantine took advantage of Christ's substantial influence and importance. And in doing so, he shaped the face of Christianity as we know it today.'

Sophie glanced at the art book before her, eager to move on and see the Da Vinci painting of the Holy Grail.

'The twist is this,' Teabing said, talking faster now. 'Because Constantine upgraded Jesus' status almost four centuries *after* Jesus' death, thousands of documents already existed chronicling His life as a *mortal* man. To rewrite the history books, Constantine knew he would need a bold stroke. From this sprang the most profound moment in Christian history.' Teabing paused, eyeing Sophie. 'Constantine commissioned and financed a new Bible, which omitted those gospels that spoke of Christ's *human* traits and embellished those gospels that made Him godlike. The earlier gospels were outlawed, gathered up, and burned.'

'An interesting note,' Langdon added. 'Anyone who chose the forbidden gospels over Constantine's version was deemed a heretic. The word *heretic* derives from that moment in history. The Latin word *haereticus* means "choice". Those who "chose" the original history of Christ were the world's first *heretics*.'

'Fortunately for historians,' Teabing said, 'some of the gospels that Constantine attempted to eradicate managed to survive. The Dead Sea Scrolls were found in the 1950s hidden in a cave near Qumran in the Judaean desert. And, of course, the Coptic Scrolls in 1945 at Nag Hammadi. In addition to telling the true Grail story, these documents speak of Christ's ministry in very human terms. Of course, the Vatican, in keeping with their tradition of misinformation, tried very hard to suppress the release of these scrolls. And why wouldn't they? The scrolls highlight glaring historical discrepancies and fabrications, clearly confirming that the modern Bible was compiled and edited by men who possessed a political agenda – to promote the divinity of the man Jesus Christ and use His influence to solidify their own power base.'

'And yet,' Langdon countered, 'it's important to remember that the modern Church's desire to suppress these documents comes from a sincere belief in their established view of Christ. The Vatican is made up of deeply pious men who truly believe these contrary documents could only be false testimony.'

Teabing chuckled as he eased himself into a chair opposite Sophie. 'As you can see, our professor has a far softer heart for Rome than I do. Nonetheless, he is correct about the modern clergy believing these opposing documents are false testimony. That's understandable. Constantine's Bible has been their truth for ages. Nobody is more indoctrinated than the indoctrinator.'

'What he means,' Langdon said, 'is that we worship the gods of our fathers.'

'What I mean,' Teabing countered, 'is that almost everything our fathers taught us about Christ is *false*. As are the stories about the Holy Grail.'

Sophie looked again at the Da Vinci quote before her. *Blinding ignorance does mislead us. O! Wretched mortals, open your eyes!*

Teabing reached for the book and flipped toward the centre. 'And finally, before I show you Da Vinci's paintings of the Holy Grail, I'd like you to take a quick look at this.' He opened the book to a colourful graphic that spanned both full pages. 'I assume you recognize this fresco?'

He's kidding, right? Sophie was staring at the most famous fresco of all time – *The Last Supper* – Da Vinci's legendary painting on the wall of Santa Maria delle Grazie in Milan. The decaying fresco portrayed Jesus and His disciples at the moment that Jesus announced one of them would betray Him. 'I know the fresco, yes.'

'Then perhaps you would indulge me this little game? Close your eyes if you would.'

Uncertain, Sophie closed her eyes.

'Where is Jesus sitting?' Teabing asked.

'In the centre.'

'Good. And what food are He and His disciples breaking and eating?'

'Bread.' *Obviously.*

'Superb. And what drink?'

'Wine. They drank wine.'

'Great. And one final question. How many wineglasses are on the table?'

Sophie paused, realizing it was the trick question. *And after dinner, Jesus took the cup of wine, sharing it with His disciples.* 'One cup,' she said. 'The chalice.' *The Cup of Christ. The Holy Grail.* 'Jesus passed a single chalice of wine, just as modern Christians do at communion.'

Teabing sighed. 'Open your eyes.'

She did. Teabing was grinning smugly. Sophie looked down at the painting, seeing to her astonishment that *everyone* at the table had a glass of wine, including Christ. Thirteen cups. Moreover, the cups were tiny, stemless, and made of glass. There was no chalice in the painting. No Holy Grail.

Teabing's eyes twinkled. 'A bit strange, don't you think, considering that both the Bible and our standard Grail legend celebrate this moment as the definitive arrival of the Holy Grail. Oddly, Da Vinci appears to have forgotten to paint the Cup of Christ.'

'Surely art scholars must have noted that.'

'You will be shocked to learn what anomalies Da Vinci included here that most scholars either do not see or simply choose to ignore. This fresco, in fact, is the entire key to the Holy Grail mystery. Da Vinci lays it all out in the open in *The Last Supper.*'

Sophie scanned the work eagerly. 'Does this fresco tell us *what* the Grail really is?'

'Not *what* it is,' Teabing whispered. 'But rather *who* it is. The Holy Grail is not a thing. It is, in fact, . . . a *person.*'

56

Sophie stared at Teabing a long moment and then turned to Langdon. 'The Holy Grail is a person?'

Langdon nodded. 'A woman, in fact.' From the blank look on Sophie's face, Langdon could tell they had already lost her. He recalled having a similar reaction the first time he heard the statement. It was not until he understood the *symbology* behind the Grail that the feminine connection became clear.

Teabing apparently had a similar thought. 'Robert, perhaps this is the moment for the symbologist to clarify?' He went to a nearby end table, found a piece of paper, and laid it in front of Langdon.

Langdon pulled a pen from his pocket. 'Sophie, are you familiar with the modern icons for male and female?' He drew the common male symbol ♂ and female symbol ♀.

'Of course,' she said.

'These,' he said quietly, 'are not the original symbols for male and female. Many people incorrectly assume the male symbol is derived from a shield and spear, while the female symbol represents a mirror reflecting beauty. In fact, the symbols originated as ancient astronomical symbols for the planet-god Mars and planet-goddess Venus. The original symbols are far simpler.' Langdon drew another icon on the paper.

'This symbol is the original icon for *male*,' he told her. 'A rudimentary phallus.'

'Quite to the point,' Sophie said.

'As it were,' Teabing added.

Langdon went on. 'This icon is formally known as the *blade*, and it represents aggression and manhood. In fact, this exact phallus symbol is still used today on modern military uniforms to denote rank.'

'Indeed.' Teabing grinned. 'The more penises you have, the higher your rank. Boys will be boys.'

Langdon winced. 'Moving on, the female symbol, as you might imagine, is the exact opposite.' He drew another symbol on the page. 'This is called the *chalice*.'

Sophie glanced up, looking surprised.

Langdon could see she had made the connection. 'The chalice,' he said, 'resembles a cup or vessel, and more important, it resembles the shape of a woman's womb. This symbol communicates femininity, womanhood and fertility.' Langdon looked directly at her now. 'Sophie, legend tells us the Holy Grail is a chalice – a cup. But the Grail's description as a *chalice* is actually an allegory to protect the true nature of the Holy Grail. That is to say, the legend uses the chalice as a *metaphor* for something far more important.'

'A woman,' Sophie said.

'Exactly.' Langdon smiled. 'The Grail is literally the ancient symbol for womanhood, and the *Holy* Grail represents the sacred feminine and the goddess, which of course has now been lost, virtually eliminated by the Church. The power of the female and her ability to produce life was once very sacred, but it posed a threat to the rise of the predominantly male Church, and so the sacred feminine was demonized and called unclean. It was *man*, not God, who created the concept of "original sin", whereby Eve tasted of the apple and caused the downfall of the human race. Woman, once the sacred giver of life, was now the enemy.'

'I should add,' Teabing chimed, 'that this concept of woman as life-bringer was the foundation of ancient religion. Childbirth was mystical and powerful. Sadly, Christian philosophy decided to embezzle the female's creative power by ignoring biological truth and making *man* the Creator. Genesis tells us that Eve was created from Adam's rib. Woman became an offshoot of man. And a sinful one at that. Genesis was the beginning of the end for the goddess.'

'The Grail,' Langdon said, 'is symbolic of the lost goddess. When Christianity came along, the old pagan religions did not die easily. Legends of chivalric quests for the lost Grail were in fact stories of forbidden quests to find the lost sacred feminine. Knights who claimed to be "searching for the chalice" were speaking in code as a way to protect themselves from a Church that had subjugated women, banished the Goddess, burned non-believers and forbidden the pagan reverence for the sacred feminine.'

Sophie shook her head. 'I'm sorry, when you said the Holy Grail was a person, I thought you meant it was an actual person.'

'It is,' Langdon said.

'And not just *any* person,' Teabing blurted, clambering excitedly to his feet. 'A woman who carried with her a secret so powerful that, if revealed, it threatened to devastate the very foundation of Christianity!'

Sophie looked overwhelmed. 'Is this woman well known in history?'

'Quite.' Teabing collected his crutches and motioned down the hall. 'And if we adjourn to the study, my friends, it would be my honour to show you Da Vinci's painting of her.'

Two rooms away, in the kitchen, manservant Rémy Legaludec stood in silence before a television. The news station was broadcasting photos of a man and woman . . . the same two individuals to whom Rémy had just served tea.

57

Standing at the roadblock outside the Depository Bank of Zurich, Lieutenant Collet wondered what was taking Fache so long to come up with the search warrant. The bankers were obviously hiding something. They claimed Langdon and Neveu had arrived earlier and were turned away from the bank because they did not have proper account identification.

So why won't they let us inside for a look?

Finally, Collet's cellular phone rang. It was the command post at the Louvre. 'Do we have a search warrant yet?' Collet demanded.

'Forget about the bank, Lieutenant,' the agent told him. 'We just got a tip. We have the exact location where Langdon and Neveu are hiding.'

Collet sat down hard on the hood of his car. 'You're kidding.'

'I have an address in the suburbs. Somewhere near Versailles.'

'Does Captain Fache know?'

'Not yet. He's busy on an important call.'

'I'm on my way. Have him call as soon as he's free.' Collet took down the address and jumped in his car. As he peeled away from the bank, Collet realized he had forgotten to ask *who* had tipped DCPJ off to Langdon's location. Not that it mattered. Collet had been blessed with a chance to redeem his skepticism and earlier blunders. He was about to make the most high-profile arrest of his career.

Collet radioed the five cars accompanying him. 'No sirens, men. Langdon can't know we're coming.'

Forty kilometres away, a black Audi pulled off a rural road and parked in the shadows on the edge of a field. Silas got out and peered through the rungs of the wrought-iron fence that encircled the vast compound before him. He gazed up the long moonlit slope to the château in the distance.

The downstairs lights were all ablaze. *Odd for this hour,* Silas thought, smiling. The information the Teacher had given him was obviously accurate. *I will not leave this house without the keystone,* he vowed. *I will not fail the bishop and the Teacher.*

Checking the thirteen-round clip in his Heckler Koch, Silas pushed it through the bars and let it fall onto the mossy ground inside the compound. Then, gripping the top of the fence, he heaved himself up and over, dropping to the ground on the other side. Ignoring the slash of pain from his *cilice*, Silas retrieved his gun and began the long trek up the grassy slope.

58

Teabing's 'study' was like no study Sophie had ever seen. Six or seven times larger than even the most luxurious of office spaces, the knight's *cabinet de travail* resembled an ungainly hybrid of science laboratory, archival library and indoor flea market. Lit by three overhead chandeliers, the boundless tile floor was dotted with clustered islands of worktables buried beneath books, artwork, artefacts and a surprising amount of electronic gear – computers, projectors, microscopes, copy machines and flatbed scanners.

'I converted the ballroom,' Teabing said, looking sheepish as he shuffled into the room. 'I have little occasion to dance.'

Sophie felt as if the entire night had become some kind of twilight zone where nothing was as she expected. 'This is all for your work?'

'Learning the truth has become my life's love,' Teabing said. 'And the Sangreal is my favourite mistress.'

The Holy Grail is a woman, Sophie thought, her mind a collage of inter-related ideas that seemed to make no sense. 'You said you have a *picture* of this woman who you claim is the Holy Grail.'

'Yes, but it is not I who *claim* she is the Grail. Christ Himself made that claim.'

'Which one is the painting?' Sophie asked, scanning the walls.

'Hmmm . . .' Teabing made a show of seeming to have forgotten. 'The Holy Grail. The Sangreal. The Chalice.' He wheeled suddenly and pointed to the far wall. On it hung an eight-foot-long print of *The Last Supper,* the same exact image Sophie had just been looking at. 'There she is!'

Sophie was certain she had missed something. 'That's the same painting you just showed me.'

He winked. 'I know, but the enlargement is so much more exciting. Don't you think?'

Sophie turned to Langdon for help. 'I'm lost.'

Langdon smiled. 'As it turns out, the Holy Grail *does* indeed make an appearance in *The Last Supper.* Leonardo included her prominently.'

'Hold on,' Sophie said. 'You told me the Holy Grail is a *woman. The Last Supper* is a painting of thirteen men.'

'Is it?' Teabing arched his eyebrows. 'Take a closer look.'

Uncertain, Sophie made her way closer to the painting, scanning the thirteen figures – Jesus Christ in the middle, six disciples on His left, and six on His right. 'They're all men,' she confirmed.

'Oh?' Teabing said. 'How about the one seated in the place of honour, at the right hand of the Lord?'

Sophie examined the figure to Jesus' immediate right, focusing in. As she studied the person's face and body, a wave of astonishment rose within her. The individual had flowing red hair, delicate folded hands, and the hint of a bosom. It was, without a doubt . . . female.

'That's a woman!' Sophie exclaimed.

Teabing was laughing. 'Surprise, surprise. Believe me, it's no mistake. Leonardo was skilled at painting the difference between the sexes.'

Sophie could not take her eyes from the woman beside Christ. *The Last Supper is supposed to be thirteen men. Who is this woman?* Although Sophie had seen this classic image many times, she had not once noticed this glaring discrepancy.

'Everyone misses it,' Teabing said. 'Our preconceived notions of this scene are so powerful that our mind blocks out the incongruity and overrides our eyes.'

'It's known as *scotoma*,' Langdon added. 'The brain does it sometimes with powerful symbols.'

'Another reason you might have missed the woman,' Teabing said, 'is that many of the photographs in art books were taken before 1954, when the details were still hidden beneath layers of grime and several restorative repaintings done by clumsy hands in the eighteenth century. Now, at last, the fresco has been cleaned down to Da Vinci's original layer of paint.' He motioned to the photograph. '*Et voilà!*'

Sophie moved closer to the image. The woman to Jesus' right was young and pious-looking, with a demure face, beautiful red hair and hands folded quietly. *This is the woman who singlehandedly could crumble the Church?*

'Who is she?' Sophie asked.

'That, my dear,' Teabing replied, 'is Mary Magdalene.'

Sophie turned. 'The prostitute?'

Teabing drew a short breath, as if the word had injured him personally. 'Magdalene was no such thing. That unfortunate misconception is the legacy of a smear campaign launched by the early Church. The Church needed to defame Mary Magdalene in order to cover up her dangerous secret – her role as the Holy Grail.'

'Her *role*?'

'As I mentioned,' Teabing clarified, 'the early Church needed to convince the world that the mortal prophet Jesus was a *divine* being. Therefore, any gospels that described *earthly* aspects of Jesus' life had to be omitted from the Bible. Unfortunately for the early editors, one particularly troubling earthly theme kept recurring in the gospels. Mary

Magdalene.' He paused. 'More specifically, her marriage to Jesus Christ.'

'I beg your pardon?' Sophie's eyes moved to Langdon and then back to Teabing.

'It's a matter of historical record,' Teabing said, 'and Da Vinci was certainly aware of that fact. *The Last Supper* practically shouts at the viewer that Jesus and Magdalene were a pair.'

Sophie glanced back to the fresco.

'Notice that Jesus and Magdalene are clothed as mirror images of one another.' Teabing pointed to the two individuals in the centre of the fresco.

Sophie was mesmerized. Sure enough, their clothes were inverse colours. Jesus wore a red robe and blue cloak; Mary Magdalene wore a blue robe and red cloak. *Yin and yang.*

'Venturing into the more bizarre,' Teabing said, 'note that Jesus and His bride appear to be joined at the hip and are leaning away from one another as if to create this clearly delineated negative space between them.'

Even before Teabing traced the contour for her, Sophie saw it – the indisputable $\vee$ shape at the focal point of the painting. It was the same symbol Langdon had drawn earlier for the Grail, the chalice and the female womb.

'Finally,' Teabing said, 'if you view Jesus and Magdalene as compositional elements rather than as people, you will see another obvious shape leap out at you.' He paused. 'A *letter* of the alphabet.'

Sophie saw it at once. To say the letter leapt out at her was an understatement. The letter was suddenly all Sophie could see. Glaring in the centre of the painting was the unquestionable outline of an enormous, flawlessly formed letter M.

'A bit too perfect for coincidence, wouldn't you say?' Teabing asked.

Sophie was amazed. 'Why is it there?'

Teabing shrugged. 'Conspiracy theorists will tell you it stands for *Matrimonio* or *Mary Magdalene*. To be honest, nobody is certain. The only certainty is that the hidden M is no mistake. Countless Grail-related works contain the hidden letter M – whether as watermarks, underpaintings, or compositional allusions. The most blatant M, of course, is emblazoned on the altar at Our Lady of Paris in London, which was designed by a former Grand Master of the Priory of Sion, Jean Cocteau.'

Sophie weighed the information. 'I'll admit, the hidden M's are intriguing, although I assume nobody is claiming they are proof of Jesus' marriage to Magdalene.'

'No, no,' Teabing said, going to a nearby table of books. 'As I said earlier, the marriage of Jesus and Mary Magdalene is part of the historical record.' He began pawing through his book collection. 'Moreover, Jesus as a married man makes infinitely more sense than our standard biblical view of Jesus as a bachelor.'

'Why?' Sophie asked.

'Because Jesus was a Jew,' Langdon said, taking over while Teabing searched for his book, 'and the social decorum during that time virtually forbade a Jewish man to be unmarried. According to Jewish custom, celibacy was condemned, and the obligation for a Jewish father was to find a suitable wife for his son. If Jesus were not married, at least one of the Bible's gospels would have mentioned it and offered some explanation for His unnatural state of bachelorhood.'

Teabing located a huge book and pulled it toward him across the table. The leather-bound edition was poster-sized, like a huge atlas. The cover read: *The Gnostic Gospels.* Teabing heaved it open, and Langdon and Sophie joined him. Sophie could see it contained photographs of what appeared to be magnified passages of ancient documents – tattered papyrus with handwritten text. She did not recognize the ancient language, but the facing pages bore typed translations.

'These are photocopies of the Nag Hammadi and Dead Sea scrolls, which I mentioned earlier,' Teabing said. 'The earliest Christian records. Troublingly, they do not match up with the gospels in the Bible.' Flipping toward the middle of the book, Teabing pointed to a passage. 'The Gospel of Philip is always a good place to start.'

Sophie read the passage:

And the companion of the Saviour is Mary Magdalene. Christ loved her more than all the disciples and used to kiss her often on her mouth. The rest of the disciples were offended by it and expressed disapproval. They said to him, 'Why do you love her more than all of us?'

The words surprised Sophie, and yet they hardly seemed conclusive. 'It says nothing of marriage.'

'*Au contraire.*' Teabing smiled, pointing to the first line. 'As any Aramaic scholar will tell you, the word *companion*, in those days, literally meant *spouse.*'

Langdon concurred with a nod.

Sophie read the first line again. *And the companion of the Saviour is Mary Magdalene.*

Teabing flipped through the book and pointed out several other passages that, to Sophie's surprise, clearly suggested Magdalene and Jesus had a romantic relationship. As she read the passages, Sophie recalled an angry priest who had banged on her grandfather's door when she was a schoolgirl.

'Is this the home of Jacques Saunière?' the priest had demanded, glaring down at young Sophie when she pulled open the door. 'I want to talk to him about this editorial he wrote.' The priest held up a newspaper.

Sophie summoned her grandfather, and the two men disappeared into his study and closed the door. *My grandfather wrote something in the paper?* Sophie immediately ran to the kitchen and flipped through that morning's paper. She found her grandfather's name on an article on the second page. She read it. Sophie didn't understand all of what was said, but it sounded like the French government, under pressure from priests, had agreed to ban an American film called *The Last Temptation of Christ*, which was about Jesus having sex with a lady called Mary Magdalene. Her grandfather's article said the Church was arrogant and wrong to ban it.

No wonder the priest is mad, Sophie thought.

'It's pornography! Sacrilege!' the priest yelled, emerging from the study and storming to the front door. 'How can you possibly endorse that! This American Martin Scorsese is a blasphemer, and the Church will permit him no pulpit in France!' The priest slammed the door on his way out.

When her grandfather came into the kitchen, he saw Sophie with the paper and frowned. 'You're quick.'

Sophie said, 'You think Jesus Christ had a girlfriend?'

'No, dear, I said the Church should not be allowed to tell us what notions we can and can't entertain.'

'Did Jesus have a girlfriend?'

Her grandfather was silent for several moments. 'Would it be so bad if He did?'

Sophie considered it and then shrugged. 'I wouldn't mind.'

Sir Leigh Teabing was still talking. 'I shan't bore you with the countless references to Jesus and Magdalene's union. That has been explored ad nauseam by modern historians. I would, however, like to point out the following.' He motioned to another passage. 'This is from the Gospel of Mary Magdalene.'

Sophie had not known a gospel existed in Magdalene's words. She read the text:

> *And Peter said, 'Did the Saviour really speak with a woman without our knowledge? Are we to turn about and all listen to her? Did he prefer her to us?'*
> *And Levi answered, 'Peter, you have always been hot-tempered. Now I see you contending against the woman like an adversary. If the Saviour made her worthy, who are you indeed to reject her? Surely the Saviour knows her very well. That is why he loved her more than us.'*

'The woman they are speaking of,' Teabing explained, 'is Mary Magdalene. Peter is jealous of her.'

'Because Jesus preferred Mary?'

'Not only that. The stakes were far greater than mere affection. At this point in the gospels, Jesus suspects He will soon be captured and crucified. So He gives Mary Magdalene instructions on how to carry on His Church after He is gone. As a result, Peter expresses his discontent over playing second fiddle to a woman. I daresay Peter was something of a sexist.'

Sophie was trying to keep up. 'This is *Saint* Peter. The rock on which Jesus built His Church.'

'The same, except for one catch. According to these unaltered gospels, it was not *Peter* to whom Christ gave directions with which to establish the Christian Church. It was *Mary Magdalene*.'

Sophie looked at him. 'You're saying the Christian Church was to be carried on by a *woman*?'

'That was the plan. Jesus was the original feminist. He intended for the future of His Church to be in the hands of Mary Magdalene.'

'And Peter had a problem with that,' Langdon said, pointing to *The Last Supper*. 'That's Peter there. You can see that Da Vinci was well aware of how Peter felt about Mary Magdalene.'

Again, Sophie was speechless. In the painting, Peter was leaning menacingly toward Mary Magdalene and slicing his blade-like hand across her neck. The same threatening gesture as in *Madonna of the Rocks*!

'And here too,' Langdon said, pointing now to the crowd of disciples near Peter. 'A bit ominous, no?'

Sophie squinted and saw a hand emerging from the crowd of disciples. 'Is that hand wielding a *dagger*?'

'Yes. Stranger still, if you count the arms, you'll see that this hand belongs to . . . no one at all. It's disembodied. Anonymous.'

Sophie was starting to feel overwhelmed. 'I'm sorry, I still don't understand how all of this makes Mary Magdalene the Holy Grail.'

'Aha!' Teabing exclaimed again. 'Therein lies the rub!' He turned once more to the table and pulled out a large chart, spreading it out for her. It was an elaborate genealogy. 'Few people realize that Mary Magdalene, in addition to being Christ's right hand, was a powerful woman already.'

Sophie could now see the title of the family tree.

THE TRIBE OF BENJAMIN

'Mary Magdalene is here,' Teabing said, pointing near the top of the genealogy.

Sophie was surprised. 'She was of the House of Benjamin?'

'Indeed,' Teabing said. 'Mary Magdalene was of royal descent.'

'But I was under the impression Magdalene was poor.'

Teabing shook his head. 'Magdalene was recast as a whore in order to erase evidence of her powerful family ties.'

Sophie found herself again glancing at Langdon, who again nodded. She turned back to Teabing. 'But why would the early Church *care* if Magdalene had royal blood?'

The Briton smiled. 'My dear child, it was not Mary Magdalene's royal blood that concerned the Church so much as it was her consorting with Christ, who *also* had royal blood. As you know, the Book of Matthew tells us that Jesus was of the House of David. A descendant of King Solomon – King of the Jews. By marrying into the powerful House of Benjamin, Jesus fused two royal bloodlines, creating a potent political union with the

662

potential of making a legitimate claim to the throne and restoring the line of kings as it was under Solomon.'

Sophie sensed he was at last coming to his point.

Teabing looked excited now. 'The legend of the Holy Grail is a legend about royal blood. When Grail legend speaks of "the chalice that held the blood of Christ" . . . it speaks, in fact, of Mary Magdalene – the female womb that carried Jesus' royal bloodline.'

The words seemed to echo across the ballroom and back before they fully registered in Sophie's mind. *Mary Magdalene carried the royal bloodline of Jesus Christ?* 'But how could Christ have a bloodline unless . . . ?' She paused and looked at Langdon.

Langdon smiled softly. 'Unless they had a child.'

Sophie stood transfixed.

'Behold,' Teabing proclaimed, 'the greatest cover-up in human history. Not only was Jesus Christ married, but He was a father. My dear, Mary Magdalene was the Holy Vessel. She was the chalice that bore the royal bloodline of Jesus Christ. She was the womb that bore the lineage, and the vine from which the sacred fruit sprang forth!'

Sophie felt the hairs stand up on her arms. 'But how could a secret *that* big be kept quiet all of these years?'

'Heavens!' Teabing said. 'It has been anything but *quiet!* The royal bloodline of Jesus Christ is the source of the most enduring legend of all time – the Holy Grail. Magdalene's story has been shouted from the rooftops for centuries in all kinds of metaphors and languages. Her story is everywhere once you open your eyes.'

'And the Sangreal documents?' Sophie said. 'They allegedly contain proof that Jesus had a royal bloodline?'

'They do.'

'So the entire Holy Grail legend is all about royal blood?'

'Quite literally,' Teabing said. 'The word *Sangreal* derives from *San Greal* – or Holy Grail. But in its most ancient form, the word *Sangreal* was divided in a different spot.' Teabing wrote on a piece of scrap paper and handed it to her.

She read what he had written.

Sang Real

Instantly, Sophie recognized the translation.
Sang Real literally meant *Royal Blood*.

59

The male receptionist in the lobby of the Opus Dei headquarters on Lexington Avenue in New York City was surprised to hear Bishop Aringarosa's voice on the line. 'Good evening, sir.'

'Have I had any messages?' the bishop demanded, sounding unusually anxious.

'Yes, sir. I'm very glad you called in. I couldn't reach you in your apartment. You had an urgent phone message about half an hour ago.'

'Yes?' He sounded relieved by the news. 'Did the caller leave a name?'

'No, sir, just a number.' The operator relayed the number.

'Prefix thirty-three? That's France, am I right?'

'Yes, sir. Paris. The caller said it was critical you contact him immediately.'

'Thank you. I have been waiting for that call.' Aringarosa quickly severed the connection.

As the receptionist hung up the receiver, he wondered why Aringarosa's phone connection sounded so crackly. The bishop's daily schedule showed him in New York this weekend, and yet he sounded a world away. The receptionist shrugged it off. Bishop Aringarosa had been acting very strangely the last few months.

My cellular phone must not have been receiving, Aringarosa thought as the Fiat approached the exit for Rome's Ciampino Charter Airport. *The Teacher was trying to reach me.* Despite Aringarosa's concern at having missed the call, he felt encouraged that the Teacher felt confident enough to call Opus Dei headquarters directly.

Things must have gone well in Paris tonight.

As Aringarosa began dialling the number, he felt excited to know he would soon be in Paris. *I'll be on the ground before dawn.* Aringarosa had a chartered turbo prop awaiting him here for the short flight to France. Commercial carriers were not an option at this hour, especially considering the contents of his briefcase.

The line began to ring.

A female voice answered. '*Direction Centrale Police Judiciaire.*'

Aringarosa felt himself hesitate. This was unexpected. 'Ah, yes . . . I was asked to call this number?'

'*Qui êtes-vous?*' the woman said. 'Your name?'

Aringarosa was uncertain if he should reveal it. *The French Judicial Police?*

'Your *name*, monsieur?' the woman pressed.

'Bishop Manuel Aringarosa.'

'*Un moment.*' There was a click on the line.

After a long wait, another man came on, his tone gruff and concerned. 'Bishop, I am glad I finally reached you. You and I have much to discuss.'

60

Sangreal . . . *Sang Real* . . . *San Greal* . . . *Royal Blood* . . . *Holy Grail.*
It was all intertwined.
The Holy Grail is Mary Magdalene . . . the mother of the royal bloodline of Jesus Christ. Sophie felt a new wave of disorientation as she stood in the silence of the ballroom and stared at Robert Langdon. The more pieces Langdon and Teabing laid on the table tonight, the more unpredictable this puzzle became.

'As you can see, my dear,' Teabing said, hobbling toward a bookshelf, 'Leonardo is not the only one who has been trying to tell the world the truth about the Holy Grail. The royal bloodline of Jesus Christ has been chronicled in exhaustive detail by scores of historians.' He ran a finger down a row of several dozen books.

Sophie tilted her head and scanned the list of titles:

THE TEMPLAR REVELATION:
Secret Guardians of the True Identity of Christ

THE WOMAN WITH THE ALABASTER JAR:
Mary Magdalene and the Holy Grail

THE GODDESS IN THE GOSPELS
Reclaiming the Sacred Feminine

'Here is perhaps the best-known tome,' Teabing said, pulling a tattered hardcover from the stack and handing it to her.

The cover read:

HOLY BLOOD, HOLY GRAIL
The Acclaimed International Bestseller

Sophie glanced up. 'An international bestseller? I've never heard of it.'
'You were young. This caused quite a stir back in the nineteen eighties. To my taste, the authors made some dubious leaps of faith in their

analysis, but their fundamental premise is sound, and to their credit, they finally brought the idea of Christ's bloodline into the mainstream.'

'What was the Church's reaction to the book?'

'Outrage, of course. But that was to be expected. After all, this was a secret the Vatican had tried to bury in the fourth century. That's part of what the Crusades were about. Gathering and destroying information. The threat Mary Magdalene posed to the men of the early Church was potentially ruinous. Not only was she the woman to whom Jesus had assigned the task of founding the Church, but she also had physical proof that the Church's newly proclaimed *deity* had spawned a mortal bloodline. The Church, in order to defend itself against the Magdalene's power, perpetuated her image as a whore and buried evidence of Christ's marriage to her, thereby defusing any potential claims that Christ had a surviving bloodline and was a mortal prophet.'

Sophie glanced at Langdon, who nodded. 'Sophie, the historical evidence supporting this is substantial.'

'I admit,' Teabing said, 'the assertions are dire, but you must understand the Church's powerful motivations to conduct such a cover-up. They could never have survived public knowledge of a bloodline. A child of Jesus would undermine the critical notion of Christ's divinity and therefore the Christian Church, which declared itself the sole vessel through which humanity could access the divine and gain entrance to the kingdom of heaven.'

'The five-petal rose,' Sophie said, pointing suddenly to the spine of one of Teabing's books. *The same exact design inlaid on the rosewood box.*

Teabing glanced at Langdon and grinned. 'She has a good eye.' He turned back to Sophie. 'That is the Priory symbol for the Grail. Mary Magdalene. Because her name was forbidden by the Church, Mary Magdalene became secretly known by many pseudonyms – the Chalice, the Holy Grail, and the Rose.' He paused. 'The Rose has ties to the five-pointed pentacle of Venus and the guiding Compass Rose. By the way, the word *rose* is identical in English, French, German, and many other languages.'

'Rose,' Langdon added, 'is also an anagram of Eros, the Greek god of sexual love.'

Sophie gave him a surprised look as Teabing ploughed on.

'The Rose has always been the premiere symbol of female sexuality. In primitive goddess cults, the five petals represented the five stations of female life – birth, menstruation, motherhood, menopause, and death. And in modern times, the flowering rose's ties to womanhood are considered more visual.' He glanced at Robert. 'Perhaps the symbologist could explain?'

Robert hesitated. A moment too long.

'Oh, heavens!' Teabing huffed. 'You Americans are such prudes.' He looked back at Sophie. 'What Robert is fumbling with is the fact that the blossoming flower resembles the female genitalia, the sublime blossom from which all mankind enters the world. And if you've ever seen any paintings by Georgia O'Keeffe, you'll know exactly what I mean.'

'The point here,' Langdon said, motioning back to the bookshelf, 'is that all of these books substantiate the same historical claim.'

'That Jesus was a father.' Sophie was still uncertain.

'Yes,' Teabing said. 'And that Mary Magdalene was the womb that carried His royal lineage. The Priory of Sion, to this day, still worships Mary Magdalene as the Goddess, the Holy Grail, the Rose and the Divine Mother.'

Sophie again flashed on the ritual in the basement.

'According to the Priory,' Teabing continued, 'Mary Magdalene was pregnant at the time of the crucifixion. For the safety of Christ's unborn child, she had no choice but to flee the Holy Land. With the help of Jesus' trusted uncle, Joseph of Arimathea, Mary Magdalene secretly traveled to France, then known as Gaul. There she found safe refuge in the Jewish community. It was here in France that she gave birth to a daughter. Her name was Sarah.'

Sophie glanced up. 'They actually know the child's *name?*'

'Far more than that. Magdalene's and Sarah's lives were scrupulously chronicled by their Jewish protectors. Remember that Magdalene's child belonged to the lineage of Jewish kings – David and Solomon. For this reason, the Jews in France considered Magdalene sacred royalty and revered her as the progenitor of the royal line of kings. Countless scholars of that era chronicled Mary Magdalene's days in France, including the birth of Sarah and the subsequent family tree.'

Sophie was startled. 'There exists a *family tree* of Jesus Christ?'

'Indeed. And it is purportedly one of the cornerstones of the Sangreal documents. A complete genealogy of the early descendants of Christ.'

'But what good is a documented genealogy of Christ's bloodline?' Sophie asked. 'It's not proof. Historians could not possibly confirm its authenticity.'

Teabing chuckled. 'No more so than they can confirm the authenticity of the Bible.'

'Meaning?'

'Meaning that history is always written by the winners. When two cultures clash, the loser is obliterated, and the winner writes the history books – books which glorify their own cause and disparage the conquered foe. As Napoleon once said, "What is history, but a fable agreed upon?"' He smiled. 'By its very nature, history is always a one-sided account.'

Sophie had never thought of it that way.

'The Sangreal documents simply tell the *other* side of the Christ story. In the end, which side of the story you believe becomes a matter of faith and personal exploration, but at least the information has survived. The Sangreal documents include tens of thousands of pages of information.

Eyewitness accounts of the Sangreal treasure describe it as being carried in four enormous trunks. In those trunks are reputed to be the *Purist Documents* – thousands of pages of unaltered, pre-Constantine documents, written by the early followers of Jesus, revering Him as a wholly human teacher and prophet. Also rumoured to be part of the treasure is the legendary "*Q*" *Document* – a manuscript that even the Vatican admit they believe exists. Allegedly, it is a book of Jesus' teachings, possibly written in His own hand.'

'Writings by Christ Himself?'

'Of course,' Teabing said. 'Why wouldn't Jesus have kept a chronicle of His ministry? Most people did in those days. Another explosive document believed to be in the treasure is a manuscript called *The Magdalene Diaries* – Mary Magdalene's personal account of her relationship with Christ, His crucifixion and her time in France.'

Sophie was silent for a long moment. 'And these four chests of documents were the treasure that the Knights Templar found under Solomon's Temple?'

'Exactly. The documents that made the Knights so powerful. The documents that have been the object of countless Grail quests throughout history.'

'But you said the Holy Grail was *Mary Magdalene*. If people are searching for documents, why would you call it a search for the Holy Grail?'

Teabing eyed her, his expression softening. 'Because the hiding place of the Holy Grail includes a sarcophagus.'

Outside, the wind howled in the trees.

Teabing spoke more quietly now. 'The quest for the Holy Grail is literally the quest to kneel before the bones of Mary Magdalene. A journey to pray at the feet of the outcast one, the lost sacred feminine.'

Sophie felt an unexpected wonder. 'The hiding place of the Holy Grail is actually . . . a *tomb*?'

Teabing's hazel eyes got misty. 'It is. A tomb containing the body of Mary Magdalene and the documents that tell the true story of her life. At its heart, the quest for the Holy Grail has always been a quest for the Magdalene – the wronged Queen, entombed with proof of her family's rightful claim to power.'

Sophie waited a moment as Teabing gathered himself. So much about her grandfather was still not making sense. 'Members of the Priory,' she finally said, 'all these years have answered the charge of protecting the Sangreal documents and the tomb of Mary Magdalene?'

'Yes, but the brotherhood had another, more important duty as well – to protect the *bloodline* itself. Christ's lineage was in perpetual danger. The early Church feared that if the lineage were permitted to grow, the secret of Jesus and Magdalene would eventually surface and challenge the fundamental Catholic doctrine – that of a divine Messiah who did not consort with women or engage in sexual union.' He paused. 'Nonetheless, Christ's line grew quietly under cover in France until making a bold move in the fifth century, when it intermarried with French royal blood and created a lineage known as the Merovingian bloodline.'

This news surprised Sophie. Merovingian was a term learned by every student in France. 'The Merovingians founded Paris.'

'Yes. That's one of the reasons the Grail legend is so rich in France. Many of the Vatican's Grail quests here were in fact stealth missions to erase members of the royal bloodline. Have you heard of King Dagobert?'

Sophie vaguely recalled the name from a grisly tale in history class. 'Dagobert was a Merovingian king, wasn't he? Stabbed in the eye while sleeping?'

'Exactly. Assassinated by the Vatican in collusion with Pepin d'Heristal. Late seventh century. With Dagobert's murder, the Merovingian bloodline was almost exterminated. Fortunately, Dagobert's son, Sigisbert, secretly escaped the attack and carried on the lineage, which later included Godefroi de Bouillon – founder of the Priory of Sion.'

'The same man,' Langdon said, 'who ordered the Knights Templar to recover the Sangreal documents from beneath Solomon's Temple and thus provide the Merovingians proof of their hereditary ties to Jesus Christ.'

Teabing nodded, heaving a ponderous sigh. 'The modern Priory of Sion has a momentous duty. Theirs is a threefold charge. The brotherhood must protect the Sangreal documents. They must protect the tomb of Mary Magdalene. And, of course, they must nurture and protect the bloodline of Christ – those few members of the royal Merovingian bloodline who have survived into modern times.'

The words hung in the huge space, and Sophie felt an odd vibration, as if her bones were reverberating with some new kind of truth. *Descendants of Jesus who survived into modern times.* Her grandfather's voice again was whispering in her ear. *Princess, I must tell you the truth about your family.*

A chill raked her flesh.

Royal blood.

She could not imagine.

Princess Sophie.

'Sir Leigh?' The manservant's words crackled through the intercom on the wall, and Sophie jumped. 'If you could join me in the kitchen a moment?'

Teabing scowled at the ill-timed intrusion. He went over to the intercom and pressed the button. 'Rémy, as you know, I am busy with my guests. If we need anything else from the kitchen tonight, we will help ourselves. Thank you and good night.'

'A word with you before I retire, sir. If you would.'

Teabing grunted and pressed the button. 'Make it quick, Rémy.'

'It is a household matter, sir, hardly fare for guests to endure.'

Teabing looked incredulous. 'And it cannot wait until morning?'

'No, sir. My question won't take a minute.'

Teabing rolled his eyes and looked at Langdon and Sophie. 'Sometimes I wonder who is serving whom?' He pressed the button again. 'I'll be right there, Rémy. Can I bring you anything when I come?'

'Only freedom from oppression, sir.'

'Rémy, you realize your *steak au poivre* is the only reason you still work for me.'

'So you tell me, sir. So you tell me.'

61

Princess Sophie.

Sophie felt hollow as she listened to the clicking of Teabing's crutches fade down the hallway. Numb, she turned and faced Langdon in the deserted ballroom. He was already shaking his head as if reading her mind.

'No, Sophie,' he whispered, his eyes reassuring. 'The same thought crossed my mind as soon as you told me your grandfather was in the Priory, and when I realized you said he wanted to tell you a secret about your family. But it's impossible.' Langdon paused. 'Saunière is not a Merovingian name.'

Sophie wasn't sure whether to feel relieved or disappointed. Earlier, Langdon had asked an unusual passing question about Sophie's mother's maiden name. Chauvel. The question now made sense. 'And Chauvel?' she asked, anxious.

Again he shook his head. 'I'm sorry. I know that would have answered some questions for you. Only two direct lines of Merovingians remain. Their family names are Plantard and Saint-Clair. Both families live in hiding, probably protected by the Priory.'

Sophie repeated the names silently in her mind and then shook her head. There was no one in her family named Plantard or Saint-Clair. A weary undertow was pulling at her now. She realized she was no closer than she had been at the Louvre to understanding what truth her grandfather had wanted to reveal to her. Sophie wished her grandfather had never mentioned her family this afternoon. He had torn open old wounds that felt as painful now as ever. *They are dead, Sophie. They are not coming back.* She thought of her mother singing her to sleep at night, of her father giving her rides on his shoulders, and of her grandmother and younger brother smiling at her with their fervent green eyes. All that was stolen. And all she had left was her grandfather.

And now he is gone too. I am alone.

Sophie turned quietly back to *The Last Supper* and gazed at Mary Magdalene's long red hair and quiet eyes. There was something in the woman's expression that echoed the loss of a loved one. Sophie could feel it too.

'Robert?' she said softly.

He stepped closer.

'I know Leigh said the Grail story is all around us, but tonight is the first time I've ever heard any of this.'

Langdon looked as if he wanted to put a comforting hand on her shoulder, but he refrained. 'You've heard her story before, Sophie. Everyone has. We just don't realize it when we hear it.'

'I don't understand.'

'The Grail story is everywhere, but it is hidden. When the Church outlawed speaking of the shunned Mary Magdalene, her story and importance had to be passed on through more discreet channels . . . channels that supported metaphor and symbolism.'

'Of course. The arts.'

Langdon motioned to *The Last Supper*. 'A perfect example. Some of today's most enduring art, literature and music secretly tell the history of Mary Magdalene and Jesus.'

Langdon quickly told her about works by Da Vinci, Botticelli, Poussin, Bernini, Mozart and Victor Hugo that all whispered of the quest to restore the banished sacred feminine. Enduring legends like Sir Gawain and the Green Knight, King Arthur and Sleeping Beauty were Grail allegories. Victor Hugo's *Hunchback of Notre Dame* and Mozart's *Magic Flute* were filled with Masonic symbolism and Grail secrets.

'Once you open your eyes to the Holy Grail,' Langdon said, 'you see her everywhere. Paintings. Music. Books. Even in cartoons, theme parks, and popular movies.'

Langdon held up his Mickey Mouse watch and told her that Walt Disney had made it his quiet life's work to pass on the Grail story to future generations. Throughout his entire life, Disney had been hailed as 'the Modern-Day Leonardo da Vinci'. Both men were generations ahead of their times, uniquely gifted artists, members of secret societies and, most notably, avid pranksters. Like Leonardo, Walt Disney loved implanting hidden messages and symbolism in his art. For the trained symbologist, watching an early Disney movie was like being barraged by an avalanche of allusion and metaphor.

Most of Disney's hidden messages dealt with religion, pagan myth and stories of the subjugated goddess. It was no mistake that Disney retold tales like *Cinderella*, *Sleeping Beauty* and *Snow White* – all of which dealt with the incarceration of the sacred feminine. Nor did one need a background in symbolism to understand that Snow White – a princess who fell from grace after partaking of a poisoned apple – was a clear allusion to the downfall of Eve in the Garden of Eden. Or that *Sleeping Beauty*'s Princess Aurora – code-named 'Rose' and hidden deep in the forest to protect her from the clutches of the evil witch – was the Grail story for children.

Despite its corporate image, Disney still had a savvy, playful element among its employees, and their artists still amused themselves by inserting hidden symbolism in Disney products. Langdon would never forget one of his students bringing in a DVD of *The Lion King* and pausing the film to reveal a freeze-frame in which the word SEX was clearly visible, spelled out by floating dust particles over Simba's head. Although Langdon suspected this was more of a cartoonist's sophomoric prank than any kind of enlightened allusion to pagan human sexuality, he had learned not to underestimate Disney's grasp of symbolism. *The Little Mermaid* was a spellbinding tapestry of spiritual symbols so specifically goddess-related that they could not be coincidence.

When Langdon had first seen *The Little Mermaid,* he had actually gasped aloud when he noticed that the painting in Ariel's underwater home was none other than seventeenth-century artist Georges de la Tour's *The Penitent Magdalene* – a famous homage to the banished Mary Magdalene – fitting decor considering the movie turned out to be a ninety-minute collage of blatant symbolic references to the lost sanctity of Isis, Eve, Pisces the fish goddess and, repeatedly, Mary Magdalene. The Little Mermaid's name, Ariel, possessed powerful ties to the sacred feminine and, in the Book of Isaiah, was synonymous with 'the Holy City besieged'. Of course, the Little Mermaid's flowing red hair was certainly no coincidence either.

The clicking of Teabing's crutches approached in the hallway, his pace unusually brisk. When their host entered the study, his expression was stern.

'You'd better explain yourself, Robert,' he said coldly. 'You have not been honest with me.'

62

'I'm being framed, Leigh,' Langdon said, trying to stay calm. *You know me. I wouldn't kill anyone.*

Teabing's tone did not soften. 'Robert, you're on television, for Christ's sake. Did you know you were wanted by the authorities?'

'Yes.'

'Then you abused my trust. I'm astonished you would put me at risk by coming here and asking me to ramble on about the Grail so you could hide out in my home.'

'I didn't kill anyone.'

'Jacques Saunière is dead, and the police say you did it.' Teabing looked saddened. 'Such a contributor to the arts . . .'

'Sir?' The manservant had appeared now, standing behind Teabing in the study doorway, his arms crossed. 'Shall I show them out?'

'Allow me.' Teabing hobbled across the study, unlocked a set of wide glass doors, and swung them open onto a side lawn. 'Please find your car, and leave.'

Sophie did not move. 'We have information about the *clef de voûte. The Priory keystone.*'

Teabing stared at her for several seconds and scoffed derisively. 'A desperate ploy. Robert knows how I've sought it.'

'She's telling the truth,' Langdon said. 'That's why we came to you tonight. To talk to you about the keystone.'

The manservant intervened now. 'Leave, or I shall call the authorities.'

'Leigh,' Langdon whispered, 'we know where it is.'

Teabing's balance seemed to falter a bit.

Rémy now marched stiffly across the room. 'Leave at once! Or I will forcibly—'

'Rémy!' Teabing spun, snapping at his servant. 'Excuse us for a moment.'

The servant's jaw dropped. 'Sir? I must protest. These people are—'

'I'll handle this.' Teabing pointed to the hallway.

After a moment of stunned silence, Rémy skulked out like a banished dog.

In the cool night breeze coming through the open doors, Teabing turned back to Sophie and Langdon, his expression still wary. 'This had better be good. What do you know of the keystone?'

In the thick brush outside Teabing's study, Silas clutched his pistol and gazed through the glass doors. Only moments ago, he had circled the house and seen Langdon and the woman talking in the large study. Before he could move in, a man on crutches entered, yelled at Langdon, threw open the doors, and demanded his guests leave. *Then the woman mentioned the keystone, and everything changed.* Shouts turned to whispers. Moods softened. And the glass doors were quickly closed.

Now, as he huddled in the shadows, Silas peered through the glass. *The keystone is somewhere inside the house.* Silas could feel it.

Staying in the shadows, he inched closer to the glass, eager to hear what was being said. He would give them five minutes. If they did not reveal where they had placed the keystone, Silas would have to enter and persuade them with force.

Inside the study, Langdon could sense their host's bewilderment.

'Grand Master?' Teabing choked, eyeing Sophie. 'Jacques Saunière?'

Sophie nodded, seeing the shock in his eyes.

'But you could not possibly know that!'

'Jacques Saunière was my grandfather.'

Teabing staggered back on his crutches, shooting a glance at Langdon, who nodded. Teabing turned back to Sophie. 'Miss Neveu, I am speechless. If this is true, then I am truly sorry for your loss. I should admit, for my research, I have kept lists of men in Paris whom I thought might be good candidates for involvement in the Priory. Jacques Saunière was on that list along with many others. But Grand Master, you say? It's hard to fathom.' Teabing was silent a moment and then shook his head. 'But it still makes no sense. Even if your grandfather were the Priory Grand Master and created the keystone himself, he would never tell you how to find it. The keystone reveals the pathway to the brotherhood's ultimate treasure. Granddaughter or not, you are not eligible to receive such knowledge.'

'Mr Saunière was dying when he passed on the information,' Langdon said. 'He had limited options.'

'He didn't *need* options,' Teabing argued. 'There exist three *sénéchaux* who also know the secret. That is the beauty of their system. One will rise to Grand Master and they will induct a new *sénéchal* and share the secret of the keystone.'

'I presume you didn't see the entire news broadcast,' Sophie said. 'In addition to my grandfather, *three* other prominent Parisians were murdered today. All in similar ways. All looked like they had been interrogated.'

Teabing's jaw fell. 'And you think they were . . .'

'The *sénéchaux*,' Langdon said.

'But how? A murderer could not possibly learn the identities of *all* four top members of the Priory of Sion! Look at *me*, I have been researching them for decades, and I can't even name *one* Priory member. It seems inconceivable that all three *sénéchaux* and the Grand Master could be discovered and killed in one day.'

'I doubt the information was gathered in a single day,' Sophie said. 'It sounds like a well-planned *décapiter*. It's a technique we use to fight organized crime syndicates. If DCPJ wants to move on a certain group, they will silently listen and watch for months, identify all the main players, and then move in and take them all at the same moment. Decapitation. With no leadership, the group falls into chaos and divulges other information. It's possible someone patiently watched the Priory and then attacked, hoping the top people would reveal the location of the keystone.'

Teabing looked unconvinced. 'But the brothers would never talk. They are sworn to secrecy. Even in the face of death.'

'Exactly,' Langdon said. 'Meaning, if they never divulged the secret, *and* they were killed . . .'

Teabing gasped. 'Then the location of the keystone would be lost for ever!'

'And with it,' Langdon said, 'the location of the Holy Grail.'

Teabing's body seemed to sway with the weight of Langdon's words. Then, as if too tired to stand another moment, he flopped in a chair and stared out the window.

Sophie walked over, her voice soft. 'Considering my grandfather's predicament, it seems possible that in total desperation he tried to pass the secret on to someone outside the brotherhood. Someone he thought he could trust. Someone in his family.'

Teabing was pale. 'But someone capable of such an attack . . . of discovering so much about the brotherhood . . .' He paused, radiating a new fear. 'It could only be one force. This kind of infiltration could only have come from the Priory's oldest enemy.'

Langdon glanced up. 'The Church.'

'Who else? Rome has been seeking the Grail for centuries.'

Sophie was sceptical. 'You think the *Church* killed my grandfather?'

Teabing replied, 'It would not be the first time in history the Church has killed to protect itself. The documents that accompany the Holy Grail are explosive, and the Church has wanted to destroy them for years.'

Langdon was having trouble buying Teabing's premise that the Church would blatantly murder people to obtain these documents. Having met the new Pope and many of the cardinals, Langdon knew they were deeply spiritual men who would never condone assassination. *Regardless of the stakes.*

Sophie seemed to be having similar thoughts. 'Isn't it possible that these Priory members were murdered by someone *outside* the Church? Someone who didn't understand what the Grail really is? The Cup of Christ, after all, would be quite an enticing treasure. Certainly treasure hunters have killed for less.'

'In my experience,' Teabing said, 'men go to far greater lengths to avoid what they fear than to obtain what they desire. I sense a desperation in this assault on the Priory.'

'Leigh,' Langdon said, 'the argument is paradoxical. Why would members of the Catholic clergy *murder* Priory members in an effort to find and destroy documents they believe are false testimony anyway?'

Teabing chuckled. 'The ivory towers of Harvard have made you soft, Robert. Yes, the clergy in Rome are blessed with potent faith, and because of this, their beliefs can weather any storm, including documents that contradict everything they hold dear. But what about the rest of the world? What about those who are not blessed with absolute certainty? What about those who look at the cruelty in the world and say, where is God today? Those who look at Church scandals and ask, who *are* these men who claim to speak the truth about Christ and yet lie to cover up the sexual abuse of children by their own priests?' Teabing paused. 'What happens to those people, Robert, if persuasive scientific evidence comes out that the Church's version of the Christ story is inaccurate, and that the greatest story ever told is, in fact, the greatest story ever *sold?*'

Langdon did not respond.

'I'll tell you what happens if the documents get out,' Teabing said. 'The Vatican faces a crisis of faith unprecedented in its two-millennia history.'

After a long silence, Sophie said, 'But if it *is* the Church who is responsible for this attack, why would they act now? After all these years? The Priory keeps the Sangreal documents hidden. They pose no immediate threat to the Church.'

Teabing heaved an ominous sigh and glanced at Langdon. 'Robert, I assume you are familiar with the Priory's final charge?'

Langdon felt his breath catch at the thought. 'I am.'

'Miss Neveu,' Teabing said, 'the Church and the Priory have had a tacit understanding for years. That is, the Church does not attack the Priory, and the Priory keeps the Sangreal documents hidden.' He paused. 'However, part of the Priory history has always included a plan to unveil the secret. With the arrival of a specific date in history, the brotherhood plans to break the silence and carry out its ultimate triumph by unveiling the Sangreal documents to the world and shouting the true story of Jesus Christ from the mountaintops.'

Sophie stared at Teabing in silence. Finally, she too sat down. 'And you think that date is approaching? And the Church knows it?'

'A speculation,' Teabing said, 'but it would certainly provide the Church motivation for an all-out attack to find the documents before it was too late.'

Langdon had the uneasy feeling that Teabing was making good sense. 'Do you think the Church would actually be capable of uncovering hard evidence of the Priory's date?'

'Why not – if we're assuming the Church was able to uncover the identities of the Priory members, then certainly they could have learned of their plans. And even if they don't have the exact date, their superstitions may be getting the better of them.'

'Superstitions?' Sophie asked.

'In terms of prophecy,' Teabing said, 'we are currently in an epoch of enormous change. The millennium has recently passed, and with it has ended the two-thousand-year-long astrological Age of Pisces – the fish, which is also the sign of Jesus. As any astrological symbologist will tell you, the Piscean ideal believes that man must be *told* what to do by higher powers because man is incapable of thinking for himself. Hence it has been a time of fervent religion. Now, however, we are entering the Age of Aquarius – the water bearer – whose ideals claim that man will learn the *truth* and be able to think for himself. The ideological shift is enormous, and it is occurring right now.'

Langdon felt a shiver. Astrological prophecy never held much interest or credibility for him, but he knew there were those in the Church who followed it very closely. 'The Church calls this transitional period the End of Days.'

Sophie looked skeptical. 'As in the end of the world? The Apocalypse?'

'No.' Langdon replied. 'That's a common misconception. Many religions speak of the End of Days. It refers not to the end of the world, but rather the end of our current age – Pisces, which began at the time of Christ's birth, spanned two thousand years, and waned with the passing of the millennium. Now that we've passed into the Age of Aquarius, the End of Days has arrived.'

'Many Grail historians,' Teabing added, 'believe that *if* the Priory is indeed planning to release this truth, *this* point in history would be a symbolically apt time. Most Priory academics, myself included, anticipated the brotherhood's release would coincide precisely with the millennium. Obviously, it did not. Admittedly, the Roman calendar does not mesh perfectly with astrological markers, so there is some grey area in the prediction. Whether the Church now has inside information that an exact date is looming, or whether they are just getting nervous on account of astrological prophecy, I don't know. Anyway, it's immaterial. Either scenario explains how the Church might be motivated to launch a preemptive attack against the Priory.' Teabing frowned. 'And believe me, if the Church finds the Holy Grail, they will destroy it. The documents and the relics of the blessed Mary Magdalene as well.' His eyes grew heavy. 'Then, my dear, with the Sangreal documents gone, all evidence will be lost. The Church will have won their age-old war to rewrite history. The past will be erased for ever.'

Slowly, Sophie pulled the cruciform key from her sweater pocket and held it out to Teabing.

Teabing took the key and studied it. 'My goodness. The Priory seal. Where did you get this?'

'My grandfather gave it to me tonight before he died.'

Teabing ran his fingers across the cruciform. 'A key to a church?'

She drew a deep breath. 'This key provides access to the keystone.'

Teabing's head snapped up, his face wild with disbelief. 'Impossible! What church did I miss? I've searched every church in France!'

'It's not in a church,' Sophie said. 'It's in a Swiss depository bank.'

Teabing's look of excitement waned. 'The keystone is in a bank?'

'A vault,' Langdon offered.

'A *bank* vault?' Teabing shook his head violently. 'That's impossible. The keystone is supposed to be hidden beneath the sign of the Rose.'

'It is,' Langdon said. 'It was stored in a rosewood box inlaid with a five-petal Rose.'

Teabing looked thunderstruck. 'You've *seen* the keystone?'

Sophie nodded. 'We visited the bank.'

Teabing came over to them, his eyes wild with fear. 'My friends, we must do something. The keystone is in danger! We have a duty to protect it. What if there are other keys? Perhaps stolen from the murdered *sénéchaux*? If the Church can gain access to the bank as you have—'

'Then they will be too late,' Sophie said. 'We removed the keystone.'

'What! You removed the keystone from its hiding place?'

'Don't worry,' Langdon said. 'The keystone is well hidden.'

'*Extremely* well hidden, I hope!'

'Actually,' Langdon said, unable to hide his grin, 'that depends on how often you dust under your couch.'

The wind outside Château Villette had picked up, and Silas's robe danced in the breeze as he crouched near the window. Although he had been unable to hear much of the conversation, the word *keystone* had sifted through the glass on numerous occasions.

It is inside.

The Teacher's words were fresh in his mind. *Enter Château Villette. Take the keystone. Hurt no one.*

Now, Langdon and the others had adjourned suddenly to another room, extinguishing the study lights as they went. Feeling like a panther stalking prey, Silas crept to the glass doors. Finding them unlocked, he slipped inside and closed the doors silently behind him. He could hear muffled voices from another room. Silas pulled the pistol from his pocket, turned off the safety and inched down the hallway.

63

Lieutenant Collet stood alone at the foot of Leigh Teabing's driveway and gazed up at the massive house. *Isolated. Dark. Good ground cover.* Collet watched his half-dozen agents spreading silently out along the length of the fence. They could be over it and have the house surrounded in a matter of minutes. Langdon could not have chosen a more ideal spot for Collet's men to make a surprise assault.

Collet was about to call Fache himself when at last his phone rang.

Fache sounded not nearly as pleased with the developments as Collet would have imagined. 'Why didn't someone tell me we had a lead on Langdon?'

'You were on a phone call and—'

'Where exactly are you, Lieutenant Collet?'

Collet gave him the address. 'The estate belongs to a British national named Teabing. Langdon drove a fair distance to get here, and the vehicle is inside the security gate, with no signs of forced entry, so chances are good that Langdon knows the occupant.'

'I'm coming out,' Fache said. 'Don't make a move. I'll handle this personally.'

Collet's jaw dropped. 'But Captain, you're twenty minutes away! We should act immediately. I have him staked out. I'm with eight men total. Four of us have field rifles and the others have sidearms.'

'Wait for me.'

'Captain, what if Langdon has a hostage in there? What if he sees us and decides to leave on foot? We need to move *now!* My men are in position and ready to go.'

'Lieutenant Collet, you will wait for me to arrive before taking action. That is an order.' Fache hung up.

Stunned, Lieutenant Collet switched off his phone. *Why the hell is Fache asking me to wait?* Collet knew the answer. Fache, though famous for his instinct, was notorious for his pride. *Fache wants credit for the arrest.* After putting the American's face all over the television, Fache wanted to be sure his own face got equal time. Collet's job was simply to hold down the fort until the boss showed up to save the day.

As he stood there, Collet flashed on a second possible explanation for this delay. *Damage control.* In law enforcement, hesitating to arrest a fugitive only occurred when uncertainty had arisen regarding the suspect's guilt. *Is Fache having second thoughts that Langdon is the right man?* The thought was frightening. Captain Fache had gone out on a limb tonight to arrest Robert Langdon – *surveillance cachée,* Interpol, and now television. Not even the great Bezu Fache would survive the political fallout if he had mistakenly splashed a prominent American's face all over French television, claiming he was a murderer. If Fache now realized he'd made a mistake, then it made perfect sense that he would tell Collet not to make a move. The last thing Fache needed was for Collet to storm an innocent Brit's private estate and take Langdon at gunpoint.

Moreover, Collet realized, if Langdon were innocent, it explained one of this case's strangest paradoxes: Why had Sophie Neveu, the *granddaughter* of the victim, helped the alleged killer escape? Unless Sophie knew Langdon was falsely charged. Fache had posited all kinds of explanations tonight to explain Sophie's odd behaviour, including that Sophie, as Saunière's sole heir, had persuaded her secret lover Robert Langdon to kill off Saunière for the inheritance money. Saunière, if he had suspected this, might have left the police the message *P.S. Find Robert Langdon.* Collet was fairly certain something else was going on here. Sophie Neveu seemed of far too solid a character to be mixed up in something that sordid.

'Lieutenant?' One of the field agents came running over. 'We found a car.'

Collet followed the agent about fifty yards past the driveway. The agent pointed to a wide shoulder on the opposite side of the road. There, parked in the brush, almost out of sight, was a black Audi. It had rental plates. Collet felt the hood. Still warm. Hot even.

'That must be how Langdon got here,' Collet said. 'Call the rental company. Find out if it's stolen.'

'Yes, sir.'

Another agent waved Collet back over in the direction of the fence. 'Lieutenant, have a look at this.' He handed Collet a pair of night vision binoculars. 'The grove of trees near the top of the driveway.'

Collet aimed the binoculars up the hill and adjusted the image intensifier dials. Slowly, the greenish shapes came into focus. He located the curve of the driveway and slowly followed it up, reaching the grove of trees. All he could do was stare. There, shrouded in the greenery, was an armoured truck. A truck identical to the one Collet had permitted to leave the Depository Bank of Zurich earlier tonight. He prayed this was some kind of bizarre coincidence, but he knew it could not be.

'It seems obvious,' the agent said, 'that this truck is how Langdon and Neveu got away from the bank.'

Collet was speechless. He thought of the armoured truck driver he had stopped at the roadblock. The Rolex. His impatience to leave. *I never checked the cargo hold.*

Incredulous, Collet realized that someone in the bank had actually lied to DCPJ about Langdon and Sophie's whereabouts and then helped them escape. *But who? And why?* Collet wondered if maybe *this* were the reason Fache had told him not to take action yet. Maybe Fache realized there were more people involved tonight than just Langdon and Sophie. *And if Langdon and Neveu arrived in the armoured truck, then who drove the Audi?*

Hundreds of miles to the south, a chartered Beechcraft Baron 58 raced northward over the Tyrrhenian Sea. Despite calm skies, Bishop Aringarosa clutched an airsickness bag, certain he could be ill at any moment. His conversation with Paris had not at all been what he had imagined.

Alone in the small cabin, Aringarosa twisted the gold ring on his finger and tried to ease his overwhelming sense of fear and desperation. *Everything in Paris has gone terribly wrong.* Closing his eyes, Aringarosa said a prayer that Bezu Fache would have the means to fix it.

64

Teabing sat on the divan, cradling the wooden box on his lap and admiring the lid's intricate inlaid Rose. *Tonight has become the strangest and most magical night of my life.*

'Lift the lid,' Sophie whispered, standing over him, beside Langdon.

Teabing smiled. *Do not rush me.* Having spent over a decade searching for this keystone, he wanted to savour every millisecond of this moment. He ran a palm across the wooden lid, feeling the texture of the inlaid flower.

'The Rose,' he whispered. *The Rose is Magdalene is the Holy Grail. The Rose is the compass that guides the way.* Teabing felt foolish. For years he had travelled to cathedrals and churches all over France, paying for special access, examining hundreds of archways beneath rose windows, searching for an encrypted keystone. *La clef de voûte – a stone key beneath the sign of the Rose.*

Teabing slowly unlatched the lid and raised it.

As his eyes finally gazed upon the contents, he knew in an instant it could only be the keystone. He was staring at a stone cylinder, crafted of interconnecting lettered dials. The device seemed surprisingly familiar to him.

'Designed from Da Vinci's diaries,' Sophie said. 'My grandfather made them as a hobby.'

Of course, Teabing realized. He had seen the sketches and blueprints. *The key to finding the Holy Grail lies inside this stone.* Teabing lifted the heavy cryptex from the box, holding it gently. Although he had no idea how to open the cylinder, he sensed his own destiny lay inside. In moments of failure, Teabing had questioned whether his life's quest would ever be rewarded. Now those doubts were gone for ever. He could hear the ancient words . . . the foundation of the Grail legend:

Vous ne trouvez pas le Saint-Graal, c'est le Saint-Graal qui vous trouve.

You do not find the Grail, the Grail finds you.

And tonight, incredibly, the key to finding the Holy Grail had walked right through his front door.

*

While Sophie and Teabing sat with the cryptex and talked about the vinegar, the dials and what the password might be, Langdon carried the rosewood box across the room to a well-lit table to get a better look at it. Something Teabing had just said was now running through Langdon's mind.

The key to the Grail is hidden beneath the sign of the Rose.

Langdon held the wooden box up to the light and examined the inlaid symbol of the Rose. Although his familiarity with art did not include woodworking or inlaid furniture, he had just recalled the famous tiled ceiling of the Spanish monastery outside of Madrid, where, three centuries after its construction, the ceiling tiles began to fall out, revealing sacred texts scrawled by monks on the plaster beneath.

Langdon looked again at the Rose.

Beneath the Rose.

Sub Rosa.

Secret.

A bump in the hallway behind him made Langdon turn. He saw nothing but shadows. Teabing's manservant most likely had passed through. Langdon turned back to the box. He ran his finger over the smooth edge of the inlay, wondering if he could pry the Rose out, but the craftsmanship was perfect. He doubted even a razor blade could fit in between the inlaid Rose and the carefully carved depression into which it was seated.

Opening the box, he examined the inside of the lid. It was smooth. As he shifted its position, though, the light caught what appeared to be a small hole on the underside of the lid, positioned in the exact centre. Langdon closed the lid and examined the inlaid symbol from the top. No hole.

It doesn't pass through.

Setting the box on the table, he looked around the room and spied a stack of papers with a paper clip on it. Borrowing the clip, he returned to the box, opened it, and studied the hole again. Carefully, he unbent the paper clip and inserted one end into the hole. He gave a gentle push. It took almost no effort. He heard something clatter quietly onto the table. Langdon closed the lid to look. It was a small piece of wood, like a puzzle piece. The wooden Rose had popped out of the lid and fallen onto the desk.

Speechless, Langdon stared at the bare spot on the lid where the Rose had been. There, engraved in the wood, written in an immaculate hand, were four lines of text in a language he had never seen.

The characters look vaguely Semitic, Langdon thought to himself, *and yet I don't recognize the language!*

A sudden movement behind him caught his attention. Out of nowhere, a crushing blow to the head knocked Langdon to his knees.

As he fell, he thought for a moment he saw a pale ghost hovering over him, clutching a gun. Then everything went black.

65

Sophie Neveu, despite working in law enforcement, had never found herself at gunpoint until tonight. Almost inconceivably, the gun into which she was now staring was clutched in the pale hand of an enormous albino with long white hair. He looked at her with red eyes that radiated a frightening, disembodied quality. Dressed in a wool robe with a rope tie, he resembled a medieval cleric. Sophie could not imagine who he was, and yet she was feeling a sudden newfound respect for Teabing's suspicions that the Church was behind this.

'You know what I have come for,' the monk said, his voice hollow.

Sophie and Teabing were seated on the divan, arms raised as their attacker had commanded. Langdon lay groaning on the floor. The monk's eyes fell immediately to the keystone on Teabing's lap.

Teabing's tone was defiant. 'You will not be able to open it.'

'My Teacher is very wise,' the monk replied, inching closer, the gun shifting between Teabing and Sophie.

Sophie wondered where Teabing's manservant was. *Didn't he hear Robert fall?*

'Who is your teacher?' Teabing asked. 'Perhaps we can make a financial arrangement.'

'The Grail is priceless.' He moved closer.

'You're bleeding,' Teabing noted calmly, nodding to the monk's right ankle where a trickle of blood had run down his leg. 'And you're limping.'

'As do you,' the monk replied, motioning to the metal crutches propped beside Teabing. 'Now, hand me the keystone.'

'You know of the keystone?' Teabing said, sounding surprised.

'Never mind what I know. Stand up slowly, and give it to me.'

'Standing is difficult for me.'

'Precisely. I would prefer nobody attempt any quick moves.'

Teabing slipped his right hand through one of his crutches and grasped the keystone in his left. Lurching to his feet, he stood erect, palming the heavy cylinder in his left hand and leaning unsteadily on his crutch with his right.

The monk closed to within a few feet, keeping the gun aimed directly at

Teabing's head. Sophie watched, feeling helpless as the monk reached out to take the cylinder.

'You will not succeed,' Teabing said. 'Only the worthy can unlock this stone.'

God alone judges the worthy, Silas thought.

'It's quite heavy,' the man on crutches said, his arm wavering now. 'If you don't take it soon, I'm afraid I shall drop it!' He swayed perilously.

Silas stepped quickly forward to take the stone, and as he did, the man on crutches lost his balance. The crutch slid out from under him, and he began to topple sideways to his right. *No!* Silas lunged to save the stone, lowering his weapon in the process. But the keystone was moving away from him now. As the man fell to his right, his left hand swung backward, and the cylinder tumbled from his palm onto the couch. At the same instant, the metal crutch that had been sliding out from under the man seemed to accelerate, cutting a wide arc through the air toward Silas's leg.

Splinters of pain tore up Silas's body as the crutch made perfect contact with his *cilice*, crushing the barbs into his already raw flesh. Buckling, Silas crumpled to his knees, causing the belt to cut deeper still. The pistol discharged with a deafening roar, the bullet burying itself harmlessly in the floorboards as Silas fell. Before he could raise the gun and fire again, the woman's foot caught him square beneath the jaw.

At the bottom of the driveway, Collet heard the gunshot. The muffled pop sent panic through his veins. With Fache on the way, Collet had already relinquished any hopes of claiming personal credit for finding Langdon tonight. But Collet would be damned if Fache's ego landed him in front of a Ministerial Review Board for negligent police procedure.

A weapon was discharged inside a private home! And you waited at the bottom of the driveway?

Collet knew the opportunity for a stealth approach had long since passed. He also knew if he stood idly by for another second, his entire career would be history by morning. Eyeing the estate's iron gate, he made his decision.

'Tie on, and pull it down.'

In the distant recesses of his groggy mind, Robert Langdon had heard the gunshot. He'd also heard a scream of pain. His own? A jackhammer was boring a hole into the back of his cranium. Somewhere nearby, people were talking.

'Where the devil were you?' Teabing was yelling.

The manservant hurried in. 'What happened? Oh my God! Who is that? I'll call the police!'

'Bloody hell! Don't call the police. Make yourself useful and get us something with which to restrain this monster.'

'And some ice!' Sophie called after him.

Langdon drifted out again. More voices. Movement. Now he was seated on the divan. Sophie was holding an ice pack to his head. His skull ached. As Langdon's vision finally began to clear, he found himself staring at a body on the floor. *Am I hallucinating?* The massive body of an albino monk lay bound and gagged with duct tape. His chin was split open, and the robe over his right thigh was soaked with blood. He too appeared to be just now coming to.

Langdon turned to Sophie. 'Who is that? What . . . happened?'

Teabing hobbled over. 'You were rescued by a knight brandishing an Excalibur made by Acme Orthopaedic.'

Huh? Langdon tried to sit up.

Sophie's touch was shaken but tender. 'Just give yourself a minute, Robert.'

'I fear,' Teabing said, 'that I've just demonstrated for your lady friend the unfortunate benefit of my condition. It seems everyone underestimates you.'

From his seat on the divan, Langdon gazed down at the monk and tried to imagine what had happened.

'He was wearing a *cilice*,' Teabing explained.

'A what?'

Teabing pointed to a bloody strip of barbed leather that lay on the floor. 'A discipline belt. He wore it on his thigh. I took careful aim.'

Langdon rubbed his head. He knew of discipline belts. 'But how . . . did you know?'

Teabing grinned. 'Christianity is my field of study, Robert, and there are certain sects who wear their hearts on their sleeves.' He pointed his crutch at the blood soaking through the monk's cloak. 'As it were.'

'Opus Dei,' Langdon whispered, recalling recent media coverage of several prominent Boston businessmen who were members of Opus Dei. Apprehensive coworkers had falsely and publicly accused the men of wearing *cilice* belts beneath their three-piece suits. In fact, the three men did no such thing. Like many members of Opus Dei, these businessmen were at the 'supernumerary' stage and practised no corporal mortification at all. They were devout Catholics, caring fathers to their children, and deeply dedicated members of the community. Not surprisingly, the media spotlighted their spiritual commitment only briefly before moving on to the shock value of the sect's more stringent 'numerary' members . . . members like the monk now lying on the floor before Langdon.

Teabing was looking closely at the bloody belt. 'But why would Opus Dei be trying to find the Holy Grail?'

Langdon was too groggy to consider it.

'Robert,' Sophie said, walking to the wooden box. 'What's this?' She was holding the small Rose inlay he had removed from the lid.

'It covered an engraving on the box. I think the text might tell us how to open the keystone.'

Before Sophie and Teabing could respond, a sea of blue police lights and sirens erupted at the bottom of the hill and began snaking up the half-mile driveway.

Teabing frowned. 'My friends, it seems we have a decision to make. And we'd better make it fast.'

66

Collet and his agents burst through the front door of Sir Leigh Teabing's estate with their guns drawn. Fanning out, they began searching all the rooms on the first level. They found a bullet hole in the drawing room floor, signs of a struggle, a small amount of blood, a strange, barbed leather belt and a partially used roll of duct tape. The entire level seemed deserted.

Just as Collet was about to divide his men to search the basement and grounds behind the house, he heard voices on the level above them.

'They're upstairs!'

Rushing up the wide staircase, Collet and his men moved room by room through the huge home, securing darkened bedrooms and hallways as they closed in on the sounds of voices. The sound seemed to be coming from the last bedroom on an exceptionally long hallway. The agents inched down the corridor, sealing off alternate exits.

As they neared the final bedroom, Collet could see the door was wide open. The voices had stopped suddenly, and had been replaced by an odd rumbling, like an engine.

Sidearm raised, Collet gave the signal. Reaching silently around the door frame, he found the light switch and flicked it on. Spinning into the room with men pouring in after him, Collet shouted and aimed his weapon at . . . nothing.

An empty guest bedroom. Pristine.

The rumbling sounds of an automobile engine poured from a black electronic panel on the wall beside the bed. Collet had seen these elsewhere in the house. Some kind of intercom system. He raced over. The panel had about a dozen labelled buttons:

STUDY . . . KITCHEN . . . LAUNDRY . . . CELLAR . . .

So where the hell do I hear a car?

MASTER BEDROOM . . . SUN ROOM . . . BARN . . . LIBRARY . . .

Barn! Collet was downstairs in seconds, running toward the back door, grabbing one of his agents on the way. The men crossed the rear lawn and arrived breathless at the front of a weathered grey barn. Even before they entered, Collet could hear the fading sounds of a car engine. He drew his weapon, rushed in, and flicked on the lights.

The right side of the barn was a rudimentary workshop – lawnmowers, automotive tools, gardening supplies. A familiar intercom panel hung on the wall nearby. One of its buttons was flipped down, transmitting.

GUEST BEDROOM II.

Collet wheeled, anger brimming. *They lured us upstairs with the intercom!* Searching the other side of the barn, he found a long line of horse stalls. No horses. Apparently the owner preferred a different kind of horsepower; the stalls had been converted into an impressive automotive parking facility. The collection was astonishing – a black Ferrari, a pristine Rolls-Royce, an antique Aston Martin sports coupé, a vintage Porsche 356.

The last stall was empty.

Collet ran over and saw oil stains on the stall floor. *They can't get off the compound.* The driveway and gate were barricaded with two patrol cars to prevent this very situation.

'Sir?' The agent pointed down the length of the stalls.

The barn's rear slider was wide open, giving way to a dark, muddy slope of rugged fields that stretched out into the night behind the barn. Collet ran to the door, trying to see out into the darkness. All he could make out was the faint shadow of a forest in the distance. No headlights. This wooded valley was probably crisscrossed by dozens of unmapped fire roads and hunting trails, but Collet was confident his quarry would never make the woods. 'Get some men spread out down there. They're probably already stuck somewhere nearby. These fancy sports cars can't handle terrain.'

'Um, sir?' The agent pointed to a nearby pegboard on which hung several sets of keys. The labels above the keys bore familiar names.

DAIMLER . . . ROLLS-ROYCE . . . ASTON MARTIN . . .
PORSCHE . . .

The last peg was empty.

When Collet read the label above the empty peg, he knew he was in trouble.

67

The Range Rover was Java Black Pearl, four-wheel drive, standard transmission, with high-strength polypropylene lamps, rear light cluster fittings and the steering wheel on the right.

Langdon was pleased he was not driving.

Teabing's manservant Rémy, on orders from his master, was doing an impressive job of manoeuvring the vehicle across the moonlit fields behind Château Villette. With no headlights, he had crossed an open knoll and was now descending a long slope, moving farther away from the estate. He seemed to be heading toward a jagged silhouette of wooded land in the distance.

Langdon, cradling the keystone, turned in the passenger seat and eyed Teabing and Sophie in the back seat.

'How's your head, Robert?' Sophie asked, sounding concerned.

Langdon forced a pained smile. 'Better, thanks.' It was killing him.

Beside her, Teabing glanced over his shoulder at the bound and gagged monk lying in the cramped luggage area behind the back seat. Teabing had the monk's gun on his lap and looked like an old photo of a British safari chap posing over his kill.

'So glad you popped in this evening, Robert,' Teabing said, grinning as if he were having fun for the first time in years.

'Sorry to get you involved in this, Leigh.'

'Oh, please, I've waited my entire life to be involved.' Teabing looked past Langdon out the windshield at the shadow of a long hedgerow. He tapped Rémy on the shoulder from behind. 'Remember, no brake lights. Use the emergency brake if you need it. I want to get into the woods a bit. No reason to risk them seeing us from the house.'

Rémy coasted to a crawl and guided the Range Rover through an opening in the hedge. As the vehicle lurched onto an overgrown pathway, almost immediately the trees overhead blotted out the moonlight.

I can't see a thing, Langdon thought, straining to distinguish any shapes at all in front of them. It was pitch black. Branches rubbed against the left side of the vehicle, and Rémy corrected in the other direction. Keeping the wheel more or less straight now, he inched ahead about thirty yards.

'You're doing beautifully, Rémy,' Teabing said. 'That should be far enough. Robert, if you could press that little blue button just below the vent there. See it?'

Langdon found the button and pressed it.

A muted yellow glow fanned out across the path in front of them, revealing thick underbrush on either side of the pathway. *Fog lights*, Langdon realized. They gave off just enough light to keep them on the path, and yet they were deep enough into the woods now that the lights would not give them away.

'Well, Rémy,' Teabing chimed happily. 'The lights are on. Our lives are in your hands.'

'Where are we going?' Sophie asked.

'This trail continues about three kilometers into the forest,' Teabing said. 'Cutting across the estate and then arching north. Provided we don't hit any standing water or fallen trees, we shall emerge unscathed on the shoulder of highway five.'

Unscathed. Langdon's head begged to differ. He turned his eyes down to his own lap, where the keystone was safely stowed in its wooden box. The inlaid Rose on the lid was back in place, and although his head felt muddled, Langdon was eager to remove the inlay again and examine the engraving beneath more closely. He unlatched the lid and began to raise it when Teabing laid a hand on his shoulder from behind.

'Patience, Robert,' Teabing said. 'It's bumpy and dark. God save us if we break anything. If you didn't recognize the language in the light, you won't do any better in the dark. Let's focus on getting away in one piece, shall we? There will be time for that very soon.'

Langdon knew Teabing was right. With a nod, he relatched the box.

The monk in the back was moaning now, struggling against his trusses. Suddenly, he began kicking wildly.

Teabing spun around and aimed the pistol over the seat. 'I can't imagine your complaint, sir. You trespassed in my home and planted a nasty welt on the skull of a dear friend. I would be well within my rights to shoot you right now and leave you to rot in the woods.'

The monk fell silent.

'Are you sure we should have brought him?' Langdon asked.

'Bloody well positive!' Teabing exclaimed. 'You're wanted for murder, Robert. This scoundrel is your ticket to freedom. The police apparently want you badly enough to have tailed you to my home.'

'My fault,' Sophie said. 'The armoured car probably had a transmitter.'

'Not the point,' Teabing said. 'I'm not surprised the *police* found you, but I *am* surprised that this Opus Dei character found you. From all you've told me, I can't imagine how this man could have tailed you to my home unless he had a contact either within the Judicial Police or within the Zurich Depository.'

Langdon considered it. Bezu Fache certainly seemed intent on finding a scapegoat for tonight's murders. And Vernet had turned on them rather suddenly, although considering Langdon was being charged with four murders, the banker's change of heart seemed understandable.

'This monk is not working alone, Robert,' Teabing said, 'and until you learn *who* is behind all this, you both are in danger. The good news, my friend, is that you are now in the position of power. This monster behind me holds that information, and whoever is pulling his strings has got to be quite nervous right now.'

Rémy was picking up speed, getting comfortable with the trail. They splashed through some water, climbed a small rise, and began descending again.

'Robert, could you be so kind as to hand me that phone?' Teabing pointed to the car phone on the dash. Langdon handed it back, and Teabing dialled a number. He waited for a very long time before someone answered. 'Richard? Did I wake you? Of course, I did. Silly question. I'm sorry. I have a small problem. I'm feeling a bit off. Rémy and I need to pop up to the Isles for my treatments. Well, right away, actually. Sorry for the short notice. Can you have Elizabeth ready in about twenty minutes? I know, do the best you can. See you shortly.' He hung up.

'Elizabeth?' Langdon said.

'My plane. She cost me a Queen's ransom.'

Langdon turned full around and looked at him.

'What?' Teabing demanded. 'You two can't expect to stay in France with the entire Judicial Police after you. London will be much safer.'

Sophie had turned to Teabing as well. 'You think we should leave the country?'

'My friends, I am far more influential in the civilized world than here in France. Furthermore, the Grail is believed to be in Great Britain. If we unlock the keystone, I am certain we will discover a map that indicates we have moved in the proper direction.'

'You're running a big risk,' Sophie said, 'by helping us. You won't make any friends with the French police.'

Teabing gave a wave of disgust. 'I am finished with France. I moved here to find the keystone. That work is now done. I shan't care if I ever again see Château Villette.'

Sophie sounded uncertain. 'How will we get through airport security?'

Teabing chuckled. 'I fly from Le Bourget – an executive airfield not far from here. French doctors make me nervous, so every fortnight, I fly north to take my treatments in England. I pay for certain special privi-leges at both ends. Once we're airborne, you can make a decision as to whether or not you'd like someone from the US Embassy to meet us.'

Langdon suddenly didn't want anything to do with the embassy. All he could think of was the keystone, the inscription and whether it would all lead to the Grail. He wondered if Teabing was right about Britain. Admittedly most modern legends placed the Grail somewhere in the

United Kingdom. Even King Arthur's mythical, Grail-rich Isle of Avalon was now believed to be none other than Glastonbury, England. Wherever the Grail lay, Langdon never imagined he would actually be looking for it. *The Sangreal documents. The true history of Jesus Christ. The tomb of Mary Magdalene.* He suddenly felt as if he were living in some kind of limbo tonight . . . a bubble where the real world could not reach him.

'Sir?' Rémy said. 'Are you truly thinking of returning to England for good?'

'Rémy, you needn't worry,' Teabing assured. 'Just because I am returning to the Queen's realm does not mean I intend to subject my palate to bangers and mash for the rest of my days. I expect you will join me there permanently. I'm planning to buy a splendid villa in Devon, and we'll have all your things shipped out immediately. An adventure, Rémy. I say, an adventure!'

Langdon had to smile. As Teabing railed on about his plans for a triumphant return to Britain, Langdon felt himself caught up in the man's infectious enthusiasm.

Gazing absently out the window, Langdon watched the woods passing by, ghostly pale in the yellow blush of the fog lights. The side mirror was tipped inward, brushed askew by branches, and Langdon saw the reflection of Sophie sitting quietly in the back seat. He watched her for a long while and felt an unexpected upwelling of contentment. Despite his troubles tonight, Langdon was thankful to have landed in such good company.

After several minutes, as if suddenly sensing his eyes on her, Sophie leaned forward and put her hands on his shoulders, giving him a quick rub. 'You okay?'

'Yeah,' Langdon said. 'Somehow.'

Sophie sat back in her seat, and Langdon saw a quiet smile cross her lips. He realized that he too was now grinning.

Wedged in the back of the Range Rover, Silas could barely breathe. His arms were wrenched backward and heavily lashed to his ankles with kitchen twine and duct tape. Every bump in the road sent pain shooting through his twisted shoulders. At least his captors had removed the *cilice.* Unable to inhale through the strip of tape over his mouth, he could only breathe through his nostrils, which were slowly clogging up due to the dusty rear cargo area into which he had been crammed. He began coughing.

'I think he's choking,' the French driver said, sounding concerned.

The British man who had struck Silas with his crutch now turned and peered over the seat, frowning coldly at Silas. 'Fortunately for you, we British judge man's civility not by his compassion for his friends, but by his compassion for his enemies.' The Brit reached down and grabbed the duct tape on Silas's mouth. In one fast motion, he tore it off.

Silas felt as if his lips had just caught fire, but the air pouring into his lungs was sent from God.

'Whom do you work for?' the British man demanded.

'I do the work of God,' Silas spat back through the pain in his jaw where the woman had kicked him.

'You belong to Opus Dei,' the man said. It was not a question.

'You know nothing of who I am.'

'Why does Opus Dei want the keystone?'

Silas had no intention of answering. The keystone was the link to the Holy Grail, and the Holy Grail was the key to protecting the faith.

I do the work of God. The Way is in peril.

Now, in the Range Rover, struggling against his bonds, Silas feared he had failed the Teacher and the bishop for ever. He had no way even to contact them and tell them the terrible turn of events. *My captors have the keystone! They will reach the Grail before we do!* In the stifling darkness, Silas prayed. He let the pain of his body fuel his supplications.

A miracle, Lord. I need a miracle. Silas had no way of knowing that hours from now, he would get one.

'Robert?' Sophie was still watching him. 'A funny look just crossed your face.'

Langdon glanced back at her, realizing his jaw was firmly set and his heart was racing. An incredible notion had just occurred to him. *Could it really be that simple an explanation?* 'I need to use your cell phone, Sophie.'

'Now?'

'I think I just figured something out.'

'What?'

'I'll tell you in a minute. I need your phone.'

Sophie looked wary. 'I doubt Fache is tracing, but keep it under a minute just in case.' She gave him her phone.

'How do I dial the States?'

'You need to reverse the charges. My service doesn't cover transatlantic.'

Langdon dialled zero, knowing that the next sixty seconds might answer a question that had been puzzling him all night.

68

New York editor Jonas Faukman had just climbed into bed for the night when the telephone rang. *A little late for callers,* he grumbled, picking up the receiver.

An operator's voice asked him, 'Will you accept charges for a collect call from Robert Langdon?'

Puzzled, Jonas turned on the light. 'Uh . . . sure, okay.'

The line clicked. 'Jonas?'

'Robert? You wake me up *and* you charge me for it?'

'Jonas, forgive me,' Langdon said. 'I'll keep this very short. I really need to know. The manuscript I gave you. Have you—'

'Robert, I'm sorry, I know I said I'd send the edits out to you this week, but I'm swamped. Next Monday. I promise.'

'I'm not worried about the edits. I need to know if you sent any copies out for blurbs without telling me?'

Faukman hesitated. Langdon's newest manuscript – an exploration of the history of goddess worship – included several sections about Mary Magdalene that were going to raise some eyebrows. Although the material was well documented and had been covered by others, Faukman had no intention of printing Advance Reading Copies of Langdon's book without at least a few endorsements from serious historians and art luminaries. Jonas had chosen ten big names in the art world and sent them all sections of the manuscript along with a polite letter asking if they would be willing to write a short endorsement for the jacket. In Faukman's experience, most people jumped at the opportunity to see their name in print.

'Jonas?' Langdon pressed. 'You sent out my manuscript, didn't you?'

Faukman frowned, sensing Langdon was not happy about it. 'The manuscript was clean, Robert, and I wanted to surprise you with some terrific blurbs.'

A pause. 'Did you send one to the curator of the Paris Louvre?'

'What do you think? Your manuscript referenced his Louvre collection several times, his books are in your bibliography, and the guy has some serious clout for foreign sales. Saunière was a no-brainer.'

The silence on the other end lasted a long time. 'When did you send it?'

697

'About a month ago. I also mentioned you would be in Paris soon and suggested you two chat. Did he ever call you to meet?' Faukman paused, rubbing his eyes. 'Hold on, aren't you supposed to *be* in Paris this week?'

'I *am* in Paris.'

Faukman sat upright. 'You called me collect from *Paris?*'

'Take it out of my royalties, Jonas. Did you ever hear back from Saunière? Did he like the manuscript?'

'I don't know. I haven't yet heard from him.'

'Well, don't hold your breath. I've got to run, but this explains a lot. Thanks.'

'Robert—'

But Langdon was gone.

Faukman hung up the phone, shaking his head in disbelief. *Authors,* he thought. *Even the sane ones are nuts.*

Inside the Range Rover, Leigh Teabing let out a guffaw. 'Robert, you're saying you wrote a manuscript that delves into a secret society, and your editor *sent* a copy to that secret society?'

Langdon slumped. 'Evidently.'

'A cruel coincidence, my friend.'

Coincidence has nothing to do with it, Langdon knew. Asking Jacques Saunière to endorse a manuscript on goddess worship was as obvious as asking Tiger Woods to endorse a book on golf. Moreover, it was virtually guaranteed that any book on goddess worship would have to mention the Priory of Sion.

'Here's the million–dollar question,' Teabing said, still chuckling. 'Was your position on the Priory favourable or unfavourable?'

Langdon could hear Teabing's true meaning loud and clear. Many historians questioned why the Priory was still keeping the Sangreal documents hidden. Some felt the information should have been shared with the world long ago. 'I took no position on the Priory's actions.'

'You mean lack thereof.'

Langdon shrugged. Teabing was apparently on the side of making the documents public. 'I simply provided history on the brotherhood and described them as a modern goddess worship society, keepers of the Grail and guardians of ancient documents.'

Sophie looked at him. 'Did you mention the keystone?'

Langdon winced. He had. Numerous times. 'I talked about the supposed keystone as an example of the lengths to which the Priory would go to protect the Sangreal documents.'

Sophie looked amazed. 'I guess that explains *P.S. Find Robert Langdon.*'

Langdon sensed it was actually something *else* in the manuscript that had piqued Saunière's interest, but that topic was something he would discuss with Sophie when they were alone.

'So,' Sophie said, 'you lied to Captain Fache.'

'What?' Langdon demanded.

'You told him you had never corresponded with my grandfather.'

'I didn't! My editor sent him a manuscript.'

'Think about it, Robert. If Captain Fache didn't find the envelope in which your editor sent the manuscript, he would have to conclude that *you* sent it.' She paused. 'Or worse, that you hand-delivered it and lied about it.'

When the Range Rover arrived at Le Bourget Airfield, Rémy drove to a small hangar at the far end of the airstrip. As they approached, a tousled man in wrinkled khakis hurried from the hangar, waved, and slid open the enormous corrugated metal door to reveal a sleek white jet within.

Langdon stared at the glistening fuselage. '*That's* Elizabeth?'

Teabing grinned. 'Beats the bloody Chunnel.'

The man in khakis hurried toward them, squinting into the headlights. 'Almost ready, sir,' he called in a British accent. 'My apologies for the delay, but you took me by surprise and—' He stopped short as the group unloaded. He looked at Sophie and Langdon, and then Teabing.

Teabing said, 'My associates and I have urgent business in London. We've no time to waste. Please prepare to depart immediately.' As he spoke, Teabing took the pistol out of the vehicle and handed it to Langdon.

The pilot's eyes bulged at the sight of the weapon. He walked over to Teabing and whispered, 'Sir, my humble apologies, but my diplomatic flight allowance provides only for you and your manservant. I cannot take your guests.'

'Richard,' Teabing said, smiling warmly, 'two thousand pounds sterling and that loaded gun say you *can* take my guests.' He motioned to the Range Rover. 'And the unfortunate fellow in the back.'

69

The Hawker 731's twin Garrett TFE-731 engines thundered, powering the plane skyward with gut-wrenching force. Outside the window, Le Bourget Airfield dropped away with startling speed.

I'm fleeing the country, Sophie thought, her body forced back into the leather seat. Until this moment, she had believed her game of cat and mouse with Fache would be somehow justifiable to the Ministry of Defence. *I was attempting to protect an innocent man. I was trying to fulfil my grandfather's dying wishes.* That window of opportunity, Sophie knew, had just closed. She was leaving the country, without documentation, accompanying a wanted man and transporting a bound hostage. If a 'line of reason' had ever existed, she had just crossed it. *At almost the speed of sound.*

Sophie was seated with Langdon and Teabing near the front of the cabin – the *Fan Jet Executive Elite Design*, according to the gold medallion on the door. Their plush swivel chairs were bolted to tracks on the floor and could be repositioned and locked around a rectangular hardwood table. A mini-boardroom. The dignified surroundings, however, did little to camouflage the less than dignified state of affairs in the rear of the plane where, in a separate seating area near the toilet, Teabing's manservant Rémy sat with the pistol in hand, begrudgingly carrying out Teabing's orders to stand guard over the bloody monk who lay trussed at his feet like a piece of luggage.

'Before we turn our attention to the keystone,' Teabing said, 'I was wondering if you would permit me a few words.' He sounded apprehensive, like a father about to give the birds-and-the-bees lecture to his children. 'My friends, I realize I am but a guest on this journey, and I am honoured as such. And yet, as someone who has spent his life in search of the Grail, I feel it is my duty to warn you that you are about to step onto a path from which there is no return, regardless of the dangers involved.' He turned to Sophie. 'Miss Neveu, your grandfather gave you this cryptex in hopes you would keep the secret of the Holy Grail alive.'

'Yes.'

'Understandably, you feel obliged to follow the trail wherever it leads.'

Sophie nodded, although she felt a second motivation still burning within her. *The truth about my family.* Despite Langdon's assurances that the keystone had nothing to do with her past, Sophie still sensed something deeply personal entwined within this mystery, as if this cryptex, forged by her grandfather's own hands, were trying to speak to her and offer some kind of resolution to the emptiness that had haunted her all these years.

'Your grandfather and three others died tonight,' Teabing continued, 'and they did so to keep this keystone away from the Church. Opus Dei came within inches tonight of possessing it. You understand, I hope, that this puts you in a position of exceptional responsibility. You have been handed a torch. A two-thousand-year-old flame that cannot be allowed to go out. This torch cannot fall into the wrong hands.' He paused, glancing at the rosewood box. 'I realize you have been given no choice in this matter, Miss Neveu, but considering what is at stake here, you must either fully embrace this responsibility . . . or you must pass that responsibility to someone else.'

'My grandfather gave the cryptex to me. I'm sure he thought I could handle the responsibility.'

Teabing looked encouraged but unconvinced. 'Good. A strong will is necessary. And yet, I am curious if you understand that successfully unlocking the keystone will bring with it a far greater trial.'

'How so?'

'My dear, imagine that you are suddenly holding a map that reveals the location of the Holy Grail. In that moment, you will be in possession of a truth capable of altering history for ever. You will be the keeper of a truth that man has sought for centuries. You will be faced with the responsibility of revealing that truth to the world. The individual who does so will be revered by many and despised by many. The question is whether you will have the necessary strength to carry out that task.'

Sophie paused. 'I'm not sure that is *my* decision to make.'

Teabing's eyebrows arched. 'No? If not the possessor of the keystone, then who?'

'The brotherhood who has successfully protected the secret for so long.'

'The Priory?' Teabing looked skeptical. 'But how? The brotherhood was shattered tonight. *Decapitated,* as you so aptly put it. Whether they were infiltrated by some kind of eavesdropping or by a spy within their ranks, we will never know, but the fact remains that someone got to them and uncovered the identities of their four top members. I would not trust anyone who stepped forward from the brotherhood at this point.'

'So what do you suggest?' Langdon asked.

'Robert, you know as well as I do that the Priory has not protected the truth all these years to have it gather dust until eternity. They have been waiting for the right moment in history to share their secret. A time when the world is ready to handle the truth.'

'And you believe that moment has arrived?' Langdon asked.

'Absolutely. It could not be more obvious. All the historical signs are in place, and if the Priory did not intend to make their secret known very soon, why has the Church now attacked?'

Sophie argued, 'The monk has not yet told us his purpose.'

'The monk's purpose is the Church's purpose,' Teabing replied, 'to destroy the documents that reveal the great deception. The Church came closer tonight than they have ever come, and the Priory has put its trust in you, Miss Neveu. The task of saving the Holy Grail clearly includes carrying out the Priory's final wishes of sharing the truth with the world.'

Langdon intervened. 'Leigh, asking Sophie to make that decision is quite a load to drop on someone who only an hour ago learned the Sangreal documents exist.'

Teabing sighed. 'I apologize if I am pressing, Miss Neveu. Clearly I have always believed these documents should be made public, but in the end the decision belongs to you. I simply feel it is important that you begin to think about what happens should we succeed in opening the keystone.'

'Gentlemen,' Sophie said, her voice firm, 'to quote your words, "You do not find the Grail, the Grail finds you." I am going to trust that the Grail has found me for a reason, and when the time comes, I will know what to do.'

Both of them looked startled.

'So then,' she said, motioning to the rosewood box. 'Let's move on.'

70

Standing in the drawing room of Château Villette, Lieutenant Collet watched the dying fire and felt despondent. Captain Fache had arrived moments earlier and was now in the next room, yelling into the phone, trying to coordinate the failed attempt to locate the missing Range Rover.

It could be anywhere by now, Collet thought.

Having disobeyed Fache's direct orders and lost Langdon for a second time, Collet was grateful that PTS had located a bullet hole in the floor, which at least corroborated Collet's claims that a shot had been fired. Still, Fache's mood was sour, and Collet sensed there would be dire repercussions when the dust settled.

Unfortunately, the clues they were turning up here seemed to shed no light at all on what was going on or who was involved. The black Audi outside had been rented in a false name with false credit card numbers, and the prints in the car matched nothing in the Interpol database.

Another agent hurried into the living room, his eyes urgent. 'Where's Captain Fache?'

Collet barely looked up from the burning embers. 'He's on the phone.'

'I'm off the phone,' Fache snapped, stalking into the room. 'What have you got?'

The second agent said, 'Sir, Central just heard from André Vernet at the Depository Bank of Zurich. He wants to talk to you privately. He is changing his story.'

'Oh?' Fache said.

Now Collet looked up.

'Vernet is admitting that Langdon and Neveu spent time inside his bank tonight.'

'We figured that out,' Fache said. 'Why did Vernet lie about it?'

'He said he'll talk only to you, but he's agreed to cooperate fully.'

'In exchange for what?'

'For our keeping his bank's name out of the news and also for helping him recover some stolen property. It sounds like Langdon and Neveu stole something from Saunière's account.'

'What?' Collet blurted. 'How?'

Fache never flinched, his eyes riveted on the second agent. 'What did they steal?'

'Vernet didn't elaborate, but he sounds like he's willing to do anything to get it back.'

Collet tried to imagine how this could happen. Maybe Langdon and Neveu had held a bank employee at gunpoint? Maybe they forced Vernet to open Saunière's account and facilitate an escape in the armoured truck. As feasible as it was, Collet was having trouble believing Sophie Neveu could be involved in anything like that.

From the kitchen, another agent yelled to Fache. 'Captain? I'm going through Mr Teabing's speed dial numbers, and I'm on the phone with Le Bourget Airfield. I've got some bad news.'

Thirty seconds later, Fache was packing up and preparing to leave Château Villette. He had just learned that Teabing kept a private jet nearby at Le Bourget Airfield and that the plane had taken off about a half hour ago.

The Bourget representative on the phone had claimed not to know who was on the plane or where it was headed. The takeoff had been unscheduled, and no flight plan had been logged. Highly illegal, even for a small airfield. Fache was certain that by applying the right pressure, he could get the answers he was looking for.

'Lieutenant Collet,' Fache barked, heading for the door, 'I have no choice but to leave you in charge of the PTS investigation here. Try to do something right for a change.'

71

As the Hawker levelled off, with its nose aimed for England, Langdon carefully lifted the rosewood box from his lap, where he had been protecting it during takeoff. Now, as he set the box on the table, he could sense Sophie and Teabing leaning forward with anticipation.

Unlatching the lid and opening the box, Langdon turned his attention not to the lettered dials of the cryptex, but rather to the tiny hole on the underside of the box lid. Using the tip of a pen, he carefully removed the inlaid Rose on top and revealed the text beneath it. *Sub Rosa,* he mused, hoping a fresh look at the text would bring clarity. Focusing all his energies, Langdon studied the strange text.

After several seconds, he began to feel the initial frustration resurfacing. 'Leigh, I just can't seem to place it.'

From where Sophie was seated across the table, she could not yet see the text, but Langdon's inability to immediately identify the language surprised her. *My grandfather spoke a language so obscure that even a symbologist can't identify it?* She quickly realized she should not find this surprising. This would not be the first secret Jacques Saunière had kept from his granddaughter.

*

Opposite Sophie, Leigh Teabing felt ready to burst. Eager for his chance to see the text, he quivered with excitement, leaning in, trying to see around Langdon, who was still hunched over the box.

'I don't know,' Langdon whispered intently. 'My first guess is a Semitic, but now I'm not so sure. Most primary Semitics include *nikkudim*. This has none.'

'Probably ancient,' Teabing offered.

'*Nikkudim?*' Sophie inquired.

Teabing never took his eyes from the box. 'Most modern Semitic alphabets have no vowels and use *nikkudim* – tiny dots and dashes written either below or within the consonants – to indicate what vowel sound accompanies them. Historically speaking, *nikkudim* are a relatively modern addition to language.'

Langdon was still hovering over the script. 'A Sephardic transliteration, perhaps . . . ?'

Teabing could bear it no longer. 'Perhaps if I just . . .' Reaching over, he edged the box away from Langdon and pulled it toward himself. No doubt Langdon had a solid familiarity with the standard ancients – Greek, Latin, the Romances – but from the fleeting glance Teabing had of *this* language, he thought it looked more specialized, possibly a Rashi script or a STA'M with crowns.

Taking a deep breath, Teabing feasted his eyes upon the engraving. He said nothing for a very long time. With each passing second, Teabing felt his confidence deflating. 'I'm astonished,' he said. 'This language looks like nothing I've ever seen!'

Langdon slumped.

'Might I see it?' Sophie asked.

Teabing pretended not to hear her. 'Robert, you said earlier that you thought you'd *seen* something like this before?'

Langdon looked vexed. 'I thought so. I'm not sure. The script looks familiar somehow.'

'Leigh?' Sophie repeated, clearly not appreciating being left out of the discussion. 'Might I have a look at the box my grandfather made?'

'Of course, dear,' Teabing said, pushing it over to her. He hadn't meant to sound belittling, and yet Sophie Neveu was light-years out of her league. If a British Royal Historian and a Harvard symbologist could not even identify the language –

'Aah,' Sophie said, seconds after examining the box. 'I should have guessed.'

Teabing and Langdon turned in unison, staring at her.

'Guessed *what?*' Teabing demanded.

Sophie shrugged. 'Guessed that *this* would be the language my grandfather would have used.'

'You're saying you can *read* this text?' Teabing exclaimed.

706

'Quite easily,' Sophie chimed, obviously enjoying herself now. 'My grandfather taught me this language when I was only six years old. I'm fluent.' She leaned across the table and fixed Teabing with an admonishing glare. 'And frankly, sir, considering your allegiance to the Crown, I'm a little surprised you didn't recognize it.'

In a flash, Langdon knew.

No wonder the script looks so damned familiar!

Several years ago, Langdon had attended an event at Harvard's Fogg Museum. Harvard dropout Bill Gates had returned to his alma mater to lend to the museum one of his priceless acquisitions – eighteen sheets of paper he had recently purchased at auction from the Armand Hammar Estate.

His winning bid – a cool $30.8 million.

The author of the pages – Leonardo da Vinci.

The eighteen folios – now known as Leonardo's *Codex Leicester* after their famous owner, the Earl of Leicester – were all that remained of one of Leonardo's most fascinating notebooks: essays and drawings outlining Da Vinci's progressive theories on astronomy, geology, archaeology and hydrology.

Langdon would never forget his reaction after waiting in line and finally viewing the priceless parchment. Utter letdown. The pages were unintelligible. Despite being beautifully preserved and written in an impeccably neat penmanship – crimson ink on cream paper – the codex looked like gibberish. At first Langdon thought he could not read them because Da Vinci wrote his notebooks in an archaic Italian. But after studying them more closely, he realized he could not identify a single Italian word, or even one letter.

'Try this, sir,' whispered the female docent at the display case. She motioned to a hand mirror affixed to the display on a chain. Langdon picked it up and examined the text in the mirror's surface.

Instantly it was clear.

Langdon had been so eager to peruse some of the great thinker's ideas that he had forgotten one of the man's numerous artistic talents was an ability to write in a mirrored script that was virtually illegible to anyone other than himself. Historians still debated whether Da Vinci wrote this way simply to amuse himself or to keep people from peering over his shoulder and stealing his ideas, but the point was moot. Da Vinci did as he pleased.

Sophie smiled inwardly to see that Robert understood her meaning. 'I can read the first few words,' she said. 'It's English.'

Teabing was still sputtering. 'What's going on?'

'Reverse text,' Langdon said. 'We need a mirror.'

'No we don't,' Sophie said. 'I bet this veneer is thin enough.' She lifted the rosewood box up to a canister light on the wall and began examining the underside of the lid. Her grandfather couldn't actually write in reverse, so he always cheated by writing *normally* and then flipping the paper over and tracing the reversed impression. Sophie's guess was that he had wood-burned *normal* text into a block of wood and then run the back of the block through a sander until the wood was paper thin and the wood-burning could be seen *through* the wood. Then he'd simply flipped the piece over, and laid it in.

As Sophie moved the lid closer to the light, she saw she was right. The bright beam sifted through the thin layer of wood, and the script appeared in reverse on the underside of the lid.

Instantly legible.

'English,' Teabing croaked, hanging his head in shame. 'My native tongue.'

At the rear of the plane, Rémy Legaludec strained to hear beyond the rumbling engines, but the conversation up front was inaudible. Rémy did not like the way the night was progressing. Not at all. He looked down at the bound monk at his feet. The man lay perfectly still now, as if in a trance of acceptance or, perhaps, in silent prayer for deliverance.

72

Fifteen thousand feet in the air, Robert Langdon felt the physical world fade away as all of his thoughts converged on Saunière's mirror-image poem, which was illuminated through the lid of the box.

Sophie quickly found some paper and copied it down longhand. When she was done, the three of them took turns reading the text. It was like some kind of archaeological crossword . . . a riddle that promised to reveal how to open the cryptex. Langdon read the verse slowly.

An ancient word of wisdom frees this scroll . . . and helps us keep her scatter'd family whole . . . a headstone praised by templars is the key . . . and atbash will reveal the truth to thee.

Before Langdon could even ponder what ancient password the verse was trying to reveal, he felt something far more fundamental resonate within him – the metre of the poem. *Iambic pentameter.*

Langdon had come across this metre often over the years while researching secret societies across Europe, including just last year in the Vatican Secret Archives. For centuries, iambic pentameter had been a preferred poetic metre of outspoken literati across the globe, from the ancient Greek writer Archilochus to Shakespeare, Milton, Chaucer and Voltaire – bold souls who chose to write their social commentaries in a metre that many of the day believed had mystical properties. The roots of iambic pentameter were deeply pagan.

Iambs. Two syllables with opposite emphasis. Stressed and unstressed. Yin yang. A balanced pair. Arranged in strings of five. Pentameter. Five for the pentacle of Venus and the sacred feminine.

'It's pentameter!' Teabing blurted, turning to Langdon. 'And the verse is in English! *La lingua pura!*'

Langdon nodded. The Priory, like many European secret societies at odds with the Church, had considered English the only European *pure* language for centuries. Unlike French, Spanish and Italian, which were rooted in Latin – *the tongue of the Vatican* – English was linguistically removed from Rome's propaganda machine, and therefore became a sacred, secret tongue for those brotherhoods educated enough to learn it.

'This poem,' Teabing gushed, 'references not only the Grail, but the Knights Templar and the scattered family of Mary Magdalene! What more could we ask for?'

'The password,' Sophie said, looking again at the poem. 'It sounds like we need some kind of ancient word of wisdom?'

'Abracadabra?' Teabing ventured, his eyes twinkling.

A word of five letters, Langdon thought, pondering the staggering number of ancient words that might be considered *words of wisdom* – selections from mystic chants, astrological prophecies, secret society inductions, Wicca incantations, Egyptian magic spells, pagan mantras – the list was endless.

'The password,' Sophie said, 'appears to have something to do with the Templars.' She read the text aloud. '"A headstone praised by Templars is the key."'

'Leigh,' Langdon said, 'you're the Templar specialist. Any ideas?'

Teabing was silent for several seconds and then sighed. 'Well, a headstone is obviously a grave marker of some sort. It's possible the poem is referencing a gravestone the Templars praised at the tomb of Magdalene, but that doesn't help us much because we have no idea where her tomb is.'

'The last line,' Sophie said, 'says that *Atbash* will reveal the truth. I've heard that word. Atbash.'

'I'm not surprised,' Langdon replied. 'You probably heard it in Cryptology 101. The Atbash Cipher is one of the oldest codes known to man.'

Of course! Sophie thought. *The famous Hebrew encoding system.*

The Atbash Cipher had indeed been part of Sophie's early cryptology training. The cipher dated back to 500 BC and was now used as a classroom example of a basic rotational substitution scheme. A common form of Jewish cryptogram, the Atbash Cipher was a simple substitution code based on the twenty-two-letter Hebrew alphabet. In Atbash, the first letter was substituted by the last letter, the second letter by the next to last letter, and so on.

'Atbash is sublimely appropriate,' Teabing said. 'Text encrypted with Atbash is found throughout the Kabbala, the Dead Sea Scrolls and even the Old Testament. Jewish scholars and mystics are *still* finding hidden meanings using Atbash. The Priory certainly would include the Atbash Cipher as part of their teachings.'

'The only problem,' Langdon said, 'is that we don't have anything on which to apply the cipher.'

Teabing sighed. 'There must be a code word on the headstone. We must find this headstone praised by Templars.'

Sophie sensed from the grim look on Langdon's face that finding the Templar headstone would be no small feat.

Atbash is the key, Sophie thought. *But we don't have a door.*

It was three minutes later that Teabing heaved a frustrated sigh and shook his head. 'My friends, I'm stymied. Let me ponder this while I get us some nibbles and check on Rémy and our guest.' He stood up and headed for the back of the plane.

Sophie felt tired as she watched him go.

Outside the window, the blackness of the predawn was absolute. Sophie felt as if she were being hurtled through space with no idea where she would land. Having grown up solving her grandfather's riddles, she had the uneasy sense right now that this poem before them contained information they still had not seen.

There is more there, she told herself. *Ingeniously hidden . . . but present nonetheless.*

Also plaguing her thoughts was a fear that what they eventually found inside this cryptex would not be as simple as 'a map to the Holy Grail'. Despite Teabing's and Langdon's confidence that the truth lay just within the marble cylinder, Sophie had solved enough of her grandfather's treasure hunts to know that Jacques Saunière did not give up his secrets easily.

73

Bourget Airfield's night shift air traffic controller had been dozing before a blank radar screen when the captain of the Judicial Police practically broke down his door.

'Teabing's jet,' Bezu Fache blared, marching into the small tower, 'where did it go?'

The controller's initial response was a babbling, lame attempt to protect the privacy of their British client – one of the airfield's most respected customers. It failed miserably.

'Okay,' Fache said, 'I am placing you under arrest for permitting a private plane to take off without registering a flight plan.' Fache motioned to another officer, who approached with handcuffs, and the traffic controller felt a surge of terror. He thought of the newspaper articles debating whether the nation's police captain was a hero or a menace. That question had just been answered.

'Wait!' the controller heard himself whimper at the sight of the handcuffs. 'I can tell you this much. Sir Leigh Teabing makes frequent trips to London for medical treatments. He has a hangar at Biggin Hill Executive Airport in Kent. On the outskirts of London.'

Fache waved off the man with the cuffs. 'Is Biggin Hill his destination tonight?'

'I don't know,' the controller said honestly. 'The plane left on its usual tack, and his last radar contact suggested the United Kingdom. Biggin Hill is an extremely likely guess.'

'Did he have others onboard?'

'I swear, sir, there is no way for me to know that. Our clients can drive directly to their hangars, and load as they please. Who is onboard is the responsibility of the customs officials at the receiving airport.'

Fache checked his watch and gazed out at the scattering of jets parked in front of the terminal. 'If they're going to Biggin Hill, how long until they land?'

The controller fumbled through his records. 'It's a short flight. His plane could be on the ground by . . . around six-thirty. Fifteen minutes from now.'

Fache frowned and turned to one of his men. 'Get a transport up here. I'm going to London. And get me the Kent local police. Not British MI5. I want this quiet. Kent *local*. Tell them I want Teabing's plane to be permitted to land. Then I want it surrounded on the tarmac. Nobody deplanes until I get there.'

74

'You're quiet,' Langdon said, gazing across the Hawker's cabin at Sophie.

'Just tired,' she replied. 'And the poem. I don't know.'

Langdon was feeling the same way. The hum of the engines and the gentle rocking of the plane were hypnotic, and his head still throbbed where he'd been hit by the monk. Teabing was still in the back of the plane, and Langdon decided to take advantage of the moment alone with Sophie to tell her something that had been on his mind. 'I think I know part of the reason why your grandfather conspired to put us together. I think there's something he wanted me to explain to you.'

'The history of the Holy Grail and Mary Magdalene isn't enough?'

Langdon felt uncertain how to proceed. 'The rift between you. The reason you haven't spoken to him in ten years. I think maybe he was hoping I could somehow make that right by explaining what drove you apart.'

Sophie squirmed in her seat. 'I haven't told you what drove us apart.'

Langdon eyed her carefully. 'You witnessed a sex rite. Didn't you?'

Sophie recoiled. 'How do you know that?'

'Sophie, you told me you witnessed something that convinced you your grandfather was in a secret society. And whatever you saw upset you enough that you haven't spoken to him since. I know a fair amount about secret societies. It doesn't take the brains of Da Vinci to guess what you saw.'

Sophie stared.

'Was it in the spring?' Langdon asked. 'Sometime around the equinox? Mid-March?'

Sophie looked out the window. 'I was on spring break from university. I came home a few days early.'

'You want to tell me about it?'

'I'd rather not.' She turned suddenly back to Langdon, her eyes welling with emotion. 'I don't know what I saw.'

'Were both men and women present?'

After a beat, she nodded.

'Dressed in white and black?'

She wiped her eyes and then nodded, seeming to open up a little. 'The women were in white gossamer gowns . . . with golden shoes. They held golden orbs. The men wore black tunics and black shoes.'

Langdon strained to hide his emotion, and yet he could not believe what he was hearing. Sophie Neveu had unwittingly witnessed a two-thousand-year-old sacred ceremony. 'Masks?' he asked, keeping his voice calm. 'Androgynous masks?'

'Yes. Everyone. Identical masks. White on the women. Black on the men.'

Langdon had read descriptions of this ceremony and understood its mystic roots. 'It's called Hieros Gamos,' he said softly. 'It dates back more than two thousand years. Egyptian priests and priestesses performed it regularly to celebrate the reproductive power of the female.' He paused, leaning toward her. 'And if you witnessed Hieros Gamos without being properly prepared to understand its meaning, I imagine it would be pretty shocking.'

Sophie said nothing.

'Hieros Gamos is Greek,' he continued. 'It means *sacred marriage*.'

'The ritual I saw was no marriage.'

'Marriage as in *union*, Sophie.'

'You mean as in sex.'

'No.'

'No?' she said, her olive eyes testing him.

Langdon backpedalled. 'Well . . . yes, in a manner of speaking, but not as we understand it today.' He explained that although what she saw probably *looked* like a sex ritual, Hieros Gamos had nothing to do with eroticism. It was a spiritual act. Historically, intercourse was the act through which male and female experienced God. The ancients believed that the male was spiritually incomplete until he had carnal knowledge of the sacred feminine. Physical union with the female remained the sole means through which man could become spiritually complete and ultimately achieve *gnosis* – knowledge of the divine. Since the days of Isis, sex rites had been considered man's only bridge from earth to heaven. 'By communing with woman,' Langdon said, 'man could achieve a climactic instant when his mind went totally blank and he could see God.'

Sophie looked skeptical. 'Orgasm as prayer?'

Langdon gave a noncommittal shrug, although Sophie was essentially correct. Physiologically speaking, the male climax was accompanied by a split second entirely devoid of thought. A brief mental vacuum. A moment of clarity during which God could be glimpsed. Meditation gurus achieved similar states of thoughtlessness without sex and often described Nirvana as a never-ending spiritual orgasm.

'Sophie,' Langdon said quietly, 'it's important to remember that the ancients' view of sex was entirely opposite from ours today. Sex begot new life – the ultimate miracle – and miracles could be performed only by a god. The ability of the woman to produce life from her womb made her sacred. A god. Intercourse was the revered union of the two halves of the human spirit – male and female – through which the male could find spiritual wholeness and communion with God. What you saw was not about sex, it was about spirituality. The Hieros Gamos ritual is not a perversion. It's a deeply sacrosanct ceremony.'

His words seemed to strike a nerve. Sophie had been remarkably poised all evening, but now, for the first time, Langdon saw the aura of composure beginning to crack. Tears materialized in her eyes again, and she dabbed them away with her sleeve.

He gave her a moment. Admittedly, the concept of sex as a pathway to God was mind-boggling at first. Langdon's Jewish students always looked flabbergasted when he first told them that the early Jewish tradition involved ritualistic sex. *In the Temple, no less.* Early Jews believed that the Holy of Holies in Solomon's Temple housed not only God but also His powerful female equal, Shekinah. Men seeking spiritual wholeness came to the Temple to visit priestesses – or *hierodules* – with whom they made love and experienced the divine through physical union. The Jewish tetragrammaton YHWH – the sacred name of God – in fact derived from Jehovah, an androgynous physical union between the masculine *Jah* and the pre-Hebraic name for Eve, *Havah.*

'For the early Church,' Langdon explained in a soft voice, 'mankind's use of sex to commune directly with God posed a serious threat to the Catholic power base. It left the Church out of the loop, undermining their self-proclaimed status as the *sole* conduit to God. For obvious reasons, they worked hard to demonize sex and recast it as a disgusting and sinful act. Other major religions did the same.'

Sophie was silent, but Langdon sensed she was starting to understand her grandfather better. Ironically, Langdon had made this same point in a class lecture earlier this semester. 'Is it surprising we feel conflicted about sex?' he asked his students. 'Our ancient heritage and our very physiologies tell us sex is natural – a cherished route to spiritual fulfilment – and yet modern religion decries it as shameful, teaching us to fear our sexual desire as the hand of the devil.'

Langdon decided not to shock his students with the fact that more than a dozen secret societies around the world – many of them quite influential – still practised sex rites and kept the ancient traditions alive. Tom Cruise's character in the film *Eyes Wide Shut* discovered this the hard way when he sneaked into a private gathering of ultra-elite Manhattanites only to find himself witnessing Hieros Gamos. Sadly, the filmmakers had got most of the specifics wrong, but the basic gist was there – a secret society communing to celebrate the magic of sexual union.

'Professor Langdon?' A male student at the back raised his hand, sounding hopeful. 'Are you saying that instead of going to chapel, we should have more sex?'

Langdon chuckled, not about to take the bait. From what he'd heard about Harvard parties, these kids were having more than enough sex. 'Gentlemen,' he said, knowing he was on tender ground, 'might I offer a suggestion for all of you. Without being so bold as to condone premarital sex, and without being so naive as to think you're all chaste angels, I will give you this bit of advice about your sex lives.'

All the men in the audience leaned forward, listening intently.

'The next time you find yourself with a woman, look in your heart and see if you cannot approach sex as a mystical, spiritual act. Challenge yourself to find that spark of divinity that man can only achieve through union with the sacred feminine.'

The women smiled knowingly, nodding.

The men exchanged dubious giggles and off-colour jokes.

Langdon sighed. College men were still boys.

Sophie's forehead felt cold as she pressed it against the plane's window and stared blankly into the void, trying to process what Langdon had just told her. She felt a new regret well within her. *Ten years.* She pictured the stacks of unopened letters her grandfather had sent her. *I will tell Robert everything.* Without turning from the window, Sophie began to speak. Quietly. Fearfully.

As she began to recount what had happened that night, she felt herself drifting back . . . alighting in the woods outside her grandfather's Normandy château . . . searching the deserted house in confusion . . . hearing the voices below her . . . and then finding the hidden door. She inched down the stone staircase, one step at a time, into that basement grotto. She could taste the earthy air. Cool and light. It was March. In the shadows of her hiding place on the staircase, she watched as the strangers swayed and chanted by flickering orange candles.

I'm dreaming, Sophie told herself. *This is a dream. What else could this be?*

The women and men were staggered, black, white, black, white. The women's beautiful gossamer gowns billowed as they raised in their right hands golden orbs and called out in unison, '*I was with you in the beginning, in the dawn of all that is holy, I bore you from the womb before the start of day.*'

The women lowered their orbs, and everyone rocked back and forth as if in a trance. They were revering something in the centre of the circle.

What are they looking at?

The voices accelerated now. Louder. Faster.

'*The woman whom you behold is love!*' The women called, raising their orbs again.

The men responded, '*She has her dwelling in eternity!*'

The chanting grew steady again. Accelerating. Thundering now. Faster. The participants stepped inward and knelt.

In that instant, Sophie could finally see what they were all watching.

On a low, ornate altar in the centre of the circle lay a man. He was naked, positioned on his back, and wearing a black mask. Sophie instantly recognized his body and the birthmark on his shoulder. She almost cried out. *Grand-père!* This image alone would have shocked Sophie beyond belief, and yet there was more.

Straddling her grandfather was a naked woman wearing a white mask, her luxuriant silver hair flowing out behind it. Her body was plump, far from perfect, and she was gyrating in rhythm to the chanting – making love to Sophie's grandfather.

Sophie wanted to turn and run, but she couldn't. The stone walls of the grotto imprisoned her as the chanting rose to a fever pitch. The circle of participants seemed almost to be singing now, the noise rising in crescendo to a frenzy. With a sudden roar, the entire room seemed to erupt in climax. Sophie could not breathe. She suddenly realized she was quietly sobbing. She turned and staggered silently up the stairs, out of the house, and drove trembling back to Paris.

75

The chartered turboprop was just passing over the twinkling lights of Monaco when Aringarosa hung up on Fache for the second time. He reached for the airsickness bag again but felt too drained even to be sick.

Just let it be over!

Fache's newest update seemed unfathomable, and yet almost nothing tonight made sense anymore. *What is going on?* Everything had spiralled wildly out of control. *What have I got Silas into? What have I got myself into!*

On shaky legs, Aringarosa walked to the cockpit. 'I need to change destinations.'

The pilot glanced over his shoulder and laughed. 'You're joking, right?'

'No. I have to get to London immediately.'

'Father, this is a charter flight, not a taxi.'

'I will pay you extra, of course. How much? London is only one hour farther north and requires almost no change of direction, so—'

'It's not a question of money, Father, there are other issues.'

'Ten thousand euros. Right now.'

The pilot turned, his eyes wide with shock. 'How much? What kind of priest carries that kind of cash?'

Aringarosa walked back to his black briefcase, opened it, and removed one of the bearer bonds. He handed it to the pilot.

'What is this?' the pilot demanded.

'A ten-thousand-euro bearer bond drawn on the Vatican Bank.'

The pilot looked dubious.

'It's the same as cash.'

'Only cash is cash,' the pilot said, handing the bond back.

Aringarosa felt weak as he steadied himself against the cockpit door. 'This is a matter of life or death. You must help me. I need to get to London.'

The pilot eyed the bishop's gold ring. 'Real diamonds?'

Aringarosa looked at the ring. 'I could not possibly part with this.'

The pilot shrugged, turning and focusing back out of the windshield.

Aringarosa felt a deepening sadness. He looked at the ring. Everything it represented was about to be lost to the bishop anyway. After a long moment, he slid the ring from his finger and placed it gently on the instrument panel.

Aringarosa slunk out of the cockpit and sat back down. Fifteen seconds later, he could feel the pilot banking a few more degrees to the north.

Even so, Aringarosa's moment of glory was in shambles.

It had all begun as a holy cause. A brilliantly crafted scheme. Now, like a house of cards, it was collapsing in on itself . . . and the end was nowhere in sight.

76

Langdon could see Sophie was still shaken from recounting her experience of Hieros Gamos. For his part, Langdon was amazed to have heard it. Not only had Sophie witnessed the full-blown ritual, but her own grandfather had been the celebrant . . . the Grand Master of the Priory of Sion. It was heady company. *Da Vinci, Botticelli, Isaac Newton, Victor Hugo, Jean Cocteau . . . Jacques Saunière.*

'I don't know what else I can tell you,' Langdon said softly.

Sophie's eyes were a deep green now, tearful. 'He raised me like his own daughter.'

Langdon now recognized the emotion that had been growing in her eyes as they spoke. It was remorse. Distant and deep. Sophie Neveu had shunned her grandfather and was now seeing him in an entirely different light.

Outside, the dawn was coming fast, its crimson aura gathering off the starboard. The earth was still black beneath them.

'Victuals, my dears?' Teabing rejoined them with a flourish, presenting several cans of Coke and a box of old crackers. He apologized profusely for the limited fare as he doled out the goods. 'Our friend the monk isn't talking yet,' he chimed, 'but give him time.' He bit into a cracker and eyed the poem. 'So, my lovely, any headway?' He looked at Sophie. 'What is your grandfather trying to tell us here? Where the devil is this headstone? This headstone praised by Templars.'

Sophie shook her head and remained silent.

While Teabing again dug into the verse, Langdon popped a Coke and turned to the window, his thoughts awash with images of secret rituals and unbroken codes. *A headstone praised by Templars is the key*. He took a long sip from the can. *A headstone praised by Templars*. The cola was warm.

The dissolving veil of night seemed to evaporate quickly, and as Langdon watched the transformation, he saw a shimmering ocean stretch out beneath them. *The English Channel*. It wouldn't be long now.

Langdon willed the light of day to bring with it a second kind of illumination, but the lighter it became outside, the further he felt from the truth. He heard the rhythms of iambic pentameter and chanting, Hieros Gamos and sacred rites, resonating with the rumble of the jet.

A headstone praised by Templars.

The plane was over land again when a flash of enlightenment struck him. Langdon set down his empty can of Coke hard. 'You won't believe this,' he said, turning to the others. 'The Templar headstone – I figured it out.'

Teabing's eyes turned to saucers. 'You *know* where the headstone is?'

Langdon smiled. 'Not *where* it is. *What* it is.'

Sophie leaned in to hear.

'I think the headstone references a literal *stone head*,' Langdon explained, savouring the familiar excitement of academic breakthrough. 'Not a grave marker.'

'A stone head?' Teabing demanded.

Sophie looked equally confused.

'Leigh,' Langdon said, turning, 'during the Inquisition, the Church accused the Knights Templar of all kinds of heresies, right?'

'Correct. They fabricated all kinds of charges. Sodomy, urination on the cross, devil worship, quite a list.'

'And on that list was the worship of *false idols*, right? Specifically, the Church accused the Templars of secretly performing rituals in which they prayed to a carved stone head . . . the pagan god—'

'Baphomet!' Teabing blurted. 'My heavens, Robert, you're right! A headstone praised by Templars!'

Langdon quickly explained to Sophie that Baphomet was a pagan fertility god associated with the creative force of reproduction. Baphomet's head was represented as that of a ram or goat, a common symbol of procreation and fecundity. The Templars honoured Baphomet by encircling a stone replica of his head and chanting prayers.

'Baphomet,' Teabing tittered. 'The ceremony honoured the creative magic of sexual union, but Pope Clement convinced everyone that Baphomet's head was in fact that of the devil. The Pope used the head of Baphomet as the linchpin in his case against the Templars.'

Langdon concurred. The modern belief in a *horned* devil known as Satan could be traced back to Baphomet and the Church's attempts to recast the horned fertility god as a symbol of evil. The Church had obviously succeeded, although not entirely. Traditional American Thanksgiving tables still bore pagan, horned fertility symbols. The cornucopia or 'horn of plenty' was a tribute to Baphomet's fertility and dated back to Zeus being suckled by a goat whose horn broke off and magically filled with fruit. Baphomet also appeared in group photographs when some joker raised two fingers behind a friend's head in the V-symbol of horns; certainly few of the pranksters realized their mocking gesture was in fact advertising their victim's robust sperm count.

'Yes, yes,' Teabing was saying excitedly. 'Baphomet must be what the poem is referring to. A headstone praised by Templars.'

'Okay,' Sophie said, 'but if Baphomet is the headstone praised by Templars, then we have a new dilemma.' She pointed to the dials on the cryptex. 'Baphomet has eight letters. We only have room for five.'

Teabing grinned broadly. 'My dear, this is where the Atbash Cipher comes into play.'

77

Langdon was impressed. Teabing had just finished writing out the entire twenty-two-letter Hebrew alphabet – *alef-beit* – from memory. Granted, he'd used Roman equivalents rather than Hebrew characters, but even so, he was now reading through them with flawless pronunciation.

A B G D H V Z Ch T Y K L M N S O P Tz Q R Sh Th

'*Alef, Beit, Gimel, Dalet, Hei, Vav, Zayin, Chet, Tet, Yud, Kaf, Lamed, Mem, Nun, Samech, Ayin, Pei, Tzadik, Kuf, Reish, Shin and Tav.*' Teabing dramatically mopped his brow and plowed on. 'In formal Hebrew spelling, the vowel sounds are not written. Therefore, when we write the word *Baphomet* using the Hebrew alphabet, it will lose its three vowels in translation, leaving us—'

'Five letters,' Sophie blurted.

Teabing nodded and began writing again. 'Okay, here is the proper spelling of Baphomet in Hebrew letters. I'll sketch in the missing vowels for clarity's sake.

<u>B</u> a <u>P</u> <u>V</u> o <u>M</u> e <u>Th</u>

'Remember, of course,' he added, 'that Hebrew is normally written in the opposite direction, but we can just as easily use Atbash this way. Next, all we have to do is create our substitution scheme by rewriting the entire alphabet in reverse order opposite the original alphabet.'

'There's an easier way,' Sophie said, taking the pen from Teabing. 'It works for all reflectional substitution ciphers, including the Atbash. A little trick I learned at the Royal Holloway.' Sophie wrote the first half of the alphabet from left to right, and then, beneath it, wrote the second half, right to left. 'Cryptanalysts call it the fold-over. Half as complicated. Twice as clean.'

A	B	G	D	H	V	Z	Ch	T	Y	K
Th	Sh	R	Q	Tz	P	O	S	N	M	L

Teabing eyed her handiwork and chuckled. 'Right you are. Glad to see those boys at the Holloway are doing their job.'

Looking at Sophie's substitution matrix, Langdon felt a rising thrill that he imagined must have rivalled the thrill felt by early scholars when they first used the Atbash Cipher to decrypt the now famous *Mystery of Sheshach*. For years, religious scholars had been baffled by biblical references to a city called *Sheshach*. The city did not appear on any map nor in any other documents, and yet it was mentioned repeatedly in the Book of Jeremiah – the king of Sheshach, the city of Sheshach, the people of Sheshach. Finally, a scholar applied the Atbash Cipher to the word, and his results were mind-numbing. The cipher revealed that Sheshach was in fact a *code word* for another very well-known city. The decryption process was simple.

Sheshach, in Hebrew, was spelled: Sh-Sh-K.

Sh-Sh-K, when placed in the substitution matrix, became B-B-L.

B-B-L, in Hebrew, spelled *Babel*.

The mysterious city of Sheshach was revealed as the city of Babel, and a frenzy of biblical examination ensued. Within weeks, several more Atbash code words were uncovered in the Old Testament, unveiling myriad hidden meanings that scholars had no idea were there.

'We're getting close,' Langdon whispered, unable to control his excitement.

'Inches, Robert,' Teabing said. He glanced over at Sophie and smiled. 'You ready?'

She nodded.

'Okay, Baphomet in Hebrew without the vowels reads: *B-P-V-M-Th*. Now we simply apply your Atbash substitution matrix to translate the letters into our five-letter password.'

Langdon's heart pounded. *B-P-V-M-Th*. The sun was pouring through the windows now. He looked at Sophie's substitution matrix and slowly began to make the conversion. *B is Sh . . . P is V . . .*

Teabing was grinning like a schoolboy at Christmas. 'And the Atbash Cipher reveals . . .' He stopped short. 'Good God!' His face went white.

Langdon's head snapped up.

'What's wrong?' Sophie demanded.

'You won't believe this.' Teabing glanced at Sophie. 'Especially you.'

'What do you mean?' she said.

'This is . . . ingenious,' he whispered. 'Utterly ingenious!' Teabing wrote again on the paper. 'Drumroll, please. Here is your password.' He showed them what he had written.

Sh-V-P-Y-A

Sophie scowled. 'What is it?'

Langdon didn't recognize it either.

Teabing's voice seemed to tremble with awe. 'This, my friend, is actually an ancient word of wisdom.'

Langdon read the letters again. *An ancient word of wisdom frees this scroll.* An instant later he got it. He had never seen this coming. 'An ancient word of wisdom!'

Teabing was laughing. 'Quite literally!'

Sophie looked at the word and then at the dial. Immediately she realized Langdon and Teabing had failed to see a serious glitch. 'Hold on! This can't be the password,' she argued. 'The cryptex doesn't have an Sh on the dial. It uses a traditional Roman alphabet.'

'*Read* the word,' Langdon urged. 'Keep in mind two things. In Hebrew, the symbol for the sound Sh can also be pronounced as S, depending on the accent. Just as the letter P can be pronounced F.'

SVFYA? she thought, puzzled.

'Genius!' Teabing added. 'The letter Vav is often a placeholder for the vowel sound O!'

Sophie again looked at the letters, attempting to sound them out. '*S . . . o . . . f . . . y . . . a.*'

She heard the sound of her voice, and could not believe what she had just said. 'Sophia? This spells Sophia?'

Langdon was nodding enthusiastically. 'Yes! *Sophia* literally means *wisdom* in Greek. The root of your name, Sophie, is literally a "word of wisdom".'

Sophie suddenly missed her grandfather immensely. *He encrypted the Priory keystone with my name.* A knot caught in her throat. It all seemed so perfect. But as she turned her gaze to the five lettered dials on the cryptex, she realized a problem still existed. 'But wait . . . the word Sophia has *six* letters.'

Teabing's smile never faded. 'Look at the poem again. Your grandfather wrote, "An *ancient* word of wisdom." '

'Yes?'

Teabing winked. 'In ancient Greek, wisdom is spelled S-O-F-I-A.'

78

Sophie felt a wild excitement as she cradled the cryptex and began dialling in the letters. *An ancient word of wisdom frees this scroll.* Langdon and Teabing seemed to have stopped breathing as they looked on.

S . . . O . . . F . . .

'Carefully,' Teabing urged. 'Ever so carefully.'

. . . I . . . A.

Sophie aligned the final dial. 'Okay,' she whispered, glancing up at the others. 'I'm going to pull it apart.'

'Remember the vinegar,' Langdon whispered with fearful exhilaration. 'Be careful.'

Sophie knew that if this cryptex were like those she had opened in her youth, all she would need to do is grip the cylinder at both ends, just beyond the dials, and pull, applying slow, steady pressure in opposite directions. If the dials were properly aligned with the password, then one of the ends would slide off, much like a lens cap, and she could reach inside and remove the rolled papyrus document, which would be wrapped around the vial of vinegar. However, if the password they had entered were *incorrect*, Sophie's outward force on the ends would be transferred to a hinged lever inside, which would pivot downward into the cavity and apply pressure to the glass vial, eventually shattering it if she pulled too hard.

Pull gently, she told herself.

Teabing and Langdon both leaned in as Sophie wrapped her palms around the ends of the cylinder. In the excitement of deciphering the code word, Sophie had almost forgotten what they expected to find inside. *This is the Priory keystone.* According to Teabing, it contained a map to the Holy Grail, unveiling the tomb of Mary Magdalene and the Sangreal treasure . . . the ultimate treasure trove of secret truth.

Now gripping the stone tube, Sophie double-checked that all of the letters were properly aligned with the indicator. Then, slowly, she pulled. Nothing happened. She applied a little more force. Suddenly, the stone slid apart like a well-crafted telescope. The heavy end piece detached in her hand. Langdon and Teabing almost jumped to their feet. Sophie's heart rate climbed as she set the end cap on the table and tipped the cylinder to peer inside.

A scroll!

Peering down the hollow of the rolled paper, Sophie could see it had been wrapped around a cylindrical object – the vial of vinegar, she assumed. Strangely, though, the paper around the vinegar was not the customary delicate papyrus but rather, vellum. *That's odd,* she thought, *vinegar can't dissolve a lambskin vellum.* She looked again down the hollow of the scroll and realized the object in the centre was not a vial of vinegar after all. It was something else entirely.

'What's wrong?' Teabing asked. 'Pull out the scroll.'

Frowning, Sophie grabbed the rolled vellum and the object around which it was wrapped, pulling them both out of the container.

'That's not papyrus,' Teabing said. 'It's too heavy.'

'I know. It's padding.'

'For what? The vial of vinegar?'

'No.' Sophie unrolled the scroll and revealed what was wrapped inside. 'For *this*.'

When Langdon saw the object inside the sheet of vellum, his heart sank.

'God help us,' Teabing said, slumping. 'Your grandfather was a pitiless architect.'

Langdon stared in amazement. *I see Saunière has no intention of making this easy.*

On the table sat a second cryptex. Smaller. Made of black onyx. It had been nested within the first. Saunière's passion for dualism. *Two cryptexes.* Everything in pairs. *Double-entendres. Male female. Black nested within white.* Langdon felt the web of symbolism stretching onward. *White gives birth to black.*

Every man sprang from woman.

White – female.

Black – male.

Reaching over, Langdon lifted the smaller cryptex. It looked identical to the first, except half the size and black. He heard the familiar gurgle. Apparently, the vial of vinegar they had heard earlier was inside this smaller cryptex.

'Well, Robert,' Teabing said, sliding the page of vellum over to him. 'You'll be pleased to hear that at least we're flying in the right direction.'

Langdon examined the thick vellum sheet. Written in ornate penmanship was another four-line verse. Again, in iambic pentameter. The verse was cryptic, but Langdon needed to read only as far as the first line to realize that Teabing's plan to come to Britain was going to pay off.

IN LONDON LIES A KNIGHT A POPE INTERRED.

The remainder of the poem clearly implied that the password for opening the second cryptex could be found by visiting this knight's tomb, somewhere in the city.

Langdon turned excitedly to Teabing. 'Do you have any idea what knight this poem is referring to?'

Teabing grinned. 'Not the foggiest. But I know in precisely which crypt we should look.'

At that moment, fifteen miles ahead of them, six Kent police cars streaked down rain-soaked streets toward Biggin Hill Executive Airport.

79

Lieutenant Collet helped himself to a Perrier from Teabing's refrigerator and strode back out through the drawing room. Rather than accompanying Fache to London where the action was, he was now baby-sitting the PTS team that had spread out through Château Villette.

So far, the evidence they had uncovered was unhelpful: a single bullet buried in the floor; a paper with several symbols scrawled on it along with the words *blade* and *chalice;* and a bloody spiked belt that PTS had told Collet was associated with the conservative Catholic group Opus Dei, which had caused a stir recently when a news programme exposed their aggressive recruiting practices in Paris.

Collet sighed. *Good luck making sense of this unlikely mélange.*

Moving down a lavish hallway, Collet entered the vast ballroom study, where the chief PTS examiner was busy dusting for fingerprints. He was a corpulent man in braces.

'Anything?' Collet asked, entering.

The examiner shook his head. 'Nothing new. Multiple sets matching those in the rest of the house.'

'How about the prints on the *cilice* belt?'

'Interpol is still working. I uploaded everything we found.'

Collet motioned to two sealed evidence bags on the desk. 'And this?'

The man shrugged. 'Force of habit. I bag anything peculiar.'

Collet walked over. *Peculiar?*

'This Brit's a strange one,' the examiner said. 'Have a look at this.' He sifted through the evidence bags and selected one, handing it to Collet.

The photo showed the main entrance of a Gothic cathedral – the traditional, recessed archway, narrowing through multiple, ribbed layers to a small doorway.

Collet studied the photo and turned. 'This is peculiar?'

'Turn it over.'

On the back, Collet found notations scrawled in English, describing a cathedral's long hollow nave as a secret pagan tribute to a woman's womb. This was strange. The notation describing the cathedral's doorway, however, was what startled him. 'Hold on! He thinks a cathedral's entrance represents a woman's . . .'

The examiner nodded. 'Complete with receding labial ridges and a nice little cinquefoil clitoris above the doorway.' He sighed. 'Kind of makes you want to go back to church.'

Collet picked up the second evidence bag. Through the plastic, he could see a large glossy photograph of what appeared to be an old document. The heading at the top read:

Les Dossiers Secrets – Number 4° lm[1] 249

'What's this?' Collet asked.

'No idea. He's got copies of it all over the place, so I bagged it.'

Collet studied the document.

PRIEURE DE SION – LES NAUTONIERS/ GRAND MASTERS

JEAN DE GISORS	*1188–1220*
MARIE DE SAINT-CLAIR	*1220–1266*
GUILLAUME DE GISORS	*1266–1307*
EDOUARD DE BAR	*1307–1336*
JEANNE DE BAR	*1336–1351*
JEAN DE SAINT-CLAIR	*1351–1366*
BLANCE D'EVREUX	*1366–1398*
NICOLAS FLAMEL	*1398–1418*
RENE D'ANJOU	*1418–1480*
IOLANDE DE BAR	*1480–1483*
SANDRO BOTTICELLI	*1483–1510*
LEONARDO DA VINCI	*1510–1519*
CONNETABLE DE BOURBON	*1519–1527*
FERDINAND DE GONZAQUE	*1527–1575*
LOUIS DE NEVERS	*1575–1595*
ROBERT FLUDD	*1595–1637*
J. VALENTIN ANDREA	*1637–1654*
ROBERT BOYLE	*1654–1691*
ISAAC NEWTON	*1691–1727*
CHARLES RADCLYFFE	*1727–1746*
CHARLES DE LORRAINE	*1746–1780*
MAXIMILIAN DE LORRAINE	*1780–1801*
CHARLES NODIER	*1801–1844*
VICTOR HUGO	*1844–1885*
CLAUDE DEBUSSY	*1885–1918*
JEAN COCTEAU	*1918–1963*

Prieuré de Sion? Collet wondered.

'Lieutenant?' Another agent stuck his head in. 'The switchboard has an urgent call for Captain Fache, but they can't reach him. Will you take it?'

Collet returned to the kitchen and took the call.

It was André Vernet.

The banker's refined accent did little to mask the tension in his voice. 'I thought Captain Fache said he would call me, but I have not yet heard from him.'

'The captain is quite busy,' Collet replied. 'May I help you?'

'I was assured I would be kept abreast of your progress tonight.'

For a moment, Collet thought he recognized the timbre of the man's voice, but he couldn't quite place it. 'Monsieur Vernet, I am currently in charge of the Paris investigation. My name is Lieutenant Collet.'

There was a long pause on the line. 'Lieutenant, I have another call coming in. Please excuse me. I will call you later.' He hung up.

For several seconds, Collet held the receiver. Then it dawned on him. *I knew I recognized that voice!* The revelation made him gasp.

The armoured truck driver.

With the fake Rolex.

Collet now understood why the banker had hung up so quickly. Vernet had remembered the name Lieutenant Collet – the officer he blatantly lied to earlier tonight.

Collet pondered the implications of this bizarre development. *Vernet is involved.* Instinctively, he knew he should call Fache. Emotionally, he knew this lucky break was going to be his moment to shine.

He immediately called Interpol and requested every shred of information they could find on the Depository Bank of Zurich and its president, André Vernet.

80

'Seat belts, please,' Teabing's pilot announced as the Hawker 731 descended into a gloomy morning drizzle. 'We'll be landing in five minutes.'

Teabing felt a joyous sense of homecoming when he saw the misty hills of Kent spreading wide beneath the descending plane. England was less than an hour from Paris, and yet a world away. This morning, the damp, spring green of his homeland looked particularly welcoming. *My time in France is over. I am returning to England victorious. The keystone has been found.* The question remained, of course, as to *where* the keystone would ultimately lead. *Somewhere in the United Kingdom.* Where exactly, Teabing had no idea, but he was already tasting the glory.

As Langdon and Sophie looked on, Teabing got up and went to the far side of the cabin, then slid aside a wall panel to reveal a discreetly hidden wall safe. He dialled in the combination, opened the safe, and extracted two passports. 'Documentation for Rémy and myself.' He then removed a thick stack of fifty-pound notes. 'And documentation for you two.'

Sophie looked leery. 'A bribe?'

'Creative diplomacy. Executive airfields make certain allowances. A British customs official will greet us at my hangar and ask to board the plane. Rather than permitting him to come on, I'll tell him I'm travelling with a French celebrity who prefers that nobody knows she is in England – press considerations, you know – and I'll offer the official this generous tip as gratitude for his discretion.'

Langdon looked amazed. 'And the official will *accept?*'

'Not from *anyone*, they won't, but these people all know me. I'm not an arms dealer, for heaven's sake. I was knighted.' Teabing smiled. 'Membership has its privileges.'

Rémy approached up the aisle now, the Heckler Koch pistol cradled in his hand. 'Sir, my agenda?'

Teabing glanced at his servant. 'I'm going to have you stay onboard with our guest until we return. We can't very well drag him all over London with us.'

Sophie looked wary. 'Leigh, I was serious about the French police finding your plane before we return.'

Teabing laughed. 'Yes, imagine their surprise if they board and find Rémy.'

Sophie looked surprised by his cavalier attitude. 'Leigh, you transported a bound hostage across international borders. This is serious.'

'So are my lawyers.' He scowled toward the monk in the rear of the plane. 'That animal broke into my home and almost killed me. That is a fact, and Rémy will corroborate.'

'But you tied him up and flew him to London!' Langdon said.

Teabing held up his right hand and feigned a courtroom oath. 'Your honour, forgive an eccentric old knight his foolish prejudice for the British court system. I realize I should have called the French authorities, but I'm a snob and do not trust those *laissez-faire* French to prosecute properly. This man almost murdered me. Yes, I made a rash decision forcing my manservant to help me bring him to England, but I was under great stress. Mea culpa. Mea culpa.'

Langdon looked incredulous. 'Coming from you, Leigh, that just might fly.'

'Sir?' the pilot called back. 'The tower just radioed. They've got some kind of maintenance problem out near your hangar, and they're asking me to bring the plane directly to the terminal instead.'

Teabing had been flying to Biggin Hill for over a decade, and this was a first. 'Did they mention what the problem is?'

'The controller was vague. Something about a petrol leak at the pumping station? They asked me to park in front of the terminal and keep everyone onboard until further notice. Safety precaution. We're not supposed to deplane until we get the all clear from airport authorities.'

Teabing was sceptical. *Must be one hell of a petrol leak.* The pumping station was a good half mile from his hangar.

Rémy also looked concerned. 'Sir, this sounds highly irregular.'

Teabing turned to Sophie and Langdon. 'My friends, I have an unpleasant suspicion that we are about to be met by a welcoming committee.'

Langdon gave a bleak sigh. 'I guess Fache still thinks I'm his man.'

'Either that,' Sophie said, 'or he is too deep into this to admit his error.'

Teabing was not listening. Regardless of Fache's mind-set, action needed to be taken fast. *Don't lose sight of the ultimate goal. The Grail. We're so close.* Below them, the landing gear descended with a clunk.

'Leigh,' Langdon said, sounding deeply remorseful, 'I should turn myself in and sort this out legally. Leave you all out of it.'

'Oh, heavens, Robert!' Teabing waved it off. 'Do you really think they're going to let the rest of us go? I just transported you illegally. Miss Neveu assisted in your escape from the Louvre, and we have a man tied up in the back of the plane. Really now! We're all in this together.'

'Maybe a different airport?' Sophie said.

Teabing shook his head. 'If we pull up now, by the time we get clearance anywhere else, our welcoming party will include army tanks.'

Sophie slumped.

Teabing sensed that if they were to have any chance of postponing confrontation with the British authorities long enough to find the Grail, bold action had to be taken. 'Give me a minute,' he said, hobbling toward the cockpit.

'What are you doing?' Langdon asked.

'Sales meeting,' Teabing said, wondering how much it would cost him to persuade his pilot to perform one highly irregular manoeuvre.

81

The Hawker *is on final approach.*

Simon Edwards – Executive Services Officer at Biggin Hill Airport – paced the control tower, squinting nervously at the rain-drenched runway. He never appreciated being awoken early on a Saturday morning, but it was particularly distasteful that he had been called in to oversee the arrest of one of his most lucrative clients. Sir Leigh Teabing paid Biggin Hill not only for a private hangar but a 'per landing fee' for his frequent arrivals and departures. Usually, the airfield had advance warning of his schedule and was able to follow a strict protocol for his arrival. Teabing liked things just so. The custom-built Jaguar stretch limousine that he kept in his hangar was to be fully tanked, polished, and the day's *Times* laid out on the back seat. A customs official was to be waiting for the plane at the hangar to expedite the mandatory documentation and luggage check. Occasionally, customs agents accepted large tips from Teabing in exchange for turning a blind eye to the transport of harmless organics – mostly luxury foods – French escargots, a particularly ripe unprocessed Roquefort, certain fruits. Many customs laws were absurd, anyway, and if Biggin Hill didn't accommodate its clients, certainly competing airfields would. Teabing was provided with what he wanted here at Biggin Hill, and the employees reaped the benefits.

Edwards's nerves felt frayed now as he watched the jet coming in. He wondered if Teabing's penchant for spreading the wealth had got him in trouble somehow; the French authorities seemed very intent on containing him. Edwards had not yet been told what the charges were, but they were obviously serious. At the French authorities' request, Kent police had ordered the Biggin Hill air traffic controller to radio the Hawker's pilot and order him directly to the terminal rather than to the client's hangar. The pilot had agreed, apparently believing the far-fetched story of a petrol leak.

Though the British police did not generally carry weapons, the gravity of the situation had brought out an armed response team. Now, eight policemen with handguns stood just inside the terminal building, awaiting the moment when the plane's engines powered down. The instant this happened, a runway attendant would place safety wedges under the tyres so the plane could no longer move. Then the police would step into view and hold the occupants at bay until the French police arrived to handle the situation.

The Hawker was low in the sky now, skimming the treetops to their right. Simon Edwards went downstairs to watch the landing from tarmac level. The Kent police were poised, just out of sight, and the maintenance man waited with his wedges. Out on the runway, the Hawker's nose tipped up, and the tyres touched down in a puff of smoke. The plane settled in for deceleration, streaking from right to left in front of the terminal, its white hull glistening in the wet weather. But rather than braking and turning into the terminal, the jet coasted calmly past the access lane and continued on toward Teabing's hangar in the distance.

All the police spun and stared at Edwards. 'I thought you said the pilot agreed to come to the terminal!'

Edwards was bewildered. 'He *did*!'

Seconds later, Edwards found himself wedged in a police car racing across the tarmac toward the distant hangar. The convoy of police was still a good five hundred yards away as Teabing's Hawker taxied calmly into the private hangar and disappeared. When the cars finally arrived and skidded to a stop outside the gaping hangar door, the police poured out, guns drawn.

Edwards jumped out too.

The noise was deafening.

The Hawker's engines were still roaring as the jet finished its usual rotation inside the hangar, positioning itself nose-out in preparation for later departure. As the plane completed its 180-degree turn and rolled toward the front of the hangar, Edwards could see the pilot's face, which understandably looked surprised and fearful to see the barricade of police cars.

The pilot brought the plane to a final stop, and powered down the engines. The police streamed in, taking up positions around the jet. Edwards joined the Kent chief inspector, who moved warily toward the hatch. After several seconds, the fuselage door popped open.

Leigh Teabing appeared in the doorway as the plane's electronic stairs smoothly dropped down. As he gazed out at the sea of weapons aimed at him, he propped himself on his crutches and scratched his head. 'Simon, did I win the policemen's lottery while I was away?' He sounded more bewildered than concerned.

Simon Edwards stepped forward, swallowing the frog in his throat. 'Good morning, sir. I apologize for the confusion. We've had a petrol leak and your pilot said he was coming to the terminal.'

'Yes, yes, well, I told him to come here instead. I'm late for an appointment. I pay for this hangar, and this rubbish about avoiding a petrol leak sounded overcautious.'

'I'm afraid your arrival has taken us a bit off guard, sir.'

'I know. I'm off my schedule, I am. Between you and me, the new medication gives me the tinkles. Thought I'd come over for a tune-up.'

The policemen all exchanged looks. Edwards winced. 'Very good, sir.'

'Sir,' the Kent chief inspector said, stepping forward. 'I need to ask you to stay onboard for another half hour or so.'

Teabing looked unamused as he hobbled down the stairs. 'I'm afraid that is impossible. I have a medical appointment.' He reached the tarmac. 'I cannot afford to miss it.'

The chief inspector repositioned himself to block Teabing's progress away from the plane. 'I am here at the orders of the French Judicial Police. They claim you are transporting fugitives from the law on this plane.'

Teabing stared at the chief inspector a long moment, and then burst out laughing. 'Is this one of those hidden camera programmes? Jolly good!'

The chief inspector never flinched. 'This is serious, sir. The French police claim you also may have a hostage onboard.'

Teabing's manservant Rémy appeared in the doorway at the top of the stairs. 'I *feel* like a hostage working for Sir Leigh, but he assures me I am free to go.' Rémy checked his watch. 'Master, we really are running late.' He nodded toward the Jaguar stretch limousine in the far corner of the hangar. The enormous automobile was ebony with smoked glass and whitewall tyres. 'I'll bring the car.' Rémy started down the stairs.

'I'm afraid we cannot let you leave,' the chief inspector said. 'Please return to your aircraft. Both of you. Representatives from the French police will be landing shortly.'

Teabing looked now toward Simon Edwards. 'Simon, for heaven's sake, this is ridiculous! We don't have anyone else on board. Just the usual – Rémy, our pilot, and myself. Perhaps you could act as an intermediary? Go and have a look onboard, and verify that the plane is empty.'

Edwards knew he was trapped. 'Yes, sir. I can have a look.'

'The devil you will!' the Kent chief inspector declared, apparently knowing enough about executive airfields to suspect Simon Edwards might well lie about the plane's occupants in an effort to keep Teabing's business at Biggin Hill. 'I will look myself.'

Teabing shook his head. 'No you won't, Inspector. This is private property and until you have a search warrant, you will stay off my plane. I am offering you a reasonable option here. Mr Edwards can perform the inspection.'

'No deal.'

Teabing's demeanour turned frosty. 'Inspector, I'm afraid I don't have time to indulge in your games. I'm late, and I'm leaving. If it is that important to you to stop me, you'll just have to shoot me.' With that, Teabing and Rémy walked around the chief inspector and headed across the hangar toward the parked limousine.

*

The Kent chief inspector felt only distaste for Leigh Teabing as the man hobbled around him in defiance. Men of privilege always felt like they were above the law.

They are not. The chief inspector turned and aimed at Teabing's back. 'Stop! I will fire!'

'Go ahead,' Teabing said without breaking stride or glancing back. 'My lawyers will fricassee your testicles for breakfast. And if you dare board my plane without a warrant, your spleen will follow.'

No stranger to power plays, the chief inspector was unimpressed. Technically, Teabing was correct and the police needed a warrant to board his jet, but because the flight had originated in France, and because the powerful Bezu Fache had given his authority, the Kent chief inspector felt certain his career would be far better served by finding out what it was on this plane that Teabing seemed so intent on hiding.

'Stop them,' the inspector ordered. 'I'm searching the plane.'

His men raced over, guns levelled, and physically blocked Teabing and his servant from reaching the limousine.

Now Teabing turned. 'Inspector, this is your last warning. Do not even think of boarding that plane. You will regret it.'

Ignoring the threat, the chief inspector gripped his sidearm and marched up the plane's gangway. Arriving at the hatch, he peered inside. After a moment, he stepped into the cabin. *What the devil?*

With the exception of the frightened-looking pilot in the cockpit, the aircraft was empty. Entirely devoid of human life. Quickly checking the bathroom, the chairs, and the luggage areas, the inspector found no traces of anyone hiding . . . much less multiple individuals.

What the hell was Bezu Fache thinking? It seemed Leigh Teabing had been telling the truth.

The Kent chief inspector stood alone in the deserted cabin and swallowed hard. *Shit.* His face flushed, he stepped back onto the gangway, gazing across the hangar at Leigh Teabing and his servant, who were now under gunpoint near the limousine. 'Let them go,' the inspector ordered. 'We received a bad tip.'

Teabing's eyes were menacing even across the hangar. 'You can expect a call from my lawyers. And for future reference, the French police cannot be trusted.'

With that, Teabing's manservant opened the door at the rear of the stretch limousine and helped his crippled master into the back seat. Then the servant walked the length of the car, climbed in behind the wheel, and gunned the engine. Policemen scattered as the Jaguar peeled out of the hangar.

'Well played, my good man,' Teabing chimed from the rear seat as the limousine accelerated out of the airport. He turned his eyes now to the dimly lit front recesses of the spacious interior. 'Everyone comfy?'

Langdon gave a weak nod. He and Sophie were still crouched on the floor beside the bound and gagged albino.

Moments earlier, as the Hawker taxied into the deserted hangar, Rémy had popped the hatch as the plane jolted to a stop halfway through its turn. With the police closing in fast, Langdon and Sophie dragged the monk down the gangway to ground level and out of sight behind the limousine. Then the jet engines had roared again, rotating the plane and completing its turn as the police cars came skidding into the hangar.

Now, as the limousine raced toward Kent, Langdon and Sophie clambered toward the rear of the limo's long interior, leaving the monk bound on the floor. They settled onto the long seat facing Teabing. The Englishman gave them both a roguish smile and opened the cabinet on the limo's bar. 'Could I offer you a drink? Some nibbles? Crisps? Nuts? Seltzer?'

Sophie and Langdon both shook their heads.

Teabing grinned and closed the bar. 'So then, about this knight's tomb . . .'

'Fleet Street?' Langdon asked, eyeing Teabing in the back of the limo. *There's a crypt on Fleet Street?* So far, Leigh was being playfully cagey about where he thought they would find the 'knight's tomb', which, according to the poem, would provide the password for opening the smaller cryptex.

Teabing grinned and turned to Sophie. 'Miss Neveu, give the Harvard boy one more shot at the verse, will you?'

Sophie fished in her pocket and pulled out the black cryptex, which was wrapped in the vellum. Everyone had decided to leave the rosewood box and larger cryptex behind in the plane's strongbox, carrying with them only what they needed, the far more portable and discreet black cryptex. Sophie unwrapped the vellum and handed the sheet to Langdon.

Although Langdon had read the poem several times onboard the jet, he had been unable to extract any specific location. Now, as he read the words again, he processed them slowly and carefully, hoping the pentametric rhythms would reveal a clearer meaning now that he was on the ground.

> In London lies a knight a Pope interred.
> His labour's fruit a Holy wrath incurred.
> You seek the orb that ought be on his tomb.
> It speaks of Rosy flesh and seeded womb.

The language seemed simple enough. There was a knight buried in London. A knight who laboured at something that angered the Church. A knight whose tomb was missing an orb that *should* be present. The poem's final reference – *Rosy flesh and seeded womb* – was a clear allusion to Mary Magdalene, the Rose who bore the seed of Jesus.

Despite the apparent straightforwardness of the verse, Langdon still had no idea *who* this knight was or where he was buried. Moreover, once they located the tomb, it sounded as if they would be searching for something that was absent. *The orb that ought be on his tomb?*

'No thoughts?' Teabing clucked in disappointment, although Langdon sensed the Royal Historian was enjoying being one up. 'Miss Neveu?'

She shook her head.

'What would you two do without me?' Teabing said. 'Very well, I will walk you through it. It's quite simple really. The first line is the key. Would you read it please?'

Langdon read aloud. "In London lies a knight a Pope interred."

'Precisely. A knight a *Pope* interred.' He eyed Langdon. 'What does that mean to you?'

Langdon shrugged. 'A knight buried by a Pope? A knight whose funeral was presided over by a Pope?'

Teabing laughed loudly. 'Oh, that's rich. Always the optimist, Robert. Look at the second line. This knight obviously did something that incurred the holy wrath of the Church. Think again. Consider the dynamic between the Church and the Knights Templar. A knight a Pope interred?'

'A knight a Pope *killed?*' Sophie asked.

Teabing smiled and patted her knee. 'Well done, my dear. A knight a Pope *buried*. Or killed.'

Langdon thought of the notorious Templar round-up in 1307 – unlucky Friday the thirteenth – when Pope Clement killed and interred hundreds of Knights Templar. 'But there must be endless graves of "knights killed by Popes".'

'Aha, not so!' Teabing said. 'Many of them were burned at the stake and tossed unceremoniously into the Tiber River. But this poem refers to a *tomb*. A tomb in London. And there are few knights buried in London.' He paused, eyeing Langdon as if waiting for light to dawn. Finally he huffed. 'Robert, for heaven's sake! The church built in London by the Priory's military arm – the Knights Templar themselves!'

'The Temple Church?' Langdon drew a startled breath. 'It has a crypt?'

'Ten of the most frightening tombs you will ever see.'

Langdon had never actually visited the Temple Church, although he'd come across numerous references in his Priory research. Once the epicentre of all Templar/Priory activities in the United Kingdom, the Temple Church had been so named in honour of Solomon's Temple, from which the Knights Templar had extracted their own title, as well as the Sangreal documents that gave them all their influence in Rome. Tales abounded of knights performing strange, secretive rituals within the Temple Church's unusual sanctuary. 'The Temple Church is on Fleet Street?'

'Actually, it's just off Fleet Street on Inner Temple Lane.' Teabing looked mischievous. 'I wanted to see you sweat a little more before I gave it away.'

'Thanks.'

'Neither of you has ever been there?'

Sophie and Langdon shook their heads.

'I'm not surprised,' Teabing said. 'The church is hidden now behind much larger buildings. Few people even know it's there. Eerie old place. The architecture is pagan to the core.'

Sophie looked surprised. 'Pagan?'

'Pantheonically pagan!' Teabing exclaimed. 'The church is *round*. The Templars ignored the traditional Christian cruciform layout and built a perfectly circular church in honour of the sun.' His eyebrows did a devilish dance. 'A not so subtle howdy-do to the boys in Rome. They might as well have resurrected Stonehenge in central London.'

Sophie eyed Teabing. 'What about the rest of the poem?'

The historian's mirthful air faded. 'I'm not sure. It's puzzling. We will need to examine each of the ten tombs carefully. With luck, one of them will have a conspicuously absent orb.'

Langdon realized how close they really were. If the missing orb revealed the password, they would be able to open the second cryptex. He had a hard time imagining what they might find inside.

Langdon eyed the poem again. It was like some kind of primordial crossword puzzle. *A five-letter word that speaks of the Grail?* On the plane, they had already tried all the obvious passwords – GRAIL, GRAAL, GREAL, VENUS, MARIA, JESUS, SARAH – but the cylinder had not budged. *Far too obvious.* Apparently there existed some other five-letter reference to the Rose's seeded womb. The fact that the word was eluding a specialist like Leigh Teabing signified to Langdon that it was no ordinary Grail reference.

'Sir Leigh?' Rémy called over his shoulder. He was watching them in the rearview mirror through the open divider. 'You said Fleet Street is near Blackfriars Bridge?'

'Yes, take Victoria Embankment.'

'I'm sorry. I'm not sure where that is. We usually go only to the hospital.'

Teabing rolled his eyes at Langdon and Sophie and grumbled, 'I swear, sometimes it's like baby-sitting a child. One moment, please. Help yourself to a drink and savoury snacks.' He left them, clambering awkwardly toward the open divider to talk to Rémy.

Sophie turned to Langdon now, her voice quiet. 'Robert, nobody knows you and I are in England.'

Langdon realized she was right. The Kent police would tell Fache the plane was empty, and Fache would have to assume they were still in France. *We are invisible.* Leigh's little stunt had just bought them a lot of time.

'Fache will not give up easily,' Sophie said. 'He has too much riding on this arrest now.'

Langdon had been trying not to think about Fache. Sophie had promised she would do everything in her power to exonerate Langdon once this was over, but Langdon was starting to fear it might not matter. *Fache could easily be part of this plot.* Although Langdon could not imagine the Judicial Police tangled up in the Holy Grail, he sensed too much coincidence tonight to disregard Fache as a possible accomplice. *Fache is religious, and he is intent on pinning these murders on me.* Then again, Sophie had argued that Fache might simply be overzealous to make the arrest. After all, the evidence against Langdon was substantial. In addition to Langdon's name scrawled on the Louvre floor and in Saunière's date book, Langdon now appeared to have lied about his manuscript and then run away. *At Sophie's suggestion.*

'Robert, I'm sorry you're so deeply involved,' Sophie said, placing her hand on his knee. 'But I'm very glad you're here.'

The comment sounded more pragmatic than romantic, and yet Langdon felt an unexpected flicker of attraction between them. He gave her a tired smile. 'I'm a lot more fun when I've slept.'

Sophie was silent for several seconds. 'My grandfather asked me to trust you. I'm glad I listened to him for once.'

'Your grandfather didn't even know me.'

'Even so, I can't help but think you've done everything he would have wanted. You helped me find the keystone, explained the Sangreal, told me about the ritual in the basement.' She paused. 'Somehow I feel closer to my grandfather tonight than I have for years. I know he would be happy about that.'

In the distance, now, the skyline of London began to materialize through the dawn drizzle. Once dominated by Big Ben and Tower Bridge, the horizon now bowed to the Millennium Eye – a colossal, ultramodern Ferris wheel that climbed five hundred feet and afforded breathtaking views of the city. Langdon had attempted to board it once, but the 'viewing capsules' reminded him of sealed sarcophagi, and he opted to keep his feet on the ground and enjoy the view from the airy banks of the Thames.

Langdon felt a squeeze on his knee, pulling him back, and Sophie's green eyes were on him. He realized she had been speaking to him. 'What do *you* think we should do with the Sangreal documents if we ever find them?' she whispered.

'What I think is immaterial,' Langdon said. 'Your grandfather gave the cryptex to you, and you should do with it what your instinct tells you he would want done.'

'I'm asking for your opinion. You obviously wrote something in that manuscript that made my grandfather trust your judgment. He scheduled a private meeting with you. That's rare.'

'Maybe he wanted to tell me I have it all wrong.'

'Why would he tell me to find you unless he liked your ideas? In your manuscript, did you support the idea that the Sangreal documents should be revealed or stay buried?'

'Neither. I made no judgment either way. The manuscript deals with the symbology of the sacred feminine – tracing her iconography throughout history. I certainly didn't presume to know where the Grail is hidden or whether it should ever be revealed.'

'And yet you're writing a book about it, so you obviously feel the information should be shared.'

'There's an enormous difference between hypothetically discussing an alternative history of Christ, and . . .' He paused.

'And what?'

'And presenting to the world thousands of ancient documents as scientific evidence that the New Testament is false testimony.'

'But you told me the New Testament is based on fabrications.'

Langdon smiled. 'Sophie, *every* faith in the world is based on fabrication. That is the definition of *faith* – acceptance of that which we imagine to be true, that which we cannot prove. Every religion describes God through metaphor, allegory and exaggeration, from the early Egyptians through modern Sunday school. Metaphors are a way to help our minds process the unprocessible. The problems arise when we begin to believe literally in our own metaphors.'

'So you are in favour of the Sangreal documents staying buried for ever?'

'I'm a historian. I'm opposed to the destruction of documents, and I would love to see religious scholars have more information to ponder the exceptional life of Jesus Christ.'

'You're arguing both sides of my question.'

'Am I? The Bible represents a fundamental guidepost for millions of people on the planet, in much the same way the Koran, Torah and Pali Canon offer guidance to people of other religions. If you and I could dig up documentation that contradicted the holy stories of Islamic belief, Judaic belief, Buddhist belief, pagan belief, should we do that? Should we wave a flag and tell the Buddhists that we have proof the Buddha did not come from a lotus blossom? Or that Jesus was not born of a *literal* virgin birth? Those who truly understand their faiths understand the stories are metaphorical.'

Sophie looked skeptical. 'My friends who are devout Christians definitely believe that Christ *literally* walked on water, *literally* turned water into wine and was born of a *literal* virgin birth.'

'My point exactly,' Langdon said. 'Religious allegory has become a part of the fabric of reality. And living in that reality helps millions of people cope and be better people.'

'But it appears their reality is false.'

Langdon chuckled. 'No more false than that of a mathematical cryptographer who believes in the imaginary number "*i*" because it helps her break codes.'

Sophie frowned. 'That's not fair.'

A moment passed.

'What was your question again?' Langdon asked.

'I can't remember.'

He smiled. 'Works every time.'

83

Langdon's Mickey Mouse wristwatch read almost seven-thirty when he emerged from the Jaguar limousine onto Inner Temple Lane with Sophie and Teabing. The threesome wound through a maze of buildings to a small courtyard outside the Temple Church. The rough-hewn stone shimmered in the rain, and doves cooed in the architecture overhead.

London's ancient Temple Church was constructed entirely of Caen stone. A dramatic, circular edifice with a daunting façade, a central turret and a protruding nave off one side, the church looked more like a military stronghold than a place of worship. Consecrated on the tenth of February in 1185 by Heraclius, Patriarch of Jerusalem, the Temple Church survived eight centuries of political turmoil, the Great Fire of London and the First World War, only to be heavily damaged by Luftwaffe incendiary bombs in 1940. After the war, it was restored to its original, stark grandeur.

The simplicity of the circle, Langdon thought, admiring the building for the first time. The architecture was coarse and simple, more reminiscent of Rome's rugged Castel Sant'Angelo than the refined Pantheon. The boxy annex jutting out to the right was an unfortunate eyesore, although it did little to shroud the original pagan shape of the primary structure.

'It's early on a Saturday,' Teabing said, hobbling toward the entrance, 'so I'm assuming we won't have services to deal with.'

The church's entryway was a recessed stone niche inside which stood a large wooden door. To the left of the door, looking entirely out of place, hung a bulletin board covered with concert schedules and religious service announcements.

Teabing frowned as he read the board. 'They don't open to sightseers for another couple of hours.' He moved to the door and tried it. The door didn't budge. Putting his ear to the wood, he listened. After a moment, he pulled back, a scheming look on his face as he pointed to the bulletin board. 'Robert, check the service schedule, will you? Who is presiding this week?'

Inside the church, an altar boy was almost finished vacuuming the communion kneelers when he heard a knocking on the sanctuary door. He ignored it. The Reverend Harvey Knowles had his own keys and was not due for another couple of hours. The knocking was probably a curious tourist or indigent. The altar boy kept vacuuming, but the knocking continued. *Can't you read?* The sign on the door clearly stated that the church did not open until nine-thirty on Saturday. The altar boy remained with his chores.

Suddenly, the knocking turned to a forceful banging, as if someone were hitting the door with a metal rod. The young man switched off his vacuum cleaner and marched angrily toward the door. Unlatching it from within, he swung it open. Three people stood in the entryway. Tourists, he grumbled. 'We open at nine-thirty.'

The heavyset man, apparently the leader, stepped forward using metal crutches. 'I am Sir Leigh Teabing,' he said, his accent highbrow British. 'As you are no doubt aware, I am escorting Mr and Mrs Christopher Wren the Fourth.' He stepped aside, flourishing his arm toward the attractive couple behind them. The woman was soft-featured, with lush burgundy hair. The man was tall, dark-haired and looked vaguely familiar.

The altar boy had no idea how to respond. Sir Christopher Wren was the Temple Church's most famous benefactor. He had made possible all the restorations following damage caused by the Great Fire. He had also been dead since the early eighteenth century. 'Um . . . an honour to meet you?'

The man on crutches frowned. 'Good thing you're not in sales, young man, you're not very convincing. Where is the Reverend Knowles?'

'It's Saturday. He's not due in until later.'

The crippled man's scowl deepened. 'There's gratitude. He assured us he would be here, but it looks as though we'll do it without him. It won't take long.'

The altar boy remained blocking the doorway. 'I'm sorry, *what* won't take long?'

The visitor's eyes sharpened now, and he leaned forward whispering as if to save everyone some embarrassment. 'Young man, apparently you are new here. Every year Sir Christopher Wren's descendants bring a pinch of the old man's ashes to scatter in the Temple sanctuary. It is part of his last will and testament. Nobody is particularly happy about making the trip, but what can we do?'

The altar boy had been here a couple of years but had never heard of this custom. 'It would be better if you waited until nine-thirty. The church isn't open yet, and I'm not finished hoovering.'

The man on crutches glared angrily. 'Young man, the only reason there's anything left of this building for you to hoover is on account of the gentleman in that woman's pocket.'

'I'm sorry?'

'Mrs Wren,' the man on crutches said, 'would you be so kind as to show this impertinent young man the reliquary of ashes?'

The woman hesitated a moment and then, as if awaking from a trance, reached in her sweater pocket and pulled out a small cylinder wrapped in protective fabric.

'There, you see?' the man on crutches snapped. 'Now, you can either grant his dying wish and let us sprinkle his ashes in the sanctuary, or I tell Mr Knowles how we've been treated.'

The altar boy hesitated, well acquainted with Mr Knowles' deep observance of church tradition . . . and, more importantly, with his foul temper when anything cast this time-honoured shrine in anything but favourable light. Maybe Mr Knowles had simply forgotten these family members were coming. If so, then there was far more risk in turning them away than in letting them in. *After all, they said it would only take a minute. What harm could it do?*

When the altar boy stepped aside to let the three people pass, he could have sworn Mr and Mrs Wren looked just as bewildered by all of this as he was. Uncertain, the boy returned to his chores, watching them out of the corner of his eye.

Langdon had to smile as the threesome moved deeper into the church. 'Leigh,' he whispered, 'you lie entirely too well.'

Teabing's eyes twinkled. 'Oxford Theatre Club. They still talk of my Julius Caesar. I'm certain nobody has ever performed the first scene of Act Three with more dedication.'

Langdon glanced over. 'I thought Caesar was *dead* in that scene.'

Teabing smirked. 'Yes, but my toga tore open when I fell, and I had to lie on stage for half an hour with my todger hanging out. Even so, I never moved a muscle. I was brilliant, I tell you.'

Langdon cringed. *Sorry I missed it.*

As the group moved through the rectangular annex toward the archway leading into the main church, Langdon was surprised by the barren austerity. Although the altar layout resembled that of a linear Christian chapel, the furnishings were stark and cold, bearing none of the traditional ornamentation. 'Bleak,' he whispered.

Teabing chuckled. 'Church of England. Anglicans drink their religion straight. Nothing to distract from their misery.'

Sophie motioned through the vast opening that gave way to the circular section of the church. 'It looks like a fortress in there,' she whispered.

Langdon agreed. Even from here, the walls looked unusually robust.

'The Knights Templar were warriors,' Teabing reminded, the sound of his aluminium crutches echoing in this reverberant space. 'A religio-military society. Their churches were their strongholds and their banks.'

'Banks?' Sophie asked, glancing at Leigh.

'Heavens, yes. The Templars *invented* the concept of modern banking. For European nobility, travelling with gold was perilous, so the Templars allowed nobles to deposit gold in their nearest Temple Church and then draw it from any *other* Temple Church across Europe. All they needed was proper documentation.' He winked. 'And a small commission. They were the original ATMs.' Teabing pointed toward a stained-glass window where the breaking sun was refracting through a white-clad knight riding a rose-coloured horse. 'Alanus Marcel,' Teabing said, 'Master of the Temple in the early twelve hundreds. He and his successors actually held the Parliamentary chair of Primus Baro Angiae.'

Langdon was surprised. 'First Baron of the Realm?'

Teabing nodded. 'The Master of the Temple, some claim, held more influence than the king himself.' As they arrived outside the circular chamber, Teabing shot a glance over his shoulder at the altar boy, who was vacuuming in the distance. 'You know,' Teabing whispered to Sophie, 'the Holy Grail is said to once have been stored in this church overnight while the Templars moved it from one hiding place to another. Can you imagine the four chests of Sangreal documents sitting right here with Mary Magdalene's sarcophagus? It gives me gooseflesh.'

Langdon was feeling gooseflesh too as they stepped into the circular chamber. His eye traced the curvature of the chamber's pale stone perimeter, taking in the carvings of gargoyles, demons, monsters and pained human faces, all staring inward. Beneath the carvings, a single stone pew curled around the entire circumference of the room.

'Theatre in the round,' Langdon whispered.

Teabing raised a crutch, pointing toward the far left of the room and then to the far right. Langdon had already seen them.

Ten stone knights.

Five on the left. Five on the right.

Lying supine on the floor, the carved, life-sized figures rested in peaceful poses. The knights were depicted wearing full armour, shields, and swords, and the tombs gave Langdon the uneasy sensation that someone had sneaked in and poured plaster over the knights while they were sleeping. All of the figures were deeply weathered, and yet each was clearly unique – different armoury pieces, distinct leg and arm positions, facial features, and markings on their shields.

In London lies a knight a Pope interred.

Langdon felt shaky as he inched deeper into the circular room.

This had to be the place.

84

In a rubbish-strewn alley very close to Temple Church, Rémy Legaludec pulled the Jaguar limousine to a stop behind a row of industrial waste bins. Killing the engine, he checked the area. Deserted. He got out of the car, walked toward the rear, and climbed back into the limousine's main cabin where the monk was.

Sensing Rémy's presence, the monk in the back emerged from a prayer-like trance, his red eyes looking more curious than fearful. All evening Rémy had been impressed with this trussed man's ability to stay calm. After some initial struggles in the Range Rover, the monk seemed to have accepted his plight and given over his fate to a higher power.

Loosening his bow tie, Rémy unbuttoned his high, starched, wing-tipped collar and felt as if he could breathe for the first time in years. He went to the limousine's wet bar, where he poured himself a Smirnoff vodka. He drank it in a single swallow and followed it with a second.

Soon I will be a man of leisure.

Searching the bar, Rémy found a standard service wine-opener and flicked open the sharp blade. The knife was usually employed to slice the lead foil from corks on fine bottles of wine, but it would serve a far more dramatic purpose this morning. Rémy turned and faced Silas, holding up the glimmering blade.

Now those red eyes flashed fear.

Rémy smiled and moved toward the back of the limousine. The monk recoiled, struggling against his bonds.

'Be still,' Rémy whispered, raising the blade.

Silas could not believe that God had forsaken him. Even the physical pain of being bound Silas had turned into a spiritual exercise, asking the throb of his blood-starved muscles to remind him of the pain Christ endured. *I have been praying all night for liberation.* Now, as the knife descended, Silas clenched his eyes shut.

A slash of pain tore through his shoulder blades. He cried out, unable to believe he was going to die here in the back of this limousine, unable to defend himself. *I was doing God's work. The Teacher said he would protect me.*

Silas felt the biting warmth spreading across his back and shoulders and could picture his own blood, spilling out over his flesh. A piercing pain cut through his thighs now, and he felt the onset of that familiar undertow of disorientation – the body's defence mechanism against the pain.

As the biting heat tore through all of his muscles now, Silas clenched his eyes tighter, determined that the final image of his life would not be of his own killer. Instead he pictured a younger Bishop Aringarosa, standing before the small church in Spain . . . the church that he and Silas had built with their own hands. *The beginning of my life.*

Silas felt as if his body were on fire.

'Take a drink,' the tuxedoed man whispered, his accent French. 'It will help with your circulation.'

Silas's eyes flew open in surprise. A blurry image was leaning over him, offering a glass of liquid. A mound of shredded duct tape lay on the floor beside the bloodless knife.

'Drink this,' he repeated. 'The pain you feel is the blood rushing into your muscles.'

Silas felt the fiery throb transforming now to a prickling sting. The vodka tasted terrible, but he drank it, feeling grateful. Fate had dealt Silas a healthy share of bad luck tonight, but God had solved it all with one miraculous twist.

God has not forsaken me.

Silas knew what Bishop Aringarosa would call it.

Divine intervention.

'I had wanted to free you earlier,' the servant apologized, 'but it was impossible. With the police arriving at Château Villette, and then at Biggin Hill airport, this was the first possible moment. You understand, don't you, Silas?'

Silas recoiled, startled. 'You know my name?'

The servant smiled.

Silas sat up now, rubbing his stiff muscles, his emotions a torrent of incredulity, appreciation and confusion. 'Are you . . . the Teacher?'

Rémy shook his head, laughing at the proposition. 'I wish I had that kind of power. No, I am not the Teacher. Like you, I serve him. But the Teacher speaks highly of you. My name is Rémy.'

Silas was amazed. 'I don't understand. If you work for the Teacher, why did Langdon bring the keystone to *your* home?'

'Not my home. The home of the world's foremost Grail historian, Sir Leigh Teabing.'

'But *you* live there. The odds . . .'

Rémy smiled, seeming to have no trouble with the apparent coincidence of Langdon's chosen refuge. 'It was all utterly predictable. Robert Langdon was in possession of the keystone, and he needed help. What more logical place to run than to the home of Leigh Teabing? That I happen to live there is why the Teacher approached me in the first place.' He paused. 'How do you think the Teacher knows so much about the Grail?'

Now it dawned, and Silas was stunned. The Teacher had recruited a servant who had access to all of Sir Leigh Teabing's research. It was brilliant.

'There is much I have to tell you,' Rémy said, handing Silas the loaded Heckler Koch pistol. Then he reached through the open partition and retrieved a small, palm-sized revolver from the glove box. 'But first, you and I have a job to do.'

Captain Fache descended from his transport plane at Biggin Hill and listened in disbelief to the Kent chief inspector's account of what had happened in Teabing's hangar.

'I searched the plane myself,' the inspector insisted, 'and there was no one inside.' His tone turned haughty. 'And I should add that if Sir Leigh Teabing presses charges against me, I will—'

'Did you interrogate the pilot?'

'Of course not. He is French, and our jurisdiction requires—'

'Take me to the plane.'

Arriving at the hangar, Fache needed only sixty seconds to locate an anomalous smear of blood on the pavement near where the limousine had been parked. Fache walked up to the plane and rapped loudly on the fuselage.

'This is the captain of the French Judicial Police. Open the door!'

The terrified pilot opened the hatch and lowered the stairs.

Fache ascended. Three minutes later, with the help of his sidearm, he had a full confession, including a description of the bound albino monk. In addition, he learned that the pilot saw Langdon and Sophie leave something behind in Teabing's safe, a wooden box of some sort. Although the pilot denied knowing what was in the box, he admitted it had been the focus of Langdon's full attention during the flight to London.

'Open the safe,' Fache demanded.

The pilot looked terrified. 'I don't know the combination!'

'That's too bad. I was going to offer to let you keep your pilot's licence.'

The pilot wrung his hands. 'I know some men in maintenance here. Maybe they could drill it?'

'You have half an hour.'

The pilot leapt for his radio.

Fache strode to the back of the plane and poured himself a hard drink. It was early, but he had not yet slept, so this hardly counted as drinking before noon. Sitting in a plush bucket seat, he closed his eyes, trying to sort out what was going on. *The Kent police's blunder could cost me dearly.* Everyone was now on the lookout for a black Jaguar limousine.

Fache's phone rang, and he wished for a moment's peace. '*Allo?*'

'I'm en route to London.' It was Bishop Aringarosa. 'I'll be arriving in an hour.'

Fache sat up. 'I thought you were going to Paris.'

'I am deeply concerned. I have changed my plans.'

'You should not have.'

'Do you have Silas?'

'No. His captors eluded the local police before I landed.'

Aringarosa's anger rang sharply. 'You assured me you would stop that plane!'

Fache lowered his voice. 'Bishop, considering your situation, I recommend you not test my patience today. I will find Silas and the others as soon as possible. Where are you landing?'

'One moment.' Aringarosa covered the receiver and then came back. 'The pilot is trying to get clearance at Heathrow. I'm his only passenger, but our redirect was unscheduled.'

'Tell him to come to Biggin Hill Executive Airport in Kent. I'll get him clearance. If I'm not here when you land, I'll have a car waiting for you.'

'Thank you.'

'As I expressed when we first spoke, Bishop, you would do well to remember that you are not the only man on the verge of losing everything.'

85

You seek the orb that ought be on his tomb.

Each of the carved knights within the Temple Church lay on his back with his head resting on a rectangular stone pillow. Sophie felt a chill. The poem's reference to an 'orb' conjured images of the night in her grandfather's basement.

Hieros Gamos. The orbs.

Sophie wondered if the ritual had been performed in this very sanctuary. The circular room seemed custom-built for such a pagan rite. A stone pew encircled a bare expanse of floor in the middle. *A theatre in the round,* as Robert had called it. She imagined this chamber at night, filled with masked people, chanting by torchlight, all witnessing a 'sacred communion' in the centre of the room.

Forcing the image from her mind, she advanced with Langdon and Teabing toward the first group of knights. Despite Teabing's insistence that their investigation should be conducted meticulously, Sophie felt eager and pushed ahead of them, making a cursory walk-through of the five knights on the left.

Scrutinizing these first tombs, Sophie noted the similarities and differences between them. Every knight was on his back, but three of the knights had their legs extended straight out while two had their legs crossed. The oddity seemed to have no relevance to the missing orb. Examining their clothing, Sophie noted that two of the knights wore tunics over their armour, while the other three wore ankle-length robes. Again, utterly unhelpful. Sophie turned her attention to the only other obvious difference – their hand positions. Two knights clutched swords, two prayed, and one had his arms at his sides. After a long moment looking at the hands, Sophie shrugged, having seen no hint anywhere of a conspicuously absent orb.

Feeling the weight of the cryptex in her sweater pocket, she glanced back at Langdon and Teabing. The men were moving slowly, still only at the third knight, apparently having no luck either. In no mood to wait, she turned away from them toward the second group of knights. As she crossed the open space, she quietly recited the poem she had read so many times now that it was committed to memory.

> In London lies a knight a Pope interred.
> His labour's fruit a Holy wrath incurred.
> You seek the orb that ought be on his tomb.
> It speaks of Rosy flesh and seeded womb.

When Sophie arrived at the second group of knights, she found that this second group was similar to the first. All lay with varied body positions, wearing armour and swords.

That was, all except the tenth and final tomb.

Hurrying over to it, she stared down.

No pillow. No armour. No tunic. No sword.

'Robert? Leigh?' she called, her voice echoing around the chamber. 'There's something missing over here.'

Both men looked up and immediately began to cross the room toward her.

'An orb?' Teabing called excitedly. His crutches clicked out a rapid staccato as he hurried across the room. 'Are we missing an orb?'

'Not exactly,' Sophie said, frowning at the tenth tomb. 'We seem to be missing an entire knight.'

Arriving beside her, both men gazed down in confusion at the tenth tomb. Rather than a knight lying in the open air, this tomb was a sealed stone coffin. The coffin was trapezoidal, tapered at the feet, widening toward the top, with a peaked lid.

'Why isn't this knight shown?' Langdon asked.

'Fascinating,' Teabing said, stroking his chin. 'I had forgotten about this oddity. It's been years since I was here.'

'This coffin,' Sophie said, 'looks like it was carved at the same time and by the same sculptor as the other nine tombs. So why is this knight in a coffin rather than in the open?'

Teabing shook his head. 'One of this church's mysteries. To the best of my knowledge, nobody has ever found any explanation for it.'

'Hello?' the altar boy said, arriving with a perturbed look on his face. 'Forgive me if this seems rude, but you told me you wanted to spread ashes, and yet you seem to be sightseeing.'

Teabing scowled at the boy and turned to Langdon. 'Mr Wren, apparently your family's philanthropy does not buy you the time it used to, so perhaps we should take out the ashes and get on with it.' Teabing turned to Sophie. 'Mrs Wren?'

Sophie played along, pulling the vellum-wrapped cryptex from her pocket.

'Now then,' Teabing snapped at the boy, 'if you would give us some privacy?'

The altar boy did not move. He was eyeing Langdon closely now. 'You look familiar.'

Teabing huffed. 'Perhaps that is because Mr Wren comes here every year!'

Or perhaps, Sophie now feared, *because he saw Langdon on television at the Vatican last year.*

'I have never met Mr Wren,' the altar boy declared.

'You're mistaken,' Langdon said politely. 'I believe you and I met in passing last year. Mr Knowles failed to formally introduce us, but I recognized your face as we came in. Now, I realize this is an intrusion, but if you could afford me a few more minutes, I have travelled a great distance to scatter ashes amonst these tombs.' Langdon spoke his lines with Teabing-esque believability.

The altar boy's expression turned even more sceptical. 'These are not *tombs.*'

'I'm sorry?' Langdon said.

'Of course they are tombs,' Teabing declared. 'What are you talking about?'

The altar boy shook his head. 'Tombs contain bodies. These are effigies. Stone tributes to real men. There are no bodies beneath these figures.'

'This is a crypt!' Teabing said.

'Only in outdated history books. This was believed to be a crypt but was revealed as nothing of the sort during the 1950 renovation.' He turned back to Langdon. 'And I imagine Mr Wren would *know* that. Considering it was his family that uncovered that fact.'

An uneasy silence fell.

It was broken by the sound of a door slamming out in the annex.

'That must be Mr Knowles,' Teabing said. 'Perhaps you should go and see?'

The altar boy looked doubtful but stalked back toward the annex, leaving Langdon, Sophie and Teabing to eye one another gloomily.

'Leigh,' Langdon whispered. 'No bodies? What is he talking about?'

Teabing looked distraught. 'I don't know. I always thought . . . certainly, this *must* be the place. I can't imagine he knows what he is talking about. It makes no sense!'

'Can I see the poem again?' Langdon said.

Sophie pulled the cryptex from her pocket and carefully handed it to him.

Langdon unwrapped the vellum, holding the cryptex in his hand while he examined the poem. 'Yes, the poem definitely references a *tomb*. Not an effigy.'

'Could the poem be wrong?' Teabing asked. 'Could Jacques Saunière have made the same mistake I just did?'

Langdon considered it and shook his head. 'Leigh, you said it yourself. This church was built by Templars, the military arm of the Priory. Something tells me the Grand Master of the Priory would have a pretty good idea if there were knights buried here.'

Teabing looked flabbergasted. 'But this place is perfect.' He wheeled back toward the knights. 'We must be missing something!'

Entering the annex, the altar boy was surprised to find it deserted. 'Mr Knowles?' *I know I heard the door,* he thought, moving forward until he could see the entryway.

A thin man in a tuxedo stood near the doorway, scratching his head and looking lost. The altar boy gave an irritated huff, realizing he had forgotten to relock the door when he let the others in. Now some pathetic sod had wandered in off the street, looking for directions to some wedding from the looks of it. 'I'm sorry,' he called out, passing a large pillar, 'we're closed.'

A flurry of cloth ruffled behind him, and before the altar boy could turn, his head snapped backward, a powerful hand clamping hard over his mouth from behind, muffling his scream. The hand over the boy's mouth was snow-white, and he smelled alcohol.

The prim man in the tuxedo calmly produced a very small revolver, which he aimed directly at the boy's forehead.

The altar boy felt his groin grow hot and realized he had wet himself.

'Listen carefully,' the tuxedoed man whispered. 'You will exit this church silently, and you will run. You will not stop. Is that clear?'

The boy nodded as best he could with the hand over his mouth.

'If you call the police . . .' The tuxedoed man pressed the gun to his skin. 'I will find you.'

The next thing the boy knew, he was sprinting across the outside courtyard with no plans of stopping until his legs gave out.

86

Like a ghost, Silas drifted silently behind his target. Sophie Neveu sensed him too late. Before she could turn, Silas pressed the gun barrel into her spine and wrapped a powerful arm across her chest, pulling her back against his hulking body. She yelled in surprise. Teabing and Langdon both turned now, their expressions astonished and fearful.

'What . . . ?' Teabing choked out. 'What did you do to Rémy!'

'Your only concern,' Silas said calmly, 'is that I leave here with the keystone.' This recovery mission, as Rémy had described it, was to be clean and simple: *Enter the church, take the keystone, and walk out; no killing, no struggle.*

Holding Sophie firm, Silas dropped his hand from her chest, down to her waist, slipping it inside her deep sweater pockets, searching. He could smell the soft fragrance of her hair through his own alcohol-laced breath. 'Where is it?' he whispered. *The keystone was in her sweater pocket earlier. So where is it now?*

'It's over here,' Langdon's deep voice resonated from across the room.

Silas turned to see Langdon holding the black cryptex before him, waving it back and forth like a matador tempting a dumb animal.

'Set it down,' Silas demanded.

'Let Sophie and Leigh leave the church,' Langdon replied. 'You and I can settle this.'

Silas pushed Sophie away from him and aimed the gun at Langdon, moving toward him.

'Not a step closer,' Langdon said. 'Not until they leave the building.'

'You are in no position to make demands.'

'I disagree.' Langdon raised the cryptex high over his head. 'I will not hesitate to smash this on the floor and break the vial inside.'

Although Silas sneered outwardly at the threat, he felt a flash of fear. This was unexpected. He aimed the gun at Langdon's head and kept his voice as steady as his hand. 'You would never break the keystone. You want to find the Grail as much as I do.'

'You're wrong. You want it much more. You've proven you're willing to kill for it.'

Forty feet away, peering out from the annex pews near the archway, Rémy Legaludec felt a rising alarm. The manoeuvre had not gone as planned, and even from here, he could see Silas was uncertain how to handle the situation. At the Teacher's orders, Rémy had forbidden Silas to fire his gun.

'Let them go,' Langdon again demanded, holding the cryptex high over his head and staring into Silas's gun.

The monk's red eyes filled with anger and frustration, and Rémy tightened with fear that Silas might actually shoot Langdon while he was holding the cryptex. *The cryptex cannot fall!*

The cryptex was to be Rémy's ticket to freedom and wealth. A little over a year ago, he was simply a fifty-five-year-old manservant living within the walls of Château Villette, catering to the whims of the insufferable cripple Sir Leigh Teabing. Then he was approached with an extraordinary proposition. Rémy's association with Sir Leigh Teabing – the pre-eminent Grail historian on earth – was going to bring Rémy everything he had ever dreamed of in life. Since then, every moment he had spent inside Château Villette had been leading him to this very instant.

I am so close, Rémy told himself, gazing into the sanctuary of the Temple Church and the keystone in Robert Langdon's hand. If Langdon dropped it, all would be lost.

Am I willing to show my face? It was something the Teacher had strictly forbidden. Rémy was the only one who knew the Teacher's identity.

'Are you certain you want *Silas* to carry out this task?' Rémy had asked the Teacher less than half an hour ago, upon getting orders to steal the keystone. 'I myself am capable.'

The Teacher was resolute. 'Silas served us well with the four Priory members. He will recover the keystone. *You* must remain anonymous. If others see you, they will need to be eliminated, and there has been enough killing already. Do not reveal your face.'

My face will change, Rémy thought. *With what you've promised to pay me, I will become an entirely new man.* Surgery could even change his fingerprints, the Teacher had told him. Soon he would be free – another unrecognizable, beautiful face soaking up the sun on the beach. 'Understood,' Rémy said. 'I will assist Silas from the shadows.'

'For your own knowledge, Rémy,' the Teacher had told him, 'the tomb in question is not in the Temple Church. So have no fear. They are looking in the wrong place.'

Rémy was stunned. 'And you know where the tomb is?'

'Of course. Later, I will tell you. For the moment, you must act quickly. If the others figure out the true location of the tomb and leave the church before you take the cryptex, we could lose the Grail for ever.'

Rémy didn't give a damn about the Grail, except that the Teacher refused to pay him until it was found. Rémy felt giddy every time he thought of the money he soon would have. *One third of twenty million euros. Plenty to disappear for ever.* Rémy had pictured the beach towns on the Côte d'Azur, where he planned to live out his days basking in the sun and letting others serve him for a change.

Now, however, here in the Temple Church, with Langdon threatening to break the keystone, Rémy's future was at risk. Unable to bear the thought of coming this close only to lose it all, Rémy made the decision to take bold action. The gun in his hand was a concealable, small-calibre, J-frame Medusa, but it would be very deadly at close range.

Stepping from the shadows, Rémy marched into the circular chamber and aimed the gun directly at Teabing's head. 'Old man, I've been waiting a long time to do this.'

Sir Leigh Teabing's heart practically stalled to see Rémy aiming a gun at him. *What is he doing!* Teabing recognized the tiny Medusa revolver as his own, the one he kept locked in the limousine glove box for safety.

'Rémy?' Teabing sputtered in shock. 'What is going on?'

Langdon and Sophie looked equally dumbstruck.

Rémy circled behind Teabing and rammed the pistol barrel into his back, high and on the left, directly behind his heart.

Teabing felt his muscles seize with terror. 'Rémy, I don't—'

'I'll make it simple,' Rémy snapped, eyeing Langdon over Teabing's shoulder. 'Set down the keystone, or I pull the trigger.'

Langdon seemed momentarily paralysed. 'The keystone is worthless to you,' he stammered. 'You cannot possibly open it.'

'Arrogant fools,' Rémy sneered. 'Have you not noticed that I have been listening tonight as you discussed these poems? Everything I heard, I have shared with others. Others who know more than you. You are not even looking in the right place. The tomb you seek is in another location entirely!'

Teabing felt panicked. *What is he saying!*

'Why do you want the Grail?' Langdon demanded. 'To destroy it? Before the End of Days?'

Rémy called to the monk. 'Silas, take the keystone from Mr Langdon.'

As the monk advanced, Langdon stepped back, raising the keystone high, looking fully prepared to hurl it at the floor.

'I would rather break it,' Langdon said, 'than see it in the wrong hands.'

Teabing now felt a wave of horror. He could see his life's work evaporating before his eyes. All his dreams about to be shattered.

'Robert, no!' Teabing exclaimed. 'Don't! That's the Grail you're holding! Rémy would *never* shoot me. We've known each other for ten—'

Rémy aimed at the ceiling and fired the Medusa. The blast was enormous for such a small weapon, the gunshot echoing like thunder inside the stone chamber.

Everyone froze.

'I am not playing games,' Rémy said. 'The next one is in his back. Hand the keystone to Silas.'

Langdon reluctantly held out the cryptex. Silas stepped forward and took it, his red eyes gleaming with the self-satisfaction of vengeance. Slipping the keystone in the pocket of his robe, Silas backed off, still holding Langdon and Sophie at gunpoint.

Teabing felt Rémy's arm clamp hard around his neck as the servant began backing out of the building, dragging Teabing with him, the gun still pressed in his back.

'Let him go,' Langdon demanded.

'We're taking Mr Teabing for a drive,' Rémy said, still backing up. 'If you call the police, he will die. If you do anything to interfere, he will die. Is that clear?'

'Take me,' Langdon demanded, his voice cracking with emotion. 'Let Leigh go.'

Rémy laughed. 'I don't think so. He and I have such a nice history. Besides, he still might prove useful.'

Silas was backing up now, keeping Langdon and Sophie at gunpoint as Rémy pulled Leigh toward the exit, his crutches dragging behind him.

Sophie's voice was unwavering. 'Who are you working for?'

The question brought a smirk to the departing Rémy's face. 'You would be surprised, Mademoiselle Neveu.'

87

The fireplace in Château Villette's drawing room was cold, but Collet paced before it nonetheless as he read the faxes from Interpol.

Not at all what he expected.

André Vernet, according to official records, was a model citizen. No police record – not even a parking ticket. Educated at a good lycée and the Sorbonne, he had a *cum laude* degree in international finance. Interpol said Vernet's name appeared in the newspapers from time to time, but always in a positive light. Apparently the man had helped design the security parameters that kept the Depository Bank of Zurich a leader in the ultramodern world of electronic security. Vernet's credit card records showed a penchant for art books, expensive wine and classical CD's – mostly Brahms – which he apparently enjoyed on an exceptionally high-end stereo system he had purchased several years ago.

Zero, Collet sighed.

The only red flag tonight from Interpol had been a set of fingerprints that apparently belonged to Teabing's servant. The chief PTS examiner was reading the report in a comfortable chair across the room.

Collet looked over. 'Anything?'

The examiner shrugged. 'Prints belong to Rémy Legaludec. Wanted for petty crime. Nothing serious. Looks like he got kicked out of university for rewiring phone jacks to get free service . . . later did some petty theft. Breaking and entering. Skipped out on a hospital bill once for an emergency tracheotomy.' He glanced up, chuckling. 'Peanut allergy.'

Collet nodded, recalling a police investigation into a restaurant that had failed to note on its menu that the chili recipe contained peanut oil. An unsuspecting patron had died of anaphylactic shock at the table after a single bite.

'Legaludec is probably a live-in here to avoid getting picked up.' The examiner looked amused. 'His lucky night.'

Collet sighed. 'All right, you better forward this info to Captain Fache.'

The examiner headed off just as another PTS agent burst into the living room. 'Lieutenant! We found something in the barn.'

From the anxious look on the agent's face, Collet could only guess. 'A body.'

'No, sir. Something more . . .' He hesitated. 'Unexpected.'

Rubbing his eyes, Collet followed the agent out to the barn. As they entered the musty, cavernous space, the agent motioned toward the centre of the room, where a wooden ladder now ascended high into the rafters, propped against the ledge of a hayloft suspended high above them.

'That ladder wasn't there earlier,' Collet said.

'No, sir. I set that up. We were dusting for prints near the Rolls when I saw the ladder lying on the floor. I wouldn't have given it a second thought except the rungs were worn and muddy. This ladder gets regular use. The height of the hayloft matched the ladder, so I raised it and climbed up to have a look.'

Collet's eyes climbed the ladder's steep incline to the soaring hayloft. *Someone goes up there regularly?* From down here, the loft appeared to be a deserted platform, and yet admittedly most of it was invisible from this line of sight.

A senior PTS agent appeared at the top of the ladder, looking down. 'You'll definitely want to see this, Lieutenant,' he said, waving Collet up with a latex-gloved hand.

Nodding tiredly, Collet walked over to the base of the old ladder and grasped the bottom rungs. The ladder was an antique tapered design and narrowed as Collet ascended. As he neared the top, Collet almost lost his footing on a thin rung. The barn below him spun. Alert now, he moved on, finally reaching the top. The agent above him reached out, offering his wrist. Collet grabbed it and made the awkward transition onto the platform.

'It's over there,' the PTS agent said, pointing deep into the immaculately clean loft. 'Only one set of prints up here. We'll have an ID shortly.'

Collet squinted through the dim light toward the far wall. *What the hell?* Nestled against the far wall sat an elaborate computer workstation – two tower CPUs, a flat-screen video monitor with speakers, an array of hard drives, and a multichannel audio console that appeared to have its own filtered power supply.

Why in the world would anyone work all the way up here? Collet moved toward the gear. 'Have you examined the system?'

'It's a listening post.'

Collet spun. 'Surveillance?'

The agent nodded. 'Very advanced surveillance.' He motioned to a long project table strewn with electronic parts, manuals, tools, wires, soldering irons and other electronic components. 'Someone clearly knows what he's doing. A lot of this gear is as sophisticated as our own equipment. Miniature microphones, photoelectric recharging cells, high-capacity RAM chips. He's even got some of those new nano drives.'

Collet was impressed.

'Here's a complete system,' the agent said, handing Collet an assembly not much larger than a pocket calculator. Dangling off the contraption was a foot-long wire with a stamp-sized piece of wafer-thin foil stuck on the end. 'The base is a high-capacity hard disk audio recording system with rechargeable battery. That strip of foil at the end of the wire is a combination microphone and photoelectric recharging cell.'

Collet knew them well. These foil-like, photocell microphones had been an enormous breakthrough a few years back. Now, a hard disk recorder could be affixed behind a lamp, for example, with its foil microphone molded into the contour of the base and dyed to match. As long as the microphone was positioned such that it received a few hours of sunlight per day, the photo cells would keep recharging the system. Bugs like this one could listen indefinitely.

'Reception method?' Collet asked.

The agent signalled to an insulated wire that ran out of the back of the computer, up the wall, through a hole in the barn roof. 'Simple radio wave. Small antenna on the roof.'

Collet knew these recording systems were generally placed in offices, were voice-activated to save hard disk space, and recorded snippets of conversation during the day, transmitting compressed audio files at night to avoid detection. After transmitting, the hard drive erased itself and prepared to do it all over again the next day.

Collet's gaze moved now to a shelf on which were stacked several hundred audio cassettes, all labelled with dates and numbers. *Someone has been very busy.* He turned back to the agent. 'Do you have any idea what target is being bugged?'

'Well, Lieutenant,' the agent said, walking to the computer and launching a piece of software. 'It's the strangest thing. . . .'

88

Langdon felt utterly spent as he and Sophie hurdled a turnstile at the Temple tube station and dashed deep into the grimy labyrinth of tunnels and platforms. The guilt ripped through him.

I involved Leigh, and now he's in enormous danger.

Rémy's involvement had been a shock, and yet it made sense. Whoever was pursuing the Grail had recruited someone on the inside. *They went to Teabing's for the same reason I did.* Throughout history, those who held knowledge of the Grail had always been magnets for thieves and scholars alike. The fact that Teabing had been a target all along should have made Langdon feel less guilty about involving him. It did not. *We need to find Leigh and help him. Immediately.*

Langdon followed Sophie to the westbound District and Circle Line platform, where she hurried to a pay phone to call the police, despite Rémy's warning to the contrary. Langdon sat on a grungy bench nearby, feeling remorseful.

'The best way to help Leigh,' Sophie reiterated as she dialled, 'is to involve the London authorities immediately. Trust me.'

Langdon had not initially agreed with this idea, but as they had hatched their plan, Sophie's logic began to make sense. Teabing was safe at the moment. Even if Rémy and the others knew where the knight's tomb was located, they still might need Teabing's help deciphering the orb reference. What worried Langdon was what would happen *after* the Grail map had been found. *Leigh will become a huge liability.*

If Langdon were to have any chance of helping Leigh, or of ever seeing the keystone again, it was essential that he find the tomb first. *Unfortunately, Rémy has a big head start.*

Slowing Rémy down had become Sophie's task.

Finding the right tomb had become Langdon's.

Sophie would make Rémy and Silas fugitives of the London police, forcing them into hiding or, better yet, catching them. Langdon's plan was less certain – to take the tube to nearby King's College, which was renowned for its electronic theological database. *The ultimate research tool,* Langdon had heard. *Instant answers to any religious historical question.* He wondered what the database would have to say about 'a knight a Pope interred'.

He stood up and paced, wishing the train would hurry.

At the pay phone, Sophie's call finally connected to the London police.

'Snow Hill Division,' the dispatcher said. 'How may I direct your call?'

'I'm reporting a kidnapping.' Sophie knew to be concise.

'Name please?'

Sophie paused. 'Agent Sophie Neveu with the French Judicial Police.'

The title had the desired effect. 'Right away, ma'am. Let me get a detective on the line for you.'

As the call went through, Sophie began wondering if the police would even believe her description of Teabing's captors. *A man in a tuxedo.* How much easier to identify could a suspect be? Even if Rémy changed clothes, he was partnered with an albino monk. *Impossible to miss.* Moreover, they had a hostage and could not take public transportation. She wondered how many Jaguar stretch limos there could be in London.

Sophie's connection to the detective seemed to be taking for ever. *Come on!* She could hear the line clicking and buzzing, as if she was being transferred.

Fifteen seconds passed.

Finally a man came on the line. 'Agent Neveu?'

Stunned, Sophie registered the gruff tone immediately.

'Agent Neveu,' Bezu Fache demanded. 'Where the hell are you?'

Sophie was speechless. Captain Fache had apparently requested the London police dispatcher alert him if Sophie called in.

'Listen,' Fache said, speaking to her in terse French. 'I made a terrible mistake tonight. Robert Langdon is innocent. All charges against him have been dropped. Even so, both of you are in danger. You need to come in.'

Sophie's jaw fell slack. She had no idea how to respond. Fache was not a man who apologized for anything.

'You did not tell me,' Fache continued, 'that Jacques Saunière was your grandfather. I fully intend to overlook your insubordination last night on account of the emotional stress you must be under. At the moment, however, you and Langdon need to go to the nearest London police headquarters for refuge.'

He knows I'm in London? What else does Fache know? Sophie heard what sounded like drilling or machinery in the background. She also heard an odd clicking on the line. 'Are you tracing this call, Captain?'

Fache's voice was firm now. 'You and I need to cooperate, Agent Neveu. We both have a lot to lose here. This is damage control. I made errors in judgment last night, and if those errors result in the deaths of an American professor and a DCPJ cryptologist, my career will be over. I've been trying to pull you back into safety for the last several hours.'

A warm wind was now pushing through the station as a train approached with a low rumble. Sophie had every intention of being on it.

Langdon apparently had the same idea; he was gathering himself together and moving toward her now.

'The man you want is Rémy Legaludec,' Sophie said. 'He is Teabing's servant. He just kidnapped Teabing inside the Temple Church and—'

'Agent Neveu!' Fache bellowed as the train thundered into the station. 'This is not something to discuss on an open line. You and Langdon will come in now. For your own well-being! That is a direct order!'

Sophie hung up and dashed with Langdon onto the train.

89

The immaculate cabin of Teabing's Hawker was now covered with steel shavings and smelled of compressed air and propane. Bezu Fache had sent everyone away and sat alone with his drink and the heavy wooden box found in Teabing's safe.

Running his finger across the inlaid Rose, he lifted the ornate lid. Inside he found a stone cylinder with lettered dials. The five dials were arranged to spell SOFIA. Fache stared at the word a long moment and then lifted the cylinder from its padded resting place and examined every inch. Then, pulling slowly on the ends, Fache slid off one of the end caps. The cylinder was empty.

Fache set it back in the box and gazed absently out the jet's window at the hangar, pondering his brief conversation with Sophie, as well as the information he'd received from PTS in Château Villette. The sound of his phone shook him from his daydream.

It was the DCPJ switchboard. The dispatcher was apologetic. The president of the Depository Bank of Zurich had been calling repeatedly, and although he had been told several times that the captain was in London on business, he just kept calling. Begrudgingly Fache told the operator to forward the call.

'Monsieur Vernet,' Fache said, before the man could even speak, 'I am sorry I did not call you earlier. I have been busy. As promised, the name of your bank has not appeared in the media. So what precisely is your concern?'

Vernet's voice was anxious as he told Fache how Langdon and Sophie had extracted a small wooden box from the bank and then persuaded Vernet to help them escape. 'Then when I heard on the radio that they were criminals,' Vernet said, 'I pulled over and demanded the box back, but they attacked me and stole the truck.'

'You are concerned for a wooden box,' Fache said, eyeing the Rose inlay on the cover and again gently opening the lid to reveal the white cylinder. 'Can you tell me what was in the box?'

'The contents are immaterial,' Vernet fired back. 'I am concerned with the reputation of my bank. We have never had a robbery. *Ever*. It will ruin us if I cannot recover this property on behalf of my client.'

'You said Agent Neveu and Robert Langdon had a password and a key. What makes you say they stole the box?'

'They *murdered* people tonight. Including Sophie Neveu's grand-father. The key and password were obviously ill-gotten.'

'Mr Vernet, my men have done some checking into your background and your interests. You are obviously a man of great culture and refinement. I would imagine you are a man of honour, as well. As am I. That said, I give you my word as commanding officer of the *Police Judiciaire* that your box, along with your bank's reputation, is in the safest of hands.'

90

High in the hayloft at Château Villette, Collet stared at the computer monitor in amazement. 'This system is eavesdropping on *all* these locations?'

'Yes,' the agent said. 'It looks like data has been collected for over a year now.'

Collet read the list again, speechless.

COLBERT SOSTAQUE – Chairman of the Conseil Constitutionnel
JEAN CHAFFÉE – Curator, Musée du Jeu de Paume
EDOUARD DESROCHERS – Senior Archivist, Mitterrand Library
JACQUES SAUNIÈRE – Curator, Musée du Louvre
MICHEL BRETON – Head of DAS (French Intelligence)

The agent pointed to the screen. 'Number four is of obvious concern.'

Collet nodded blankly. He had noticed it immediately. *Jacques Saunière was being bugged.* He looked at the rest of the list again. *How could anyone possibly manage to bug these prominent people?* 'Have you heard any of the audio files?'

'A few. Here's one of the most recent.' The agent clicked a few computer keys. The speakers crackled to life. '*Capitaine, un agent du Département de Cryptographie est arrivé.*'

Collet could not believe his ears. 'That's me! That's my voice!' He recalled sitting at Saunière's desk and radioing Fache in the Grand Gallery to alert him of Sophie Neveu's arrival.

The agent nodded. 'A lot of our Louvre investigation tonight would have been audible if someone had been interested.'

'Have you sent anyone in to sweep for the bug?'

'No need. I know exactly where it is.' The agent went to a pile of old notes and blueprints on the worktable. He selected a page and handed it to Collet. 'Look familiar?'

Collet was amazed. He was holding a photocopy of an ancient schematic diagram, which depicted a rudimentary machine. He was unable to read the handwritten Italian labels, and yet he knew what he was looking at. A model for a fully articulated medieval French knight.

The knight sitting on Saunière's desk!

Collet's eyes moved to the margins, where someone had scribbled notes on the photocopy in red felt-tipped marker. The notes were in French and appeared to be ideas outlining how best to insert a listening device into the knight.

91

Silas sat in the passenger seat of the parked Jaguar limousine near the Temple Church. His hands felt damp on the keystone as he waited for Rémy to finish tying and gagging Teabing in the back with the rope they had found in the trunk.

Finally, Rémy climbed out of the rear of the limo, walked around, and slid into the driver's seat beside Silas.

'Secure?' Silas asked.

Rémy chuckled, shaking off the rain and glancing over his shoulder through the open partition at the crumpled form of Leigh Teabing, who was barely visible in the shadows in the rear. 'He's not going anywhere.'

Silas could hear Teabing's muffled cries and realized Rémy had used some of the old duct tape to gag him.

'*Ferme ta gueule!*' Rémy shouted over his shoulder at Teabing. Reaching to a control panel on the elaborate dash, Rémy pressed a button. An opaque partition raised behind them, sealing off the back. Teabing disappeared, and his voice was silenced. Rémy glanced at Silas. 'I've been listening to his miserable whimpering long enough.'

Minutes later, as the Jaguar stretch limo powered through the streets, Silas's cell phone rang. *The Teacher*. He answered excitedly. 'Hello?'

'Silas,' the Teacher's familiar French accent said, 'I am relieved to hear your voice. This means you are safe.'

Silas was equally comforted to hear the Teacher. It had been hours, and the operation had veered wildly off course. Now, at last, it seemed to be back on track. 'I have the keystone.'

'This is superb news,' the Teacher told him. 'Is Rémy with you?'

Silas was surprised to hear the Teacher use Rémy's name. 'Yes. Rémy freed me.'

'As I ordered him to do. I am only sorry you had to endure captivity for so long.'

'Physical discomfort has no meaning. The important thing is that the keystone is ours.'

'Yes. I need it delivered to me at once. Time is of the essence.'

Silas was eager to meet the Teacher face-to-face at last. 'Yes, sir, I would be honoured.'

'Silas, I would like *Rémy* to bring it to me.'

Rémy? Silas was crestfallen. After everything Silas had done for the Teacher, he had believed he would be the one to hand over the prize. *The Teacher favours Rémy?*

'I sense your disappointment,' the Teacher said, 'which tells me you do not understand my meaning.' He lowered his voice to a whisper. 'You must believe that I would much prefer to receive the keystone from *you* – a man of God rather than a criminal – but Rémy must be dealt with. He disobeyed my orders and made a grave mistake that has put our entire mission at risk.'

Silas felt a chill and glanced over at Rémy. Kidnapping Teabing had not been part of the plan, and deciding what to do with him posed a new problem.

'You and I are men of God,' the Teacher whispered. 'We cannot be deterred from our goal.' There was an ominous pause on the line. 'For this reason alone, I will ask Rémy to bring me the keystone. Do you understand?'

Silas sensed anger in the Teacher's voice and was surprised the man was not more understanding. *Showing his face could not be avoided*, Silas thought. *Rémy did what he had to do. He saved the keystone.* 'I understand,' Silas managed.

'Good. For your own safety, you need to get off the street immediately. The police will be looking for the limousine soon, and I do not want you caught. Opus Dei has a residence in London, no?'

'Of course.'

'And you are welcome there?'

'As a brother.'

'Then go there and stay out of sight. I will call you the moment I am in possession of the keystone and have attended to my current problem.'

'You are in London?'

'Do as I say, and everything will be fine.'

'Yes, sir.'

The Teacher heaved a sigh, as if what he now had to do was profoundly regrettable. 'It's time I speak to Rémy.'

Silas handed Rémy the phone, sensing it might be the last call Rémy Legaludec ever took.

As Rémy took the phone, he knew this poor, twisted monk had no idea what fate awaited him now that he had served his purpose.

The Teacher used you, Silas.

And your bishop is a pawn.

Rémy still marvelled at the Teacher's powers of persuasion. Bishop Aringarosa had trusted everything. He had been blinded by his own desperation. *Aringarosa was far too eager to believe.* Although Rémy did not particularly like the Teacher, he felt pride at having gained the man's trust and helped him so substantially. *I have earned my payday.*

'Listen carefully,' the Teacher said. 'Take Silas to the Opus Dei residence hall and drop him off a few streets away. Then drive to St. James's Park. It is adjacent to The Mall. You can park the limousine on Horse Guards Parade. We'll talk there.'

With that, the connection went dead.

92

King's College, established by King George IV in 1829, houses its Department of Theology and Religious Studies adjacent to Parliament on property granted by the Crown. King's College Religion Department boasts not only 150 years' experience in teaching and research, but the 1982 establishment of the Research Institute in Systematic Theology, which possesses one of the most complete and electronically advanced religious research libraries in the world.

Langdon still felt shaky as he and Sophie came in from the rain and entered the library. The primary research room was as Teabing had described it – a dramatic octagonal chamber dominated by an enormous round table around which King Arthur and his knights might have been comfortable were it not for the presence of twelve flat-screen computer workstations. On the far side of the room, a reference librarian was just pouring a pot of tea and settling in for her day of work.

'Lovely morning,' she said cheerfully, leaving the tea and walking over. 'May I help you?'

'Thank you, yes,' Langdon replied. 'My name is—'

'Robert Langdon.' She gave a pleasant smile. 'I know who you are.'

For an instant, he feared Fache had put him on English television as well, but the librarian's smile suggested otherwise. Langdon still had not got used to these moments of unexpected celebrity. Then again, if anyone on earth were going to recognize his face, it would be a librarian in a Religious Studies reference facility.

'Pamela Gettum,' the librarian said, offering her hand. She had a genial, erudite face and a pleasingly fluid voice. The horn-rimmed glasses hanging around her neck were thick.

'A pleasure,' Langdon said. 'This is my friend Sophie Neveu.'

The two women greeted one another, and Gettum turned immediately back to Langdon. 'I didn't know you were coming.'

'Neither did we. If it's not too much trouble, we could really use your help finding some information.'

Gettum shifted, looking uncertain. 'Normally our services are by petition and appointment only, unless of course you're the guest of someone at the college?'

Langdon shook his head. 'I'm afraid we've come unannounced. A friend of mine speaks very highly of you. Sir Leigh Teabing?' Langdon felt a pang of gloom as he said the name. 'The British Royal Historian.'

Gettum brightened now, laughing. 'Heavens, yes. What a character. Fanatical! Every time he comes in, it's always the same search strings. Grail. Grail. Grail. I swear that man will die before he gives up on that quest.' She winked. 'Time and money afford one such lovely luxuries, wouldn't you say? A regular Don Quixote, that one.'

'Is there any chance you can help us?' Sophie asked. 'It's quite important.'

Gettum glanced around the deserted library and then winked at them both. 'Well, I can't very well claim I'm too busy, now can I? As long as you sign in, I can't imagine anyone being too upset. What did you have in mind?'

'We're trying to find a tomb in London.'

Gettum looked dubious. 'We've got about twenty thousand of them. Can you be a little more specific?'

'It's the tomb of a *knight*. We don't have a name.'

'A knight. That tightens the net substantially. Much less common.'

'We don't have much information about the knight we're looking for,' Sophie said, 'but this is what we know.' She produced a slip of paper on which she had written only the first two lines of the poem.

Hesitant to show the entire poem to an outsider, Langdon and Sophie had decided to share just the first two lines, those that identified the knight. *Compartmentalized cryptography*, Sophie had called it. When an intelligence agency intercepted a code containing sensitive data, cryptographers each worked on a discrete section of the code. This way, when they broke it, no single cryptographer possessed the entire deciphered message.

In this case, the precaution was probably excessive; even if this librarian saw the entire poem, identified the knight's tomb and knew what orb was missing, the information was useless without the cryptex.

Gettum sensed an urgency in the eyes of this famed American scholar, almost as if his finding this tomb quickly were a matter of critical importance. The green-eyed woman accompanying him also seemed anxious.

Puzzled, Gettum put on her glasses and examined the paper they had just handed her.

> In London lies a knight a Pope interred.
> His labour's fruit a Holy wrath incurred.

She glanced at her guests. 'What is this? Some kind of Harvard treasure hunt?'

Langdon's laugh sounded forced. 'Yeah, something like that.'

Gettum paused, feeling she was not getting the whole story. Nonetheless, she felt intrigued and found herself pondering the verse carefully. 'According to this rhyme, a knight did something that incurred displeasure with God, and yet a Pope was kind enough to bury him in London.'

Langdon nodded. 'Does it ring any bells?'

Gettum moved toward one of the workstations. 'Not offhand, but let's see what we can pull up in the database.'

Over the past two decades, King's College Research Institute in Systematic Theology had used optical character recognition software in unison with linguistic translation devices to digitize and catalogue an enormous collection of texts – encyclopedias of religion, religious biographies, sacred scriptures in dozens of languages, histories, Vatican letters, diaries of clerics, anything at all that qualified as writings on human spirituality. Because the massive collection was now in the form of bits and bytes rather than physical pages, the data were infinitely more accessible.

Settling into one of the workstations, Gettum eyed the slip of paper and began typing. 'To begin, we'll run a straight Boolean with a few obvious keywords and see what happens.'

'Thank you.'

Gettum typed in a few words:

London, Knight, Pope

As she clicked the SEARCH button, she could feel the hum of the massive mainframe downstairs scanning data at a rate of 500 MB/sec. 'I'm asking the system to show us any documents whose complete text contains all three of these keywords. We'll get more hits than we want, but it's a good place to start.'

The screen was already showing the first of the hits now.

```
Painting the Pope. The Collected Portraits of
Sir Joshua Reynolds. London University Press.
```

Gettum shook her head. 'Obviously not what you're looking for.' She scrolled to the next hit.

```
The London Writings of Alexander Pope
             by G. Wilson Knight.
```

Again she shook her head.

As the system churned on, the hits came up more quickly than usual. Dozens of texts appeared, many of them referencing the eighteenth-century English writer Alexander Pope, whose counterreligious, mock-epic poetry apparently contained plenty of references to knights and London.

Gettum shot a quick glance to the numeric field at the bottom of the screen. This computer, by calculating the current number of hits and multiplying by the percentage of the database left to search, provided a rough guess of how much information would be found. This particular search looked like it was going to return an obscenely large amount of data.

Estimated number of total hits: 2,692

'We need to refine the parameters further,' Gettum said, stopping the search. 'Is this all the information you have regarding the tomb? There's nothing else to go on?'

Langdon glanced at Sophie Neveu, looking uncertain.

This is no treasure hunt, Gettum sensed. She had heard the whisperings of Robert Langdon's experience in Rome last year. This American had been granted access to the most secure library on earth – the Vatican Secret Archives. She wondered what kinds of secrets Langdon might have learned inside and if his current desperate hunt for a mysterious London tomb might relate to information he had gained within the Vatican. Gettum had been a librarian long enough to know the most common reason people came to London to look for knights. *The Grail.*

Gettum smiled and adjusted her glasses. 'You are friends with Leigh Teabing, you are in England, and you are looking for a knight.' She folded her hands. 'I can only assume you are on a Grail quest.'

Langdon and Sophie exchanged startled looks.

Gettum laughed. 'My friends, this library is a base camp for Grail seekers. Leigh Teabing among them. I wish I had a shilling for every time I'd run searches for the Rose, Mary Magdalene, Sangreal, Merovingian, Priory of Sion, et cetera, et cetera. Everyone loves a conspiracy.' She took off her glasses and eyed them. 'I need more information.'

In the silence, Gettum sensed her guests' desire for discretion was quickly being outweighed by their eagerness for a fast result.

'Here,' Sophie Neveu blurted. 'This is everything we know.' Borrowing a pen from Langdon, she wrote two more lines on the slip of paper and handed it to Gettum.

You seek the orb that ought be on his tomb.
It speaks of Rosy flesh and seeded womb.

Gettum gave an inward smile. *The Grail indeed,* she thought, noting the references to the Rose and her seeded womb. 'I can help you,' she said, looking up from the slip of paper. 'Might I ask where this verse came from? And why you are seeking an orb?'

'You might ask,' Langdon said, with a friendly smile, 'but it's a long story and we have very little time.'

'Sounds like a polite way of saying "mind your own business".'

'We would be for ever in your debt, Pamela,' Langdon said, 'if you could find out who this knight is and where he is buried.'

'Very well,' Gettum said, typing again. 'I'll play along. If this is a Grail-related issue, we should cross-reference against Grail keywords. I'll add a proximity parameter and remove the title weighting. That will limit our hits only to those instances of textual keywords that occur *near* a Grail-related word.'

Search for:
KNIGHT, LONDON, POPE, TOMB

Within 100 word proximity of:
GRAIL, ROSE, SANGREAL, CHALICE

'How long will this take?' Sophie asked.

'A few hundred terabytes with multiple cross-referencing fields?' Gettum's eyes glimmered as she clicked the SEARCH key. 'A mere fifteen minutes.'

Langdon and Sophie said nothing, but Gettum sensed this sounded like an eternity to them.

'Tea?' Gettum asked, standing and walking toward the pot she had made earlier. 'Leigh always loves my tea.'

93

London's Opus Dei Centre is a modest brick building at 5 Orme Court, overlooking the North Walk at Kensington Gardens. Silas had never been here, but he felt a rising sense of refuge and asylum as he approached the building on foot. Despite the rain, Rémy had dropped him off a short distance away in order to keep the limousine off the main streets. Silas didn't mind the walk. The rain was cleansing.

At Rémy's suggestion, Silas had wiped down his gun and disposed of it through a sewer grate. He was glad to get rid of it. He felt lighter. His legs still ached from being bound all that time, but Silas had endured far greater pain. He wondered, though, about Teabing, whom Rémy had left bound in the back of the limousine. The Briton certainly had to be feeling the pain by now.

'What will you do with him?' Silas had asked Rémy as they drove over here.

Rémy had shrugged. 'That is a decision for the Teacher.' There was an odd finality in his tone.

Now, as Silas approached the Opus Dei building, the rain began to fall harder, soaking his heavy robe, stinging the wounds of the day before. He was ready to leave behind the sins of the last twenty-four hours and purge his soul. His work was done.

Moving across a small courtyard to the front door, Silas was not surprised to find the door unlocked. He opened it and stepped into the minimalist foyer. A muted electronic chime sounded upstairs as Silas stepped onto the carpet. The bell was a common feature in these halls where the residents spent most of the day in their rooms in prayer. Silas could hear movement above on the creaky wood floors.

A man in a cloak came downstairs. 'May I help you?' He had kind eyes that seemed not even to register Silas's startling physical appearance.

'Thank you. My name is Silas. I am an Opus Dei numerary.'

'American?'

Silas nodded. 'I am in town only for the day. Might I rest here?'

'You need not even ask. There are two empty rooms on the third floor. Shall I bring you some tea and bread?'

'Thank you.' Silas was famished.

Silas went upstairs to a modest room with a window, where he took off his wet robe and knelt down to pray in his undergarments. He heard his host come up and lay a tray outside his door. Silas finished his prayers, ate his food and lay down to sleep.

Three stories below, a phone was ringing. The Opus Dei numerary who had welcomed Silas answered the line.

'This is the London police,' the caller said. 'We are trying to find an albino monk. We've had a tip-off that he might be there. Have you seen him?'

The numerary was startled. 'Yes, he is here. Is something wrong?'

'He is there *now?*'

'Yes, upstairs praying. What is going on?'

'Leave him precisely where he is,' the officer commanded. 'Don't say a word to anyone. I'm sending officers over right away.'

94

St James's Park is a sea of green in the middle of London, a public park bordering the palaces of Westminster, Buckingham and St James's. Once enclosed by King Henry VIII and stocked with deer for the hunt, St James's Park is now open to the public. On sunny afternoons, Londoners picnic beneath the willows and feed the pond's resident pelicans, whose ancestors were a gift to Charles II from the Russian ambassador.

The Teacher saw no pelicans today. The stormy weather had brought instead seagulls from the ocean. The lawns were covered with them – hundreds of white bodies all facing the same direction, patiently riding out the damp wind. Despite the morning fog, the park afforded splendid views of the Houses of Parliament and Big Ben. Gazing across the sloping lawns, past the duck pond and the delicate silhouettes of the weeping willows, the Teacher could see the spires of the building that housed the knight's tomb – the real reason he had told Rémy to come to this spot.

As the Teacher approached the front passenger door of the parked limousine, Rémy leaned across and opened the door. The Teacher paused outside, taking a pull from the flask of cognac he was carrying. Then, dabbing his mouth, he slid in beside Rémy and closed the door.

Rémy held up the keystone like a trophy. 'It was almost lost.'

'You have done well,' the Teacher said.

'*We* have done well,' Rémy replied, laying the keystone in the Teacher's eager hands.

The Teacher admired it a long moment, smiling. 'And the gun? You wiped it down?'

'Back in the glove box where I found it.'

'Excellent.' The Teacher took another drink of cognac and handed the flask to Rémy. 'Let's toast our success. The end is near.'

Rémy accepted the bottle gratefully. The cognac tasted salty, but Rémy didn't care. He and the Teacher were truly partners now. He could feel himself ascending to a higher station in life. *I will never be a servant again.* As Rémy gazed down the embankment at the duck pond below, Château Villette seemed miles away.

Taking another swig from the flask, Rémy could feel the cognac warming his blood. The warmth in Rémy's throat, however, mutated quickly to an uncomfortable heat. Loosening his bow tie, Rémy tasted an unpleasant grittiness and handed the flask back to the Teacher. 'I've probably had enough,' he managed, weakly.

Taking the flask, the Teacher said, 'Rémy, as you are aware, you are the only one who knows my face. I placed enormous trust in you.'

'Yes,' he said, feeling feverish as he loosened his tie further. 'And your identity shall go with me to the grave.'

The Teacher was silent a long moment. 'I believe you.' Pocketing the flask and the keystone, the Teacher reached for the glove box and pulled out the tiny Medusa revolver. For an instant, Rémy felt a surge of fear, but the Teacher simply slipped it in his trousers pocket.

What is he doing? Rémy felt himself sweating suddenly.

'I know I promised you freedom,' the Teacher said, his voice now sounding regretful. 'But considering your circumstances, this is the best I can do.'

The swelling in Rémy's throat came on like an earthquake, and he lurched against the steering column, grabbing his throat and tasting vomit in his narrowing trachea. He let out a muted croak of a scream, not even loud enough to be heard outside the car. The saltiness in the cognac now registered.

I'm being murdered!

Incredulous, Rémy turned to see the Teacher sitting calmly beside him, staring straight ahead through the windshield. Rémy's eyesight blurred, and he gasped for breath. *I made everything possible for him! How could he do this!* Whether the Teacher had intended to kill Rémy all along or whether it had been Rémy's actions in the Temple Church that had made the Teacher lose faith, Rémy would never know. Terror and rage coursed through him now. Rémy tried to lunge for the Teacher, but his stiffening body could barely move. *I trusted you with everything!*

Rémy tried to lift his clenched fists to blow the horn, but instead he slipped sideways, rolling onto the seat, lying on his side beside the Teacher, clutching at his throat. The rain fell harder now. Rémy could no longer see, but he could sense his oxygen-deprived brain straining to cling to his last faint shreds of lucidity. As his world slowly went black, Rémy Legaludec could have sworn he heard the sounds of the soft Riviera surf.

The Teacher stepped from the limousine, pleased to see that nobody was looking in his direction. *I had no choice,* he told himself, surprised how little remorse he felt for what he had just done. *Rémy sealed his own fate.* The Teacher had feared all along that Rémy might need to be eliminated when the mission was complete, but by brazenly showing himself in the Temple Church, Rémy had accelerated the necessity dramatically. Robert Langdon's unexpected visit to Château Villette had brought the Teacher both a fortuitous windfall and an intricate dilemma. Langdon had delivered the keystone directly to the heart of the operation, which was a pleasant surprise, and yet he had brought the police on his tail. Rémy's prints were all over Château Villette, as well as in the barn's listening post, where Rémy had carried out the surveillance. The Teacher was grateful he had taken so much care in preventing any ties between Rémy's activities and his own. Nobody could implicate the Teacher unless Rémy talked, and that was no longer a concern.

One more loose end to tie up here, the Teacher thought, moving now toward the rear door of the limousine. *The police will have no idea what happened . . . and no living witness left to tell them.* Glancing around to ensure nobody was watching, he pulled open the door and climbed into the spacious rear compartment.

Minutes later, the Teacher was crossing St James's Park. *Only two people now remain. Langdon and Neveu.* They were more complicated. But manageable. At the moment, however, the Teacher had the cryptex to attend to.

Gazing triumphantly across the park, he could see his destination. *In London lies a knight a Pope interred.* As soon as the Teacher had heard the poem, he had known the answer. Even so, that the others had not figured it out was not surprising. *I have an unfair advantage.* Having listened to Saunière's conversations for months now, the Teacher had heard the Grand Master mention this famous knight on occasion, expressing esteem almost matching that he held for Da Vinci. The poem's reference to the knight was brutally simple once one saw it – a credit to Saunière's wit – and yet how this tomb would reveal the final password was still a mystery.

You seek the orb that ought be on his tomb.

The Teacher vaguely recalled photos of the famous tomb and, in particular, its most distinguishing feature. *A magnificent orb.* The huge sphere mounted atop the tomb was almost as large as the tomb itself. The presence of the orb seemed both encouraging and troubling to the Teacher. On one hand, it felt like a signpost, and yet, according to the poem, the missing piece of the puzzle was an orb that *ought* to be on his tomb . . . not one that was already there. He was counting on his closer inspection of the tomb to unveil the answer.

The rain was getting heavier now, and he tucked the cryptex deep in his right-hand pocket to protect it from the dampness. He kept the tiny Medusa revolver in his left, out of sight. Within minutes, he was stepping into the quiet sanctuary of London's grandest nine-hundred-year-old building.

Just as the Teacher was stepping out of the rain, Bishop Aringarosa was stepping into it. On the rainy tarmac at Biggin Hill Executive Airport, Aringarosa emerged from his cramped plane, bundling his cassock against the cold damp. He had hoped to be greeted by Captain Fache. Instead a young British police officer approached with an umbrella.

'Bishop Aringarosa? Captain Fache had to leave. He asked me to look after you. He suggested I take you to Scotland Yard. He thought it would be safest.'

Safest? Aringarosa looked down at the heavy briefcase of Vatican bonds clutched in his hand. He had almost forgotten. 'Yes, thank you.'

Aringarosa climbed into the police car, wondering where Silas could be. Minutes later, the police scanner crackled with the answer.

5 Orme Court.

Aringarosa recognized the address instantly.

The Opus Dei Centre in London.

He spun to the driver. 'Take me there at once!'

95

Langdon's eyes had not left the computer screen since the search began.

Five minutes. Only two hits. Both irrelevant.

He was starting to get worried.

Pamela Gettum was in the adjoining room, preparing hot drinks. Langdon and Sophie had inquired unwisely if there might be some *coffee* brewing alongside the tea Gettum had offered, and from the sound of the microwave beeps in the next room, Langdon suspected their request was about to be rewarded with instant Nescafé.

Finally, the computer pinged happily.

'Sounds like you got another,' Gettum called from the next room. 'What's the title?'

Langdon eyed the screen.

Grail Allegory in Medieval Literature:
A Treatise on Sir Gawain and the Green Knight.

'Allegory of the Green Knight,' he called back.

'No good,' Gettum said. 'Not many mythological green giants buried in London.'

Langdon and Sophie sat patiently in front of the screen and waited through two more dubious returns. When the computer pinged again, though, the offering was unexpected.

DIE OPERN VON RICHARD WAGNER

'The operas of Wagner?' Sophie asked.

Gettum peeked back in the doorway, holding a packet of instant coffee. 'That seems like a strange match. Was Wagner a knight?'

'No,' Langdon said, feeling a sudden intrigue. 'But he was a well-known Freemason.' *Along with Mozart, Beethoven, Shakespeare, Gershwin, Houdini and Disney.* Volumes had been written about the ties between the Masons and the Knights Templar, the Priory of Sion, and the Holy Grail. 'I want to look at this one. How do I see the full text?'

'You don't want the full text,' Gettum called. 'Click on the hypertext title. The computer will display your keyword hits along with mono prelogs and triple postlogs for context.'

Langdon had no idea what she had just said, but he clicked anyway. A new window popped up.

```
        . . . mythological knight named Parsifal
                    who . . .
            . . . metaphorical Grail quest that
                    arguably . . .
        . . . the London Philharmonic in 1855 . . .
    Rebecca Pope's opera anthology 'Diva's . . .
        . . . Wagner's tomb in Bayreuth, Germany . . .
```

'Wrong Pope,' Langdon said, disappointed. Even so, he was amazed by the system's ease of use. The keywords with context were enough to remind him that Wagner's opera *Parsifal* was a tribute to Mary Magdalene and the bloodline of Jesus Christ, told through the story of a young knight on a quest for truth.

'Just be patient,' Gettum urged. 'It's a numbers game. Let the machine run.'

Over the next few minutes, the computer returned several more Grail references, including a text about *troubadours* – France's famous wandering minstrels. Langdon knew it was no coincidence that the word *minstrel* and *minister* shared an etymological root. The troubadours were the travelling servants or 'ministers' of the Church of Mary Magdalene, using music to disseminate the story of the sacred feminine among the common folk. To this day, the troubadours sang songs extolling the virtues of 'our Lady' – a mysterious and beautiful woman to whom they pledged themselves for ever.

Eagerly, he checked the hypertext but found nothing.

The computer pinged again.

KNIGHTS, KNAVES, POPES, AND PENTACLES:
THE HISTORY OF THE HOLY GRAIL THROUGH TAROT

'Not surprising,' Langdon said to Sophie. 'Some of our keywords have the same names as individual cards.' He reached for the mouse to click on a hyperlink. 'I'm not sure if your grandfather ever mentioned it when you played Tarot with him, Sophie, but this game is a "flash-card catechism" into the story of the Lost Bride and her subjugation by the evil Church.'

Sophie eyed him, looking incredulous. 'I had no idea.'

'That's the point. By teaching through a metaphorical game, the followers of the Grail disguised their message from the watchful eye of the Church.' Langdon often wondered how many modern card players had any clue that their four suits – spades, hearts, clubs, diamonds – were Grail-related symbols that came directly from Tarot's four suits of swords, cups, sceptres and pentacles.

Spades were Swords – The blade. Male.
Hearts were Cups – The chalice. Feminine.
Clubs were Sceptres – The Royal Line. The flowering staff.
Diamonds were Pentacles – The goddess. The sacred feminine.

Four minutes later, as Langdon began feeling fearful they would not find what they had come for, the computer produced another hit.

The Gravity of Genius:
Biography of a Modern Knight.

'*Gravity of Genius?*' Langdon called out to Gettum. 'Bio of a modern knight?'

Gettum stuck her head around the corner. 'How modern? Please don't tell me it's your Sir Rudy Giuliani. Personally, I found that one a bit off the mark.'

Langdon had his own qualms about the newly knighted Sir Mick Jagger, but this hardly seemed the moment to debate the politics of modern British knighthood. 'Let's have a look.' Langdon summoned up the hypertext keywords.

```
. . . honourable knight, Sir Isaac Newton . . .
        . . . in London in 1727 and . . .
     . . . his tomb in Westminster Abbey . . .
 . . . Alexander Pope, friend and colleague . . .
```

'I suppose "modern" is a relative term,' Sophie called to Gettum. 'It's an old book. About Sir Isaac Newton.'

Gettum shook her head in the doorway. 'No good. Newton was buried in Westminster Abbey, the seat of English Protestantism. There's no way a Catholic Pope was present. Cream and sugar?'

Sophie nodded.

Gettum waited. 'Robert?'

Langdon's heart was hammering. He pulled his eyes from the screen and stood up. 'Sir Isaac Newton is our knight.'

Sophie remained seated. 'What are you talking about?'

'Newton is buried in London,' Langdon said. 'His labours produced new sciences that incurred the wrath of the Church. And he was a Grand Master of the Priory of Sion. What more could we want?'

'What more?' Sophie pointed to the poem. 'How about a knight a Pope interred? You heard Ms Gettum. Newton was not buried by a Catholic Pope.'

Langdon reached for the mouse. 'Who said anything about a *Catholic* Pope?' He clicked on the 'Pope' hyperlink, and the complete sentence appeared.

```
   Sir Isaac Newton's burial, attended by kings
and nobles, was presided over by Alexander Pope,
friend and colleague, who gave a stirring eulogy
     before sprinkling dirt on the tomb.
```

Langdon looked at Sophie. 'We had the correct Pope on our second hit. Alexander.' He paused. 'A. Pope.'

In London lies a knight A. Pope interred.

Sophie stood up, looking stunned.

Jacques Saunière, the master of double-entendres, had proven once again that he was a frighteningly clever man.

96

Silas awoke with a start.

He had no idea what had awoken him or how long he had been asleep. *Was I dreaming?* Sitting up now on his straw mat, he listened to the quiet breathing of the Opus Dei residence hall, the stillness textured only by the soft murmurs of someone praying aloud in a room below him. These were familiar sounds and should have comforted him.

And yet he felt a sudden and unexpected wariness.

Standing, wearing only his undergarments, Silas walked to the window. *Was I followed?* The courtyard below was deserted, exactly as he had seen it when he entered. He listened. Silence. *So why am I uneasy?* Long ago Silas had learned to trust his intuition. Intuition had kept him alive as a child on the streets of Marseilles long before prison . . . long before he was born again by the hand of Bishop Aringarosa. Peering out the window, he now saw the faint outline of a car through the hedge. On the car's roof was a police siren. A floorboard creaked in the hallway. A door latch moved.

Silas reacted on instinct, surging across the room and sliding to a stop just behind the door as it crashed open. The first police officer stormed through, swinging his gun left then right at what appeared an empty room. Before he realized where Silas was, Silas had thrown his shoulder into the door, crushing a second officer as he came through. As the first officer wheeled to shoot, Silas dove for his legs. The gun went off, the bullet sailing above Silas's head, just as he connected with the officer's shins, driving his legs out from under him, and sending the man down, his head hitting the floor. The second officer staggered to his feet in the doorway, and Silas drove a knee into his groin, then went clambering over the writhing body into the hall.

Almost naked, Silas hurled his pale body down the staircase. He knew he had been betrayed, but by whom? When he reached the foyer, more officers were surging through the front door. Silas turned the other way and dashed deeper into the residence hall. *The women's entrance. Every Opus Dei building has one.* Winding down narrow hallways, Silas snaked through a kitchen, past terrified workers, who left to avoid the naked albino as he knocked over bowls and silverware, bursting into a dark hallway near the boiler room. He now saw the door he sought, an exit light gleaming at the end.

Running full speed through the door out into the rain, Silas leapt off the low landing, not seeing the officer coming the other way until it was too late. The two men collided, Silas's broad, naked shoulder grinding into the man's sternum with crushing force. He drove the officer backward onto the pavement, landing hard on top of him. The officer's gun clattered away. Silas could hear men running down the hall shouting. Rolling, he grabbed the loose gun just as the officers emerged. A shot rang out on the stairs, and Silas felt a searing pain below his ribs. Filled with rage, he opened fire at all three officers, their blood spraying.

A dark shadow loomed behind, coming out of nowhere. The angry hands that grabbed at his bare shoulders felt as if they were infused with the power of the devil himself. The man roared in his ear. *SILAS, NO!*

Silas spun and fired. Their eyes met. Silas was already screaming in horror as Bishop Aringarosa fell.

97

More than three thousand people are entombed or enshrined within Westminster Abbey. The colossal stone interior burgeons with the remains of kings, statesmen, scientists, poets and musicians. Their tombs, packed into every last niche and alcove, range in grandeur from the most regal of mausoleums – that of Queen Elizabeth I, whose canopied sarcophagus inhabits its own private, apsidal chapel – down to the most modest etched floor tiles whose inscriptions have worn away with centuries of foot traffic, leaving it to one's imagination whose relics might lie below the tile in the undercroft.

Designed in the style of the great cathedrals of Amiens, Chartresand Canterbury, Westminster Abbey is considered neither cathedral nor parish church. It bears the classification of *royal peculiar*, subject only to the Sovereign. Since hosting the coronation of William the Conqueror on Christmas Day in 1066, the dazzling sanctuary has witnessed an endless procession of royal ceremonies and affairs of state – from the canonization of Edward the Confessor to the marriage of Prince Andrew and Sarah Ferguson to the funerals of Henry V, Queen Elizabeth I and Princess Diana.

Even so, Robert Langdon currently felt no interest in any of the abbey's ancient history, save one event – the funeral of the British knight Sir Isaac Newton.

In London lies a knight a Pope interred.

Hurrying through the grand portico on the north transept, Langdon and Sophie were met by guards who politely ushered them through the abbey's newest addition – a large walk-through metal detector – now present in most historic buildings in London. They both passed through without setting off the alarm and continued to the abbey entrance.

Stepping across the threshold into Westminster Abbey, Langdon felt the outside world evaporate with a sudden hush. No rumble of traffic. No hiss of rain. Just a deafening silence, which seemed to reverberate back and forth as if the building were whispering to itself.

Langdon's and Sophie's eyes, like those of almost every visitor, shifted immediately skyward, where the abbey's great abyss seemed to explode overhead. Grey stone columns ascended like redwoods into the shadows, arching gracefully over dizzying expanses, and then shooting back down to the stone floor. Before them, the wide alley of the north transept stretched out like a deep canyon, flanked by sheer cliffs of stained glass. On sunny days, the abbey floor was a prismatic patchwork of light. Today, the rain and darkness gave this massive hollow a wraithlike aura . . . more like that of the crypt it truly was.

'It's practically empty,' Sophie whispered.

Langdon felt disappointed. He had hoped for a lot more people. *A more public place.* Their earlier experience in the deserted Temple Church was not one Langdon wanted to repeat. He had been anticipating a certain feeling of security in the popular tourist destination, but Langdon's recollections of bustling throngs in a well-lit abbey had been formed during the peak summer tourist season. Today was a rainy April morning. Rather than crowds and shimmering stained glass, all Langdon saw was acres of desolate floor and shadowy, empty alcoves.

'We passed through metal detectors,' Sophie reminded, apparently sensing Langdon's apprehension. 'If anyone is in here, they can't be armed.'

Langdon nodded but still felt circumspect. He had wanted to bring the London police with them, but Sophie's fears of who might be involved put a damper on any contact with the authorities. *We need to recover the cryptex,* Sophie had insisted. *It is the key to everything.*

She was right, of course.

The key to getting Leigh back alive.

The key to finding the Holy Grail.

The key to learning who is behind this.

Unfortunately, their only chance to recover the keystone seemed to be here and now . . . at the tomb of Isaac Newton. Whoever held the cryptex would have to pay a visit to the tomb to decipher the final clue, and if they had not already come and gone, Sophie and Langdon intended to intercept them.

Striding toward the left wall to get out of the open, they moved into an obscure side aisle behind a row of pilasters. Langdon couldn't shake the image of Leigh Teabing being held captive, probably tied up in the back of his own limousine. Whoever had ordered the top Priory members killed would not hesitate to eliminate others who stood in the way. It seemed a cruel irony that Teabing – a modern British knight – was a hostage in the search for his own countryman, Sir Isaac Newton.

'Which way is it?' Sophie asked, looking around.

The tomb. Langdon had no idea. 'We should find a docent and ask.'

Langdon knew better than to wander aimlessly in here. Westminster Abbey was a tangled warren of mausoleums, perimeter chambers and walk-in burial niches. Like the Louvre's Grand Gallery, it had a lone point of entry – the door through which they had just passed – easy to find your way in, but impossible to find your way out. *A literal tourist trap,* one of

Langdon's befuddled colleagues had called it. Keeping architectural tradition, the abbey was laid out in the shape of a giant crucifix. Unlike most churches, however, it had its entrance on the *side*, rather than the standard rear of the church via the narthex at the bottom of the nave. Moreover, the abbey had a series of sprawling cloisters attached. One false step through the wrong archway, and a visitor was lost in a labyrinth of outdoor passageways surrounded by high walls.

'Docents wear crimson robes,' Langdon said, approaching the centre of the church. Peering obliquely across the towering gilded altar to the far end of the south transept, Langdon saw several people crawling on their hands and knees. This prostrate pilgrimage was a common occurrence in Poets' Corner, although it was far less holy than it appeared. *Tourists doing grave rubbings.*

'I don't see any docents,' Sophie said. 'Maybe we can find the tomb on our own?'

Without a word, Langdon led her another few steps to the centre of the abbey and pointed to the right.

Sophie drew a startled breath as she looked down the length of the abbey's nave, the full magnitude of the building now visible. 'Aah,' she said. 'Let's find a docent.'

At that moment, a hundred yards down the nave, out of sight behind the choir screen, the stately tomb of Sir Isaac Newton had a lone visitor. The Teacher had been scrutinizing the monument for ten minutes now.

Newton's tomb consisted of a massive black-marble sarcophagus on which reclined the sculpted form of Sir Isaac Newton, wearing classical costume, and leaning proudly against a stack of his own books – *Divinity, Chronology, Opticks* and *Philosophiae Naturalis Principia Mathematica*. At Newton's feet stood two winged boys holding a scroll. Behind Newton's recumbent body rose an austere pyramid. Although the pyramid itself seemed an oddity, it was the giant shape mounted halfway *up* the pyramid that most intrigued the Teacher.

An orb.

The Teacher pondered Saunière's beguiling riddle. *You seek the orb that ought be on his tomb.* The massive orb protruding from the face of the pyramid was carved in basso-relievo and depicted all kinds of heavenly bodies – constellations, signs of the zodiac, comets, stars and planets. Above it, the image of the Goddess of Astronomy beneath a field of stars.

Countless orbs.

The Teacher had been convinced that once he found the tomb, discerning the missing orb would be easy. Now he was not so sure. He was gazing at a complicated map of the heavens. Was there a missing planet? Had some astronomical orb been omitted from a constellation? He had no idea. Even so, the Teacher could not help but suspect that the solution would be ingeniously clean and simple – 'a knight a pope interred.' *What orb am I looking for?* Certainly, an advanced knowledge of astrophysics was not a prerequisite for finding the Holy Grail, was it?

It speaks of Rosy flesh and seeded womb.

The Teacher's concentration was broken by several approaching tourists. He slipped the cryptex back in his pocket and watched warily as the visitors went to a nearby table, left a donation in the cup and restocked on the complimentary grave-rubbing supplies set out by the abbey. Armed with fresh charcoal pencils and large sheets of heavy paper, they headed off toward the front of the abbey, probably to the popular Poets' Corner to pay their respects to Chaucer, Tennyson and Dickens by rubbing furiously on their graves.

Alone again, he stepped closer to the tomb, scanning it from bottom to top. He began with the clawed feet beneath the sarcophagus, moved upward past Newton, past his books on science, past the two boys with their mathematical scroll, up the face of the pyramid to the giant orb with its constellations, and finally up to the niche's star-filled canopy.

What orb ought to be here . . . and yet is missing? He touched the cryptex in his pocket as if he could somehow divine the answer from Saunière's crafted marble. *Only five letters separate me from the Grail.*

Pacing now near the corner of the choir screen, he took a deep breath and glanced up the long nave toward the main altar in the distance. His gaze dropped from the gilded altar down to the bright crimson robe of an abbey docent who was being waved over by two very familiar individuals.

Langdon and Neveu.

Calmly, the Teacher moved two steps back behind the choir screen. *That was fast.* He had anticipated Langdon and Sophie would eventually decipher the poem's meaning and come to Newton's tomb, but this was sooner than he had imagined. Taking a deep breath, the Teacher considered his options. He had grown accustomed to dealing with surprises.

I am holding the cryptex.

Reaching down to his pocket, he touched the second object that gave him his confidence: the Medusa revolver. As expected, the abbey's metal detectors had blared as the Teacher passed through with the concealed gun. Also as expected, the guards had backed off at once when the Teacher glared indignantly and flashed his identification card. Official rank always commanded the proper respect.

Although initially the Teacher had hoped to solve the cryptex alone and avoid any further complications, he now sensed that the arrival of Langdon and Neveu was actually a welcome development. Considering the lack of success he was having with the 'orb' reference, he might be able to use their expertise. After all, if Langdon had deciphered the poem to find the tomb, there was a reasonable chance he also knew something about the orb. And if Langdon knew the password, then it was just a matter of applying the right pressure.

Not here, of course.

Somewhere private.

The Teacher recalled a small announcement sign he had seen on his way into the abbey. Immediately he knew the perfect place to lure them. The only question now . . . what to use as bait.

98

Langdon and Sophie moved slowly down the north aisle, keeping to the shadows behind the ample pillars that separated it from the open nave. Despite having travelled more than halfway down the nave, they still had no clear view of Newton's tomb. The sarcophagus was recessed in a niche, obscured from this oblique angle.

'At least there's nobody over there,' Sophie whispered.

Langdon nodded, relieved. The entire section of the nave near Newton's tomb was deserted. 'I'll go over,' he whispered. 'You should stay hidden just in case someone—'

Sophie had already stepped from the shadows and was headed across the open floor.

'—is watching,' Langdon sighed, hurrying to join her.

Crossing the massive nave on a diagonal, Langdon and Sophie remained silent as the elaborate sepulchre revealed itself in tantalizing increments . . . a black-marble sarcophagus . . . a reclining statue of Newton . . . two winged boys . . . a huge pyramid . . . and . . . *an enormous orb.*

'Did you know about that?' Sophie said, sounding startled.

Langdon shook his head, also surprised.

'Those look like constellations carved on it,' Sophie said.

As they approached the niche, Langdon felt a slow sinking sensation. Newton's tomb was *covered* with orbs – stars, comets, planets. *You seek the orb that ought be on his tomb?* It could turn out to be like trying to find a missing blade of grass on a golf course.

'Astronomical bodies,' Sophie said, looking concerned. 'And a lot of them.'

Langdon frowned. The only link between the planets and the Grail that Langdon could imagine was the pentacle of Venus, and he had already tried the password 'Venus' en route to the Temple Church.

Sophie moved directly to the sarcophagus, but Langdon hung back a few feet, keeping an eye on the abbey around them.

'*Divinity,*' Sophie said, tilting her head and reading the titles of the books on which Newton was leaning. '*Chronology. Opticks. Philosophiae Naturalis Principia Mathematica?*' She turned to him. 'Ring any bells?'

Langdon stepped closer, considering it. '*Principia Mathematica,* as I remember, has something to do with the gravitation pull of planets . . . which admittedly are orbs, but it seems a little far-fetched.'

'How about the signs of the zodiac?' Sophie asked, pointing to the constellations on the orb. 'You were talking about Pisces and Aquarius earlier, weren't you?'

The End of Days, Langdon thought. 'The end of Pisces and the beginning of Aquarius was allegedly the historical marker at which the Priory planned to release the Sangreal documents to the world.' *But the millennium came and went without incident, leaving historians uncertain when the truth was coming.*

'It seems possible,' Sophie said, 'that the Priory's plans to reveal the truth might be related to the last line of the poem.'

It speaks of Rosy flesh and seeded womb. Langdon felt a shiver of potential. He had not considered the line that way before.

'You told me earlier,' she said, 'that the timing of the Priory's plans to unveil the truth about "the Rose" and her fertile womb was linked directly to the position of planets – orbs.'

Langdon nodded, feeling the first faint wisps of possibility materializing. Even so, his intuition told him astronomy was not the key. The Grand Master's previous solutions had all possessed an eloquent, symbolic significance – the *Mona Lisa, Madonna of the Rocks,* SOFIA. This eloquence was definitely lacking in the concept of planetary orbs and the zodiac. Thus far, Jacques Saunière had proven himself a meticulous code writer, and Langdon had to believe that his final password – those five letters that unlocked the Priory's ultimate secret – would prove to be not only symbolically fitting but also crystal clear. If this solution were anything like the others, it would be painfully obvious once it dawned.

'Look!' Sophie gasped, jarring his thoughts as she grabbed his arm. From the fear in her touch Langdon sensed someone must be approaching, but when he turned to her, she was staring aghast at the top of the black marble sarcophagus. 'Someone was here,' she whispered, pointing to a spot on the sarcophagus near Newton's outstretched right foot.

Langdon did not understand her concern. A careless tourist had left a charcoal, grave-rubbing pencil on the sarcophagus lid near Newton's foot. *It's nothing.* Langdon reached out to pick it up, but as he leaned toward the sarcophagus, the light shifted on the polished black-marble slab, and Langdon froze. Suddenly, he saw why Sophie was afraid.

Scrawled on the sarcophagus lid, at Newton's feet, shimmered a barely visible charcoal-pencil message:

I have Teabing.
Go through Chapter House,
out south exit, to public garden.

Langdon read the words twice, his heart pounding wildly.

Sophie turned and scanned the nave.

Despite the pall of trepidation that settled over him upon seeing the words, Langdon told himself this was good news. *Leigh is still alive.* There was another implication here too. 'They don't know the password either,' he whispered.

Sophie nodded. Otherwise why make their presence known?

'They may want to trade Leigh for the password.'

'Or it's a trap.'

Langdon shook his head. 'I don't think so. The garden is *outside* the abbey walls. A very public place.' Langdon had once visited the abbey's famous College Garden – a small fruit orchard and herb garden – left over from the days when monks grew natural pharmacological remedies here. Boasting the oldest living fruit trees in Great Britain, College Garden was a popular spot for tourists to visit without having to enter the abbey. 'I think sending us outside is a show of faith. So we feel safe.'

Sophie looked dubious. 'You mean outside, where there are no metal detectors?'

Langdon scowled. She had a point.

Gazing back at the orb-filled tomb, Langdon wished he had some idea about the cryptex password . . . something with which to negotiate. *I got Leigh involved in this, and I'll do whatever it takes if there is a chance to help him.*

'The note says to go through the Chapter House to the south exit,' Sophie said. 'Maybe from the exit we would have a view of the garden? That way we could assess the situation before we walked out there and exposed ourselves to any danger?'

The idea was a good one. Langdon vaguely recalled the Chapter House as a huge octagonal hall where the original British Parliament convened in the days before the modern Parliament building existed. It had been years since he had been there, but he remembered it being out through the cloister somewhere. Taking several steps back from the tomb, Langdon peered around the choir screen to his right, across the nave to the side opposite that which they had descended.

A gaping vaulted passageway stood nearby, with a large sign.

THIS WAY TO:
CLOISTERS
DEANERY
COLLEGE HALL
MUSEUM
PYX CHAMBER
ST FAITH'S CHAPEL
CHAPTER HOUSE

Langdon and Sophie were jogging as they passed beneath the sign, moving too quickly to notice the small announcement apologizing that certain areas were closed for renovations.

They emerged immediately into a high-walled, open-roof courtyard through which morning rain was falling. Above them, the wind howled across the opening with a low drone, like someone blowing over the mouth of a bottle. Entering the narrow, low-hanging walkways that bordered the courtyard perimeter, Langdon felt the familiar uneasiness he always felt in enclosed spaces. These walkways were called *cloisters,* and Langdon noted with uneasiness that these particular *cloisters* lived up to their Latin ties to the word *claustrophobic.*

Focusing his mind straight ahead toward the end of the tunnel, Langdon followed the signs for the Chapter House. The rain was spitting now, and the walkway was cold and damp with gusts of rain that blew through the lone pillared wall that was the cloister's only source of light. Another couple scurried past them the other way, hurrying to get out of the worsening weather. The cloisters looked deserted now, admittedly the abbey's least enticing section in the wind and rain.

Forty yards down the east cloister, an archway materialized on their left, giving way to another hallway. Although this was the entrance they were looking for, the opening was cordoned off by a swag and an official-looking sign.

CLOSED FOR RENOVATION
PYX CHAMBER
ST FAITH'S CHAPEL
CHAPTER HOUSE

The long, deserted corridor beyond the swag was littered with scaffolding and drop cloths. Immediately beyond the swag, Langdon could see the entrances to the Pyx Chamber and St Faith's Chapel on the right and left. The entrance to the Chapter House, however, was much farther away, at the far end of the long hallway. Even from here, Langdon could see that its heavy wooden door was wide open, and the spacious octagonal interior was bathed in a greyish natural light from the room's enormous windows that looked out on College Garden. *Go through Chapter House, out south exit, to public garden.*

'We just left the east cloister,' Langdon said, 'so the south exit to the garden must be through there and to the right.'

Sophie was already stepping over the swag and moving forward.

As they hurried down the dark corridor, the sounds of the wind and rain from the open cloister faded behind them. The Chapter House was a kind of satellite structure – a freestanding annex at the end of the long hallway to ensure the privacy of the Parliament proceedings housed there.

'It looks huge,' Sophie whispered as they approached.

Langdon had forgotten just how large this room was. Even from outside the entrance, he could gaze across the vast expanse of floor to the breathtaking windows on the far side of the octagon, which rose five stories to a vaulted ceiling. They would certainly have a clear view of the garden from in here.

Crossing the threshold, both Langdon and Sophie found themselves having to squint. After the gloomy cloisters, the Chapter House felt like a solarium. They were a good ten feet into the room, searching the south wall, when they realized the door they had been promised was not there.

They were standing in an enormous dead end.

The creaking of a heavy door behind them made them turn, just as the door closed with a resounding thud and the latch fell into place. The lone man who had been standing behind the door looked calm as he aimed a small revolver at them. He was portly and was propped on a pair of aluminium crutches.

For a moment Langdon thought he must be dreaming.

It was Leigh Teabing.

99

Sir Leigh Teabing felt rueful as he gazed out over the barrel of his Medusa revolver at Robert Langdon and Sophie Neveu. 'My friends,' he said, 'since the moment you walked into my home last night, I have done everything in my power to keep you out of harm's way. But your persistence has now put me in a difficult position.'

He could see the expressions of shock and betrayal on Sophie's and Langdon's faces, and yet he was confident that soon they would both understand the chain of events that had guided the three of them to this unlikely crossroads.

There is so much I have to tell you both . . . so much you do not yet understand.

'Please believe,' Teabing said, 'I never had any intention of your being involved. You came to my home. *You* came searching for *me*.'

'Leigh?' Langdon finally managed. 'What the hell are you doing? We thought you were in trouble. We came here to help you!'

'As I trusted you would,' he said. 'We have much to discuss.'

Langdon and Sophie seemed unable to tear their stunned gazes from the revolver aimed at them.

'It is simply to ensure your full attention,' Teabing said. 'If I had wanted to harm you, you would be dead by now. When you walked into my home last night, I risked everything to spare your lives. I am a man of honour, and I vowed in my deepest conscience only to sacrifice those who had betrayed the Sangreal.'

'What are you talking about?' Langdon said. 'Betrayed the Sangreal?'

'I discovered a terrible truth,' Teabing said, sighing. 'I learned *why* the Sangreal documents were never revealed to the world. I learned that the Priory had decided not to release the truth after all. That's why the millennium passed without any revelation, why nothing happened as we entered the End of Days.'

Langdon drew a breath, about to protest.

'The Priory,' Teabing continued, 'was given a sacred charge to share the truth. To release the Sangreal documents when the End of Days arrived. For centuries, men like Da Vinci, Botticelli and Newton risked everything to protect the documents and carry out that charge. And now, at the ultimate moment of truth, Jacques Saunière changed his mind. The man honoured with the greatest responsibility in Christian history eschewed his duty. He decided the time was not right.' Teabing turned to Sophie. 'He failed the Grail. He failed the Priory. And he failed the memory of all the generations that had worked to make that moment possible.'

'You?' Sophie declared, glancing up now, her green eyes boring into him with rage and realization. '*You* are the one responsible for my grandfather's murder?'

Teabing scoffed. 'Your grandfather and his *sénéchaux* were traitors to the Grail.'

Sophie felt a fury rising from deep within. *He's lying!*

Teabing's voice was relentless. 'Your grandfather sold out to the Church. It is obvious they pressured him to keep the truth quiet.'

Sophie shook her head. 'The Church had no influence on my grandfather!'

Teabing laughed coldly. 'My dear, the Church has two thousand years of experience pressuring those who threaten to unveil its lies. Since the days of Constantine, the Church has successfully hidden the truth about Mary Magdalene and Jesus. We should not be surprised that now, once again, they have found a way to keep the world in the dark. The Church may no longer employ crusaders to slaughter nonbelievers, but their influence is no less persuasive. No less insidious.' He paused, as if to punctuate his next point. 'Miss Neveu, for some time now your grandfather has wanted to tell you the truth about your family.'

Sophie was stunned. 'How could you know that?'

'My methods are immaterial. The important thing for you to grasp right now is this.' He took a deep breath. 'The deaths of your mother, father, grandmother and brother were *not* accidental.'

The words sent Sophie's emotions reeling. She opened her mouth to speak but was unable.

Langdon shook his head. 'What are you saying?'

'Robert, it explains everything. All the pieces fit. History repeats itself. The Church has a precedent of murder when it comes to silencing the Sangreal. With the End of Days imminent, killing the Grand Master's loved ones sent a very clear message. Be quiet, or you and Sophie are next.'

'It was a car accident,' Sophie stammered, feeling the childhood pain welling inside her. 'An *accident!*'

'Bedtime stories to protect your innocence,' Teabing said. 'Consider that only two family members went untouched – the Priory's Grand Master and his lone granddaughter – the perfect pair to provide the Church with control over the brotherhood. I can only imagine the terror the Church wielded over your grandfather these past years, threatening to kill you if he dared release the Sangreal secret, threatening to finish the job they started unless Saunière influenced the Priory to reconsider its ancient vow.'

'Leigh,' Langdon argued, now visibly riled, 'certainly you have no proof that the Church had anything to do with those deaths, or that it influenced the Priory's decision to remain silent.'

'Proof?' Teabing fired back. 'You want proof the Priory was influenced? The new millennium has arrived, and yet the world remains ignorant! Is that not proof enough?'

In the echoes of Teabing's words, Sophie heard another voice speaking. *Sophie, I must tell you the truth about your family.* She realized she was trembling. Could *this* possibly be that truth her grandfather had wanted to tell her? That her family had been *murdered*? What did she truly know about the crash that took her family? Only sketchy details. Even the stories in the newspaper had been vague. An accident? Bedtime stories? Sophie flashed suddenly on her grandfather's overprotectiveness, how he never liked to leave her alone when she was young. Even when Sophie was grown and away at university, she had the sense her grandfather was watching over. She wondered if there had been Priory members in the shadows throughout her entire life, looking after her.

'You suspected he was being manipulated,' Langdon said, glaring with disbelief at Teabing. 'So you *murdered* him?'

'I did not pull the trigger,' Teabing said. 'Saunière was dead years ago, when the Church stole his family from him. He was compromised. Now he is free of that pain, released from the shame caused by his inability to carry out his sacred duty. Consider the alternative. Something had to be done. Shall the world be ignorant for ever? Shall the Church be allowed to cement its lies into our history books for all eternity? Shall the Church be permitted to influence indefinitely with murder and extortion? No, something needed to be done! And now we are poised to carry out Saunière's legacy and right a terrible wrong.' He paused. 'The three of us. Together.'

Sophie felt only incredulity. 'How could you *possibly* believe that we would help you?'

'Because, my dear, *you* are the reason the Priory failed to release the documents. Your grandfather's love for you prevented him from challenging the Church. His fear of reprisal against his only remaining family crippled him. He never had a chance to explain the truth because you rejected him, tying his hands, making him wait. Now you owe the world the truth. You owe it to the memory of your grandfather.'

Robert Langdon had given up trying to get his bearings. Despite the torrent of questions running through his mind, he knew only one thing mattered now – getting Sophie out of here alive. All the guilt Langdon had mistakenly felt earlier for involving Teabing had now been transferred to Sophie.

I took her to Château Villette. I am responsible.

Langdon could not fathom that Leigh Teabing would be capable of killing them in cold blood here in the Chapter House, and yet Teabing certainly had been involved in killing others during his misguided quest. Langdon had the uneasy feeling that gunshots in this secluded, thick-walled chamber would go unheard, especially in this rain. *And Leigh just admitted his guilt to us.*

Langdon glanced at Sophie, who looked shaken. *The Church murdered Sophie's family to silence the Priory?* Langdon felt certain the modern Church did not murder people. There had to be some other explanation.

'Let Sophie leave,' Langdon declared, staring at Leigh. 'You and I should discuss this alone.'

Teabing gave an unnatural laugh. 'I'm afraid that is one show of faith I cannot afford. I can, however, offer you *this*.' He propped himself fully on his crutches, gracelessly keeping the gun aimed at Sophie, and removed the keystone from his pocket. He swayed a bit as he held it out for Langdon. 'A token of trust, Robert.'

Robert felt wary and didn't move. *Leigh is giving the keystone back to us?*

'Take it,' Teabing said, thrusting it awkwardly toward Langdon.

Langdon could imagine only one reason Teabing would give it back. 'You opened it already. You removed the map.'

Teabing was shaking his head. 'Robert, if I had solved the keystone, I would have disappeared to find the Grail myself and kept you uninvolved. No, I do not know the answer. And I can admit that freely. A true knight learns humility in the face of the Grail. He learns to obey the signs placed before him. When I saw you enter the abbey, I understood. You were here for a reason. To help. I am not looking for singular glory here. I serve a far greater master than my own pride. The Truth. Mankind deserves to know that truth. The Grail found us all, and now she is begging to be revealed. We must work together.'

Despite Teabing's pleas for cooperation and trust, his gun remained trained on Sophie as Langdon stepped forward and accepted the cold marble cylinder. The vinegar inside gurgled as Langdon grasped it and stepped backward. The dials were still in random order, and the cryptex remained locked.

Langdon eyed Teabing. 'How do you know I won't smash it right now?'

Teabing's laugh was an eerie chortle. 'I should have realized your threat to break it in the Temple Church was an empty one. Robert Langdon would never break the keystone. You are an historian, Robert. You are holding the key to two thousand years of history – the lost key to the Sangreal. You can feel the souls of all the knights burned at the stake to protect her secret. Would you have them die in vain? No, you will vindicate them. You will join the ranks of the great men you admire – Da Vinci, Botticelli, Newton – each of whom would have been honoured to be in your shoes right now. The contents of the keystone are crying out to us. Longing to be set free. The time has come. Destiny has led us to this moment.'

'I cannot help you, Leigh. I have no idea how to open this. I only saw Newton's tomb for a moment. And even if I knew the password . . .' Langdon paused, realizing he had said too much.

'You would not tell me?' Teabing sighed. 'I am disappointed and surprised, Robert, that you do not appreciate the extent to which you are in my debt. My task would have been far simpler had Rémy and I eliminated you both when you walked into Château Villette. Instead I risked everything to take the nobler course.'

'This is *noble?*' Langdon demanded, eyeing the gun.

'Saunière's fault,' Teabing said. 'He and his *sénéchaux* lied to Silas. Otherwise, I would have obtained the keystone without complication. How was I to imagine the Grand Master would go to such ends to deceive me and bequeath the keystone to an estranged granddaughter?' Teabing looked at Sophie with disdain. 'Someone so unqualified to hold this knowledge that she required a symbologist baby-sitter.' Teabing glanced back at Langdon. 'Fortunately, Robert, your involvement turned out to be my saving grace. Rather than the keystone remaining locked in the depository bank for ever, you extracted it and walked into my home.'

Where else would I run? Langdon thought. *The community of Grail historians is small, and Teabing and I have a history together.*

Teabing now looked smug. 'When I learned Saunière left you a dying message, I had a pretty good idea you were holding valuable Priory information. Whether it was the keystone itself, or information on where to find it, I was not sure. But with the police on your heels, I had a sneaking suspicion you might arrive on my doorstep.'

Langdon glared. 'And if we had not?'

'I was formulating a plan to extend you a helping hand. One way or another, the keystone was coming to Château Villette. The fact that you delivered it into my waiting hands only serves as proof that my cause is just.'

'What!' Langdon was appalled.

'Silas was supposed to break in and steal the keystone from you in Château Villette – thus removing you from the equation without hurting you, and exonerating me from any suspicion of complicity. However, when I saw the intricacy of Saunière's codes, I decided to include you both in my quest a bit longer. I could have Silas steal the keystone later, once I knew enough to carry on alone.'

'The Temple Church,' Sophie said, her tone awash with betrayal.

Light begins to dawn, Teabing thought. The Temple Church was the perfect location to steal the keystone from Robert and Sophie, and its apparent relevance to the poem made it a plausible decoy. Rémy's orders had been clear – stay out of sight while Silas recovers the keystone. Unfortunately, Langdon's threat to smash the keystone on the chapel floor had caused

Rémy to panic. *If only Rémy had not revealed himself,* Teabing thought rue-fully, recalling his own mock kidnapping. *Rémy was the sole link to me, and he showed his face!*

Fortunately, Silas remained unaware of Teabing's true identity and was easily fooled into taking him from the church and then watching naively as Rémy pretended to tie their hostage in the back of the limousine. With the soundproof divider raised, Teabing was able to phone Silas in the front seat, use the fake French accent of the Teacher, and direct Silas to go straight to Opus Dei. A simple anonymous tip to the police was all it would take to remove Silas from the picture.

One loose end tied up.

The other loose end was harder. *Rémy.*

Teabing struggled deeply with the decision, but in the end Rémy had proven himself a liability. *Every Grail quest requires sacrifice.* The cleanest solution had been staring Teabing in the face from the limousine's wet bar – a flask, some cognac, and a can of peanuts. The powder at the bottom of the can would be more than enough to trigger Rémy's deadly allergy. When Rémy parked the limo on Horse Guards Parade, Teabing climbed out of the back, walked to the side passenger door, and sat in the front next to Rémy. Minutes later, Teabing got out of the car, climbed into the rear again, cleaned up the evidence, and finally emerged to carry out the final phase of his mission.

Westminster Abbey had been a short walk, and although Teabing's leg braces, crutches and gun had set off the metal detector, the rent-a-cops never knew what to do. *Do we ask him to remove his braces and crawl through? Do we frisk his deformed body?* Teabing presented the flustered guards a far easier solution – an embossed card identifying him as Knight of the Realm. The poor fellows practically tripped over one another ushering him in.

Now, eyeing the bewildered Langdon and Neveu, Teabing resisted the urge to reveal how he had brilliantly implicated Opus Dei in the plot that would soon bring about the demise of the entire Church. That would have to wait. Right now there was work to do.

'*Mes amis,*' Teabing declared in flawless French, '*vous ne trouvez pas le Saint-Graal, c'est le Saint-Graal qui vous trouve.*' He smiled. 'Our paths together could not be more clear. The Grail has found us.'

Silence.

He spoke to them in a whisper now. 'Listen. Can you hear it? The Grail is speaking to us across the centuries. She is begging to be saved from the Priory's folly. I implore you both to recognize this opportunity. There could not possibly be three more capable people assembled at this moment to break the final code and open the cryptex.' Teabing paused, his eyes alight. 'We need to swear an oath together. A pledge of faith to one another. A knight's allegiance to uncover the truth and make it known.'

Sophie stared deep into Teabing's eyes and spoke in a steely tone. 'I will never swear an oath with my grandfather's murderer. Except an oath that I will see you go to prison.'

Teabing's heart turned grave, then resolute. 'I am sorry you feel that way, mademoiselle.' He turned and aimed the gun at Langdon. 'And you, Robert? Are you with me, or against me?'

100

Bishop Manuel Aringarosa's body had endured many kinds of pain, and yet the searing heat of the bullet wound in his chest felt profoundly foreign to him. Deep and grave. Not a wound of the flesh . . . but closer to the soul.

He opened his eyes, trying to see, but the rain on his face blurred his vision. *Where am I?* He could feel powerful arms holding him, carrying his limp body like a rag doll, his black cassock flapping.

Lifting a weary arm, he mopped his eyes and saw the man holding him was Silas. The great albino was struggling down a misty sidewalk, shouting for a hospital, his voice a heartrending wail of agony. His red eyes were focused dead ahead, tears streaming down his pale, blood-spattered face.

'My son,' Aringarosa whispered, 'you're hurt.'

Silas glanced down, his visage contorted in anguish. 'I am so very sorry, Father.' He seemed almost too pained to speak.

'No, Silas,' Aringarosa replied. 'It is I who am sorry. This is my fault.' *The Teacher promised me there would be no killing, and I told you to obey him fully.* 'I was too eager. Too fearful. You and I were deceived.' *The Teacher was never going to deliver us the Holy Grail.*

Cradled in the arms of the man he had taken in all those years ago, Bishop Aringarosa felt himself reel back in time. To Spain. To his modest beginnings, building a small Catholic church in Oviedo with Silas. And later, to New York City, where he had proclaimed the glory of God with the towering Opus Dei Center on Lexington Avenue.

Five months ago, Aringarosa had received devastating news. His life's work was in jeopardy. He recalled, with vivid detail, the meeting inside Castel Gandolfo that had changed his life . . . the news that had set this entire calamity into motion.

Aringarosa had entered Gandolfo's Astronomy Library with his head held high, fully expecting to be lauded by throngs of welcoming hands, all eager to pat him on the back for his superior work representing Catholicism in America.

But only three people were present.

The Vatican secretarius. Obese. Dour.

Two high-ranking Italian cardinals. Sanctimonious. Smug.

'Secretarius?' Aringarosa said, puzzled.

The rotund overseer of legal affairs shook Aringarosa's hand and motioned to the chair opposite him. 'Please, make yourself comfortable.'

Aringarosa sat, sensing something was wrong.

'I am not skilled in small talk, Bishop,' the secretarius said, 'so let me be direct about the reason for your visit.'

'Please. Speak openly.' Aringarosa glanced at the two cardinals, who seemed to be measuring him with self-righteous anticipation.

'As you are well aware,' the secretarius said, 'His Holiness and others in Rome have been concerned lately with the political fallout from Opus Dei's more controversial practices.'

Aringarosa felt himself bristle instantly. He already had been through this on numerous occasions with the new pontiff, who, to Aringarosa's great dismay, had turned out to be a distressingly fervent voice for liberal change in the Church.

'I want to assure you,' the secretarius added quickly, 'that His Holiness does not seek to change anything about the way you run your ministry.'

I should hope not! 'Then why am I here?'

The enormous man sighed. 'Bishop, I am not sure how to say this delicately, so I will state it directly. Two days ago, the Secretariat Council voted unanimously to revoke the Vatican's sanction of Opus Dei.'

Aringarosa was certain he had heard incorrectly. 'I beg your pardon?'

'Plainly stated, six months from today, Opus Dei will no longer be considered a prelature of the Vatican. You will be a church unto yourself. The Holy See will be disassociating itself from you. His Holiness agrees and we are already drawing up the legal papers.'

'But . . . that is impossible!'

'On the contrary, it is quite possible. And necessary. His Holiness has become uneasy with your aggressive recruiting policies and your practices of corporal mortification.' He paused. 'Also your policies regarding women. Quite frankly, Opus Dei has become a liability and an embarrassment.'

Bishop Aringarosa was stupefied. 'An embarrassment?'

'Certainly you cannot be surprised it has come to this.'

'Opus Dei is the only Catholic organization whose numbers are growing! We now have over eleven hundred priests!'

'True. A troubling issue for us all.'

Aringarosa shot to his feet. 'Ask His Holiness if Opus Dei was an embarrassment in 1982 when we helped the Vatican Bank!'

'The Vatican will always be grateful for that,' the secretarius said, his tone appeasing, 'and yet there are those who still believe your financial munificence in 1982 is the only reason you were granted prelature status in the first place.'

'That is not true!' The insinuation offended Aringarosa deeply.

'Whatever the case, we plan to act in good faith. We are drawing up severance terms that will include a reimbursement of those monies. It will be paid in five instalments.'

'You are buying me off?' Aringarosa demanded. 'Paying me to go quietly? When Opus Dei is the only remaining voice of reason!'

One of the cardinals glanced up. 'I'm sorry, did you say *reason?*'

Aringarosa leaned across the table, sharpening his tone to a point. 'Do you really wonder why Catholics are leaving the Church? Look around you, Cardinal. People have lost respect. The rigours of faith are gone. The doctrine has become a buffet table. Abstinence, confession, communion, baptism, mass – take your pick – choose whatever combination pleases you and ignore the rest. What kind of spiritual guidance is the Church offering?'

'Third-century laws,' the second cardinal said, 'cannot be applied to the modern followers of Christ. The rules are not workable in today's society.'

'Well, they seem to be working for Opus Dei!'

'Bishop Aringarosa,' the secretarius said, his voice conclusive. 'Out of respect for your organization's relationship with the previous Pope, His Holiness will be giving Opus Dei six months to *voluntarily* break away from the Vatican. I suggest you cite your differences of opinion with the Holy See and establish yourself as your own Christian organization.'

'I refuse!' Aringarosa declared. 'And I'll tell him that in person!'

'I'm afraid His Holiness no longer cares to meet you.'

Aringarosa stood up. 'He would not *dare* abolish a personal prelature established by a previous Pope!'

'I'm sorry.' The secretarius's eyes did not flinch. 'The Lord giveth and the Lord taketh away.'

Aringarosa had staggered from that meeting in bewilderment and panic. Returning to New York, he stared out at the skyline in disillusionment for days, overwhelmed with sadness for the future of Christianity.

It was several weeks later that he received the phone call that changed all that. The caller sounded French and identified himself as *the Teacher* – a title common in the prelature. He said he knew of the Vatican's plans to pull support from Opus Dei.

How could he know that? Aringarosa wondered. He had hoped only a handful of Vatican power brokers knew of Opus Dei's impending annulment. Apparently the word was out. When it came to containing gossip, no walls in the world were as porous as those surrounding Vatican City.

'I have ears everywhere, Bishop,' the Teacher whispered, 'and with these ears I have gained certain knowledge. With your help, I can uncover the hiding place of a sacred relic that will bring you enormous power . . . enough power to make the Vatican bow before you. Enough power to save the Faith.' He paused. 'Not just for Opus Dei. But for all of us.'

The Lord taketh away . . . and the Lord giveth. Aringarosa felt a glorious ray of hope. 'Tell me your plan.'

Bishop Aringarosa was unconscious when the doors of St Mary's Hospital hissed open. Silas lurched into the entryway delirious with exhaustion. Dropping to his knees on the tile floor, he cried out for help. Everyone in the reception area gaped in wonderment at the half-naked albino offering forth a bleeding clergyman.

The doctor who helped Silas heave the delirious bishop onto a trolley looked gloomy as he felt Aringarosa's pulse. 'He's lost a lot of blood. I am not hopeful.'

Aringarosa's eyes flickered, and he returned for a moment, his gaze locating Silas. 'My child . . .'

Silas's soul thundered with remorse and rage. 'Father, if it takes my lifetime, I will find the one who deceived us, and I will kill him.'

Aringarosa shook his head, looking sad as they prepared to wheel him away. 'Silas . . . if you have learned nothing from me, please . . . learn this.' He took Silas's hand and gave it a firm squeeze. 'Forgiveness is God's greatest gift.'

'But Father . . .'

Aringarosa closed his eyes. 'Silas, you must pray.'

101

Robert Langdon stood beneath the lofty cupola of the deserted Chapter House and stared into the barrel of Leigh Teabing's gun.

Robert, are you with me, or against me? The Royal Historian's words echoed in the silence of Langdon's mind.

There was no viable response, Langdon knew. Answer yes, and he would be selling out Sophie. Answer no, and Teabing would have no choice but to kill them both.

Langdon's years in the classroom had not imbued him with any skills relevant to handling confrontations at gunpoint, but the classroom *had* taught him something about answering paradoxical questions. *When a question has no correct answer, there is only one honest response.*

The grey area between yes and no.

Silence.

Staring at the cryptex in his hands, Langdon chose simply to walk away.

Without ever lifting his eyes, he stepped backward, out into the room's vast empty spaces. *Neutral ground.* He hoped his focus on the cryptex signalled to Teabing that collaboration might be an option, and that his silence signalled to Sophie he had not abandoned her.

All the while buying time to think.

The act of thinking, Langdon suspected, was exactly what Teabing wanted him to do. *That's why he handed me the cryptex. So I could feel the weight of my decision.* The British historian hoped the touch of the Grand Master's cryptex would make Langdon fully grasp the magnitude of its contents, coaxing his academic curiosity to overwhelm all else, forcing him to realize that failure to unlock the keystone would mean the loss of history itself.

With Sophie at gunpoint across the room, Langdon feared that discovering the cryptex's elusive password would be his only remaining hope of bartering for her release. *If I can free the map, Teabing will negotiate.* Forcing his mind to this critical task, Langdon moved slowly toward the far windows . . . allowing his mind to fill with the numerous astronomical images on Newton's tomb.

You seek the orb that ought be on his tomb.
It speaks of Rosy flesh and seeded womb.

Turning his back to the others, he walked toward the towering windows, searching for any inspiration in their stained-glass mosaics. There was none.

Place yourself in Saunière's mind, he urged, gazing outward now into College Garden. *What would he believe is the orb that ought be on Newton's tomb?* Images of stars, comets and planets twinkled in the falling rain, but Langdon ignored them. Saunière was not a man of science. He was a man of humanity, of art, of history. *The sacred feminine . . . the chalice . . . the Rose . . . the banished Mary Magdalene . . . the decline of the goddess . . . the Holy Grail.*

Legend had always portrayed the Grail as a cruel mistress, dancing in the shadows just out of sight, whispering in your ear, luring you one more step and then evaporating into the mist.

Gazing out at the rustling trees of College Garden, Langdon sensed her playful presence. The signs were everywhere. Like a taunting silhouette emerging from the fog, the branches of Britain's oldest apple tree burgeoned with five-petalled blossoms, all glistening like Venus. The goddess was in the garden now. She was dancing in the rain, singing songs of the ages, peeking out from behind the bud-filled branches as if to remind Langdon that the fruit of knowledge was growing just beyond his reach.

Across the room, Sir Leigh Teabing watched with confidence as Langdon gazed out the window as if under a spell.

Exactly as I hoped, Teabing thought. *He will come round.*

For some time now, Teabing had suspected Langdon might hold the key to the Grail. It was no coincidence that Teabing launched his plan into action on the same night Langdon was scheduled to meet Jacques Saunière. Listening in on the curator, Teabing was certain the man's eagerness to meet Langdon privately could mean only one thing. *Langdon's mysterious manuscript has touched a nerve with the Priory. Langdon has stumbled onto a truth, and Saunière fears its release.* Teabing felt certain the Grand Master was summoning Langdon to silence him.

The Truth has been silenced long enough!

Teabing knew he had to act quickly. Silas's attack would accomplish two goals. It would prevent Saunière from persuading Langdon to keep quiet, and it would ensure that once the keystone was in Teabing's hands, Langdon would be in Paris for recruitment should Teabing need him.

Arranging the fatal meeting between Saunière and Silas had been almost too easy. *I had inside information about Saunière's deepest fears.* Yesterday afternoon, Silas had phoned the curator and posed as a distraught priest. 'Monsieur Saunière, forgive me, I must speak to you at once. I should never breach the sanctity of the confessional, but in this case, I feel I must. I just took confession from a man who claimed to have murdered members of your family.'

Saunière's response was startled but wary. 'My family died in an accident. The police report was conclusive.'

'Yes, a *car* accident,' Silas said, baiting the hook. 'The man I spoke to said he forced their car off the road into a river.'

Saunière fell silent.

'Monsieur Saunière, I would never have phoned you directly except this man made a comment which makes me now fear for *your* safety.' He paused. 'The man also mentioned your granddaughter, Sophie.'

The mention of Sophie's name had been the catalyst. The curator leapt into action. He ordered Silas to come and see him immediately in the safest location Saunière knew – his Louvre office. Then he phoned Sophie to warn her she might be in danger. Drinks with Robert Langdon were instantly abandoned.

Now, with Langdon separated from Sophie on the far side of the room, Teabing sensed he had successfully alienated the two companions from one another. Sophie Neveu remained defiant, but Langdon clearly saw the larger picture. He was trying to figure out the password. *He understands the importance of finding the Grail and releasing her from bondage.*

'He won't open it for you,' Sophie said coldly. 'Even if he can.'

Teabing was glancing at Langdon as he held the gun on Sophie. He was fairly certain now he was going to have to use the weapon. Although the idea troubled him, he knew he would not hesitate if it came to that. *I have given her every opportunity to do the right thing. The Grail is bigger than any one of us.*

At that moment, Langdon turned from the window. 'The tomb . . .' he said suddenly, facing them with a faint glimmer of hope in his eyes. 'I know where to look on Newton's tomb. Yes, I think I can find the password!'

Teabing's heart soared. 'Where, Robert? Tell me!'

Sophie sounded horrified. 'Robert, no! You're not going to help him, *are* you?'

Langdon approached with a resolute stride, holding the cryptex before him. 'No,' he said, his eyes hardening as he turned to Leigh. 'Not until he lets you go.'

Teabing's optimism darkened. 'We are so close, Robert. Don't you dare start playing games with me!'

'No games,' Langdon said. 'Let her go. Then I'll take you to Newton's tomb. We'll open the cryptex together.'

'I'm not going anywhere,' Sophie declared, her eyes narrowing with rage. 'That cryptex was given to me by my grandfather. It is not *yours* to open.'

Langdon wheeled, looking fearful. 'Sophie, please! You're in danger. I'm trying to help you!'

'How? By unveiling the secret my grandfather died trying to protect? He trusted you, Robert. *I* trusted you!'

Langdon's blue eyes showed panic now, and Teabing could not help but smile to see the two of them working against one another. Langdon's attempts to be gallant were more pathetic than anything. *On the verge of unveiling one of history's greatest secrets, and he troubles himself with a woman who has proven herself unworthy of the quest.*

'Sophie,' Langdon pleaded. 'Please . . . you must leave.'

She shook her head. 'Not unless you either hand me the cryptex or smash it on the floor.'

'What?' Langdon gasped.

'Robert, my grandfather would prefer his secret lost for ever than see it in the hands of his murderer.' Sophie's eyes looked as if they would well with tears, but they did not. She stared directly back at Teabing. 'Shoot me if you have to. I am not leaving my grandfather's legacy in your hands.'

Very well. Teabing aimed the weapon.

'No!' Langdon shouted, raising his arm and suspending the cryptex precariously over the hard stone floor. 'Leigh, if you even think about it, I will drop this.'

Teabing laughed. 'That bluff worked on Rémy. Not on me. I know you better than that.'

'Do you, Leigh?'

Yes I do. Your poker face needs work, my friend. It took me several seconds, but I can see now that you are lying. You have no idea where on Newton's tomb the answer lies. 'Truly, Robert? You know where on the tomb to look?'

'I do.'

The falter in Langdon's eyes was fleeting but Leigh caught it. There was a lie there. A desperate, pathetic ploy to save Sophie. Teabing felt a profound disappointment in Robert Langdon.

I am a lone knight, surrounded by unworthy souls. And I will have to decipher the keystone on my own.

Langdon and Neveu were nothing but a threat to Teabing now . . . and to the Grail. As painful as the solution was going to be, he knew he could carry it out with a clean conscience. The only challenge would be to persuade Langdon to set down the keystone so Teabing could safely end this charade.

'A show of faith,' Teabing said, lowering the gun from Sophie. 'Set down the keystone, and we'll talk.'

Langdon knew his lie had failed.

He could see the dark resolve in Teabing's face and knew the moment was upon them. *When I set this down, he will kill us both.* Even without looking at Sophie, he could hear her heart beseeching him in silent desperation. *Robert, this man is not worthy of the Grail. Please do not place it in his hands. No matter what the cost.*

Langdon had already made his decision several minutes ago, while standing alone at the window overlooking College Garden.

Protect Sophie.

Protect the Grail.

Langdon had almost shouted out in desperation. *But I cannot see how!*

The stark moments of disillusionment had brought with them a clarity unlike any he had ever felt. *The Truth is right before your eyes, Robert.* He knew not from where the epiphany came. *The Grail is not mocking you, she is calling out to a worthy soul.*

Now, bowing down like a subject several yards in front of Leigh Teabing, Langdon lowered the cryptex to within inches of the stone floor.

'Yes, Robert,' Teabing whispered, aiming the gun at him. 'Set it down.'

Langdon's eyes moved heavenward, up into the gaping void of the Chapter House cupola. Crouching lower, Langdon lowered his gaze to Teabing's gun, aimed directly at him.

'I'm sorry, Leigh.'

In one fluid motion, Langdon leapt up, swinging his arm skyward, launching the cryptex straight up toward the dome above.

Leigh Teabing did not feel his finger pull the trigger, but the Medusa discharged with a thundering crash. Langdon's crouched form was now vertical, almost airborne, and the bullet exploded in the floor near Langdon's feet. Half of Teabing's brain attempted to adjust his aim and fire again in rage, but the more powerful half dragged his eyes upward into the cupola.

The keystone!

Time seemed to freeze, morphing into a slow-motion dream as Teabing's entire world became the airborne keystone. He watched it rise to the apex of its climb . . . hovering for a moment in the void . . . and then tumbling downward, end over end, back toward the stone floor.

All of Teabing's hopes and dreams were plummeting toward earth. *It cannot strike the floor! I can reach it!* Teabing's body reacted on instinct. He released the gun and heaved himself forward, dropping his crutches as he reached out with his soft, manicured hands. Stretching his arms and fingers, he snatched the keystone from midair.

Falling forward with the keystone victoriously clutched in his hand, Teabing knew he was falling too fast. With nothing to break his fall, his outstretched arms hit first, and the cryptex collided hard with the floor.

There was a sickening crunch of glass within.

For a full second, Teabing did not breathe. Lying there outstretched on the cold floor, staring the length of his outstretched arms at the marble cylinder in his bare palms, he implored the glass vial inside to hold. Then the acrid tang of vinegar cut the air, and Teabing felt the cool liquid flowing out through the dials onto his palm.

Wild panic gripped him. *NO!* The vinegar was streaming now, and

Teabing pictured the papyrus dissolving within. *Robert, you fool! The secret is lost!*

Teabing felt himself sobbing uncontrollably. *The Grail is gone. Everything destroyed.* Shuddering in disbelief over Langdon's actions, Teabing tried to force the cylinder apart, longing to catch a fleeting glimpse of history before it dissolved for ever. To his shock, as he pulled the ends of the keystone, the cylinder separated.

He gasped and peered inside. It was empty except for shards of wet glass. No dissolving papyrus. Teabing rolled over and looked up at Langdon. Sophie stood beside him, aiming the gun down at Teabing.

Bewildered, Teabing looked back at the keystone and saw it. The dials were no longer at random. They spelled a five-letter word: APPLE.

'The orb from which Eve partook,' Langdon said coolly, 'incurring the Holy wrath of God. Original sin. The symbol of the fall of the sacred feminine.'

Teabing felt the truth come crashing down on him in excruciating austerity. The orb that ought be on Newton's tomb could be none other than the Rosy apple that fell from heaven, struck Newton on the head, and inspired his life's work. *His labour's fruit! The Rosy flesh with a seeded womb!*

'Robert,' Teabing stammered, overwhelmed. 'You opened it. Where . . . is the map?'

Without blinking, Langdon reached into the breast pocket of his tweed coat and carefully extracted a delicate rolled papyrus. Only a few yards from where Teabing lay, Langdon unrolled the scroll and looked at it. After a long moment, a knowing smile crossed Langdon's face.

He knows! Teabing's heart craved that knowledge. His life's dream was right in front of him. 'Tell me!' Teabing demanded. 'Please! Oh God, please! It's not too late!'

As the sound of heavy footsteps thundered down the hall toward the Chapter House, Langdon quietly rolled the papyrus and slipped it back in his pocket.

'No!' Teabing cried out, trying in vain to stand.

When the doors burst open, Bezu Fache entered like a bull into a ring, his feral eyes scanning, finding his target – Leigh Teabing – helpless on the floor. Exhaling in relief, Fache holstered his Manurhin sidearm and turned to Sophie. 'Agent Neveu, I am relieved you and Mr. Langdon are safe. You should have come in when I asked.'

The British police entered on Fache's heels, seizing the anguished prisoner and placing him in handcuffs.

Sophie seemed stunned to see Fache. 'How did you find us?'

Fache pointed to Teabing. 'He made the mistake of showing his ID when he entered the abbey. The guards heard a police broadcast about our search for him.'

'It's in Langdon's pocket!' Teabing was screaming like a madman. 'The map to the Holy Grail!'

As they hoisted Teabing and carried him out, he threw back his head and howled. 'Robert! Tell me where it's hidden!'

As Teabing passed, Langdon looked him in the eye. 'Only the worthy find the Grail, Leigh. You taught me that.'

102

The mist had settled low on Kensington Gardens as Silas limped into a quiet hollow out of sight. Kneeling on the wet grass, he could feel a warm stream of blood flowing from the bullet wound below his ribs. Still, he stared straight ahead.

The fog made it look like heaven here.

Raising his bloody hands to pray, he watched the raindrops caress his fingers, turning them white again. As the droplets fell harder across his back and shoulders, he could feel his body disappearing bit by bit into the mist.

I am a ghost.

A breeze rustled past him, carrying the damp, earthy scent of new life. With every living cell in his broken body, Silas prayed. He prayed for forgiveness. He prayed for mercy. And, above all, he prayed for his mentor . . . Bishop Aringarosa . . . that the Lord would not take him before his time. *He has so much work left to do.*

The fog was swirling around him now, and Silas felt so light that he was sure the wisps would carry him away. Closing his eyes, he said a final prayer.

From somewhere in the mist, the voice of Manuel Aringarosa whispered to him.

Our Lord is a good and merciful God.

Silas's pain at last began to fade, and he knew the bishop was right.

103

It was late afternoon when the London sun broke through and the city began to dry. Bezu Fache felt weary as he emerged from the interrogation room and hailed a cab. Sir Leigh Teabing had vociferously proclaimed his innocence, and yet from his incoherent rantings about the Holy Grail, secret documents, and mysterious brotherhoods, Fache suspected the wily historian was setting the stage for his lawyers to plead an insanity defence.

Sure, Fache thought. *Insane.* Teabing had displayed ingenious precision in formulating a plan that protected his innocence at every turn. He had exploited both the Vatican and Opus Dei, two groups that turned out to be completely innocent. His dirty work had been carried out unknowingly by a fanatical monk and a desperate bishop. More clever still, Teabing had situated his electronic listening post in the *one* place a man with polio could not possibly reach. The actual surveillance had been carried out by his manservant, Rémy – the lone person privy to Teabing's true identity – now conveniently dead of an allergic reaction.

Hardly the handiwork of someone lacking mental faculties, Fache thought.

The information coming from Collet out of Château Villette suggested that Teabing's cunning ran so deep that Fache himself might even learn from it. To successfully hide bugs in some of Paris's most powerful offices, the British historian had turned to the Greeks. *Trojan horses.* Some of Teabing's intended targets received lavish gifts of artwork, others unwittingly bid at auctions in which Teabing had placed specific lots. In Saunière's case, the curator had received a dinner invitation to Château Villette to discuss the possibility of Teabing's funding a new Da Vinci Wing at the Louvre. Saunière's invitation had contained an innocuous postscript expressing fascination with a robotic knight that Saunière was rumoured to have built. *Bring him to dinner,* Teabing had suggested. Saunière apparently had done just that and left the knight unattended long enough for Rémy Legaludec to make one inconspicuous addition.

Now, sitting in the back of the cab, Fache closed his eyes. *One more thing to attend to before I return to Paris.*

*

The St Mary's Hospital recovery room was sunny.

'You've impressed us all,' the nurse said, smiling down at him. 'Nothing short of miraculous.'

Bishop Aringarosa gave a weak smile. 'I have always been blessed.'

The nurse finished puttering, leaving the bishop alone. The sunlight felt welcome and warm on his face. Last night had been the darkest night of his life.

Despondently, he thought of Silas, whose body had been found in the park.

Please forgive me, my son.

Aringarosa had longed for Silas to be part of his glorious plan. Last night, however, Aringarosa had received a call from Bezu Fache, questioning the bishop about his apparent connection to a nun who had been murdered in Saint-Sulpice. Aringarosa realized the evening had taken a horrifying turn. News of the four additional murders transformed his horror to anguish. *Silas, what have you done!* Unable to reach the Teacher, the bishop knew he had been cut loose. *Used.* The only way to stop the horrific chain of events he had helped put in motion was to confess everything to Fache, and from that moment on, Aringarosa and Fache had been racing to catch up with Silas before the Teacher persuaded him to kill again.

Feeling bone weary, Aringarosa closed his eyes and listened to the television coverage of the arrest of a prominent British knight, Sir Leigh Teabing. *The Teacher laid bare for all to see.* Teabing had caught wind of the Vatican's plans to disassociate itself from Opus Dei. He had chosen Aringarosa as the perfect pawn in his plan. *After all, who more likely to leap blindly after the Holy Grail than a man like myself with everything to lose? The Grail would have brought enormous power to anyone who possessed it.*

Leigh Teabing had protected his identity shrewdly – feigning a French accent and a pious heart, and demanding as payment the one thing he did not need – money. Aringarosa had been far too eager to be suspicious. The price tag of twenty million euros was paltry when compared with the prize of obtaining the Grail, and with the Vatican's separation payment to Opus Dei, the finances had worked nicely. *The blind see what they want to see.* Teabing's ultimate insult, of course, had been to demand payment in Vatican bonds, such that if anything went wrong, the investigation would lead to Rome.

'I am glad to see you're well, My Lord.'

Aringarosa recognized the gruff voice in the doorway, but the face was unexpected – stern, powerful features, slicked-back hair and a broad neck that strained against his dark suit. 'Captain Fache?' Aringarosa asked. The compassion and concern the captain had shown for Aringarosa's plight last night had conjured images of a far gentler physique.

The captain approached the bed and hoisted a familiar, heavy black briefcase onto a chair. 'I believe this belongs to you.'

Aringarosa looked at the briefcase filled with bonds and immediately looked away, feeling only shame. 'Yes . . . thank you.' He paused while working his fingers across the seam of his bedsheet, then continued. 'Captain, I have been giving this deep thought, and I need to ask a favour of you.'

'Of course.'

'The families of those in Paris who Silas . . .' He paused, swallowing the emotion. 'I realize no sum could possibly serve as sufficient restitution, and yet, if you could be kind enough to divide the contents of this briefcase among them . . . the families of the deceased.'

Fache's dark eyes studied him a long moment. 'A virtuous gesture, My Lord. I will see to it your wishes are carried out.'

A heavy silence fell between them.

On the television, a lean French police officer was giving a press conference in front of a sprawling mansion. Fache saw who it was and turned his attention to the screen.

'Lieutenant Collet,' a BBC reporter said, her voice accusing. 'Last night, your captain publicly charged two innocent people with murder. Will Robert Langdon and Sophie Neveu be seeking accountability from your department? Will this cost Captain Fache his job?'

Lieutenant Collet's smile was tired but calm. 'It is my experience that Captain Bezu Fache seldom makes mistakes. I have not yet spoken to him on this matter, but knowing how he operates, I suspect his public manhunt for Agent Neveu and Mr Langdon was part of a ruse to lure out the real killer.'

The reporters exchanged surprised looks.

Collet continued. 'Whether or not Mr Langdon and Agent Neveu were willing participants in the sting, I do not know. Captain Fache tends to keep his more creative methods to himself. All I can confirm at this point is that the captain has successfully arrested the man responsible, and that Mr Langdon and Agent Neveu are both innocent and safe.'

Fache had a faint smile on his lips as he turned back to Aringarosa. 'A good man, that Collet.'

Several moments passed. Finally, Fache ran his hand over his forehead, slicking back his hair as he gazed down at Aringarosa. 'My Lord, before I return to Paris, there is one final matter I'd like to discuss – your impromptu flight to London. You bribed a pilot to change course. In doing so, you broke a number of international laws.'

Aringarosa slumped. 'I was desperate.'

'Yes. As was the pilot when my men interrogated him.' Fache reached in his pocket and produced a purple amethyst ring with a familiar hand-tooled mitre-crozier appliqué.

Aringarosa felt tears welling as he accepted the ring and slipped it back on his finger. 'You've been so kind.' He held out his hand and clasped Fache's. 'Thank you.'

Fache waved off the gesture, walking to the window and gazing out at the city, his thoughts obviously far away. When he turned, there was an uncertainty about him. 'My Lord, where do you go from here?'

Aringarosa had been asked the exact same question as he left Castel Gandolfo the night before. 'I suspect my path is as uncertain as yours.'

'Yes.' Fache paused. 'I suspect I will be retiring early.'

Aringarosa smiled. 'A little faith can do wonders, Captain. A little faith.'

104

Rosslyn Chapel – often called the Cathedral of Codes – stands seven miles south of Edinburgh, on the site of an ancient Mithraic temple. Built by the Knights Templar in 1446, the chapel is engraved with a mind-boggling array of symbols from the Jewish, Christian, Egyptian, Masonic and pagan traditions.

The chapel's geographic coordinates fall precisely on the north-south meridian that runs through Glastonbury. This longitudinal Rose Line is the traditional marker of King Arthur's Isle of Avalon and is considered the central pillar of Britain's sacred geometry. It is from this hallowed Rose Line that Rosslyn – originally spelled Roslin – takes its name.

Rosslyn's rugged spires were casting long evening shadows as Robert Langdon and Sophie Neveu pulled their rental car into the grassy parking area at the foot of the bluff on which the chapel stood. Their short flight from London to Edinburgh had been restful, although neither of them had slept for the anticipation of what lay ahead. Gazing up at the stark edifice framed against a cloud-swept sky, Langdon felt like Alice falling headlong into the rabbit hole. *This must be a dream.* And yet he knew the text of Saunière's final message could not have been more specific.

The Holy Grail 'neath ancient Roslin waits.

Langdon had fantasized that Saunière's 'Grail map' would be a diagram – a drawing with an X-marks-the-spot – and yet the Priory's final secret had been unveiled in the same way Saunière had spoken to them from the beginning. *Simple verse.* Four explicit lines that pointed without a doubt to this very spot. In addition to identifying Rosslyn by name, the verse made reference to several of the chapel's renowned architectural features.

Despite the clarity of Saunière's final revelation, Langdon had been left feeling more off balance than enlightened. To him, Rosslyn Chapel seemed far too obvious a location. For centuries, this stone chapel had echoed with whispers of the Holy Grail's presence. The whispers had turned to shouts in recent decades when ground-penetrating radar revealed the presence of an astonishing structure *beneath* the chapel – a massive subterranean chamber. Not only did this deep vault dwarf the chapel atop it, but it appeared to have no entrance or exit. Archaeologists petitioned to begin blasting through the bedrock to reach the mysterious chamber, but the Rosslyn Trust expressly forbade any excavation of the sacred site. Of course, this only fuelled the fires of speculation. What was the Rosslyn Trust trying to hide?

Rosslyn had now become a pilgrimage site for mystery seekers. Some claimed they were drawn here by the powerful magnetic field that emanated inexplicably from these coordinates, some claimed they came to search the hillside for a hidden entrance to the vault, but most admitted they had come simply to wander the grounds and absorb the lore of the Holy Grail.

Although Langdon had never been to Rosslyn before now, he always chuckled when he heard the chapel described as the current home of the Holy Grail. Admittedly, Rosslyn *once* might have been home to the Grail, long ago . . . but certainly no longer. Far too much attention had been drawn to Rosslyn in past decades, and sooner or later someone would find a way to break into the vault.

True Grail academics agreed that Rosslyn was a decoy – one of the devious dead ends the Priory crafted so convincingly. Tonight, however, with the Priory's keystone offering a verse that pointed directly to this spot, Langdon no longer felt so smug. A perplexing question had been running through his mind all day:

Why would Saunière go to such effort to guide us to so obvious a location?

There seemed only one logical answer.

There is something about Rosslyn we have yet to understand.

'Robert?' Sophie was standing outside the car, looking back at him. 'Are you coming?' She was holding the rosewood box, which Captain Fache had returned to them. Inside, both cryptexes had been reassembled and nested as they had been found. The papyrus verse was locked safely at its core – minus the shattered vial of vinegar.

Making their way up the long gravel path, Langdon and Sophie passed the famous west wall of the chapel. Casual visitors assumed this oddly protruding wall was a section of the chapel that had not been finished. The truth, Langdon recalled, was far more intriguing.

The west wall of Solomon's Temple.

The Knights Templar had designed Rosslyn Chapel as an exact architectural blueprint of Solomon's Temple in Jerusalem – complete with a west wall, a narrow rectangular sanctuary, and a subterranean vault like the Holy of Holies, in which the original nine knights had first unearthed their priceless treasure. Langdon had to admit, there existed an intriguing symmetry in the idea of the Templars building a modern Grail repository that echoed the Grail's original hiding place.

Rosslyn Chapel's entrance was more modest than Langdon expected. The small wooden door had two iron hinges and a simple, oak sign.

This ancient spelling, Langdon explained to Sophie, derived from the Rose Line meridian on which the chapel sat; or, as Grail academics preferred to believe, from the 'Line of Rose' – the ancestral lineage of Mary Magdalene.

The chapel would be closing soon, and as Langdon pulled open the door, a warm puff of air escaped, as if the ancient edifice were heaving a weary sigh at the end of a long day. Her entry arches burgeoned with carved cinquefoils.

Roses. The womb of the goddess.

Entering with Sophie, Langdon felt his eyes reaching across the famous sanctuary and taking it all in. Although he had read accounts of Rosslyn's arrestingly intricate stonework, seeing it in person was an overwhelming encounter.

Symbology heaven, one of Langdon's colleagues had called it.

Every surface in the chapel had been carved with symbols – Christian cruciforms, Jewish stars, Masonic seals, Templar crosses, cornucopias, pyramids, astrological signs, plants, vegetables, pentacles and roses. The Knights Templar had been master stonemasons, erecting Templar churches all over Europe, but Rosslyn was considered their most sublime labour of love and veneration. The master masons had left no stone uncarved. Rosslyn Chapel was a shrine to all faiths . . . to all traditions . . . and, above all, to nature and the goddess.

The sanctuary was empty except for a handful of visitors listening to a young man giving the day's last tour. He was leading them in a single-file line along a well-known route on the floor – an invisible pathway linking six key architectural points within the sanctuary. Generations of visitors had walked these straight lines, connecting the points, and their countless footsteps had engraved an enormous symbol on the floor.

The Star of David, Langdon thought. *No coincidence there.* Also known as Solomon's Seal, this hexagram had once been the secret symbol of the stargazing priests and was later adopted by the Israelite kings – David and Solomon.

The guide had seen Langdon and Sophie enter, and although it was closing time, offered a pleasant smile and motioned for them to feel free to look around.

Langdon nodded his thanks and began to move deeper into the sanctuary. Sophie, however, stood riveted in the entryway, a puzzled look on her face.

'What is it?' Langdon asked.

Sophie stared out at the chapel. 'I think . . . I've been here.'

Langdon was surprised. 'But you said you hadn't even *heard* of Rosslyn.'

'I hadn't . . .' She scanned the sanctuary, looking uncertain. 'My grand-father must have brought me here when I was very young. I don't know. It feels familiar.' As her eyes scanned the room, she began nodding with more certainty. 'Yes.' She pointed to the front of the sanctuary. 'Those two pillars . . . I've seen them.'

Langdon looked at the pair of intricately sculpted columns at the far end of the sanctuary. Their white lacework carvings seemed to smoulder with a ruddy glow as the last of the day's sunlight streamed in through the west window. The pillars – positioned where the altar would normally stand – were an oddly matched pair. The pillar on the left was carved with simple, vertical lines, while the pillar on the right was embellished with an ornate, flowering spiral.

Sophie was already moving toward them. Langdon hurried after her, and as they reached the pillars, Sophie was nodding with incredulity. 'Yes, I'm positive I have seen these!'

'I don't doubt you've seen them,' Langdon said, 'but it wasn't necessarily *here*.'

She turned. 'What do you mean?'

'These two pillars are the most duplicated architectural structures in history. Replicas exist all over the world.'

'Replicas of Rosslyn?' She looked skeptical.

'No. Of the pillars. Do you remember earlier that I mentioned Rosslyn *itself* is a copy of Solomon's Temple? Those two pillars are exact replicas of the two pillars that stood at the head of Solomon's Temple.' Langdon pointed to the pillar on the left. 'That's called *Boaz* – or the Mason's Pillar. The other is called *Jachin* – or the Apprentice Pillar.' He paused. 'In fact, virtually every Masonic temple in the world has two pillars like these.'

Langdon had already explained to her about the Templars' powerful historic ties to the modern Masonic secret societies, whose primary degrees – Apprentice Freemason, Fellowcraft Freemason and Master Mason – harked back to early Templar days. Sophie's grandfather's final verse made direct reference to the Master Masons who adorned Rosslyn with their carved artistic offerings. It also noted Rosslyn's central ceiling, which was covered with carvings of stars and planets.

'I've never been in a Masonic temple,' Sophie said, still eyeing the pillars. 'I am almost positive I saw these *here*.' She turned back into the chapel, as if looking for something else to jog her memory.

The rest of the visitors were now leaving, and the young verger made his way across the chapel to them with a pleasant smile. He was a handsome young man in his late twenties, with a Scottish brogue and strawberry blond hair. 'I'm about to close up for the day. May I help you find anything?'

How about the Holy Grail? Langdon wanted to say.

'The code,' Sophie blurted, in sudden revelation. 'There's a code here!'

The verger looked pleased by her enthusiasm. 'Yes, there is, ma'am.'

'It's on the ceiling,' she said, turning to the right-hand wall. 'Somewhere over . . . there.'

He smiled. 'Not your first visit to Rosslyn, I see.'

The code, Langdon thought. He had forgotten that little bit of lore. Among Rosslyn's numerous mysteries was a vaulted archway from which hundreds of stone blocks protruded, jutting down to form a bizarre multi-faceted surface. Each block was carved with a symbol, seemingly at random, creating a cipher of unfathomable proportion. Some people believed the code revealed the entrance to the vault beneath the chapel. Others believed it told the true Grail legend. Not that it mattered – cryptographers had been trying for centuries to decipher its meaning. To this day the Rosslyn Trust offered a generous reward to anyone who could unveil the secret meaning, but the code remained a mystery.

'I'd be happy to show . . .'

The verger's voice trailed off.

My first code, Sophie thought, moving alone, in a trance, toward the encoded archway. Having handed the rosewood box to Langdon, she could feel herself momentarily forgetting all about the Holy Grail, the Priory of Sion, and all the mysteries of the past day. When she arrived beneath the encoded ceiling and saw the symbols above her, the memories came flooding back. She was recalling her first visit here, and strangely, the memories conjured an unexpected sadness.

She was a little girl . . . a year or so after her family's death. Her grandfather had brought her to Scotland on a short vacation. They had come to see Rosslyn Chapel before going back to Paris. It was late evening, and the chapel was closed. But they were still inside.

'Can we go home, *Grand-père?*' Sophie begged, feeling tired.

'Soon, dear, very soon.' His voice was melancholy. 'I have one last thing I need to do here. How about if you wait in the car?'

'You're doing another big person thing?'

He nodded. 'I'll be fast. I promise.'

'Can I do the archway code again? That was fun.'

'I don't know. I have to step outside. You won't be frightened in here alone?'

'Of course not!' she said in a huff. 'It's not even dark yet!'

He smiled. 'Very well then.' He led her over to the elaborate archway he had shown her earlier.

Sophie immediately plopped down on the stone floor, lying on her back and staring up at the collage of puzzle pieces overhead. 'I'm going to break this code before you get back!'

'It's a race then.' He bent over, kissed her forehead, and walked to the nearby side door. 'I'll be right outside. I'll leave the door open. If you need me, just call.' He exited into the soft evening light.

Sophie lay there on the floor, gazing up at the code. Her eyes felt sleepy. After a few minutes, the symbols got fuzzy. And then they disappeared.

When Sophie awoke, the floor felt cold.

'*Grand-père?*'

There was no answer. Standing up, she brushed herself off. The side door was still open. The evening was getting darker. She walked outside and could see her grandfather standing on the porch of a nearby stone house directly behind the church. Her grandfather was talking quietly to a person barely visible inside the screened door.

'*Grand-père?*' she called.

Her grandfather turned and waved, motioning for her to wait just a moment. Then, slowly, he said some final words to the person inside and blew a kiss toward the screened door. He came to her with tearful eyes.

'Why are you crying, *Grand-père?*'

He picked her up and held her close. 'Oh, Sophie, you and I have said good-bye to a lot of people this year. It's hard.'

Sophie thought of the accident, of saying good-bye to her mother and father, her grandmother and baby brother. 'Were you saying good-bye to *another* person?'

'To a dear friend whom I love very much,' he replied, his voice heavy with emotion. 'And I fear I will not see her again for a very long time.'

Standing with the verger, Langdon had been scanning the chapel walls and feeling a rising wariness that a dead end might be looming. Sophie had wandered off to look at the code and left Langdon holding the rosewood box, which contained a Grail map that now appeared to be no help at all. Although Saunière's poem clearly indicated Rosslyn, Langdon was not sure what to do now that they had arrived. The poem made reference to a 'blade and chalice', which Langdon saw nowhere.

The Holy Grail 'neath ancient Roslin waits.
The blade and chalice guarding o'er Her gates.

Again Langdon sensed there remained some facet of this mystery yet to reveal itself.

'I hate to pry,' the verger said, eyeing the rosewood box in Langdon's hands. 'But this box . . . might I ask where you got it?'

Langdon gave a weary laugh. 'That's an exceptionally long story.'

The young man hesitated, his eyes on the box again. 'It's the strangest thing – my grandmother has a box *exactly* like that – a jewelry box. Identical polished rosewood, same inlaid rose, even the hinges look the same.'

Langdon knew the young man must be mistaken. If ever a box had been one of a kind, it was *this* one – the box custom-made for the Priory keystone. 'The two boxes may be similar but—'

The side door closed loudly, drawing both of their gazes. Sophie had exited without a word and was now wandering down the bluff toward a fieldstone house nearby. Langdon stared after her. *Where is she going?* She had been acting strangely ever since they entered the building. He turned to the guide. 'Do you know what that house is?'

He nodded, also looking puzzled that Sophie was going down there. 'That's the chapel rectory. The chapel curator lives there. She also happens to be the head of the Rosslyn Trust.' He paused. 'And my grandmother.'

'Your grandmother heads the Rosslyn Trust?'

The young man nodded. 'I live with her in the rectory and help keep up the chapel and give tours.' He shrugged. 'I've lived here my whole life. My grandmother brought me up in that house.'

Concerned for Sophie, Langdon moved across the chapel toward the door to call out to her. He was only halfway there when he stopped short. Something the young man said just registered.

My grandmother brought me up.

Langdon looked out at Sophie on the bluff, then down at the rosewood box in his hand. *Impossible.* Slowly, Langdon turned back to the young man. 'You said your grandmother has a box like this one?'

'Almost identical.'

'Where did she get it?'

'My grandfather made it for her. He died when I was a baby, but my grandmother still talks about him. She says he was a genius with his hands. He made all kinds of things.'

Langdon glimpsed an unimaginable web of connections emerging. 'You said your grandmother brought you up. Do you mind my asking what happened to your parents?'

The young man looked surprised. 'They died when I was young.' He paused. 'The same day as my grandfather.'

Langdon's heart pounded. 'In a car accident?'

The guide recoiled, a look of bewilderment in his olive-green eyes. 'Yes. In a car accident. My entire family died that day. I lost my grandfather, my parents, and . . .' He hesitated, glancing down at the floor.

'And your sister,' Langdon said.

Out on the bluff, the fieldstone house was exactly as Sophie remembered it. Night was falling now, and the house exuded a warm and inviting aura. The smell of bread wafted through the open screened door, and a golden light shone in the windows. As Sophie approached, she could hear the quiet sounds of sobbing from within.

Through the screened door, Sophie saw an elderly woman in the hallway. Her back was to the door, but Sophie could see she was crying. The woman had long, luxuriant, silver hair that conjured an unexpected wisp of memory. Feeling herself drawn closer, Sophie stepped onto the porch stairs. The woman was clutching a framed photograph of a man and touching her fingertips to his face with loving sadness.

It was a face Sophie knew well.

Grand-père.

The woman had obviously heard the sad news of his death last night.

A board squeaked beneath Sophie's feet, and the woman turned slowly, her sad eyes finding Sophie's. Sophie wanted to run, but she stood transfixed. The woman's fervent gaze never wavered as she set down the photo and approached the screened door. An eternity seemed to pass as the two women stared at one another through the thin mesh. Then, like the slowly gathering swell of an ocean wave, the woman's visage transformed from one of uncertainty . . . to disbelief . . . to hope . . . and finally, to cresting joy.

Throwing open the door, she came out, reaching with soft hands, cradling Sophie's thunderstruck face. 'Oh, dear child . . . look at you!'

Although Sophie did not recognize her, she knew who this woman was. She tried to speak but found she could not even breathe.

'Sophie,' the woman sobbed, kissing her forehead.

Sophie's words were a choked whisper. 'But . . . *Grand-père* said you were . . .'

'I know.' The woman placed her tender hands on Sophie's shoulders and gazed at her with familiar eyes. 'Your grandfather and I were forced to say so many things. We did what we thought was right. I'm so sorry. It was for your own safety, princess.'

Sophie heard her final word, and immediately thought of her grandfather, who had called her princess for so many years. The sound of his voice seemed to echo now in the ancient stones of Rosslyn, settling through the earth and reverberating in the unknown hollows below.

The woman threw her arms around Sophie, the tears flowing faster. 'Your grandfather wanted so badly to tell you everything. But things were difficult between you two. He tried so hard. There's so much to explain. So very much to explain.' She kissed Sophie's forehead once again, then whispered in her ear. 'No more secrets, princess. It's time you learn the truth about our family.'

Sophie and her grandmother were seated on the porch stairs in a tearful hug when the young guide dashed across the lawn, his eyes shining with hope and disbelief.

'Sophie?'

Through her tears, Sophie nodded, standing. She did not know the young man's face, but as they embraced, she could feel the power of the blood coursing through his veins . . . the blood she now understood they shared.

When Langdon walked across the lawn to join them, Sophie could not imagine that only yesterday she had felt so alone in the world. And now, somehow, in this foreign place, in the company of three people she barely knew, she felt at last that she was home.

105

Night had fallen over Rosslyn.

Robert Langdon stood alone on the porch of the fieldstone house enjoying the sounds of laughter and reunion drifting through the screened door behind him. The mug of potent Brazilian coffee in his hand had granted him a hazy reprieve from his mounting exhaustion, and yet he sensed the reprieve would be fleeting. The fatigue in his body went to the core.

'You slipped out quietly,' a voice behind him said.

He turned. Sophie's grandmother emerged, her silver hair shimmering in the night. Her name, for the last twenty-eight years at least, was Marie Chauvel.

Langdon gave a tired smile. 'I thought I'd give your family some time together.' Through the window, he could see Sophie talking with her brother.

Marie came over and stood beside him. 'Mr Langdon, when I first heard of Jacques's murder, I was terrified for Sophie's safety. Seeing her standing in my doorway tonight was the greatest relief of my life. I cannot thank you enough.'

Langdon had no idea how to respond. Although he had offered to give Sophie and her grandmother time to talk in private, Marie had asked him to stay and listen. *My husband obviously trusted you, Mr Langdon, so I do as well.*

And so Langdon had remained, standing beside Sophie and listening in mute astonishment while Marie told the story of Sophie's late parents. Incredibly, both had been from Merovingian families – direct descendants of Mary Magdalene and Jesus Christ. Sophie's parents and ancestors, for protection, had changed their family names of Plantard and Saint-Clair. Their children represented the most direct surviving royal bloodline and therefore were carefully guarded by the Priory. When Sophie's parents were killed in a car accident whose cause could not be determined, the Priory feared the identity of the royal line had been discovered.

'Your grandfather and I,' Marie had explained in a voice choked with pain, 'had to make a grave decision the instant we received the phone call. Your parents' car had just been found in the river.' She dabbed at the tears in her eyes. 'All six of us – including you two grandchildren – were supposed to be travelling together in that car that very night. Fortunately we changed our plans at the last moment, and your parents were alone. Hearing of the accident, Jacques and I had no way to know what had really happened . . . or if this was truly an *accident*.' Marie looked at Sophie. 'We knew we had to protect our grandchildren, and we did what we thought was best. Jacques reported to the police that your brother and I had been in the car . . . our two bodies apparently washed off in the current. Then your brother and I went underground with the Priory. Jacques, being a man of prominence, did not have the luxury of disappearing. It only made sense that Sophie, being the eldest, would stay in Paris to be taught and raised by Jacques, close to the heart and protection of the Priory.' Her voice fell to a whisper. 'Separating the family was the hardest thing we ever had to do. Jacques and I saw each other only very infrequently, and always in the most secret of settings . . . under the protection of the Priory. There are certain ceremonies to which the brotherhood always stays faithful.'

Langdon had sensed the story went far deeper, but he also sensed it was not for him to hear. So he had stepped outside. Now, gazing up at the spires of Rosslyn, Langdon could not escape the hollow gnaw of Rosslyn's unsolved mystery. *Is the Grail really here at Rosslyn? And if so, where are the blade and chalice that Saunière mentioned in his poem?*

'I'll take that,' Marie said, motioning to Langdon's hand.

'Oh, thank you.' Langdon held out his empty coffee cup.

She stared at him. 'I was referring to your *other* hand, Mr Langdon.'

Langdon looked down and realized he was holding Saunière's papyrus. He had taken it from the cryptex once again in hopes of seeing something he had missed earlier. 'Of course, I'm sorry.'

Marie looked amused as she took the paper. 'I know of a man at a bank in Paris who is probably very eager to see the return of this rosewood box. André Vernet was a dear friend of Jacques, and Jacques trusted him explicitly. André would have done anything to honour Jacques's requests for the care of this box.'

Including shooting me, Langdon recalled, deciding not to mention that he had probably broken the poor man's nose. Thinking of Paris, Langdon flashed on the three *sénéchaux* who had been killed the night before. 'And the Priory? What happens now?'

'The wheels are already in motion, Mr Langdon. The brotherhood has endured for centuries, and it will endure this. There are always those waiting to move up and rebuild.'

All evening Langdon had suspected that Sophie's grandmother was closely tied to the operations of the Priory. After all, the Priory had always had women members. Four Grand Masters had been women. The *sénéchaux* were traditionally men – the guardians – and yet women held far more honoured status within the Priory and could ascend to the highest post from virtually any rank.

Langdon thought of Leigh Teabing and Westminster Abbey. It seemed a lifetime ago. 'Was the Church pressuring your husband not to release the Sangreal documents at the End of Days?'

'Heavens no. The End of Days is a legend of paranoid minds. There is nothing in the Priory doctrine that identifies a date at which the Grail should be unveiled. In fact the Priory has always maintained that the Grail should *never* be unveiled.'

'Never?' Langdon was stunned.

'It is the mystery and wonderment that serve our souls, not the Grail itself. The beauty of the Grail lies in her ethereal nature.' Marie Chauvel gazed up at Rosslyn now. 'For some, the Grail is a chalice that will bring them everlasting life. For others, it is the quest for lost documents and secret history. And for most, I suspect the Holy Grail is simply a grand idea . . . a glorious unattainable treasure that somehow, even in today's world of chaos, inspires us.'

'But if the Sangreal documents remain hidden, the story of Mary Magdalene will be lost for ever,' Langdon said.

'Will it? Look around you. Her story is being told in art, music and books. More so every day. The pendulum is swinging. We are starting to sense the dangers of our history . . . and of our destructive paths. We are beginning to sense the need to restore the sacred feminine.' She paused. 'You mentioned you are writing a manuscript about the symbols of the sacred feminine, are you not?'

'I am.'

She smiled. 'Finish it, Mr Langdon. Sing her song. The world needs modern troubadours.'

Langdon fell silent, feeling the weight of her message upon him. Across the open spaces, a new moon was rising above the tree line. Turning his eyes toward Rosslyn, Langdon felt a boyish craving to know her secrets. *Don't ask*, he told himself. *This is not the moment.* He glanced at the papyrus in Marie's hand, and then back at Rosslyn.

'Ask the question, Mr Langdon,' Marie said, looking amused. 'You have earned the right.'

Langdon felt himself flush.

'You want to know if the Grail is here at Rosslyn.'

'Can you tell me?'

She sighed in mock exasperation. 'Why is it that men simply *cannot* let the Grail rest?' She laughed, obviously enjoying herself. 'Why do you think it's here?'

Langdon motioned to the papyrus in her hand. 'Your husband's poem speaks specifically of Rosslyn, except it also mentions a blade and chalice watching over the Grail. I didn't see any symbols of the blade and chalice up there.'

'The blade and chalice?' Marie asked. 'What exactly do they look like?'

Langdon sensed she was toying with him, but he played along, quickly describing the symbols.

A look of vague recollection crossed her face. 'Ah, yes, of course. The blade represents all that is masculine. I believe it is drawn like this, no?' Using her index finger, she traced a shape on her palm.

'Yes,' Langdon said. Marie had drawn the less common 'closed' form of the blade, although Langdon had seen the symbol portrayed both ways.

'And the inverse,' she said, drawing again on her palm, 'is the chalice, which represents the feminine.'

'Correct,' Langdon said.

'And you are saying that in all the hundreds of symbols we have here in Rosslyn Chapel, these two shapes appear nowhere?'

'I didn't see them.'

'And if I show them to you, will you get some sleep?'

Before Langdon could answer, Marie Chauvel had stepped off the porch and was heading toward the chapel. Langdon hurried after her. Entering the ancient building, Marie turned on the lights and pointed to the centre of the sanctuary floor. 'There you are, Mr Langdon. The blade and chalice.'

Langdon stared at the scuffed stone floor. It was blank. 'There's nothing here. . . .'

Marie sighed and began to walk along the famous path worn into the chapel floor, the same path Langdon had seen the visitors walking earlier this evening. As his eyes adjusted to see the giant symbol, he still felt lost. 'But that's the Star of Dav—'

Langdon stopped short, mute with amazement as it dawned on him.

The blade and chalice.

Fused as one.

The Star of David . . . the perfect union of male and female . . . Solomon's Seal . . . marking the Holy of Holies, where the male and female deities – Yahweh and Shekinah – were thought to dwell.

Langdon needed a minute to find his words. 'The verse does point here to Rosslyn. Completely. Perfectly.'

Marie smiled. 'Apparently.'

The implications chilled him. 'So the Holy Grail is in the vault beneath us?'

She laughed. 'Only in spirit. One of the Priory's most ancient charges was one day to return the Grail to her homeland of France where she could rest for eternity. For centuries, she was dragged across the countryside to keep her safe. Most undignified. Jacques's charge when he became Grand Master was to restore her honour by returning her to France and building her a resting place fit for a queen.'

'And he succeeded?'

Now her face grew serious. 'Mr Langdon, considering what you've done for me tonight, and as curator of the Rosslyn Trust, I can tell you for certain that the Grail is no longer here.'

Langdon decided to press. 'But the keystone is supposed to point to the place where the Holy Grail is hidden *now*. Why does it point to Rosslyn?'

'Maybe you're misreading its meaning. Remember, the Grail can be deceptive. As could my late husband.'

'But how much clearer could he be?' he asked. 'We are standing over an underground vault marked by the blade and chalice, underneath a ceiling of stars, surrounded by the art of Master Masons. Everything speaks of Rosslyn.'

'Very well, let me see this mysterious verse.' She unrolled the papyrus and read the poem aloud in a deliberate tone.

> The Holy Grail 'neath ancient Roslin waits.
> The blade and chalice guarding o'er Her gates.
> Adorned in masters' loving art, She lies.
> She rests at last beneath the starry skies.

When she finished, she was still for several seconds, until a knowing smile crossed her lips. 'Aah, Jacques.'

Langdon watched her expectantly. 'You *understand* this?'

'As you have witnessed on the chapel floor, Mr Langdon, there are many ways to see simple things.'

Langdon strained to understand. Everything about Jacques Saunière seemed to have double meanings, and yet Langdon could see no further.

Marie gave a tired yawn. 'Mr Langdon, I will make a confession to you. I have never officially been privy to the present location of the Grail. But, of course, I was married to a person of enormous influence . . . and my woman's intuition is strong.' Langdon started to speak but Marie continued. 'I am sorry that after all your hard work, you will be leaving Rosslyn without any real answers. And yet, something tells me you will eventually find what you seek. One day it will dawn on you.' She smiled. 'And when it does, I trust that you, of all people, can keep a secret.'

There was a sound of someone arriving in the doorway. 'Both of you disappeared,' Sophie said, entering.

'I was just leaving,' her grandmother replied, walking over to Sophie at the door. 'Good night, princess.' She kissed Sophie's forehead. 'Don't keep Mr Langdon out too late.'

Langdon and Sophie watched her grandmother walk back toward the fieldstone house. When Sophie turned to him, her eyes were awash in deep emotion. 'Not exactly the ending I expected.'

That makes two of us, he thought. Langdon could see she was overwhelmed. The news she had received tonight had changed everything in her life. 'Are you okay? It's a lot to take in.'

She smiled quietly. 'I have a family. That's where I'm going to start. Who we are and where we came from will take some time.'

Langdon remained silent.

'Beyond tonight, will you stay with us?' Sophie asked. 'At least for a few days?'

Langdon sighed, wanting nothing more. 'You need some time here with your family, Sophie. I'm going back to Paris in the morning.'

She looked disappointed but seemed to know it was the right thing to do. Neither of them spoke for a long time. Finally Sophie reached over and, taking his hand, led him out of the chapel. They walked to a small rise on the bluff. From here, the Scottish countryside spread out before them, suffused in a pale moonlight that sifted through the departing clouds. They stood in silence, holding hands, both of them fighting the descending shroud of exhaustion.

The stars were just now appearing, but to the west, a single point of light glowed brighter than any other. Langdon smiled when he saw it. It was Venus. The ancient Goddess shining down with her steady and patient light.

The night was growing cooler, a crisp breeze rolling up from the lowlands. After a while, Langdon looked over at Sophie. Her eyes were closed, her lips relaxed in a contented smile. Langdon could feel his own eyes growing heavy. Reluctantly, he squeezed her hand. 'Sophie?'

Slowly, she opened her eyes and turned to him. Her face was beautiful in the moonlight. She gave him a sleepy smile. 'Hi.'

Langdon felt an unexpected sadness to realize he would be returning to Paris without her. 'I may be gone before you wake up.' He paused, a knot growing in his throat. 'I'm sorry, I'm not very good at—'

Sophie reached out and placed her soft hand on the side of his face. Then, leaning forward, she kissed him tenderly on the cheek. 'When can I see you again?'

Langdon reeled momentarily, lost in her eyes. 'When?' He paused, curious if she had any idea how much he had been wondering the same thing. 'Well, actually, next month I'm lecturing at a conference in Florence. I'll be there a week without much to do.'

'Is that an invitation?'

'We'd be living in luxury. They're giving me a room at the Brunelleschi.'

Sophie smiled playfully. 'You presume a lot, Mr Langdon.'

He cringed at how it had sounded. 'What I meant—'

'I would love nothing more than to meet you in Florence, Robert. But on *one* condition.' Her tone turned serious. 'No museums, no churches, no tombs, no art, no relics.'

'In Florence? For a week? There's nothing else to do.'

Sophie leaned forward and kissed him again, now on the lips. Their bodies came together, softly at first, and then completely. When she pulled away, her eyes were full of promise.

'Right,' Langdon managed. 'It's a date.'

Epilogue

Robert Langdon awoke with a start. He had been dreaming. The bathrobe beside his bed bore the monogram *HOTEL RITZ PARIS*. He saw a dim light filtering through the blinds. *Is it dusk or dawn?* he wondered.

Langdon's body felt warm and deeply contented. He had slept the better part of the last two days. Sitting up slowly in bed, he now realized what had awoken him . . . the strangest thought. For days he had been trying to sort through a barrage of information, but now Langdon found himself fixed on something he'd not considered before.

Could it be?

He remained motionless a long moment.

Getting out of bed, he walked to the marble shower. Stepping inside, he let the powerful jets message his shoulders. Still, the thought enthralled him.

Impossible.

Twenty minutes later, Langdon stepped out of the Hotel Ritz into Place Vendôme. Night was falling. The days of sleep had left him disoriented . . . and yet his mind felt oddly lucid. He had promised himself he would stop in the hotel lobby for a café au lait to clear his thoughts, but instead his legs carried him directly out of the front door into the gathering Paris night.

Walking east on Rue des Petits Champs, Langdon felt a growing excitement. He turned south onto Rue Richelieu, where the air grew sweet with the scent of blossoming jasmine from the stately gardens of the Palais Royal.

He continued south until he saw what he was looking for – the famous royal arcade – a glistening expanse of polished black marble. Moving onto it, Langdon scanned the surface beneath his feet. Within seconds, he found what he knew was there – several bronze medallions embedded in the ground in a perfectly straight line. Each disk was five inches in diameter and embossed with the letters N and S.

Nord. Sud.

He turned due south, letting his eye trace the extended line formed by the medallions. He began moving again, following the trail, watching the pavement as he walked. As he cut across the corner of the Comédie-Française, another bronze medallion passed beneath his feet. *Yes!*

The streets of Paris, Langdon had learned years ago, were adorned with 135 of these bronze markers, embedded in sidewalks, courtyards, and streets, on a north–south axis across the city. He had once followed the line from Sacré-Coeur, north across the Seine, and finally to the ancient Paris Observatory. There he discovered the significance of the sacred path it traced.

The earth's original prime meridian.
The first zero longitude of the world.
Paris's ancient Rose Line.

Now, as Langdon hurried across Rue de Rivoli, he could feel his destination within reach. Less than a block away.

The Holy Grail 'neath ancient Roslin waits.

The revelations were coming now in waves. Saunière's ancient spelling of Roslin . . . the blade and chalice . . . the tomb adorned with masters' art.

Is that why Saunière needed to talk with me? Had I unknowingly guessed the truth?

He broke into a jog, feeling the Rose Line beneath his feet, guiding him, pulling him toward his destination. As he entered the long tunnel of Passage Richelieu, the hairs on his neck began to bristle with anticipation. He knew that at the end of this tunnel stood the most mysterious of Parisian monuments – conceived and commissioned in the 1980s by the Sphinx himself, François Mitterrand, a man rumoured to move in secret circles, a man whose final legacy to Paris was a place Langdon had visited only days before.

Another lifetime.

With a final surge of energy, Langdon burst from the passageway into the familiar courtyard and came to a stop. Breathless, he raised his eyes, slowly, disbelieving, to the glistening structure in front of him.

The Louvre Pyramid.

Gleaming in the darkness.

He admired it only a moment. He was more interested in what lay to his right. Turning, he felt his feet again tracing the invisible path of the ancient Rose Line, carrying him across the courtyard to the Carrousel du Louvre – the enormous circle of grass surrounded by a perimeter of neatly trimmed hedges – once the site of Paris's primeval nature-worshipping festivals . . . joyous rites to celebrate fertility and the Goddess.

Langdon felt as if he were crossing into another world as he stepped over the bushes to the grassy area within. This hallowed ground was now marked by one of the city's most unusual monuments. There in the centre, plunging into the earth like a crystal chasm, gaped the giant inverted pyramid of glass that he had seen a few nights ago when he entered the Louvre's subterranean entresol.

La Pyramide Inversée.

Tremulous, Langdon walked to the edge and peered down into the Louvre's sprawling underground complex, aglow with amber light. His eye was trained not just on the massive inverted pyramid, but on what lay directly beneath it. There, on the floor of the chamber below, stood the tiniest of structures . . . a structure Langdon had mentioned in his manuscript.

Langdon felt himself awaken fully now to the thrill of unthinkable possibility. Raising his eyes again to the Louvre, he sensed the huge wings of the museum enveloping him . . . hallways that burgeoned with the world's finest art.

Da Vinci . . . Botticelli . . .

Adorned in masters' loving art, She lies.

Alive with wonder, he stared once again downward through the glass at the tiny structure below.

I must go down there!

Stepping out of the circle, he hurried across the courtyard back toward the towering pyramid entrance of the Louvre. The day's last visitors were trickling out of the museum.

Pushing through the revolving door, Langdon descended the curved staircase into the pyramid. He could feel the air grow cooler. When he reached the bottom, he entered the long tunnel that stretched beneath the Louvre's courtyard, back toward *La Pyramide Inversée.*

At the end of the tunnel, he emerged into a large chamber. Directly before him, hanging down from above, gleamed the inverted pyramid – a breathtaking V-shaped contour of glass.

The Chalice.

Langdon's eyes traced its narrowing form downward to its tip, suspended only six feet above the floor. There, directly beneath it, stood the tiny structure.

A miniature pyramid. Only three feet tall. The only structure in this colossal complex that had been built on a small scale.

Langdon's manuscript, while discussing the Louvre's elaborate collection of goddess art, had made passing note of this modest pyramid. '*The miniature structure itself protrudes up through the floor as though it were the tip of an iceberg – the apex of an enormous, pyramidical vault, submerged below like a hidden chamber.*'

Illuminated in the soft lights of the deserted entresol, the two pyramids pointed at one another, their bodies perfectly aligned, their tips almost touching.

The Chalice above. The Blade below.

The blade and chalice guarding o'er Her gates.

Langdon heard Marie Chauvel's words. *One day it will dawn on you.*

He was standing beneath the ancient Rose Line, surrounded by the work of masters. *What better place for Saunière to keep watch?* Now at last, he sensed he understood the true meaning of the Grand Master's verse. Raising his eyes to heaven, he gazed upward through the glass to a glorious, star-filled night.

She rests at last beneath the starry skies.

Like the murmurs of spirits in the darkness, forgotten words echoed. *The quest for the Holy Grail is the quest to kneel before the bones of Mary Magdalene. A journey to pray at the feet of the outcast one.*

With a sudden upwelling of reverence, Robert Langdon fell to his knees.

For a moment, he thought he heard a woman's voice . . . the wisdom of the ages . . . whispering up from the chasms of the earth.